SLOAN WILSON

The Man
in the
Gray Flannel Suit

SIMON AND SCHUSTER

1955

EIGHTH PRINTING

LIBRARY OF CONGRESS CATALOG CARD NUMBER: 54–9811
MANUFACTURED IN THE UNITED STATES OF AMERICA
BY H. WOLFF BOOK MFG. CO., INC., NEW YORK, N.Y.

This book is dedicated by my wife and me
to her father,
CARL E. PICKHARDT

ACKNOWLEDGMENTS

I'm grateful to Elise Pickhardt Wilson, my wife, for the help she gave me in writing this book. She mowed the lawn, took care of the children, and managed the family finances so that I could find time to write. She never made me feel that writing is justifiable only if it is successful. During a two-year period of almost all work and no play, she made life worth living for everyone in my house. Many of the thoughts on which this book is based are hers.

Both she and I are thankful for assistance rendered by many others. During dark hours when there was no realistic reason to suppose that the manuscript was ever going to get finished, Richard L. Simon, my publisher, administered miraculous transfusions of skill and courage. He emboldened me to have a try at this book in the first place, and now that the work is done, leaves me feeling as though he had fought at my side through a long war. There is no greater friendship.

For editorial advice and encouragement, I'm also deeply indebted to Norman Cousins. My mother, Mrs. Ruth Danenhower Wilson, proved that she is, among other things, a good editor. Kenneth Payson Kempton at Harvard was the first teacher to show me that a writer doesn't necessarily have to be a fool. Lester Anderson at The University of Buffalo helped in many ways. And last but not least, I'm grateful to the people in my office at The University of Buffalo. They did much of my University work while I was otherwise occupied.

S.W.

So I said
To the man who knew:
"Where are they going?
And what do they carry?
And why do they hurry so?"

A.F.W.

The Man
in the
Gray Flannel Suit

1

By THE TIME they had lived seven years in the little house on Green-tree Avenue in Westport, Connecticut, they both detested it. There were many reasons, none of them logical, but all of them compelling. For one thing, the house had a kind of evil genius for displaying proof of their weaknesses and wiping out all traces of their strengths. The ragged lawn and weed-filled garden proclaimed to passers-by and the neighbors that Thomas R. Rath and his family disliked "working around the place" and couldn't afford to pay someone else to do it. The interior of the house was even more vengeful. In the living room there was a big dent in the plaster near the floor, with a huge crack curving up from it in the shape of a question mark. That wall was damaged in the fall of 1952, when, after struggling for months to pay up the back bills, Tom came home one night to find that Betsy had bought a cut-glass vase for forty dollars. Such an extravagant gesture was utterly unlike her, at least since the war. Betsy was a conscientious household manager, and usually when she did something Tom didn't like, they talked the matter over with careful reasonableness. But on that particular night, Tom was tired and worried because he himself had just spent seventy dollars on a new suit he felt he needed to dress properly for his business, and at the climax

-3-

of a heated argument, he picked up the vase and heaved it against the wall. The heavy glass shattered, the plaster cracked, and two of the lathes behind it broke. The next morning, Tom and Betsy worked together on their knees to patch the plaster, and they repainted the whole wall, but when the paint dried, the big dent near the floor with the crack curving up from it almost to the ceiling in the shape of a question mark was still clearly visible. The fact that the crack was in the shape of a question mark did not seem symbolic to Tom and Betsy, nor even amusing—it was just annoying. Its peculiar shape caused people to stare at it abstractedly, and once at a cocktail party one of the guests who had had a little too much to drink said, "Say, that's funny. Did you ever notice that big question mark on your wall?"

"It's only a crack," Tom replied.

"But why should it be in the form of a question mark?"

"It's just coincidence."

"That's funny," the guest said.

Tom and Betsy assured each other that someday they would have the whole wall replastered, but they never did. The crack remained as a perpetual reminder of Betsy's moment of extravagance, Tom's moment of violence, and their inability either to fix walls properly or to pay to have them fixed. It seemed ironic to Tom that the house should preserve a souvenir of such things, while allowing evenings of pleasure and kindness to slip by without a trace.

The crack in the living room was not the only reminder of the worst. An ink stain with hand marks on the wallpaper in Janey's room commemorated one of the few times Janey ever willfully destroyed property, and the only time Betsy ever lost her temper with her and struck her. Janey was five, and the middle one of the three Rath children. She did everything hard: she screamed when she cried, and when she was happy her small face seemed to hold for an instant all the joy in the world. Upon deciding that she wanted to play with ink, she carefully poured ink over both her hands and made neat imprints on the wallpaper, from the floor to as high as she could reach. Betsy was so angry that she slapped both her hands, and Janey, feeling she had simply been interrupted in

-4-

the midst of an artistic endeavor, lay on the bed for an hour sobbing and rubbing her hands in her eyes until her whole face was covered with ink. Feeling like a murderess, Betsy tried to comfort her, but even holding and rocking her didn't seem to help, and Betsy was shocked to find that the child was shuddering. When Tom came home that night he found mother and daughter asleep on the bed together, tightly locked in each other's arms. Both their faces were covered with ink. All this the wall remembered and recorded.

A thousand petty shabbinesses bore witness to the negligence of the Raths. The front door had been scratched by a dog which had been run over the year before. The hot-water faucet in the bathroom dripped. Almost all the furniture needed to be refinished, reupholstered, or cleaned. And besides that, the house was too small, ugly, and almost precisely like the houses on all sides of it.

The Raths had bought the house in 1946, shortly after Tom had got out of the army and, at the suggestion of his grandmother, become an assistant to the director of the Schanenhauser Foundation, an organization which an elderly millionaire had established to help finance scientific research and the arts. They had told each other that they probably would be in the house only one or two years before they could afford something better. It took them five years to realize that the expense of raising three children was likely to increase at least as fast as Tom's salary at a charitable foundation. If Tom and Betsy had been entirely reasonable, this might have caused them to start painting the place like crazy, but it had the reverse effect. Without talking about it much, they both began to think of the house as a trap, and they no more enjoyed refurbishing it than a prisoner would delight in shining up the bars of his cell. Both of them were aware that their feelings about the house were not admirable.

"I don't know what's the matter with us," Betsy said one night. "Your job is plenty good enough. We've got three nice kids, and lots of people would be glad to have a house like this. We shouldn't be so *discontented* all the time."

"Of course we shouldn't!" Tom said.

Their words sounded hollow. It was curious to believe that that house with the crack in the form of a question mark on the wall and the ink stains on the wallpaper was probably the end of their personal road. It was impossible to believe. Somehow something would have to happen.

Tom thought about his house on that day early in June 1953, when a friend of his named Bill Hawthorne mentioned the possibility of a job at the United Broadcasting Corporation. Tom was having lunch with a group of acquaintances in The Golden Horseshoe, a small restaurant and bar near Rockefeller Center.

"I hear we've got a new spot opening up in our public-relations department," Bill, who wrote promotion for United Broadcasting, said. "I think any of you would be crazy to take it, mind you, but if you're interested, there it is. . . ."

Tom unfolded his long legs under the table and shifted his big body on his chair restlessly. "How much would it pay?" he asked casually.

"I don't know," Bill said. "Anywhere from eight to twelve thousand, I'd guess, according to how good a hold-up man you are. If you try for it, ask fifteen. I'd like to see somebody stick the bastards good."

It was fashionable that summer to be cynical about one's employers, and the promotion men were the most cynical of all.

"You can have it," Cliff Otis, a young copy writer for a large advertising agency, said. "I wouldn't want to get into a rat race like that."

Tom glanced into his glass and said nothing. Maybe I could get ten thousand a year, he thought. If I could do that, Betsy and I might be able to buy a better house.

2

WHEN TOM STEPPED OFF the train at Westport that night, he stood among a crowd of men and looked toward the corner of the station where Betsy usually waited for him. She was there, and involuntarily his pace quickened at the sight of her. After almost twelve years of marriage, he was still not quite used to his good fortune at having acquired such a pretty wife. Even with her light-brown hair somewhat tousled, as it was now, she looked wonderful to him. The slightly rumpled cotton house dress she was wearing innocently displayed her slim-waisted but full figure to advantage, and although she looked a little tired, her smile was bright and youthful as she waved to him. Because he felt it so genuinely, there was always a temptation for him to say to her, "How beautiful you are!" when he saw her after being away for the day, but he didn't, because long ago he had learned that she was perhaps the one woman in the world who didn't like such compliments. "Don't keep telling me I'm pretty," she had said to him once with real impatience in her voice. "I've been told that ever since I was twelve years old. If you want to compliment me, tell me I'm something I'm not. Tell me that I'm a marvelous housekeeper, or that I don't have a selfish bone in my body."

Now he hurried toward her. "Hi!" he said. "It's good to get home. How did things go with you today?"

"Not so well," she replied ruefully. "Brace yourself."

"Why, what happened?" he said, and kissed her lightly.

"Barbara's got the chicken pox, and the washing machine broke down."

"Chicken pox!" Tom said. "Do they get very sick with that?"

"No, but according to Dr. Spock, it's messy. The other two will probably get it. Poor Barbara feels awful. And I think we're going to have to buy a new washing machine."

They climbed into their old Ford. On the way home they stopped at a drugstore, and Tom bought Barbara a toy lamb. Barbara was six and wanted nothing but toy lambs. When they got to Greentree Avenue, the little house looked more monotonous than ever, and Tom saw that the front lawn needed cutting. Janey, followed by his son, Pete, ran to meet him as he opened the front door. "Barbara's got the chicken pox, and we're *all* going to get it!" she said delightedly. "Mother says so!"

Lucy Hitchcock, who lived next door and who had been staying with the children while Betsy drove to the station, was sitting in the living room watching a puppet show on television. She got up to go, and while Tom was thanking her, Janey saw the parcel he was holding in his hand. "What's that?" she demanded.

"A present for Barbara because she's sick."

"Did you bring anything for me?"

"No. You're not sick yet."

"That's not *fair!*" Janey said, and began to howl. Without making any inquiries, Pete began to howl too.

"Barbara's *sick!*" Tom said.

"You always bring her presents and you never bring me any," Janey retorted.

"That's not true," Tom said.

"No television!" Betsy said. "If you children don't stop this nonsense immediately, no television for a week."

"Not *fair!*" Janey said.

"This is your last chance!" Betsy said. "Be quiet."

". . . fair," Janey murmured.

"All right, that does it," Betsy said. "No television for a week!"

Redoubled howls came from Janey and Pete, until Betsy relented on condition that they both be quiet for the rest of the evening. Mournfully the children followed Tom upstairs. He found Barbara in bed, with her small face already a mass of sores. "Did you bring me a present?" she asked eagerly.

He gave her the parcel. "A lamb!" she said delightedly when she unwrapped it. "Another lamb!"

"I didn't want another lamb anyway," Janey said. "Lambs are silly."

"They're not silly!"

-8-

"Quiet! Not another word!" Betsy said, coming into the room with a glass of water and medicine for Barbara.

Tom went downstairs and mixed a Martini for Betsy and himself. When Betsy came down, they sat in the kitchen, sipping their drinks gratefully while the children played in the living room and watched television. The linoleum on the kitchen floor was beginning to wrinkle. Originally it had been what the builder described as a "bright, basket-weave pattern," but now it was scuffed, and by the sink it was worn through to the wood underneath. "We ought to get some new linoleum," Betsy said. "We could lay it ourselves."

"I heard about a new job today," Tom said. "Public relations. United Broadcasting Corporation."

"How much does it pay?"

"Probably a good deal more than I'm getting now."

There was an instant of silence before she said, "Are you going to try for it?"

"I might."

Betsy finished her drink and poured herself another. "I've never thought of you as a public-relations man," she said soberly. "Would you like it?"

"I'd like the money."

Betsy sighed. "It would be wonderful to get out of this house," she said.

3

THE NEXT MORNING, Tom put on his best suit, a freshly cleaned and pressed gray flannel. On his way to work he stopped in Grand Central Station to buy a clean white handkerchief and to have his shoes shined. During his luncheon hour he set out to visit the United

Broadcasting Corporation. As he walked across Rockefeller Plaza, he thought wryly of the days when he and Betsy had assured each other that money didn't matter. They had told each other that when they were married, before the war, and during the war they had repeated it in long letters. "The important thing is to find a kind of work you really like, and something that is useful," Betsy had written him. "The money doesn't matter."

The hell with that, he thought. The real trouble is that up to now we've been kidding ourselves. We might as well admit that what we want is a big house and a new car and trips to Florida in the winter, and plenty of life insurance. When you come right down to it, a man with three children has no damn right to say that money doesn't matter.

There were eighteen elevators in the lobby of the United Broadcasting building. They were all brass colored and looked as though they were made of money. The receptionist in the personnel office was a breathtakingly beautiful girl with money-colored hair—a sort of copper gold. "Yes?" she said.

"I want to apply for a position in the public-relations department."

"If you will sit down in the reception room, I'll arrange an interview for you," she said.

The company had a policy of giving all job applicants an interview. Every year about twenty thousand people, most of them wildly unqualified, applied for jobs there, and it was considered poor public relations to turn them away too abruptly. Beyond the receptionist's desk was a huge waiting room. A rich wine-red carpet was on the floor, and there were dozens of heavy leather armchairs filled with people nervously smoking cigarettes. On the walls were enormous colored photographs of the company's leading radio and television stars. They were all youthful, handsome, and unutterably rich-appearing as they smiled down benignly on the job applicants. Tom picked a chair directly beneath a picture of a big-bosomed blonde. He had to wait only about twenty minutes before the receptionist told him that a Mr. Everett would see him. Mr. Everett's office was a cubicle with walls of opaque glass brick, only about three times as big as a priest's confessional. Everett himself was a man about Tom's age and was also dressed in a gray flannel suit. The uniform of the day, Tom thought. Somebody must have put out an order.

"I understand that you are interested in a position in the public-relations department," Everett said.

"I just want to explore the situation," Tom replied. "I already have a good position with the Schanenhauser Foundation, but I'm considering a change."

It took Everett only about a minute to size Tom up as a "possibility." He gave him a long printed form to fill out and told him he'd hear from the United Broadcasting Corporation in a few days. Tom spent almost an hour filling out all the pages of the form, which, among other things, required a list of the childhood diseases he had had and the names of countries he had visited. When he had finished, he gave it to the girl with the hair of copper gold and rang for one of the golden elevators to take him down.

Five days later Tom got a letter from Everett saying an interview had been arranged for him with Mr. Gordon Walker in Room 3672 the following Monday at 11:00 A.M. In the letter Walker was given no title. Tom didn't know whether he were going to have another routine interview, or whether he were actually being considered for a position. He wondered whether he should tell Dick Haver, the director of the Schanenhauser Foundation, that he was looking for another job. The danger of not telling him was that the broadcasting company might call him for references any time, and Dick wouldn't be pleased to find that Tom was applying for another job behind his back. It was important to keep Dick's good will, because the broadcasting company's decision might depend on the recommendation Dick gave him. In any one of a thousand ways, Dick could damn him, without Tom's ever learning about it. All Dick would have to do when the broadcasting company telephoned him would be to say, "Tom Rath? Well, I don't know. I don't think I'd want to go on record one way or the other on Mr. Rath. He's a nice person, you understand, an awfully nice person. I'd be perfectly willing to say that!"

On the other hand, it would be embarrassing to tell Dick he was seeking another job and then be unable to find one. Tom decided to delay seeing Dick until after he had had his next interview.

Walker's outer office was impressive. As soon as Tom saw it, he knew he was being seriously considered for a job, and maybe a pretty good one. Walker had two secretaries, one chosen for looks, apparently, and one for utility. A pale-yellow carpet lay on the floor, and there was a yellow leather armchair for callers. Walker himself was closeted in an inner office which was separated from the rest of the room by a partition of opaque glass brick.

The utilitarian secretary told Tom to wait. It was extremely quiet. Neither of the two girls was typing, and although each had two telephones on her desk and an interoffice communication box, there was no ringing or buzzing. Both the secretaries sat reading typewritten sheets in black notebooks. After Tom had waited about half an hour, the pretty secretary, with no audible or visible cue, suddenly looked up brightly and said, "Mr. Walker will see you now. Just open the door and go in."

Tom opened the door and saw a fat pale man sitting in a high-backed upholstered chair behind a kidney-shaped desk with nothing on it but a blotter and pen. He was in his shirt sleeves, and he weighed about two hundred and fifty pounds. His face was as white as a marshmallow. He didn't stand up when Tom came in, but he smiled. It was a surprisingly warm, spontaneous smile, as though he had unexpectedly recognized an old friend. "Thomas Rath?" he said. "Sit down! Make yourself comfortable! Take off your coat!"

Tom thanked him and, although it wasn't particularly warm, took off his coat. There wasn't anyplace to put it, so, sitting down in the comfortable chair in front of Walker's desk, he laid the coat awkwardly across his lap.

"I've read the application forms you filled out, and it seems to me you might be qualified for a new position we may have opening up here," Walker said. "There are just a few questions I want to ask you." He was still smiling. Suddenly he touched a button on the arm of his chair and the back of the chair dropped, allowing him to recline, as though he were in an airplane seat. Tom could see only his face across the top of the desk.

"You will excuse me," Walker said, still smiling. "The doctor says I must get plenty of rest, and this is the way I do it."

Tom couldn't think of anything more appropriate to say than "It looks comfortable. . . ."

"Why do you want to work for the United Broadcasting Corporation?" Walker asked abruptly.

"It's a good company . . ." Tom began hesitantly, and was suddenly impatient at the need for hypocrisy. The sole reason he wanted to work for United Broadcasting was that he thought he might be able to make a lot of money there fast, but he felt he couldn't say that. It was sometimes considered fashionable for the employees of foundations to say that they were in it for the money, but people were supposed to work at advertising agencies and broadcasting companies for spiritual reasons.

"I believe," Tom said, "that television is developing into the greatest medium for mass education and entertainment. It has always fascinated me, and I would like to work with it. . . ."

"What kind of salary do you have in mind?" Walker asked. Tom hadn't expected the question that soon. Walker was still smiling.

"The salary isn't the primary consideration with me," Tom said, trying desperately to come up with stock answers to stock questions. "I'm mainly interested in finding something useful and worth while to do. I have personal responsibilities, however, and I would hope that something could be worked out to enable me to meet them. . . ."

"Of course," Walker said, beaming more cheerily than ever. "I understand you applied for a position in the public-relations department. Why did you choose that?"

Because I heard there was an opening, Tom wanted to say, but quickly thought better of it and substituted a halting avowal of lifelong interest in public relations. "I think my experience in working with *people* at the Schanenhauser Foundation would be helpful," he concluded lamely.

"I see," Walker said kindly. There was a short silence before he added, "Can you write?"

"I do most of the writing at the Schanenhauser Foundation," Tom said. "The annual report to the trustees is my job, and so are most of the reports on individual projects. I used to be editor of my college paper."

"That sounds fine," Walker said casually. "I have a little favor I want to ask of you. I want you to write me your autobiography."

"What?" Tom asked in astonishment.

"Nothing very long," Walker said. "Just as much as you can manage to type out in an hour. One of my girls will give you a room with a typewriter."

"Is there anything in particular you want me to tell you about?"

"Yourself," Walker said, looking hugely pleased. "Explain yourself to me. Tell me what kind of person you are. Explain why we should hire you."

"I'll try," Tom said weakly.

"You'll have precisely an hour," Walker said. "You see, this is a device I use in employing people—I find it most helpful. For this particular job, I have twenty or thirty applicants. It's hard to tell from a brief interview whom to choose, so I ask them all to write about themselves for an hour. You'd be surprised how revealing the results are. . . ."

He paused, still smiling. Tom said nothing.

"Just a few hints," Walker continued. "Write anything you want, but at the end of your last page, I'd like you to finish this sentence: 'The most significant fact about me is . . .' "

"The most significant fact about me is . . ." Tom repeated idiotically.

"The results, of course, will be entirely confidential." Walker lifted a bulky arm and inspected his wrist watch. "It's now five minutes to twelve," he concluded. "I'll expect your paper on my desk at precisely one o'clock."

Tom stood up, put on his coat, said, "Thank you," and went out of the room. The utilitarian secretary already had a stack of typewriting paper ready for him. She led him to a small room a few doors down the hall in which were a typewriter and a hard office chair. There was a large clock on the wall. The room had no windows. Across the ceiling was a glaring fluorescent light which made the bare white plaster walls look yellow. The secretary walked out without a word, shutting the door silently behind her.

Tom sat down in the chair, which had been designed for a stenog-

rapher and was far too small for him. Son of a bitch, he thought—
I guess the laws about cruel and unusual punishment don't apply to
personnel men. He tried to think of something to write, but all he
could remember was Betsy and the drab little house and the need to
buy a new washing machine, and the time he had thrown a vase that
cost forty dollars against the wall. "The most significant fact about
me is that I once threw a vase costing forty dollars against a wall."
That would be as sensible as anything else he could think of, but he
doubted whether it would get him the job. He thought of Janey saying, "It isn't *fair!*" and the worn linoleum on the kitchen floor. "The
most significant fact about me is . . ." It was a stupid sentence to
ask a man to finish.

I have children, he thought—that's probably the most significant
fact about me, the only one that will have much importance for
long. Anything about a man can be summed up in numbers. Thomas
R. Rath, thirty-three years old, making seven thousand dollars a
year, owner of a 1939 Ford, a six-room house, and ten thousand
dollars' worth of G.I. Life Insurance which, in case of his death,
would pay his widow about forty dollars a month. Six feet one and
a half inches tall; weight, 198 pounds. He served four and a half
years in the Army, most of it in Europe and the rest in the South
Pacific.

Another statistical fact came to him then, a fact which he knew
would be ridiculously melodramatic to put into an application for a
job at the United Broadcasting Corporation, or to think about at all.
He hadn't thought about this for a long while. It wasn't a thing he
had deliberately tried to forget—he simply hadn't thought about it
for quite a few years. It was the unreal-sounding, probably irrelevant,
but quite accurate fact that he had killed seventeen men.

It had been during the war, of course. He had been a paratrooper.
Lots of other people had killed more men than he had. Lots of
bomber crews and artillerymen had, but, of course, they never really
knew it. Lots of infantrymen and lots of paratroopers had, and most
of them knew it. Plenty of men had been dropped behind the enemy
lines, as Tom had been on five different occasions, and they had had
to do some of their killing silently, with blackjacks and knives. They

had known what they were doing, and most of them were healthy enough not to be morbid about it, and not to be proud of it, and not to be ashamed of it. Such things were merely part of the war, the war before the Korean one. It was no longer fashionable to talk about the war, and certainly it had never been fashionable to talk about the number of men one had killed. Tom couldn't forget the number, "seventeen," but it didn't seem real any more; it was just a small, isolated statistic that nobody wanted. His mind went blank. Suddenly the word "Maria" flashed into it.

"The most significant fact about me is that I . . . ."

Nonsense, he thought, and brought himself back to the present with a jerk. Only masochists can get along without editing their own memories. Maria was a girl he had known in Italy during the war, a long time ago, and he never thought about her any more, just as he never thought about the seventeen men he had killed. It wasn't always easy to forget, but it was certainly necessary to try.

"The most significant fact about me is that for four and a half years my profession was jumping out of airplanes with a gun, and now I want to go into public relations."

That probably wouldn't get him the job, Tom thought. "The most significant fact about me is that I detest the United Broadcasting Corporation, with all its soap operas, commercials, and yammering studio audiences, and the only reason I'm willing to spend my life in such a ridiculous enterprise is that I want to buy a more expensive house and a better brand of gin."

That certainly wouldn't get him the job.

"The most significant fact about me is that I've become a cheap cynic."

That would not be apt to get him the job.

"The most significant fact about me is that as a young man in college, I played the mandolin incessantly. I, champion mandolin player, am applying to you for a position in the public-relations department!"

That would not be likely to get him far. Impatiently he sat down at the typewriter and glanced at his wrist watch. It was a big loud-ticking wrist watch with a black face, luminous figures, and a red sweep hand that rapidly ticked off the seconds. He had bought it years ago at an Army post exchange and had worn it all through the war. The watch was the closest thing to a good-luck charm he had ever had, although he never thought of it as such. Now it was more reassuring to look at than the big impersonal clock on the wall, though both said it was almost twelve-thirty. So far he had written nothing. What the hell, he thought. I was a damn fool to think I wanted to work here anyway. Then he thought of Betsy asking, as she would be sure to, "Did you get the job? How did it go?" And he decided to try.

"Anybody's life can be summed up in a paragraph," he wrote. "I was born on November 20, 1920, in my grandmother's house in South Bay, Connecticut. I was graduated from Covington Academy in 1937, and from Harvard College in 1941. I spent four and a half years in the Army, reaching the rank of captain. Since 1946, I have been employed as an assistant to the director of the Schanenhauser Foundation. I live in Westport, Connecticut, with my wife and three children. From the point of view of the United Broadcasting Corporation, the most significant fact about me is that I am applying for a position in its public-relations department, and after an initial period of learning, I probably would do a good job. I will be glad to answer any questions which seem relevant, but after considerable thought, I have decided that I do not wish to attempt an autobiogra phy as part of an application for a job."

He typed this paragraph neatly in the precise center of a clean piece of paper, added his name and address, and carried it into Walker's office. It was only quarter to one, and Walker was obviously surprised to see him. "You've still got fifteen minutes!" he said.

"I've written all I think is necessary," Tom replied, and handed him the almost empty page.

Walker read it slowly, his big pale face expressionless. When he had finished it, he dropped it into a drawer. "We'll let you know our decision in a week or so," he said.

4

"How did the interview go?" Betsy asked him that night as soon as he got off the train. "Tell me *all* about it!"

"I don't know," Tom said. "I wouldn't get my hopes up. I'm one of about forty people being considered."

"You'll get it," she said. "I'm *sure* you will."

"Don't get your hopes up."

"I talked to a real-estate agent today," she replied. "He said we could probably get fifteen thousand dollars for our house, maybe more. And he's got some *wonderful* places selling for about thirty thousand!"

"For Pete's sake!" Tom said. "Aren't you rushing things a little?"

"It doesn't do any harm to *plan*, does it?" she asked with an injured air.

"You better just pretend nothing's happened at all," he said. "Then you won't be disappointed if nothing does happen."

Tom tried not to think about the interview with Walker. Probably it would be a week or two before he heard from United Broadcasting, he figured, but as things turned out, a letter from Walker arrived at Westport only three days later. Betsy took it from the mailman, ripped it open, and immediately called Tom at the Schanenhauser Foundation. "It's here!" she said. "The mailman just brought it! Walker wants to see you at eleven o'clock next Tuesday for another interview."

"Fine," Tom said noncommittally.

"That means things must be getting pretty serious, doesn't it? I mean, they wouldn't want to see you again if you didn't make a pretty good impression last time."

"Maybe."

"Don't be stuffy," Betsy said. "I feel like celebrating. Tonight we're going to have steak and sparkling Burgundy, and to hell with the cost."

She hung up before he could object. She's probably right about one thing, he thought—I don't think Walker would want to see me if he didn't have anything for me. It was time to talk to Dick Haver, his boss at the foundation, Tom concluded.

Dick Haver was a tall, tweedy man who had been a college professor. "Why do you want to leave?" he asked Tom that afternoon when Tom had explained the situation.

"Money," Tom said. "I have three children and I need more money than I think I can make here in the immediate future."

Haver smiled wanly. "How much do you think you need?" he asked.

"I'd like ten thousand," Tom said. "And later, I'd like to think I could make more."

"You could here—in time," Haver said.

"How much time?"

"Five or six years maybe. Up to now, you've been doing fairly well."

"I'd like a place where there would be more opportunity for rapid advancement," Tom said.

"Don't make your decision too quickly," Haver replied. "I'll talk the matter over with some of the others here, and we'll see if we can do a little more for you. I'm not at all sure you'd like it over at United Broadcasting."

"Why not?"

"It's just a feeling I have," Haver said. "Think it over and make your own decision, of course."

"Nuts!" Betsy exclaimed that night when Tom told her about his conversation with Haver. "The old goat is just trying to hang onto you! He'll come up with an offer of some piddling raise you should have gotten two years ago, and every time you want another one, you'll have to threaten to quit!"

She sipped her sparkling Burgundy reflectively a moment. "You know what you ought to do now?" she said. "You ought to go have a talk with Grandmother. After all, she told you about the job at the foundation in the first place, and she might have ways of finding out whether Haver really will have anything big for you. Anyway, she ought to know you're thinking about leaving—she'd be hurt if she found out about it from anyone else."

"I guess so," Tom said reluctantly. "I'll take a run up to see her Saturday."

Early Saturday morning he drove to South Bay alone, because by that time all three of the children had chicken pox and Betsy had to stay with them. South Bay is a small town not far from Stamford. When Tom approached it, he got a curious feeling of home-coming which was still strong, despite all the years that had passed since he had lived there. The wide, elm-shaded main street had changed since the war. Brightly painted one-story houses filled the fields where Tom had hunted rabbits as a boy, and even the old nine-hole golf course had miraculously become something called "Shoreline Estates," in spite of the fact that it was a good two miles inland. The road leading from the main street to his grandmother's house had changed little, however. The great brick and stone mansions were not quite so well kept as they had been when Tom had ridden his bicycle past them, but they still seemed comfortable, solid, and much more permanent than the recently built structures on the golf course, which looked as though they were quite capable of disappearing as quickly as they had come. At the end of a row of big houses, the road narrowed and started up a steep hill. The old Ford groaned as Tom shifted it into second gear. There were two sharp turns in the road made necessary by massive outcroppings of rock which gave the hill the appearance of a mountain. It was on the second of these turns that Tom's father, Stephen Rath, had been killed thirty years ago, before Tom was old enough to remember him. Stephen Rath had been driving down the road very late one night at what must have been a vicious speed and had slammed into the rock so hard that his automobile had been completely demolished. Tom had never found why his father had been driving down that narrow road so fast at such an odd hour, and long ago he had learned to stop wondering about it. Now as he passed the rock, he glanced away from it, as he had ever since, at the age of five, he learned that it was the place where his father had been killed.

Stone posts topped by iron urns three feet high marked the entrance to the driveway of his grandmother's house. Beyond them were the carriage house, which itself was bigger than Tom's home in Westport, and the rock garden in which his mother and he had spent so many sunny mornings long ago. In the corner of the rock garden stood a heavy stone bench, now almost entirely surrounded by bushes which once had been kept neatly trimmed. At the sight of it, Tom was beset by the same old mixture of emotions from which he always suffered when he visited the place, as though each object there were possessed of a special ghost which leaped out at him as soon as he passed through the gates. His mother had spent countless afternoons sitting on that bench and watching him as he played. Once, when he was about seven years old, he had noticed two lines of verse carved in bold script across the back of the bench. With his forefinger he had traced out the letters grooved in the warm stone and had asked his mother what they meant. Now, almost thirty years later, he could still remember the bitterness in her voice as she read: "The lark's on the wing; the snail's on the thorn: God's in his heaven—all's right with the world!"

He looked quickly away from the bench which had become so strangely surrounded by bushes, and continued along the driveway. It led to the top of the hill, on the highest point of which was the old mansion itself, a tall Victorian structure with a tower at one end that had been designed to appear even larger and more grandiose than it was. The wind that almost always blew there seemed full of voices.

"It's a dwarfed castle," he remembered his mother saying bitterly the year before she died of pneumonia, when he was fifteen years old. "When your father first took me here before we were engaged, he joked about dwarfs in armor behind the parapets at the top of the tower. . . ."

"Here, it's for you!" he remembered another voice saying, the voice of his grandmother. She had been holding a beautifully polished, old-fashioned, deep-bellied mandolin out to him—he couldn't have been more than ten or twelve years old at the time. "Your father used to play it," she had said. "Maybe you'd like to learn."

Now Tom paused at the top of the hill. There was a breath-taking view of Long Island Sound, with the bright water mottled by the shadows of clouds. The grass on both sides of the driveway had grown long. Looking at it, Tom remembered the days when it had been kept as carefully as a putting green and felt the first pang of the rising annoyance he feared every time he went there, the rage at his grandmother's refusal to sell the place, and her calm willingness to pour into it what little was left of the money she had inherited from her husband and father.

"I love this place, and I'll keep it as long as I can pay the taxes on it," she had said when, shortly after the war, Tom had suggested that she move.

He left his car by the front door. Edward, a tall old man who long ago had served as her butler and now acted as a man of all work, let him in. "Good morning, Mr. Rath," he said deferentially. "Mrs. Rath is waiting for you in the sunroom."

Tom found his grandmother seated in an armchair, dressed in a long white gown. In her hand was a gnarled black walnut cane which looked almost like an extension of her withered fingers. She was ninety-three years old.

"Tommy!" she said when she saw him, and leaned eagerly forward in her chair.

"Don't get up, Grandmother," he said. "It's good to see you."

The old lady peered at him sharply. He was shocked at how much she had aged during the past two months, or perhaps it was just that he persisted in remembering her as a younger woman and was surprised now, each time he saw her. And she in turn was shocked to see Tom, whom she remembered as a young boy. She continued to stare at him, her old eyes bright and disarmingly kind.

"You look tired, Tommy," she said suddenly.

"I feel fine."

"You're getting a little stout," she said bluntly.

"I'm getting older, Grandmother."

"You ought to go riding more," she said. "The Senator always said riding is the best exercise. He used to ride for an hour almost every morning."

There it was, her terrible projection of the past into the present, which was more a deliberate refusal to face change than a passive acquiescence to senility. And there too was her elaborate myth about the Rath family's accomplishments. "The Senator" was the phrase she always used for her dead husband, Tom's grandfather, who had served one term as a State Senator in Hartford during his early youth, and who had spent most of the rest of his life doing absolutely nothing.

"I've got a few things I want to talk over with you," Tom began, trying to change the subject.

"You mustn't get stout," the old lady went on relentlessly. "Your father never got stout. Stephen was always slender."

"Yes, Grandmother," he said. Sometimes he imagined that she deliberately dwelt upon painful subjects, for she enjoyed talking about his father with him, presenting a caricature of a hero, elaborated by all kinds of distorted facts, hidden among which Tom often caught glimpses of what he suspected were unpleasant truths. What were the facts about his father? Tom had had to piece them together from trifles. "I don't know why, but Stephen never played the mandolin after the war," the old lady had told him once long ago. "At college he was in the Mandolin Club, and even as a boy he played beautifully, but after the war he never did it any more."

His father had been a second lieutenant during the First World War. He had been sent home from France several weeks before the Armistice for unexplained reasons and had for a while worked with a large investment firm in New York. As far as Tom could make out from the dim echoes of rumor which survived, Stephen Rath had either quit work or been fired about two years before he died, and during his remaining days had simply lived a life of leisure in the big house with his wife, mother, and son. Presumably he had not been happy; he had never played the mandolin any more. Tom suspected that there must have been quite a chain of events leading up to the night when Stephen had backed his Packard out of the carriage house and careened down the road to the waiting rocks at the turn. But of all this Tom could learn nothing from his grandmother's conversation. According to the old lady, Stephen had been a great military hero, and over the years she had advanced him by her own automatic laws of seniority to the rank of major.

"I hear you're getting ahead very well at the foundation," the old lady was saying now.

"I think I may leave the foundation, Grandmother," he said. "That's what I want to talk to you about."

"Leave? Why?"

How difficult it was to explain to an old lady who had never earned a penny in her life, and who had never even bothered to conserve what she had inherited, that he needed more money! He said, "I may have an opportunity offered me that's too good to turn down."

"I was telling Mrs. Gliden the other day how well you're doing at the foundation," the old lady said. "I told her it might not be long before you were chosen as director. I hear that man Haver may be leaving."

"Where did you hear that?"

"I don't remember," the old lady said. "There is a rumor. . . ."

That was the trouble—he never could be sure whether his grandmother was simply ensnaring him in her dreams of family glory, or whether the old connections with prominent people which she treasured so carefully actually resulted in useful information. But on the face of it, the thought that he might be chosen to head the Schanenhauser Foundation was ridiculous, regardless of whether Haver was leaving or not. There were at least twenty people who would be chosen first.

"Are you thinking of going into government?" the old lady asked unexpectedly.

"No—I'm thinking of going into business."

"Your great-grandfather was very successful in business," she said. "At one time he owned a fleet of twenty-eight vessels. Are you going into shipping?"

"No," Tom said. "This will be a little different, Grandmother. There's nothing definite about it yet, but I've mentioned it to Dick Haver, and I thought you ought to know."

"I'm sorry you have to go into business," she said soberly, "but I suppose it's necessary. Business is such a bore—The Major never could stand it, and neither could The Senator. But I suppose it's necessary. Come, let's talk about something more cheerful. How do you think the place looks?"

"Fine," he said.

"I can't afford to keep the lawns up, but the house itself is in as good repair as ever."

"It looks beautiful."

"I hope that when I go, you and Betsy will be able to live here," she said. "I'm trying to keep it up for you. I don't want you to mention it to a soul, but I had to take a small mortgage on the place to have the roof fixed and to have an oil furnace put in. Edward is getting old, and he can't shovel coal any more."

A furnace, Tom thought—I'll bet that the price of a furnace for this place would send all three of my kids through a year of college. He felt the old double, contradictory anger rising in him, the familiar fury at his grandmother for dissipating money which ordinarily would come to him eventually, and the accompanying disgust at himself for lusting after an old lady's money. He tried to feel the gratitude which, after all, was due the person who had brought him up, and paid for his education, and treated him with kindness and love.

"She's selfish, but I could forgive her that," Tom remembered his mother saying about the old lady. "What I can't forgive is the arrogance, and the deliberate pretenses she inflicted on her son, and everyone around her. Poor Steve was raised on lies. . . ."

His mother hadn't been talking to him when she had said that; she had been talking to a minister who visited her quite often after her husband's death, and the minister had noticed that Tom, who was only twelve years old then, had come into the room, and he had said, "Hush—the boy's here. How are you, Tom? It won't be long before you'll be going to high school!"

Now Tom wondered whether he should try to work with the old lady's lawyer to straighten out whatever might be left of her estate. When he had come home from the war, he had, after tortuous examination of his own motives, asked his grandmother whether he could help manage things for her, and she had turned him down abruptly. She had never mentioned money to him in all the years he had lived with her, except to say that it didn't matter, that it was a frightful bore.

"If you want any help, let me know," he said now. "I don't think it's wise for you to be taking out mortgages—there might be ways to avoid it."

"The bank was very helpful," she said. "I haven't got many more years to go, and I think the lawyer has arranged for me to be taken care of quite nicely. The important thing is to keep this house in shape for you and Betsy."

"I doubt whether we'll be able to afford such a place," he said. "Not many people can these days."

"Nonsense!" she replied. "You're going into business, aren't you? Perhaps you'll be able to improve it. The Senator always wanted to put another wing on the south side of the house. Come, and I'll show you where."

She walked with astonishing agility and pointed with her cane to show just where the billiard room should go, and a glass-walled conservatory for raising orchids.

There were really four completely unrelated worlds in which he lived, Tom reflected as he drove the old Ford back to Westport. There was the crazy, ghost-ridden world of his grandmother and his dead parents. There was the isolated, best-not-remembered world in which he had been a paratrooper. There was the matter-of-fact, opaque-glass-brick-partitioned world of places like the United Broadcasting Company and the Schanenhauser Foundation. And there was the entirely separate world populated by Betsy and Janey and Barbara and Pete, the only one of the four worlds worth a damn. There must be some way in which the four worlds were related, he thought, but it was easier to think of them as entirely divorced from one another.

5

THE FOLLOWING TUESDAY Tom left the Schanenhauser Foundation at ten-thirty in the morning to keep his appointment with Walker. It was not necessary for him to give any excuse for leaving his desk, but he felt vaguely guilty as he told his secretary he probably wouldn't be back until noon. He walked quickly up Fifth Avenue and across Rockefeller Plaza, so preoccupied with his own thoughts that he hardly noticed the people he passed. When he got inside the United Broadcasting building, a starter wearing a fancy, silver-braided cap directed him into one of the waiting gold-colored elevators.

"Floor please?" the elevator operator said. He spoke in a deep voice with a slight Italian accent. Tom glanced at him. The man was wearing a plum-colored uniform and had his back turned toward him. He was a stout, dark-complexioned man about thirty years old with thick black hair only partly covered by a plum-colored cap shaped like an army overseas cap. Across the back of his thick neck, just visible above his collar, was a long, thin white scar. There was something startlingly familiar about the slope of his narrow shoulders and the deep voice. Tom stepped to one side to get a better look at him, but the elevator was getting crowded, and he couldn't see the front of the man's face.

"Floor please?" the elevator man repeated as people filed into the car. "Floor please?"

"Thirty-six," Tom said. The man turned toward him, and their eyes met. The elevator operator's face was fat, almost round, and he had a thin, incongruously dapper mustache. His eyes were black and unblinking. He stared at Tom for several seconds. There might have been a quickly suppressed flicker of recognition, but Tom couldn't be sure. The face seemed impassive. Tom looked away. The elevator doors rumbled shut, and the machine shot upward. There was an instant of silence before it stopped, and the doors rumbled open. Tom started to get out.

"This is twenty," the operator said in his deep voice.

Tom edged back into the elevator. When he got out at his floor, he felt oddly flustered. Down the hall he saw a men's room and went there to wash his face and comb his hair before going to see Walker. It was absurd to attach such importance to a chance encounter with an elevator man. Even if it were someone he had known, what possible difference could it make?

A few minutes later Tom found Walker reclining as usual in his adjustable chair. Sitting in front of Walker's desk was a handsome, angular man whom Walker introduced as Bill Ogden. Ogden shook hands with Tom rather stiffly and said almost nothing during the remainder of the interview. Apparently he was there simply as an observer.

"We've gone over your qualifications and are now prepared to talk in more specific terms," Walker said, smiling cheerily. "I think I should begin by saying that this isn't just an ordinary job in the public-relations department we're considering. What we're looking for is a young man to work with Mr. Hopkins, the president of the company, on a special project. . . ."

He paused, apparently expecting Tom to say something. "That sounds very interesting," Tom said.

Walker nodded. "As a matter of fact, this position wouldn't really be with United Broadcasting at all, except in a purely technical sense," he continued. "You would be working directly for Mr. Hopkins on an outside project completely unrelated to the company. One reason we think you might be suited for the job is that you would be working quite closely with the foundations. We hope that the project will eventually be sponsored by the foundations."

"Just what kind of a project is it?"

"Mr. Hopkins has been asked to start a national committee on mental health," Walker said.

There was a brief silence, during which Tom heard a fire engine, deprived of its siren because of the need to reserve the sirens for air raid warnings, go chortling down the street far below, uttering shrill but unsirenlike mechanical screams. "A committee on mental health?" he asked stupidly.

"Mr. Hopkins plans to get together forty or fifty national leaders from many different fields and devise a program to encourage people all over the United States to work for mental health," Walker said.

"What kind of a program?" Tom asked incredulously.

"We don't know yet. Perhaps it will be a drive for better mental hospitals, or community guidance clinics. Something which would do for mental disease what the March of Dimes has done for polio."

"Sounds like a good idea," Tom said, realizing he was expected to register enthusiasm.

"What Mr. Hopkins wants now is a young man to begin helping him with research for the speeches he will have to make to kick the project off. Later he will want someone to help him draw up a prospectus for an organization and to start getting the people together. Are you interested?"

"I certainly am!" Tom said heartily. "I've always been interested in mental health!" That sounded a little foolish, but he could think of nothing to rectify it.

"This wouldn't be a very high-paying job," Walker continued. "We were thinking of a figure somewhere near seven thousand dollars."

Tom knew then that Walker had talked to Dick Haver at the foundation and learned what he had been making. The union of bosses is the most powerful union in the world.

"I'd been hoping for more than that," he said. "Ordinarily, salary wouldn't be an important consideration for me, especially in connection with a job of this kind, but I have increasing personal responsibilities. I feel I should be making ten thousand dollars a year."

"Wouldn't that be quite a jump from your present position?" Walker asked bluntly. Ogden, who had been sitting almost motionless, put his hand in his pocket and took out a package of cigarettes.

"It would," Tom said, "but there would have to be considerable incentive for me to leave the foundation."

Walker, lolling comfortably in his chair, glanced at Ogden, who had just finished lighting a cigarette.

"We don't have to make any decisions now," Ogden said, in a casual, almost bored voice.

Walker nodded. "Perhaps the next step would be to have him meet Mr. Hopkins," he said to Ogden, as though Tom were not in the room.

"All right," Ogden said.

"Could you have lunch with Mr. Hopkins at twelve-thirty, day after tomorrow?" Walker asked.

"Certainly," Tom said.

"Meet me here, and I'll take you up and introduce you," Walker concluded.

Tom thanked him and hurried out of his office. When he got in the elevator, he glanced at the operator, but it was a thin man he had never seen before. In a telephone booth in the enormous lobby downstairs he called Bill Hawthorne, who had told him about the job in the first place. "Come on down and give me some briefing," he said. "I'm supposed to have lunch with Hopkins day after tomorrow!"

"With Hopkins!" Bill said in an awed voice. "Say, for a guy who hasn't even been hired yet, you're doing all right!"

They went to a bar two doors down the street and ordered Martinis. "Now tell me all about your boy Hopkins," Tom said. "Walker tells me he's starting a project on mental health. What's it all about?"

Bill sipped his drink thoughtfully. "What do you already know about Hopkins?" he asked.

"Not much," Tom said. "I've hardly heard of him. Somebody told me he started with nothing and he's making two hundred thousand a year now. That's about all I know—I don't think I've ever even seen a picture of him."

"Precisely," Bill said professionally. "Precisely."

"What the hell do you mean by that?"

"I mean it looks like the public-relations boys have cooked up a big deal to put Hopkins on the map, and you've stumbled into it."

"I don't get it," Tom said.

"Figure it out for yourself. Here's Hopkins, about fifty years old, and the president of the United Broadcasting Corporation. As you say, he makes about two hundred thousand dollars a year, and that doesn't count stock deals and all the rest of it. Inside the company he's the biggest shot in the world. The top comedians and all the famous actors are scared to death of him. But outside the company he's nothing. Taxi drivers don't call him "Sir." Waiters in restaurants more than five blocks from Radio Center don't give him a special table. Little boys don't gape at him. Don't you see how tough it must be?"

"I'm weeping," Tom said.

"All right. Here's a guy who works fifteen or twenty hours a day —inside the company he's famous for it. He's a regular *machine* for work. And he's competent. Give him almost any business, and he'd double the profit in a year. And people like him—he knows how to drive people and still make them like him. But what's he get out of life?"

"Money."

"Of course! But if he made only a quarter as much money, he'd still be able to buy everything he wants. Hopkins is a guy of simple tastes. He has only one or two places in the country, and a small yacht, and three automobiles. He was able to afford all that long ago and could go on affording it if he quit work tomorrow. So what's he keep working fifteen or twenty hours a day for?"

"Must be nuts," Tom said.

"Nuts nothing! The poor son of a bitch wants fame! And he's in a position to buy it. So he calls in Ogden and Walker and says, 'Boys, make me famous. One year from today I want to be famous, or you're fired!' "

"Oh come on," Tom said, laughing. "You know damn well that's nonsense."

"Perhaps it wouldn't work that way exactly," Bill said, obviously enjoying himself. "He'd say, 'Gentlemen, I believe that for the sake of the company, the major executives must direct more attention to their personal public relations, and I hope that in the immediate future we can work something out.' "

"I doubt like hell that a man in his position would say that either."

"Okay—be a stickler for detail. What would really happen is that somebody would suggest that Hopkins head a committee on mental health—these guys are asked to do that sort of thing all the time

Usually they refuse. But this time Hopkins figures he's got a chance for the national spotlight. You're right about one thing—he'd never say anything about it. He wouldn't have to. He'd call in Walker and Ogden, and they're paid enough to *know* what he's thinking without being told. The only thing they'd all say is that it's every citizen's duty to do something about mental-health problems. They'd be nauseatingly noble about it. But all the time they'd know damn well they were doing it to give Hopkins a shot of publicity, and that's the reason why you, my boy, will be on the United Broadcasting Corporation's pay roll, and why every cent that Hopkins spends on this project will come off his company expense account!"

"Why mental health?" Tom asked. "Why a subject like that?"

"Figure it out for yourself. What would you do to make Hopkins famous? You can't play up the success he's had in business, because nobody much cares, and because newspapers and magazines don't like to publicize radio and television companies any more than they have to—they're all in competition for advertising. You've got to play up something about his personal life, not his business. And you can't have him marrying chorus girls, or winning a prize for water skiing—you've got to keep it dignified. What would you do?"

"All right, I'll give the answer you want," Tom said. "I'd advise him to start a national committee on mental health, or some other public-service thing, and I'd publicize hell out of it."

"Precisely," Bill replied, finishing his drink and ordering another one. "You would follow the newest maxim of the public-relations boys: 'If you want good publicity, do something good!' It's all very profound. Want another drink?"

"I think I'd better stay sober," Tom said. "And I also think there's something wrong in your theory."

"You're going to be a *good* public-relations man!" Bill said admiringly. "You're defending him already!"

"Nuts!" Tom replied. "I just want to take all the possibilities into account. You say he's doing this because he wants publicity—yet all his life, he's apparently detested publicity. Certainly he could have had it long before now if he'd wanted it. Why has he waited all this time, and what's made him change?"

"All right, all right, there may be more to all this than meets the eye," Bill said. "Maybe he personally doesn't want publicity. But maybe the board of directors is worried about the bad name the company's getting by making the television shows just as bad as the radio programs. There's been a rumor going around lately that United Broadcasting is just trying to make money and is half-hearted about improving people's minds. One thing the company could do is actually to improve the programs, but it would be cheaper to tell all the company's top executives, and particularly the president, to go out and acquire a reputation for doing good. After all, Hopkins will always be identified as the president of the United Broadcasting Corporation, and if he's doing something good, and kind of intellectual, that would be about the least expensive way the company could get respectable."

"Maybe," Tom said.

"Or perhaps it's more complicated," Bill continued. "Hopkins has had a taste of power inside the company. Maybe he likes it and wants more. He can't get any more inside the company. So it's just possible that he's made up his mind to go into politics. He'd have to do some public-service thing first—right now he'd be political poison. But after he was known all over the country as the man who started the very successful mental-health committee, who knows? You may be the first campaign man in the Hopkins-for-President drive!"

"Haven't we left one possibility out?" Tom asked.

"What?"

"That he might be sincere. That he might want to do some good. That after concentrating on his personal fortune all these years, he may have come to the point where he wants to do something for the public welfare, with no strings attached."

"It's possible," Bill said doubtfully. "But it would be awfully dull if it were true!"

"Do you really know him?" Tom asked. "Do you really know what kind of a guy he is?"

"Hell," Bill said. "I've been working for this damn outfit for four years, and I've never laid eyes on the guy. There are all kinds of stories about him—they used to say he had two children and had been home twice in the last twenty years. I think his son was killed during the war—anyway, nobody talks about that any more. They say he needs less sleep than Edison did. They say he's got his whole filing system memorized, practically, and can quote from any important letter or contract in it. Some say he's got a little blond girl on Park Avenue. Some say he's sleeping with some actress who flies in from Hollywood once a month. I've even heard it said that he's queer. But nobody who passes that stuff around really knows him. The only people I know who actually work with him are Walker and Ogden, and of course they never talk about him. To tell the honest truth, I have no idea in the world what kind of man he is, except he must be pretty damn smart to be where he is."

"He ought to be interesting to work for," Tom said.

"Maybe," Bill replied, "but I ought to tell you one more thing: everybody says he's tough as hell. If you can't do what he wants, he'll fire you without batting an eye. I don't *know* that's true, mind you, but it's what everybody says."

"Sounds fair enough, if you can do what he wants," Tom said. "If you do it real well, is he quick with the raises?"

"I don't know. You'd be surprised how a company this size can pinch pennies—they even got an order out the other day cautioning us all to put our office lights out when we weren't using them and asking us to quit stealing pencils. But I'd say it's always a good bet to work for a man making two hundred thousand a year. At least you've got a long way to go before you start competing with the boss!"

"If I can get the job, I think I'll take it," Tom said.

Bill finished his drink and lit a cigarette. "If you don't, you're crazy," he said.

6

Tom thought Betsy would be excited when she heard he had a luncheon date with the president of United Broadcasting, but as soon as he stepped into his house that night he knew something was wrong. The house looked as though a herd of wild horses had stampeded through it. Soiled laundry was scattered about the living room. In the kitchen a mixture of dirty luncheon and breakfast dishes littered the table and counters.

"Betsy!" he called from the living room. "Where are you?"

"Up here," she said in a weak voice.

He raced up the stairs and found her lying fully clothed on the bed. "What's the matter?" he asked.

"I feel awful," she replied. "It hit me right after you left this morning, but I didn't want to call you up and bother you. Go see if the kids are all right."

He stepped into the room the three children shared. The beds were unmade, and a tangle of clothes and toys littered the floor. The three children were crouched over a glass of water paint. Pete was naked, and Barbara and Janey wore only underclothes. All three showed the ravages of chicken pox on both their faces and bodies, but they glanced up at Tom cheerfully.

"Momma's sick," Janey said delightedly. "We've been taking care of her."

"You're not very well yourself," Tom said. "You're supposed to be in bed."

"We're *painting!*" Janey said indignantly.

Tom went through some drawers and got them pajamas. He helped them put the pajamas on and tucked them into bed before returning to Betsy.

"I went to sleep," Betsy said. "I was trying to keep an eye on them, but I went to sleep. They've really been angels—I told them I wasn't feeling well, and they've been talking in whispers all day."

Tom felt her forehead and found it was dry and hot. He searched through the medicine cabinet in the bathroom and returned carrying a thermometer.

"You're sure that's the one you're supposed to put in your *mouth?*" Betsy asked suspiciously.

"Sure," he said. "Stick it under your tongue."

While they were waiting the required two minutes, Janey suddenly called in a loud clear voice, "Daddy, is Momma going to die?"

"No," he said.

"Well, if she *does* die," Janey continued speculatively, "who will take care of us?"

"She's not going to die!" Tom said.

"But if she did . . ."

"I'm not going to!" Betsy blurted, trying to keep her lips closed around the thermometer.

"Anyway," Janey said, "I guess Grandmother would take care of us, wouldn't she?"

"Don't worry about me, kids," Betsy said. "I'm going to be fine." She held the thermometer up to the light.

"What is it?" Tom asked.

"A hundred and three."

"Have you ever had chicken pox?"

"Oh, God!" she said. "Of course, I must have had it! All children get it!"

"Do you remember having it?"

"Not exactly," she said. "I just assumed . . ."

"We better call the doctor," he said.

He telephoned Dr. Grantland. He always disliked calling him, because although Dr. Grantland was only about forty-five years old, he suffered from rheumatism and asthma, and it always seemed a shame to bother him. After the telephone had buzzed for a long while, the doctor answered wheezily.

"Do you want me to come over?" he asked after Tom had described Betsy's symptoms.

"If it isn't too much trouble," Tom said.

The doctor wheezed alarmingly before saying bravely, "All right, all right. I guess I can make it."

While they were waiting for the doctor, Tom told Betsy he had a luncheon engagement with Hopkins. "Who's he?" she asked.

"The president of United Broadcasting."

"That's nice," she said weakly. "Oh, Tommy, my head hurts!"

"What are we going to have for supper?" Barbara called. "Mother just gave us soup for lunch and we're hungry!"

"I'll get you supper in a few minutes," Tom said. "The doctor is coming to see Mother."

"Is he going to give her a needle?" Janey asked enthusiastically.

"I don't know."

"If he does, can we watch?"

"No!" Tom said. "You stay in bed."

"I can't stand it," Betsy said. "Chicken pox! Why didn't I get it when I was a child?"

"You won't be very sick," Tom said.

"I will too! And I know why I didn't get it when I was a child— because Mother took such damn good care of me. She never let me play with other children because she was afraid I'd catch something."

"I don't see why we can't watch her get the needle," Janey called. "She always watches when the doctor gives it to *us!*"

"Quiet!" Tom said. "I'm going downstairs and pick up a little before the doctor comes."

He threw the dirty laundry down the cellar stairs, then went to the kitchen and mixed himself a Martini. Before he had finished it, the doorbell rang, and Dr. Grantland was there.

"Oh, dear," he said as Tom let him in, "I think this asthma of mine is getting worse every day."

"I'm terribly sorry," Tom said. "Betsy's upstairs. Can I carry your bag for you?"

"No," he said bravely. "I can manage."

Tom followed him upstairs. The doctor sat down on a chair beside the bed, opened his bag, and took out a nebulizer with which he sprayed his own throat. "Ah," he said gratefully. "That certainly helps."

"My head hurts and I have a temperature of a hundred and three and I feel awful," Betsy said. "Tom thinks I have chicken pox."

"Have you ever had it before?" the doctor asked.

At that moment the three children came into the room, their scabbed faces wreathed in smiles. "Are you going to give her a needle?" Janey asked.

"Heavens!" the doctor said, and started to wheeze. "You certainly have been exposed!"

"I guess I never had chicken pox," Betsy said grumpily. "Mother always kept me away from other children, and I never got *anything.*"

"Remove your upper clothing," the doctor said.

"Are you going to give her a needle?" Janey repeated.

"Go back to bed!" Betsy ordered. "This minute!"

"I'll stay in your room with you and tell you a story," Tom said to the children. "Get in there now, and I'll be right in."

The children withdrew to their own room. Tom ducked downstairs, grabbed his drink, and joined them.

"Tell us about Bubbley," Barbara said.

Long ago he had made up a story about a little dog named Bubbley who swallowed a cake of soap and blew bubbles when he barked. Barbara always wanted it recited over and over again in precisely the same words he had used the first time.

"There was this little dog named Bubbley," he began wearily, after taking a long sip from his glass.

"No!" Barbara said. *"Once upon a time* there was a little dog named Bubbley."

"All right," he said irritably. "Don't interrupt."

"Well, tell it *right!*" Barbara said.

Pete, who was only four years old, looked at his father solemnly with his thumb in his mouth. "I *hate* the story about Bubbley," he said quietly to himself.

"You keep still!" Barbara said venomously to him.

"One day he swallowed a cake of soap," Tom said. "And ever after that . . ."

Before he had finished the story, the door opened, and Dr. Grantland came in. "I guess she's got chicken pox all right," he said. "Could you give me a glass of water?"

"Sure," Tom said, "but before you go, could you take a look at the kids?"

The doctor glanced at the children with distaste. "I'm not a pediatrician," he said.

"I know," Tom replied. "We had a pediatrician look at them two days ago, but I thought that since you were here . . ."

"I only look at children in emergencies," the doctor said. "All my patients have to be twelve years old or more."

"I'll get you a glass of water," Tom said.

The doctor followed him downstairs. When Tom gave him a glass of water, he slipped a pill into his mouth and swallowed it.

"Thank you," he said gravely. "Now about Mrs. Rath. All we can do is let this thing run its course. Here are some prescriptions which will help a little, but there's not a great deal we can do. Make sure she gets plenty of rest. She should stay in bed for a week, maybe more."

"I'll try to find someone to look after the kids," Tom said.

Two hours later, when the children had had their supper and the house was cleaned up, Tom started telephoning to find a woman to act as housekeeper. No one he knew was available, but an elderly woman named Mrs. Manter who was recommended by a friend said that as a special favor she would come for sixty dollars a week, provided Tom would call for her in his car not earlier than nine in the morning and take her home not later than six in the afternoon. That would mean he would not be able to get to work until eleven in the morning and would have to leave the office at four o'clock in the afternooon, and it would also mean that the family budget would have to be scrapped, but there was no choice. He hoped Dick Haver wouldn't think he was just taking it easy because he expected to get a new job.

The next morning Mrs. Manter turned out to be a stern-faced farm woman about sixty-five years old who weighed at least two hundred pounds and had a voice without any volume control.

"I'm awfully glad you could come," Tom said when he picked her up. "You know how it is when the woman of a family gets sick and there are sick children to be cared for."

"DON'T TELL ME!" she thundered. "I HAD EIGHT KIDS MYSELF, AND ONCE WHEN THEY WAS ALL DOWN WITH MEASLES, I BROKE MY LEG!"

"Why, that's terrible," Tom said.

"MY HUSBAND WAS AWAY," she said so loudly that he immediately made up his mind she was deaf and couldn't hear herself.

"WHAT DID YOU DO?" he yelled.

"YOU DON'T HAVE TO SPEAK SO LOUDLY!" she shouted back. "I can hear! I just put my knee on a chair and tied it that way. Found I could get around the house quite well, dragging the chair with me."

Tom drove her quickly to his house, introduced her to Betsy, who looked dazed, and rushed for the train.

7

WHEN HE GOT TO HIS OFFICE he explained to Dick Haver why he was going to have to keep the hours of the semiretired during the next two weeks.

"That's all right, Tom," Dick said pleasantly. "I understand. By the way, some of the people over at United Broadcasting called me up the other day to ask about you. Anything definite developed there yet?"

"I haven't made up my mind what to do," Tom said, figuring he'd better leave an opportunity to say he didn't want to go to United Broadcasting if Hopkins ended by not wanting to hire him.

"We'd like to keep you here if we could," Dick said, "but I don't want to try to influence you too much. There are a few things you might want to take into account when you make your decision, however."

"I certainly would appreciate any advice. . . ."

"If you stay here, you can expect fairly steady small salary increases," Dick said. "If you go there, you might make a great deal in a short while, and on the other hand, you might find yourself without a job. It's extremely unlikely you'll remain in your present financial position for long if you go to United Broadcasting—you'll either go up or down. . . ."

"It's hard to figure," Tom said tentatively.

"I happen to know Mr. Hopkins," Dick said.

So they told him all about the job, Tom thought. Probably he knows more about it than I do—a whole lot more.

"He's a fine man," Dick continued. "He's one of the few authentic business geniuses in New York today. If you get a chance to work with him, it will be a great privilege."

"That's what I think," Tom said.

"On the other hand," Dick went on thoughtfully, "I understand that they don't really want you to work for United Broadcasting—they want you for some private project Ralph Hopkins is dreaming up. There are some dangers for you there. . . ."

Dick paused. "What do you mean?" Tom asked.

"He might get sick of his project and abandon it—a man like Ralph Hopkins is always starting things, trying them out, and discarding the ones that don't work. If that happened, he might drop you—or he might let you try out at United Broadcasting. But the important thing for you to remember is that when you start work on a private project for a man like Hopkins, you don't have any clearly defined ladder to climb. You're just going to have to play it by ear, hoping Hopkins will not lose interest. You won't have any real profession—your profession will be pleasing Hopkins. And if you fail in that, the experience you've had with Hopkins won't necessarily prepare you for a very good job anywhere else."

"I can see that," Tom said.

"What I'm trying to say," Dick continued, "is that working for Great Men is a profession in itself, and the trouble is that when you're through with one Great Man, you can't always find another."

He's making it sound as though I'm going to be a professional toady, Tom thought. He's trying to persuade me not to go. He said nothing.

"I think I ought to add," Dick said, "that when you leave, if you leave, we'll have to replace you, and it might not be possible for us to find a position here for you if you returned to look for a job."

"Of course," Tom said.

Dick smiled. "Make your own decision," he said. "Whatever you do, I wish you luck."

Tom thanked him and went to his own desk. If he had really wanted to keep me he could have offered me a big raise, but that would have encouraged everybody else to threaten to leave, he thought. He couldn't do that. Or, if he wanted to keep me, all he would have to do would be to give me a bad reference. He could do it over the telephone and I'd never know about it, but Dick would never even think of that. The union of bosses is powerful, but, within its self-prescribed limits, marvelously scrupulous. Tom glanced at his watch and saw it was almost time for lunch. On his desk was a long report from a college trying to explain what it had done with a half-million-dollar grant the Schanenhauser Foundation had given it a year ago. Tom started to read it. He decided he wouldn't go to lunch. He worked right through the day, unobtrusively making sure that Dick Haver knew it.

When Tom got back to Westport that night he found the house spotless, and an enormous steak dinner in the oven awaiting him.

"THERE'S AN APPLE PIE IN THE BREAD BOX," Mrs. Manter shouted. "THE CHILDREN HAVE ET THEIR SUPPER AND ARE IN BED."

"Fine," Tom said. "How is everybody?"

"YOUR WIFE'S NOT REALLY SICK AT ALL," Mrs. Manter said. "TAKE ME HOME NOW—IT'S ALMOST SIX O'CLOCK."

Before taking her home, Tom ran up the stairs to see Betsy, who was lying on a neatly made bed looking wilted. "How are you?" he asked.

"Exhausted," she said. "Just watching that woman makes me exhausted. Do you know what she did? She washed clothes by hand in the bathtub, and she scrubbed all the woodwork in the kitchen. She mowed the lawn. She made cookies. And the children mind her like trained seals. She tells them to keep quiet and they don't say a word."

"Maybe we can learn something," Tom said.

"The children are in their room now keeping quiet."

"I'll take her home," Tom said. "Can you manage till I get back?"

"I won't tell the children she's gone," Betsy said weakly.

At seven the next morning Tom awoke with the knowledge that he had to prepare breakfast for the children, get Mrs. Manter, and go into New York to have lunch with the president of the United Broadcasting Corporation. He was dismayed to find that no freshly pressed suit was in his closet, and that the one shirt in his drawer which didn't have a frayed collar lacked two buttons.

"Betsy!" he said. "I can't go in to see Hopkins looking like a bum!"

"I forgot!" Betsy replied. "I was supposed to pick up your things at the cleaners the day before yesterday. So much has been going on!"

"What will I do?"

"Go down and get breakfast," Betsy said. "I'll be pressing your gray flannel suit and sewing on buttons."

"Are you strong enough?"

Betsy struggled out of bed. "You don't have to be very strong to lift a button," she said.

Dressed only in his shoes, socks, and underpants, Tom went to the kitchen and fried eggs. The children, feeling much better in spite of the fact that their faces had not yet healed, insisted on having breakfast in the kitchen, instead of in bed. Tom remembered the formal breakfasts his grandmother's butler had served during his own childhood, with silver covers on dishes of eggs and sausage, and, seeing himself in his underwear serving his children, he thought, Things sure are different for them—one thing they won't have to get over is gracious living.

By the time he was dressed, Tom found himself surprisingly nervous at the prospect of meeting Hopkins. He felt almost the way he had before combat jumps during the war. "Wish me luck," he said to Betsy, after he had delivered Mrs. Manter and was leaving to catch his train.

"You'll get the job," Betsy said confidently.

That was the way she always was. During the war, he was sure, she had never worried about him—she was perfectly confident that he'd come back unhurt. Her confident letters, which sometimes had arrived when he was certain he would never survive the next jump, had made him acutely lonely, and he felt the same way now as he bent over and kissed her.

There's no damn reason in the world to be nervous, he thought, later in the morning, as he walked toward the United Broadcasting building. After all I've been through, why should I be nervous now? He wondered what Hopkins was like. What did a man have to be like to make so damn much money? It's never just luck that lets them make it, he thought, and it isn't just who they know—I won't let myself fall into the trap of thinking that. Hopkins has got something, something special, or he wouldn't be making two hundred thousand a year. What is it?

All I have to do is be myself, he thought. Just treat him like anybody else. I wonder what it's like to have all that money? I wonder what it's like never to have to worry about frayed shirt collars, and cracks in the living-room wall, and holes in the kitchen linoleum, and how to pay a woman to take care of your children when your wife is sick? I wonder what it's like to know there's plenty of money to send your kids to college? What's it like to be a success?

Buck fever, he thought—I've got buck fever. I've got my sights on the guy, and my hands are beginning to shake. The son of a bitch. Why shouldn't he like me? He may be tough all right, but I wish he'd been along with me a few years ago; I would like to have seen how tough he was when the sergeant opened the door of the airplane two thousand feet up and said, "Guess we're getting close, sir. Are you ready?"

I'll bet old Hopkins has fought battles, Tom thought, but his battles paid off. Suddenly the ridiculous old resentment rose in him, the crazy anger he had felt so many times when he'd been scared and seen some poor inoffensive colonel who never had to jump sitting behind a desk, drinking coffee maybe, and wisecracking with a sergeant about when they were going to get their next leave. When he'd seen something like that, especially when he'd seen it a few hours before he knew he had to take off, this crazy anger had risen in him, and for no reason at all he felt the same way now. Then he was in the gold elevator, going up, high into the sky. He looked

at the operator and was absurdly relieved to find it was not the man whose face and voice had been so strangely familiar.

"Hello!" Walker said as Tom entered his office. "You're right on time!"

Tom smiled. "I try to be punctual," he said primly, and felt absurd.

Walker put his small puffy white hands on his desk and painfully eased his enormous bulk from his reclining chair. "We'll pick up Bill Ogden and go on up to see Mr. Hopkins," he said.

Ogden looked more like a fashion plate than ever. "Glad to see you," he said to Tom, but he didn't sound glad at all—he didn't sound as though he had ever been glad about anything except the happy circumstances which had caused him to be handsome and slender and well dressed and in a position of at least a little authority.

With Ogden leading the way, and Walker puffing along behind, Tom got back into the gold elevator. Following Ogden, he stepped out at the fifty-sixth floor. The corridors there were wider, he immediately noticed. The floors were carpeted more richly, and even the light fixtures on the ceiling were of a heavier brass than on the floors below. In the air, he felt, there was almost the smell of money, impregnating everything, like musk.

Hopkins' outer office was a large room, in which two pretty girls and one gray-haired woman sat at big typewriters which looked like cash registers. There were five comfortable chairs made of molded plywood arranged in a circle around an ash tray on a pedestal. Three doors, all of them shut, led from this outer office. One of these doors was especially broad and obviously led to the final retreat of Hopkins himself.

"Mr. Hopkins is busy," the gray-haired woman said to Walker, and smiled. Everybody in this building smiles, Tom thought—even Ogden managed a thin little twinge of the lips whenever he spoke. It must be a company rule.

They sat in the chairs surrounding the ash tray, and Tom saw a row of carefully framed photographs on the wall in front of him. One was of Winston Churchill debarking from an airplane. Something was written in a bold script across the bottom of the photo-

graph, but Tom was not close enough to read it, and somehow it would have been unthinkable to get up and inspect the photograph closely.

"He has Mr. Givens with him," the gray-haired woman said. "They'll be through in a moment." She smiled again, and both Ogden and Walker smiled back at her.

Ten minutes later a tall, distinguished-looking man emerged from the largest of the three doors and walked briskly through the outer office toward the elevators.

"You can go in now," the gray-haired woman said.

Following Ogden, Tom entered a large rectangular room with big windows on two sides of it. The view of the city was breath-taking— the floor seemed almost like a platform suspended in mid-air. At the far end of the room, behind a huge rectangular desk, sat Hopkins. He was small, not more than five feet three or four—somehow Tom had expected him to be seven feet tall. He was pale, slender, and partly bald. His eyes were deep set, the face narrow, and the nose short like the nose of a child. His smile was curiously boyish. He was dressed in a brown worsted suit.

"Hello!" he said, getting up from his chair and walking briskly around the end of the desk. "Good morning, Gordon! How are you, Bill! And you're Tom Rath! I certainly do appreciate your taking the time to have lunch with us!"

His manner was both warm and deferential. He shook Tom's hand heartily, and without making it necessary for him to say more than "How do you do?" kept up a steady patter of conversation.

"I hear you're working with the Schanenhauser Foundation," he said. "My, that's a fine outfit! I've done a little work with Dick Haver on committees. . . ."

He moved toward the door and, after insisting that everyone precede him out, walked beside Tom to the elevator, still talking. Gradually, Tom found himself relaxing. It was ridiculous to be nervous with this friendly little man who seemed so anxious to please him. Now that Tom had met him, the conversations he had had with Bill Hawthorne seemed absurd.

When they got on the elevator, Tom saw immediately that the operator was the familiar-appearing man he had seen before. The elevator man glanced at him, then quickly looked toward Hopkins.

"Good morning, Mr. Hopkins!" he said in his deep voice, and shot down to the ground floor without any intermediate stops. Hopkins insisted on being the last man out of the elevator. As they walked out of the building, Tom glanced over his shoulder and saw the elevator operator standing there at the door of his car watching them. Tom looked away quickly. Hopkins led the way across Rockefeller Plaza to another building, at the top of which was a club with a large dining room overlooking the city. They sat down at a corner table, and a waitress took orders for cocktails.

"I understand that Bill and Gordon here have told you something about the new project we're thinking of starting," Hopkins said when the drinks had arrived. "What do you think of it?"

"I don't know any of the details yet, but it certainly sounds interesting," Tom replied, trying to combine wariness, sagacity, and enthusiasm.

"We don't know the details ourselves yet," Hopkins said. "It all started when a group of doctors called on me a few months ago. They apparently felt that there is too little public understanding of the whole question of mental illness, and that a campaign like the fight against cancer or polio is needed. I was impressed by the statistics they gave me. Do you know that more hospital beds are occupied by the mentally ill than by all the cancer, heart, and polio patients put together?"

"I've heard that," Tom said. "Did the doctors have any specific program to suggest?"

Hopkins smiled. "I'm afraid it's up to us to develop a program," he said. "What would you do?"

"I suppose we could, in general, divide the operation into two parts," Tom said, "publicity and action."

"Which do you feel is the more important?" Hopkins asked mildly.

"I don't think their importance can be rated," Tom said, "for the purpose of publicity would be to get action."

"That's very true," Hopkins said, as though he had just heard something very profound. "What kind of action do you think we should try to get?"

A waitress came and replaced the empty cocktail glasses on the table with full ones. "Of course, I'm just talking off the top of my head," Tom began, "but theoretically I suppose we could urge people to donate more money for research on mental illness, we could try to get them to vote more state and federal funds for mental hospitals, and we could suggest some kind of direct action at the local level, such as the organization of community psychiatric clinics."

"How would we do that?" Ogden asked in an unmistakably bored voice which contrasted sharply with Hopkins' enthusiasm.

"I suppose we'd have to consult with a lot of people to determine that," Tom said quickly. "I certainly couldn't tell you now."

"Of course," Hopkins said reassuringly. "None of us can spell anything out at this stage."

Walker sat looking amused and saying nothing. Tom's nervousness was returning. A waiter took orders for food.

"I hear you live out in Westport," Hopkins said to Tom. "I live out that way myself—I just got a place in South Bay."

"South Bay!" Tom said. "I was born there. My Grandmother lives out there now."

It was ridiculous, but Tom found it somehow impossible to think of Hopkins in South Bay. It seemed to Tom that everyone in South Bay either was something like his grandmother and her friends, or was a buyer of one of the unlikely-looking houses which had been built on the golf course. Certainly Hopkins fitted neither category.

"We just built a little place down by the water," Hopkins said. "It's a beautiful town, isn't it?"

He must have bought the old yacht club's land—I heard it was for sale, Tom thought. I wonder what kind of a place he's got. Aloud he said, "I think you'll like it there—I've always thought South Bay the nicest town within commuting distance."

"Stop in next time you visit your grandmother," Hopkins said. "We'd be delighted to see you."

He sounded as though he meant it. Tom suddenly saw himself and

– 48 –

Betsy and the three children, all with the chicken pox, descending on the Hopkins household. What kind of a wife did Hopkins have? Bill Hawthorne had mentioned all sorts of rumors, but it didn't seem possible that they could be true.

"Do you play croquet?" Hopkins asked.

"Yes," Tom said, though he hadn't played for fifteen years. He had a vision of himself playing croquet with Hopkins, using solid gold balls and silver mallets.

"We'll have to have a game sometime," Hopkins said. "I used to play tennis, but I'm getting a little too old for it. . . ."

Throughout the meal, Hopkins continued to chat as though the luncheon were strictly a social occasion, rather than an opportunity for him to inspect a prospective employee. Before dessert was served, however, he glanced at his watch. "My!" he said. "I've got to be getting back to the office! Would you people excuse me?"

Before the others could stand up, he waved cheerily and dashed toward the elevators.

"Coffee?" Walker asked Tom.

"Please," Tom said.

There was a heavy silence, while Tom wondered what, if anything, had been decided. What was the next step? Would Hopkins and Walker and Ogden all get together now and decide whether to hire him, and if so, when would he hear?

"Cigarette?" Ogden asked.

Tom accepted one. It seemed funny they didn't give him some kind of hint about what to expect. Maybe Hopkins hadn't liked him and had kept up the friendly patter just to get through a difficult lunch. Maybe he would get a letter in a couple of days which would begin, "We tremendously enjoyed talking with you, but we're sorry to say there have been some changes of plan. . . ."

Walker painfully pulled himself to his feet. "Got to be getting back," he said. "Nice to have seen you, Mr. Rath."

He sounded friendly, but noncommittal. Ogden made no motion to get up. "See you," he said to Walker and poured himself another cup of coffee.

Maybe he'll tell me now, Tom thought. Maybe he'll just be frank

– 49 –

and say, "I'm awfully sorry it didn't work out. . . ." Still, how could he know what Hopkins had thought? He hadn't had a chance to speak to Hopkins while Tom wasn't there. Maybe they have some signal, Tom thought. Thumbs down.

"It was a very nice lunch," Tom said tentatively. "Thank you very much. . . ."

"Glad you could come," Ogden said. "More coffee?"

Coffee was the last thing Tom wanted, but apparently Ogden didn't want him to leave yet. He accepted the coffee and waited. Ogden sat staring expressionlessly out the window, and for a long while said absolutely nothing. The tension mounted. Tom couldn't make up his mind whether Ogden was just being completely matter-of-fact about the luncheon, or whether this was an act of deliberate cruelty.

"We'll be in touch with you before long," Ogden said finally. "Mr. Hopkins has got to go to the West Coast tomorrow, and we may have to wait until he gets back before making any final decision. Meanwhile, I wouldn't count too heavily on anything. It's not entirely definite yet that we're even going to tackle this mental-health project."

"I understand that," Tom said, and hurriedly added, "I've got to be getting back to my office now—thanks again for the lunch."

He almost fled from the table. When he thought of Hopkins, it seemed certain that he would get the job, for if Hopkins hadn't liked him, why would he have been so friendly? But Ogden had been careful to pave the way for a letter ending the whole thing. Anyway, I met Hopkins, he thought. He seems like a nice guy pretty much like anybody else. Whatever it is that makes him worth two hundred thousand dollars a year is certainly well hidden.

8

When Tom got back to his office he found a slip of paper on his desk saying that his wife had called and that it was important for him to call her back. He put the call through immediately.

"It's your grandmother," she said. "She fell and broke her thigh. At her age, Tommy, bones don't knit. She wants to see you, and you better go out there right away. I would have gone myself, but I still feel pretty rocky, and the doctor's with her—it's not a real emergency."

"I'll go right out," Tom said.

The next train to South Bay was a local one, which stopped almost every five minutes. Tom sat on a soiled green seat in the smoker staring out the window. He didn't want to think. At first there were only the dark caverns of Grand Central Station to see, with the dim figures of tired-appearing men in overalls occasionally illuminated by naked electric-light bulbs. Then the train emerged into the bright sunlight and was surrounded by the littered streets and squalid brick tenements of Harlem. Tom had passed them twice a day for years, and usually he didn't look at them, but now he didn't want to think about his grandmother and he didn't want to think about Hopkins, and the tenements absorbed his attention. There was one grimy brick building with a huge billboard showing a beautiful girl thirty feet long lying under a palm tree. "Fly to Miami," the sign said. Directly under the girl's head, about six feet below the edge of the billboard, was an open window, outside of which an orange crate had been tied. In the orange crate was a flowerpot with a withered geranium, and as the train passed it, an aged colored woman with sunken cheeks leaned out of the window and poured some water from a milk bottle into the flowerpot.

"Ticket?" the conductor asked. He was a stout, red-faced man. Tom gave him his commuter's ticket.

"We don't go as far as Westport," the conductor said.

"I'm getting off at South Bay."

"Westport tickets are no good on this train," the conductor said. "You'll have to buy a ticket to South Bay."

"But South Bay is on the way to Westport," Tom objected.

"I don't make the rules," the conductor said.

Tom paid for a ticket to South Bay. The whole damn world is crazy, he thought. Grandmother is hurt and probably dying, and she brought me up, and I should be thinking only the kindest thoughts about her, and I can't.

She's dying, he thought. She's lived ninety-three years, and it's all been a free ride. She's never cooked a meal, or made a bed, or washed a diaper, or done a damn thing for herself or anybody else. She's spent at least three million dollars, and her only comment has been that money is boring. She's had a free ride for ninety-three years, and I'm damned if I'll cry about the end of it.

Yet to his astonishment he suddenly felt like crying. She doesn't want to die, he thought. I'll bet the poor old lady's scared.

Suddenly he remembered a night soon after his mother had died when a particularly violent thunder squall had struck the old house. Although he had been fifteen years old then, he had been afraid to stay in his room alone. He had gone to his grandmother's room, and she had played double solitaire with him half the night. If she wants me to, I'll stay with her, he thought. I guess Betsy can get along without me for a few days.

As soon as the taxi let him out at the front door of the big house, old Edward opened the front door for him. "The doctor's in the living room, Mr. Rath," he said. "He was hoping to see you before he went."

"Tell him to wait," Tom said, and raced up the stairs to his grandmother's room. The door was closed. Cautiously he opened it, in order not to awaken her if she were asleep. There was her big four-poster bed, with the old-fashioned crocheted canopy. The old lady was lying in the precise center of the bed, propped up on pillows. She was looking out the window at the Sound, where a fleet of small sailboats was racing in the distance. She turned her head quickly and smiled at him. "I'm glad you're here," she said "They're trying to take me to the hospital."

"I'll talk to them," he said.

"My leg broke. I didn't fall and break it—it just broke, and then I fell."

"I'm sorry, Grandmother," he said. "We'll get you fixed up in no time."

"Don't be ridiculous," she said. "I'm going to die, and I prefer to die here. I detest hospitals."

"I'll talk to the doctor," he said.

"Never mind that. I want you to make sure they don't take me to the hospital. They keep giving me drugs, and I don't want to wake up in some iron cot with a lot of supercilious nurses telling me what to do."

"I'll do my best," Tom said.

"The Senator died in this bed, and I want to die here too."

"I'll talk to the doctor now," Tom said.

"Stay here. There's plenty of time. I've got lots of things I want to tell you and I may be asleep when you come back up. Do you know I've left everything I've got to you?"

"I didn't, Grandmother," he said. "I'm very grateful."

"There's not much," she said. "For the last ten years I've been living off capital. And there's a small mortgage on the house. You won't get much."

"Try to sleep now," he said. "We can talk about business later."

"We might as well get it over with now. Did you know that most of your grandfather's estate was lost long ago?"

"Yes, Grandmother."

"How did you know?"

"I guess you must have told me. I think I've always known it."

"I'm sorry things have happened this way," she said. "The Senator and I had so much. I've always been sorry we couldn't do more for you."

"You've given me a great deal," he said.

There was a long moment of silence during which she seemed to be breathing with difficulty, but she kept her eyes intently on his face, and he saw she didn't want him to go.

"I want you to do something for Edward," she said. "He has to be kept in his place, but he's been loyal. He's old and should be provided for."

"I'll try, Grandmother," he said.

She closed her eyes. "How do you think the house looks?" she asked drowsily.

"Beautiful."

"I have tried to keep it up for you," she said. "The west wing . . ."

The sentence trailed off, and Tom saw she was asleep. After waiting a few minutes to be sure, he went downstairs. His grandmother's doctor, an elderly man named Worthington, was waiting.

"I'm afraid your grandmother isn't very well," he began.

"How long do you think she can live?"

The doctor took off his glasses and started polishing them with his handkerchief. "She's broken her thigh," he said, "and I think the pelvis may be fractured too. She took a bad fall. She says her leg just snapped and she fell, and it may actually have happened that way. We won't be able to tell about the pelvis till we take her to the hospital and get her X-rayed."

"She doesn't want to go to the hospital," Tom said. "Is there really much point to it?"

"We've got to get X rays," the doctor replied, sounding shocked. "And we can't give her proper care here!"

"Won't she die pretty soon, anyway?"

"She will if she doesn't get proper care!" the doctor said angrily. "With the proper care, we might be able to keep her going for quite a little while."

"She'll be miserable in a hospital."

"I'll call an ambulance," the doctor said. "There's no question that she has to go."

"I don't think she'll allow you to take her."

"We'll fix it so she won't know a thing about it," the doctor said. Picking up a black bag, he climbed the stairs to the old lady's room. Tom didn't try to stop him. So she's going to wake up in an iron bed in a strange room after all, he thought.

9

FLORENCE RATH DIED only eight days later, complaining not so much of a broken thigh and a fractured pelvis as of the refusal of the doctors to obey her.

"They *know* they can't cure me, so why don't they send me home?" she asked Tom every day, and he was never able to invent a plausible answer.

Perhaps on the theory that she might be sent home if she made herself unpleasant enough, she made as much trouble as possible and constantly insulted everyone.

"The nurses are so *common!*" she said loudly to Tom, "and the doctors aren't much better. They all look like a lot of *druggists!*" She made the word sound like an unpardonable obscenity.

For the entire eight days, she constantly demanded services of everyone. Every few minutes she called a nurse to ask her to smooth her covers, or to change the water in the many vases of flowers with which she had surrounded herself. She asked doctors to make telephone calls for her and even asked one elderly physician to go out and buy her a paper. The night nurse simply disconnected her call bell.

Never once, however, did the old lady complain of pain or show any fear of death. She made no attempt to solicit pity, and it would have been impossible to feel truly sorry for so imperious a figure. Tom wasn't much surprised to find that in spite of the demands and insults she hurled at them, the doctors and nurses loved her. Tired and harried as they were, they ran errands for her and sat listening to the endless stories she told of the exploits of "The Senator" and Tom's father, "The Major."

She died in her sleep, two hours after Tom had left the hospital to go back to Westport. He had visited her every evening on the way home from work, after having arranged for a taxi to take Mrs. Manter home. By that time Betsy was able to care for the children a few hours by herself.

When the hospital called him to say the old lady had died, Tom said, "Thank you for calling," very quietly, and put the telephone receiver carefully back on its hook.

"What is it?" Betsy asked.

"Grandmother's dead," he said.

He went into the kitchen and got himself a drink. He was tired— for the last eight nights he hadn't been getting to bed until after midnight, and even then he hadn't been able to sleep. Everything seemed uncertain. He hadn't heard a word from United Broadcasting. He had no idea whether his grandmother would leave even enough money to cover her debts. While she was in the hospital, he had asked her for the name of her lawyer, but she had seemed offended.

"Wait," she had said. "I'll tell you when the time comes."

And she had told him, the afternoon before she died. The lawyer was Alfred J. Sims, a name Tom had never heard before in his life.

Now the thought that there was a large house with an old man in it who had worked for his grandmother half his life and who now presumably expected a pension from him worried Tom. The thought that Hopkins might decide not to hire him worried him, and the fact that Dick Haver seemed to be growing increasingly impatient over the whole situation worried him. Every day Dick asked him whether he had heard anything from United Broadcasting—he seemed to take a wry pleasure from the question. And beyond these worries, Tom faced accumulating small debts. Mrs. Manter's wages, the down payment on a new washing machine, and the daily taxi bill had wiped out his cash on hand, and he was charging everything he could, from groceries to medicine. Soon there would be his grandmother's hospital bill and funeral expenses. He wondered how long it would take to settle her estate.

"Isn't it funny she never told you her lawyer's name before?" Betsy asked.

"She never talked about business."

"Don't you think you should get a complete accounting from the lawyer? I mean an accounting for all the money she lost—it seems awfully funny that she lost so much. For all we know, the lawyer's been cheating her for years."

"I'll get a complete accounting," he said.

That night he slept hardly at all. In the morning he telephoned Sims, who apparently had only a residence in New York and no office. The lawyer's voice was high pitched, with a pronounced Boston accent. "I've been expecting to hear from you," he said. "Your grandmother's death was a great shock to me. Her papers are all in order, and I don't think you need expect any difficulty."

Sims's house was a brownstone structure on Fifty-third Street. After telling Dick Haver he wouldn't be in all day because of his grandmother's death, Tom took a taxi there. A uniformed maid opened the door and ushered him into a dimly lit study lined with books. Sims, a gaunt-faced man about sixty years old, was sitting in a wheel chair behind a desk littered with papers.

"I'm glad to see you, Tom," he said. "Excuse me for not getting up. And excuse me for using your first name—I've known your family far too long to use anything else."

"I'm glad to meet you," Tom replied.

"Your grandmother was a great woman," Sims said. "She's the last of her kind."

"I know," Tom replied abstractedly. He was staring at a photograph of a young man, a rather faded photograph which he was quite sure was of his father. The photograph was in a leather frame on Sims's desk.

"You recognize the picture?"

"My father?"

"Of course. Your father and I were good friends. We were classmates at college, and we were in France together."

"I never saw that picture before," Tom said. He picked the frame up and inspected the photograph more closely. It showed a man five or six years younger than himself. The man wore a tweed cap, and he was smiling boyishly. Tom put the photograph down. Somewhere in the back of the house a clock struck the quarter hour.

"Now about your grandmother's estate," Sims said, picking up a folder with a blue cover from his desk. "As I presume you know, you are the sole heir."

"She told me," Tom said.

"And I presume you also know that there isn't much in the estate."

"How much?"

"This may come as something of a shock to you, but when the estate is completely settled, I don't think you'll have much except for the house. There are some securities of course, but there's also a mortgage on the house, and there'll be an inheritance tax. And I suppose you'll want to do something about Edward."

"I'll have to see," Tom said. "Just what is the value of the securities?"

"I haven't checked the current market value recently, but there will be about twenty thousand dollars. Not much more. If your grandmother had lived a few more years, I don't know what we would have done."

"And the mortgage? How much is that?"

"Ten thousand dollars."

"I don't understand it!" Tom blurted out. "Do you have any idea how much Grandmother inherited from her father and from Grandfather, and how she managed to lose it?"

"What has she told you?"

"Nothing!"

"But you knew she had lost a great deal."

"She told me just before she died, and I guess I've always assumed it, from the way she had to economize."

Sims sighed. "What do you know about your father?" he asked. "What kind of man was he?"

"He was delightful," Sims said. "He was possibly the most charming, talented man ever born. That's why I wish you could have known him—you would be proud of him."

"What happened to him?"

"I don't know—it's pretty hard to explain what happens to people. When we were in college together, Steve could do anything. During the first few weeks we were overseas, he was the best officer I've ever seen. He was the last man I'd ever expect to have a nervous breakdown, but that's what he had. In those days we called it shell shock. They sent him home, and after he had spent a few months in a hospital, he got a job with Irvington and Wells—that used to be just about the best brokerage house on the street. He tried awfully hard there—I guess I'm one of the few people who really knows how hard he tried, and how much he wanted to succeed—but he wasn't well. He couldn't concentrate on anything, and sometimes he got so nervous during conferences that he'd have to get up and walk out of the room. Old Wells loved him like a son—everyone loved your father—but finally he had to ask him to take some time off and try to get himself under control. Your father had just been married a few months, and it was a great blow to him. He and your mother lived with your grandmother, and the idleness didn't do him any good. He asked your grandmother if he could handle her estate, and your grandmother thought it might give him confidence to let him try. He made some bad mistakes—that can happen to anyone. Your grandmother was patient, but he got panicky—he was determined to get back everything he'd lost. He started taking long shots on the stock market and losing more and more. I tried to reason with him, but getting back all the money he had lost seemed a matter of life and death with him. I talked it over with your grandmother, and she finally decided she had to take what was left of her estate out of his hands. The night she told him that, he started driving off somewhere and was killed."

"Was it suicide?"

"I don't know. He left no notes. When we looked into things, we found he had recently taken out some life insurance that had a suicide clause in it. The insurance company paid. We also found that his losses had been worse than we knew. Four fifths of your grandmother's estate was gone."

Sims paused. "In 1928, I managed to build up the estate a good deal, and we were lucky enough to get out before the crash," he continued. "I must admit, though, that I never could get your grandmother to live on a budget—she aways felt that she was entitled to a certain standard of living, and that she would maintain it as long as she had a cent. I don't know what she would have done if she had been forced to sell that house—I'm glad I never had to find out."

"Thanks for telling me all this," Tom said. "I don't know why, but I feel a lot better knowing."

"Your father's death was a great shock to your grandmother," Sims said. "She was determined never to tell you about it. And she never wanted any member of her family to have anything to do with her money after that, either. That's understandable, of course, but she carried it to extremes. She never wanted you to meet me—she was afraid I'd tell you about your father. I think she'd be angry if she knew I was telling you now."

"She gave me your name," Tom said.

"She knew you finally had to know. Anyway, there's nothing for you to be ashamed of. He was a fine man."

Sims wheeled his chair to a cupboard near his desk and took out a bottle of sherry. Tom noticed that his hand shook as he poured it into two glasses. Suddenly the older man looked up and smiled. "You see," he said, "I understand your father. The war hit me too. Not only my legs—my hands."

"It almost happened to me," Tom said.

"You were in the last one?"

"Not Korea. The one before that."

"But you came out all right."

"I wasn't in sustained action," Tom said. "We didn't have trench warfare. I don't think I could have taken that. I was usually thrown in for a few days and then taken out."

"I remember now," Sims said. "I know what you were in. It scares hell out of me just to think of it."

The sherry tasted good. When they had finished it, Sims said, "I've prepared a dossier on the whole estate—a complete history of it, in fact. I'll have it typed up and mailed to you. It may take several months to get the will through the probate court. If you need cash in the meantime, I can arrange for a bank to give you a loan on the securities."

"I may need cash," Tom said. "I'm broke. And until the house is sold, things are going to be tough."

"Don't sell it too fast," Sims said. "Your grandmother has twenty-three acres of the best land in South Bay. It ought to be worth something."

10

THAT NIGHT when he got home to Westport, Tom found a letter from United Broadcasting. "We're sorry to have taken so long before getting in touch with you," it said, "but Mr. Hopkins has been on an extended trip to the West Coast, and it has not been until now that we have been in a position to discuss final arrangements with you. Mr. Hopkins enjoyed meeting you, and if you would care to drop into my office Friday at 11 A.M., I hope we can work something out." The letter was signed by Ogden.

"It's good news, isn't it?" Betsy asked.

"I guess so."

"You don't sound very excited."

"I'm confused," Tom said. "I don't see how we can do everything we're supposed to do."

He had already told Betsy about his conversation with Sims. They both sat thinking about the necessity to make some sort of decision about old Edward, and how to sell the big house most advantageously, and how to keep it up meanwhile, and how at the same time to start a new job.

"The trouble is," Tom said, "I have no idea what we're going to net on the estate, and it may be months before we know. That old house is pretty much a white elephant, I'm sure, but until we sell it we won't have any idea whether we're going to end up in the hole, or with quite a lot."

"You worry about United Broadcasting," Betsy said. "I'm feeling pretty well now. I don't need Mrs. Manter any more, and I'll make all the arrangements about your grandmother's house. Don't worry about it for the next month. I've already talked to Edward and told him we wanted him to stay on for another month, until we know what arrangements can be made. He's going to live there as a care-taker."

"You've already spoken to him?"

"He telephoned here for instructions."

Tom sighed. "The funeral's tomorrow," he said, "and the next day, I'll see Ogden and make some kind of decision there. After that I'll worry about Grandmother's house."

The day after the funeral when Tom went into the United Broad-casting building, he did not think at all about the familiar-appearing elevator operator until he saw the man standing outside his elevator, smoking a cigarette. Instinctively wishing to avoid him, Tom quickly walked into another elevator. When he got to Ogden's outer office, a secretary told him he might have to wait quite a long while, because someone from out of town had come in unexpectedly to see Ogden. Tom sat in a comfortable leather chair. His thoughts kept returning to the elevator operator. It was ridiculous to be preoccupied with such a matter, he told himself; what possible meaning could it have? Still, it was maddening not to be able to place the man's face and that deep, familiar voice. With an effort Tom forced himself to think about his coming interview with Ogden.

"Have you made up your mind whether you want to work with us?" Ogden asked when Tom finally got in to see him.

"I don't really know enough details to make a decision," Tom said. "We haven't discussed salary."

"We discussed it, but I guess we didn't reach an agreement," Ogden said casually. "I understand your salary at the Schanenhauser Foundation has been seven thousand a year. We are prepared to offer you eight."

Tom hesitated. It didn't seem feasible for him to bargain with United Broadcasting, but it also didn't seem possible that Hopkins would worry about two thousand dollars more a year if he really wanted him. "I've had a long talk with Dick Haver," Tom said finally, "and I understand my prospects are fairly good at the foundation. . . ."

"We don't believe in starting people at high salaries," Ogden said. "If new employees prove themselves here, their compensation is adjusted accordingly."

Tom visualized himself going back to Dick Haver and saying he had decided not to go to United Broadcasting. Dick would probably let him wait a long while for a raise after that. Still, if Hopkins really wanted him, now was the time to hold out.

"I'm sorry," Tom said. "There is always a certain amount of risk in starting a new position, and I feel I should be compensated for it. I want ten thousand a year."

"We wouldn't feel justified in giving you that," Ogden said easily. "We don't like to quibble about these things, for we feel that if a man really wants to work for United Broadcasting, it isn't necessary. Nevertheless, we might stretch a point and give you nine thousand. I'm afraid we couldn't do more than that now."

If I still held out, I might be able to get more, Tom thought, but he dreaded the possibility of another week's indecision while Ogden and the others conferred. "All right," he said. "I'm very pleased to accept the position. I feel it will be a great privilege to work for Mr. Hopkins."

"Fine!" Ogden said. "We're delighted to have you. Can you start in a week?"

"I ought to give the foundation at least two weeks' notice."

"We need you right away—Mr. Hopkins has a speech he has to prepare. I'll see if we can fix it up with Dick Haver."

"If Dick approves, it's all right with me," Tom replied.

"One more thing," Ogden said. "You'll be working with Mr. Hopkins, but you'll be responsible directly to me. And for the first six months you'll be on a temporary basis."

"I understand."

"Good luck," Ogden said, concluding the interview. "We're looking forward to a very happy relationship."

When Tom got home that night there was a long bright-red Jaguar convertible parked in the driveway of the little house in Westport. In the living room Betsy was seated on the sofa, talking to a short thin man dressed in a soft tweed suit.

"This is Mr. Swanson Howard," she said to Tom as he came in the front door. "He wants to talk to you."

"How do you do, Mr. Swanson," Tom said.

"It's Swanson Howard, not Howard Swanson," the man said, getting to his feet. He was almost a foot shorter than Tom.

"Of course," Tom said. "I'm glad to meet you."

"Anybody want a drink?" Betsy asked.

"Martini?" Tom suggested to Howard.

"A little Scotch on the rocks," Howard said.

"I'm afraid we don't have any Scotch," Betsy said.

"A Martini will be fine then," Howard replied, and lit a cigarette. "I was very sorry to hear of Mrs. Rath's death."

"You knew her?" Tom asked.

"I knew of her." Howard looked around the room, and Tom imagined that his eyes dwelt on the crack in the wall, and the soiled upholstery on one of the chairs. "I understand she left you her house," Howard said.

"That's right."

"Do you plan to move into it?"

Betsy came from the kitchen, carrying a tray with a pitcher of Martinis and three glasses. "I'm sorry, but there aren't any olives or pickled onions or lemon peels or *anything* to go in it," she said. "Anyway, we've got the essentials."

Howard accepted a drink, but kept his eyes on Tom.

"We expect to sell it," Tom said.

"I might be interested in buying the place," Howard said casually, and took the first sip of his drink. Betsy sat down suddenly in the nearest chair.

"The estate won't be settled for quite a while," Tom said.

"I understand that. Of course, a place like that isn't easy to sell, as

I'm sure you know. The property needs a lot of work. The house is old-fashioned, and far too big for most people. The taxes are about twenty-two hundred dollars a year, and it would cost about twenty-four hundred a year to heat the place. And of course it couldn't be run without servants. You won't find many prospective purchasers for a property like that, and it will be expensive for you to hold for long."

"You seem to know a lot about it," Tom said.

"I like the place. I like the view. We might be able to work something out."

"Do you want to make an offer?"

"My offer would probably sound low to you," Howard said. "It would be based solely on the value of the land. Although I might live in the house, I'd figure it had almost no market value."

"How much would you offer?"

"Twenty thousand dollars."

"I'll have to consider it," Tom said. "I won't be able to give you an answer for a long while."

"I'm afraid I'd have to know within a week or so," Howard said. "We're considering several properties." He took an engraved card from his pocket and handed it to Tom. "Hearthside Restaurants, Inc.," it said in large letters, and in smaller letters at the left-hand bottom corner, "Mr. Swanson Howard." In the right-hand corner was an address on Thirty-third Street in New York and a telephone number.

"Would you be buying the house as a residence for yourself?" Tom asked.

"Of course. If we can get a decision within a week or so."

"I'll be in touch with you," Tom said.

Howard thanked him for the drink, smiled mechanically, and left. A moment later the engine of the Jaguar roared—apparently he had a cutout on the exhaust.

"What do you think?" Betsy asked excitedly. "You'll hold out for more, won't you?"

"I don't know," Tom said, stretching out exhaustedly on the couch. "By the way, United Broadcasting hired me today. The salary's nine thousand, and I'm on a temporary basis for six months. I'm supposed to start in a week."

"That's wonderful!" Betsy said. "Oh, Tommy, let's put this damn little house on the market tomorrow! Everything's going to be wonderful for us—I can just feel it!"

The front door slammed, and Barbara rushed in, followed by Janey and Pete. "Momma!" Janey said excitedly. "There are some boys across the street with knives, and they said they're going to *stick* us!"

"They're probably rubber knives," Betsy said.

"They're *real knives!*"

"Play upstairs then," Betsy said. "Your father and I are talking."

"They said they were going to chop off our hands and our legs and our heads and everything!"

"They were just fooling," Betsy said. "Upstairs!"

"But they *weren't* fooling!"

"UPSTAIRS, or I'll call Mrs. Manter!"

The three children immediately went upstairs.

"The name Mrs. Manter still works," Betsy said gratefully. "I don't think you ought to sell Grandmother's house to that man. He's in too much of a hurry. With a salary of nine thousand we could afford to hold it for a while."

"I don't know," Tom said. Unaccountably, he felt depressed and pessimistic. "Suppose we turn down this offer," he said, "and suppose that after six months, they tell me I'm through at United Broadcasting. And suppose we can't sell Grandmother's place. Then what do we do?"

"Don't be absurd," Betsy said. "I'll bet that at the end of six months you get a big raise at United Broadcasting. Hopkins seemed to like you, didn't he?"

"Sure, he seemed to like me. Hopkins seems to like everybody. With the money he makes, why shouldn't he? I tell you, Betsy, I'm uneasy. I don't like this guy Ogden, and it's him I'm really going to be working for. I don't like being responsible for old Edward. What are we supposed to do, pay him a salary for the rest of his life, or give him a lump sum? You can't throw an old man like that out on the street. And I'm worried about Grandmother's house. It would cost us at least six thousand a year to hang onto it, counting mortgage, taxes, minimum repairs, and a caretaker of some kind. You'd have to have a caretaker there, or it would go to hell in no time. Are you going to keep a house that costs you six thousand dollars a year on a salary of nine thousand? And what happens when you lose the job paying you the nine thousand?"

"You can't look at things like that," Betsy said. "You've got to plan on things going all right. I've never seen you lose your self-confidence!"

"I haven't lost it, but maybe it's time we started being sensible. All we've ever thought about is getting out of this house. The more I think about it, the more I think that's crazy. This house is plenty comfortable enough. With nine thousand a year, we could afford some life insurance. Did you ever stop and think what would happen to you if I dropped dead some morning?"

"Don't think about it!" Betsy said. "I'd drop dead right alongside you."

"Then what would happen to the children?"

"What's gotten into you, Tommy? I've never heard you talk like this before!"

"I think we've both always assumed that Grandmother would be waiting to catch us if we tripped," he said. "Maybe it's time we grew up. She's not there any more."

"All right, get some more insurance," Betsy said, "but when we sell Grandmother's place, we can still afford a better home."

"Can we? Let's say that after we take care of old Edward, we net twenty thousand dollars out of Grandmother's house. Let's say I hang onto my job, and over the years get a few small raises—I'm beginning to doubt like hell I'm going to get rich quick on a mental-health project. Let's say, though, that in ten years I'm making fifteen thousand. How are we going to send the kids to college?"

"On fifteen thousand it would be easy!"

"Maybe—but we've never lived on a budget yet. For a while, all three kids will be in college at the same time. We ought to figure at least three thousand dollars a year for each child at college. That's nine thousand a year, *after* taxes. That means we'll need thirty-six thousand dollars to send three kids through college. Do you think you could take that out of my salary?"

"We'd manage it somehow. Anyway, they wouldn't need three thousand a year."

"I needed it, and that was fifteen years ago, almost. We've never talked about this, Betsy, but I figure we owe our kids the same kind of education we got, and that's what Grandmother's money really should be used for."

"You plan to live the rest of our lives *here?*"

"We could do worse."

"I don't give a damn," she said. "I won't be noble. Not unless you make me."

"Think it over," he said.

"I *have* thought it over. It's not fair to the children to bring them up in a neighborhood like this!"

"What's wrong with this neighborhood?"

"It's *dull.*"

"You mean 'The Senator' wouldn't like it?"

"That's cruel," she said. "Anyway, 'The Senator' is your ancestor, not mine. I mean that I don't like it, and I'm not ashamed to admit it!"

"It's time we forgot the Rath family's dreams of glory, and *your* family's dreams of glory too," he said. "It's time we started being sensible."

"My family never had any dreams of glory!"

"Didn't your father borrow ten thousand dollars to throw that coming-out party where I met you?"

Betsy flushed. "Where did you hear that?"

"He told me himself. He was very honest about explaining to me that I wasn't marrying any money."

"Dad borrowed it to keep a promise," she said. "Ever since I was a little girl, he promised me a big coming-out party, and when the time came, he couldn't afford it. So he borrowed the money. That's the kind of a man he was. And he paid every cent back."

"It was nice of him," Tom said, "but don't you think that was a crazy promise to make to a little girl? Hell, when you were a little girl, you didn't care! He was making a promise to himself."

"It was a lovely party," Betsy said. "I'll never forget it. And if I hadn't had it, I might never have met you."

"Most expensive damn introduction in the world!" Tom said. "We've got to get that kind of stuff out of our minds."

"I haven't even *mentioned* a coming-out party for Barbara and Janey," Betsy said. "All I want is a decent house, without a damn-fool crack in the wall like a question mark, and without everything coming apart."

"We can have the wall replastered," Tom said. "I'm going to bed."

He took a half tumblerful of Martinis up with him and lay for a long while sipping it in the dark. When it was finished, he went to sleep. He had no idea how much later it was when Betsy awoke him by shaking his shoulders hard. "Go away," he said. "I'm asleep."

"Wake up!" she said. "I've got a wonderful idea!"

She almost rolled him out of bed. The light was bright in his eyes. "Tell me in the morning!" he said.

"No!" she said. "Now!"

He struggled to a sitting position and rubbed his eyes. "What time is it?"

"It's only about one o'clock. Ever since you've been asleep, I've been sitting downstairs thinking, and suddenly I got it!"

"Got what?"

"This idea!"

"Go to sleep."

"No! You've got to listen to me!"

"I will if you get me a drink," he said.

She rushed downstairs and came back with a glass half full of gin and ice. "There's no more vermouth," she said, "but this ought to fix you."

He sipped it and made a face.

"Now!" she said. "Will you listen?"

"Is there a choice?"

"What I want to do," she said, "is to sell this house and move into Grandmother's house. Not for good, you understand—just until we can figure out what to do with it."

"That's wonderful," he said. "Grandmother wanted us to add another wing. Do you plan to do that too?"

"Be quiet. Now you stop and figure, Tommy. We've got twenty-three acres in South Bay, the only twenty-three acres with a view anything like that. Even around here, good one-acre lots sell for as much as five thousand dollars apiece. If we divided that land up, we might get as high as a hundred thousand dollars!"

"Sure," he said. "But there are a few other things to consider. Things like zoning restrictions. Things like building roads, so people could get to their lots. Things like wells and sewers."

"Exactly," she said. "And we couldn't figure all that out while we were living in Westport and you were working in New York. But if I were living in Grandmother's house, I could *see* the zoning board, and show contractors the place, and all the rest of it."

"And what if it didn't work?"

"We'd still be there to sell Grandmother's place. And we'd have the money from selling this house. And we could let Edward stay with us."

"Let's talk about it in the morning," Tom said.

"We can't give Edward a pension—we never could afford it. And I bet he'd rather stay right in the old house."

"Talk about it in the morning," Tom repeated.

"And there are even more possibilities! Let's say we took all our available money, from selling this place and from Grandmother's estate and everything. Let's say we took it all and converted Grandmother's carriage house into a dwelling. It could be a *charming* place. Let's say we did that and sold it with one acre of land for forty thousand dollars. Places like that go for *at least* that, and I bet we could fix the old carriage house up for twenty thousand. That would give us a profit of twenty thousand. We could use that to build *another* house and sell that for profit. We could put up a whole housing development, one house at a time. Maybe we could make *more* than a hundred thousand!"

"I'm dizzy," Tom said. "To do that, you'd need capital. You'd have to know the real-estate business and the building business. And you should be able to devote full time to it."

"I can learn, and I will devote full time to it."

"And in the end we'd lose our shirts," Tom said. "I know it."

"In the end we might have a hundred thousand dollars and the pick of the new houses for ourselves."

"Dreams of glory," he said. "I've spent my whole life getting over them."

"Look, Tommy," she said. "You said I should think, and I did. You know what you are? You're spoiled. You've spent most of your life feeling sorry for yourself because you knew Grandmother wasn't going to leave you a lot of money. You're spoiled and you're licked before you start. In spite of all you did in the war, you're not really willing to go out and fight for what you want. You came back from the war, and you took an easy job, and we both bellyached all the time because you didn't get more money. And what's more, you're a coward. You're afraid to risk a god-damn thing!"

"Thanks for the character reference," he said.

"You've gotten to the point where you disrespect anybody who does what you can't do," she said. "You sneer at the United Broadcasting men, and everybody else. You think you're something special because a hell of a long while ago you were a good paratrooper. And now all you want is security, and life insurance, and money in the bank to send the kids to college twelve or fifteen years from now, and you're scared because for six months you'll be on trial on a new job, and you always look at the dark side of everything, and you've got *no guts!*"

Suddenly she broke into tears. "I love you, Tommy," she said between sobs. "I just had to say it."

For several minutes the room was quiet.

"You're partly right," he said suddenly.

"I exaggerated," she said. "And, Tommy, you've got more guts than any man I ever saw. Do you know why I love you, Tommy? It's a funny thing—it's childish. It's because I never saw a man I thought could get away with making you really angry."

"Plenty have," he said.

"It's not just strength," she said. "It's something in you. When you really want something, I don't think anything in the world can stand in your way. That's why you were so damned good in the war."

"It was luck," he said. "Whether you get out of a war or not is ninety per cent luck."

"Maybe," she said, "but since you've gotten back, you haven't really wanted much. You've worked hard, but at heart you've never been really trying."

"We'll have a go at this real-estate thing if you want," he said. "I still doubt like hell that it will work. If we wind up broke, can you take it?"

"I can take it," she said. "And you can too. I know what you're thinking about."

"My father."

"I know. But it's better to think of Barbara and Janey and Pete, and a new life. I haven't been really trying, either. From now on I'm going to change."

11

WHEN TOM AWOKE in the morning, Betsy was already dressed. Her hair was combed and she had put on lipstick.

"What time is it?" he asked.

"Six-thirty."

"Good God," he said. "Go away. I've another hour to sleep."

"No you *don't*," she said. "No more rushing for the train."

"What?"

"This is the new regime. We're going to have a leisurely breakfast before you go to work."

"Oh, God!" he said.

The three children came in and stood by the bed staring at him. Their hair was all combed, and they had on freshly ironed clothes. "Momma got us up early," Janey said mournfully. "Are you going to get up too?"

"He certainly is!" Betsy said. "Tom, I've got a lot of important things I want to say to you. Get up this minute!"

There didn't seem to be much chance of getting any more sleep, so Tom climbed out of bed, groped his way to the bathroom, and started to shave. When he went downstairs, he heard a coffeepot percolating. The coffee smelled good. In the kitchen he found the breakfast table fully set and waffles cooking. "What's going on?" he asked Betsy.

"Breakfast," she said. "No more instant coffee. No more grabbing a piece of toast to eat on the way to the station. We're going to start living *sanely*."

He sat down and poured some maple sirup on a waffle.

"No more hotdogs and hamburgers for dinner," Betsy said. "I'm going to start making stews and casseroles and roasts and things."

"Just watch the grocery bill," he said.

"No more television."

"What?"

"No more television. I'm going to give the damn set away."

"What for?"

"Bad for the kids," she said. "Instead of shooing them off to the television set, we're going to sit in a family group and read aloud. And you ought to get your mandolin fixed up. We could have friends in and sing—we've been having too much passive entertainment."

Tom poured himself a fragrant cup of coffee. "I'll need the television for my work," he said.

Betsy ignored him. "No more homogenized milk," she said. "We're going to save two cents a quart and shake the bottle ourselves."

"Fine."

"And we're going to church every Sunday. We're going to stop lying around Sunday mornings, drinking Martinis. We're going to church in a family group."

"All right."

"*Peter!*" Betsy said.

Pete had just slowly and deliberately poured half the bottle of maple sirup over his waffle. The sirup had overflowed the plate and was now dripping on the floor. "You *know* you shouldn't do that!"

"Don't be cross," Janey said. "It was an accident."

"It was *not* an accident," Barbara said. "He did it on purpose. I saw him."

"Don't be a tattletale," Betsy said, wiping up the sirup with a damp rag. "You children are going to learn some table manners. No waffles for you, Pete."

Pete immediately began to howl at the top of his lungs. "Give him his waffle," Tom said hastily. "It was an accident."

"No," Betsy said. "We're going to start having some consistent punishment around here."

Pete put his thumb in his mouth and stared at her solemnly.

"It's almost time for me to catch my train," Tom said. "Are you going to drive me to the station, or can I take the car?"

"You're going to walk!" she said. "It's time you started getting some exercise."

"I'm going to take the car," he said. "Unless you want to drive me."

"*Can't* you walk?"

"I'm tired this morning," he said. "Are you going to drive, or shall I take the car?"

"I'll drive," she said judiciously. "Get in the car, kids!"

The children scrambled into the car. All the way to the station, Betsy sat uncomfortably erect. Hardly any cars were at the station when they got there, and they saw they had ten minutes to wait for the train. They sat in silence.

"You think I'm being silly, don't you?" Betsy said suddenly.

"I'm just a little startled."

"We ought to start doing the things we believe in," she said. "We've got a lot of hard work ahead of us, and we better start now."

He kissed her and went to buy his paper. On the train it was both cool and quiet. He sank down in a blue plush-covered seat. All up and down the aisle men were sitting, motionless and voiceless, reading their papers. Tom opened his and read a long story about negotiations in Korea. A columnist debated the question of when Russia would have hydrogen bombs to drop on the United States. Tom folded his paper and stared out the window at the suburban stations gliding by. He wondered what it would be like to work for Ogden and Hopkins, and he wondered whether Betsy's schemes could possibly turn out successfully. What would happen if he got fired by Hopkins and Betsy's real-estate deals turned into a fiasco?

"It doesn't really matter." The words came to his mind so clearly that he half thought someone had spoken them in his ear.

"Here goes nothing."

The sentence sounded in his mind, flat and emotionless. Suddenly the tension drained out of him, and he felt relaxed. It will be interesting to see what happens, he thought. Then he had a sudden impulse to laugh. The man across the aisle from him peered over his paper suspiciously, and Tom turned his face toward the window. A railroad track alongside the ones on which he was speeding gleamed brightly in the sun.

"It doesn't really matter." During the war that had been a kind of key phrase for him, almost a magical charm, an incantation. He had always been tense before a jump. He had always started worrying about Betsy—that was the first stage, as soon as he learned he had another jump coming up. He had had a clear picture in his mind of a Western Union boy delivering a telegram to her beginning, "The War Department regrets to inform you . . ." Betsy would open the telegram, and then she'd go upstairs to the big bedroom in Grandmother's house, and she'd show it to Grandmother, and Grandmother would say, "You should be proud. He died for his country." And then Betsy would start to swear—he had always been able to see her staring at his grandmother, crying and swearing, exactly as his mother had long ago.

That vision had always given way to another, on the eve of a combat jump. He'd start thinking about how he'd never go to bed with Betsy again. And he'd start thinking about all the cold beer he was never going to drink, and the rare steaks he was never going to eat. Then he'd start getting mad.

By the time he'd got his parachute on, or had "chuted up," as they had called it in the 'troops, he had usually widened his self-pity to embrace all the others aboard the plane. The poor bastards, he had thought. The men had sat in their bucket seats on each side of the aisle of the plane, as expressionless as the men on the commuter train —about the only difference was that during the war they had had no newspapers. Tom had often sat there, expressionless as the others, thinking of a whole platoon of Western Union boys delivering the War Department's regrets. He had heard men talk about premonitions of death before a battle, and often when someone was killed, it would turn out that he had told someone about a premonition, but Tom had had premonitions all the time.

The worst part of the whole nightmare had always come just a few minutes before the jump. A sharp image of a compound fracture of the right thigh would suddenly flash into his mind. During his first combat jump the man beside him had landed wrong and suffered a compound fracture of the right thigh. A long jagged splinter of bone had come through the trouser leg, and the man had sat there staring at it until someone had given him a shot of morphine. Tom had never seen him again, because the Germans had started moving in on them, and it had been necessary to abandon the man with the broken thigh, lying there doped up, still staring at the splinter of bone. Tom had never been able to forget it, and almost every time after that he'd catch himself gripping his own right thigh a few minutes before he had to jump. It was at such times that this silly sentence would come into his mind, and he'd start to relax.

"It doesn't really matter."

The words had had a marvelous effect on him. He had often repeated them to himself, until they began to sound like some kind of revelation. By the time it had been necessary to stand up and walk toward the open door of the airplane, he had always been able to move as casually as though he were just going to step into the next room.

"Geronimo!" a lot of the men used to yell as they jumped, trying to sound fierce as hell. Tom used to yell it too when it was expected of him, but what he was really thinking, with a curiously comforting air of detachment, was "It doesn't really matter." And then, just as Tom went through the door into the prop blast, the second part of the charm had always come to him: "Here goes nothing." And when the parachute had opened, with its terrific wallop at the back of his neck, and he found himself floating down in that curious moment of complete quiet and calm which immediately precedes a combat landing, the third part of his incantation had always come to him: "It will be interesting to see what happens."

All this seemed incredible to Tom as he looked back at it, but those three catch phrases still had the power to soothe him as he sat on the train, one of many men holding newspapers on their laps, and thought about a new job and what Betsy called "the start of a new regime."

By the time he got to New York, he felt relaxed. What the hell is all the crisis about? he thought. After the whole damn war, why am I scared now? I always thought peace would be peaceful, he thought, and laughed. As he walked through Grand Central Station, he looked up and for the first time in years noticed the stars painted on the blue ceiling there. They seemed to be shining brightly, and feeling slightly theatrical, he wondered if it were legitimate to wish on a painted star. He decided it would be all right to make a phony wish, so he wished he could make a million dollars and add a new wing to his grandmother's house, with a billiard room and a conservatory in which to grow orchids.

12

I<small>T WAS</small> while he was walking up Forty-second Street from Grand Central Station to his office at the Schanenhauser Foundation that he saw the man with a leather jacket. It was an ordinary brown leather jacket with a sheepskin collar—it was only unusual that the man should be wearing it in the summer. The man was a swarthy, rather rumpled individual, wearing dungarees, a T-shirt, and the leather jacket, unzipped. Somehow the jacket nagged at Tom's mind—he had seen one like it somewhere a long while ago. It was ridiculous to have one's mind keep returning to a leather jacket when there was work to be done. The memory of the leather jacket was like a riddle, the answer to which had been half forgotten, obscurely important, as though someone had told him a secret he was never to repeat, a secret with some hidden meaning, but now he couldn't remember it.

Trying to put the jacket out of his mind, he hurried along the street. While he was waiting to cross Fifth Avenue, a man standing beside him coughed painfully. Then Tom remembered about the leather jacket—remembered everything about it as clearly as though he had never forgotten.

It had been back in 1943, not many months before Germany started to disintegrate. Only he hadn't known then that Germany would fall to pieces—it had seemed as though the war would go on forever. It had been in December, early in December, that he killed the man in the leather jacket, simply because he needed the jacket for himself.

No, it hadn't been like that at all. There was no use making it worse than it was. The man in the leather jacket had been armed, he had been an enemy, legally decreed such by several governments. He had been a German, and the Germans were different from other people, or at least it had seemed so at the time. How hard it was to remember what the Germans had seemed like then! They had been unconquerable. They had been efficient. They had been professionals at war, while everybody else was an amateur. They had been cold and pitiless. They had been Jew beaters. They had shot, burned, and gassed millions of innocent people. They had laughed at weakness, they had taken joy in cruelty, they had been methodical, they had done things According to Plan. They had started the war, they had been infinitely guilty. The man with the leather jacket had been eighteen years old.

Jesus Christ, that doesn't make any difference! Tom looked up at the traffic light on Fifth Avenue. The man beside him coughed again. The boy with the leather jacket should not have coughed; it had been his cough which had given him away.

"Now listen. One thing you've got to get through your heads is we're not playing games!"

That was a curious sentence to remember. It had been spoken in a harsh voice, matter-of-fact rather than fierce, perhaps a little exasperated, the voice of a teacher confronted by slightly stupid pupils, the voice of the old master sergeant who had prepared Tom for his assault on the boy with the leather jacket, the old master sergeant to whom, in a sense, Tom owed his life, for if he had not learned the lesson, he himself, rather than the boy with the leather jacket, might now be only a painful memory.

"Now listen. One thing you've got to get through your heads is we're not playing games! When you're behind the enemy lines, you don't take prisoners—if you do, you have to stay awake all night to watch them, and the odds are they'll trip you up someway, anyhow. There's no use taking a chance. You see a Jerry, you don't go through this cowboy crap of telling him to put up his hands; you just shoot the bastard, in the back if possible, because you take less chances that way. We ain't playing games. And let's not have any tend-the-wounded crap. The wounded can get you with a hand grenade or a pistol—I've seen it happen a hundred times. There's no use taking a chance. Either don't go near the wounded, or finish them off before you go near them. We ain't playing games."

Well, Tom thought as he entered the office of the Schanenhauser Foundation and sat down at his desk, he had played no games back in 1943, when he had met the boy in the leather jacket. There had been no time for games. Tom and Hank Mahoney had been alone—

the whole company had been busted up, it had been snafu from the beginning—situation normal, all fouled up, only they hadn't used the word "fouled" in those days; no word had been anywhere near bad enough to express the way they felt. They had jumped at the wrong time at the wrong place, and a quarter of the company had been killed by rifle and machine-gun fire before they hit the ground. That had been no time to have sad thoughts about eighteen-year-old German boys. They had jumped and been jumped, by a whole damn division, it had seemed like, and Tom had had just one idea: I'm going to get out of this alive and *don't* try to stop me. No, he hadn't thought that; it had been different from that. He had thought: I'm going to try to get out of this, I'm going to try; I'm not going to die for lack of trying.

Everything had been confusion. They had jumped from the planes just at nightfall, about a hundred men dropped behind the German lines to destroy a bridge. They had been supposed to land in a field near a copse of woods without opposition and proceed to the bridge under cover of darkness, but it hadn't been like that at all. The Germans had been waiting; they had sent up flares and turned searchlights on the men dangling from the glistening white parachutes in the air. And those who survived had panicked as soon as they hit the ground. They had been green troops, many of them, boys who had never been on a combat jump before, and as soon as they saw that things weren't going according to plan, they panicked and went running across the field toward the trees, and the Germans had really had it that time; they had simply lowered their antiaircraft guns and had a real turkey shoot right there at the edge of the forest. The paratroopers had been trained to crawl like snakes at a time like that, to hide like lizards on the ground, but most of them had forgotten, and had dashed toward the woods, running scared, big as snowmen in the searchlights and the flares. It hadn't been necessary for a man to be very bright to be a soldier; all he had had to do was to remember a few basic rules, the most obvious one being to crawl when under fire, to slide like a snake, to live like a lizard, but that time the green troops had panicked and most of them, instead of living like lizards, had died like men.

Tom had gathered twelve men around him, lying on their bellies in the snow and the mud. He and Hank Mahoney and ten other men who kept their heads had crawled in a wide circle and made the woods, all right, at about ten o'clock in the evening. Going into the woods, they had crawled single file, one man thirty feet behind the other, leaving a track like a great snake through the snow and the mud, with Tom as lead man, fifty feet ahead of the others, because the woods might be mined, and it would just be foolish to let a mine kill more than one man. They had been wet to the skin long before they reached the woods, and it had been cold, very cold, as a half moon climbed above the naked trees. Tom and Hank Mahoney and the other ten men had sat huddled together in the woods for a few minutes, until Tom, thinking of the great snake's trail they had left behind, had ordered them to disperse and try to get back to their own lines by different routes, traveling in pairs because it would be just foolishness to let the Germans catch them all at once.

So they had split up, and Tom had never seen most of the men again, nor heard what happened to them. Mahoney had gone with him. The two of them had walked as fast as they could through the woods, planning to circle home eventually, but hoping soon to find dry clothes, or an abandoned hut, or someway to escape the cold.

Shortly before dawn they had reached the edge of the woods and, shivering violently, had hidden behind an ice-glazed rock and looked at what they finally made out to be a German tank depot, with orderly rows of barracks topped by chimneys out of which wisps of smoke had been curling, black and velvety against the frosty sky. It had been then that they heard a man cough only a few hundred yards away from them, and they had crawled back into the trees and along the edge of the woods, keeping under cover, until they saw two sentries in leather, sheepskin-lined jackets, the dry collars turned snugly up around their ears. The younger and slighter of the two sentries had been the one doing the coughing. He had been standing about thirty feet outside the woods, looking down at his feet and coughing. With his right hand he had been negligently holding his rifle, and with his left he had been clutching his chest. The other sentry had been standing about twenty feet from him, his rifle cradled in one arm, watching his companion cough, and looking worried.

It had not been necessary for Tom and Hank Mahoney to talk. They had crawled toward the sentries over the hard crust of old snow in the dim light of the setting moon. It hadn't been difficult. They had been able to crawl within ten feet of the sentries before jumping them silently—it hadn't been difficult at all, and only one small cry had been made, not a very loud sound, the sort of noise a man might make in his sleep, not the sort of cry to alarm the whole camp. Tom hadn't even had to use his knife at first—he had choked the sentry to prevent him from shouting, and when he had taken his hands away, the boy had seemed dead. Tom and Mahoney had stripped the bodies of the warm clothes, and the sheepskin collars had felt delicious against their own cold ears and necks. Before daylight, they had effaced all signs of the struggle and dragged the bodies into the woods behind a fallen tree in the hope that the Germans would think for a little while that their sentries had just gone over the hill. They had been about to leave the bodies lying stretched in the snow when the sentry Tom had choked groaned and moved one arm.

"I made sure of mine with my knife," Hank had said. "Better finish yours off, or he'll come to and rouse the whole camp."

Tom had taken out his sheath knife and had hesitated. The young German sentry had lain at his feet, helpless as a patient on an operating table.

"Hurry up," Hank had said nervously. "We've got to get out of here."

Tom had knelt beside the sentry. He had not thought it would be difficult, but the tendons of the boy's neck had proved tough, and suddenly the sentry had started to sit up. In a rage Tom had plunged the knife repeatedly into his throat, ramming it home with all his strength until he had almost severed the head from the body.

"Come on, that's enough," Hank had said in a shocked voice. "Let's get out of here."

Trembling, Tom had stood up and followed Hank out of the woods. They had skirted the tank depot, until on the other side of the gully they found a burned-out tank which apparently had been left there to await shipment back to Germany as scrap. They had climbed into the wrecked tank and huddled in the cinders until nightfall.

In the pockets of his newly acquired leather jacket Tom had found chocolate and cough drops and a wallet with no money, and an identification card with a picture of a thin, serious-looking youth eighteen years old named Hans Engelhart, and there had also been a letter written in a fine feminine script on thin, blue, slightly scented paper, but the letter had been in German, and Tom hadn't been able to read it. On the upper-left-hand corner of the envelope had been printed what obviously was a return address. The absurd idea of writing the sender of the letter had flashed into Tom's mind. What would he say? "This morning I killed your boy, and I would like to send my condolences. He was in the wrong army, but he seemed like a nice boy, and I'm sorry it had to happen like this." Impulsively he had torn the letter into small bits, together with its envelope, and, trying to forget the feeling of the plunging knife in his hand, had lain in the ashes to sleep.

After dark, Tom and Hank Mahoney had crawled out of the wrecked tank and had begun the long, circuitous journey back to their own lines. Skirting the tank depot, they had returned to the woods. In the darkness they had tried to head west, but they had soon become confused and after about two hours had realized that they were retracing their steps.

"In a few minutes the moon will be up, and we can see better," Hank had said. "Let's sit down for a breather."

They had continued to walk until they found a tree trunk to sit upon. Through naked branches they had seen the moon climbing above the crest of a distant hill. Gradually the darkness had dissolved. They had just started to walk again when Tom noticed the two bodies they had left there that morning and realized that they had come full circle. The bodies had been lying just as they had left them, except that their faces had acquired the sardonic grin of death.

"I guess they have the last laugh," Hank had said. "I don't think we're ever going to get out of here. The dead always have the last laugh."

"Come on," Tom had replied. "We've got to try."

Together they had resumed their journey, making better progress in the moonlight. At about midnight they had come to the field where they had landed. It was still strewn with equipment, and the dead. Stealing from body to body, they had collected six boxes of K-rations and five full canteens of water. After eating and drinking their fill, they had pressed on. Just before dawn exhaustion and the continuous cold had combined to make them lightheaded, and they had staggered along, holding each other up like drunks returning from a party. There had been no more woods—only fields affording little protection. "Before it gets any lighter, we've got to find a place to hide out," Tom had said. At sunrise they had found a crater gouged in the earth by a crashing plane. Eagerly they had slid into the tangle of wreckage within it, only to be greeted by a fearful stench. "I can't stand this," Mahoney had said. "Let's keep going."

"No," Tom had said, nodding toward the endless fields which lay in front of them. "We'd be picked up sure. You'll get used to the smell."

Mahoney had gagged.

"Anyway, it's going to be a nice day," Tom had said. "We're better off than if it were raining, and we've got plenty to eat and drink. Look at those clouds over there—they look warm. It's a nice morning."

He had paused, suddenly and incongruously remembering the lines of verse carved on the bench in his grandmother's garden so far away: "The lark's on the wing; the snail's on the thorn: God's in his heaven—all's right with the world." He had started to laugh. Collapsing into the mud at the bottom of the hole, he had given himself over to almost maniacal laughter.

"You nuts?" Mahoney had said.

"No. I just thought of something—something I can't explain," Tom had replied. Mahoney had been too tired to question him further. They had curled up in the mud at the bottom of the crater full of wreckage and immediately had slept, not awakening until dusk. The sun had warmed them, and they had both felt refreshed and rested. "I think we're going to make it," Tom had said. "For the first time, I really think we're going to make it."

They had made it all right, six days later, and upon rejoining their company had been looked upon as heroes by the young recruits who replaced the men who didn't come back. There had been one young corporal who had been in the army only a few months, a thin boy of Italian ancestry, who had wanted to buy the German jacket, and Tom had given it to him. Gardella, the corporal's name had been— "Caesar" Gardella, the boys had called him. He had had a deep voice. Now, Tom suddenly froze at his desk in the offices of the Schanenhauser Foundation. Caesar Gardella! That was the elevator man at the United Broadcasting building! It was Caesar Gardella, grown fat and with a mustache! And the leather jacket wouldn't be all he'd remember; he'd remember everything that had happened after that—the jump on the island of Karkow and, before that, Rome and Maria. Tom found he was gripping his thigh and sweating.

Maria.

It is not my fault, he thought; it was not my fault; it was nobody's fault at all. It happened a long while ago.

Maria.

I have forgotten her, he thought. I haven't thought about her for a long time; I really haven't thought about her; she never entered my head for a long time.

It really wasn't my fault, he thought. It was no one's fault. I am not to blame.

How curious it was to find that apparently nothing was ever really forgotten, that the past was never really gone, that it was always lurking, ready to destroy the present, or at least to make the present seem absurd, or if not that, to make Tom himself seem absurd, the perpetuator of an endless and rather hideous masquerade.

I am a good man, he thought, and I have never done anything of which I am truly ashamed. Curiously, he seemed to be mimicking himself. "I am a good man," he seemed to be saying in a high, effeminate, prissy voice, "and I have never done anything of which I am truly ashamed." A gust of ghostly and derisive laughter seemed to ring out in reply.

It's the way things happen, he thought, and if I were to go through it all again, they would happen the same way.

It's funny, but I can think about it now, he thought—I can see what happened, after all these years, I can finally see what happened, and it's absurd to be ashamed.

Maria. The time was December 1944. The place, Rome. And everything was different. Now, as he sat behind his desk at the Schanenhauser Foundation in the year 1953, Tom felt again the blind helpless fury that had started it all, back in December 1944, when, after fighting one war and getting it almost won, he and Mahoney and Caesar Gardella and all the rest of them had got orders to go to the Pacific, without even a day of leave in the States between wars. The whole company had got those orders, after having made two combat jumps in France and two in Italy. Someone had got the idea that the way to save lives in the invasion of the islands of the Pacific was to use more paratroopers. Take the islands from the air instead of going in on the beaches, somebody had said—send us more jump boys; we want to get this thing over in a hurry and all go home.

"Another day, another war," Mahoney had said when he heard it.

Tom had said nothing. I got through one war, he had thought. I won't get through another. The odds build up against you. They throw you in once, and you fight your way out. You do it twice, you can do it three times. But sooner or later the odds catch up with you. It's like throwing dice—sooner or later you get snake eyes. If they're going to send me out to the Pacific, I won't come back.

He had had a clear picture then, as soon as he heard where he was going, of a Japanese soldier, a caricature of one, with a small evil face, grinning, and holding a bayonet poised. That's my boy, he had thought. That's the one who's waiting for me. I've had the Germans and I've had the Italians, and now the Japs are going to have me.

"Anyway," Hank had said, "they say they're going to give us a week here before we go, and it won't even be counted as leave."

"A week?" Tom had said.

"Sure! How much money you got?"

"I'm broke," Tom had said. His allotment to Betsy had never left him much. Since the beginning of the war, he had allotted her two thirds of his salary, and she had put it all into a savings bank, so that they could buy a house after the war. He had never minded being broke before.

"Don't worry," Hank had said. "I'm loaded. I got six hundred bucks I won in a crap game, and I'll give you half. This will be a week to remember!"

Betsy, Tom had thought, but somehow she had dissolved into nothing more than an ironic and rather painful memory, something to be kept out of his mind. I've got a week, he had thought, a week in Rome, a week on the town. And to Mahoney he had said, "Okay, Hank, let's go."

It had been a week to remember, all right. They had started in a small bar in the basement of a cheap hotel. In the corner there had been a piano painted white, with a thin, bald, blind man playing old American jazz very badly. It had been there he had met Maria. She had come into the bar hesitantly with painfully obvious intention, and every man in the room had glanced up and looked at her, a pretty girl, eighteen years old, in a worn black dress and a coat that had once belonged to a soldier. She had walked over to the bar meekly and ordered a glass of vermouth. She had sat on a stool in front of the bar and had taken off her coat, which had been clumsily retailored to fit her, and she had laid it across her lap while she sipped her vermouth slowly to make it last a long time. Tom had looked at her coldly. Young, with a good figure, and a face which, if it were relaxed, could be beautiful—it might as well be this one as any other. When you've only got a week, you can't look around forever. He had walked over and sat down beside her. "Can I buy you a drink?" he had asked.

It had been real romantic. She had glanced up at him with a forced smile on her lips. "Thank you," she had said in a strong Italian accent. Her voice had been soft and timid.

"Well, I see you're fixed up," Hank had said, coming over and leaning on the bar beside Tom. "I'm going to shove on—there's nothing else around here. Let's meet here tomorrow morning."

"All right," Tom had said.

He had sat beside Maria sipping his sweet vermouth, the picture of the grinning little man with the bayonet still in his mind. "You'll be all right," Betsy had written him in her last letter. "I'm absolutely sure you'll come home to me all right."

Pretty Betsy, he had thought, as he sat sipping the sweet vermouth. Pretty Betsy, with the pretty shoulders and the soft skin tanned by the summer sun. I will not think of Betsy.

I have a week, he had thought, seven days and seven nights, the amount of time the world was created in. He had glanced then at Maria, who also had been sitting sipping her vermouth and looking down thoughtfully, and he had seen that she was prettier than he had thought, that her face, when in repose, was still the face of a young girl, and that her body was as beautiful as the body of any woman, and much more beautiful than most.

"Do you speak English?"

"A little," she had replied in her strong accent. "My father spoke English. Sometimes he used to be a guide for tourists."

"My name's Bill Brown," Tom had said, "William T. Brown from Kansas City, Iowa. What's your name?"

She had shrugged. "Maria," she had said.

"How about a meal, Maria? Let's get out of here and get a real dinner! You like champagne?"

"Yes."

They had gone to a big restaurant with white table linen and waiters in dinner coats, as though there had never been a war at all. For an enormous price they had eaten roast chicken and fried potatoes and pastries, and they had had champagne, all right, champagne which the Germans had brought to Rome from France. She had eaten greedily and drunk little. When the meal was over, and the waiter paid, she had quietly asked him to go to her room with her; he hadn't even had to hint at all. They had got into a taxi and ridden a long way, down dimly lit streets, with the silhouettes of tall buildings ruined by time rather than war black and jagged against the moonlit sky. They had not talked. In the taxi he had kissed her once, finding that her lips were unbelievably soft and that he had forgotten what a kiss was like. The despair, the fury of having to fly to another war, and the cold loneliness that had been sitting in his stomach so many months, through so many battles and the intervals between battles, had left him, and somehow the sense of cheapness and sordidness had gone, and he had felt relaxed and completely happy for the first time in two years, for the first time since he had got aboard the slate-gray troopship which had carried him from New York into the fog of the North Atlantic an endless number of months ago.

"You are beautiful," he had said.

The taxi had stopped in front of a tenement house. An old woman had leaned out a window and watched them with open curiosity. After paying the driver, Tom had followed the girl through a courtyard jammed with debris, into a dark hall. There had been no light. The girl had taken his hand and led him up five winding flights of stairs, littered with cardboard boxes and bottles. Moonlight had streamed through the window at each landing. The pitch-darkness of the stairs between landings had not been like the darkness of a battlefield, an impenetrable wall concealing only danger and death. It had been a protecting darkness, friendly, warm, almost soft and caressing. She had led him to her room, and he had snapped a light switch, but no light had come on, and she had lit a candle, bending over it seriously as the flame from the match in her cupped hands grew, first showing her silhouette, and then her face, with shadows flickering in the candlelight. He had kissed her again, and with the tips of her fingers she had caressed the back of his head, and his neck and his shoulders, very gently, hardly touching him at all, and when the kiss was over, she had smiled, and the look of strain had gone from her face, and it hadn't been sordid any more. She had taken off her clothes and stood there golden in the candlelight, incredibly beautiful.

He hadn't gone to meet Mahoney in the bar in the morning. He had lived with Maria for a week, shunning everyone he knew, and in that week he and Maria had built a small, temporary world for themselves, full of delights and confidences, a completely self-sufficient world, packed with private jokes, and memories, a whole lifetime with silver and golden anniversaries, Christmases and birthdays, fifty years compressed into a week. They had kept no secrets from each other. He had told her his real name. Lying on the bed naked, taking great pleasure in nakedness even when their passion was spent, they had talked endlessly, discussing all troubles, all angers, all fears, and for that week, nothing had seemed very bad any more, even the inevitable prospect of the grinning little man with the bayonet, whom he introduced to her, and whom she acknowledged sadly, as a person she knew well. They had understood each other, the three of them, Tom and Maria and the caricature of the man waiting with a gun.

At the end of the week, Tom had said good-by to her and reported back to his unit, only to be told that transportation wasn't available yet and that he could live wherever he wanted as long as he checked in, or at least telephoned headquarters, every morning at eight o'clock. He had returned to her room, and it had been exactly as though he had returned from a long absence, the young husband coming home from the wars: they had both felt that way, they had both experienced all the happiness of a reunion, without the awkwardness which follows long absence.

He had lived in the room with her, thinking that each day was the last, thinking that tomorrow at eight o'clock the sergeant who answered the telephone would say, "Oh, yes, Captain Rath—we've got a plane leaving in two hours. You better get right down here." He had kept his bags packed, and every morning at seven o'clock he had kissed her and crept out of bed and got himself fully dressed, in case it would be necessary to hurry, and each morning for seven weeks, for forty-nine days in all, the sergeant had said, "Nothing yet, Captain—the colonel asks me to tell you to be sure to check in tomorrow."

There had been forty-nine last days, and the greatest pleasure in the world had been to walk back to her room from the restaurant where he made his telephone calls at eight o'clock in the morning, shivering a little in the dampness, and to hear her say delightedly, "Not yet?"

"Not yet!" he had said forty-nine times and, still shivering from the coldness of early morning, had jumped into the warm bed beside her.

During those forty-nine last days, they had grown old together, patient of each other's weaknesses, and they had even acquired old family friends, men in bars who nodded to them and recognized them as a couple who belonged together, old ladies on street corners who addressed Maria as a married woman, respectable as themselves. And in particular, they had acquired one friend, almost an uncle, or perhaps a brother, a melancholy man who owned a bakery, where hot coffee was served, a wonderful place to have breakfast. The man's name had been Lapa, Louis Lapa, and he had fought with the Germans against the Americans and, a little later, with the Americans against the Germans, fighting both times well, but without enthusiasm. Finally he had been wounded and had returned to his bakery with his foot in a cast, and when Tom and Maria sat down to have breakfast in his shop, he brought hot rolls and coffee, limping badly and coughing, but always smiling. After the first few days he had often sat down to join them, drinking a cup of coffee himself, of course knowing without being told a great deal about Tom and Maria, knowing that they had just met, and that they would soon part, and feeling sad about this, but also companionable. They had come to know Louis well and on one occasion had even invited him to visit them in their room, and they had had a quiet family evening together, with Louis admiring Maria's beauty the way a friendly brother or uncle might admire the beauty of a young wife. He had called her the most beautiful girl in Rome and had told Tom he was lucky, and Tom had replied that he was indeed lucky, and he had felt this to be true.

They had had many friends, other Americans living with Italian girls, and one of them had been Caesar Gardella, who had turned out to be intensely religious, who had tried to get an audience with the Pope, and who told everyone he was going to come back to Rome and marry his girl after the war was over. His girl's name had been Gina—she was a cousin of Maria's or some sort of distant relative. Tom and Caesar and Gina and Maria had sat drinking together on several evenings, and it had been almost like a suburban community, with the men all working for the same big corporation. But after seven weeks, the sergeant at headquarters had told Tom he had to hurry, transportation was available—the plane was due to leave in three hours. After hearing that over the telephone, Tom had raced back to Maria's room, and it had been then she had told him she thought she was pregnant, she wasn't sure, but she thought she probably was. There had been no recriminations. She had asked nothing, and he had denied nothing. She, knowing he was married, and knowing he was flying to the Pacific to meet his grinning little man with a gun, had assumed he could do nothing much for her and had been surprised and grateful when he borrowed five hundred dollars from his friends and gave it to her, along with a jeepful of canned goods and cigarettes and chewing gum, all of which was worth a great deal.

"If you are pregnant," he had said, "will you have the child?"

"God willing," she had replied, and he had been glad, absurdly glad that in flying to meet his evil, grinning little man with the bayonet, he was leaving a child behind, even if it were to be a child with no father to care for it; a ragamuffin child dancing in the street for pennies, perhaps, but at least a child, which was better than to die and leave nothing, as though he had never been born.

But of course he hadn't been sure about the child; it had been only a possibility. He had been sure about nothing, as he boarded the plane and sat in the hard, uncomfortable bucket seat, waiting to take off for the long flight to the Pacific. How strange to think that he might have a child, never to see, never to hold, but a child just the same! How strange that after all the long months of killing, there would be finally, perhaps, the birth of a child, and that this would be the one thing he had done in the last two years which could conceivably lead to trouble. This, of all he had done, would be the one deed which could lead to a court-martial, and stern disapproving looks on the part of commanding officers, and colonels shaking fingers in his face, and social ostracism at home, if he ever got home, and divorce, and a very bad name, instead of medals.

How strange, he had thought, as he sat in the plane: what a curious inversion, how to the despair of the chaplains is the inclination of the young soldiers to forget their job of killing and to run off and make love!

He had started to laugh as the plane took off, and above the roar of the engines Mahoney had shouted, "What the hell is funny?"

"We're all nuts!" Tom had said, with a feeling that he had at last discovered the great fundamental truth. "We're all nuts, every god-damn one of us—we're all absolutely nuts!"

"You're god-damn right!" Mahoney had replied.

"Ever hear of Karkow?" Caesar Gardella had asked an hour later.

Tom had heard of it vaguely, a small island not far from the Philippines, a very small island which the British had held for two months against strong Japanese attack at the beginning of the war, but had finally lost. "What about it?" he had replied.

"I hear," Caesar had said above the roar of the engines, "I hear they're going to drop us on it."

It was just a rumor, Tom had thought, but at such times the rumors are always right. Karkow! What a curious name for a place to die!

The plane had stopped at many places, hurrying to refuel, always in a hurry to get to its destination, until finally it had deposited Tom and Mahoney in a transient officers' camp in Hollandia, New Guinea, where there was nothing to do but lie all day on cots under mosquito netting and wait for the attack on Karkow. Lying there, drinking heavily chlorinated water or warm beer when he could get it, Tom had wondered what he would do if he were not killed at Karkow, or wherever he was going. What did one do when one had a wife in the States and a woman and maybe a child in Italy? Did one simply take one's choice? After he had been in New Guinea about two weeks, the letters Betsy had written him almost every night had caught up with him. In the first one he opened she had said:

Tommy my darling,

Gosh, what a day this has been! At eight-thirty this morning—*eight-thirty,* mind you—Dotty Kimble telephoned me and wanted me to play bridge in the afternoon. It seems that Nancy Gorton had promised that she would be her partner in a tournament at the club, and at the last minute Nancy got a telegram that John was getting a week-end pass, so of course she simply took off for South Carolina. That left Dotty without a partner in this tournament which she seemed to think was awfully important—you know how seriously she takes things like that. Well, anyway, I said all right, and guess who we played in the very first game? Lillie Barton and Jessie Willis! You'd die if you saw Jessie now—she's gained about *fifty* pounds, and she's worried to death that she won't be able to take it off after the baby comes. She's due next month. Anyway, I thought I'd die when I found we were going to play her and Lillie, because you know what sharks they are. Well, to make a long story short, you would have been proud of me, darling—I won't even try to be modest. Dotty and I won! We each got a perfectly adorable majolica bowl for a prize. I've wrapped mine up and stored it with our wedding presents, and after the war, when we buy our house, I'm going to put it right in the middle of our dining-room table, and every morning you can take an orange out of it and think how smart I am!

Can't think of anything more to say now, except I miss you like anything. If I sent all the kisses I'd like to give you, this letter would have to go parcel post!

I love you forever and forever and forever and forever!

BETSY

Her other letters had been much the same. They had contained descriptions of movies she had seen, and dreams of the future, when he would have a job with J. H. Nottingsby, Incorporated, or some firm with a name which would have to sound like that. Along with the easy optimism, the cheerfulness, and long, involved jokes, Betsy had sent him pictures of herself, snapshots of a slender, fresh-faced girl, hearty, healthy, and smiling, a girl he had seen someplace sometime, long ago, a real beauty.

Perhaps I shall go back to Italy, if I go anywhere at all, he had thought. If I go back to Italy I shall betray one person, but if I go home to Betsy, perhaps I shall betray two. It had been strange to lie on the narrow canvas cot in New Guinea and think of a son, perhaps, the grandson of "The Major," his own son, the great-grandson of "The Senator," the likeness of himself, dancing for pennies in the streets of Rome. If he did not go back to Rome, what would happen to such a son? He would go wandering barefoot, begging for chew-chew gum, a child without a father, the son of a harlot grown ugly and bitter. That's my boy, he had thought while lying on the hard canvas cot in New Guinea; that's my boy. If I get it on Karkow, that will be the only part of me I'll leave behind.

He had decided that if he survived the war he would go back to Italy, at least to see how Maria was making out, and he envied Caesar Gardella, who got long letters in Italian from his girl in Rome, and who considered himself formally engaged and talked constantly about getting married after the war. Maria had never written Tom at all. It had been her kind of faithfulness not to write, to allow herself to be forgotten. But apparently Gina had written something to Caesar about her, for Caesar's attitude toward Tom had changed—he had become reserved and disapproving, and with an edge to his voice, he had for the first time begun to call Tom "Sir."

Now in his office at the Schanenhauser Foundation, Tom got up and stared out the window at the city below. He had not thought of Karkow for years. If Karkow had not cauterized his mind, he might not have forgotten Maria so easily, and things might have been different between him and Caesar. How had it started? He had first heard the name Karkow as a rumor, while flying from Europe. After he had lain for weeks in a transient officers' camp in New Guinea, the rumor had grown until it was substantiated by a colonel who had called Tom and Mahoney and many other officers into his matter-of-fact office, with a matter-of-fact map on the wall, to brief them.

Karkow was a small, jagged island, with steep rocky cliffs on all but one side. The Japs, like the British before them, had had many guns trained on the gravel beach on that one side, waiting for an invasion, and they had honeycombed the island with tunnels and caves. The island lay in the mouth of a large bay, and it had to be taken —no one had doubted that. The plan for taking it was simple, the colonel had explained in his matter-of-fact way: three thousand paratroopers would be dropped on it.

"Damn it to hell!" Mahoney had said that night after the colonel had explained the plan. "Don't they know anything about how paratroopers work? You don't jump on top of the god-damn enemy! You don't throw three thousand men right down on top of nests of antiaircraft artillery and machine guns and thousands of armed men, ready and waiting!"

"Well, this time I guess they do," Caesar had said bitterly. "The colonel's sure the Navy will have blasted every gun off the island before we get there. Didn't you hear him?"

"I wonder," Tom had said, "how many of us will even hit the god-damn island? It's pretty small. I bet they dump half of us in the water."

The idea had been to take off for the jump at four o'clock in the morning and to start landing troops on the island with the first light of dawn. The plan had been for the Navy to start shelling the place two days beforehand and to have landing craft approach to make the Japs think the invasion was coming from the sea.

I will be sensible, Tom had thought late on the afternoon before the invasion. I will be sensible and go to bed early, and get a good rest. He had lain down on his cot and tried hard to think of nothing, to make his mind a complete blank. He had not wanted to think of the small island, Karkow, lying now under shellfire from the Navy, with the Japs in their caves. He had not wanted to think of Betsy, and he had not wanted to think of Maria. How painful had been the memory of a kiss or of anything good he would never have again! He had lain still, pretending to be asleep when Mahoney came in and stretched out on the cot near him.

"Tom?" Mahoney had asked after a few minutes.

"Yes."

"It's funny," Mahoney had said. "I was just thinking, we got nothing to worry about. I mean, we either don't get it tomorrow, and we got nothing to worry about, or we do get it tomorrow, and we got nothing to worry about."

"That's wonderful."

"No, I mean it. I been worrying a lot about what kind of job I'll get after the war. Now I'm not worrying about it."

"No worries," Tom had said.

They had both lain there on the canvas cots, unable to sleep, and a curious lightheaded mood had taken possession of them, almost gaiety. At about one o'clock they had given up trying to sleep and had gone to a near-by dispensary, where some doctors were playing poker. They had joined the game and had accepted a few drinks of medicinal alcohol from the doctors, but they had not got drunk; they would have been crazy to do that. It had not really been necessary to get drunk. The jokes had all seemed astonishingly funny, in fact everything had seemed funny. The doctors had not known that he and Mahoney were supposed to take off in a few hours for Karkow. One of them had complained bitterly about having to be on duty all night, and about what a great financial sacrifice a doctor in the Army makes, because he could be making ten times more money at home. Mahoney had sympathized with the doctor, his great face morose and understanding, without a hint of irony, and Tom had laughed inside until his stomach hurt.

At about three o'clock Mahoney had said, "Well, I guess we got to be going. How about it, Tom?"

"I guess so," Tom had said.

"Hey, you can't quit while you're ahead," one of the doctors had objected.

"Sorry," Mahoney had said. He and Tom had left the doctors without saying where they were going, not so much because they weren't supposed to tell as because it was more bitter and more funny to hear the doctors complain about breaking up the game too early.

Tom and Mahoney had gone from the card game to the mess hall and had had a big breakfast. They had sat together, looking at the young boys, the members of their companies, fresh recruits, most of them, filing into the mess hall, the sleep still in their eyes. More than half of them had never been in a combat jump, and they had looked incredibly young, almost like schoolboys as they filed into the mess hall to get a good breakfast before taking off.

"We've got five or six years on most of them," Mahoney had said, and Tom had understood that he said it in sorrow for the young boys, for at times like that, each year of age, each year behind you, seemed like a million dollars in the bank that could never be taken away, and the old were to be envied more than anyone on earth, for they had lived their lives, but the young were vulnerable—their lives could be stolen from them.

Breakfast had been over quickly. The men had lined up outside the mess hall, and trucks had taken them to the air strip where the big planes waited, their engines quiet, their propellers motionless. The men had strapped on their parachutes and checked their equipment. It had still been dark. The moon had been almost full, a lopsided moon, and the warm tropic night had been stroked by a breeze as soft as the touch of a woman's fingertips. The sky, even before dawn, had been full of peaceful birds, and the jungle beyond the air strip had hummed with life. Tom and Mahoney had walked out on the air strip together, but they had been assigned to different planes. As they parted in the middle of the air strip, Mahoney had said, "Take it easy, boy—and when you hit, close up with my boys fast. And keep those damn kids of yours from shooting my men up—it's going to be close quarters when we get there."

"You better not be worrying about that," Tom had said. "Don't let your kids freeze up—they'll do it every time. I'm telling my boys to go in shooting and to keep shooting until nobody shoots back."

Mahoney had grinned. "You're a tough bastard," he had said. "I'm glad you're on our side."

Tom had walked up the ramp of his plane, and Caesar Gardella had helped him to check to make sure his men were all there and that they were fully equipped. Tom had been cheerful and bluff—he had learned to do that by then. And as he had told Mahoney, he had given his troops one parting piece of advice. "Just keep firing," he had said. "Start firing when you hit the ground and don't stop till the place is ours. Remember just one thing: The trouble with most green troops is they don't fire their guns, especially when things are mixed up. They remember too much about 'Safety First.' Don't shoot each other if you can help it and don't shoot up the other companies, but keep firing. You're not going to be blamed if somebody gets hurt."

Tom had sat in the airplane, like the young boys on all sides of him, chewing gum and looking out the window in a matter-of-fact way. A sergeant had shut the door of the plane. Tom had swallowed twice as the engines coughed, then roared, and had fastened his safety belt as the plane started to taxi down the runway, rushing faster and faster, until it finally soared over the gleaming sea. He had grinned at the boys around him, and they had grinned back—that had been part of the ritual. The plane had gained altitude, and gradually it had begun to grow cold. Caesar had walked down the aisle passing out blankets. Out the windows of the plane, Tom had seen the pale stars, already beginning to fade before the approach of dawn. Anyway, I will leave a child, he had thought. It had been a curiously comforting thought.

The flight to Karkow had seemed short, far too short. It had been comparatively comfortable to huddle in a bucket seat under a blanket, with the engine droning drowsily. Far below, the moon had made a path on the sea, and there had been nothing else to look at until the flash of big guns at Karkow became visible. By the time the plane reached Karkow, it had been light enough to see—the whole operation had been behind schedule from the start. Thousands of feet below, the island had looked no bigger than a pebble on the ruffled surface of the sea. What had seemed to be only a few inches from the pebble, about twenty tiny-appearing ships had lain, and from both the ships and the island puffs of smoke occasionally lit by pale flashes of flame had floated upward. The planes carrying the paratroopers had circled at a high altitude, waiting for the ships to finish their bombardment. Suddenly the smoke from the ships had stopped. A squadron of bombers had roared in low over the island, and the whole place had seemed to explode into smoke and fire.

"Boy!" Gardella had said. "This isn't going to be so bad! By the time we get down, there isn't going to be anybody alive!"

"It won't be so bad," Tom had said, thinking of the Japs hanging on in their caves, waiting for the interval between the bombing and the landing of their enemies to come out and man their guns. He had wondered what it was like to hang on in a cave, with the bombs crashing overhead, waiting. Suddenly the Japs had not seemed so much like caricatures of little yellow men grinning and holding bayonets any more—he had found himself feeling more in common with the Japs hanging on in their caves down below, and waiting, as he was waiting, than with all the safe people in the world, the people at home, safe, and the sailors far below, safe aboard their ships, and the crews of the bombers, who were flying home right now to have hot coffee and a morning nap, their part of the invasion over. It must be tough to wait in a cave, he had thought, knowing that soon the whole works is going to be thrown at you. It must be tough, it must be like waiting up here. And yet, I will leave a child, he had thought.

The sky had begun to grow bright and blue, with an intense quality, almost like a stained-glass window. The surface of the sea had become jade green, flecked with white over the shoals to the south of Karkow. As the plane circled lower, it had become obvious that the sea was rough. It's blowing pretty hard down there, Tom had thought. I'll bet more than half of us will be blown clean over the island. I hope they have enough rescue boats down there.

A big gray transport near the north end of the island was unloading landing craft, Tom had seen, and these now began to circle as though in preparation for a landing, but the element of surprise must be diminished, he had thought, by the big planes circling overhead. Below him Tom could see the first of the planes carrying paratroopers begin to level off and head for the island. For the first time the guns on the island had opened fire, and almost immediately one of the big planes had begun to smoke and quietly, almost as if by plan, had slanted into the sea. The men in Tom's plane had already stood up, and the door had already been opened in preparation for the jump. Standing near the door as the plane slanted lower and lower, Tom had seen the men from the planes ahead bail out, had seen a few plummet down without the flutter of a parachute, had seen others drift over the island or fall short of it into the sea. He had seen hundreds land on the smoking island, which was already crisscrossed by tracers; he had seen more than one thousand men spilled into the air by the prodigal planes, and then he himself had been in the air, falling. There had been the jerk of the parachute opening, and he had swung like a violent pendulum back and forth, the great lip of the cliff down below, men all around him in the air, and, just below, one man also swinging like a pendulum in the wind had crashed into the jagged side of the cliff and was being dragged over the sea, his parachute still full of wind, like the sails of a sloop in summer. Tom had twisted, working the risers of his parachute with all the strength of his wrists, spilling wind from it, angling in over the edge of the cliff. From below tracer bullets had arched up at him, slowly, like candle flames in the air. Then there had been a sudden impact, and he had been dragged over rocks, fighting his harness, until he had found himself lying in a gully, free of his parachute, a gun in his hand, and all around him gunfire and the hoarse shouts of men.

Everywhere there had been Japs, and the paratroopers had been coming down like rain all over the island. There had been no clear line of battle, only a melee, the Japs and paratroopers all mixed up together. And as Tom had known would happen, a lot of the green troops had been afraid to fire, for fear of killing their own men. They had frozen, and Tom had crawled from his gully, rounding up his men, cursing at them and shoving their guns into their hands. The Japs had not been afraid to fire—they had taken it as a matter of course that they would kill some of their own men. It had been necessary for the paratroopers to fire too.

Hank Mahoney had been behind a rock, near the ravine where Tom had landed, and there had been three Japs with a mortar just to the left of him. Tom had found Gardella, and the two of them had got part of the company together and had just managed to clean out the Jap mortar when Mahoney ran out from behind his rock. Tom, barely seeing a moving figure out of the corner of his eye, had whirled and thrown a hand grenade. "No!" Gardella had yelled, just too late. In the instant while the grenade had been poised in mid-air, and Mahoney had still been running, like a schoolboy about to receive a forward pass, Tom had seen who it was, but then the grenade had exploded, Mahoney had crumpled, and at the same time a machine gun had opened up on Tom and his men. Tom had motioned to Gardella and the others to withdraw to the shelter of a near-by shell hole. He himself had flattened his body against the earth and had crawled over to Hank. Mahoney had been lying on his belly, and no injury had been visible on his back. "Hank?" Tom had said. There had been no answer. Tom had put his hand under Mahoney's arm and turned him over. Mahoney's entire chest had been torn away, leaving the naked lungs and splintered ribs exposed. His face had been unsoiled and serene. Perhaps that, in addition to the panic-stricken torrent of self-accusation, had contributed to Tom's madness. With courage and surprising lucidity of mind, he had undertaken the rescue of a corpse. Picking up Hank's blood-drenched body, he had run, cleverly dodging from rock to rock. When confronted by a cave full of Japs, he had carefully propped Hank up in a shell hole and under heavy machine-gun fire had crawled to within fifteen feet of the mouth of the cave and tossed in two hand grenades. When the smoke and dust had cleared, he had gone into the cave with a knife, finding six Japs dead and one half alive. With grim pleasure he had finished that one off and calmly returned to Hank's body. Picking it up as if it were a child, he had continued across the island. He had fought his way almost to the beach on the opposite side when it occurred to him that he didn't know where he was going, for there was nothing on the beach, and no doctors had yet been landed anywhere on the island. Carrying Hank's body into a pillbox which had been cracked open by bombs, he had knelt astride it and had committed his ultimate act of agony and madness: he had tried to give Hank's pitifully torn body artificial respiration. Remembering fragments of lessons in lifesaving he had taken as a boy, he had pumped Hank's stiffening arms up and down relentlessly, succeeding only in forcing blood through Hank's nose and mouth. He had had no idea how long he applied artificial respiration, but after a long time he had become aware that the shooting outside the pillbox had stopped. The whole island had suddenly hummed with silence. Picking up Hank's body, which had stopped bleeding, he had run to the top of a knoll. "Medic!" he had shouted. "Medic! Medic!"

A sergeant halfway down the knoll had called to him and pointed toward a medical corpsman bandaging a man's knee a hundred yards away. Tom had run there and gently put Hank's body on the ground near the man with the injured knee. "This is an emergency case," he had said to the medical corpsman. The man had glanced briefly at Hank's body, then walked over and examined it closely.

"You don't need no medic for this guy," he had said casually. "He's been dead for hours. Put him with the other dead over there." The corpsman had gestured toward an irregularly shaped pile covered by a torn parachute. Flies had been crawling on the white cloth.

"No," Tom had said.

"He's dead," the corpsman had replied.

"He's not."

The corpsman had glanced at Tom sharply and sighed. "I'll do it for you," he had said and, leaning forward, had unceremoniously started to drag Hank's body away.

"Don't touch him. I want a real doctor for him," Tom had said.

The corpsman had straightened up and stared at Tom. Then he had called over his shoulder to a group of soldiers who had sat down in the dirt and already started a card game. "Hey, come over here," the corpsman had said. The soldiers had wearily got to their feet. Holding a knife in one hand, Tom had stood astride Mahoney's body. The soldiers had approached him slowly and stopped a few yards away.

"Captain, that man you've got there is dead," the corpsman had said. "Let these men take care of him, and you get a rest." The soldiers had spread out around him, but had kept their distance. Tom had said nothing, but his big body had been tense and alert, and some of the soldiers had started to back away. After a moment of silence Tom had said calmly and reasonably, "I just want this man here to see a real doctor."

"Let him go," a fat corporal had said to the corpsman. "The captain looks like a mighty big man, and somebody's going to get hurt if we rush him."

"The guy's psycho," the corpsman had said.

"Let him go find a doctor if he wants," the fat corporal had replied.

While they were arguing, Tom had suddenly stooped, picked up

Mahoney's body, and burst through the loose circle they had formed. He had run hard, without feeling the great weight of Mahoney's body. After a few minutes he had felt gravel under his feet and had heard many voices. Looking up, he had found himself standing only a few hundred feet from the sea, surrounded by Negro troops pouring from a landing barge. "What's the matter, Captain?" a gigantic Negro master sergeant had said. "You looking for the medics?"

"Yes."

"They're taking some wounded out to the hospital ship right over there," the enormous sergeant had said, gesturing toward another landing craft several hundred yards down the beach. Tom had started off, but had felt a big hand on his shoulder. "Let me carry him for you, Captain," the sergeant had said. "You must be beat."

"I'll take him."

The sergeant had already put one great arm around Hank's body. In a shocked voice he had suddenly said, "Captain, this man's dead. Look at his chest."

"Let him alone."

"Ain't no use, Captain," the sergeant had replied in a soft voice. "Put him down and take yourself a rest."

"I'm not going to put him with the dead."

"Of course not. Let me put him right down here." The big sergeant had put gentle and respectful hands on Hank's body, and Tom had not objected. Carefully the sergeant had put Hank's body on the gravel a hundred yards from the other men. "Sit down now, Captain," the sergeant had said.

Dazedly Tom had sat down. The sergeant had given him a cigarette and lit it for him. Tom had sat staring at the sergeant's shoes, tremendous muddy shoes, the tops of which were still highly polished. After looking at the shoes for a long while, he had brought himself to glance at Mahoney and had seen that on Hank's face was the sardonic grin of a dead man. The dead always have the last laugh, Hank had said. A wave of nausea had overtaken Tom, and he had been sick. For several minutes he had lain there retching. The big sergeant had put cool hands on his forehead, the way a mother holds the head of a sick child. Gradually the nausea had gone, and with it the madness. Tom had stood up slowly, and the sergeant had handed him a canteen. After taking a drink, Tom had poured water into his hands and splashed his face. "Thanks, Sergeant," he had said.

"Let me help you find a burial detail," the sergeant had replied. "You look mighty tired."

"I'd like to find one with a chaplain."

The sergeant had picked Mahoney up. They had walked a long while before finding a priest with a detachment of men preparing for funeral services. The big sergeant had put Mahoney down, and the chaplain had immediately come over and had gently laid a blanket over him.

"Take care of him, Father," Tom had said, and had strode across the island to rejoin his company. He had found his men lying exhausted on the ground waiting for landing craft to take them off the island. Caesar had been wounded. Seeing him being carried off in a stretcher, Tom had hurried over to him. "You're going to be all right," he had said, but Caesar had just turned his face away, as though the sight of Tom were painful to him.

Tom had helped get the other wounded to the hospital ship, and then had thrown himself on the ground to try to sleep. Only a fitful half-sleep had come, and he had been aware of men moving all around him. All kinds of things had happened that night. Some of the troops who arrived after the fighting had searched the tangled earth for souvenirs, making necklaces of teeth and fingernails from corpses. Pitched battles had been fought over Japanese swords, pistols, and flags. At two o'clock in the morning a Jap had been found cowering in a clump of underbrush and had been joyfully bayoneted and castrated by a company of supply troops who had thought they would have to finish out the war without meeting the enemy.

Finally an LST had picked up Tom and most of the paratroopers who were uninjured. As it backed away from the island, Tom had sat in a dark corner of its hold, thinking of Mahoney running with the grenade in mid-air, poised there forever like Keats's lovers on a Grecian urn, Hank always young and alive, the grenade always outlined clearly against the sky, just a few feet above his shoulder.

A major, coming to squat beside him, said, "Some of these god-damn sailors got heads. They went ashore and got Jap heads, and they tried to boil them in the galley to get the skulls for souvenirs."

Tom had shrugged and said nothing. The fact that he had been too quick to throw a hand grenade and had killed Mahoney, the fact that some young sailors had wanted skulls for souvenirs, and the fact that a few hundred men had lost their lives to take the island of Karkow—all these facts were simply incomprehensible and had to be forgotten. That, he had decided, was the final truth of the war, and he had greeted it with relief, greeted it eagerly, the simple fact that it was incomprehensible and had to be forgotten. Things just happen, he had decided; they happen and they happen again, and anybody who tries to make sense out of it goes out of his mind. Suddenly he had longed to go home, home to Betsy and the serenity of Grandmother's house. "How long do you think they'll give us before the next jump?" he had asked the major.

Now, in his office in the Schanenhauser Foundation in the year 1953, Tom wondered whether Caesar Gardella actually had gone back to Rome to marry Gina, or whether he had simply returned to New York when the war was over and tried to forget the whole thing, as Tom had. And most of all he wondered if Gardella had recognized him, and if he were still resentful of the abandonment of Maria. It was strange that there was only Maria to worry about, Tom thought—certainly Caesar wouldn't hold the death of Mahoney against him. It had been an accident—Caesar had certainly realized that. Probably Caesar wouldn't even remember Mahoney. But if Maria had a son or a daughter, and if Caesar told her where Tom was, that conceivably could be quite another thing. A birth usually has more consequences than a death.

Suddenly Tom's telephone rang. It was Dick Haver calling from the office across the hall. "Tom, can you step in here a minute?" he asked.

"Sure," Tom said. "Be glad to."

13

"Mr. Hopkins telephoned me a few minutes ago," Dick said, "and asked if I could let you start work over there next week. I take it you've reached a decision."

"I was going to tell you this morning," Tom said. "I haven't had a chance to see you. . . ."

"I understand. I told Hopkins that as far as we were concerned, you could start work over there right away."

Tom didn't like that at all—Dick hadn't made him sound very valuable. "All right," he said reluctantly. "I certainly appreciate everything you've done for me here."

"We don't have to say good-by," Dick said. "Let's have lunch together once in a while."

Tom went back to his office to clean out his desk. There are a few things I've got to get straight with myself, he thought. The fact that Caesar Gardella is running an elevator over at United Broadcasting doesn't make any difference at all. It changes nothing. The past is just as it was, and I can't get myself into a state of nerves every time I step into an elevator. My nerves have held out until now, and I guess they'll keep on holding out. Whether Caesar recognizes me or not doesn't make any difference. I've got nothing to be ashamed of, or at least no more than I had before I knew Caesar was running an elevator. Mahoney wasn't the first man to be killed by mistake by his own men in the heat of battle—Old Hank would understand that if anyone would. And Maria held nothing against me. We understood each other. I wonder if she had the child, he thought. I wonder if Caesar knows. If he recognized me, why didn't he say anything?

No, Tom thought, I mustn't go on like this. Between peace and war a clear line must be drawn. The past is something best forgotten; only in theory is it the father of the present. In practice, it is only a wildly unrelated dream, a chamber of horrors. And most of the time the present is unrelated to the future. It is a disconnected world, or it is better to believe it that way if you can, and an elevator man has no business popping up to form a connecting link. The past is gone, Tom thought, and I will not brood about it. I've got to be tough. I am not the type to have a nervous breakdown. I can't afford it. I have too many responsibilities. This is a time of peace, and I will forget about the war.

It's funny, Tom thought—it's funny, the way the world goes. You take your children and with all honesty you teach them, "Thou Shalt Not Kill." You give them dancing lessons, and tennis lessons, and music lessons. You teach them Latin, and how to dress properly. You teach them self-respect, if you can. All these things my father must have learned when he was young, and all these things I learned, and if I can, I will teach all these things to my son. And if I can, I will also teach him to defend his country. If he has to, I hope he'll be a tough bastard too.

"All right, men, this is a rifle. Any of you never seen a rifle before?"

Tom remembered the sergeant who had given him basic training, a hollow-cheeked man with a flat voice, who had taught him back in the year 1942. The recruits had laughed when he said, "Any of you never seen a rifle before?" All sergeants in all generations talk the same, and all recruits laugh at the same jokes.

"All right. This is a rifle, and here in my other hand I'm holding a bayonet. Any of you never seen a bayonet before?"

This time, no laughter. The recruits, standing in a circle around the sergeant, had shuffled nervously.

"Now you take this bayonet and you fit it onto the barrel of your rifle like this. Shove it down until it clicks. Stand back a little. I'm going to run through this once for you now, and then you try it. There are three basic motions in the use of a bayonet. You stick it in like this, you pull it out, using your foot or knee to shove the enemy away, and then you bring the stock of your rifle down hard on his head like this, all in one smooth motion. . . ."

It is necessary to forget all that and everything it led to, Tom thought; it is as necessary to forget it now as it was to learn it in the first place. They ought to begin wars with a course in basic training and end them with a course in basic forgetting. The trick is to learn to believe that it's a disconnected world, a lunatic world, where what is true now was not true then; where Thou Shalt Not Kill and the fact that one has killed a great many men mean nothing, absolutely nothing, for now is the time to raise legitimate children, and make money, and dress properly, and be kind to one's wife, and admire one's boss, and learn not to worry, and think of oneself as what? That makes no difference, he thought—I'm just a man in a gray flannel suit. I must keep my suit neatly pressed like anyone else, for I am a very respectable young man. If Caesar recognizes me, we might go out and have a drink together, and that would be that. It doesn't make any difference whether he recognizes me or not. It is ridiculous to live in fear of an elevator man. I will go to my new job, and I will be cheerful, and I will be industrious, and I will be matter-of-fact. I will keep my gray flannel suit spotless. I will have a sense of humor. I will have guts—I'm not the type to start crying now.

An hour later Tom stepped into the United Broadcasting building. The elevator operator who took him up to Ogden's office was a thin boy not more than eighteen years old.

14

A SECRETARY in a tight pink sweater told Tom that Ogden couldn't see him for another hour, but that he had asked her to show him to the office he was to occupy. Tom thanked her and followed her down the hall. The passageway ran out of carpet by the time they got to his door, but Tom was surprised at the size of his quarters. He had a room about fifteen feet square entirely to himself, and there was a small alcove where a pert brown-haired secretary sat at a small desk copying letters. "Mr. Rath, this is Miss Lawrence," the girl in the pink sweater said. "She will be your secretary."

"It's nice to meet you," Miss Lawrence said. She stood up, and smiled.

Tom's desk was fancily shaped, much like the one behind which Walker had given him his first interview, but he had an ordinary swivel chair instead of a reclining one. He sat down in it. There were two telephones on the desk, an interoffice communication box, and a small panel with three red buttons on it. Experimentally he pushed one of the buttons. Almost immediately, the door to his office opened and a distinguished and statuesque blond girl in a dark-green blouse and expensive-looking tweed skirt came in. "You buzzed, sir?" she asked in a rather upstage Boston accent.

"Who are you?"

"I'm the office girl. I deliver the interoffice mail. Did you buzz for me?"

"By mistake," Tom said. "Thank you very much."

She left, and he sat examining the other buttons with interest. Maybe the second one's for a redhead and the third one's for a brunette, he thought. After a moment of hesitation, he pushed the second one. This time Miss Lawrence came in. "Yes?" she asked.

"What's the third button for?"

"Nothing," she said, grinning. "It's for men who have two secretaries. Do you know how to use the interoffice communication system?"

He said no, and she showed him. She also explained the telephone system and brought from her desk a stack of papers for him to sign which placed him officially on the pay roll and insured him against almost everything in the world but getting fired. Just as he finished signing them, his interoffice communication box uttered some ominous crackling sounds, like a radio in a thunderstorm. He flicked a switch on it, and Ogden's voice suddenly shouted at him so loudly that he jumped, "Are you there, Rath?"

Tom turned the volume down to make Ogden more polite. "Just got here," he said.

"Come up and see me in half an hour," Ogden almost whispered. There were more noises like static.

"I'll be there," Tom said.

There was no reply, and he shut off the box. For a moment he busied himself looking through the drawers of his desk, inspecting with admiration a typewriter which pulled out on a special shelf. Then he turned his chair around and stared out the window. Below him, the city stretched like a map. Far away in the Hudson River a flotilla of destroyers was getting up steam. One of them was using a signal light. Tom could still read Morse Code. "Where in hell is the liberty boat?" the signalman was asking.

Twenty minutes later Tom started toward Ogden's office. Down the hall he took a wrong turn at a junction of corridors and wound up at the entrance to an enormous room in which about thirty clerks worked at desks in neat rows as in a schoolroom. When he found Ogden's office it was five minutes past the time set for the appointment, but that didn't make any difference. because Ogden kept him waiting another hour.

"Glad you could start work today," Ogden said when he finally had the girl in the pink sweater show him in. "Is your office all right?"

"It's fine," Tom said casually.

"About a title for you," Ogden said. "I suppose we should give you a title. You'll be responsible directly to me, of course, but I think we'll call you 'Special Assistant to Mr. Hopkins.' There will be times when that title will be useful."

Ogden paused, and Tom said, "That sounds like a fine title."

"Just remember that it doesn't apply to company business," Ogden said. "You're special assistant to Mr. Hopkins on this special project —nothing else. That will be made clear inside the company, but of course there will be no need to spell it out anywhere else."

"Of course," Tom said.

"Can you have dinner with Mr. Hopkins tonight?"

"Yes," Tom said, trying not to sound surprised. "I think I can arrange it."

"Meet us at seven-thirty at his apartment," Ogden said, and gave a Park Avenue address, which Tom wrote down on a pad and put in his pocket.

"Now let me give you the pitch," Ogden continued. "There's a . . ." Before he could go on, his telephone rang. "No," Ogden said into the receiver. "Absolutely not." He listened for a full minute before adding, "I'm still not convinced. Contact me on it later. Good-by."

He hung up and shifted his gaze to Tom. With hardly a pause, he said, "The pitch is this. There's a big convention of medical men in Atlantic City on September 15. Hopkins has been asked to speak, and he figures it will be a good time for him to send up a trial balloon on this whole project. He can't mention the small group of doctors who got him interested in all this. We've got to help him with the speech."

"Does that mean you want me to write it?"

Ogden looked at Tom with distaste. "We don't write speeches for Mr. Hopkins," he said. "He writes his own speeches. We just help him with the research and try to get something on paper for him to work with."

"I see," Tom said, feeling he had made a strategic error.

"Tonight we're going to kick the speech around," Ogden said. "You better be thinking about what he should say. He'll want your ideas."

Tom didn't have any idea in the world what the president of United Broadcasting should say to a convention of physicians about mental health. "Did the doctors suggest any topic when they invited him?" he asked.

"No."

"I suppose he could talk about increasing public understanding of the mental-illness problem," Tom said tentatively. He was tired of that thought already.

"Maybe. But keep in mind the purpose of the speech. If we achieve our purpose one hundred per cent, the audience should rise as one man when he's through and demand that he start a national committee on mental health immediately. He shouldn't propose such a thing, understand—they should suggest it to him. If this is the kind of speech it should be, every newspaper in the country should have it on the front page the next morning. Requests for him to form a national committee on mental health should pour in from all over the nation."

"It'll have to be quite a speech," Tom said.

"Perhaps we can't expect to achieve our purpose one hundred per cent, but we ought to keep the goal clearly in mind. And we also must not forget the possibility of a one hundred per cent failure. Do you know what that would be?"

"No response at all," Tom said.

"No—a negative response. If the speech went one hundred per cent wrong, the doctors would all get together to *prevent* the formation of a national committee on mental health. Mr. Hopkins would be accused of meddling in things he didn't know anything about. United Broadcasting would be described as a sinister influence trying to muscle in on the doctors for mysterious reasons. People would say we want socialized medicine, or that we are reactionaries fighting co-operative health plans. Hopkins would be accused of being a publicity hound. Rumors would start that he had political ambitions. If that sort of thing happened, the whole project would of course have to be abandoned."

There goes my job, Tom thought. Bill Ogden's already chipping away at it. He said, "I don't think there's much danger of that happening. After all, the doctors invited him to speak."

"That was arranged by a small group," Ogden said. "If the speech backfired, they'd be the first to claim they had nothing to do with it."

As soon as he got back to his own office, Tom telephoned Betsy. "I've already started work for United Broadcasting and I won't be home for dinner tonight," he said. "I'm having dinner with Hopkins in his Park Avenue apartment."

"You're going up in the world fast," Betsy said. "I haven't been moving so slowly, either. I've put this house on the market. The agents are sure we can get at least fifteen thousand for it. And I've checked our mortgage—we've paid off all but about seven thousand of that."

"Don't commit yourself on anything without talking to me," Tom said nervously.

She laughed. "I don't guarantee anything," she replied.

Late that afternoon Tom steeled himself when he rang for the elevator to take him down, and he did not admit to himself how relieved he was when the operator turned out to be an old man he had never seen before. When they got to the lobby, Tom hurried to get a taxicab.

The Park Avenue address proved to be a tall apartment house with a long dark-red awning extending over the sidewalk in front of it, under which a doorman who looked like an unemployed general stood guard. The man stepped quickly in front of him, but ceremoniously pushed the button for the elevator inside when Tom explained he had an appointment with Mr. Hopkins. When the elevator, which was operated by a young girl, arrived, the doorman said, "Take this gentleman to Mr. Hopkins' apartment."

The elevator moved slowly upward for what seemed a long while. Finally it stopped, and Tom stepped into a small marble vestibule with three black doors, on one of which was a simple brass knocker. There were no name plates on the doors. Tom turned to ask the elevator operator which door was Mr. Hopkins', but the elevator had already started down. He lifted the brass knocker and let it fall. The door was opened almost immediately by Hopkins himself. He was smiling and looked more affable than ever. "Come in!" he said. "So nice of you to come!"

Tom stepped into a high-ceilinged room. Two walls were entirely lined with bookcases. A third wall had glass shelves holding a collection of fancy hand-painted lead soldiers. The fourth wall had a large window and two glass doors leading to a neatly kept lawn on the roof, some twenty floors above the street.

"Won't you sit down?" Hopkins said. "What can I get you to drink?"

"Anything. What are you having?"

Hopkins walked over to a table near one of the windows on which stood a small forest of bottles, a trayful of glasses, and an ice bucket.

"It looks as though we have quite a collection here," he said, as though that were the first time he had seen it. "I think I'll have Scotch on the rocks. Will that suit you?"

"That'll be fine."

Hopkins took a pair of silver ice tongs in his hand and delicately dropped ice cubes into a glass. After splashing whisky over them, he placed the glass on a small tray, ceremoniously walked over and handed it to Tom. "Thanks," Tom said, figuring he was getting served by the highest-paid bartender in the world. "Is there anything I can do to help?"

"Just sit down and make yourself comfortable. Bill Ogden will be along any minute."

Tom sat in a small, hard leather chair. Hopkins poured himself a drink and, acting for all the world like an anxious housewife entertaining the rector, fussed about the room, offering Tom first a plate of crackers spread with caviar, and then a porcelain box of cigarettes. Finally he sat down near Tom and sipped his drink thoughtfully. "This is an exciting new project we're going to be working on together," he said, making Tom a partner. "I think there's a real need for it, and it certainly is a challenge!"

He sounded as though the thing he wanted most in the world was a challenge. Tom, feeling called upon to match his enthusiasm, said, "I can't think of anything more needed!"

Luckily, there was a knock on the door before he had to elaborate on that theme. Hopkins jumped springily from his chair, dashed to the door, and let Ogden in. *"Hello,* Bill!" he said, as though he hadn't seen Ogden for three months. *"So* good of you to give up your evening for this!"

"Glad to, Ralph," Ogden said urbanely, exchanged greetings briefly with Tom, and strolled over to the liquor table. "Mind if I mix myself a drink?"

"Take what you like—take what you like!"

Ogden poured himself a Scotch on the rocks and sat down on a hassock. "How are Helen and Susan?" he asked Hopkins.

"Fine! Susan is entering Vassar this fall!"

Tom glanced around the apartment. It didn't look like a place where a family lived. Did Hopkins and his family gather to play croquet on the lawn on the roof? Then he remembered that Hopkins had just built a place in South Bay. Hopkins must keep this place just for business meetings, he figured.

Ogden glanced at his wrist watch. "I've been giving a good deal of thought to this speech you've got scheduled in Atlantic City," he began. "I figure we ought to pitch it chiefly on the need for more public understanding. . . ."

For half an hour Ogden elaborated on this, saying about what he had told Tom that morning. Hopkins sat listening and nodding his head appreciatively, but saying little. His chief preoccupation seemed to be keeping everybody's glass full. At about a quarter after eight, a uniformed maid came in from the door near the shelves of lead soldiers and announced dinner. They all went into a small dining room and were served cherry-stone clams, rare roast beef, and apple pie. All through dinner, Ogden kept talking about the speech. When they returned to the living room, Hopkins cleared his throat and said, "That's very helpful, Bill. Now let me see if I can draw some of it together."

"Take notes," Ogden hissed at Tom.

Tom quickly took a pad from his pocket and sat with pencil poised. "Point number one," Hopkins said. "'The medical profession has done a wonderful job on mental-health problems. Point number two: the public must supply more money and understanding. Put in a lot of 'Too few people realize this' and 'Too few people realize that.' Point out that there are special funds for polio and cancer and heart disease. Say too few realize there's no such fund for research on mental illness and that the mentally ill fill more than half the hospital beds. Mention the publicity job that made it respectable to talk about venereal disease. Talk about the amount of money a mentally ill patient costs the state a year. Say someone should start a national committee on mental health. Say it should be a doctor— use the phrase, 'some fully qualified person. . . .'"

He paused. "No, darn it," he said. "I think we're hitting it too directly. Maybe we could start with some sort of historical parallel. What do you . . ."

There was a knock at the door, and Hopkins leaped to his feet to open it. Two imposing-looking men carrying briefcases entered. "*So* nice of you to come!" Hopkins said heartily. "Sit down! We'll be through here in just a minute. Brandy? A liqueur?"

"Thanks, Ralph," the bigger of the two men said. "Anything you've got. Good evening, Bill."

After brief introductions, and after everyone had a drink, Hopkins said, "Now, Tom, do you think you have the hang of what I want to say in Atlantic City?"

"I guess so," Tom said.

"Would it be putting you to too much trouble to ask for a rough draft in, say, three or four days?"

"I'll have something for you," Tom said.

"Fine! Thanks *so* much for coming up. I know how hard it is to stay in town late when you live in Connecticut. I certainly appreciate it!"

Bill Ogden stood up. "Thanks for everything, Ralph," he said. "I've got to be running."

"Thank *you*, Bill!" Hopkins said.

This is the most polite damn bunch of people I've ever met, Tom thought. As he and Bill Ogden went out the door he heard Hopkins say to the other two men, "I *certainly* appreciate your giving up your evening for this! Have you got some of those promotion plans we were discussing last week spelled out a little more?"

It turned out that Ogden lived in Stamford, and he rode to Grand Central Station in a taxi with Tom. They had just missed the nine-thirty-five train, and there wasn't another one for more than an hour. They went to the bar on the lower level of the station and ordered highballs.

"I can't help being curious," Tom said. "Does Mr. Hopkins work every night?"

"He often takes long week ends on an island he has up in Maine," Ogden said.

Tom reflected upon this for a few moments. "You mean he just lives alone in that apartment and has business appointments every evening?" he asked incredulously.

"Oh, he goes out to his place at South Bay quite often," Ogden said. "He sees a lot of his family—especially around Christmas time."

Tom took a few swallows of his drink.

"He never gets tired," Ogden said. "Lots of guys work hard, but he's always fresh. I've never seen him tired in my life."

When Tom got back to Westport, the first thing he noticed when he stepped in the front door of his house was that everything looked suspiciously neat, and a table with a large vase of hollyhocks had been moved against the living-room wall to obscure the crack in the plaster. Betsy was waiting. "How did it go?" she asked.

"Fine," he said. "I got to write a speech. I mean, I have to help Mr. Hopkins with a speech. I might as well get the terminology of this thing straight from the beginning."

To his surprise, Betsy looked hurt. "I wish you'd stop being so damn bright and cynical," she said. "It's no way to start a new job. You ought to be enthusiastic. Damn it, Tommy, try being naïve!"

"What's got into you?" he asked, looking puzzled.

"I'll bet Hopkins doesn't go around making wisecracks!" she said. "Does he?"

"No."

"Nobody does who gets anywhere. You've got to be positive and enthusiastic!"

"How come you know so much all of a sudden about how to get ahead?"

"I just *know*," she said. "I'm sick of being smart and broke."

"Okay," he said. "I'll be owl-faced. My whole interest in life is working for mental health. I care nothing for myself. I am a dedicated human being."

"All right, be witty. But I've been worried about this for a long time. You've always been talking about Hopkins' mental-health project with your tongue in your cheek, and if you feel that way about it, you ought not work for the man. You ought to be thinking it's

the best idea in the world! And why isn't it a good idea, when you come right down to it? What's wrong with trying to do something about mental illness? Why do you have to be so damn *cynical* about it?"

"From now on I'll be pious," he said, "if you promise to stop being insufferable."

"I just want you to start off on the right foot," she said. "Do you like Mr. Hopkins?"

"I guess so."

"You should *try* to like him! Give him the benefit of every doubt. Or quit working for him right now!"

"I love him," he said simply. "I adore him. My heart is his."

"You scare me, Tommy," she said. "I'm dead serious. You scare hell out of me when you're like that. To me it means you're going to be unenthusiastic about everything for the rest of your life."

"I'm going to try to do this job right," he said. "You don't have to worry about that. I'm going to try."

"Sit down now and have a drink," she said. "Three people looked at the house today, and one may be coming back."

15

JUST as Tom and Betsy were preparing to go to bed, the telephone rang. It was Lucy Hitchcock, who lived next door. "Hi!" she said with slightly alcoholic jubilation in her voice. "Could you and Tom come over for cocktails tomorrow night? Bob just got a wonderful raise, and we're going to celebrate."

"Congratulations," Betsy said. "We'll be there."

"I've got to call twenty other people," Lucy said. "Good-by!"

Filled with sudden distaste, Betsy put the telephone down. In this invitation tendered so late in the evening to a party for the celebration of an increase in salary received by the host, Betsy found concentrated everything she disliked about Greentree Avenue. The intensity of her displeasure surprised her, and long after she had gone to bed, she lay awake trying to analyze it.

It's not that I'm a snob—it's more than that, she thought fiercely. There are all kinds of reasons. Slowly she counted them off.

The first reason the invitation annoyed her was that she felt obligated to accept it. She and Tom had already declined invitations to two of the Hitchcocks' parties, and Lucy would interpret a third refusal as a slight, regardless of what excuse were given.

The second reason was that like most cocktail parties on Greentree Avenue, this one would be an exhausting exercise. On Greentree Avenue cocktail parties started at seven-thirty, when the men came home from New York, and they usually continued without any dinner until three or four o'clock in the morning. It was almost impossible for the owners of the small houses to provide dinner for their guests—on that street the custom of asking people in for dinner had almost disappeared. The kitchens were small, dining rooms were almost nonexistent, and after the women had put the children to bed, they were in no mood to fix company meals. Cocktail parties were an easier form of hospitality, and the only trouble was that anyone who went home for dinner was considered a spoilsport. Somewhere around nine-thirty in the evening, Martinis and Manhattans would give way to highballs, but the formality of eating anything but hors d'oeuvres in between had been entirely omitted.

It can't be true that the whole street is like that, Betsy thought—it must be just the people we know. For a long while after she went to bed, she lay thinking of the various families up and down the street. Almost all the houses were occupied by couples with young children, and few people considered Greentree Avenue a permanent stop—the place was just a crossroads where families waited until they could afford to move on to something better. The finances of almost every household were an open book. Budgets were frankly discussed, and the public celebration of increases in salary was common. The biggest parties of all were moving-out parties, given by those who finally were able to buy a bigger house. Of course there were a few men in the area who had given up hope of rising in the world, and a few who had moved from worse surroundings and considered Greentree Avenue a desirable end of the road, but they and their families suffered a kind of social ostracism. On Greentree Avenue, contentment was an object of contempt.

No one here is evil, Betsy thought defensively. In spite of all the drinking, the young couples were usually well enough behaved at the cocktail parties. Sure, there were sometimes a few kitchen kisses and an occasional high-pitched argument, but usually the men and their wives just sat talking about the modern houses they would like to build, or the old barns they would like to convert into dwellings. The price the small houses on Greentree Avenue were currently bringing and the question of how big a mortgage the local banks were offering on larger places were constantly discussed. As the evening wore on, the men generally fell to divulging dreams of escaping to an entirely different sort of life—to a dairy farm in Vermont, or to the management of a motel in Florida—but for the most part, the cocktail parties simply gave everyone a chance to prove he considered Greentree Avenue no more than a stepping stone to the same kind of life on a bigger scale. There's nothing wrong with that, Betsy tried to tell herself. This isn't a bad place to be, it's just . . .

Dull. That was the word she usually used for Greentree Avenue, but tonight she rejected it. If this were just a dull place, I wouldn't mind it so much, she thought. The trouble is, it's not dull enough—it's tense and it's frantic. Or, to be honest, Tom and I are tense and frantic, and I wish to heaven I knew why.

Betsy sat up in bed and, in the dim light from the window, glanced at Tom. He was asleep and, at least for the moment, looked entirely serene. She fumbled on the bedside table, found a cigarette, and lit it. A feeling of black pessimism and self-reproach overtook her. With Betsy, such moods were extremely rare, but when she fell victim to them, every humiliating experience she had suffered since early childhood sprang to life, and all comforting thoughts fell from beneath her, as though she had been standing on a trap door. At such times, the big brick house on Beacon Street in which she had been brought up came back to her memory not as a cheerful place, with pine logs roaring in the living-room fireplace on winter afternoons, but as a cavernous building with a long dark staircase with a creak in every step which she had been obliged to climb alone early each evening, leaving her older sister, Alice, to bask in the warmth below. Betsy had had a rather lonely childhood—her sister was eight years older than she, and her parents had been quite old when she was born and had lacked the energy, if not the will, to give much time to a small child. Almost from the beginning, Betsy had been a rather adult child. She had rarely cried, and although she had been terrified by the shadows on the wall of the stairs and the darkness in the hall above, she had never confided her fears to anyone. Instead she had hummed to herself determinedly while going up to bed, with lips compressed and fists tightly clenched as she edged along the shadows and into the blackness of the hall, where anything could lurk. Because her parents had not approved of night lights for children, she had slept in the dark, with her ears straining for the comforting sound of voices on the floor below and the occasional laugh of her older sister. Now, lying in the dark beside Tom, Betsy found herself half expecting to hear the sound of that laughter again.

"*Mark my words . . .*" her sister Alice had said. That had been much later, when Betsy had told her family she wanted to marry Tom. "*Mark my words,*" she had said. "If you get married now, you'll regret it. You're too young. Someday you'll remember I told you that and wish you had taken my advice. Wait till after the war. A girl your age who marries a man just about to go in the service is crazy."

"*But I've known him for three years,*" Betsy had said.

"*But you don't know how either of you will feel after he gets back.*"

"*We'll always feel the same as we do now!*"

How bravely the words came back to her! Why should I think of Alice now? Betsy thought. She leaned over to an ash tray and extinguished her cigarette. Beside her, Tom stirred restlessly in the bed.

Nothing's wrong with our marriage, or at least nothing permanent, Betsy thought. We can't be like a couple of children gaily playing house forever.

That's the way it had been before the war—*like children playing house,* she thought, but even the sarcasm of the phrase couldn't tarnish the memory. They had had only three months together before Tom went into the Army. How exciting those days had been! He had spent an absurd proportion of his savings on her engagement ring and a diamond-sprinkled wedding ring to match. At the time she had remonstrated with him, and it was curious to remember now that that jewelry, bought with a brave gesture of gallantry, had turned out to be the only shrewd investment they had ever made. The last time she had had the rings cleaned, the jeweler had offered her far more than Tom had paid for them, because diamonds had increased in value a great deal since the war.

That somehow seemed typical of the way everything had turned out, Betsy thought. The foolish gesture had turned out to be a shrewd investment, and most of their careful planning had led to nothing. I would like to go back to the beginning, and follow the years along, and find out what went wrong, Betsy thought. After she and Tom had been married, they had moved into a tiny apartment in Boston, and upon her request, Tom had immediately bought a Saint Bernard puppy and a white Angora kitten with blue eyes, because in the old house on Beacon Hill, her family had never allowed her to have pets. Now her clearest memory of those three months before the war was of the great clumsy puppy and the wide-eyed kitten and Tom and herself, all rolling and tumbling and playing together on the floor, with the sunshine streaming in the window on a big red and gold oriental rug someone had given them for a wedding present.

Like children playing house, she thought. During the first two days they lived in that apartment, she had ordered milk from two milkmen, because the second one had been a very aggressive salesman, and the icebox had been jammed with milk bottles until Tom straightened the matter out. The kitchenette had been fragrant with spices thoughout those three months—she had experimented with almost every recipe in the cookbook. Meals had not seemed simply a chore to get through as quickly as possible then.

We weren't too young to be married in those days, she thought—I think the trouble is that although only twelve years have gone by, we are somehow too old to be married now. I suppose that's really why I want to move out of this house so much, Betsy thought—I don't want a bigger place so much; I want that old three months before the war back. It's as though Tom and I had been married twice, once before the war and once afterward, and what I want is my first marriage back.

"Now mark my words," Alice had said.

Damn Alice, Betsy thought now. I'm still not sorry I got married, and I'm glad I didn't take her advice. Ever since the war, poor Tom has just had to work awfully hard, and he has lots of worries on his mind. And I've been tired, what with taking care of the kids and all. We're both exhausted most of the time—the Tired Thirties, the doctor called it once, the time when people have children, and have to make good at jobs, and buy houses, and all the rest of it. We're both just tired out. That's why nothing seems to be much fun any more.

There, I've said it, she thought, and it sounds absurd, but it's true. Nothing seems to be much fun any more. There's nothing wrong with our house, really, and nothing wrong with Greentree Avenue, or Tom or me. It's just that nothing seems to be much fun any more, and that's horrible, for when you've said that, there's nothing more to say.

Why? she thought.

It probably would take a psychiatrist to answer that. Maybe Tom and I both ought to visit one, she thought. What's the matter? the psychiatrist would say, and I would reply, I don't know—nothing seems to be much fun any more. All of a sudden the music stopped, and it didn't start again. Is that strange, or does it happen to everyone about the time when youth starts to go?

The psychiatrist would have an explanation, Betsy thought, but I don't want to hear it. People rely too much on explanations these days, and not enough on courage and action. Why make such a complicated thing out of selling this house? We don't like Greentree Avenue, so we'll move. Tom has a good job, and he'll get his enthusiasm back, and be a success at it. Everything's going to be fine. It does no good to wallow in night thoughts. In God we trust, and that's that.

Betsy's fists were clenched, and her lips pressed tightly together, just as they had been when, as a little girl, she had gone up through the shadows to bed, determined not to admit her fear or her jealousy of her sister, sitting by the fire and laughing below. She glanced at Tom, and seeing that the blankets had slipped from his shoulders, she carefully covered him up. Then she went to sleep, and when she awoke in the morning, she was as energetic and cheerful as ever, humming a tuneless song under her breath as she got breakfast and drove her husband to the station.

Four days after he had visited Hopkins' apartment, Tom typed for the fifth time his final draft of a first draft of Hopkins' speech. From the first sentence (It's a great pleasure for me to be here this evening.) to the last sentence (It's a job that *can* be done.), it seemed to Tom to go quite well. True, it all had a rather otherworldly ring to it, but no matter how hard Tom tried, he couldn't make it appear quite natural for the president of United Broadcasting to be talking about mental health at all. When he had polished the speech as much as he could, he handed it to his secretary, who retyped it neatly with three carbon copies. Two of these Tom filed and took the original with one copy to Ogden. He didn't expect Ogden to throw up his hands and cheer when he read the speech, but he was totally unprepared when Ogden, after finishing the first two pages, slammed the speech down on his desk and said, "Christ! This is awful! It isn't what we want at all!"

For the first time in years, Tom felt his face turning red.

"You can do better than this!" Ogden said contemptuously, before Tom had a chance to say anything. "Take it back and do it over. See if you can have something ready by tonight. Mr. Hopkins wants to see you at his apartment at eight-thirty. And this time, really try."

"I'll try," Tom said in an unnaturally quiet voice. He had a sud den, immediately controlled impulse to kill Ogden. He knew just how he could do it—he'd clench both hands together, raise them high above his head, and, using the full strength of his back, bring them down hard on the back of Ogden's neck. Shaken by his own thoughts, he picked the speech up and walked back to his office. Glancing at his familiar, thick old wrist watch, he saw he had nine hours in which to work. He rolled a clean piece of paper into his typewriter. "It's a great pleasure to be here this evening," he began, and crossed it out. "I'm deeply grateful for this opportunity to talk to you this evening," he substituted. No, damn it! he thought, and crossed that out. "It gives me the greatest pleasure . . ."

At eight-thirty that night he knocked blearily at the door of Hopkins' apartment, clutching the retyped speech in a manila envelope in his hand. Hopkins let him in, again thanked him for coming, and gave him a drink. Tom handed him the speech and, unable to watch him read it, walked self-consciously across the room to inspect the lead soldiers. They were hand-painted, in astonishing detail. On the top shelf was a small group of knights in armor. He wondered how long it would take Hopkins to read the speech. At least he hadn't thrown it down yet, and he must have finished the first page. On the second shelf was a company of English archers, apparently aiming their long arrows at a platoon of soldiers waiting for the American Revolution. Behind him, Tom heard a page rustle, and Hopkins cleared his throat. On the middle shelf were Civil War infantrymen of both North and South, apparently teaming up against some World War I artillerymen. Behind him, Tom heard a match scratch, and Hopkins' chair squeaked. He must be half through it, Tom thought. On the bottom shelf were several squads of World War II marines, all standing at attention. Somewhere in the room a clock ticked.

"Wonderful!" Hopkins suddenly boomed.

Tom turned around.

"*Marvelous,*" Hopkins said, even louder. His whole face was beaming with satisfaction. "You've really got the feel for it!"

"I'm glad you like it," Tom said modestly.

"This really *sings*," Hopkins said enthusiastically. "It's remarkable that you could do so well the first time around!"

"It's a second draft, actually," Tom said. "Mr. Ogden gave me some suggestions."

"The *heart* of the thing is just right!" Hopkins said. "Now let's just go over it together. Did you bring a copy?"

Tom took one from the manila envelope.

"Let's look at this introduction," Hopkins said. "Do you think we could make it a little more natural? How about, 'Good evening. It's good of you gentlemen to give your attention to a layman. . . .'"

Sentence by sentence Hopkins took the whole speech apart. When he finished, he had asked for changes in almost every paragraph. "Well!" he concluded. "You certainly did a grand job! Just fix up the details we've worked out and let's see it again in a few days. Would Wednesday be too early?"

"That will be plenty of time," Tom said.

"Can I fill your glass for you?"

"Sure."

"You've really got the feel for this sort of thing," Hopkins said, while putting fresh ice cubes in his glass. "You've made a grand beginning!"

"Thanks," Tom said.

There was a knock at the door, and Hopkins let in a thin man holding an enormous blueprint, rolled up like a rug.

"Good *evening*, Bruce," Hopkins said. "So nice of you to give up your evening!"

Tom gulped his drink and excused himself as rapidly as possible. He was halfway to Grand Central Station before he fully realized that Ogden and Hopkins had simply told him the same thing in two different ways: to rewrite the speech. In spite of this, Hopkins had somehow left him eager to try. Well, he thought admiringly, I always heard he could drive men and make them like it.

16

A WEEK LATER, just when Tom was forgetting his apprehension about meeting Caesar Gardella, it happened. He had been working late on the speech, and it was about seven-thirty when he rang for the elevator. The corridor by the elevators was empty. When he pressed the button there was the prolonged hum which always preceded the coming of the elevator. The doors rumbled open, and there was Caesar, standing alone in the entrance to the car, his big round face impassive. "Going down," he said in his deep voice. Tom stepped into the elevator. Caesar turned toward the controls, and the door rumbled shut behind him. Caesar stood with his back toward Tom. The elevator dropped sickeningly fast. Then Caesar turned toward Tom. His face was without emotion. "You're Captain Rath, aren't you?" he said.

"Yes," Tom replied, and, trying to feign surprise, added, "Why, you're Caesar Gardella!" He stuck out his hand, but just then a light flashed on the control board of the elevator, and Caesar brought the car to a halt at the nineteenth floor. The door rumbled open, and two pretty secretaries stepped in. "We'll be late, I know we're going to be late, and they'll *never* wait!" one said.

"They'll wait, all right," her companion replied. "It's a good thing to keep them waiting." The elevator started down, and both girls laughed.

When they got to the ground floor, the secretaries hurried out of the elevator. Tom stayed behind awkwardly. He wanted to say, *Did you go back to Rome? Did you ever hear what happened to Maria?* But instead, sounding foolish to himself and talking very fast, he said, "It certainly is nice to run into you, Caesar! It's been a long time! Gosh, I guess it's been almost ten years, eight or nine, anyway! You're looking good, boy! Sure looks as though civilian life is agreeing with you!"

Caesar smiled. "You're not doing so bad yourself," he said. "I seen you riding down with Mr. Hopkins. You an assistant of his or something?"

"Yes," Tom said. "I'm working for him."

There was an awkward silence, during which the smile disappeared from Caesar's face.

"I've got to be running," Tom said, edging toward the door. "Got a train to catch. Sure is nice to have seen you!"

"Could we get together sometime?" Caesar blurted out quickly. He suddenly seemed nervous and pushed his purple cap back on his head. "Just for a drink or something," he said. "I'd kind of like to talk to you."

"Sure," Tom said hesitantly. "Sure, I'd love to!" Seized with a desire to get the meeting over, he added, "How about now? I could catch a later train."

"No," Caesar replied. "I'm on duty for another two hours. Can I give you a call sometime when I'm not on duty?"

"Sure!" Tom said. "Any time! Give me a call!"

Lights were flashing on the elevator's control panel, and the starter was walking toward them. Tom hurried out of the elevator, waved cheerily, and walked rapidly toward Grand Central Station. He wants to see me, he thought. What about? To talk over old times, perhaps—that's a perfectly normal thing to do. We meet and have a drink and we make jokes about the war. That's all there is to it. What else could he do?

Blackmail. The word flashed into his mind suddenly. That's absurd, he thought. In the first place, Caesar would never do a thing like that. He was always a decent guy. And in the second place, there's a statute of limitations. And in the third place, he couldn't prove anything, especially after all this time. When you come right down to it, I haven't done anything illegal anyway, or at least nothing anyone could do anything about. Maria wouldn't turn on me now.

Still, Caesar could make things rather awkward for me, Tom thought. Publicity—if he made any charges, the publicity alone could ruin me. And he probably thinks I'm rich, seeing me with Hopkins and all. I wonder what he's got on his mind? Maybe he knows something about Maria, something he wants to tell me.

No, Tom thought as he got to Grand Central Station, it's not that. Two old buddies meet and have a drink together, that's all—that's the convention, and Caesar's just trying to play it according to the script. It's ridiculous to worry. I've got to learn simply to relax and take things as they come. I'm tough and I'm not going to get weak-kneed now.

The next day he expected Caesar to call and was tense whenever his telephone rang, as well as whenever he got on an elevator, but he neither saw nor heard from Caesar. The day after that nothing happened, and the day after that. Probably he never will call me, Tom thought—probably this is the way it's going to end. It's quite possible, in fact, it's probable that the poor guy was just trying to be polite. As more days went by with no word from Caesar, Tom's conviction that this was so deepened. He's probably embarrassed to call me, he thought. After all, the gulf between an elevator operator and an assistant to the president of a large corporation is greater than that between a corporal and a captain in the Army. He was trying to be polite, Tom told himself over and over, and I'll probably never hear from him again. If we meet in the elevator, we'll just nod at each other, and that will be that.

During the next week, Tom did four more drafts of the speech, each of which Ogden vilified and Hopkins praised highly before asking for a rewrite. Tom got to the point where he mumbled phrases from the speech in his sleep. "It's a great pleasure . . ." he groaned at three o'clock one morning.

"What?" Betsy asked, startled.

"A real pleasure to be here with this distinguished company this evening. . . ."

"Wake up!" Betsy said. "Wake up! You're talking in your sleep!"

The fear that he was proving an utter failure in his new job grew. He would have quit in discouragement if it hadn't been for Hopkins' praise, which grew in warmth as the number of discarded efforts multiplied, and which somehow never failed to sound utterly sincere. Maybe he just goes on like that till he definitely makes up his mind to fire you and then lets you have it between the eyes, Tom thought. But why should a guy like that lie? Maybe he *does* think I'm doing a good job. Maybe he expects a speech to be written a thousand times.

Tom didn't know. Every time Hopkins built him up, Ogden tore him down. "It's getting *worse*," Ogden said when he read the third draft. "Give it a fresh approach! Put some *oomph* into it!"

There was only one comforting thought. The speech would have to be completed before many weeks went by, if Hopkins were going to give it at all—it wouldn't really be possible to go on rewriting it forever.

A week later, when Tom was in the middle of his sixth draft of the speech, and apparently no closer to an acceptable final draft than ever, his mind was distracted by a simple event: Betsy sold the house in Westport and agreed to get out of it within two days. Tom had been falsely reassured by the fact that not many people had inspected the house, and he had figured it probably would take some time for Betsy to put her plans into action. "But why did you agree to get out in *two days?*" he asked in dismay when she told him she had accepted an offer of sixteen thousand dollars.

"He wanted to move his family in—he's just come from Chicago," Betsy said. "It was such a good price he offered, and I was afraid he'd get away."

"How can we do it?" Tom asked. "We've got to pack china, and clothes, and *everything!* And I'm going to be working day and night on this speech!"

"Don't worry about the packing," Betsy said. "I'll have everything ready. The movers will come Saturday morning, and Saturday afternoon we'll all pile in the car and drive to South Bay."

The next evening when Tom got home from New York, every room in the house was cluttered with cardboard boxes and barrels.

"Daddy!" Janey said delightedly. "Momma said not to mind about keeping things neat!"

Tom looked around the disordered house, and suddenly it was unutterably dear to him. The crack like a question mark in the living-room wall, the shabby furniture, the worn linoleum on the kitchen floor—all seemed part of something precious that was slipping fast, something already gone which never could be retrieved. He went to the kitchen cupboard where the liquor was usually kept, but it was gone, and the empty cupboard was neatly lined with clean white paper.

"The liquor's in the big red wastepaper basket," Betsy said cheerfully.

Quietly Tom poured himself a drink.

"That Mr. Howard called again today," Betsy said. "I told him we were moving into Grandmother's house. He seemed quite disappointed—and no wonder. I found something out about him."

"What?" Tom asked somberly.

"He's a professional real-estate man—that's a lot of malarky he gave us about wanting to buy the place for his own use. He's the real-estate man for that restaurant company. Mrs. Reid, the agent who sold this place for us, recognized his name and told me."

"He wouldn't want to put a restaurant way up on that hill," Tom said. "They build that kind of restaurant near highways."

"Mrs. Reid says he probably didn't want it for a restaurant—he speculates on real estate for himself on the side. He probably wanted to do just what we're going to do with it. I think that's a good sign."

A good sign, Tom thought—that's what I need. The old premonition of disaster was sneaking up on him. I've had it a million times before, he thought—it doesn't mean a thing. I'm doing all right on my job. Hopkins likes me. We're really being smart to sell this place and move to Grandmother's house. We're going to make a damn good thing of it!

He couldn't convince himself. Even if I do get fired, it won't matter, he thought. We've got a little cash now. I'll get into some kind of business for myself. I'll work full time on selling Grandmother's house.

Suddenly he had a picture of himself hanging around his grandmother's house, precisely as his father had, with nothing to do. He glanced down and found he was gripping his right thigh so hard that his knuckles were white. He hadn't done that for some time. Why the hell should I get scared in peacetime? he thought. Deliberately he stood up. It doesn't really matter, he thought. Here goes nothing. It will be interesting to see what happens.

"Betsy!" he said. "Is there any packing I can help you with?"

"Not a thing! Say, guess what I found today while I was cleaning out the attic!"

"What?"

"Your old mandolin—I packed it in one of the boxes. You ought to get it fixed up. It would be fun."

"I will sometime," he said.

"Daddy," Janey said, "tell us a story about Bubbley."

"All right," Tom said. "Once upon a time there was a little dog named Bubbley. He swallowed a cake of soap, and . . ."

"Don't tell it so fast!" Barbara said.

". . . every time he barked, he blew bubbles," Tom said, spacing the words evenly. "One day a man from a circus saw him. . . ."

He told the story well and repeated it twice upon request.

17

"WILL GRANDMOTHER BE THERE when we get there?" Janey asked.

It was late Saturday afternoon. They were droning along the Merritt Parkway from Westport to South Bay, with the car packed tightly with suitcases and paper cartons of clothes. Tom had just signed the deed transferring the little house on Greentree Avenue to its new owner, who had seemed overjoyed to get it.

"Grandmother is dead," Betsy said gently. She had already explained this to the children several times.

"Do dead people ever come back?" Barbara asked.

"No," Tom said.

"Do they *like* being dead?" Janey inquired.

"I don't know," Tom said.

"Grandmother is in heaven," Betsy said. "I'm sure she's happy there."

The engine of the old Ford was knocking, and the indicator on the dashboard showed it was heating up. Tom slowed down to twenty-five miles an hour and stayed at the extreme right edge of the highway. He had always had a horror of breaking down on the Merritt Parkway with the children along, and of not being able to get the old car off the pavement. Now other cars regularly blared their horns as they flashed by.

"We'll have to get a new car pretty soon," Betsy said. Tom didn't answer.

"Where is Grandmother now?" Janey asked. "What did they do with her when she got dead?"

"Her soul went to heaven," Betsy said. "Her body has been buried in the cemetery."

"Does she ever try to get out of the cemetery?"

"No," Tom said.

"She's not really in the cemetery," Betsy said. "Her *spirit* is in heaven."

"How long is it going to be before we get there?" Barbara asked.

"Get where?" Tom said.

"Grandmother's house."

"About half an hour."

"Can I have a drink of water?" Janey inquired.

The engine seemed to be knocking louder. Don't break down now, Tom thought. Not now. Somehow it would have seemed a very bad omen to have the car break down while they were moving to Grandmother's house.

When they got off the parkway, they stopped at a restaurant and had supper. By the time they reached the winding road leading up the hill to the big house, it was almost dark. The heat indicator on the dashboard of the old car touched the red line marked "danger." Tom slowed to ten miles an hour, shifted into second gear, and crawled around the sharp turns by the massive outcroppings of rock. The engine kept going. Finally he saw the stone posts, with the tall iron urns on them, turned into the driveway, and shifted into low gear as he passed the grove of oak trees, the carriage house, and the rock garden. Ahead of him the old mansion loomed, silhouetted against the sky. Tom parked the car near the house and cut off the tired engine. Old Edward opened the front door of the house and stood framed in it. "Good evening, Mr. Rath," he said.

Ever since he could remember, Tom had taken old Edward for granted—he had to think hard to remember his last name, which was Schultz. Now Tom looked at him closely, as though he had never seen him before. Edward was a tall man about sixty-five years old, thin and bent at the shoulders. Deep lines ran from the edges of his nose to the corners of his mouth, and his brow was furrowed. What kind of life has he led? Tom wondered. What has he done all these years when the supper dishes were washed? He remembered his grandmother telling him that Edward kept canaries in his room. Somehow it didn't seem possible.

Now Edward stood holding the front door open with one hand, his face stern and unwelcoming. The children, tired of being pent up in the car, dashed ahead of their parents into the big house, but, surprised by the dim and somehow eerie light of the front hall, skidded to a stop, rumpling a scatter rug. Tom and Betsy came in, carrying boxes and suitcases. Edward made no motion to help them. When they got inside, he let the front door close softly behind them. "I would like to talk to you, Mr. Rath," he said.

There was no deference in his manner—that's why he seemed like an entirely different man. There was also no friendliness. His voice was cold, almost supercilious, perhaps a little mocking, Tom thought, wondering if it were simply his imagination.

"As soon as we get these things put away," Tom said. Edward stood watching him and Betsy as they carried their bags upstairs. The children, oddly subdued, followed their parents.

"What room shall we put our things in?" Betsy asked, breathing hard.

"Grandmother's, I guess," Tom said. "We'll want the children on the same floor with us, so I guess we won't use the third floor. If the girls want to stay together we can put them in the large guest room, and Pete can have the room I used to have."

The door to his grandmother's room was not latched. Without putting his suitcases down, he pushed it with his toe. It swung open, revealing the big four-poster bed, which looked strangely wide and empty. From the walls of the room old paintings of "The Senator" and "The Major" as children stared from ornate gilt frames. Barbara and Janey, abruptly recovering their spirits, leaped onto the big bed and started jouncing up and down.

"Get off there!" Tom said sharply.

The children looked startled. "Why?" Janey asked.

"We don't want you to mess up the bed," Betsy replied kindly. She piled the boxes she had been carrying on a chair.

"I think I'll go down and talk to old Edward right away," Tom said.

"What are you going to tell him?"

"I don't know—that we won't know what we can do for him for some time, I guess."

Edward was waiting for him at the bottom of the stairs. "Let's go into the living room and sit down," Tom said.

The old man followed him silently. Tom sat in an armchair, and Edward sank negligently into the rocking chair old Mrs. Rath had always used. Somehow he looked shockingly incongruous there, as he crossed one knee over the other and leaned back.

"You wanted to talk to me?" Tom asked. He thought it would be better to let Edward start.

"When are they going to read the will?"

"Read the will? I don't know that they are going to. Mrs. Rath's lawyer has it. Why do you ask?"

"Do you know what she left me?"

"Mrs. Rath spoke to me about you shortly before she died," Tom said. "She asked me to do what I could for you, and I intend to try. You weren't mentioned in the will specifically."

"I wasn't *mentioned!*" Edward said. He leaned forward in his chair.

"I intended to talk to you about it," Tom said. "As you may know, Mrs. Rath did not leave a great deal. It will be some time before I know precisely what I can do for you, but I assure you I'll do all I can."

"I don't believe it!" Edward replied. "She said she'd remember me in her will!"

"Perhaps Mrs. Rath was a little confused . . ." Tom began.

"I don't believe it! I'll go to law! I've got proof!"

"I don't think that will be necessary," Tom said. "I don't want you to worry. I don't have much to give, but as long as we have this house, you'll at least have a place to stay, and in time I hope to work something out for you."

"I don't need your charity!" the old man said. "I've saved my money—I've probably got a lot more than you have! I only want my just due!"

"I won't be able to tell you how much I can give you until the estate is settled," Tom said.

"Never mind that! I want to see the will! I don't believe she didn't mention me. She promised she'd leave me the house."

"The *house?*"

"That's right—I've got proof!"

"You must be mistaken," Tom said. "She spoke to me often about leaving me the house. Are you sure you aren't imagining all this?"

"Of course I'm sure! Why do you think I've stayed here all these years? Why do you think I took her orders, and cooked her food, and did her laundry, and cleaned up her dirt? Do you think I loved the old woman?"

Tom stood up. He didn't mean to, but he suddenly rose out of his chair and stood towering over Edward. There was an instant of complete silence. When Tom spoke his voice was soft. "Don't talk like that about Mrs. Rath again," he said.

Edward stared up at him and said nothing. His face was white, perhaps with anger, perhaps with fear. Tom hadn't meant to lunge out of his chair so fast. Slowly Tom sat down. "Now listen," he continued quietly. "I frankly don't believe Mrs. Rath ever promised you anything. She didn't make promises like that, and if she had, she would have told me. But I'm willing to admit that you had a right to expect something, and that perhaps she said things which encouraged you. It's quite possible that as she grew older she grew confused and thought she had more than she did. Now get one thing straight: she didn't have much to leave anyone. By the time the estate is settled, and the mortgage on this house is paid, there probably won't be much more than the house and land. I intend to sell them if I can, and I intend to see you're as well cared for as possible, but I'm not going to promise you anything now. You worked here of your own free will for a salary, and you'll take what I can give you. Until I can get things organized and sell the land, you can keep your room and have your meals here if you want, and if you mind your tongue. You will not be required to do any work."

"I'll get a lawyer!" Edward said. "I'll sue! I've got proof she meant the house for me!"

"The will leaves it to me," Tom said. "The only question now is whether you're going to be reasonable and take what you can get, or whether you're going to keep on like this and get thrown out of here tonight."

"I'll leave, but you'll hear from me!"

I mustn't get angry, Tom thought. He's an old man. He had a right to expect something. Maybe she did make him promises, or at least, maybe he thought she did. I mustn't get angry. "Calm down," he said. "It's not going to do either of us any good to get excited."

"You're cheating me!" the old man said. "Either you are or she did! She was crazy! She was filthy! She never took a bath. She was . . ."

"Stop!" Tom said. His voice was like the report of a gun. The old man drew in his breath sharply.

"Now get out of here," Tom said. "Go down and pack your bags and call a taxi, and get out of here. If you're not gone in an hour I'll throw you out."

"I'll get a lawyer," Edward said. "You think I can't afford one. I can get the best. The house is mine, and I've got proof."

"Get all the lawyers you want, but right now, get out of that chair," Tom said. "And stay in the servant quarters until the taxi comes."

Edward got up. Tom waited until he had left the room before going upstairs.

"What happened?" Betsy said. "You look upset."

Tom lay down on the big double bed and stared up at the crocheted canopy stretching like a net overhead. "I got angry," he said.

"At Edward?"

"Yes—I threw him out. He's leaving in an hour."

He told her about it then, and as he talked, her indignation grew. "Of course you got mad!" she said. "I would have hit him."

Tom didn't move. He felt limp and utterly exhausted. "I get angry too easily," he said. "Tonight I had a real impulse to kill Edward. Often I feel as though I'd like to kill Ogden, at the office. It's strange that I am permitted to kill only strangers and friends."

"What?"

"Nothing. I'm awfully tired."

"That was such a funny thing you said about killing strangers and friends."

"I meant the war," he said.

"Did you ever kill anyone?"

"Of course."

"I mean, did you personally ever kill anyone? You've never talked to me about it at all."

"Right now I'm too tired. I want to go to sleep."

He stirred restlessly and shut his eyes. In the dim light from the window, Betsy lay looking at his big hands lying quietly folded on top of the covers. "I cannot imagine your killing anyone," she said.

There was no answer. Betsy lay looking at him for several minutes before trying to go to sleep. How strange, she thought, to know so little about one's husband. I wish he would talk to me about the war, but I should know better than try to make him. After all, a good wife isn't supposed to ask her husband questions he obviously doesn't want to answer.

18

IT TOOK both Tom and Betsy a long while to get to sleep that night. They lay in the dark, separate and silent. Neither of them commented when they heard a taxi drive up to the house and the front door slam. For some reason, each felt a necessity to feign sleep. Downstairs the old grandfather's clock which had marked the passage of Tom's boyhood continued to mourn the loss of each hour.

Only a few minutes after Tom had finally got to sleep, he was awakened by a piercing scream from the next room. He leaped out of bed and, followed by Betsy, ran to the room where the two girls were sleeping, and snapped on the light. Janey was sitting bolt upright in her bed, crying. Tears were running down her face. Betsy ran to her and picked her up. "What's the matter, baby?" she said. "Did you have a nightmare?"

Janey said nothing. She hugged her mother tightly with both arms, and gradually her cries subsided into sobs. In the bed on the other side of the room, Barbara slept peacefully, oblivious to any disturbance. Betsy took Janey into the room she and Tom were using and put her down on the big bed. Tom put the lights out, and he and Betsy lay there in the dark, with the child between them. Janey's sobs stopped. She gave a long, shuddering sigh and, still clinging tightly to her mother, went to sleep.

I wonder what she dreamed, Tom thought. What does a child have nightmares about? Did she dream that wild beasts were chasing her, or about drowning, or falling through space? What does a child fear most?

"Betsy, are you still awake?" he whispered. The steady, mingled breathing of mother and child was the only answer.

When Tom awoke in the morning, he felt drugged, as though he had been drinking heavily. No one else was in the big bed. Glancing at the familiar face of his wrist watch, he saw it was almost nine-thirty. He jumped to his feet. "Betsy!" he called. "I've missed my train!"

She was nowhere in the room. In his pajamas, Tom ran downstairs, through the living room and the dining room to the big old-fashioned kitchen, where Betsy was washing dishes. "I'll be late to work!" he said. "I've got to get another draft of the speech done!"

She looked up and smiled. "It's Sunday," she said.

"Oh," he replied ruefully, "I forgot." He stood in the middle of the big kitchen, a little confused. Bright sunlight streamed through the window. "Where are the kids?" he asked.

"Outside. That old rock garden is a wonderful place for them to play."

"I think I'll go upstairs and catch another nap," he said.

"Don't you dare! I've been up since seven o'clock unpacking, and now we're going to church! And before that we're going to make a list of all the things we have to do."

"There isn't enough paper," he said. "Not in the whole world."

He went upstairs. The first thing he saw was his old mandolin in its battered black leather case, lying on top of his bureau where Betsy had put it after unpacking it. He stood looking at it a moment, then drew the instrument from its case. It was covered with dust, and the strings were rusty and slack. Slowly he tightened one of the strings, strumming it gently with his thumb. It snapped suddenly. Tom shrugged, put the mandolin back in its case, and glanced around the room. In one corner was a built-in bookcase with a wide empty shelf at its top. He reached up and put the mandolin there. Then he walked quickly to the bathroom. There was dust in the bottom of the bathtub. Impatiently he washed it

– 141 –

out and let the tub fill while he shaved, bending almost double to see himself in the mirror.

"Hurry up!" Betsy called.

When he got downstairs, he found a plate of bacon and eggs waiting for him at one end of the big, marble-topped kitchen table. At the other end Betsy was seated, determinedly writing on a pad. "We've got to get more stuff out of the car and unpack the rest of the boxes the truck brought," she said, "and we've got to get the girls enrolled in school."

"I've got to call Sims and tell him about Edward," Tom said. "He should know, in case he makes any trouble."

"I've got to clear out Grandmother's closets," Betsy said. "Her clothes are still there. And if you want the television set in the living room, you better see about getting it hooked up."

"The main thing for me to do," he said, "is to get the information we'll need to make some sort of decision on your housing project. I've got to get a copy of the zoning regulations, and we'll probably have to find out the procedure for getting an exception to them. We ought to have at least three contractors look the place over and give us bids on rebuilding the carriage house and putting in roads. God, Betsy, there's so much! I can't go to church today. I'm going to stay here and write letters."

"You're going to church!" she said. "We're going to church every Sunday. From now on."

"You go," he said.

"Why won't you?"

"I'm sorry," he said, feeling embarrassed. "You take the kids and go to church, and I'll stay here and write letters."

Betsy put her pencil down, picked up the plate from which he had just eaten his eggs, and put it in the sink. With her back turned to him she said, "Tommy, I'm asking you a favor. Go to church with me and the kids."

"All right," he said.

"Even if you're bored," she said, "try it. Maybe someday it would help you to stop worrying all the time."

"I don't worry all the time!"

"All right. But try it. I don't know about you, but I've been miserable for a long time. I used to think it was that damn little house, and it was partly, but it was more. We can't just go on being scared all the time, Tommy. Sometime it will have to stop."

"If you want me to go to church, I'll go," he said. "I didn't know you were miserable all the time."

"You know what I mean!"

"Sure."

"There seems to be something hanging over us, something that makes it hard to be happy."

"I know," he said.

"It isn't your fault. It's just something we both have to wrestle with."

"I'm all right," he said.

"I'm all right too. I just feel I'd like to go to church."

"Okay," he said. "Before we go, I'll call Sims."

"There isn't time."

Reluctantly Tom went upstairs and put on a blue suit. When he returned to the kitchen, Betsy was combing the children's hair. The two girls wore fluffy white dresses and Pete was in gray flannel shorts and a brown jacket. "Why do we have to wear party clothes to go to church?" Barbara asked.

"We just do," Betsy said. "Get in the car."

After leaving the children at the Sunday school in the annex of the Episcopal church, Tom followed Betsy into the church itself. They sat in a back pew, and Betsy knelt gracefully to pray. Her face was drawn and serious. Tom glanced away from her, feeling somehow that he was invading her privacy. An unseen organ started to hum melodiously, and an acolyte appeared before the altar and lit fourteen candles with a long, silver-handled taper. All around Tom the pews were filled with elderly ladies, many of whom knelt. Tom glanced at Betsy and saw she was still on her knees, her eyes closed, her face rapt. How beautiful she is, he thought. He knelt uncomfortably beside her and shut his eyes.

An hour later, when Tom got home, he went right to the telephone and called Sims. When Sims heard about Edward, he swore, the oaths sounding strangely cultivated and precise as he spoke them.

"Do you think he can make any trouble for us?" Tom asked.

"It depends on what he calls 'proof'—if he has anything in writing he might make things difficult. If he tried to contest the will, it could drag on for months."

"If it were a long delay, it could break me," Tom said. "I've got to turn this place over fast—the longer we hold it, the less money anybody's going to have. Perhaps I could settle with him out of court."

"Maybe that's what he's counting on," Sims said. "I wouldn't consider it. I know damn well your grandmother meant you to have everything—we talked about it countless times. I'd hang on and see what kind of case he's got. Let him find out how hard it is to go to law before you talk to him."

"Is there anything we can do while we're waiting?"

"Not much," Sims said. "Actually, I won't be able to help you much from now on. The whole thing will be up to the Probate Judge—I've already sent him a copy of the will. He'll be the one who will have to rule on any claims Edward puts in."

"Who is he?"

"Bernstein—Saul Bernstein. He has an office on Main Street, I think—I hear he's lived in South Bay all his life. It might pay you to drop in and see him."

"Do you have any idea what kind of guy he is?"

"None," Sims said. "Never met him."

Tom thanked Sims and hung up. He decided to write Bernstein for an appointment. It was curious to think that so much depended on a man he had never met.

19

I⊤ wₐₛ nine o'clock Tuesday morning. Judge Saul Bernstein, a small stout man with a large mole on his left cheek, climbed the stairs to the third floor of the Whitelock building, the second biggest office building in the town of South Bay. Puffing a little, he walked into the bare, linoleum-floored room which was his office and smiled at his secretary, a thin girl bent intently over her typewriter. "Good morning, Sally," he said. "How are you feeling today?"

Her hands stopped fluttering over the keys, and she looked up at him gratefully. "Fine, Judge," she said. "My cold's almost gone."

He sat down behind his scarred pine desk in the corner of the room and looked at the morning mail, which his secretary had opened for him. The top letter asked for an appointment the following Saturday or any evening, if that would not be too inconvenient. "I'd like to talk to you about settling the estate of the late Mrs. Florence Rath," the letter said. "I have also been told that you might be able to advise me on the possibility of subdividing her land into one-acre lots eventually. . . ." The letter referred to the will Sims had sent to Bernstein and concluded with advance gratitude for any help Bernstein could offer. It was signed, "Thomas R. Rath."

Bernstein had just finished reading the letter when the telephone on his desk rang. His secretary answered it, using an extension on her own desk, and said, "It's for you, Judge. He won't give his name."

"Hello?" Bernstein said.

For a moment there was no answer but the humming in the receiver.

"Hello?" Bernstein repeated.

"I want to talk to the judge!" a heavy voice replied.

"This is Judge Bernstein. Who is this calling?"

"Are you the judge that handles wills?" the voice asked.

"Yes, I'm the judge of the Probate Court," Bernstein said briskly. "Give me your name, please."

"My name is Schultz, Edward Schultz," the voice said, "and I have a claim to make. . . ."

Bernstein listened to Schultz for a long time. When he had hung up, he picked up Tom's letter and reread it. His stomach was beginning to hurt, as it always did when he saw he was going to have to arbitrate a fight.

Thomas Rath, he thought—the grandson of the old lady. Saul Bernstein remembered old Florence Rath well. He had first seen her more than thirty years ago, when his own father and mother had moved from a tenement in Brooklyn to open a delicatessen in South Bay. It had been a small delicatessen, not at all the kind of establishment that Florence Rath had patronized, except on holidays when it was the only store open. Florence Rath had often telephoned the store on Sundays to ask casually for a small jar of cheese or a can of anchovies to be delivered to her house, which had been more than six miles away from the store. More than once Saul Bernstein had bicycled up the long steep hill and around the two sharp curves by the outcroppings of rock to deliver a bottle of olives, or some other item which brought a profit of about a nickel, and often the servants who received the delivery had never bothered to see that he was tipped.

Saul Bernstein remembered many things about Florence Rath. Once she had come into his family's store. That had been in 1931, when the depression had been at its worst, and his father had been almost at the point of giving up the store and going back to New York to look for a job. The heat in the store had been turned off for reasons of economy, and Saul Bernstein's parents had stood behind the little counter all day wearing heavy coats, mufflers, and gloves and slapping their hands against their shoulders to keep warm. The store had been damp and had smelled of mildew, and a few jars had broken when their contents froze. Saul Bernstein hadn't been in the store much himself in those days, for his family had insisted that he and his two brothers spend as much time as possible in the high school, where it was warm, but on this particular Sunday when Florence Rath came in, his mother had been lying in her little room upstairs ill, with her husband taking care of her, and Saul had been in charge of the store. Florence Rath had been dressed in a long fur coat, and while she waited for him to bring her a box of mixed nuts, she had complained. "Why don't you keep this place warm?" she had said. "Are you trying to freeze your customers to death?"

"No, ma'am," he had replied and had felt obliged to add, "The furnace broke—we're having it fixed."

Saul Bernstein had a long memory. He remembered when he had been a young lawyer, only a year out of school, and a hardware merchant had come to him and asked him to collect a bill from Mrs. Rath for some expensive garden tools which the merchant said she had ordered and never paid for. That had been in the days when Bernstein had been spending most of his time sitting patiently in a tiny office, hopefully listening for the footsteps of possible clients in the hall and trying to forget the advice of his best friends, who told him that he ought to go into New York to practice law, because there was no place for a Jewish attorney in a small, hidebound Connecticut town notorious for its prejudice against Jews. The hardware merchant with his claim against Mrs. Rath had been Bernstein's first client, for the simple reason that all the other lawyers in the town had refused to handle his case. Bernstein had been glad to get it, and he had burned with righteous indignation at the thought of the rich old woman at the top of the hill ordering tools from the poor merchant and refusing to pay for them. He had almost gone charging to the top of the hill to berate her, but an innate caution had stopped him, and instead, he had made inquiries around the town and discovered that Mrs. Rath was famous for paying her bills the day she received them. He had found from the hardware merchant that a gardener of Mrs. Rath's had bought the tools, and further investigation had shown that the gardener had been discharged by Mrs. Rath two days before the purchase of tools had been made. And so Bernstein had turned the case over to the police, who eventually had extracted payment from the gardener, and he had felt that on his first case he had learned a lesson: to investigate thoroughly.

All this had happened long ago. Since then Saul Bernstein had prospered in the town of South Bay, despite the predictions of his best friends. He had grown reasonably rich, and respected, and might have been happy except for one thing: he detested justice almost as much as he detested violence or cruelty of any other kind.

He had found this out in 1940, when he had been made judge of the Municipal Court. One of the first men to appear before him had been a truck driver who had got drunk and driven his truck into a tree. The man had been about forty years old, with a red face and dismayed blue eyes, and he had pleaded for mercy. He had explained that his job depended upon his driving license, which would be taken away from him if he were convicted of drunken driving, and standing there in court, full of hurt dignity, he had said his wife was pregnant, and that he didn't want to lose his job.

"But this is your second offense," Bernstein had said. "According to the record, you were convicted of driving while under the influ- ence of liquor only two years ago."

"That's why I can't be convicted now!" the man had replied desperately. "I'll never get my license back again!"

And he had asked for mercy, but Bernstein had been in the business of giving justice, and with his stomach aching, he had given justice, and the man had turned away with a look of utter despair on his red, forlorn face.

It is not an easy thing for a judge to find he detests justice, and Bernstein had not admitted his discovery to himself for a long while. He had not faced it until 1948, when he had had a choice between becoming Probate Judge in South Bay, or going on to a higher court. There had been some temptation to leave South Bay, for in spite of his new eminence, his wife had not been asked to join any of the women's clubs in town, but he had chosen differ- ently for two reasons: the idea of having to judge cases involving long prison sentences, or even the death penalty, appalled him, and he had evolved the theory that justice is bearable to the judge only when it is based on complete knowledge of the disputants as well as the law. He had a horror of sentencing men he knew almost nothing about. In South Bay, where he knew almost everyone and had plenty of time to devote to each case, Bernstein was able to withhold his decisions until he had assembled complete information. Rarely was he put in the position of having to decide what was justice for strangers.

So Bernstein had chosen to stay in South Bay and become the judge of the Probate Court, which was primarily concerned with the orderly disposal of papers rather than people. And somewhat to his own astonishment, he had become enormously powerful in the town, for people had found that hating justice as he did, he dispensed it extremely well, and they called him in on disputes of all kinds, even those which had nothing to do with the Probate Court, and when, after delaying as long as he could, Bernstein delivered his opinion, it had a weight in the town more than that of any other man. He and his wife were rarely asked to cocktail parties or dinners, but he was almost always appointed moderator at town meetings, or on any occasion, formal or informal, where impartiality was needed, and few people knew how his stomach hurt when he raised his pudgy hand and said, "Yes, yes, I understand, but let us now examine the other point of view. . . ."

Now as Judge Bernstein reread the letter he had received from Tom Rath and recalled the conversation he had just had over the telephone with Edward Schultz, the gnawing in his stomach grew worse and worse. Disputed wills were always painful, almost as painful as divorce cases. They brought out the worst in everyone, Bernstein knew from experience. On the surface this case was simple: a rich young heir was apparently trying to cut out a faithful old servant. Usually things turn out to be exactly as they appear on the surface, Bernstein had found, but not always. He wondered what young Thomas Rath was like—probably one of those commuters who did their shopping in Bermuda shorts, sporting a cigarette in a long holder, he decided—old Mrs. Rath would be apt to have a grandson like that. And this man Edward Schultz, who had sounded rather lunatic over the telephone, what sort of man was he? Which of the two men would be pleased by justice?

But more than a dispute over a will had been dropped on his desk that morning, Bernstein reflected. If Rath got the land, he apparently intended to try to subdivide it into one-acre lots. The Rath estate was in a "Triple A Zone," where no estate of less than ten acres was supposed to exist. That meant that if Rath got the land, there would be a zoning fight. Bernstein had lived in South Bay so long that he could predict the intensity of any dispute, if not its outcome, and he thought, "Not a zoning fight now—all we need is a zoning fight now!"

Sometimes it was almost a disadvantage to have lived in a town so long, because Bernstein knew all the people in the local government so well that he could foretell how they would answer almost any question, and without moving from his chair could conduct a fairly accurate public-opinion poll, a process which was often disturbing. Now he imagined what the various leaders in South Bay would say if Thomas Rath asked the Zoning Board to let him divide his land. Old John Bradbury, chairman of the Zoning Board, would explode at the very thought. He would immediately tie the whole question up with the controversy over whether to build a new public school. "Twenty acres with one house will bring in one family which will use a private school," old Bradbury would say exasperatedly. "Twenty acres with twenty houses will bring in twenty families, all of whom will expect the town to educate their children!"

And old Mr. Parkington, whose estate was near the south side of the Rath property, would have a double reason for apoplectic objections. As a member of the Zoning Board he had been one of the people who had instituted the ten-acre area in the first place, "to preserve the rural beauties of South Bay," and for more than fifteen years he had conducted a personal crusade against any effort to change the zoning ordinances. His reaction to having land so near his own converted into a housing project would be picturesque, Bernstein reflected grimly, and hoped he wouldn't have to see it.

The worst part of such a fight would be, Bernstein thought, that the arguments in favor of allowing Rath to subdivide his land would be as apoplectic as the arguments against it. Bob Murphy, who since 1931 had been a member of the Zoning Board, would use the case as an excuse to continue his unending battle against what he termed "the privileged few." And old Mrs. Allison, the fourth member of the board, would undoubtedly agree with everyone on both sides of the controversy, but would end by voting for young Rath, because she would be almost sure to judge him the underdog.

If there had been a fifth member of the Zoning Board, Bernstein could have foretold how the case would go with little possibility of error, but there was no fifth member. The post was vacant and seemed likely to remain vacant for a long time. It had been vacant ever since Harold Mathews, a tight-lipped Yankee who had decided each case on its merit, had died a month ago, for every time anyone had been suggested to take Mathews' place, a great fuss had been made by those who believed the new member would weight the board against them. Sooner or later a new member would have to be named, but meanwhile even Bernstein couldn't predict how zoning cases would be decided. All he knew was that there would be a bitter fight, the very thought of which made his stomach ache worse than ever. How violent Schultz had sounded over the telephone! *"I want justice,"* he had said. I wonder how many murders have been committed, and how many wars have been fought with that as a slogan, Bernstein thought. When they say they want justice, they always want someone else to get the sharp end of it. Justice is a thing that is better to give than to receive, but I am sick of giving it, he thought. I think it should be a prerogative of the gods.

20

THAT TUESDAY MORNING Tom perfected the latest draft of the speech he was writing for Ralph Hopkins. The whole text, which was now about thirty pages long ("We can cut it later," Hopkins said), had come to seem a sort of penance from which he would never escape, an endless tract, a meaningless lifework.

At noon Tom took the speech up to Bill Ogden. He thought he knew precisely what would happen next. Ogden would read it and say it was terrible. Tom would then rewrite it again and be asked to dinner in Hopkins' apartment. Hopkins would say it was wonderful and tell him to do it over again, and this whole process would doubtlessly be repeated over and over again until September 15, when Hopkins would presumably walk out on the speaker's platform in some big hotel in Atlantic City and tell everybody how delighted he was to be there.

But it didn't happen that way at all. Tuesday when Tom took the speech up to Ogden, Ogden laid it negligently among some other papers on his desk without even glancing at the first page.

"Thanks, Tom," he said casually. "We're going to take you off this now and give Gordon Walker a crack at it."

Tom waited, thinking there would be some other assignment for him, but apparently there was none. Ogden picked up his telephone and placed a call to someone in San Francisco. Tom got up uncertainly, thinking Ogden would tell him to wait, but Ogden just sat there, holding the telephone receiver negligently to his ear, saying nothing. I shouldn't dislike the guy so much, Tom thought. After all, he's awfully good at his job. He went back to his own office and sat down. Why had they taken him off the speech? Did that mean he had failed at it? Or was it normal procedure to pass the speech around among several of Hopkins' assistants? Tom didn't know.

There was nothing for him to do. Only a few minutes ago he had dreaded the prospect of coming back to his office and starting

to rewrite the speech, but now he would have welcomed it. There was nothing for him to do. How long would Hopkins pay him to sit in a neat little office, with a secretary outside, with nothing to do? Maybe that was the way Hopkins got rid of people. In this strange, polite world high in the sky above Rockefeller Center, maybe nobody ever really got fired. Maybe all Hopkins did was to give a man nothing to do, absolutely nothing to do, until he started to go out of his mind sitting uselessly in his office all day, and resigned. Maybe that was the polite, smooth way to get rid of a man nobody wanted.

It wouldn't work, Tom thought. If they tried that on me, I'd buy magazines and just sit here having a good time, making nine thousand dollars a year. It wouldn't be so bad to get nine thousand dollars a year for doing absolutely nothing. I'd find something to keep me busy. By God, I'd work on selling Grandmother's land.

But that state of affairs wouldn't last long—of course Hopkins would fire a man if he insisted on staying, after he had been given nothing to do for a few weeks. Giving a man nothing to do would just be a warning; it would be offering him an opportunity to get out gracefully.

Maybe that isn't it at all, Tom thought. Maybe they're just clever enough to know that a man goes stale on a speech after he's worked it over a few times. This is probably routine, and because this mental-health thing is a new project, they just don't have anything else for me at the moment. That's all it is—just routine. He got up and started pacing up and down his office, feeling much as he had during the war when he heard of another jump coming up. He glanced at his watch and nervously wound it.

I wonder if old Edward really has any proof, he thought; I wonder if Grandmother did write a later will and give it to him, but that's impossible; she wouldn't have done that without telling me. I wonder if we really will be able to sell off the land in small lots. This man Bernstein will be able to tell me—I wonder what he's like.

I shouldn't be thinking of private business, he thought. I should be showing initiative on this mental-health project. I shouldn't expect Ogden to keep giving me assignments; I should dream up

assignments of my own. I bet Ogden never has to be told what to do. I'll think of what has to be done, and I'll do it. How the hell *do* you start a national committee on mental health? You get a list of big shots for members—Hopkins undoubtedly has that in his mind already. You get the thing financed—and I bet Hopkins already has some understanding with the foundations about that. He could pay for the thing himself as another tax deduction, but he'll need the prestige of the foundations, and he wouldn't have gone this far if he didn't have it all lined up. He'll need the co-operation of the medics, and that's why he's working so hard on this speech. What else will he need? A little knowledge of what the problems in the field really are—that's the only thing nobody seems to be bothering about. If we're going to figure out a program, we ought to have a list of what the experts think the basic problems are. I ought to interview the top medics. I ought to see what the public library has on the subject. I ought to become well informed.

I can't start interviewing people without Ogden's permission, he thought—that might be tipping Hopkins' hand too soon. But I can start getting books to read, and I can ask Ogden for permission to interview people—that at least will let him know I'm on the job.

Tom pressed a button on his desk, and when his secretary came in, he dictated a memorandum to Ogden requesting permission to visit the state mental hospitals and several leading psychiatrists to gather information about mental-health problems. He added that he was planning to get together a bibliography on the subject—he thought that sounded quite impressive. He had just told his secretary he was going out to lunch, and that he would spend the afternoon at the public library, when the telephone rang. He picked up the receiver.

"Hello," a familiar deep voice said. "Is this Mr. Rath?"

"Hello, Caesar," Tom replied with sinking heart, and he thought, Here it comes. So Caesar wasn't just embarrassed at seeing me—he was biding his time. I wonder if he's been in touch with Maria.

"I'm off duty now, and I thought maybe we might have lunch together," Caesar said.

"Sure!" Tom replied with forced cheer. "Where will I meet you?"

"In the lobby by the information booth," Caesar said. "What time would be best for you?"

"Right away," Tom replied. "I'll be right down."

Caesar, still dressed in his plum-colored elevator operator's uniform, was leaning against the wall by the information booth, smoking a cigarette. He grinned diffidently when he saw Tom coming toward him.

"This is a swell idea!" Tom said heartily, ashamed that in addition to all the other strains involved in their relationship, he should find it awkward to have lunch with a man in an elevator operator's uniform. "I know a swell little place on Forty-ninth Street, up toward Sixth Avenue."

"Fine," Caesar replied, and fell in beside him. They walked rapidly across Rockefeller Plaza. Actually, Tom had no restaurant clearly in mind—he simply wanted to find a place where they wouldn't be seen. The impulse to keep his connection with Caesar completely private was overpowering. They walked in silence for several minutes. When they finally came to a dingy little Mexican restaurant and bar on Sixth Avenue which looked like an establishment none of his acquaintants ever would frequent, Tom said, "This is the place. I like Mexican food, don't you?"

"Sure," Caesar replied.

They went in and sat down at a dimly lighted table. A waiter in a stained apron came to take their orders. Over the bar a radio was playing a song in which a girl kept saying over and over again, "I love you."

"The drinks are on me," Tom said. "Order anything you want."

"I'd like Scotch," Caesar replied. "Some Black and White."

"Make it two double Black and White's," Tom said to the waiter.

"Funny, the way we just happened to run into each other," Caesar said.

"I'm falling for you," the woman on the radio sang. "Falling, falling, falling, head over heels in love."

"It is funny," Tom said. "I sure was surprised to see you."

The waiter put their drinks before them, and Tom lifted his to his lips eagerly.

"Well, this is better than that old jungle juice we used to drink in New Guinea," Caesar said.

"It sure is!" Tom replied. The phrase "jungle juice" sounded antique to him—he didn't really remember drinking any at all.

"You've sure done all right for yourself," Caesar said. "Assistant to Ralph Hopkins!"

"The breaks," Tom said. "It isn't as much of a job as you might think."

"Mind you, I'm not complaining," Caesar said. "Things have gone pretty good for us."

"You married?"

"Sure. Are you?"

"Yes," Tom said. "I was married before the war."

The girl on the radio finished her song. "And now the news," an announcer said. The bartender turned the radio off.

"Did you go back to Rome after the war?" Tom asked.

"Sure—as soon as I got out of the hospital. Gina and I got married in forty-seven. We got three kids now."

Tom said nothing. He finished his drink and motioned to the bartender to bring two more.

"Three kids," Caesar repeated. "Things were pretty tough for us for a while, but I've got a twenty per cent disability because of my back, and Gina is working now. We're making out all right. She runs an elevator over in the Empire State building. Sometimes she takes a night shift and sometimes I do—we got it worked out so one of us is always home with the kids."

"Sounds like a pretty good arrangement," Tom said.

"We got a nice apartment," Caesar replied. "It's a hell of a lot better than we'd have had if we'd stayed in Rome, the way Gina's folks wanted us to."

"I guess things are pretty tough back there," Tom said.

"I'll say! We hear from Gina's old lady every once in a while. Those people don't have it easy."

- 156 -

Tom took a long sip of his drink. "Caesar," he said, "did you ever hear anything about Maria?"

Caesar looked down at the table. "I did," he said. "That's what I wanted to talk to you about."

"How is she?"

"I haven't heard anything lately—not for more than a year. You knew she married that guy who had the bakeshop, Louis Lapa?"

"No!" Tom said. "When?"

Caesar seemed embarrassed. "She married him about two months after we left," he said.

"I'm glad to hear it," Tom said. "I certainly am glad to hear it. Louis was a nice guy."

Caesar glanced up. "You knew she had a son?" he said. "She had a son a little while later."

"No," Tom said. "I didn't know that."

"She's got a boy," Caesar said, "and things weren't going well for them. You know Louis had a bad leg, and it's given him a lot of trouble."

"I'm sorry to hear that," Tom said.

"He was in the hospital for a long while trying to get that leg fixed and they lost the store."

"I'm sorry to hear that," Tom repeated.

"Gina's folks helped them out for a while," Caesar said. "I don't know how you feel about these things, Mr. Rath, but when I saw you, and found you were doing so well and all, I got to thinking about Maria and her boy, and I wondered whether you could do anything for them."

Tom said nothing.

"Of course, I haven't heard from them lately," Caesar continued, "but if you wanted, I could find out about them—Gina's mother could tell me easy. Maria is a cousin of Gina's."

Still Tom said nothing.

"What I mean is," Caesar continued earnestly, "things are so much easier for us here than they are for them. Gina and I manage to send a little back every month. And I thought the way things worked out for you and Maria . . ."

"I've got a wife here!" Tom said. "A wife and three kids!"

"I'm not trying to make any trouble for you," Caesar said hastily. "I just thought that if you had a little money you didn't know what to do with . . ."

"But . . ." Tom began.

"I'm just trying to say it would be a blessing," Caesar interrupted. "Anything you could do would be a blessing."

"But I don't even know whether Maria would want me to do anything!" Tom said. "Maybe Louis wouldn't like it."

"I'm not even sure Louis is still alive," Caesar said. "The last I heard, he was pretty sick. And even if he is alive, it's hard for a sick man to get work in Rome."

"You don't really know, though, do you? For all you know, they might be doing fine."

"I haven't heard for over a year," Caesar said, "but I could find out."

"You don't understand," Tom said. "I'm practically broke. And I never could send Maria much of anything without my wife finding out about it, and how could I ever expect her to understand a thing like that?"

"I'm not trying to make trouble for you," Caesar said. "I just thought I'd talk to you about it. You ought to know that things are pretty tough back there."

"I can't promise anything," Tom said. "I'd like to hear how they're doing, but I can't promise anything."

"I'll write a letter," Caesar said. "It may take a little time to hear. . . ."

"All right!" Tom said. He was breathing hard. "Let's not talk about it any more now. Let's have something to eat."

"Okay," Caesar said.

Tom beckoned to the waiter, and they ordered hot Mexican chile con carne which burned their tongues. Hank Mahoney's name was in Tom's mind constantly, but Caesar never mentioned it. Maria was obviously his only concern.

An hour later Tom returned to his office, feeling exhausted. "Mr.

Ogden called while you were gone," his secretary said. "He asked you not to do anything more now."

"What?" Tom asked.

"He said he'd just gotten your memo, and he wanted you to know right away that he doesn't want you to talk about the mental-health committee with anybody. Not now, he said."

"All right," Tom replied. "Thank you." He sat down at his desk and stared out the window. After a few moments he got up and went to the library. In spite of everything, it was necessary to succeed at his job, he thought—maybe it would be more necessary than ever now.

21

"How DID IT GO TODAY?" Betsy asked when she met him at the station that night.

"Fine," Tom said, just as he always did. There's no point in carrying your troubles home with you, somebody had said. You're supposed to leave them in the office.

"There's a man named Bugala coming to see you," she said. "He's a contractor. He spent all morning looking at the carriage house."

"Bugala?" Tom asked. "He's not one of the contractors I wrote to."

"I don't know about that," she replied, "but he wants to see you. And he looks to me like a man who can get things done."

When they got back to the house, Antonio Bugala was waiting, sitting in a battered Chevrolet pickup truck. He was stocky, dark-haired, and had once been told by a girl that he looked like pictures of Napoleon as a young man. This was a compliment he had never forgotten—he much preferred it to the dubious distinction conferred upon him by his nickname, which was "Buggy." "Buggy Bugala" had been brought up in South Bay and for the past five years had been astonishing everyone by becoming almost as successful as he had always predicted. Already, at the age of twenty-eight, Bugala was a contractor with thirty-four men, including his father, on his pay roll.

Now Bugala jumped out of his pickup truck and walked cockily over to Tom. "I'm Tony Bugala," he said. "I hear you got some building and road work to be done."

"How did you hear about it?" Tom asked.

Bugala glanced at him sharply. There's no use in giving this guy a lesson in business, he thought. In point of fact, Bugala had culti-vated the affections of a secretary in the office of the leading contrac-tor in South Bay, and she obligingly told him about all jobs on which her boss was asked to bid, but obviously this was a trade secret which could not be divulged.

"Friend told me," Bugala said honestly. "Said you wanted that old barn made into a house."

"I just want some estimates," Tom said. "I won't be in a position to do anything about it for some time."

"I looked at it this morning," Bugala said. "You can't do much with it—it's just a shell. You could build a house from the ground up for what it would cost you to make anything out of that place."

"Are you sure?" Betsy asked.

Bugala thought, You figure I go around discouraging business for the fun of it? Aloud he said, "There's no basement—just a dirt floor. That stone is only a façade, and the wood under it is rotten."

Well, there goes what we thought would be a sure initial profit, Tom thought. He said, "If we divided this land into one-acre lots, how much would it cost to run in a road that would give access to all of them?"

"You figuring on doing that?"

"I'm just looking into it."

"You got permission from the Zoning Board?"

"I haven't even asked. I don't have title to the place yet."

"Your land go to that row of pines over there?"

"That's right. The stone fence marks the other boundaries."

"Let me take a look at it," Bugala said. He wanted time to think, for he had immediately perceived there might be more to do here than run in a road or convert a barn into a house. The light was fading, and the row of pines was dark against the sky. Bugala plunged into the grass, which was growing knee high, and walked rapidly toward the pines, darting quick glances in all directions. He took in everything—the astonishing view of the Sound, the gradual slope of the land which would provide a view from every lot, and the outcroppings of rock, which probably would mean expensive blasting, but no drainage problems. Putting in a road would be easy, he figured—the driveway to the old house could probably be continued right along the west boundary of the property. With a view like that, why sell acre lots? There was no place else in South Bay, almost nowhere else within commuting distance of New York, where a man could buy such a view of the Sound. Bugala's imagination, which was always at a slow simmer, suddenly began to boil over. Why not put up a whole housing project on quarter-acre lots? All right, you'd have to jump over the Zoning Board somehow, but if it could be done—the prospect was fantastic!

Bugala's mind did not plod, it soared, and he abruptly arrived at a picture of the way the land could be developed, complete with all financial details and photographs in national magazines showing what Antonio Bugala, *Mr.* Antonio Bugala, *Esquire,* had done. You'd start by running in a crooked road along the west boundary— a straight road would be cheaper, but everybody in Connecticut was crazy and liked crooked roads better. In all, Bugala judged with a practiced eye, there must be more than twenty acres of land. You wouldn't put in straight rows of houses, you'd stagger them, about eighty houses on quarter-acre lots, each with a view of the Sound— you'd set them in just like seats in a theater, the back row the highest, and the front row the lowest, only you'd be careful to avoid straight lines. You'd put planting around each house and perhaps push up some earth between houses, so in time you couldn't see one house from another, at least in the summer—maybe it would pay to transplant some fairly big bushes. The houses would be modern, very low to preserve the view, with big windows overlooking the Sound, and no cellars, to save having to blast through that ledge. It might pay to go arty and get a fancy architect to figure out enough variations on a few simple modern designs to prevent the place from looking like a low-cost housing development. The houses wouldn't have to be much—what you'd be selling would be the view. With just an adequate house, you might get twenty-five thousand dollars for a quarter acre of that view. If you brought in your materials and heavy machinery to build all eighty houses at the same time, you might be able to put up something pretty good for a base cost of no more than fifteen thousand dollars per unit, for labor and materials.

Tony Bugala began to sweat. That meant there was a potential profit of ten thousand dollars on each quarter acre of land, he figured—a possible take of $800,000 before taxes, if it were handled right, and if you could raise the initial money for labor and materials. He wondered how much money Tom Rath had, and whether Tom had any clear idea of the potentials of the place. Quickly a lot of facts came together in his mind. Tom drove an old car; the land was obviously run down; people were saying old Mrs. Rath had died broke. Obviously Tom Rath didn't have much. Bugala wondered whether Tom would sell him the land cheap—maybe the thing to do was to tell him a road couldn't be put in, the whole venture was impractical, but he'd take the place off his hands for twenty or thirty thousand dollars. No, that wouldn't work—in the long run it never paid to try that stuff, not if you planned on getting big. If you wanted to become really tops in the business, you had to forget that small-time cleverness and play it straight. Anyway, Rath had already asked other contractors for estimates on roads, and one of them would be sure to tell him he had a potential gold mine in the view.

The thing to do, Bugala decided, was just to talk the whole idea over with Rath, maybe try to form some kind of partnership, even a stock company to raise the money to put up the houses all at once. After all, there was no reason to try to cut Rath out—there would be plenty of profit to go around, a long way around, and it was more important to get part of it than to fail in a try to get it all. Tony

Bugala, a man of quick enthusiasms and fast decisions, immediately made up his mind to drive some sort of bargain with Tom. For five years he had been looking for something big, something into which he could throw all his energies, one great calculated risk that would take him out of the small stuff and put him into the big time, where no one had thought "Buggy" Bugala could go. This was it, he figured—there would have to be lots of talking and fussing around and figuring and paper signing, but if the Zoning Board didn't block them, this was it.

Bugala had jumped so far ahead in his thoughts that when he reached the row of pines and looked up to find himself standing in a bare field, with the light almost gone, he was surprised. He turned and started walking rapidly back toward Tom. If I can't get Rath's co-operation, the whole deal's off, he thought—that's the first step. His mind, however, refused to wait for the first step—it kept bounding ahead. The financing wouldn't be hard. Rath could probably raise fifty thousand dollars on the land alone, once it was re-zoned, Bugala figured. As each house went up, more could be borrowed on it. On his own heavy construction equipment, Bugala figured, he could raise twenty thousand, and maybe he could get more on a personal note—the banks were already beginning to keep a friendly eye on Antonio Bugala. It wouldn't be difficult to find a partner to throw in another twenty thousand, maybe, and with a hundred thousand in the kitty, construction could begin. Put a down payment on the materials for all eighty houses, but concentrate on completing the first four. Sell those at twenty-five thousand apiece, and you've got your initial investment back!

While he was thinking all this, Tony Bugala was walking rapidly, almost running with enthusiasm, back to the house, where Tom and Betsy were standing with the three children. Tom watched Bugala's hurried movements with astonishment. It was growing chilly, and an evening breeze was starting to ruffle the distant waters of the Sound, which lay gray and nebulous in the last glow of twilight. Bugala came striding up to Tom, perspiring with excitement.

"Mr. Rath," he said bluntly, "I've got a proposition to make."

They sat in the kitchen of the old house talking until midnight. "Buggy" Bugala slammed the table with his small thick hand and, talking a mile a minute, described the houses he wanted to build so minutely that Tom could almost look out the window and see them. Betsy leaned forward, her face flushed and her lips parted, drinking it all in. "Eight hundred thousand dollars!" she said.

"Wait a minute," Tom said. "This is all fine, but before we go any farther, there are a few hard facts we got to take into account. In the first place, the estate isn't settled yet, and the will may be contested— it may be months before we have a clear title on this land. In the second place, the whole plan depends on our getting permission from the Zoning Board. I'll know more about that Saturday when I see Judge Bernstein, but meanwhile I wouldn't count on anything too much—it's never easy to put quarter-acre lots among a lot of big estates. In the third place, even if everything else goes all right, we're going to have to look for somebody to put up more cash. Even if I can raise fifty thousand on the land, and even if you can throw in twenty or thirty thousand, we've still got twenty or thirty thousand to go—and that's assuming that a hundred thousand is enough to start a project like this. And in the fourth place, Mr. Bugala, I don't mean to be discourteous, but I just met you for the first time tonight, and I don't want to commit myself on going into a venture like this with you. Have you ever done anything like this before?"

Bugala flushed. "I built six houses last year," he said. "I can do it. I built fifteen houses since the war. And you know what? During the war I put an air strip across Kiwan in eight days! Eight days! You ever seen Kiwan?"

"Yeah," Tom said. "I've seen it. Did you put that air strip in?"

"You're damn right! In eight days! And with the Japs bombing us every night!"

"You didn't have to pay your men for overtime on Kiwan," Tom said practically. "This is a different deal."

"All right," Bugala said. "I'll tell you something else I've done. You know that big place a guy named Hopkins just put up down where the old yacht club used to be? I built almost half of that. Now let me level with you—I wasn't the contractor, but plenty of it was subcontracted to me. I did most of the outside construction work, and damn near all the landscaping. You want to see what I can do, go down and look at the place. I'll give you a list of all the people I've done work for! Ask the bank about me. Ask anybody around here about me—I got a good name!"

"I don't doubt it," Tom said. "I just don't want to have to commit myself tonight."

"You wouldn't take my ideas and go to a big outfit with them, would you?"

"I don't plan to, but I don't want to commit myself," Tom said. "There are a lot of wrinkles to be ironed out of your ideas yet. Do you really think we can make a profit of ten thousand dollars on each house and quarter-acre lot?"

"Maybe—and what if we only make half that? Would that be so bad?"

"No, but how are you going to pay interest on a hundred thousand dollars while we're building? And there'll be taxes. It might be a year before we had anything to sell. We'd be operating on an awfully slim margin."

"Hell, we can borrow a hundred and ten thousand and use ten of it to pay the interest and taxes—that would last us almost two years!"

"I don't know," Tom said. "You make it sound awfully easy. What if you run into unexpected delays? What if you can't get your materials on time, or a storm washes us out when everything's half done, and what if a depression sets in, and we can't sell our houses when we finish them? This might be an easy way to make a pile, but it's also an easy way to go bankrupt!"

"Tom always looks at the dark side of everything!" Betsy said impatiently. "Tommy, sometimes I think you just look for reasons why nothing can ever get done."

"You got to gamble," Bugala said. "Hell, everything's a gamble! It's the guys who take the chances who make the dough! If I hadn't been willing to gamble, I'd still be on a pick and shovel gang!"

"I'm willing to gamble," Tom said. "I just want to make sure we've got the odds on our side."

Bugala laughed and stood up. "We'll make it work!" he said confidently. "Get in touch with me after you've talked to Judge Bernstein about the zoning."

The next morning on the way to the train, Tom asked Betsy to circle around by the waterfront, where the old yacht club had been, so he could look at the house Hopkins had built. Involuntarily, Betsy stepped on the brakes when they saw it. Hopkins' house was low, long and enormous. The old yacht club wharf had been removed, and in its place was a carefully buttressed sea wall and an elaborate artificial harbor, in which a tall white yawl was anchored. One wing of the house reached out over the edge of the harbor. At least twelve acres of green lawn separated the house from the road. Betsy whistled. "You mean you work for *that* guy?" she said.

22

THAT SAME MORNING Ralph Hopkins awoke in his Park Avenue apartment at precisely seven o'clock. He had been working on his speech about mental health until after midnight, and as soon as he opened his eyes, his thoughts were full of it again. The latest draft written by Ogden wasn't right, and Hopkins was beginning to wonder whether he was ever going to be able to devise a speech on mental health he wanted to give. Maybe the whole idea of starting a mental-health committee was a mistake. Glancing at his wrist watch, he saw it was quarter after seven. No time to worry about the speech now, he thought—there was a busy day ahead. He jumped lightly out of bed, stepped briskly across his small, simply furnished bedroom, and slid open a door leading to a large tiled shower room. Stripping off his white silk pajamas, he stepped into a booth and pulled a curtain. He turned an elaborate chromium dial on the wall in front of him, and hot water shot against him at a high velocity from a dozen nozzles placed in the booth above and on all sides of him. Gradually Hopkins turned the dial until the water was lukewarm—the doctor had forbidden him to take cold showers. He stood there in the lukewarm water for thirty seconds before turning the shower off and stepped out of the booth. From a special slot in the wall he drew an enormous, warm turkish towel. Wrapping himself in this, he walked to the other side of the room and stepped on a set of scales which had been built into the floor. He weighed a hundred and thirty-eight pounds, including the towel. That was three pounds too much, he figured, and made a mental note to cut down on his eating. It was stupid to get fat, he thought—half his friends were eating themselves into their graves.

After he had brushed his teeth and shaved, Hopkins went into his dressing room, where his valet had laid out his clothes. The valet was not there—Hopkins liked to have his clothes laid out for him, but hated to have people fussing about him. He dressed himself.

At quarter to eight Hopkins walked downstairs to the living room of his apartment, just as his personal secretary, Miss MacDonald, the elderly gray-haired woman Tom had observed in Hopkins' outer office, was arriving. She always began her working day at a quarter to eight in Hopkins' apartment and went to the office with him.

"Good morning, Miss MacDonald," he said cheerily. "What have you got on the docket for me today?"

"Mr. Albert Pierce is coming in to have breakfast with you," she said. "Mr. Pierce owns three television stations in Texas and two in Oklahoma. He has some programming suggestions he wants to discuss with you—remember his letters?"

"Yes," Hopkins said.

The breakfast business appointment was routine; it had been routine for ten years. So many people wanted to see Hopkins that it was necessary to fit them in wherever possible. First there were all the people who wanted to see him on company business—production people, research men, the top entertainers who had to be flattered, advertising executives with big contracts, the owners of affiliated stations, promotion men, publicity experts, sponsors, writers who were great artists and had never written for television, but now were going to. There were also bankers, real-estate men, investment experts, and lawyers who, under Hopkins' guidance, administered the holdings of the United Broadcasting Corporation. And in addition to all these people who wanted to see Hopkins, there were executives of the many corporations of which he was a director, and the men and women connected with the good works of which he was a trustee. Hopkins was a trustee of two universities, five hospitals, three public libraries, one fund for orphaned children, two foundations for the advancement of the arts and sciences, a home for the blind, a haven for crippled children, and a snug harbor for retired seamen. In addition to that, he was a member of committees and commissions studying, variously, conditions in South India, Public Health in the United States, Racial Segregation, Higher Standards for Advertising, the Parking Problem in New York City, Farm Subsidies, Safety on the Highways, Freedom of the Press, Atomic Energy, the House Rules of the City Club, and a Code of Decency for Comic Books.

"After Mr. Pierce, Dr. Andrews is coming up—it's time for your quarterly check-up," Miss MacDonald said.

Hopkins frowned slightly. It was only common sense to have a quarterly check-up, but he detested it. "All right, what next?" he asked.

"Because of Dr. Andrews, I haven't scheduled you for anything at the office before ten o'clock this morning. At that time Mr. Hebbard wants a conference with you—he's got some new cost estimates and time schedules. At eleven there's a board meeting, lasting through lunch. . . ."

She was interrupted by the doorbell. Hopkins opened the door. Albert Pierce, a large potbellied man wearing a wide cream-colored sombrero, walked in.

"Hello!" Hopkins said, shaking his hand heartily. "*So* good of you to come so early. I had hoped to have lunch with you, but my board is meeting today, and you know how it is! I *certainly* appreciate this chance to see you!"

The big man beamed. "Right nice of you to put yourself out for me!" he said.

Miss MacDonald slipped out a side door, and Hopkins led Pierce to the dining room. A waitress served Pierce a bowl of fresh fruit, waffles, and sausage patties. Hopkins had only a bowl of dry cereal with skim milk and a cup of black coffee. "I wish I had your appetite!" he said to his guest. "It's this city air that takes it away from a man!"

Throughout the meal Pierce expounded his views on television programs, which consisted mostly of the thought that more *old-fashioned* shows, such as square dances, rodeos, and hymn sings, would be welcomed by rural audiences. Hopkins agreed with him heartily. At a quarter of nine, the doorbell rang again, and Hopkins jumped up to answer it. That was one of the advantages in not having a servant open the door—it gave Hopkins an opportunity to conclude interviews without being impolite. Dr. Andrews, an urbane man with prematurely white hair, walked in, carrying a small black bag. *"Thank* you for coming up," Hopkins said. "I'll be with you in a few moments. Mr. Pierce, this is Dr. Andrews—*don't* go, Mr. Pierce —I had hoped to chat with you longer. Well, if you *have* to go, I understand. I *certainly* do appreciate your advice on the programs, and you can be sure it will have effect!"

When Pierce had left, Hopkins and the doctor sat down in the living room. "How have you been feeling?" the doctor asked.

"Fine—better than ever!"

"Trouble getting to sleep?"

"Not a bit!"

The doctor opened his bag and took out a stethoscope. Hopkins took off his coat and opened his shirt. The doctor listened to his heart intently for several seconds. "It sounds pretty good," he said finally. "Had any more dizziness lately?"

"Not a trace of it!"

"Difficulty breathing?"

"No."

The doctor put his stethoscope back in his bag and took out his equipment for measuring blood pressure. Hopkins rolled up his sleeve and looked out the window at the green lawn on the roof while the doctor strapped the device to his arm. There was an interval of silence. "It's up a little," the doctor said finally. "Not badly—nothing to worry about."

"That's good," Hopkins said, relieved.

"It's a warning, though," the doctor continued. "I guess there's no use in my repeating it: you ought to slow down."

"I've been getting plenty of rest," Hopkins said.

"I'll say it to satisfy my own conscience," the doctor continued. "You ought to take a long vacation—a couple of months, just lying in the sun. You ought to get yourself a hobby, something to help you relax."

Hopkins looked at him intently, but said nothing.

"You ought to cut way down on your schedule," the doctor went on. "Start getting into your office about ten-thirty or eleven and leaving about three or four in the afternoon—there's no reason why a man in your position can't do that. In the long run, you'd be ensuring yourself more working hours. And cut out all these outside activities of yours—take it easy for a few years. You've got to slow down!"

"Are you advising me to retire, Doctor?" Hopkins asked dryly.

"No—I'd be satisfied if you just followed a normal, human routine!"

"I will," Hopkins said courteously. "I certainly appreciate your advice, Doctor, and I'll take it. Thanks *so* much for coming up so early this morning!"

When the doctor had gone, Miss MacDonald called for Hopkins' car, a black Cadillac five years old, driven by an aging Negro chauffeur. They started driving toward the United Broadcasting building. Before they had gone three blocks the car got caught in a bad traffic jam and could barely crawl. Hopkins put his head back on the soft gray upholstery and closed his eyes. "You've got to slow down!" the doctor had said. It seemed to Hopkins that people had been telling him that all his life.

It had started when he was a boy in public school. He had been editor of the school paper, and though he had been too small to excel at athletics, he had been manager of the football and basketball teams. He had stood at the top of his class scholastically, and whenever there had been a dance or a school play, he had always been chairman of the arrangements committee. "You've got to slow down!" the teachers had told him. "Take it easy, boy—you'll wear yourself out!"

At Princeton, where he had gone on a scholarship, it had been more of the same. He had headed the debating team, managed the football team, and engaged in a dozen other activities in addition to maintaining an almost straight A average in his studies. "You've got to slow down!" his faculty adviser had told him. "Take it easy!"

But he had not slowed down. Summers he had worked at all kinds of jobs, always astonishing his employers with his energy. After college had come a brief stint in the Army, a period during which his friends had kidded him about wanting to be a general. Upon being released from service in 1919, he had worked for a few years at a brokerage house before going to the United Broadcasting Corporation, which had just been started. A year later he had met Helen Perry, who had at the time been a fashionable beauty in New York. He had pursued her with all the zeal he always devoted to anything he wanted, and on June 3, 1921, he had married her. Up to that time, Hopkins had never had a failure in his life.

"You've got to slow down!" Helen had started saying, even before they were married, but unlike the teachers and faculty advisers, she had not let it go at that. As she discovered that it was Hopkins' habit to spend most of his evenings and week ends at his office, she had become first annoyed, then indignant, and, finally, hurt and bewildered.

"Life isn't worth living like this," she had said. "I never see you! You've got to slow down!"

He had tried. Especially when their first child, Robert, had come, during the second year of their marriage, he had tried. He had come home every evening at six o'clock and conscientiously played with the baby and sat talking with his wife, and he had been genuinely appalled to find that the baby made him nervous, and that while he was talking to his wife, it was almost impossible for him to sit quietly. He had felt impelled to get up and pace up and down the room, jingling his change in his pockets and glancing at the clock. For the first time in his life he had started to drink heavily during those long evenings at home. Gradually he had started staying late at the office again—by that time he had already had a fairly important job at the United Broadcasting Corporation. Helen had remonstrated with him. There had been recriminations, high-pitched arguments, and threats of divorce.

All right, it's a problem, he had said to himself after a particularly bitter scene—it's a problem that must be met head on, like all other problems. To Helen he had said, in a quiet voice, "I don't want to have any more scenes—they wear us both out. I'm prepared to admit that whatever is wrong is entirely my fault. I am preoccupied with my work—I've been that way all my life, and it is nothing for which you should blame yourself."

She had gone pale. "Do you want a divorce?" she had asked.

"No," he had said. "Do you?"

"No."

They had never talked about divorce again, but she had begun to refer to his preoccupation with work as a disease. "You've got to do something about it," she had said, and had suggested a psychiatrist.

For two years Hopkins had submitted to psychoanalysis. Five times a week he had lain on a couch in the psychoanalyst's apartment on Sixty-ninth Street and recalled his childhood. His father had been a cheerful, rather ineffectual man who, each afternoon upon returning from his job as assistant manager of a small paper mill in an upstate New York village, had spent most of his time rocking on the front porch of their shabby but comfortable house. His mother had been disappointed by the modesty of her husband's achievements and aspirations and had been bitterly condescending to him. Leaving her family to fend for itself most of the time, she had thrown all her energy into working for the local garden club and a bewildering variety of social and civic organizations. As she gained positions of leadership in these groups, her resentment at her serenely undistinguished husband had grown. Finally she had established herself in a separate room on the third floor of their house and, throughout most of Ralph's boyhood, had conducted herself like a great lady temporarily forced to live with poor relatives.

Hopkins was not an introspective man, but in recounting all this to the psychoanalyst, he had said, "I always felt sorry for my father because my mother treated him so badly. She never gave me much time, either, except when I did something she thought was outstanding. Whenever I got a particularly good report card, or won anything, she'd take me up to her room to have tea alone with her. 'We're two of a kind,' she used to say. 'We get things done.' I suppose I got the impression from her that achievement means everything."

Hopkins had felt quite proud of his efforts at self-diagnosis and had been surprised when the psychoanalyst had disgarded his suggestions in favor of much more bizarre "explanations of neurosis." He had said that Hopkins probably had a deep guilt complex, and that his constant work was simply an effort to punish and perhaps kill himself. The guilt complex was probably based on a fear of homosexuality, he had said. To Hopkins, who had never consciously worried about homosexuality, or guilt, this had seemed like so much rubbish, but he had tried to believe it, for the psychoanalyst had said it was necessary for him to believe to be cured, and Hopkins had wanted to be cured, in order to make his wife happy.

The trouble had been that every time he left the psychoanalyst's office the temptation to return to his own office and bury himself in work had been irresistible. At the end of two years he had become the youngest vice-president of United Broadcasting and had told his wife he simply wouldn't have time for psychoanalysis any longer.

It had been shortly after this that he had rented an apartment to use for business meetings in New York and had drifted into the habit of staying away from his home, which had then been in Darien, for weeks at a time. His wife had not objected. She had gone in for horses for a while and, tiring of that, had become a relentless giver of parties. After Susan had been born in 1935, she had abruptly stopped the parties and had thrown herself into motherhood with abandon, firing the nursemaid who had taken care of her son and surrounding herself with *avant-garde* parents who discussed their children the way psychiatrists discuss their patients. Hopkins had never complained—he had been too grateful to her for letting him alone and, as he saw it, making up for his deficiencies as a parent.

Things had gone pretty well until 1943, when Robert, their son, had been killed in the war. Hopkins had hurried home when his wife telephoned to tell him and had tried to sympathize with her, but all she had said was, "You never knew him! You never knew him!" Hopkins had stayed with her for three days, at the end of which time he had returned to his office and thrown himself harder than ever into his work.

"Slow down!" the doctors had been saying regularly ever since. "You've got to slow down!" But Helen, his wife, had stopped saying that to him. After Robert had been killed, she had gone for a brief time to a sanitarium, leaving Susan, her daughter, with the servants. After returning from the sanitarium, Helen had started to give parties again, and had begun to plan the great show place in South Bay, and had bought the yawl, and had seemed happier than she ever had in her life.

"This traffic!" Hopkins said now, as he sat in his limousine and looked out the window at the pedestrians on the sidewalk, who were making better time. "This traffic is terrible!" He sat back and consciously tried to relax, but it was impossible A policeman blew his whistle sharply, and a taxi driver ahead started to curse. Hopkins shut his eyes. It was ridiculous to worry, it was unproductive. It would be better to think of the future, of things to be done. There was, for instance, the mental-health speech to revise. Hopkins took a cigarette out of his pocket and lit it. "Miss MacDonald," he said, "it looks as though we're going to be stuck in this traffic for quite a while. Would you mind taking dictation?"

23

"THEY WANT TO USE the top of the tower for sky watchers," Betsy said to Tom when he returned from work Friday night.

"What?" he asked in astonishment.

"It's Civilian Defense—they're making a plan for Civilian Defense here. They want to use our tower for airplane spotters until they get a permanent place for themselves."

"Oh, Lord," Tom groaned.

"Don't you approve?"

"I guess so," he said. "I don't know, it sounds so absurd. What do they want us to do?"

"Just let them use the tower for a few weeks. It's the highest place in South Bay, they said, and has the best view. Why is it absurd?"

"It's not," he said. "I'm just tired, and I don't like thinking about another war. I have a million other things to do."

"Sit down and have a drink," Betsy said. "Dinner will be ready in a few minutes."

That night Tom lay awake a long time worrying about Maria, about old Edward's claim on the estate, about zoning laws, and about the meeting he was to have with Bernstein in the morning. When he awoke he felt exhausted and so irritable that the high-pitched voices of the children at the breakfast table annoyed him. "Be quiet!" he said sharply to Janey when she said, "Daddy, can I have the milk? Can I have the milk? Can I have the milk?" She looked so hurt that he hastily added, "I'm sorry," gave her the milk, and himself kept quiet for the rest of the meal.

"I'll drop you off at Judge Bernstein's office," Betsy said after he had finished his second cup of coffee. "I'll take the kids with me and enroll the girls at school."

"I don't want to go to school," Janey said. "I *never* want to go."

"It's not so bad," Barbara said thoughtfully. "I only hate it a little."

"Can I go?" Pete asked.

"Nobody has to go for another month," Betsy said.

They got in the car and drove slowly to the main street of South Bay.

"Now don't take any nonsense from him," Betsy said as Tom got out of the car in front of the building in which Bernstein had his office. "We ought to have our first ten houses for sale next spring, and if we're going to do that, we should start right away."

Bernstein was sitting behind his scarred pine desk when Tom came in. He glanced up at Tom sharply—somehow he hadn't expected Mrs. Rath's grandson to be so tall. "Sit down, Mr. Rath," he said cordially. "What can I do for you?"

"I want to get some idea of how long it will take for Mrs. Rath's estate to go through the Probate Court," Tom said, "and I want to learn about zoning laws around here. We've got an idea we may want to put up some kind of a housing development."

"I see," Bernstein said, and waited.

"How long does it generally take for an estate to be settled?"

"Not long, if there are no complications. A man by the name of Schultz was in here to see me a few days ago. Edward Schultz. Name mean anything to you?"

"He used to work for my grandmother. I want to do what I can for him, but I have to wait until the estate is settled."

"Mr. Schultz tells me he believes Mrs. Rath meant the entire estate to go to him," Bernstein said quietly.

"That's absurd! My grandmother talked to me about him shortly before she died."

"Apparently he believes he's entitled to the house," Bernstein said dryly.

"That's ridiculous!'"

"Why do you suppose he thinks he has a claim?"

"I think he must be a little crazy," Tom said. "I don't know—I feel pretty badly about this. Mrs. Rath was ninety-three years old when she died, and possibly she gave him some reason for hoping she would leave him everything."

"Do you think she could have promised him the estate in return for his services for the rest of her life?" Bernstein asked mildly.

"No! She would have told me! Just before she died she told me she

- 176 -

was leaving everything to me, and that's the way the will is written."

"Mr. Schultz claims that he asked Mrs. Rath for a salary increase about a year before she died, and that she said she couldn't afford to give him one, but that if he'd stay as long as she lived, she'd leave everything to him."

"I want to try to be fair about this," Tom said. "We can't prove whether she said that or not. She was old and confused, and I suppose it's possible she said that and forgot it. All I know is she used to talk all the time about saving the house for me, and that's the way the will is written."

"Mr. Schultz seems to feel an attempt is being made to cheat him."

"I can't help the way the old man feels!" Tom said. "I can't afford to have the settling of the estate delayed indefinitely! How can he hold things up? He hasn't got any proof!"

"He says he has," Bernstein said.

"What kind?"

"He told me he has everything in writing from her, postdating the will Mr. Sims sent me."

"I don't believe it!"

"That's what he says. I have asked him to have a photostat of his document sent to me, and he agreed to."

"Have you received it yet?"

"No—there hasn't been time."

"I can't understand it!" Tom said. "She wasn't like that. She never would have done a thing like that without telling me!"

"The court will have to examine both documents and make a decision."

"How long will it take?"

"That depends on a lot of things. It may be necessary to get a lot of information together. It could be a matter of months, or even more."

"Meanwhile, I'm living in my grandmother's place. What would happen if the court awarded it to him?"

"He could dispossess you and perhaps charge you rent retroactively, I suppose."

"Is it legal for me to be there now?"

"When a property is in dispute, it's hard to tell what to do with it. I don't think Mr. Schultz is trying to dispossess you before the court makes a decision."

"That's nice of him," Tom said bitterly. There was a moment of silence before he added, "I guess I should ask Mr. Sims to represent me—I'll need a lawyer, won't I?"

"That would be advisable."

"You wouldn't take the case for me?"

"Hardly. I'm the judge."

"Has Edward, I mean Mr. Schultz, got a lawyer?"

"Yes. A big outfit in New York is representing him. Frankly, I don't think he could have got them to take the case if he didn't have a legitimate claim in their opinion."

"That's fine," Tom said.

"All you can do is put the case in the hands of your lawyer and wait," Bernstein said.

Tom looked at him helplessly for an instant before getting to his feet abruptly. "I guess there's nothing more I can do," he said. "There doesn't seem to be much point in asking about zoning laws now."

"You're in a ten-acre zone," Bernstein said. "If you wanted to put a housing development there, you'd have quite a fight on your hands. I wouldn't go into it until the estate is settled."

"Thanks," Tom said, feeling a rush of unreasonable resentment against Bernstein. "Anyway, thanks." He left the room.

As soon as he had gone, Bernstein walked to the window of his office and stood looking down at the street, where Betsy and the children were waiting in the parked car. His stomach was beginning to ache.

"Why, that school is *terrible!*" Betsy said as soon as Tom got into the car, before he could say anything. "It's dingy and overcrowded, and I don't think it's safe. I *hate* to send the kids there! When we get going, I'm going to send them to a private school!"

"Betsy," Tom said, "I've got some news that isn't very good."

"What?"

"Edward has put in a claim for the whole estate, and he says he has a will Grandmother signed after she wrote the one we have. He's got a big firm of lawyers working on it."

"Oh, no! She *told* you . . ."

"I know."

"What's going to happen?"

"We just have to put Sims to work on it and let the court decide."

Betsy said nothing. "What's the matter?" Janey asked.

"Everything's all right, baby," Betsy said.

"What did Daddy say?"

"Nothing important," Tom said. "We're going home now."

He started the car. On the way up the hill to the old house they were all silent. When they came to the rock ledge against which his father had slammed the old Packard, Tom stared at it deliberately—it was ridiculous to look away. The rocks were massive and craggy, some of them tinged with a dull red hue, which was probably iron ore.

"Either Edward or your grandmother lied!" Betsy said suddenly, as Tom stopped the car in front of the house. "I know it was Edward! Everything's going to turn out all right!"

"Don't count on it, baby," he said.

For some reason he didn't want to go into the dim old house. Instead, he walked alone into the tall grass toward the distant row of pines. In the distance the smooth surface of the Sound glittered. The children bounded after him until Betsy called them back. "Leave your father alone," she said.

It's funny, he thought. I'm always sure things are going to turn out badly, and, damn it, they usually do.

"Everything's going to turn out all right!" Betsy always said.

Sure, he thought, we'll live here a year or so while this case is being decided, and then Edward will get the house and slap a bill for back rent on us. And we'll have lawyers' bills and court costs to pay. And the only job I've got now is sitting all day behind a desk doing nothing.

What will happen if we lose this place, and run up a lot of bills, and I get fired? he thought. What will we do? And what will happen if Maria makes trouble?

I can always get a job, he thought. Dick Haver would give me a job again. I can always get a job somewhere.

Maybe, he thought. If Hopkins fired me six months after I was hired, people would want to know why. And if there were any publicity about Maria—if she made any charges—none of the foundations would touch me. And what the hell other kind of work am I trained for?

I could go back in the Army, he thought. They'd make me a major. Good pay, travel, education, and security. Grandmother could look down from heaven and be real proud of me—she could talk to the angels about the family major and be honest.

Grandmother, he thought—by God, what kind of woman was she? Did she promise Edward her estate just to make sure she would have service the rest of her life? And was she afraid to tell me, unwilling to suffer the slightest unpleasantness? Did she play it both ways, getting the fun of telling me she was leaving me everything and at the same time wringing the last drop of ease out of life? Was she, when you come right down to it, only an evil, pretentious, lying old woman who could be expected to beget nothing but evil, a suicide, and a . . .

This is ridiculous, he thought—that's one thing I won't do. Money isn't that important. I'm tough. I can always get a job. I can go back to the Army. Travel, education, security. Times like these are made for me—a tough bastard who knows how to handle a gun. And I wouldn't even have to do that. If worse came to worst, I could dig a ditch, I could operate an elevator like Caesar, and in heaven Grandmother could say, "My grandson is in the transportation business."

It's absurd to think of these things, he thought. I could get a job in an advertising agency. I'll write copy telling people to eat more corn flakes and smoke more and more cigarettes and buy more refrigerators and automobiles, until they explode with happiness.

I shouldn't get excited, he thought. It doesn't really matter. Here goes nothing. It will be interesting to see what happens.

Maybe it will turn out all right, he thought; maybe it really will. Betsy says you have to believe everything will turn out all right, even if it doesn't. You can't go on worrying all the time; it has to stop someday. You can't really believe the world is insane; you have to believe everything's going to turn out all right. The Lord is my Shepherd, I shall not want. I shall grow old gracefully, and my children will all grow up happily and healthily, and everything's going to be fine; it is ridiculous that optimism should always sound false.

He wondered suddenly whether the young German in the leather jacket who had stood negligently holding his rifle and coughing had been an optimist. And he wondered whether the girl or woman who had written the man in the leather jacket the letter on thin, blue, faintly scented stationery had had faith that everything was going to turn out all right. And how about the other men he had killed? How about the man who had run zigzagging across the beach, while Tom moved the machine gun up on him, the bullets kicking up the sand behind him, until the man had sagged with the blood pouring out of his mouth like a long tongue? Had he had faith? In what? And how about Mahoney? And Maria, who right now, perhaps, might be trying to raise her son alone?

Maybe they had no faith, Tom thought. Maybe they were like me, always expecting disaster, surprised only when it doesn't hit. Maybe we are all, the killers and the killed, equally damned; not guilty, not somehow made wise by war, not heroes, just men who are either dead or convinced that the world is insane.

He felt someone pulling his trouser leg and looked down. Janey was there, telling him that lunch was ready. She had a worried expression on her face. Her hand was soft as a dove in his as he led her into the house.

24

THE IMPORTANT THING is to make money, Tom thought as he took the train into New York on the following Monday. The important thing is to create an island of order in a sea of chaos—somebody very bright had said that, somebody whose name he had forgotten, but whose writings he had studied at college. And an island of order obviously must be made of money, for one doesn't bring up children in an orderly way without money, and one doesn't even have one's meals in an orderly way, or dress in an orderly way, or think in an orderly way without money. Money is the root of all order, he told himself, and the only trouble with it is, it's so damn hard to get, especially when one has a job which consists of sitting behind a desk all day doing absolutely nothing.

On his way up to his office in the elevator that morning, he did not see Caesar—he was grateful for that. And he hadn't been sitting behind his desk doing nothing for more than fifteen minutes when the interoffice communication box crackled and buzzed. He switched it on.

"Rath?" Ogden's voice whispered hoarsely.

Tom turned up the volume control. "Good morning," he said. "What can I do for you?"

"Can you fly down to Atlantic City this afternoon—the Stockton House Hotel? I've just heard that the place is filling up with conventions, and I want to make sure we have the proper accommodations for Mr. Hopkins on the fifteenth."

"Sure I can go," Tom said. He was so grateful to be given something to do that his voice sounded ridiculously eager.

"I want you to make all the arrangements, both for the rooms and the speech. Check the speaker's platform. Find out just what room his speech is scheduled for, exactly where it is, and what door he should enter."

"I will!" Tom said. He found himself speaking with exclamation points, like Ralph Hopkins.

"Check the amplifying equipment, and if it isn't good, make the hotel fix it. Be sure there's a lectern—Mr. Hopkins likes to stand behind a lectern with enough space on it to open a ten-by-twelve-inch notebook. Are you taking notes?"

"Right!" said Tom, scribbling furiously.

"He likes the lectern four feet five inches from the floor," Ogden continued, "and he likes the mike the same height, to the right of the lectern, not in front of it. There will be only the mike for the loud-speaker—this won't be broadcast."

Tom was not surprised at that. For the president of a broadcasting company to have his speech broadcast, even if he wanted maximum publicity, would be shooting fish in a barrel. The executives of broad-casting companies yearn for space in magazines and newspapers, and the publishers of magazines and newspapers yearn for radio and tele-vision coverage.

"I've got it," Tom said.

"Now about his rooms. Get a suite of three. He likes a hard mat-tress. Try out the mattress—he hates a soft one."

"Right," Tom said.

"But it shouldn't be lumpy. Don't hesitate to make the hotel get you a good one—hard but smooth."

"Check," Tom said.

"Immediately after the speech, a bartender should be on duty in the living room of Mr. Hopkins' suite, and he should be equipped to serve fifty people anything they want. He should remain on duty for the rest of the evening if necessary."

"Got it," Tom said.

"Now about flowers. Mr. Hopkins sometimes gets hay fever, so be sure there's no goldenrod or anything like that around—sometimes they put it in fall decorations. And he detests chrysanthemums. He likes roses—long-stemmed roses. Be sure there are several dozen around his rooms."

"Right," Tom said.

"And be sure he gets a good bedroom suite. Mr. Hopkins' rooms all should be facing the sea. Three rooms, with the living room big enough to hold fifty people comfortably—he detests crowded rooms.

We'll also need single rooms for you, me, and Miss MacDonald on the same floor, all reserved for September 15."

"Fine," Tom said.

"Another thing. Mr. Hopkins will want an electric refrigerator and a few bottles of Scotch in his bedroom. He doesn't like to have to keep calling room service."

"I've got it," Tom said.

"There should be a large-screen television set and a radio in his bedroom."

"I'll get them."

"We'll want a man with a wire recorder to record Mr. Hopkins' speech—he likes to hear it played back."

"Will do."

"Make sure the local press is alerted. Our public-relations department will be sending them advance releases, but it helps to drop in and chat with them."

"I'll do it," Tom said.

"I guess that's about all—in general, make sure everything's set for Mr. Hopkins. Call me when you get back. Tell the travel department to get you a plane ticket."

Before Tom could say "Right" again, Ogden snapped off his voice box. Tom started to telephone Betsy to say he wouldn't be home that night, but before he got the call through, the voice box sputtered again. This time it was Hopkins. "Tom," he said, "could you come up to the apartment for dinner tonight?"

"Bill Ogden just asked me to go to Atlantic City to arrange hotel accommodations for your speech," Tom said.

"Oh, fine, but see me when you get back, will you?"

"Sure," Tom said, hoping Hopkins would tell him what he wanted. Instead, Hopkins said cheerily, "Have a good trip," and the voice box was silent.

That afternoon Tom boarded a plane and sat down in one of the comfortably upholstered seats. As the plane gunned its engines and began the familiar headlong, all or nothing, rush down the runway, he fastened his safety belt and leaned back, still wondering what Hopkins wanted to see him about. Anyway, I won't have to jump this time, he thought—this time I'm on my way to test a mattress and arrange for long-stemmed roses. He started to laugh. I'll get roses with the longest god-damn stems in the whole world, he thought.

The hotel was a large one, twenty stories high, without a room to rent for less than twenty-two dollars a night, and please make reservations well in advance. Tom looked up the manager and found him eager to co-operate in making things satisfactory for Ralph Hopkins. The right sort of lectern was procured, and the loud-speaker system proved suitable. The manager felt that a bridal suite, ornately furnished with pictures of French courtiers on the wall, was just the thing for Mr. Hopkins. Ceremoniously Tom lay down on the large double bed and pronounced the mattress too soft. Four housemen quickly brought another. Feeling like Goldilocks in the house of the Three Bears, Tom pronounced it too lumpy. Grumbling, the four housemen brought a third mattress, which Tom decreed just right.

"I want the stems *really long*," he said to the hotel florist. "There ought to be about four dozen roses on a table in the living room and two dozen in the bedroom."

"You can rely on me," the florist said.

By seven o'clock in the evening Tom had completed his arrangements. He went to the hotel bar and ordered a Martini. It was an ornate circular bar, in the center of which a lighted pyramid of bottles revolved slowly. Somewhere in a near-by room an orchestra was playing dance music. Suddenly a group of young people in evening clothes swept into the bar and sat down at tables near Tom. "I don't *really* believe you, Harry," a young girl not more than twenty said to her escort, "but I thank you just the same."

The sight of the young couples and the sound of the dance music made Tom feel suddenly old. He looked at the couple nearest him. They're not more than twenty, or at the most twenty-one, he thought. My God, when Pearl Harbor was attacked, they couldn't have been more than ten years old! And when Betsy and I met, back in 1939, they were seven years old!

The band in the next room began to play a waltz. It had been in a hotel that Tom had met Betsy, a hotel in Boston with a big bar and a dance band and crowds of young people in evening clothes. It had been in the fall of 1939, just a few weeks before the Christmas holidays, in the best hotel in Boston, in the grand ballroom of which Betsy had had her coming-out party.

"When the deep purple falls over sleepy garden walls . . ." That had been the song that year. He had never liked it much at the time and could never have expected that his mind would choose it as one of the things to remember, probably for the rest of his life.

Nineteen thirty-nine! My God, the world has changed since then, he thought—it's enough to make a man feel a million years old! In the fall of 1939, Hitler had just invaded Poland. The experts had been saying that the Polish Lancers and General Mud would stop him, but by the time Betsy had had her coming-out party, Poland had fallen, and the experts had turned to saying that now France would stop Hitler, the French Army was the finest in the world. The experts had also been saying that the United States would not get into this war. It had been then Tom had started to acquire a permanent disrespect for all experts and to equate pessimism with wisdom. Almost ever since he could remember, he himself had been sure there would be a war, and that the United States would get into it. At Covington Academy, way back in 1935, the boys had even had an organization called "The Veterans of Future Wars" which had demanded soldiers' bonuses before death instead of after. The pacifists had been printing pictures in magazines showing a wounded soldier, and the caption had said, "Hello Sucker!" But the boys had not been confused. They had known for a long while that regardless of what anyone said, war was coming. They had been offended by the picture of the wounded soldier with the caption calling him a sucker, and they had also been horrified at a picture book in the library with the grim and then prophetic title, "The First World War," but they had not talked about it much. They had played football and baseball, they had organized a mandolin club and gone to see Ginger Rogers in the movies, and they had waited without any confusion at all. Only the experts had been confused.

But the night Tom had gone to Betsy's coming-out party he hadn't been worried about the war. He had received the formally engraved invitation about three weeks before. "Mr. and Mrs. Mathew A. Donner cordially invite you to a dance in honor of their daughter, Miss Elizabeth A. Donner," it had begun, and he had answered, "Mr. Thomas R. Rath cordially accepts . . ." Dozens of such invitations had arrived every month during those years at college, because his name had been on the right lists—old Florence Rath had seen to that.

He had never met Betsy when he got the invitation and never had heard of the Donners. The afternoon before the party he had made up his mind not to go, because he had too much studying to do, but along about eight o'clock he had grown bored with his history book and, throwing it down in disgust, had put on his dinner coat and driven his second-hand car into Boston. "Might as well get some free champagne," he had said to his roommate.

The hotel had been crowded when he came in—it was a big party, he had seen at a glance. He had pushed through the groups of young people in evening clothes who crowded around the entrance to the ballroom and made his way to the long table in an adjoining room, where the champagne was being served. It had been good, imported champagne. Sipping his drink, Tom had stood just inside the door to the ballroom surveying the dancers in a mildly predatory way. At the time, he had considered himself an expert on women; he had thought he could just glance at them and tell which ones were passionate, which were cold, which would expect a lot of money to be spent on them, and which would not. His eye had skipped over Nina Henderson, who already had become a professional beauty, pictured on a magazine cover as the debutante of the year, a girl who later, as things turned out, married the fat orchestra leader who played at most of the dances that year and bore him a son before divorcing him. Tom's eye had also passed over the plain girls sitting on the side lines or dancing with their brothers. His glance had traveled across the floor until he saw Betsy.

How strangely comforting it was to look back now and realize that the enchantment he had felt that night at the first sight of her had been, after all, as unsentimentally real and factual as any ugly emotion or truth he could recall. And it was also comforting to reflect that what he had felt that night still defied analysis. Sure, Betsy's figure had never been calculated to calm a young man's pulse, but certainly there had been other girls in the room as admirable in measurement. The grace with which Betsy moved, the way her sparkling white dress had accentuated the warm colors of her skin and hair, the curve of her cheek, the flash of her smile—of course, all these things had had their effect, but there had been more, much more which could never have been caught by a camera, even if it used all the Technicolor in the world. The moment he had seen her he wanted to marry her, a fact which sounded so banal when he told it to her months later that they both had laughed, feeling suddenly ridiculous. But it was a true fact, and that night he had felt so bewildered by it that he stood for a long while watching her dance with others before mustering the courage to make his way across the dance floor and cut in on her.

"Who are you?" he had asked.

"Betsy Donner."

"The lady of the evening!" he had replied, hoping that his voice sounded light and sophisticated. "It's a nice party."

"It's a *beautiful* party!" she had said. "I suppose I shouldn't say that, but it is."

She had seemed to be floating. He had never been a good dancer, but her feet hadn't seemed to touch the floor at all, and he had felt suddenly graceful. Then a hand had touched him on the shoulder, and she had gone to someone else.

It's natural, he had thought—she's a pretty girl, and it's her party, and everybody has to dance with her at least once. But he had been disturbed to find he was unable to be with her for more than a few minutes.

That's when it all had started. For three years after that they had gone to movies and football games and college dances and night clubs, and performed the whole ritual of entertainment preparatory to marriage. He had played the mandolin for her—she had considered it a quaint, old-fashioned instrument. They had talked. At the time, Tom had been sure he would be rich a few years after the war was over, although he hadn't given much thought to what he would get rich at. They had kissed. At the time, they had known much less about each other than any personnel man knows about a prospective stenographer, but almost casually, certainly without anything which could be described as thought, on the strength of a kiss, she had agreed to marry him and had not considered it strange at all.

I was lucky, Tom thought now, as he stared at the slowly revolving bottles in the center of the bar in the hotel at Atlantic City. That was one time I was lucky. At that age I could have fallen in love with any empty-headed girl with a good figure, but I was lucky— that's one time when everything turned out all right.

How strange it is to remember, he thought. Poor Betsy, she could have married somebody with money, somebody who would be taking her to Florida every winter now, somebody who would never worry, who would smile and be cheerful while the cook cooked dinner, and the waitress served it, and Betsy sat smiling. Back in 1939, there had been several rich young men pursuing Betsy, and without thinking, apparently, she had turned them down, because they had not appealed to her at the moment, and she had chosen Tom on the strength of a kiss and had never thought about money.

How incredibly naïve we were, he thought now as he stared at the revolving pyramid of bottles. How incredibly innocent, as we parked my car and worried because we couldn't stop making love to each other! Once while they had been parked, a policeman on a motorcycle had shone the bright beam of his flashlight on them, and Betsy had jumped as though she were burned. The policeman had grinned and said, "All right, kids, break it up!" and had gone on, patrolling his beat, his light disappearing around a bend in the road.

I wonder if she's sorry, Tom thought. It isn't just the money— I wonder if she wishes she had a husband who could be cheerful around the house.

It's funny what happens to people, he thought. We were alike in those days, Betsy and I, all our experiences had been the same, and there was nothing we found impossible to explain to each other. We were confident—my God, we never worried at all! With the whole war in front of us, we never worried at all. We were sure that I would go through the war and become a hero. He remembered a mental picture he had had of himself, a clear image of himself, a soldier in a foreign land, sad and tired-looking, but clean and un-wounded, thinking of Betsy on Christmas Day, writing sad, brave letters about his friends who had died.

It wouldn't be too bad to be a soldier, he had thought—he had seen himself sitting in some jolly French tavern, or perhaps in the corner of some romantically Spartan barracks, singing Army songs—things like "Pack Up Your Troubles in Your Old Kit Bag, and Smile, Smile, Smile." Probably he'd take his mandolin along, he had thought—it would make him popular in the Army.

The future had seemed perfectly predictable in those days. Betsy would weep in a genteel way when he sailed overseas, with his man-dolin, but he would come back unhurt and march up Fifth Avenue, and she would throw herself into his arms and say, "Darling, you have come back to me!" and it would all be sad and brave and happy, like a movie of the First World War.

And the funny thing was, it had all happened, more or less; at least in the beginning, it had followed the script. He had gone off to his basic training carrying, among other things, his mandolin, and he had actually played it a few times, and several of the men had gathered around to sing. But when he had learned he was going overseas, he had shipped the mandolin home along with other sur-plus gear—somehow the idea of a paratrooper arriving in Europe with a mandolin had already begun to appear ridiculous. That had been the beginning of the destruction of the script, although to a sur-prising degree the outline had been followed. He had been a hero, all right, and had been awarded three medals to prove it. He had not been wounded. He had come home, and Betsy had met the transport at the wharf. She had run out of the crowd as he came down the gangplank, thrown her arms around him and said, "Darling, you have come back to me!"

That's what she had said, meaning it from the heart, and it had not been her fault that the words sounded satirical to him. He had held her away from him a little, seeing that she was a woman any man would want. That day she had been wearing a new dress spe-cially bought for the occasion, a gay red dress that closely followed the lines of her figure, a flamboyant dress which she had bought in a flamboyant mood the day she heard he was actually on his way home. She had kissed him passionately, and he had felt precisely as though a beautiful woman he had never seen before had rushed out of the crowd and begun making love to him. He had felt incredulous, awkward, abashed, and unwillingly lustful. The feeling of lust had appalled him, making him feel unfaithful to Maria, and also to Betsy as he remembered her from long ago, a young girl to be taken in love, not with the sort of feeling he would have for a pretty stranger unbelievably embracing him in the street.

"I've got a hotel room all reserved," she had said. "I'm not going to take you back to Grandmother's house tonight."

They had gone to the hotel, and the love-making had been intense and brief and unsatisfactory, leaving him with a profound feeling of confusion and shame. When it was over, her cheerfulness had surprised him. She had poured drinks, and, sitting down in a big armchair with a cigarette in her hand, she had leaned back and said, "Do you mind talking about the war? There are all sorts of questions I'm dying to ask."

"There's not much to tell," he had said. "What do you want to do tomorrow?"

Betsy had never been insensitive. She had not pursued the matter, and with gratitude he had felt he would never have to tell her anything about the war, not about Maria, not about Mahoney, not about anything. It would be better that way, he had thought, far better for both of them.

She had not seemed to mind his reticence. That night she had begun to talk brightly about the future. As he listened to her, he had gradually realized that here in this pretty girl sitting across the room from him in a pair of silk pajamas was himself as of 1939. Here was a kind of antique version of himself, unchanged. Here was the casual certainty that he would get a job which would soon lead to the vice-presidency of J. H. Nottersby, Incorporated, or some firm with a name which would have to sound like that. Here was all the half-remembered optimism, the implicit belief that before long they would move into a house something like Mount Vernon, with nice old darky servants nodding and singing all the time, a place where they would grow old gracefully, not getting fat, but becoming only a little gray around the temples, a mansion where they would of course be happy, real happy for the rest of their lives.

The trouble hadn't been only that he didn't believe in the dream any more; it was that he didn't even find it interesting or sad in its improbability. Like an old man, he had been preoccupied with the past, not the future. He had changed, and she had not.

That night he had listened to her almost paternally. "I don't know what I want to do," he had said when she asked if he had any definite ideas about a job. "We'll have to figure that out."

"I know you'll succeed, no matter what you do," she had said, her whole happy dream of the future hanging almost palpably in front of her, like the pictures of dreams people have in cartoons.

But of course her dream had not come true—that seemed sad to him now for her sake. Instead of getting the house like Mount Vernon, they had moved into the little house on Greentree Avenue in Westport, and Betsy had become pregnant, and he had thrown the vase against the wall, and the washing machine had broken down. And Grandmother had died and left her house to somebody, and instead of being made vice-president of J. H. Nottersby, Incorporated, he had finally arrived at a job where he tested mattresses, was uneasy when his boss said he wanted to see him without explaining why, and lived in fear of an elevator operator.

I hope Betsy isn't sorry, he thought. If I lose this job and have to take whatever I can get, I hope she still won't be sorry. I hope she never has to learn about Maria.

"Hello," someone said.

He turned and saw a pretty, dark-haired girl in a copper-colored evening gown sitting at the bar next to him. "You look preoccupied," she said.

He smiled. "I was thinking," he replied.

"Bad practice," the girl said. "Very bad practice. My name's Marie. Want to come to our party?"

"Thank you," he said hastily. "No, I can't." He got up and walked out of the room, feeling oddly perturbed.

25

AFTER DINNER THAT NIGHT, Tom went to his room in the hotel and lay down. It isn't fair to Betsy, he thought, to keep remembering the weeks with Maria as the happiest of my life. It wasn't the difference between two women—it was simply the difference in circumstance. When he and Betsy had first met back in 1939, they had been children, and their happiness had been the pale, fragile happiness of children, full of little anxieties about getting home on time, and doing the proper thing. And after the war, there hadn't really been time for happiness—there had been budgets and bills from obstetricians and frantic planning for the future. That had been the trouble with him and Betsy: what with his brooding about the past and worrying about the future, there never had been any present at all.

But with Maria it had been different; they had both been reconciled to having no future, and the past had been something which had to be forgotten. With Maria there had been only the moment at hand, completely unshadowed, unexpected, something to be grateful for. Perhaps, Tom thought, it's a matter of expectations—he and Betsy had always expected so much! Everything would be perfect for them, they had expected from the beginning. They would be rich, they would be healthy, and they would do no wrong. Any deviation from perfection had seemed a blight which ruined the whole. But he and Maria had expected nothing; they had started with hopelessness and had been astonished to learn that for a few weeks they could be happy.

Lying there in his hotel room, Tom suddenly remembered the day of the picnic with Maria, and he smiled—even the distant memory made him smile. It had been a ridiculous day from the beginning. After having wangled the use of a jeep, he and Maria had started from Rome at nine o'clock in the morning, with a large basket full of groceries and a bottle of wine. The sky had been gray, with feathery wisps of white cloud blowing across darker, blacker clouds billowing up from the horizon, and it had been cold—the mud puddles beside the road had been crusted with ice. At nine-thirty, just as they got outside the city, it had begun to rain. It had been a ridiculous day for a picnic, but the thought of going back had not even occurred to them. He had stopped, and she had helped him to put the side curtains on the jeep, and it had been snug and warm inside, with the world appearing eerie through the dripping windshield. They had headed south and driven aimlessly—there had been a delicious sense of freedom in coming to a crossroad and turning to the left or right completely at random, without caring at all where they were going. Maria had turned up the collar of her old soldier's overcoat, but she had not worn a hat, and her dark glossy hair had got wet while they were putting the side curtains up and had stayed damp all day. She had looked contented sitting there on the hard uncomfortable seat of the jeep. She had not smiled—her face had so often been serious—but she had hummed a song almost inaudibly under her breath, and he had kept glancing at her, receiving enormous satisfaction from the sight of her sitting there beside him so serenely.

"What are you singing?" he had asked. "Sing louder, so I can hear."

She had shaken her head modestly. "I can't sing," she had said. "I know no music."

"I do," he had said. "You happen to be sitting beside the star baritone and mandolin virtuoso of the entire United States. Want to hear me?"

"Yes." She had laughed.

"You'll have to imagine the mandolin in the background," he had replied. "Pling, pling, pling—does that set the proper mood?"

"Yes."

"All right!" At the top of his lungs he had sung "Old Man River" and the "Saint Louis Blues," both of which had seemed absurdly doleful. Her laughter had formed a sort of accompaniment to the songs, and he had gone on to sing, "Way down upon the Swanee River, far, far away—there's where my heart is turning ever, there's where the old folks stay. . . ." He had been briefly conscious of the irony of the fact that at the moment he wasn't worrying much about the old folks at home, but he had brushed that thought away. He had sung all the songs whose words he knew that day while they drove aimlessly around in the rain. She had not tried to sing with him—she had just sat there and from time to time had put her hand on his knee with curious hesitation, almost as though it were dark and she were trying to make sure he was still there. Once, when he stopped at a crossroad, she had leaned over and kissed him on the mouth with almost painful intensity. That had been a curious and wonderful thing about her that he had understood only gradually: her almost constant eagerness to make love. At first, he had been surprised, and then he had thought that she was simply an ideal and probably practiced soldier's girl, and he had been a little cynical about her ardor. But after he had known her a few days he had realized that physical love was the only form of reassurance she knew, and that she was completely happy and sure of him only when she was caressing him and giving him pleasure, and that it was chiefly this that caused her constantly to entice him. She was scared, just as scared as he was, he had realized. On that day while they were driving in the rain she had told him a little about her past. The village in which she had lived with her parents had been one of the first hit by the invasion. The Germans had made a brief stand there, and the planes had dropped bombs of white phosphorus. Her parents had refused to go to a bomb shelter for fear that their house would be looted if left empty, but they had forced her to go. Crawling up from the shelter after a bomb had burst near by, she had seen her house in flames, seen her father stagger out carrying her mother, both their bodies enveloped in flames. The other people from the bomb shelter had not let her run to them. Her father had fallen after taking only a few steps, and she had seen the bodies of her parents lying at right angles to each other, burning like a fiery cross. As she told Tom about this, she had been objective, almost matter-of-fact. The tears had not come until he had impulsively stopped the jeep and put his arms around her, feeling in himself an overpowering need to try to comfort her, in spite of the knowledge that for such things there is no solace. She had cried hard for about ten minutes, and her sobs had been all the more agonizing because they came silently through clenched teeth and taut lips. After regaining control of herself, she had taken from her battered handbag a cheap imitation gold compact, opened it, and put powder on her face. For several seconds she had stared at herself in the tiny, clouded mirror. "Do you think I am beautiful?" she had asked.

"Very beautiful."

"Not beautiful enough to keep you. Everyone dies or goes away."

Not wanting to lie or to be cruelly truthful, he had not contradicted her. He had said nothing, but had kissed her, and she had returned the kiss with all the passion which had been suppressed in her silent tears. "Tell me again that I am beautiful," she had said.

He had done so. She had sighed and said, "All right. Let's drive some more."

For an hour they had driven in silence. At about noon they had grown hungry and had turned up a narrow road in hilly country, seeking a place where they could get out of the rain and eat. They had driven for perhaps another half hour before coming to an abandoned villa, the east end of which had been destroyed by artillery fire. The ground all around the villa had been badly cut up, and the buff-colored stucco walls pockmarked with machine-gun bullets. He had driven the jeep slowly around the driveway which encircled the building, past a swimming pool choked with fallen masonry. On impulse he had twisted the steering wheel suddenly and driven between two shattered pillars, across a tiled courtyard littered with rubble, under a part of the roof which projected over what must once have been an anteroom. There he had stopped, and, wondering at the marvelous convenience of the ruin which allowed them to drive out of the rain, they had stepped out of the jeep. He had lifted the hood and taken part of the distributor with him, as well as the ignition key, to make sure no one would steal the car. Carrying their picnic basket and shivering a little in the dampness, they had walked through an enormous jagged hole in a charred wall and entered a huge living room. The glass in the high windows along the right-hand side of the room had been shattered, and tattered damask draperies were being blown inward, arched by the wind into the shape of wings. There had been a puddle in the middle of the polished oak floor, and everywhere there had been bits of glass and countless pieces of paper, as though an office had exploded. In one corner there had been the wreck of a grand piano, the board with the ivory keys lying separate from the rest, like the jawbone of a prehistoric beast, and the big brass-colored frame with most of the strings still taut resting on edge, like a harp. They had crossed this room and, after walking through two utterly bare rooms, had found what must once have been a small library, with a white marble fireplace at one end. The walls had been lined with bookcases, all empty now, except for many scattered leaves and detached leather bindings. There had been only two windows in that room, and, miraculously, only a few of the lower panes had been broken. Through one of the windows they had been able to see a small circular pool, in the middle of which a white marble nymph, slim waisted and full breasted but now headless, rose, holding in one upraised arm a cornucopia, out of which a fountain must once have spouted.

"Here," he had said, putting the picnic basket down. "We'll see if the chimney works." Gathering some of the book leaves which lay on the floor, he had struck a match, ignited the paper, and dropped it into the fireplace. The smoke had gone straight up. "We can build a fire," he had said.

She had stood, holding her coat collar close around her neck and looking small and lost, while he had gone to the great living room and brought back an armful of polished fragments from the splintered top of the piano. After she had helped him to gather more paper, he had built a fire carefully, setting the sharp splinters of wood on end like a wigwam. The smoky orange flame had climbed them swiftly. Suddenly the room had been full of the acrid smell of burning varnish. She had knelt by the fire and held her hands out to it, and he had noticed for the first time that her hands were the hands of a nervous child, that she had bitten her fingernails to the quick. Her hands had been surprisingly small, fragile, and finely tapered. She had glanced up at him, and upon seeing that he was looking at her hands, she had quickly doubled them into fists, so that the fingernails were hidden, and had put them into the pockets of her coat with exactly the gesture of a child caught stealing cookies. Then she had stood up, looking flustered. Impulsively he had taken her right hand out of her pocket, smoothed it in his own hands, and kissed it. She had buried her face in his shoulder, and he had felt that she was shivering.

"You're too beautiful to worry about your hands," he had said. "Come on, you're cold—let's get more wood on that fire." He had gone to the living room and come back carrying a heavy amputated leg of the piano, the foot of which had been carved to resemble the claws of a lion clutching a round, shiny ball. This he had placed on the fire, and the flames had immediately embraced it, licking greedily at the varnish. He had returned to the living room and, grabbing one of the tattered damask draperies, had given it a hard pull and brought it down in a cloud of dust and a clatter of falling curtain rods. This he had dragged to the library and had ripped pieces from it to stuff the broken windowpanes. The remainder he had spread on the floor as a tablecloth, and she had begun to unpack the basket, placing sandwiches done up in brown paper and the bottle of wine and a cold roast chicken carefully in a row. Gradually the roaring fire had warmed the room. They had taken their overcoats off and folded them by the tablecloth to serve as pillows on which to sit.

That day she had been wearing a worn black skirt, a white blouse cut almost like a man's shirt with an open collar, and a dark-green jacket which she had made herself, trying to copy a picture in a magazine advertisement. They had eaten greedily, wiping their hands on the damask tablecloth and passing the bottle of wine back and forth between them. When they were through, she had packed the remnants of the picnic away in the basket. Carefully lighting two cigarettes, he had handed her one, and she had sat down comfortably, edging a little toward the fire and holding her hands out to the flames, this time unabashed. Outside, the rain had started coming down faster, and the rags he had stuffed in the broken windowpanes had started to drip on the floor. Far overhead a squadron of bombers had droned, going somewhere, high above the clouds. The unbroken glass in the windows had trembled. Content to sit and stare into the fire, which was already reducing the great claw of the piano leg to embers, he had said nothing. Glancing at his wrist watch, he had seen it was not yet two o'clock. That meant they would have eighteen more hours until eight o'clock the next morning, when he would have to check in with the sergeant at the transportation desk. Eighteen more hours, he had thought gratefully, and slowly had calculated: the big sweep hand on his watch would have to tick off one thousand and eighty minutes, a marvelously long time. He had glanced at her and to his surprise had found her looking hurt and forlorn. Suddenly he had realized that she had expected him to make love to her long before this, and that she was afraid that he had grown tired of her, or that she had displeased him in some way. He had smiled at her. "Come over here," he had said. Quickly she had gone to him and lain with her head in his lap, looking up at him, his smile mirrored on her face. He had stroked her hair and forehead softly, feeling, for the moment, oddly calm. Overhead another squadron of bombers had droned, followed by more and more, until the whole building trembled. He had glanced over his shoulder and through the rain-streaked glass had seen the headless nymph outside, holding her empty cornucopia high, silhouetted against the rain-drenched clouds. After a few moments he had looked back at Maria, lying with her head on his lap in the yellow firelight, and he had seen that to invite his affections, she had unbuttoned her jacket and opened the blouse, partly exposing her breasts and the deep valley between them. He had kissed her then, the kiss beginning almost as an act of kindness, but quickly becoming much more than that. "Oh, God, I love you," he had said.

They had left the villa just in time to get back to Rome before dark. When they had returned to her room, she had started cooking supper on a small primus stove he had given her, and he had lain down on the bed and glanced at his watch again. It had been only six o'clock—still fourteen more hours, eight hundred and forty more revolutions of the sweep hand before he had to check in. He had stretched out on the soft bed, full of an incredible sense of luxury, thinking of the minutes ahead as a king might think of his empire. Maria had sat, looking wise and contented, stirring a pan of soup, which slowly had begun to steam, giving a fragrance to the air.

Only a few days after that he had bought a mandolin in a little music store they had happened to pass while walking home from a restaurant, and he had spent many afternoons lying in Maria's room strumming it idly, not really trying to play it, but finding great relaxation in the feel of the smooth steel strings under his fingers. Maria had loved it—her father had played the mandolin, she had said. The mandolin had been one of the things Tom had left her, along with the jeepload of canned goods and twelve cartons of cigarettes.

Now, lying alone in his hotel room in Atlantic City, Tom involuntarily glanced at his watch, with the same old sweep hand emptily ticking off the minutes. It was just youth, he thought, and the war, which, if it did nothing else, taught the value of time. Somebody should make me and Betsy check in at a transportation desk every morning and give us just one more day—that might teach us not to waste time. How different Betsy and Maria are, he thought. Betsy's parents had not died—instead of dying, they had retired to a modern bungalow in California, from which they sent their daughter pictures of themselves smiling and picking oranges. Nobody whom Betsy loved had ever died or left her for long. Ever since she was twelve years old, Betsy had been told she was beautiful—she did not like to hear it any more. I wonder if anyone tells Maria she is beautiful now, he thought. I wonder what kind of word Caesar will bring me about Maria after Gina writes her family in Rome. I wonder what Maria will do if Caesar tells her where I am, and that I look rich.

26

THE FIRST THING Tom did when he got back to his office the next day was to call Hopkins on the interoffice communication box.

"Glad you're back!" Hopkins said cheerily, as though Tom had just returned from a voyage around the world. "Have a good trip?"

"Fine," Tom said. "Did you want to see me?"

"Yes," Hopkins replied. "I'll send a girl down with the latest draft of my speech for Atlantic City. Let's have lunch tomorrow, and you can tell me what you think of it. Would one o'clock be all right?"

So that's all he wanted, Tom thought. He said, "Fine! I'll meet you in your office tomorrow at one."

An hour later an exceptionally pretty office girl arrived and with a dazzling smile handed Tom a large manila envelope from Hopkins. Tom opened it and extracted the speech, which had grown and changed since he had worked on it. "It's a real pleasure to be here this evening," he read. "I tremendously appreciate this opportunity to discuss with this distinguished gathering what I believe to be the most crucial problem facing the world today." Having made this point, the speech went on—in fact, it went on and on and on for thirty pages, saying over and over again in different ways that mental health is important. The last ten pages were devoted to the thought that mental-health problems affect the economy of the nation. "Our wealth depends on mental health," this section concluded. "Yes, our wealth depends on mental health!"

Tom put the speech down, feeling slightly ill. Good Lord, he thought, they're going to sell mental health the way they sell cigarettes! He left the speech on his desk, walked over to the window, and stared out over the city. Standing there, he shrugged his shoulders in an oddly hopeless way.

"Let's have lunch tomorrow, and you can tell me what you think of it," Hopkins had said.

"Well, of course I'm just talking off the top of my head, but I think this draft has some fine things in it, and, on the other hand, I have some reservations," Tom imagined himself saying. That was the way it was done—always feel the boss out to find what he thinks before committing yourself. Tell the man what he wants to hear.

"I'm sorry, but I think this speech is absurd. It's an endless repetition of the obvious fact that mental health is important. You've said that over and over again and finally turned it into a cheap advertising slogan. If you want to form a mental-health committee, why don't you find out what needs to be done and offer to help do it?"

A few years ago I would have said that, Tom thought. Be honest, be yourself. If the man asks you what you think of his speech, tell him. Don't be afraid. Give him your frank opinion.

That sounds so easy when you're young, Tom thought. It sounds so easy before you learn that your frank opinion often leads directly to the street. What if Hopkins really likes this speech?

Tom shrugged again. The thing to remember is this, he thought: Hopkins would want me to be honest. But when you come right down to it, why does he hire me? To help him do what he wants to do—obviously that's why any man hires another. And if he finds that I disagree with everything he wants to do, what good am I to him? I should quit if I don't like what he does, but I want to eat, and so, like a half million other guys in gray flannel suits, I'll always pretend to agree, until I get big enough to be honest without being hurt. That's not being crooked, it's just being smart.

But it doesn't make you feel very good, Tom thought. It makes you feel lousy. For the third time, he shrugged. How strangely it all works out, he thought. The pretty girl smiles as she hands me the innocuous manila envelope with the speech. I'll go with my boss for luncheon to a nice restaurant somewhere, with music playing in the background, perhaps, and people laughing all around, and the waiters will bow, and my boss will be polite, and I'll be tactful, and there in such delicate surroundings, I'll not be rude enough to say a stupid speech is stupid. How smoothly one becomes, not a cheat, exactly, not really a liar, just a man who'll say anything for pay.

Tom remained by the window a long while, looking down at the cars crawling along the streets below. It was queer to be suspended motionless so far above the city. It was almost as though his parachute had got stuck in mid-air, halfway between the plane and the ground.

That night when Tom went home he put the speech back in the manila envelope and on impulse took it with him. Betsy and the children met him at the station in South Bay. "What's that?" Janey said, eying the big envelope. "Is it a present for us?"

"No," Tom said, and handed the envelope to Betsy. "This is Hopkins' speech. I'd like you to read it and tell me what you think of it. Hopkins wants me to have lunch with him and give him my opinion on it tomorrow."

"I'll look at it after dinner," Betsy said, and casually put the envelope down on the front seat of the car.

"Mother has a surprise for you," Barbara said. "She got it for you today."

"Hush!" Betsy said. "How is it going to be a surprise if you talk about it?"

"I can hardly wait to find out what it is," Tom said, and, realizing he had been so preoccupied that he hadn't kissed Betsy, leaned over and patted her on the shoulder. "It's good to get home," he said.

She turned toward him with a quick, vivid smile. "It's not much of a surprise, really," she said. "Don't get your hopes up."

The surprise turned out to be a large leather armchair with a matching hassock for Tom to put his feet on. Betsy had put a small table by it, with a box of cigarettes, matches, and an ash tray. She had also placed an ice bucket there, two glasses, and the mixings for cocktails. "You looked so tired when you got back from Atlantic City last night," she said. "I figured you ought to have a place where you can just sink down and rest when you get home. I'm going to try to organize things so we have a half hour of quiet before supper. Kids, go upstairs, the way you promised you would!"

Janey grinned, and with unusual obedience led the others up the stairs. "I put ginger ale up there for them," Betsy said. "They're going to have a quiet period in their room, while we have ours down here. We're going to try to do it that way for a half hour every night."

"That's wonderful," Tom said. "It's a marvelous chair." He sat down in it gratefully, put his feet up on the hassock, and lit a cigarette. Betsy mixed the cocktails and handed him one. He took a sip and said, "Did you bring that speech in from the car?"

"Yes. It's on the hall table. Why?"

"I'm anxious to see what you think of it."

"Sure," she said. "I'll go get it."

She sat in a chair across the room from Tom and took the speech from the envelope. He watched her face while she read it. Her expression was serene. At first she read slowly, but soon began to flip rapidly through the pages. Tom poured himself another drink. "What do you think of it so far?" he asked.

"Did you write this?"

"I helped. Do you like it?"

"Well," she said hesitantly, "I don't know much about the subject. My opinion wouldn't mean much."

"Come on. What do you think of it?"

"It's kind of boring," she said. "Maybe it's just me, but I find it pretty hard to keep my mind on it. It seems to keep saying the same thing over and over again."

Tom laughed. "Any other comments?"

"To be honest, some of it sounds pretty silly," Betsy said. "Is this what Hopkins wanted you to write?"

"I didn't really write it," Tom said. "I think Ogden did most of it, or maybe Hopkins himself. And now Hopkins wants me to tell him what I think of it."

"What are you going to say?"

Tom laughed again. "There's a standard operating procedure for this sort of thing," he said. "It's a little like reading fortunes. You make a lot of highly qualified contradictory statements and keep your eyes on the man's face to see which ones please him. That way you can feel your way along, and if you're clever, you can always end up by telling him exactly what he wants to hear."

"Is that what they do?" Betsy asked. She didn't laugh.

"That's what they do. For instance, I'll begin by saying, 'I think there are some *wonderful* things about this speech. . . .' If Hopkins seems pleased, I'll finish the sentence by saying, 'and I have only the most minor improvements to suggest.' But if he seems a little surprised at the word *wonderful*, I'll end the sentence with, 'but as a whole, I don't think it comes off at all, and I think major revisions are necessary.'"

"Is that what you're going to do?" Betsy asked. She wasn't even smiling.

"As I say, it's standard operating procedure," Tom replied. "The first thing the young executive must learn."

"I think it's a little sickening," Betsy said bluntly.

"Damn it, have a sense of humor. What's the matter with you?"

"Nothing's the matter with me. I'm just interested in knowing the answers to a few questions. What do you really think of that speech?"

"I think it's terrible," Tom said. "My business education, you see, is not complete. In a few years I'll be able to suspend judgment entirely until I learn what Hopkins thinks, and then I'll really and truly feel the way he does. That way I won't have to be dishonest any more."

Betsy put the speech neatly back in its envelope, handed it to Tom, and without a word went to the kitchen.

"Betsy!" he said. "Come back. I want to talk to you."

"I'm getting dinner," she said.

"What's the matter? It's not time for dinner yet."

"I've got some things that have to be put on the stove."

He went to the kitchen and found her filling a kettle with water. "You're angry with me," he said. "Can't you take a joke?"

"I don't think you were joking."

"Of course I was. I was knocking myself out with humor."

"What are you going to tell Hopkins tomorrow?"

"I don't know. Why's that so important all of a sudden?"

She put the kettle on the stove and turned toward him suddenly. "I didn't like the look of you sitting there in that big chair talking so damn smugly and cynically!" she said. "You looked disgusting! You looked like just the kind of guy you always used to hate. The guy with all the answers. The guy who has no respect for himself or anyone else!"

"What do you want me to do?" he asked quietly. "Do you want me to go in there tomorrow and tell Hopkins I think his speech is a farce?"

"I don't care what you tell him, but I don't like the idea of your becoming a cheap cynical yes-man and being so self-satisfied and analytical about it. You never used to be like that."

"All right," Tom said. "I'll tell him I think his speech is absurd.

– 205 –

And he'll decide I'm a nice honest guy who just happens to be no use to him at all."

"How do you know? Maybe he doesn't like the speech either."

"Sure, it might turn out that way. I've got a fifty-fifty chance if I play it straight, but if I feel my way along, I have a ninety per cent chance of giving him what he wants."

"Maybe he just wants an honest opinion."

"That sounds real nice," Tom said bitterly. "You don't know how guys like Hopkins are."

"No, I don't," she said.

"You haven't even met him."

"No, I haven't. What's he ever done to convince you he's dishonest?"

"I didn't say he is dishonest."

"He is if you have to agree with him all the time to keep your job."

"That's not true. A guy who disagreed with him most of the time simply wouldn't be useful to him."

"Not if you were right and he was wrong—if it were that way, you could be damn useful by disagreeing. There's no two ways about it: either you think that he'd fire you for disagreeing, even if you were right, or you're not sure you're right. Either you've got no confidence in him, or none in yourself. Which is it?"

"Don't be so righteous," Tom said. "If you really want to know, I'm not too damn sure of either him or myself. I don't really know whether that speech will do whatever he wants it to do or not— maybe all the slick advertising guys will think it's wonderful, and maybe that's what he wants. I don't know how he'd feel about a guy who disagreed with him. The point is, you'd have to take an awful chance to find out."

"And you don't want to take a chance."

"You're talking like a typical American woman," Tom said disgustedly. "You want it both ways. 'Don't play it safe,' you say, 'and can we get a new car tomorrow?'"

"You can't imagine being honest and getting a raise for it."

"My Boy Scout days are over," Tom said doggedly.

"And so you're going in there tomorrow and lie to the man if you figure that's what he wants."

"You're damn right I am."

"How long will it be before you decide it isn't necessary to tell the truth to me?"

The truth, Tom thought. The truth about what? The truth about Maria? Shall we all sit down now and tell each other the truth? Suddenly he felt immensely angry. "You've had an easy life, Betsy," he said in a deadly quiet voice. "You just stay here and take care of the kids and enjoy your moral indignation while I go in town every day to wrestle with guys like Hopkins. But don't read me lectures. The truth is I'm doing the best I can with the world as I see it."

"Go to hell," Betsy said with passion.

"Thanks," Tom replied. "Is that the last of your moral advice?"

Betsy didn't answer. She was pale and quiet all through dinner. After she had put the children to bed, Tom said to her, "Haven't we been making an awful lot out of nothing?"

"I guess we have," she said. "If you don't mind, I think I'll turn in. And if you're going to see Hopkins tomorrow, you better get a good night's rest yourself."

27

SAUL BERNSTEIN walked into the First National Bank, which was the biggest building in South Bay. As a boy he had thought "the bank" a frightful monster, for he had often heard his parents worrying about whether it would take their store away, as though it were a giant who could reach out and rip the building from its foundations, but for two years now, he had been a member of the bank's board of directors, and he no longer thought of it as anything but a rather tired group of men trying to meet their responsibilities. He walked to the rear of the bank, opened a gate in a low partition there, and approached the desk of Walter Johnson, the president. "Good morning, Walt," he said. "I'd like to find out the bank balance of two men: a Mr. Thomas R. Rath and a Mr. Edward F. Schultz."

"Just a minute," Johnson said, and picked up his telephone. Bernstein sat down. That morning he had received in the mail from Edward Schultz a photostat of a document written on the personal stationery of Mrs. Florence Rath. "To Whom It May Concern," the document said. "In exchange for his services for the rest of my life, and in place of paying him a regular salary for same from this day forward, I hereby bequeath my entire possessions, including my house and land, to Edward F. Schultz, who has served me faithfully for more than thirty years." This was typewritten, with the date, June 10, 1953. Florence Rath's signature followed, written by a quavering hand.

Bernstein had studied this and had carefully reread the long, precisely phrased will which Sims had sent him, a document which was dated January 18, 1948. Edward's document was not a legal will like the one which left everything to Tom, Bernstein saw, but it might be considered a legal contract, and quite a case might be built on that. And regardless of the legal technicalities, what had old Mrs. Rath intended?

As he waited for Johnson to get him the figures he had requested, Bernstein reviewed for the hundredth time the possibilities, the different combinations of circumstance, which theoretically could have led to contradictory documents. It was possible that old Mrs. Rath had simply been forgetful, had made her bargain with Schultz and forgotten to tell her lawyer or grandson. It was possible she had deliberately refrained from telling them, for fear that their objections might be painful. On the other hand, she might have told her grandson of the change, and young Rath might have decided simply to say nothing about it to anyone, confident that his grandmother's agreement with Schultz would be thrown out of court because of legal technicalities—because it bore the names of no witnesses to the signature. And theoretically it was just as possible that the document presented by Schultz was in some way a fake, although Bernstein was quite sure that Schultz's lawyers would have had the signature examined before accepting the case. His real responsibility, Bernstein felt, was to discover which of these circumstances had actually happened. Until he knew that, it would be impossible to tell what paragraphs in the thick law books which lined the walls of his inner office should be chosen to justify a decision in the case. It was, of course, difficult to resurrect the past, but not impossible. In a small town the past clung to the present more permanently than in a big city. People's footprints lasted longer before they were stamped out.

The bank president wrote several figures on a pad. "Mr. Rath has a savings account with approximately nine thousand dollars in it, deposited on September 2, all in one check from a real-estate outfit in Westport," he said. "Mr. Schultz has a savings account of approximately seventy-eight thousand dollars, deposited here over a period of thirty years, in varying amounts on the third of each month."

"Are you sure?" Bernstein asked in astonishment.

"Those are the figures."

"Thank you," Bernstein said.

"Not a bit," Johnson replied. He knew he was not supposed to give out such figures, but in South Bay a man who had demonstrated good intentions and the ability to keep his mouth shut could get any information he wanted.

Bernstein walked slowly up Main Street. It was surprising how often bank balances helped to point the way toward justice. The figures he had just learned might mean anything or nothing, but they at least rid his mind of the picture of the faithful impoverished old servant being cheated by a young heir. Here the servant was richer than the heir, all of which went to show, Bernstein reflected, that a man must guard himself against his own prejudices. And another thing: how could old Schultz have continued his deposits if he had had no salary for several months? And why were his monthly deposits of "varying amounts"? Wouldn't an employee with a regular salary tend to deposit the same sum every month? Perhaps he had cashed his checks, spent varying amounts, and deposited the remainder, Bernstein thought, but it would be strange if such a haphazard plan enabled a butler to save so much. How much had Mrs. Rath been paying him? Suddenly Bernstein had an idea. He hadn't worked in a delicatessen all during his boyhood without learning anything.

Quickening his pace, Bernstein walked to Hopeland's Grocery Store, which specialized in luxury items. That is where Mrs. Rath would have been almost sure to order her groceries. He went to the room on the second floor where Julius Marvella, the manager, was busy reckoning his accounts. "Morning, Julius," he said.

"What are you doing up here, Judge?" Julius replied, grinning. "Have you come to take me in?"

"Not today. I wondered if you could tell me something. Did old Mrs. Rath trade here?"

"Nope—she went to Fritz's place."

"Why?"

Julius shrugged.

"Did she ever trade here?"

"A long time ago, when I was a kid. Then she changed."

"Do you know why?"

Julius shrugged again.

"Nobody's going to get into trouble if you tell me," Bernstein said. "And you won't have to appear in court. I won't mention your name."

"Okay, Judge," Julius said. "This guy Schultz did all her buying for her, and he wanted kickbacks. He asked Pop to pad Mrs. Rath's bill. Not just a little, mind you—Schultz wanted him to add twenty per cent every month and kick back fifteen per cent to him. You know how Pop was on that stuff. He threw the bastard out."

"Thanks," Bernstein said.

"I don't know what Fritz did for him," Julius said. "I'm making no charges—I'm just telling you what happened here. I don't want to get Fritz into trouble. You know how it is, Judge—Fritz might get a chance to put me in a jam someday. It don't pay to start things in a town like this. Wouldn't be long before he found some way to knock me."

"I won't even have to talk to Fritz," Bernstein said. Six years before he had successfully represented a man bringing suit against Fritz for padding bills. He thanked Julius again and continued on his way down Main Street. That clears up one thing, he thought— Schultz is dishonest. A piece of knowledge like that was a lot more help to Bernstein than the legal reviews that came to his office each month.

Bernstein strolled around the town, chatting casually with shopkeepers, the manager of the movie theater, the keepers of taverns, the man who sold tickets at the railroad station, and many others. Within two hours he had accumulated a fairly complete dossier on Schultz. Five shopkeepers had reported that Schultz had tried to get them to pad bills. These five all had good reputations, and Schultz had not traded with them regularly. He had done most of his purchasing at stores whose proprietors Bernstein suspected, some because of rumors he had heard, others because of their record. All this was perhaps less strange, Bernstein thought, than the fact that virtually no one could remember ever having seen Schultz spend money on himself, or buy any entertainment. In the thirty years Schultz had lived in the house on the top of the hill, the taxi company had rarely been called to bring him to town. He had never been seen in the movies or taverns and had not taken regular trips on the train. What had he done on his days off? Perhaps he's a miser, Bernstein thought; perhaps he did nothing but save money. One couldn't refuse to allow a man to inherit a house simply because he had padded bills and saved money, but Bernstein felt he was beginning to see the tortuous road to justice more clearly.

28

IT WAS a little after ten o'clock in the morning. "Mrs. Hopkins is on the wire, Mr. Hopkins," Miss MacDonald said. "Will you take the call now?"

"Of course!" Hopkins said. "Put her through."

"Ralph?" Helen's voice broke in.

"Hello, dear," he said. "What can I do for you?"

"Ralph, can you come out here? I want to talk to you."

"Sure," he said. "Sure! I have some appointments, but I can break them. What time do you want me to be there?"

"Try to get here for lunch. This is important, Ralph. It's about Susan."

"Susan? What's the matter with her?"

"She just told me she refuses to go to college. I'm worried about her, Ralph. I'll talk to you about it when I see you."

"I'll come right out," he said.

After telephoning Tom to postpone their luncheon date, Hopkins had his chauffeur drive him to South Bay. As the car turned into his driveway, he tried not to look at the enormous low house, with one wing extending over the edge of the artificial harbor. His wife had had it built, had directed the architect herself, and Hopkins did not like the place—he detested anything which seemed to be made mostly for show. He had never complained about the house, however, and did not intend to.

A butler let Hopkins in, and a maid took his hat—that was another thing which bothered him about the house: there were always too many servants hanging around. He walked through the enormous living room, the entire east side of which was made of glass, to the library. Helen was sitting there alone. She was a short woman who had grown rather stout, but her face retained its delicate shape. Her graying brown hair was carefully arranged in a style a little too youthful for her, and she wore a severe black cocktail dress which had been designed for a much slimmer figure. She got up a little nervously when Hopkins came into the room. She hadn't seen him for more than a month.

"Hello, dear," he said. "You're looking grand!" He kissed her lightly.

"Thanks for coming," she said. "I've been terribly worried."

"Sit down," he said. "Let's have a drink. Do you have any liquor in here?"

"Just pull the bell cord."

He pulled it, and a moment later a maid who had never seen Hopkins before came in. She was extremely nervous. "You rang, sir?" she asked. "Did you ring?"

"Yes," Hopkins replied. "Scotch on the rocks, please."

"I'll have a Manhattan," Helen said.

The maid withdrew.

"Is Susan here?" Hopkins asked.

"No—she's at some party out on Long Island. That's what I want to talk to you about, Ralph. She's at parties all the time."

"That's natural," Hopkins said easily. "She's young. I don't see anything to worry about."

"Well, I do!" Helen paused as the maid came in to set up a stand for a tray of drinks.

"After this, please try to have a closet or something in here with some liquor in it," Hopkins said to her. "I like to mix my own drinks."

"All right," Helen said. "Anna, please see about that in the morning."

"Yes, Madam," the maid said, passed the drinks, and withdrew.

"I don't think you understand the situation," Helen said. "Have you ever *thought* about it?"

"About what?"

"About Susan! About the problems she's going to have."

"It doesn't seem to me that she's in very difficult circumstances," Hopkins said dryly. "When I was her age . . ."

"You haven't thought about it, then," Helen interrupted. "It's time you did. What do you think is going to happen to her?"

"Happen to her?" Hopkins said. "Nothing, I hope. I hope she marries and has a nice family."

"What chance do you think she has for that?"

"Not bad, I'd say. She's pretty, and she won't be exactly a pauper."

"No, she won't be a pauper," Helen said. "I'm glad you've thought about it at least that much!"

"What do you mean by that?"

"To put it bluntly, your little daughter is probably going to be one of the richest young women in the country, and we haven't done anything at all to prepare her for it. And if she keeps on the way she's started, she's going to get into a lot of trouble."

"I think you're exaggerating," he said. "Money is no reason why she has to get into trouble."

"What do you think would happen if you and I died tomorrow?"

"Susan would inherit a lot of money, but she wouldn't have to worry about it. My lawyers would take care of all that."

"For the rest of her life?"

"If she wanted."

"You're awfully willing to write her off as an incompetent," Helen said. "The fact is that sooner or later the child's going to have tremendous responsibilities, and she has enormous temptations right now. It's our job to help her handle them."

"It's too early for that," Hopkins said. "Wait till she gets older. Then I'll see that she learns something about investments and all the rest of it."

"It's not investments I'm worried about!" Helen said. "Don't you see what a difference that money makes for her already? For one thing, everything she does gets in the newspapers! 'Miss Susan Hopkins seen at the Stork Club last night.' My God, any little joke she makes gets in the gossip columns. Don't you read the papers?"

"Not the gossip columns."

"Well, try them! You'll learn a lot about your daughter. At the age of eighteen, she's a celebrity!"

"That's inevitable," he said. "She'll learn to take it in her stride."

"And the men she goes out with!" Helen said. "They're not just nice healthy schoolboys—you should see them. A man called for her here the other night who's older than I am!"

"Who?"

"Byron Holgate, his name is. He drives a ridiculous-looking automobile, he's had two wives, and he sails in ocean races."

"I know Holgate," Hopkins said. "He's a fool. What's she running around with him for?"

"She's not just running around with him in a casual way—she's with him half the time. I wouldn't be surprised if she were thinking about marrying him. And the other people she sees aren't much better—it's the whole café society crowd. Do you know what she said to me the other day? She came in here dressed in some horrible thing she'd just bought, and she said, 'Mother, do you think I'm old for my age? I think boys my age are children.'"

"All girls go through a stage like that."

"Nonsense! Most girls would like to, but they don't get the chance. You have no idea what's been going on. The other day a man who had a play opening on Broadway took her to the opening night with him. How can a college boy compete with that?"

"Who was it?"

"Michael Patterson, his name is. He's forty-three years old and has three children. His wife divorced him last year."

"His play folded after three nights," Hopkins said. "You shouldn't let her run around with a crowd like that."

"How can I stop her? Do you want me to lock her in her room?"

"Have you had a talk with her?"

"Sure I've talked with her! She says I'm old-fashioned and she says . . ." Helen paused before she finished the sentence. "It's rather funny," she continued. "She says I'm nobody to talk, because my own marriage has been a failure."

"That's not true," Hopkins said quietly. "I consider our marriage a success."

"Let's not go into that," Helen said. "The point is, I can't do anything with her. And I'll tell you exactly what's going to happen if she keeps on: she's going to be one of those women who's in and out of the divorce courts most of her life."

– 215 –

"I think you're being an alarmist," he said. "She's young and high-spirited. Give her a few years, and she'll straighten out."

"*How* is she going to straighten out?" Helen demanded. "What kind of training is she getting? In the mornings she sleeps until lunch. She spends half the afternoon getting dressed. Most of the time she's awake she's getting entertained. Is that going to straighten her out? My God, she's already complaining that she's bored all the time. Bored, at eighteen!"

"She ought to go to college," Hopkins said.

"Yesterday she flatly refused. College is for children, she said. She claimed most of the men she knows are more brilliant than college professors—I suppose she's thinking of her playwright."

Hopkins finished his drink. "Tell that girl to bring a bottle and an ice bucket in here," he said.

Helen touched the bell pull, and a moment later the maid appeared. "You rang, Madam?" she asked. "Did you ring for me?"

"Bring a bottle of Scotch and an ice bucket for Mr. Hopkins," Helen said.

"Certainly, Madam," the girl replied, and scurried from the room.

"That girl makes me nervous," Hopkins said. "Where did you get her?"

"She's just inexperienced. I think she's a little overawed by you."

"I like to mix my own drinks!"

"Don't get irritable, dear," Helen said. "It isn't like you."

"I'm sorry," Hopkins said.

After the maid had brought the bottle of Scotch and the ice bucket, Hopkins filled his glass and took a long drink. "I think you better tell Susan she simply has to go to college," he said.

"I have, and she told me not to be medieval. That's exactly what she said."

"Maybe we've got to get a little tough with her. Tell her if she doesn't go to college we'll stop her allowance."

"I've already told her that," Helen said patiently. "She said to go ahead. She said she's already been offered a job singing with a band, and that she thinks she could get a screen test. And the funny thing is, she's right: plenty of people would be willing to hire your daughter, and you might as well understand that. Simply because she's your daughter, she's not the same as other people. You've given her a problem, and it's time you started helping her to handle it."

"I don't see what I can do," Hopkins said. "She's not a child any more. If she wants to ruin her own life, there's not much either of us can do about it. All we can do is watch, and if she runs wild, I'll set up a small trust fund for her and put the rest into my foundation."

"The Ralph Hopkins Foundation!" Helen said bitterly. "That and the headlines about your daughter's divorces will perpetuate your name."

"Let's not get emotional," Hopkins said.

"I'm not emotional!" Helen replied, her voice rising. "I just want to discuss a few facts. Since they were born, you've left the upbringing of the children to me. I've done it alone, and up to now, I haven't done a bad job. Bobby was a good boy—you were never particularly aware of him, but he was. He got good marks in college, and he never got into any trouble, and he enlisted in the Marines because he thought it was the right thing to do. He didn't even want a commission—he wanted the hardest job he could get, and no favors from you!"

Tears suddenly came to Helen's eyes, as they still did quite often when she talked about her dead son. Hopkins got up and awkwardly put his arm around her. "You've done a wonderful job," he said.

"But Susan has me licked, and I need your help!"

"I'll try," he said. "I don't know what I can do. You know I'm no good at this sort of thing."

"You're not stupid! This is a problem. All I'm asking is that you *try* to do something about it. It would help if Susan just knew you were trying. Don't go back to that office of yours and just forget about her. By God, if it will help you, think of her as a business problem!"

"I'll do anything you want," he said.

"It's not anything *I* want. I don't know what to ask you to do. I just want you to figure something out for yourself."

"I'll try," he said.

He handed her a clean handkerchief, and she wiped her face.

When she straightened up in her chair she was completely composed. "I just want to tell you this," she said quietly. "I'm asking you for help. I haven't done that for twenty-five years. I've got to admit I don't think I'll get it. What I really think is that you'll go back to New York, and maybe have a talk with Susan, and then forget all about her and me too. What I want you to understand is this: if that happens, I'm through. I'll get a divorce, on grounds of desertion."

"I'm going to try," he said.

"Trying isn't enough. I don't mean you've got to succeed with Susan, but you've got to do more than just make a halfhearted effort to get yourself interested. And don't come back to me and tell me you're sorry, but you are what you are, and nothing can be done about it. You've got to give her *time*. Put her down on your calendar. Treat her as though she were something you were a trustee of!"

29

At noon of the day finally set for Tom to have lunch with Hopkins to discuss the speech, Tom's secretary came into his office and rather incredulously said, "There's an elevator man here to see you. He says his name is Gardella. Shall I tell him to come in?"

"Yes," Tom said.

A moment later Caesar entered, shut the door behind him, and rather self-consciously took off his purple cap.

"Hello, Caesar," Tom said. "Nice to see you."

"Good morning, Mr. Rath," Caesar replied. "We heard from Gina's mother. It's funny—I thought you'd want to know about it. She doesn't know where Maria is."

"Doesn't know?"

"What I mean is, Maria and Louis and the boy—they've gone somewhere. They're not in Rome any more, or at least they're not

-218-

anywhere where Gina's mother can find them. She hasn't heard a word from them for six months."

"What do you think happened?"

"I don't know. Things had been pretty hard for them for a long while. Louis was out of the hospital, but with his leg and all, he couldn't get any work. Gina's mother had been helping them out, and I guess that bothered Louis a lot. Louis's a funny guy—he's proud."

Tom glanced out the window. He found it hard to look at Caesar.

"Gina's mother thinks they may have gone to Milan to look for work, and that they didn't tell anybody they were leaving because they owed so much money," Caesar continued. "Anyway, there's no sign of them now. I thought you ought to know."

"Thanks," Tom said.

"Gina's mother has an aunt in Milan, and she's asked her to look for them," Caesar added. "She'll let me know if they find them."

"I guess there's not much we can do now," Tom said.

"They'll turn up eventually," Caesar replied. "I'm sure of that. Gina has an awful lot of relatives over there. Louis's funny—if he made some money, he'd come back and pay his debts. And if things went real bad, Maria would have to go to some relatives for help. Sooner or later she'll turn up. I'll let you know."

"Thanks," Tom said.

"Well, so long," Caesar concluded, awkwardly put on his cap, and went out the door.

Tom got up and walked over to the window. So they've disappeared, he thought. I wonder if this is the way it will end—with no ending at all, with me never knowing what happened to them. They'll turn up, Caesar said. Somewhat to his own surprise, Tom found himself hoping they would—soon. The implications of that startled him a little, and he turned quickly to sit down at his desk. What would I do? he thought: what would I do if right now I knew they were starving and knew where to reach them? I couldn't do anything without telling Betsy—we've got joint bank accounts, both the saving and the checking, and Betsy keeps much closer track of the money than I do. I could take a few dollars out and make up some kind of excuse, sure, but not much and not regularly. And even if I could find a way to get the money without her knowing, it wouldn't be fair to her. I'd have to tell her, he thought. I'd have to tell her and pray to God she'd understand.

How would you tell your wife a thing like that? he asked himself. Would you go up to her and say, "Look, honey, I'm sorry to have to say this, but during the war . . ."

What would she do? It suddenly seemed to him that his wife was a stranger whose actions he could not predict at all. I don't know her, he thought with a kind of panic, I don't really know my own wife at all. Poor Betsy! Betsy had never had anything happen to her which could possibly help her to understand a thing like that. Would she accuse him of being immoral? Would she cry? Would she be angry, jealous? Would she figure that the whole time they had spent together since the war had been a kind of living lie, and would she want a divorce? He simply could not imagine what she would do— he couldn't picture himself telling her about Maria at all. Maybe I'll never have to, he thought. Maria has disappeared as completely as though I had wished her away. She isn't there any more, or at least no one can find her—it is as though she never existed. I should be glad Caesar can't find her, he thought; I should be glad, I should feel immensely relieved. He put his hand up to his face and suddenly realized he was praying like a child: Dear God, I want Maria to be all right.

His thoughts were suddenly interrupted by the buzz of the interoffice communication box on his desk. He turned it on, and Ralph Hopkins' cheery voice said, "Good morning, Tom! Ready to go to lunch now? Bring along a copy of the speech!"

"I'll be there in a few minutes," Tom said.

Carrying the speech in its manila envelope, Tom stepped into one of the golden elevators. The secretaries in Hopkins' office all smiled at him, and he smiled back. Hopkins came out almost immediately. "Glad you could make it, Tom!" he said. "How have you been?"

"Fine," Tom said. "The hotel accommodations are all set for you in Atlantic City."

Hopkins started toward the elevators. "Did you read the speech?" he asked.

"Yes."

"I'm looking forward to talking to you about it," Hopkins replied. An elevator door rumbled open, and they both stepped in. The elevator was crowded, and on the way down they both remained silent.

"How about the University Club for lunch?" Hopkins asked when they got out on the street.

"That would be nice."

"Let's walk—it's a grand day," Hopkins said, and strode rapidly up Fifth Avenue.

I hope he doesn't ask me what I think of the speech now, walking along Fifth Avenue in the sunshine, Tom thought. It would be very difficult for me to play games with him here and now.

"Did you get a chance for a vacation this summer?" Hopkins asked.

"No—I haven't been on the job long enough," Tom said.

"I just got a couple of week ends myself," Hopkins replied. "Put in some good fishing, though. Have you ever tried landlocked salmon?"

On the way to the University Club, Hopkins continued a pleasant line of chatter about fishing. They sat at a table in the corner of a high-ceilinged dining room. All around them earnest-appearing businessmen ate and talked. A waiter bowed and took their order for cocktails.

It isn't quite as I pictured it, Tom thought. Such a respectable place for me to lie about a speech, and there really should be music.

"Well, what do you think of the speech?" Hopkins asked mildly.

Parts of it are wonderful, Tom started to say, but on the other hand . . .

He didn't say it. Instead, he glanced at Hopkins and saw that he was watching him intently. On his face was an expression of courteous attention, nothing more. There was a pause.

"Would you care to order your luncheon now, sir?" a waiter asked. He spoke in a thick Italian accent.

"I guess we might as well," Hopkins said. "What will you have, Tom?"

"Anything," Tom said. "I guess I'd like some cold salmon."

"Scrambled eggs for me," Hopkins said. "And a cup of tea."

The business of ordering luncheon took a few more minutes. A man at a near-by table laughed explosively. The hell with it, Tom thought suddenly, so clearly that he half thought he had said it. It doesn't really matter. Here goes nothing. It will be interesting to see what happens. In defiance of his intentions, he heard himself saying aloud in a remarkably casual voice, "To tell you the truth, Mr. Hopkins, I read the latest draft of your speech, and I'm afraid I question it pretty seriously."

"You do?" Hopkins asked. His face did not change expression.

"I'm afraid I just don't think it's a very good speech," Tom said flatly.

"What do you think is the trouble with it?"

"It doesn't say anything," Tom replied. "That's the main trouble I had when I was trying to write it. The only point you really make is that mental health is important, and you can't repeat that for thirty pages. And frankly, I don't think an audience of physicians will react very well to slogans."

"I see," Hopkins said. "What do you recommend that I do?"

"I think you should come up with some concrete recommendations on how to solve mental-health problems," Tom heard himself booming confidently.

"I believe that at some point Ogden already has me asking for more mental hospitals and research," Hopkins said dryly.

"But everybody knows that's necessary—it's another repetition of the obvious," Tom said. "Couldn't you give some ideas about how to get the research and the hospitals?"

"Wait a minute," Hopkins said with a trace of impatience. "Don't let's forget that I don't know anything about concrete solutions for mental-health problems, and I don't want to pretend that I do."

"But . . ." Tom began.

"Wait a minute. I think you've put your finger on something. This draft of Bill Ogden's rings false because it confuses the job of starting a mental-health campaign with carrying it out. As you say, my audience at Atlantic City certainly won't need convincing that mental-health problems are important. But it would be just as phony for me to do a little quick research and come up with all kinds of recommendations in a field I don't know anything about. Let's go back to the original purpose of this speech. What I'm trying to do is to form a committee to publicize mental-health problems—that's a subject I do know something about. I'm going down to Atlantic City, not to convince a lot of doctors that mental health is important, but to show them *I* know it's important. I'm trying to make myself a rallying point, to bring the doctors and a committee of publicity boys together. Somebody's got to do it if anything's ever really going to get done about mental health, and it looks as though the finger's been pointed at me. It won't be an easy job, but it's a necessary one."

"I see," Tom said.

"Now, I can't stand up and propose a committee right off the bat —that would be pushing it too hard and would invite misinterpretation. Never forget that there are always a million cynics ready to read the worst motives into anything we do. Before I try to start a committee, I have to demonstrate my interest and my availability. What this speech should say, in effect, is that I know the problem, and Barkus is willing if wanted. That's all. Do you get the picture?"

"I think so," Tom said.

"All right. We've been way off base on this speech. Try it for me from scratch, will you?"

"Be glad to," Tom said.

Hopkins turned his attention toward his scrambled eggs. Well, that's that, Tom thought, feeling a peculiar sensation of letdown. It all happened awfully fast, and I'm not sure where it leaves us. Hopkins finished his eggs and glanced at his watch. "Say, I've got to hurry—some people are waiting for me in my office," he said. "Can you have something for me by the end of the week?"

"I'll certainly try," Tom said, paused, and added, "I was wrong in advising you to make specific recommendations—I can see that."

Hopkins smiled. "You've helped me cut through a lot of fog on this," he said. "Can't thank you enough!" Waving cheerily, he pushed his chair sharply backward, and at his usual brisk gate almost trotted from the room.

That night when Tom got home to South Bay, Betsy immediately asked, "Did you see Hopkins?"

"Yes," Tom replied.

"I suppose you told him his speech is great," she said bitterly.

"No, I didn't."

"You didn't?" Betsy asked, her voice quickening.

"It didn't go the way I expected it to at all," Tom said. "I was completely honest with him, and I think he was with me. And what's more, he cleared up a doubt I've always had in the back of my mind—he showed me he's completely sincere about wanting to do something about mental-health problems. All this talk about his starting this committee just for a publicity build-up is a lot of nonsense —I'm sure about that now."

"You seem so astonished," she said, laughing. "You sound almost disappointed."

Tom grinned. "I don't know," he said. "Maybe I've been worrying too much about Hopkins' honesty and not enough about my own. Anyway, from now on I'm going to play it straight with him, and we'll see how it goes. I'm rather looking forward to fixing up that speech."

"Thank God!" Betsy said. "You know, for a while there, I wasn't sure *what* kind of a man I had married."

Tom glanced at her sharply. "Don't let's go into that," he said. "Let's have a drink. How about mixing up some Martinis?"

30

HOPKINS HAD TRIED to arrange to have lunch with his daughter the day after he had talked to his wife, but Susan had been busy. Now he was due to meet her in his apartment in half an hour. At quarter after twelve he said to the motion-picture producer with whom he had spent the morning, "I'm sorry, but I've got to be going. Can I see you tomorrow?"

"I've got to fly back to the Coast," the producer said. "How about lunch?"

"I'm sorry, I just can't today," Hopkins said. "I'll be in touch with you by phone."

The producer was an important man in the business, and he looked a little hurt. Hopkins shook hands with him, apologized effusively, and dashed for the elevator. Miss MacDonald had a taxi waiting for him. He gave the driver the address of his apartment and said, "Hurry."

When he got to his apartment, he let himself in and looked quickly around the big living room. No one was there. He walked through the dining room and poked his head into the kitchen, where the cook was fixing luncheon for two and the waitress was filling a silver bucket with ice cubes. "Has Miss Hopkins called?" he asked.

"No, sir," the waitress said. "No one's called all morning."

He returned to the living room and sat down. When the waitress brought in the ice, he mixed himself a drink and glanced at his watch. It was a quarter to one. He had talked over the telephone to Susan two days ago, and she had said she would be there at twelve-thirty. Well, anyone could be a quarter hour late. He glanced out the window and was suddenly seized with the fear that she simply would not come. Impatiently he got up, walked to his desk, and took out a draft of a promotion brochure. Picking a pencil from his pocket, he sat down and began to edit it.

A half hour later there was a timid knock on the door. He sprang from his chair, dashed across the room, and opened it. Susan stood there. "Hello," she said. "I'm sorry I'm late. The traffic . . ."

"It's all right!" he said. "Come in! Come in and sit down!"

She walked hesitantly into the room, which she had seen only once before, long ago, after her father had taken her and her mother to the theater. She was a slight, dark-haired girl with a good figure, who in a curiously elderly way leaned a little forward as she walked. Her face was beautiful, more because of an intense quality than any unusual symmetry of feature. She sat down and nervously lit a cigarette. "You wanted to talk to me?" she asked.

"Yes," he replied. "Have a drink. Ginger ale? Coca-Cola? Or something else? I guess you're old enough to drink now, aren't you?"

"It seems so," she said, smiling. "I'll have bourbon on the rocks."

He mixed her the drink, fussing perhaps a little too long with the silver ice tongs and the little tray on which he put the glass. After handing it to her and passing her a plate of canapés, he returned to his chair. She was glancing down into her glass with an abstracted look on her face, as though the glass were a crystal ball in which she could see her future. She is beautiful, he thought, and she's no child any more. I've got to handle this thing carefully.

"I suppose Mother told you I don't want to go to college, and now you're going to try to persuade me," she said suddenly without looking up.

"Of course I'm not!" Hopkins said without hesitation. "I don't want you to go to college if you don't want to!"

He had answered automatically, from instinct and long training in the handling of people, in spite of the fact that he had of course intended to try to persuade her. She glanced up at him, surprised. "What do you want to see me for, then?"

The arguments he had planned could not be used now. "I just want to talk to you in general about your future," he said. "Obviously, there's no point in our trying to send you to college if you don't want to go, but what are you going to do?"

"I don't know," she said, appearing a little confused. "I want to get married. Maybe before long."

"Anybody particular in mind?"

"I'm not sure yet."

"After marriage, what?"

She shrugged. "I'd like to travel," she said.

He sipped his drink slowly. "I've got a problem I've never discussed with you," he said. "It's a rather hard one to talk about, but perhaps we should."

"What kind of a problem?"

"It's difficult to describe. You are aware, I suppose, that the world has treated me pretty well. Over the years, I have gradually accumulated a good many responsibilities. I have been lucky, because they came to me gradually, and I had plenty of time to learn how to handle them. The curious thing is that all these accumulated responsibilities, or at least, a good many of them, could easily fall upon your shoulders quite suddenly, and you've had no opportunity to get ready for them. . . ."

"Are you talking about money?"

"In part."

"I'm not interested in money. I think it's a bore."

"No sane person is interested in money as such," he said.

"You've always seemed to be. I always thought it was all you were interested in. That's what everybody says."

"I'm sure they do," he said. "Susan, what's a million dollars?"

She shrugged.

"Go on—think about it and tell me."

"A lot of money, I guess."

"You'd be surprised how little. A million dollars is about half a small hospital. With a million dollars you could give all the children in a place like, say, South Korea, maybe one cupful of milk at each meal for two days. It isn't much, really, when you come to think of it, yet it represents the entire life earnings of about six average men —the whole working energy of six men during their entire lives. A million dollars is a lot of things. It's a college education for maybe a hundred boys. It's a home of their own for maybe seventy-five people. It's a pursuit plane for the Army, it's a new television station, but one thing it's not: it's not something any intelligent person can consider a bore."

"You're saying it's power," she said. "I'm not interested in power, either."

"Of course not. Neither am I. I wasn't trying to say money is power. I'm saying that when you hold a million dollars in your hand, you are in a very real sense holding the entire working lives of six men, and you better be damn careful what you do with it!"

"Are you trying to tell me you're going to leave your money to charity?"

"I don't know. I'm saying that we've got a problem we ought to start working on together, a responsibility that is mine, which someday may be yours. I got a lot of training before I was given any responsibility, and I am appalled to think what you may have to do without any training at all. Susan, do you know I have a bad heart?"

"No! No one told me."

"I never told your mother—there didn't seem to be any point in worrying her. It's not very bad, but it's at least conceivable that I could die any time. And frankly, Susan, leaving a lot of money to you would be like giving a gun to a baby!"

"I'm not going to let that part of it worry me," she said. "I hope nothing happens to you, but I'm not going to worry about money. I'm not going to let money ruin my life the way it's ruined yours and Mother's."

"Let's at least be accurate," he said dryly. "Money has not ruined your mother's life, and it has not ruined mine. I'm not willing to concede that either your mother or I have been more unhappy than most people, but if we have been, it's not because of money. The money has come as a by-product."

"It's stupid, the way you work all the time!" she said. "You don't know how to live. If I'd been Mother, I would have divorced you long ago. I don't know why you have to work all the time—ever since I can remember! I think you must have a guilt complex. You're a masochist!"

"Which of your friends is an amateur psychoanalyst? The playwright?"

"He understands people," she said in confusion.

"Tell him to stop trying to give pat explanations of men and women," Hopkins replied. "If he had learned that, his play might not have closed down so quickly."

"It was a great play!" she said. "The public just doesn't . . ."

". . . appreciate great art," Hopkins finished wryly for her. "I know. But Shakespeare didn't do badly in his time, and not many good plays today shut down as soon as they open. If you want to know what the public wants, I'll tell you: great art on the extremely rare occasions when it's available, but no phony art—they'd rather have good honest blood and thunder. The public doesn't like fakers, and neither do I. If you want to meet some playwrights, tell me, and I'll get some good ones up here for you."

There was a brief silence during which he got up and poured himself another drink. While his back was turned she said passionately, "I want to get some happiness out of life! I don't want to be like you and Mother. I want to have a good time. And no matter what you say, there's nothing wrong with that!"

He turned toward her slowly. "Of course there isn't," he said. "I just want to see that you set about it properly."

"I don't need any help. Not from you, anyway. I don't think you're anyone to be giving lessons!"

"I'm not trying to give you a lesson," he said. "I think we're getting a little off the subject. I'm talking about learning to handle responsibilities."

"I don't want to handle responsibilities. I want to get some fun out of life. It's time somebody in this family did!"

"How would you set about getting fun out of life?"

"I'd give parties. I'd give beautiful parties. I wouldn't try to change the world. I don't have any God complex. I just want to have a good time!"

"You'll get tired of parties," he said.

"Maybe. But by then I'll have had a good time!"

She was breathing hard, and he saw that she was upset. "Believe me, I want you to have a good time," he said gently, "but people who have that primarily in mind rarely accomplish it."

"What do you want me to do? You must have asked me up here alone for some reason. You never did anything like this before!"

"Look, Susan," he said. "I don't want you to continue accusing me and your mother. I'm quite ready to admit that I've made a great many mistakes, and that a great many things are the matter with me. I'm not apologizing to you—there would be no point to that. And there's no point in continuous accusations. The main thing is for us to see if we can start working together on what really are common problems. I can't undo the past, but I'm going to try to be of more help to you in the future."

"How?"

"I don't know yet. Let's think it over. I have a number of ideas. If you'd like, it might be nice if you moved into this apartment for a while—we could see each other evenings. Perhaps it would be fun for your mother and you and me to take a trip together somewhere. Someday it might be possible for me to arrange for you to get some sort of job working closely with me, if you'd like that. We both should think this whole matter over."

"I don't want to work with you!"

"You don't have to. I'm just trying to think of ways in which you might get some training if you don't want to go to college, and ways in which we might grow closer together."

"Why don't you leave me alone? You always have!"

"Susan," he said quietly, "when I was your age, I didn't have much money, and nobody paid much attention to me. I had a good chance to grow up. Now I've made a lot of money—I've never thought about it in this way before, but I suppose that if everything I have were liquidated today, there would be more than five million dollars. I know this talk of money shocks you—undoubtedly you think it vulgar. But I think this is a time for plain talking. For better or for worse, you're rich. It's nothing for you to be ashamed of, or proud of, or to worry about—it's just a fact. Now there are two kinds of rich—foolish rich and responsible rich. I've hated the foolish rich all my life, and I've never seen anybody who was foolish rich and happy for long. It seems to me that you're getting a good start on the way to being foolish rich. If you keep on the way your mother says you have been, you're going to make yourself miserable. You're going to get involved in a lot of half-baked marriages and divorces, and by the time you're thirty, you're going to find there's no way in the world for you to have a good time. A lot of this is my fault, but I refuse to go into that now. What I'm trying to do is help you and myself too. This is just as much my problem as it is yours, and I plan to do something about it. I'm asking your help."

She stared at him a moment. "Why are you doing this?" she asked finally. "Why the long speeches all of a sudden?"

"Because you're my daughter," he said. That sounded strangely inadequate, and he added awkwardly, "Because I love you."

"That's not true!" she exclaimed. "Don't be a hypocrite! You've hardly bothered to see me since I was born!"

He was shocked at her vehemence. "People love in different ways," he said.

"Why can't you be honest? You don't love me and you don't love Mother. To tell the truth, I don't think you love anyone—I don't think you love anyone in the whole world! And I don't want to be like that!"

Before he could say anything, she got up and fled from the apartment, slamming the door behind her. "Susie!" he called, getting up and following her. *"That's not true!"*

Frantically she rang for the elevator. He stood in the door of his apartment and said, "Come back and sit down. Let's be reasonable."

"I don't want to be reasonable," she replied. "You and Mother have been reasonable all your lives. I'm going to try something else."

Before he could answer, the elevator doors slid open, revealing the calm and aloof face of the girl who operated them. "Going down," she said. Susan stepped into the elevator, and the doors rumbled shut behind her. Hopkins was left alone.

31

EDWARD SCHULTZ WALKED UP the stairs to Judge Saul Bernstein's office. He wore a shabby raincoat over his uniform. He had always had his uniforms provided by his employer and for years had refused to buy a suit to wear on his day off. He walked into Bernstein's office boldly, without knocking, and stared for a moment at a man sitting in a wheel chair there. Then he turned and looked at Bernstein, who was sitting behind his desk. "You wanted me?" he asked harshly.

"Yes," Bernstein said calmly. "Sit down, Mr. Schultz."

Edward remained standing. "Who's he?" he demanded, jerking his thumb toward the man in the wheel chair.

"This is Mr. Sims, Mr. Rath's lawyer," Bernstein said. "Sit down, Mr. Schultz. We have some things we wish to talk over with you."

"Why isn't my lawyer here?"

"This isn't a trial, and you are at liberty to call your lawyer whenever you want," Bernstein said. "I suggest that you hear what we have to say first."

"We want to do you a favor," Sims said icily.

"A favor? What kind of a favor?"

"We think we can save you money."

Edward sat down in the nearest chair. "What do you mean?" he asked.

"We want to give you a preview of the hearings on this document you brought in signed by the late Mrs. Rath," Sims said quietly. "We think that might save you money—lots of it."

"She signed it!" Edward said.

"We know that," Sims replied. "But by a curious coincidence, she never told anyone about it, and there are no witnesses to her signature. Do you know why the law generally requires witnesses to a signature?"

"It doesn't always!" Edward said. "I read that any document can be considered a will if in the opinion of the court it represents the intention of the deceased." He spoke in a monotone.

"That's true," Sims replied gravely. "But there usually is some reason even for technicalities in the law. The reason that witnesses to a signature are generally required is that theoretically—theoretically, mind you—it would be possible for a man to trick an elderly woman into signing something without knowing it. I don't say that happened in this case, mind you—I just say it's theoretically possible."

"You can't prove that."

"Of course not," Sims replied soothingly. "Of course not. But if you persist in pressing your claim against the estate, there are a few facts I can prove, and I intend to bring them all before the court. For one thing, I intend to show it was part of your job to type up the checks Mrs. Rath used to pay her bills and to submit them for her signature. I also intend to prove that her eyesight was extremely poor during her later years. And finally, Mr. Schultz, I will prove that you are dishonest."

"How?"

"By presenting at least five witnesses who will swear that you asked them to pad bills," Sims said mildly.

Bernstein, who had been looking at Schultz's face, glanced away. His stomach was hurting badly.

"They're lying," Schultz said.

"I doubt that the court would think so," Sims continued evenly. "Our witnesses happen to be the most respected tradesmen in town. And there are other things we could look into. It might be interesting, for instance, to compare your bank balance with your income tax returns—that too might show you are dishonest."

Edward's face went white. "You can't . . ." he began.

"Just keep quiet a moment," Sims said. "I'm going to give you a chance to save your neck. If you withdraw this document of yours and sign a release giving up all claim to the Rath estate, you can get out of this by paying only a small fee to your lawyer for the trouble you've already caused him. It's entirely possible, of course, that your lawyer will sue you for giving him a fraudulent case, but that will be between you and him. If you continue your suit he'll be much more likely to sue you himself, and that won't be all. We may reconsider and sue for all the bills which you've been padding during the last thirty years. If you pursue this fraudulent claim, you'll walk out of here without a cent, and you may go to jail!"

"Wait a minute," Bernstein said. "You understand, Mr. Schultz, that we don't want you to sign any sort of release if you feel further investigation would clear you of the suspicions Mr. Sims has formed. If you have a clear conscience, I suggest you sign nothing and that you call your lawyer immediately. If, on the other hand, you know that Mr. Sims's suspicions are justified, you will probably be saving yourself and everyone concerned a lot of trouble if you drop your case here and now."

"I have prepared those papers," Sims said, pointing to some neatly typed documents on Bernstein's desk. "It is an ordinary release, and by signing it you will give up all claim to the Rath estate. I'd like you to sign all five copies, and we'll have a witness come in from next door."

Edward said nothing.

"If you don't sign, we'll go ahead with our case," Sims said. "I think I'll start by impounding your bank account."

"You're cheating me!" Edward said.

"Then don't sign and get out of here," Sims shot out. "If you think you're being cheated, call your lawyer, and we'll get on with the case. In the long run I think we might get more out of you that way, anyhow. We might collect forty or fifty thousand dollars."

Without a word, Edward walked to Bernstein's desk and seized the papers lying there. Standing like a speaker about to deliver an address, he read them, his lips moving slowly. Then he reached for a pen.

"Wait a minute," Bernstein said. "We want to call a witness."

He picked up the telephone, and a moment later an elderly woman who served as a Notary Public and worked in an insurance office next door stepped in. With a trembling hand Edward signed his name to all five documents. When he had finished, he stood watching the Notary impress her seal on them. Then he suddenly turned and bolted out the door.

When the Notary Public had gone, Sims said, "That's that."

"I'm glad it's over," Bernstein said, and sighed.

"I'll tell Tom Rath," Sims said. "I'll also tell him you deserve the credit for figuring this thing out."

"Oh, no!" Bernstein said in real alarm. "Don't do that—in conducting my own little investigation, I really exceeded the prerogatives of a judge. It wasn't ethical at all!"

Sims laughed. "Now if you'll help me down the stairs, I'll go up and see the Raths," he said. "I imagine they'll be happy to hear about this."

"Wait," Bernstein said. "You might as well give them the bad news with the good. I've just been appointed a member of the Zoning Board, and although I can't speak for the other members, I personally would not like to consider a housing project unless the town votes for a new school. If the people here won't build schools, we can't bring in a lot of new families. Ask Rath to hold up on his housing project, at least until the vote on the school next month."

That same morning Tom finished a new, much shorter draft of the speech. For the first time he himself liked what he had written, and he was anxious to find if Hopkins approved. Only an hour after he had sent the speech up to Hopkins, the voice box on his desk buzzed, and when Tom flipped it on, Hopkins' voice boomed, "Well, you've really done it, Tom! That's just what I wanted. Let's have lunch today by way of celebration."

"Thanks!" Tom said. "I'm glad we finally got it right."

"Come up in about ten minutes," Hopkins said. "Bill Ogden will join us, and we can talk about plans for following up the speech."

Only about five minutes after Tom had learned of this success, his telephone rang. It was Betsy, with the news that Edward had withdrawn his claim from the estate, and that in due time the house, land, and a small amount of money would be theirs. The two pieces of good news, arriving so close together, seemed extraordinary to Tom. "That's wonderful!" he said several times to Betsy, and to himself thought, Let this be a lesson to me. Sometimes things really do turn out all right. Grandmother was perfectly honest, and I never should have doubted her.

"There's only one thing for us to worry about now," Betsy said after he had told her that he had successfully completed the speech. "Bernstein says we shouldn't do anything about our housing project unless they pass a bond issue for a new school. If they vote that down next month, it may be ages. To tell the truth, I don't understand much about it—Bernstein says that in a few days there's going to be a public hearing on the whole thing that we ought to go to. Anyway, don't let's worry about that now. Tonight we're going to have a *double* celebration."

"That will be swell," Tom said. "I've got to see Hopkins now. Don't cook anything tonight—let's all go out somewhere."

He started up to Hopkins' office. As soon as he got in the elevator, he saw Caesar at the controls. "Going up," Caesar said in his deep voice. "Going up. Face the front, please."

The elevator was crowded. Tom edged toward Caesar. On this day of good luck, it seemed that anything could happen, and he half expected Caesar to tell him that he had just heard from Maria, that she was doing fine and didn't need any help at all. Instead, Caesar, who had a strong sense of propriety, barely glanced at him, and all he said was, "Floor, please. Going up. Face the front."

He couldn't have heard anything about Maria, Tom thought. If he had, he would have nodded to me or something. He hurried to Hopkins' office, feeling somewhat subdued.

Hopkins led the way to a taxi and told the driver to take them to the River Club, where they were going to meet Ogden. It was cold— the first cold day of autumn. Many of the women on the street were already wearing their fur coats. When they passed St. Patrick's Cathedral, Tom saw on the wide stone steps a worn woman with a shawl around her head leading a thin child, a little boy wearing only a light summer coat, which the wind was whipping around his legs. The cathedral looked like one which was not far from Maria's apartment in Rome. Tom remembered the first time Maria had taken him there, two days after he had met her, and before he had known her very well—he had been surprised that a girl he had picked up in a bar wanted to take him to church. She had been insistent about going, and he had agreed, feeling, if anything, indulgent. The moment he had stepped into the cathedral that had changed. Somewhere an organ had been playing softly. The ceiling had arched up so high that it disappeared in the shadows. The air had smoldered with incense. Along the walls had been life-sized statues of saints, their faces exalted and serene. In front of the saints had been racks holding tiers of many short thick candles—at first glance, the whole interior of the cathedral had seemed to be sparkling with innumerable small flames. He had never been in a Catholic church before and had watched, entranced, as one person after another stepped up to the statues of the saints, lit a candle, placed it carefully on the rack among all the others, then knelt in prayer. Taking him by the hand, Maria had led him to the statue of the Virgin and had made him kneel beside her. He had glanced from the simply carved but compassionate face of the statue to Maria, kneeling beside him with her lips moving silently, and he had felt no irony and no hypocrisy in kneeling before the Virgin with a girl he had picked up in a bar. After that he and Maria had gone to the cathedral often. He had said good-by to her there. After he had received his orders to go, and after she had told him she expected a child, she had insisted that they go to the cathedral one more time together. And she had not prayed for herself—she had prayed for him. Knowing how scared he was of death, she had knelt with him before the Virgin, and she had prayed for him. "After you have gone, I will come here often and light a candle for you," she had said. And he had cried—for the first time in his adult life he had cried when he said good-by to her.

Now, riding past St. Patrick's Cathedral in New York on this day of his good luck, Tom wondered whether she had lit many candles for him. Now he was safe, and everything was turning out beautifully for him, but where was she? He had a sudden impulse to leap out of the moving taxicab, run into the cathedral, and light a candle for her.

At luncheon Hopkins was effusive in his praise of the speech, and Ogden gave even more satisfaction by seeming pained at the compliments Tom got, but the thoughts set in motion by the glimpse of the worn woman with a thin little boy in the cold wind on the steps of St. Patrick's Cathedral robbed Tom of a feeling of victory. It is strange, he thought, that almost always there is so much irony in success.

"*A fundamental responsibility* . . ." Hopkins was saying.

"What?" Tom asked, bringing himself back to the luncheon conversation with difficulty.

"We people in the business of communications have a fundamental responsibility to bring key issues to the attention of the public," Hopkins continued. "I think this speech we've worked out is an excellent example. . . ."

Tom couldn't concentrate, and Hopkins' voice seemed to fade away. *Maria,* Tom thought, *Maria.* Somehow the very name sounded heartbreakingly lonely and forlorn. He felt as though he had been awakened suddenly in the night by the distant echo of a cry for help.

32

I⊤ was eight-fifteen on the evening of the fifteenth of September. The Grand Ballroom of the big hotel in Atlantic City had been changed into an auditorium by filling it with rows of chairs. About fifteen hundred physicians were sitting there holding printed programs on their laps. The room hummed with conversation, which gradually subsided as a tall, white-haired doctor in a dinner coat stood up behind the lectern at the head of the room. The tall man stood there smiling until the room was quiet. "Gentlemen," he said, "we have a distinguished speaker here tonight, a man whose influence is felt in almost every home in America—every home which has a radio or television set. This is a man who without ever seeking personal fame has been behind almost every public-service advertising campaign which has taken place in the past twenty years. He has been one of the leaders in marshaling public opinion in the fight against polio, heart disease, and cancer. He is not a physician himself, but I think it fair to say that indirectly he has been responsible for saving more lives than any of us. Gentlemen, I present to you Mr. Ralph Hopkins, president of the United Broadcasting Corporation!"

There was mild applause. Ralph Hopkins, who had been sitting in one of the front rows, walked to the platform and stood behind the lectern. He looked astonishingly small, almost frail. He placed a black notebook containing the speech Tom had written for him on the lectern, looked up, and coughed apologetically. Tom, sitting in a back row, thought with astonishment, He's nervous—the poor guy doesn't like to make speeches, and he's scared. Hopkins waited until the applause died down. Then in a small, unassuming voice, he said, "Dr. Stutgarten, and other distinguished physicians: it is a great pleasure for me to have this opportunity to talk to you tonight. As a layman, I feel peculiarly honored to be invited to address this gathering of doctors. I will not keep you long. . . ."

He paused. The audience waited without a sound.

"Now, we laymen look at disease somewhat differently than you doctors do," Hopkins continued in a firmer voice. "In the first place, we're scared of disease and don't like to talk about it much. When something goes wrong with us, we go to a doctor and put the whole burden on his shoulders. We don't tend to believe that there's anything *we* can do about disease ourselves, and almost the last thing which occurs to us is that the doctor might need help. Of course, there actually isn't much a patient can do to help his doctor, except to follow his advice, but there is, I think, a legitimate responsibility the public as a whole has toward its physicians. We laymen must make sure we have a broad understanding of the problems the physicians face and that the physicians have the tools they need to find solutions."

Hopkins looked up from his notebook to smile hesitantly at the audience, then glanced down again. "Now, the medical profession," he went on, "has done wonders with the conquest of the physical diseases—we all know how the human life expectancy has been extended. But while this progress has been going on, the incidence of

-239-

mental illness has been rising, as we all know. The question I want to pose here tonight is whether there is anything the public could do to help the doctors conquer this problem. It is my belief that the public has failed the medical profession worst in this area, because the public is the most scared of mental illness and understands it least of all. I am wondering if something couldn't be done to bring the problem of mental illness into the open and get together the funds necessary to make a major frontal attack upon it."

It was an odd sensation, Tom found, to sit in the audience and hear the words he had written come back to him. He did not feel very proprietary about the words. If I myself said them, they would mean little, he thought, but coming from Hopkins, they mean a lot. He listened as Hopkins continued to develop his theme. At the end of precisely twenty minutes, Hopkins concluded by saying, "There is a possibility that some organization might be formed, similar in purpose to the March of Dimes, to subsidize research on mental disease, but, beyond that, to banish unreasonable fear. In such an effort, the medical profession would have to take the lead. I think you can be sure that those of us whose business it is to transmit information to the public will do everything we can to help."

He stopped abruptly and folded his notebook. The audience clapped politely, almost enthusiastically, and several doctors walked up to the lectern to congratulate him. Hopkins stood in the middle of a small circle of physicians, shaking hands and smiling. Then he moved slowly toward the lobby and, followed by a growing group of physicians, headed toward the elevators.

Fifteen minutes later, Tom walked into the crowded living room of Hopkins' suite and found Hopkins drinking with a group of the leaders of medical associations. Several of them were urging him to start a mental-health committee. "It's nice of you to suggest it," he said. "I'm not at all sure I'm the man to take the leadership and I'm so pressed for time. . . ."

"How do you think it went?" Tom asked Ogden, who was standing in a corner sipping a highball, next to a vase of long-stemmed roses.

"Fair," Ogden said. "Just about fair, I'd say. The advance publicity wasn't much. We'll see what the morning papers do with it."

As it happened, the morning papers played the story up. Some of them put it on the front page, but Hopkins barely glanced at the clippings Ogden handed him. He seemed much more impressed by the many requests he got from doctors to start the committee. "I didn't sense a bit of opposition," he said to Tom. "I know that speech was a lot of work, but I think it's done exactly what we intended."

33

WITHOUT WARNING, on September 16, Susan Hopkins eloped with Byron Holgate, an aging playboy with an affectionate smile. Ralph Hopkins heard about it in his office on one of his own company's three o'clock news broadcasts soon after he returned from Atlantic City. He immediately called his wife in South Bay. She answered the telephone herself. "Hello," she said, and her voice sounded so dead that he knew she had heard about it and had not hurried to let him know.

"I just heard about Susan," he said. "I'll be right out."

"No," she said dully.

"I want to."

There was no response.

"I want to," he said again.

"I know."

"I'll be right out."

"I'm tired," she said. "I'm terribly tired."

"Of course. Go to bed and I'll see you in an hour."

No answer.

"I think I'll stay out there with you, Helen," he said. "I think I'll give up the apartment here in town."

There was a pause, and then, as though he hadn't spoken, she said, "Ralph, will you do me a favor?"

"Of course!"

"Have one of your secretaries get me a ticket on one of those cruises that go around the world."

"I'll go with you," he said.

There was another long pause before she said, "That's awfully nice of you, dear, but I think I want to be alone for a few months. I'm awfully tired."

"Of course," he said.

"One more thing. Could you get rid of this place out here? I don't know—with Susan gone, there doesn't seem to be much point to it any more. I don't want to have to worry about it."

"Leave it to me," he said. "I'll have it put on the market, or think of something to do with it."

"Thank you, dear," she said, and there was still another long pause.

"I'm going to start driving out now," he said. "I'll see you in an hour."

"Ralph," she replied, "would you mind waiting? I don't know, I don't want to talk to anybody right now. I just want to go to bed."

"I understand," he said.

"I'll see you in a few days. Get me on a boat that leaves as soon as possible, will you?"

"I'll make all the arrangements."

"Thank you, dear," she said quietly. "Good-by."

Later that afternoon Miss MacDonald told Tom that Hopkins would like to see him that evening at seven o'clock. At two minutes after the hour, Tom knocked at Hopkins' door. Hopkins opened it. He was alone, and to Tom's surprise, he looked tired. He was pacing restlessly up and down the room jingling the change in his pockets and gesticulating as he talked. The first thing he said after greeting Tom was, "I've definitely decided to go ahead with this mental-health committee. I want to get rolling on it now fast."

"Maybe we should start by . . ." Tom began.

"Wait a minute," Hopkins said. "Here's what I want to do. I'm

– 242 –

going to expand it beyond the publicists—I want a really representative group. Begin by asking about a dozen people to form an Exploratory Committee—choose the people we'll eventually want as trustees. For labor, Bill Krisky. For a Catholic, Fred Bellows. For a Jew, Abraham Goldberg. For a liberal, Mary Harkins. For a hard-shelled businessman, I'll do. For a Democrat, Pete Cronin. For a Republican, Nat Higgins. How many is that?"

"Seven," Tom said. He was taking notes furiously.

"All right. For a Negro, Herbert Shaw. For radio and television, I'll do. Sam Peterson for newspapers. Ted Bailey for mass circulation magazines. We should have an intellectual: make it Harold Norton, up at Harvard."

"That's eleven." Tom said.

"What are we missing? Oh, somebody from the movies. Ross Pattern. Make that the first twelve. Write letters of invitation to them tomorrow for my signature and find out a convenient day for all of us to meet at the Waldorf next month."

"Right," Tom said.

"Now an advisory medical panel. Make it seven members. The heads of all the major medical associations, and fill up the rest of it with the best psychiatrists—make sure you don't get the crackpots."

"I've got a list all made up," Tom said.

"Fine—show it to me tomorrow. Now a tentative program—enclose it with your letter of invitation. We'll start with a broad publicity barrage aimed to make people more aware of mental-health problems. We'll want spot announcements on both television and radio, all networks. Have films and records made to send out to the local stations. Get the agencies to work on the copy and bring me samples as soon as possible. I'd play up the theme, 'An enemy in the dark is more dangerous than one in the light—bring the problem of mental illness into the open!' That's not the wording, of course—I'm just thinking out loud."

"I'll get the agencies to work on it," Tom said.

"Start getting the National Mental Health Committee incorporated."

"I've done the spade work on that already."

"Good—make sure the lawyers have it done as soon as the Exploratory Committee meets."

Hopkins continued to pace as he spoke. He ordered drafts of the preliminary program readied for the foundations, lists of possible members, bylaws, and news releases announcing the formation of the committee.

"Now the program," he said. "First, your general publicity barrage —and while you're on that, make sure that mats are sent to all newspapers and that plates are made up for the magazines. See if the Advertising Association will foot the bill. The advertising boys ought to arrange for outdoor posters and car cards for buses and subways, too. Second, we'll want a small study group to develop a long-range plan for attacking the problem. I've already got foundation support lined up for that. Don't worry about the money on this—all the foundations are interested in the study part of it."

He paused, walked over to a table, and poured himself a drink. "Now Tom," he said, "I want you to carry the ball on this. You did a grand job on that speech—I think I can count on you. You've got the signal. I'm not going to be able to give this project much time, other than to arrange the financing and look over your plans just before they're final. I've got several new projects underway. Wrap this whole thing up for me. Figure out the details for yourself. Just remember that nothing can go until after the Exploratory Committee meets, but you've got to be ready to jump the next day. The Exploratory Committee won't do anything but approve what we submit to them, and you can't expect any work from them."

"We'll get everything ready," Tom said.

"And while you're making your publicity plans, don't forget the outdoor advertising boys. I want this campaign to break in all media within a week after the full committee is formed, and I want the full committee formed within a month after the Exploratory Committee meets. So you've got to work fast."

"We can do it," Tom replied.

Hopkins smiled. "Thanks, Tom," he said.

Tom stood up to go. He was surprised when Hopkins added, "Don't rush. Sit down and have a drink."

"Sure," Tom replied, sitting down again. "Sure." Expecting more directions concerning the mental-health committee, he took his pad out of his pocket and held it ready.

"Put that thing away," Hopkins said, and then with unusual hesitation in his voice, "I don't know, I just thought it might be fun to sit and talk a little while."

"Of course," Tom said, feeling curiously embarrassed. There was a moment of silence. Hopkins got up, mixed two strong highballs, and handed one to Tom. Tom was astonished to see him drink his very fast. The silence became painful.

"Do you have any children?" Hopkins asked suddenly.

"Yes," Tom said.

"How many?"

"Three."

"That's a nice family," Hopkins said. He mixed another drink for himself and to Tom's surprise stretched out comfortably on the couch. He seemed to be staring at Tom—he never turned his eyes away from him. On his face was an expression Tom had never seen there before: a look of exhaustion, confusion, and, incongruously, great kindness.

"Do you like working on this mental-health committee?" Hopkins asked after an awkward interval of silence.

"Yes," Tom said. "I like it very much."

"What are your plans?"

"I don't know," Tom replied. "I want to do my job here as well as I can, I guess, and see where it leads."

"That's the best way. When I was your age, I didn't have any plans—I was just thinking about the job at hand."

There was another interval of silence, during which Hopkins apparently was thinking, but he never took his eyes off Tom's face.

"I had a son once," Hopkins said suddenly. "He was killed in the war."

"I'm sorry to hear that," Tom said, although he had heard it before.

"Were you in the war?"

"Yes."

"Back in the First World War, I was a lieutenant, but I never got overseas. The war ended about two days after I got my commission."

"You were lucky."

"I guess I was," Hopkins said.

Tom sipped his drink. He was tense and wary, terribly conscious that it was important for Hopkins to like him.

"How did you happen to get interested in working on this mental-health project?" Hopkins asked abruptly.

Tom started to say, "I've always been interested in mental health," but he remembered how ridiculous that had sounded the last time he said it. I made up my mind I was going to play it straight with him, he thought, and I will. Aloud he said, "I was working over at the Schanenhauser Foundation. I needed more money, and a friend told me there was an opening in your public-relations department. I applied for it, and Mr. Walker steered me into this."

"That's the way I got started in radio," Hopkins said. "After I got out of the Army, I worked a few years for a brokerage house, and I hated it. A friend told me a magazine was hiring people. I walked over there, and they didn't have a place for me, but the personnel man said a new broadcasting company was being started in the same building. I walked in and was hired."

There was a pause. "When I was a boy, I wanted to be an actor," Hopkins continued, "a Shakespearean actor. That was my 'ambition for about five years. I used to try out for all the high-school plays, but I wasn't much good, and they always got me to be stage manager."

"I don't think I ever knew what I wanted to be," Tom replied.

"I wonder whether this mental-health project is right for you," Hopkins said contemplatively. "I think you have a lot of 'capabilities. You look at things straight—I like the way you brought that speech down to the ground. And you're at an important stage 'of your career. How old are you?"

"Thirty-three."

"That's an 'important age. In the next six or seven years, you should really be on your way."

"Do you think there will be many opportunities with the mental-health committee?"

"Yes—of a kind. Of course, there's always a limit to that sort of thing. Organizations which don't make money never pay much, and the top planning is done by volunteers. There's a limit to how far you can go as a staff member on that sort of thing."

"What do you think I should do?"

"I don't know," Hopkins said thoughtfully. "It depends on what you want, I guess. Is money important to you?"

"Yes."

"I could look around the company and see if I could find a spot for you."

"I'd appreciate that," Tom said. Under Hopkins' kindly but steady gaze he felt as tense as though he were waiting for a parachute jump.

"The business world is different than it was when I was young," Hopkins said. "It's tougher and more competitive."

"I guess it is."

"A young man has to get started right. The ideal thing is to find a job which always expects a little more than you can deliver, but not so much that you get snowed under. A job should always keep you straining at the limits of your abilities. That's the way men learn."

"I guess it is," Tom repeated.

"How do you assess your own abilities? What do you *like* best? If you could choose any branch of the business, what would you take?"

There was a pause while Tom wondered whether honesty should be pushed to the point of self-depreciation. I can't fool him, he thought—he's not a guy who can be fooled. I'd better go on telling him the truth. "I don't know what my abilities are," he said. "I'd like to find out. I'm afraid that the branches of the broadcasting business I'd really enjoy are probably the ones I know least about, and if I got into them, I might not like them as much as I think."

"What are they?"

"I'd like to analyze the news," Tom said, entirely to his own astonishment. "I'd like to study the news and give my views on it. I know I don't have any qualifications at all for that kind of job."

Hopkins smiled wryly. "That's like me wanting to be an actor," he said. "If you wanted to be a news commentator, I'm afraid you'd probably have to put in a long apprenticeship on a newspaper, and there might be a good deal of voice training involved. There aren't many jobs for news commentators—there are at least a hundred applicants for every opening."

"I know," Tom said, "but you asked me what I'd really like, and that came into my mind. It's not a thing I've thought about. To tell you the truth, I've always just gone along taking what I could get."

"If you really wanted to broadcast news, and were willing to devote the time and effort to it, you probably could," Hopkins said. "I'm afraid the job isn't as good as you think it is. It pays comparatively little, and unless you're something special, it's pretty routine."

"I know," Tom said. "With me, it's probably just a case of far fields looking greener."

There was a pause, during which Tom regretted his frankness. I've made a fool of myself, he thought. I should have told him what I really want to be is a good administrator. That's a field in which he could really help me. Hopkins' eyes were still upon him. It was disturbing, that steady, unabashed gaze, the eyes tired, the whole face exhausted, yet so curiously intense and kind.

"How would you like to be my personal assistant?" Hopkins asked suddenly.

"What?"

"I mean, not just on this mental-health thing—someone to help me with everything I do. I don't really have a personal assistant. Walker is in public relations, and Ogden is going to be a vice-president before long. I've never had a personal assistant—I've never wanted one. But I like the honesty of your approach, and it strikes me that you might be able to help out in many ways. The job would give you a chance to watch lots of operations in the company and see what you're best fitted for. Who knows? Maybe you could learn something." These last words were said with an attempt at jocosity and self-disparagement which was utterly unlike Hopkins. Seeming ill at ease, he got up and poured himself another drink.

"I'm sure I could learn a lot," Tom said. "It would be a great opportunity."

Hopkins stood with his back toward him, putting ice in his glass. When he turned around, his briskness had returned, and he seemed his old self again. "I'll talk to Bill Ogden about it in the morning," he said. "We'll see what we can work out. I'm afraid it's getting late—your wife will be angry at me. Thanks for coming up. It's *so* nice of you to give up your evening."

When Tom got to Grand Central Station that night, he bought a paper to read on the train home. On the front page he saw a story about the marriage of Susan Hopkins to Byron Holgate, whose age was given as forty-eight, but who, in an accompanying photograph, looked much older. After reading the article, Tom folded the paper and sat thinking about Hopkins all the way home to South Bay. When he got to his house, he found Betsy waiting up for him. "Hopkins wants me to leave the mental-health committee and become his personal assistant," he said.

"Why, that's wonderful," she replied. "What a marvelous opportunity! It must mean he likes you."

"I guess it does."

"You don't sound very excited about it."

"I don't know," Tom said. "I'm trying to figure it out. It *is* a marvelous opportunity—there's no doubt about that. But I'm not sure I want to be given a job simply because a man likes me. I'm not sure it's good business."

"What do you mean?"

"I don't want to have to depend on somebody's friendship. I want to feel that any time I want to quit a job, or any time my boss dies or retires, I can walk two doors down the street and get something as good or better. It's not smart business to depend on friendship— it's too risky."

"What makes you think he's hiring you because of friendship? He liked that speech you wrote. He must think that you're simply the best man for the job."

"I don't know," Tom said. "He's never had a personal assistant before. And the way he was tonight—it's hard to explain. He was trying to do something for me."

"Is there anything wrong with that?"

"No—I should be grateful. But I don't know what he *can* do for me. For a child, yes—a man can make sure a child gets a good education, and all the rest of it. But for another man, no. After all, what could Hopkins do for me? Keep me on as a ghost writer? I'd hate that as a full-time career. There's nothing dishonest about ghost writing, really, but the whole idea of it makes me uncomfortable. I don't like being the shadow of another man. Should I ask him to give me a top administrative job? I wouldn't know what to do with it if I had it. I must be getting old or something—I'm beginning to realize my limitations. I'm not a very good administrator—not compared to guys like Hopkins and Ogden. I never will be, and the main reason is, I don't want to be. This sounds like a silly way to put it, but I don't think you can get to be a top administrator without working every week end for half your life, and I'd just as soon spend my week ends with you and the kids."

"Some good administrators don't work all the time."

"A few—damn few. It's the fashion nowadays for them to pretend they don't work as hard as they do. After all, running any big outfit is incredibly hard work. You know what a good administrator has to do? He has to keep a million details in his mind all at the same time, and he has to know how to juggle people. Why do you think Hopkins is great? Mainly, it's because he never thinks about anything but his work, day and night, seven days a week, three hundred and sixty-five days a year. All geniuses are like that—there's no mystery about it. The great painters, the great composers, the great scientists, and the great businessmen—they all have the same capacity for total absorption in their work. I like Hopkins—I admire him. But even if I could, I wouldn't want to be like him. I don't want to get so wrapped up in a broadcasting business that I don't care about anything else. And I'm afraid that in asking me to be his personal assistant, he's trying to make me be like him, and I know that's foolish. I never could do it, and I don't want to."

"Aren't you making this awfully complicated?" Betsy asked. "He's offered you a better job. Maybe a raise will go with it."

"Maybe. But this *is* complicated! What it all comes down to is, what do we want? He asked me that tonight: what do I want? I tried to answer him straight, but I was too confused to think. He asked me whether money is important to me, and I said yes, but I forgot to say why. I want money to help us enjoy life, but that's not what a guy like Hopkins wants. He doesn't care any more about money than a good violinist does. He's totally absorbed in his work —nothing else matters to him. You could pay him in medals or in beans, you could put him in the middle of the Sahara Desert, and he'd still find some way to go on working day and night. Something about the way he acted tonight scared me. It sounds crazy, but I think he wants to try to create me in his own image and I don't want any part of it."

"What makes you think that?"

"Figure it out for yourself. Hopkins doesn't need a personal assistant—he has three secretaries and Ogden and Walker helping him already, and he's always been careful to keep his relationship with all those people anything but personal. The whole time I've known him, he's never had the slightest personal interest in me. And now all of a sudden he wants me to be his personal assistant. Why?"

"Because he likes that speech you did for him," Betsy said.

"Partly. But you know something? His daughter got married today—I read it in the paper on the way home. And his son got killed in the war—I'd heard that, and he told me about it tonight. I think the poor guy's just lonely, and he's trying to hire a son."

"If that's the way he feels, it could still be pretty good for you," Betsy said.

"I don't think so. When he found I couldn't get to be like him, he might get sick of me—he might get sick of me pretty soon, anyway. You can't tell. Playing with a guy like that is like petting a tiger—any time he wants to turn on you, he can. I don't want to be in a position like that."

"What are you going to do, turn him down?"

"No—that might hurt his feelings. As I say, this is like petting a tiger—you have to be awfully careful. And the funny part of it is, I'd like to be his personal assistant for three reasons: I might learn something, it would be a good recommendation for anything else I wanted to do later, and I like the guy. I think I better take the job, but I'm going to have to keep my fingers crossed—nobody can tell how it's going to turn out. When he finds I have no idea in the world of trying to be like him, he may get mad—and then he may fire me altogether."

34

AT QUARTER TO SEVEN the next morning Betsy came into the bathroom while Tom was shaving and said, "I don't know what to do. Janey says she won't go to school."

"She give any reason?"

"No. She just woke up and announced that she wasn't going. I told her that she had to, and she said she simply wouldn't."

"Why don't you let her stay home a day or two," Tom said. "At her age it wouldn't matter."

"If I let her stay home, Barbara will want to stay too—she's not very happy about going herself. As a matter of fact, I wouldn't be surprised if she wanted to go even less than Janey does, but she's different. She does what she thinks she has to do."

"I'll talk to Janey," Tom said.

"The trouble is, I really don't blame the child," Betsy said. "It's such an awful-looking school!"

Tom wiped the soap off his face and walked to the bedroom his daughters shared. Janey was sitting on her bed, still dressed in her pajamas. Her face was set in a determined expression, and her hands were folded stubbornly in her lap. On the other side of the room Barbara was slowly getting dressed. Her face looked strained.

"What's the matter, kids?" Tom asked. "Janey, if you don't hurry up and get dressed, you're going to be late."

"I'm not going to school," Janey said.

"Why not?"

"I'm just not going."

"You have to go," Tom said. "There's a law. Anyway, you wouldn't want to grow up without knowing anything."

"I'm not going," Janey said. From her face he saw she was about to cry.

"Did something happen at school yesterday?"

"No."

"Was someone cross to you?"

"No." She paused before adding, "I'm afraid."

"Afraid of what?"

"The hall."

"The hall? What do you mean?"

Janey said nothing.

"What's the matter with the hall?"

"Nothing," Janey said.

"I'll take you to school today and you can show me the hall. Will that help?"

Janey looked down at the floor, her face hopeless. She said nothing.

"School is fun when you get used to it," Tom said hesitantly. Still Janey said nothing.

"If you're a good girl and go nicely, I'll bring you home a present tonight. I'll bring you a surprise."

"All right," Janey said woefully. "If you'll go with me."

"I'll take you down," Tom said, and began to help her get dressed.

At breakfast Betsy said, "I can take her—you'll miss your train if you go."

"I'll take a later train," Tom said. "There's something about a hall that bothers Janey. I want to see this school."

Leaving Betsy at home with Pete, Tom put both his daughters in

– 253 –

the car and started down the road toward the school. He remembered being driven down the same road by a chauffeur during his own boyhood, only they had not stopped at the public school; they had gone beyond it to the South Bay Country Day School, where both Tom and his father had gone. The tuition had been six hundred dollars a year, even in the nineteen twenties. Tom wondered what it was now. It was ridiculous to feel that he had to send his children to a private school, he thought. In Westport, the public schools had been just as good as the private schools.

The traffic got heavy as they neared the public school. It was a weather-beaten brick building of Victorian design set in the middle of a black asphalt-covered play yard, part of which had been marked off to form a parking area. The school and its yard was surrounded by a high iron fence, as though it were a zoo. Tom drove through a gate and found a parking place adjoining the play yard, where children of widely varying age were running, jumping, and shouting together. He and his daughters walked up the front steps of the school and entered a narrow, high-ceilinged hall, the walls of which were painted a dull chocolate brown. The indefinable smell of an old school building was strong—sweat, chalk dust, and an incongruous trace of cheap perfume.

Suddenly an electric bell rang, reverberating harshly against the bare walls. Immediately a horde of children rushed through the door which Tom had just entered and dashed down the hall. They continued to funnel in from the playground, jostling and pushing each other. The hall quickly became overcrowded, and someone said, "Don't push!" in a high shrill voice. The children continued to jam in, and Tom felt a flash of claustrophobia. Janey clung tightly to his hand. She looked scared. "This is the hall," she said.

"Yesterday she got knocked down here," Barbara volunteered.

"It won't happen again," Tom said, his voice sounding false to himself.

"I guess I better go now," Barbara said. "My room's upstairs." She let go of Tom's other hand and was immediately swept away in the crowd. A few minutes later Tom caught a glimpse of her going up the stairs at the end of the hall, her small figure very erect.

"Stay with me," Janey said.

"I'll take you to your classroom," Tom said. "Where is it?"

Janey led the way to a crowded doorway and paused. Inside, Tom could see a small room with many desks jammed together. With so many children jostling by, it was hard to stand still. Janey suddenly let go of his hand. "Thanks," she said. He saw her go and sit at the very back of the room.

When Tom got outside, the fresh air felt good. He drove to the station and walked up and down the platform waiting for his train.

They shouldn't have a school building like that, he thought. They shouldn't have a school like that for *anybody's* children. It wasn't like that in Westport. It's not just that I can't afford to send my children to private school.

I wonder what kind of schools they have for the children of the poor in Rome, he thought. Suddenly he remembered how easy things had been for him in his boyhood. The old South Bay Country Day School had had ten or, at most, fifteen children in a class, and often the teachers had met with the pupils in the big living room of the old mansion which had been made into the school, and they had all sat in overstuffed chairs. How soft everything was made for me, he thought. Because his father had gone to the South Bay Country Day School, and because his grandmother had given generously to the school in the past, old Miss Trilly, the head mistress, had been especially kind to Tom and had once given a teacher a stern lecture for reprimanding him too harshly. Maybe it's better for my kids to begin the way they are, he thought, as he paced up and down the platform of the railroad station. Maybe they'll have less to learn later.

"Rowdies! Young Rowdies! They come from the public school!"

He remembered those words being spoken in a high, slightly nasal, indignant voice by Miss Trilly—she had said them often. The public-school children had frequently invaded the playground of the Country Day School to play on the slides and swings. Occasion-

– 255 –

ally they had picked fights with the Country Day children, and this is what had inspired old Miss Trilly's anger.

"They're from the *public school!*" she had said, incorporating a sly slur in the words which none of her pupils had missed.

Tom wondered whether Janey and Barbara would ever sneak into the playground of the Country Day School to play on the slides and the swings, and whether Miss Trilly, or her successor, would say, "They're from the *public school!*"

It doesn't really matter, he thought now, as he reached the end of the station platform and started to pace in the other direction. People are tough, even children. But good Lord, I ought to be able to do something. There's no particular democratic virtue in jamming so many children into a school like that. Janey isn't going to learn much by being knocked down in the hall.

Money, I need money, he thought. If they don't build a new public school, I should be able to afford a private school. I should get everything but money out of my head and really do a job for Hopkins. I ought to be at work now. He glanced at his watch and saw it was quarter after nine—the train was late.

Money, Tom thought. The housing project could make money, but it depends on re-zoning, and Bernstein says we shouldn't ask for that until they vote on a new school.

A new school, he thought—so much depends on that! Bernstein says there's going to be a hearing on it and that a lot of people are against it. I should find out all the details. I should work for a new school, and I should work harder for Hopkins, and I should be making plans for our housing project. Where did I ever get the idea that life is supposed to be anything but work? A man's work should be his pleasure—I shouldn't expect anything more.

Far up the track the train blew its whistle. He joined a throng of men pushing to get aboard the train and, with chin on his chest, sat thinking about his daughters' school.

35

Two days later, Tom moved into Hopkins' outer office. He sat at a desk in a corner—it had been necessary to move Miss MacDonald's desk and those of the two typists to make room for him. Hopkins' ffice had not been designed with accommodations for a personal as- :stant. Miss MacDonald seemed flustered by the change. She sat at her desk nervously thumbing through correspondence, and whenever Tom said anything to her, she answered with an exaggerated politeness which was almost worse than the coldness which Ogden displayed. The two stenographers kept glancing from Miss MacDonald to Tom, as though they expected a battle to start between them. Tom missed his private office and his own secretary. In its exterior aspects, the change seemed more like a demotion than a promotion.

A half hour after Tom arrived at his new desk, Hopkins came out of his inner office. "Good morning, Tom!" he said briskly. "Good to have you here!"

"Good to be here!" Tom said. He had developed a hesitancy about whether to call Hopkins by his first name. "Mr. Hopkins" now sounded impolitely formal, and "Ralph" sounded brash. He avoided using either name whenever possible.

"I've got some correspondence I'd like you to answer for me," Hopkins said. "Miss MacDonald, you can give Mr. Rath the morning's mail after I've looked it over and let him rough out the replies."

"Yes, sir," Miss MacDonald said.

Hopkins returned to his inner office. An hour later Miss MacDonald brought Tom a wire basket containing about thirty letters. Some were requests from charities, some suggested various new projects for United Broadcasting, and others concerned complex business transactions already underway. On the latter Hopkins had written in his small, neat handwriting, "See me." On some of the simple requests he had written, "Tell him no," and on others, "Tell him yes." On still others he had written, "Maybe—don't commit us."

Tom was not surprised at all this—he knew that the stage after having a girl to take dictation is to have someone to do the dictating. He had often written letters for Dick Haver at the Schanenhauser Foundation. Calling one of the stenographers over to his desk, he began the letters for Hopkins' signature. In reply to a letter from a newly formed charity on which Hopkins had scribbled, "Tell him no," he said, "I was most interested to see the information you sent me, and I certainly agree with you that this is an important and worthy endeavor, but it is necessary for us to plan ahead on this sort of thing, and I'm afraid that we've already committed ourselves so heavily on other similar projects that we won't be able to include this one on our list of contributions now. I certainly hope your program is successful, however, and at some later time we would be glad to give your needs thorough consideration. Sincerely, Ralph Hopkins, president, United Broadcasting Corporation."

When he had several similar letters typed up, he sent them into Hopkins' office. To his surprise, they came back almost immediately with carefully inked corrections on them. Most of the letters had been made a little more gracious, a little more informal, but on the letter saying no to the charity, Hopkins had written to Tom, "Don't agree with him that project is important and don't wish him success. I never heard of this outfit. They might use my letter as an endorsement, and they might be phonies."

Tom glanced up, and, seeing that Miss MacDonald was looking at him smugly, he realized that she had been the one who had answered the letters before and that she was pleased to see his work needed correction. He called the stenographer to his desk again and redictated the letters.

A few moments later, Hopkins spoke to him through the inter-office communication box. "Come in and bring the rest of the mail," he said. Tom picked up the letters on which Hopkins had written, "See me," and entered the inner office. Hopkins was pacing back and forth, looking ill at ease. "The reason I'm having you start out on this mail is that I think it's the best way for you to learn how I work and to get an idea of some of the projects we have underway," he said. "Now, take that letter from Richardson at the Henkel Manufacturing Corporation. That's a long story. They manufacture

– 258 –

television sets which go out under various brand names. For some time we've been trying to work out a deal that will let us market our own sets—United Broadcasting Corporation sets. We've got two or three other companies interested in supplying the sets, but this is more than a matter of just getting bids. We're trying to work out a deal where we tie in with some big retailing outfit. . . ."

He talked on for a long time. To Tom, the whole subject seemed hopelessly complicated. "Anyway," Hopkins concluded, "the point is, we've got to stall Richardson now without letting him think we've lost interest. Tell him that several other people here want to study the specifications he sent us and that he'll hear from us in a few days."

Hopkins went on to discuss this and other letters, while Tom took notes. By the time Tom got back to his desk, his head was whirling.

"Mr. Ogden called you," Miss MacDonald said. "He wants you to call him back."

"Thanks," Tom replied, and immediately called Ogden. "Oh, Tom," Ogden said. "Can you drop in at about ten tomorrow to review what you've done for the mental-health committee?"

"Sure," Tom said. "I'll be there."

"There was another call for you," Miss MacDonald said as soon as Tom had hung up. "A Mr. Gardella. He said it was personal."

"Gardella?"

"Yes. He left his number. He wants you to call him back."

Miss MacDonald handed him a slip of paper with an outside telephone number written on it. Tom dialed it himself. "Hello," Caesar's deep voice answered.

"This is Tom Rath. Did you call me?"

"Yes, Mr. Rath," Caesar said. "I just thought I ought to tell you. . . ."

"Did you hear anything?" Tom interrupted.

"No—not yet. I just thought I ought to tell you that I've got a new job. Gina and I got a job taking care of a new apartment building over in Brooklyn—we're going to be custodians. We get an apartment for ourselves with the deal and everything. Anyway, I probably won't be around the United Broadcasting building much any more, but I wanted to tell you that when we hear from Maria, we'll let you know."

"You think you will hear?"

"Sure, sooner or later. When Louis gets on his feet, they'll get in touch with Gina's mother. Anyway, I'll let you know."

"Thanks," Tom said, and hurriedly added, "I'm glad you've got a good job. I wish you luck."

"Same to you," Gardella said. "Good-by."

Tom put the telephone receiver down. Miss MacDonald was looking at him curiously. Quickly he picked up a letter lying on his desk and started to read it. So Caesar's got a new job, he thought—I won't be running into him on the elevators any more. Suddenly he felt sure he would never see or hear from Caesar again. So that is my punishment, he thought—I probably never will know what happened to Maria and the boy. Maybe this is just retribution. The hardest thing of all for me is going to be never to know. She and the boy could be starving. They could be dead. Or they could be getting along fine. How strange it is never to know. He picked up the piece of paper on which Miss MacDonald had written Caesar's telephone number and carefully put it in his wallet.

The next morning Ogden said to Tom, "For the time being your duties as Mr. Hopkins' personal assistant will be in addition to your work on the mental-health committee. We'll start looking for someone else for that, but until we find someone, it's still your responsibility."

Tom hoped he'd go on and discuss an increase in salary. Instead, Ogden said, "As you know, Mr. Hopkins wants to get cracking on the mental-health committee. Fill me in now. Where are we?"

"I've been getting some tentative bylaws drawn up to show the exploratory committee when it meets," Tom said.

"Good. How about a statement on the background of this committee—something to tell how it got started."

"We haven't discussed that," Tom said.

"You mean you haven't even thought of it? It's the first thing

- 260 -

Hopkins will want. How did this whole thing begin, anyhow? Everybody's going to be asking that. You've got to answer it."

"I'll work something out," Tom said.

"Have you got sample news releases announcing the formation of the committee?"

"Yes."

"Suggested budget?"

"Nothing yet," Tom said. "We haven't discussed that."

"Haven't discussed it! Hasn't it ever occurred to you that someone might inquire how much this whole operation is going to cost? What's Mr. Hopkins going to say: 'I'm sorry, but we hadn't thought of that'?"

"I'll get some cost estimates together," Tom said.

"How about plans for staff? How much of a staff is this committee going to need when it gets going? You're going to have to answer that before you can make out a tentative budget."

"I'm sorry," Tom said hotly, "but I've never been able to get a very clear idea of just how big a project Mr. Hopkins is planning!"

"We're supposed to do the planning for him! That's what we're paid for. Get some data together! How much of a staff does the polio outfit have, and what did it start with? How about the cancer outfit? What are their budgets? You've got to think these things out for yourself!"

"I'll get some data together," Tom said.

"You better get cracking. This should have been done two months ago."

"I'll do my best," Tom said.

There was an instant of silence before Ogden said, "Now listen, Tom. You wrote a darn good speech for Mr. Hopkins—I know that. And I know you're Mr. Hopkins' personal assistant now, but that doesn't mean you can forget about this mental-health committee. It's going to grow. Mr. Hopkins can't be worrying about it all the time. He's got to be able to rely on you."

Ogden paused, and Tom waited without saying anything.

"Up till now," Ogden continued, "there hasn't been much we could do, but in the future, things will be different. There's a big administrative job to be done, and a big job of promotion. I of course won't be the one to determine where you will fit into the structure—ultimately, that will be up to you. It will depend on what you've shown us you can do. But if you're going to be Hopkins' personal assistant, you should get to the point where you anticipate his needs. Don't wait for me to tell you."

"I understand," Tom said. His face was hot.

"Thanks for coming up," Ogden said, and swung around in his swivel chair. Picking up the receiver of his telephone, he said, "Now, Miss Horton, you can put that call through to Denver." He remained with his back turned while Tom got up and walked out of the room.

When Tom returned to Hopkins' outer office, the first thing he saw was a pile of about fifteen thick leather-bound books on his desk.

"Mr. Hopkins asked me to give you those," Miss MacDonald said. "They're the company's annual reports—there are two to a volume. He said he thought you'd like to go through them."

"Thanks," Tom said. He sat down, picked up one of the books, and leafed through it. The pages were full of graphs and statistics showing the progress of United Broadcasting. Of course, he thought —I should be studying these. I should have asked for them myself. I bet Hopkins knows these by heart. Anyone who seriously intended to make this company his career should study its history. I should be spending every spare minute on these. He tried to read one of the pages describing a complicated division of stock. His mind wandered —it was difficult material. I should be getting that work on the mental-health committee done first, he thought—my background reading should be done on evenings and week ends. Work in the office on Saturdays and do your background reading on Sundays—hundreds do it. He glanced at his watch. It was only eleven o'clock. Suddenly he longed for the day to be over—he was ashamed to find that for no particular reason he felt exhausted, and he wanted to go home and relax. An hour and a half until lunch, and then another five and a half hours before he could reasonably catch the train to South Bay. The big sweep hand on his wrist watch seemed to crawl with maddening slowness. Hopkins rarely left his office before seven o'clock, and Tom had sensed he was annoyed to find that Tom usually left earlier. It was embarrassing to have to compete with Hopkins' hours —it was like taking a Sunday-afternoon walk with a long-distance runner. The stereotyped notion of the earnest young man arriving early and leaving late, and the complacent boss dropping in for a few hours in the middle of the day to see how things were going was completely reversed.

Tom rolled a piece of paper into his typewriter and began to write a brief statement describing the origins of the mental-health committee. After finishing it, he glanced at his watch again. Almost an hour before lunchtime—it was ridiculous to be so restless. I'll bet Hopkins never was a clock watcher, he thought.

"Don't wish time away."

The sentence came abruptly to his mind. Who had said that? It's just an old saying, he thought. "Don't wish time away." Suddenly he remembered sittting with Maria in the abandoned villa so many years before, looking at this same wrist watch and counting each second the way a miser might count his money.

We didn't wish time away, he thought. I've got to stop thinking about Maria. Time, he thought—I need more time. I've got to get this work done for the committee, and I've got to read the annual reports, and I must get our housing project going. I've got no business wishing time away.

Time, he thought: I wonder how much more time I've got? I'm thirty-three years old; that's the halfway point, really—I'm probably halfway through my life. What am I going to do during the other half, ride the commuters' train, and read annual reports, and write endless letters for Hopkins or someone like him, and pride myself on working every week end? Shall I make a full-time career of being Hopkins' ghost? Is that what I want?

I don't know, he thought—who the hell knows what he wants? It's ridiculous to think of the next thirty-three years stretching ahead like an endless uphill road. Don't wish time away.

There's something wrong, he thought. There must be something drastically wrong when a man starts wishing time away. Time was given us like jewels to spend, and it's the ultimate sacrilege to wish it away. He glanced at his watch and again found himself thinking of

Maria. She had not liked the watch. "Take it off," she had said. "I hate to hear it ticking."

That had been in her room, only a few days before he had left Rome. "Tick tock!" she had said derisively. "Tick, tick, tick, tick, tick! I would like to break it! And the buckle scratches me."

He had taken it off and put it on the floor beside the bed. The room had been very dark, and the luminous dial had glowed like the eyes of a cat.

"I can hear your heart beating," he had said.

"Kiss me. I don't want you to hear my heart beating."

"I love the sound of your heart and the sound of your breath."

Tom's thoughts were suddenly interrupted by the telephone ringing on his desk in the United Broadcasting building. He picked up the receiver. It was Betsy. "Hello," she said cheerfully. "Can you get home a little early tonight?"

"Why?"

"The PTA is having a meeting in advance of the public hearing on the new school. We ought to go—Bernstein says rumors about our housing project have got around, and we may get involved in the discussion tomorrow. We should get boned up on all the facts tonight."

"I'm afraid I won't be able to make it tonight," Tom said. "I'm. going to have to stay here and work late this evening. I may not be home until after midnight. And don't count on me for week ends for a long while."

"Why? What's happened?"

"Nothing. I just have a lot of work to do."

"Can't you do it some other time? This meeting is *important*."

"No. Don't count on me. I'll go to the hearing tomorrow, but I can't go anywhere tonight."

"All right," Betsy said resignedly.

Tom put the receiver down and turned toward his typewriter. That school thing is important, he thought—I should be helping to work for it. How interconnected everything is! If we could get the school, maybe we could get the housing project through and really make some money. Then maybe I could find and help Maria, and maybe I could work something out with Hopkins. Maybe I could

– 264 –

find a good honest job with him which would pay me a decent living, but not require me to work day and night, pretending I want to be some kind of a tycoon. What could I say to him? Could I say, look, when you come right down to it, I'm just a nine-to-five guy, and I'm not interested in being much more, because life is too short, and I don't want to work evenings and week ends forever? Could a guy like Hopkins ever understand that? Damn it, Tom thought, I'm not lazy! If there were some cause worth working for, I might not mind so much. But what's the great missionary spirit in United Broadcasting? It seemed to Tom suddenly that he had managed to get himself into a position which made it necessary to keep secrets from both his employer and his wife—that both, if they knew the truth about him, would abandon him. Maybe that's why I'm on edge all the time, he thought—I have to keep pretending. Maybe if I could tell Betsy about Maria, and if I felt that Hopkins really understood that I don't want to get as wrapped up in my work as he is, then maybe I might relax. It's no damn fun to keep the truth from people. And it's not fair to them. Damn it, I'm really cheating Hopkins—by agreeing to become his personal assistant at all, I in effect promised him something I have no intention of delivering. Of course he'll be angry when he finds out! And I'm cheating Betsy too. I bet she doesn't like this kind of life any better than I do. It must not be much fun to have a husband as incommunicative as I've been. It's funny how hard it is for us to understand each other! But how could I ever expect her really to forgive me for Maria and her boy? What would she say: "That's all right, dear, don't give it a second thought"?

I'm wasting time, he thought—I've got to get to work. The next thing to do, he decided, was to write some introductory remarks for Hopkins to use at the first meeting of the exploratory committee on mental health. "It's very kind of you to accept my invitation to meet here to discuss one of the great problems of the day," he wrote. "It is my hope that from this meeting will stem . . ."

36

On the evening of October 8, Tom and Betsy Rath went to the Town Hall in South Bay to attend the public hearing on the proposed new school. The town hall was stuffy, and the people filing in from the commuting trains looked bored. The chair on which Tom sat was hard, and he was tired. He squirmed restlessly. Why is it that important public issues always have to be decided in places like this? he thought. Somehow the hard chairs, the smoky room, and the rumpled coats of the weary commuters didn't seem to be the right props for stirring decisions about anything. "How long do you think this meeting will take?" he asked Betsy.

At five minutes after eight, Bernstein, who had been appointed moderator, walked out on a raised platform at the front of the hall. He foresaw an evening of bitter argument, and his stomach was already beginning to ache. Sitting behind a wooden table, he picked up a gavel and tapped it lightly. Gradually the big auditorium quieted down. "Good evening," Bernstein said. "We have gathered here for a hearing on an eight-hundred-thousand-dollar bond issue which has been proposed for a new elementary school, and which we will vote on a week from today. The call for this meeting has been duly published in the newspaper, and I hereby make a motion that we dispense with reading it."

"Motion seconded," someone from the audience called.

"All in favor say 'Aye,' " Bernstein said.

"Aye!" the audience thundered.

"Nay?" Bernstein asked.

"No!" a lone, derisive voice called, and the audience laughed.

"The Ayes have it," Bernstein said, and thought, They seem good humored, but a crowd's laughter can be a symptom of tension. He cleared his throat and said, "To begin the proceedings, Dr. Clyde Eustace, Superintendent of Schools, will tell why he believes a new elementary school is necessary."

Eustace, who had been sitting in the front row, climbed to the platform. He was a large man, but his voice was surprisingly soft. "Ladies and gentlemen, it's very simple," he said. "Although the present elementary school building is badly overcrowded, the welfare of our children is only one question to be discussed tonight. Another basic issue is whether this town should be allowed to grow any more. If you build houses you have to build schools. The main thing I want to point out is that if you decide to vote *no* on this school, you are voting against any further development of this community, and . . ."

A tall, gray-haired man in the front row stood up. "I'm willing to fight it out on those grounds," he said.

Bernstein banged his gavel. "Dr. Eustace has the floor!" he said sharply.

Betsy glanced at Tom. "Who's that?" she asked.

"Parkington's his name," Tom replied. "He was an old friend of Grandmother's—they used to feud all the time."

"Eustace doesn't have to say any more," Parkington persisted. "He's named the basic issue."

"Dr. Eustace will have the floor until I as moderator recognize someone else, and I have not yet recognized you, Mr. Parkington," Bernstein said firmly, and banged his gavel again. "Dr. Eustace, please continue."

Parkington sat down. Eustace went on to give many facts and figures about the need for a new school. He talked too long, and the tone of his voice became monotonous. As soon as he was through, Parkington stood up again.

"All right, Mr. Parkington, you may have the floor now," Bernstein said.

"Let's just go back to what Dr. Eustace said a few moments ago," Parkington began in a deep voice. "If you vote *no* on this school, you vote against further development of this community—and, if I may say so, against further deterioration. What I'm trying to tell everyone here tonight is that's exactly what you should do."

"That's bad for our housing project," Tom whispered to Betsy. "Parkington's nuts, but he's pretty powerful around here."

"This has always been a good town, a beautiful town," Parkington continued passionately. "I was born and brought up here. I've never been able to understand why people move here because they like the place and then start to change it. This new school will send taxes up. That will drive the owners of big estates out. If the big estates are broken up, housing projects will come in. Housing projects bring more children than they do money. The average small house owner pays the town only about a third of what it costs to educate his children. Who's going to make up the difference?"

There was a rising murmur from the audience, and several people tried to speak at once. Bernstein slammed the table with his gavel. "Mr. Parkington still has the floor," he said. "Do you wish to continue, Mr. Parkington?"

"Yes," said Parkington. "I just want to point out that if this school is built, it won't be six months before another one is needed. I've heard a rumor that the old Rath estate is going to be made into a housing development. I'd like to come right out and ask Mr. Rath about that now. I know he's here tonight, because I saw him come in. He's sitting right there in one of the back rows. How about it, Tom? Aren't you just waiting for this school to go through, so you can get permission from the Zoning Board to cut up your land?"

"Mr. Rath, would you care to comment?" Bernstein asked. His stomach was hurting quite badly now.

Slowly Tom stood up. There was a rustling sound throughout the auditorium as people twisted in their seats to see him. He glanced at Betsy and saw she looked nervous. Mechanically he smiled at her. The hall seemed astonishingly quiet, and all faces were turned toward him. His mouth felt dry. "I didn't come prepared to give a talk . . ." he began lamely.

Somewhere in the crowd there was a snicker, which quickly grew into laughter. Bernstein tapped his gavel. "Mr. Rath, please step to the front of the hall," he said.

Awkwardly Tom edged his way to the aisle. The walk to the front of the auditorium seemed endless. Then he was on the platform facing the crowd, and the laughter subsided. The upturned faces blurred. It doesn't really matter, he thought. Here goes nothing. It will be interesting to see what happens. "All right," he said suddenly in a firm voice, "the rumor is true. I plan to ask the Zoning Board for permission to start a housing project."

He paused, and the hall was utterly silent. He couldn't find Betsy's face in the crowd. He took a deep breath. "I don't want my plans for a housing project to hurt the chances for this new school," he said. "They ought to be decided as separate issues. A new school is needed right now. I've got two children in the old one, and I've seen it—it's terrible. Let's get the new school first and fight the battle of my housing project later."

"But the school is an opening wedge!" Parkington interrupted. Bernstein banged his gavel.

"Mr. Parkington," Tom continued, "I think I see your point of view. I was born in South Bay too, and I like the town the way it is. As a matter of fact, I liked it even better the way it used to be, didn't you? It was prettier before the houses went up on the golf course. What I'm trying to say is, the town *is* changing, and we can't take a vote to stop change. If the Zoning Board lets me start a housing project, I'll do everything possible to keep it from being unsightly, or a financial drain on the town, but I don't promise to keep my grandmother's house and land unchanged. That's impossible. And I hope you won't leave the school we have today unchanged. As it stands today, it's a disgrace to all of us."

There was mild applause as Tom stepped down from the platform. Almost immediately Parkington was on his feet. "I just want to warn everybody here that breaking up the Rath estate is just the beginning," he said. "If we don't hold taxes down, other big estates will go. I've just heard that the big place the president of a broadcasting company built down by the water has been placed on the market."

"I know a little about that, and it doesn't have anything to do with schools or taxes," Tom said quickly.

"Maybe," Parkington replied, "but if the big estates go, and we keep on building schools, our taxes will be doubled!"

"I don't think the big estates will go just because we build a new school, and even if they do, I don't think we're so poor and so helpless we can't educate our children," Tom said.

"That sounds fine," Parkington retorted heatedly, "but I'm telling you here and now that if we replace the big estates with housing projects, South Bay will become a slum within ten years—a slum, I tell you, a slum!"

He paused, and the silence was impressive.

"I don't agree with you," Tom said quietly. "We won't let the town become a slum." He started walking toward the back of the hall to rejoin Betsy. Immediately a dozen people were on their feet asking Bernstein for permission to be heard. Antonio Bugala, the contractor, began an impassioned plea for increased business opportunities. For more than an hour the argument raged back and forth, the voices becoming louder and more strident. Tom glanced at Betsy. She looked scared. How curious, he thought, that we should be so dependent—that so much of our future should depend on what all these shouting people decide. His head started to ache, and he longed for the cool air outside.

Finally there was a pause. "Does anyone have anything more to add about the construction of a new school?" Bernstein asked wearily.

Parkington jumped to his feet again immediately. "To sum it all up, a vote for a school is a vote for a housing project Tom Rath admits he's planning," he said. "That's a vote to make this town a slum!"

Bernstein raised his gavel. "If there are no more opinions to be heard . . ." he said.

"A slum!" Parkington repeated portentously.

"I hereby declare this meeting at a . . ." Bernstein began.

"Wait a minute!" Betsy called impetuously, and suddenly found herself on her feet. Tom looked at her in astonishment and saw that her face was flushed.

"Mrs. Rath has the floor," Bernstein said.

For an instant Betsy hesitated. "I'm sorry," she said. "I just didn't want this meeting to end with the word *slum.*"

The audience was attentive.

"The children need a new school," Betsy continued. "Don't let our housing project be used as a weapon against . . ."

"This will be only the beginning . . ." Parkington interrupted.

"Mr. Parkington!" Betsy cut in with remarkable self-possession. "I don't think that growth will necessarily hurt the town. And although I may be taking advantage of being a woman, I refuse to let you have the last word!"

The audience laughed, and although Parkington said something, no one could hear him. Bernstein banged his gavel. Gradually the hall quieted. "I think we've heard the full expression of all relevant opinions," Bernstein said. "I remind you that a week from today we vote on this issue. This meeting stands adjourned!"

On the way out of the Town Hall, Betsy clung tightly to Tom's arm, and he saw that she had been shaken. "I was proud of you," he said.

She smiled up at him. "I was proud of you too," she replied. "You were wonderful."

Going home in the car she sat very close to him. After leaving the car in the old carriage house, they walked up to the house, arm in arm. The sitter they had left with the children met them at the door. "There was a telephone call for you, Mr. Rath," she said. "A Mr. Hopkins called from New York. He left his number and wants you to call him back."

Tom put the call through immediately. Hopkins answered the telephone himself. "Hello, Tom!" he said. "Sorry to bother you so late, but I just decided to fly out to Hollywood tomorrow, and I thought you might like to go with me."

"Hollywood?"

"Yes. We're thinking of organizing a subsidiary company out there to produce some of our programs on film, and I have to go out. I thought it might be a good chance for you to come along with me and learn something about that end of the business."

"Thanks," Tom said. "I'd love to. How long will we be gone?"

"Only four or five days. I've had reservations booked on Flight 227 leaving La Guardia at ten in the morning. Meet me there."

"Certainly!" Tom said. "Certainly! Thanks very much."

He put the telephone down and said somewhat bewilderedly to Betsy, "Hopkins wants me to fly out to Hollywood with him."

"What for?"

"I don't know. He thinks I should learn something about the company's operations out there."

"He really is trying to do something for you," Betsy said. "This is a fantastic opportunity."

"I guess it is," Tom replied. "I hope I'll be back in time for the school election."

"That's not as important as this," she said. "How long do you think you'll be gone?"

"Just four or five days, according to Hopkins. I hope it won't be any longer."

Betsy sat down, looking suddenly solemn. "Gosh, it's going to be lonely around here," she said. "Do you realize that we haven't been away from each other that long since the war?"

"It will be lonely for me too," Tom said, and sat down beside her. She had dressed up for the school meeting and was wearing a dark-blue dress with silver buttons. How young she looks, he thought—she looks almost as young as she did before the war.

"I wish we had more time together," she said. "Things have been so hectic lately."

"I know."

"When do you think you can get your vacation?"

"I guess I could get a week off any time I wanted."

"If things go well," she said, "let's see if we can get somebody like Mrs. Manter to come in and take care of the kids. I'd love to go off on a trip somewhere—just you and I alone together. We wouldn't have to go far."

"It would be fun," he said.

"Maybe we could get a cottage up in Vermont. We could just go there and swim in a lake, maybe, and talk. The way things are going now, we hardly see each other, Tommy! I hate this business of your working every week end. You're always running for a train. We ought to just go off somewhere alone together. We haven't done that for ages."

"Maybe we can." He glanced at his watch. "It's almost midnight," he said. "We better get to bed—I'll have to leave here at eight in the morning to make that plane."

"Eight hours," she said. "We've got eight hours—that's still quite a lot of time."

He glanced at her, startled. She smiled hesitantly at him. It was true: time had become precious again.

37

THE NEXT MORNING Tom got to the airport before Hopkins did. He waited at the gate where Flight 227 was posted. In a few moments he saw Hopkins walking toward him. Hopkins looked small —a short, almost frail-appearing man hurrying across the terminal, holding a huge hard leather briefcase in his hand. "Good morning, Tom!" he said briskly. "It's good of you to come on such short notice as this!"

"No trouble at all," Tom replied, still avoiding the use of Hopkins' name, because he couldn't make up his mind whether to call him "Ralph" or not. They walked aboard the plane, and Hopkins politely resisted the efforts of a stewardess to put his briefcase in the luggage compartment—it was so big that she thought it was a suitcase. No one aboard the plane recognized Hopkins. Tom had grown so used to seeing him deferred to in the United Broadcasting building that it was a shock to see him treated like anyone else. Hopkins obviously didn't mind—if anything, he appeared more diffident and more anxious to be polite than anyone else on the plane. He meekly allowed himself to be jostled away from the seat he was heading for, and when the stewardess offered him some chewing gum, he said, "Thank you—thank you very much, but I think not. I don't chew gum," and smiled apologetically, being al most absurdly careful not to hurt her feelings. She smiled back at him. What a nice little man, she thought.

Tom sat next to Hopkins. Even before the plane took off, Hopkins opened his briefcase, took out a thick report in pale-blue covers, and started to read. When the plane's engines roared, and they taxied toward the runway, he glanced up briefly. "This might interest you, Tom," he said, leaned over, and took another report from his briefcase. "This is something Bill Ogden roughed out on our plan for a subsidiary company to put programs on film—it's still just in the tentative planning stage, of course."

"Thanks," Tom said, accepting the document. As the plane rushed down the runway and lunged into the air, he opened the report. "On the basis of all available data, which is as yet incomplete, there might be considerable advantage in organizing an affiliated company, rather than trying to do the job directly ourselves," he read. He glanced out the window of the plane. Already they were at an altitude of about a thousand feet. He flexed his shoulder muscles, unconsciously trying to see if the parachute harness were strapped tight enough, then realized what he was doing, and smiled at himself. Sitting back, he tried to concentrate on Ogden's report.

After reading for two hours, Hopkins placed his briefcase on his lap and started writing memoranda with a pencil. He worked steadily throughout the long trip. When the plane finally landed in Hollywood, Tom felt tired, but Hopkins seemed energetic as ever. "We're right on time," he said with satisfaction, glancing at his watch. "Let's go to the hotel and wash up. Then we've got some meetings scheduled."

At the hotel a suite of large rooms had been reserved for Hopkins with an adjoining private room and bath for Tom. It was late, but Hopkins didn't mention dinner. They left their bags and hurried to the executive offices of the United Broadcasting Corporation's Hollywood building. Hopkins introduced Tom to a succession of men, all of whom talked fast and with apparent urgency about matters Tom could hardly understand at all. He was glad when they went into a private dining room adjoining one of the offices and sat down around a long table. In all, there were eight men present, and they all kept talking to Hopkins at once. A pretty waitress brought cocktails.

"I'll tell you, Ralph," a tall but rather paunchy man with the oddly apt name of Potkin said. "Like it or not, live shows are going out. In another ten years, the whole television business will be right here. You ought to be thinking in terms of moving your whole operation. If you don't, it's not going to be long before the tail out here starts wagging the dog in New York."

"I'm not convinced of that yet," Hopkins said. "And that's not the only consideration involved in setting up a subsidiary company. There are some legal angles to this. . . ."

On and on the conversation went. It was nine o'clock in the evening before it was over. "Come on over to my house for a drink," Potkin said.

"No," Hopkins replied. "I'm a little tired. I think I'd better go back to the hotel and get some rest. Want to come, Tom?"

"Sure," Tom said.

A taxi took them to the hotel. In the elevator Hopkins said, "Want to stop in for a nightcap before you turn in?"

"That would be fine," Tom replied.

When they entered Hopkins' suite, Tom saw that someone in the company's Hollywood office had made all the arrangements he had made at Atlantic City the month before. On a table was a large vase of long-stemmed roses, and in the bedroom was an electric refrigerator and a cabinet holding a small bar. Tom suspected suddenly that Hopkins had never asked for such elaborate fixings, that they were all the idea of Ogden or someone else trying to please him, and that Hopkins was simply too polite to object. He wished he could find out, but there didn't seem to be any way to ask. Hopkins fixed two glasses of bourbon on the rocks and sprawled out on a sofa the way he had the night he and Tom had talked in his apartment. To his increasing discomfort, Tom found that Hopkins was staring at him again. There was the same mixture of tiredness and kindness on his face, the same steady gaze. Tom sipped his drink nervously.

"Well, what do you think?" Hopkins asked suddenly.

"About what?"

"About this whole operation we've been talking about. Do you think we ought to set up a separate but affiliated organization?"

"I don't know," Tom said. "There's so much involved. . . ."

"Of course—we can't make a decision yet. How would you like to move out here and work on this end of things for a year or so?"

"What?" Tom asked in astonishment.

"You could work with Potkin. He's right about one thing—this end of the business is going to get increasingly important. If you put in a year or two on it, I think you might pick up a lot that would be useful when you came back to New York."

Several thoughts immediately flamed up in Tom's mind. This is his way of getting rid of me, he suddenly knew—this personal assistant business is making him as uncomfortable as it's made me. But he's still trying to do something for me—now he just wants to do it at a distance, by remote control. It's a great opportunity, he thought, but what would happen to our housing project? He was suddenly filled with the confusion of moving, putting his grandmother's house on the market to sell the quickest way possible, and looking for a place to live in Hollywood. Out of this welter of impressions came one word: no. He didn't say it. Instead, he said, "Gosh, that's a pretty big step. . . ."

"Don't you like the idea?"

Wait a minute, Tom thought. If I say no, he's going to wonder what the devil to do with me in New York. I'll be upsetting his whole scheme. If I buck him, he's liable to turn on me. This is like petting a tiger. "I don't know," he said carefully. "I'd like to have a little time to think it over."

"Don't you want to learn the business?" Hopkins asked quietly, but with obvious import.

"Of course . . ." Tom began. Then he paused and took a sip of his drink. The hell with it, he thought. There's no point in pretending. I've played it straight with him so far, and I might as well keep on. Anyway, he's a guy who can't be fooled. He glanced up and saw that Hopkins was smiling at him with great friendliness. Here goes nothing, Tom thought, and the words came with a rush.

"Look, Ralph," he said, using the first name unconsciously, "I don't think I do want to learn the business. I don't think I'm the kind of guy who should try to be a big executive. I'll say it frankly: I don't think I have the willingness to make the sacrifices. I don't want to give up the time. I'm trying to be honest about this. I want the money. Nobody likes money better than I do. But I'm just not the kind of guy who can work evenings and week ends and all the rest of it forever. I guess there's even more to it than that. I'm not the kind of person who can get all wrapped up in a job—I can't get myself convinced that my work is the most important thing in the world. I've been through one war. Maybe another one's coming. If one is, I want to be able to look back and figure I spent the time between wars with my family, the way it should have been spent. Regardless of war, I want to get the most out of the years I've got left. Maybe that sounds silly. It's just that if I have to bury myself in a job every minute of my life, I don't see any point to it. And I know that to do the kind of job you want me to do, I'd have to be willing to bury myself in it, and, well, I just don't want to."

He paused, out of breath, half afraid to look at Hopkins. And then it happened—Hopkins gave a funny, high, indescribable little laugh which rose in the air and was cut off immediately. It was a laugh Tom never forgot, and it was followed by a moment of complete silence. Then Hopkins said in a low voice, "I'm glad you're honest. I've always appreciated that quality in you."

It was Tom's turn to laugh nervously. "Well, there it is," he said. "I don't know what I do now. Do you still want me to work for you?"

"Of course," Hopkins said kindly, getting up and pouring himself another drink. "There are plenty of good positions where it's not necessary for a man to put in an unusual amount of work. Now it's just a matter of finding the right spot for you."

"I'm willing to look at it straight," Tom said. "There are a lot of contradictions in my own thinking I've got to face. In spite of everything I've said, I'm still ambitious. I want to get ahead as far as I possibly can without sacrificing my entire personal life."

Hopkins stood with his back turned toward Tom, and when he spoke, his voice sounded curiously remote. "I think we can find something for you," he said. "How would you like to go back to the mental-health committee? That will be developing into a small, permanent organization. I'm thinking of giving my house in South Bay to be its headquarters. That would be quite nice for you—you wouldn't even have any commuting. How would you like to be director of the outfit? That job would pay pretty well. I'd like to think I had a man with your integrity there, and I'll be making all the major decisions."

"I'd be grateful," Tom said in a low voice.

Suddenly Hopkins whirled and faced him. *"Somebody has to do the big jobs!"* he said passionately. "This world was built by men like me! To really do a job, you have to live it, body and soul! You people who just give half your mind to your work are riding on our backs!"

"I know it," Tom said.

Almost immediately Hopkins regained control of himself. A somewhat forced smile spread over his face. "Really, I don't know why we're taking all this so seriously," he said. "I think you've made a good decision. You don't have to worry about being stuck with a foundation job all your life. I'll be starting other projects. We need men like you—I guess we need a few men who keep a sense of proportion."

"Thanks," Tom said.

Hopkins smiled again, this time with complete spontaneity. "Now if you'll pardon me, I think I'll go to bed," he said. "It's been a long day."

38

THE NEXT MORNING Hopkins was friendly, but brisk and a little distant. "Good morning, Tom!" he said when they met for break-fast. "I find that I've got to stay out here a little longer than I thought. There's no reason why I should hold you up, though—you can fly back to New York any time you want."

"Thanks," Tom said. "I guess I might as well take the first plane I can."

"Certainly!" Hopkins replied, "and thanks so much for coming out with me. Don't worry about anything. In a couple of months we'll have that mental-health committee set up, and I'm sure we can work out something good. I really meant it when I said we can use a man like you. I won't keep you on the mental-health committee more than a few years—we'll work out lots of new and exciting projects. I think the two of us will make a good team."

"I'm grateful," Tom said.

"By the way," Hopkins concluded, handing him a large manila envelope. "Give this to Bill Ogden when you get back, will you? It's just a few notes I've made on some projects he has underway, and I know he's waiting to get my reaction."

"Sure," Tom said. "Glad to. See you later, Ralph—see you when you get back to New York."

Tom went to his room to pack. He glanced at the telephone. Half the night he had lain awake wanting to call Betsy to tell her about his conversation with Hopkins. He didn't know why, but he didn't want to wait any longer. Without knowing whether she would be disappointed or glad, or even whether she'd understand what had happened at all, he had an intense urge to communicate with her. On impulse, he picked up the receiver and placed the call.

"It'll be a few minutes," the operator said. "I'll ring you."

He sat down on the bed and waited. In a shorter time than he had expected, the telephone rang. "I have your call to Connecti-cut," the operator said. "Go ahead, please."

"Betsy?"

"Yes!" she replied, sounding marvelously close. "Is everything all right?"

"Yes. I'm flying home today."

"Today? That's wonderful! But why?"

"Something's happened," he said. "I had a really frank talk with Ralph and I'm going back to work on the mental-health committee. I'm going to be its director, at least for a while. Then I'll probably go on to something else with Ralph."

"Are you glad about it?" she asked, sounding bewildered.

"Yes. I think it's going to work out fine. Ralph is a good guy, Betsy—an awfully good guy. Guys like that never get appreciated enough. I'm going to go on working with him, but he understands that I'm not built the way he is. You and I will have plenty of time to ourselves. No more working every week end."

"It sounds grand," she said. "Tell me all about it when you get home. And hurry back. I miss you."

"I'll hurry," he said.

To his disappointment, he found he couldn't get a plane until evening. He was tired, and after sending a wire to Betsy to say he wouldn't be home until the next morning, he spent most of the day sleeping in his hotel room. As a result, he had difficulty sleeping on the plane. It was not a direct flight, and every few hours they landed at some big airport. During the night Tom had four cups of coffee in four different states. The plane wasn't due in La Guardia until six-thirty in the morning, and head winds made it an hour late. Tom shaved with an electric razor provided by the stewardess. It would be almost nine o'clock by the time he got to Grand Central Station, he figured, and he better stop at the office at least long enough to give Hopkins' envelope to Ogden before doing what he wanted to do, which was to rush home.

Ogden seemed surprised to see him, but accepted the envelope without comment. Tom stopped at his desk in Hopkins' office to see if there were any calls for him. Miss MacDonald also seemed surprised to see him. "There's a message on your desk," she said. "I didn't expect you back until the end of the week."

Tom went to his desk. There was a typewritten memorandum from Miss MacDonald with yesterday's date. "A Mr. Gardella called," she had written. "He said it was important and asked me to have you call him as soon as you returned." Caesar's telephone number followed. Tom dialed it.

"Hello," a woman with an Italian accent answered.

"Is Mr. Gardella there?"

"Just a minute," the woman said, and Tom heard her calling, "Caesar! Caesar! Telephone for you!" She added something in Italian. There was a moment of silence, followed by the sound of heavy footsteps approaching the telephone. "Hello," Caesar said in his deep voice.

"This is Tom Rath. Did you call me?"

"Yes, Mr. Rath. I heard from Maria. I'd like to see you."

"Is she all right?"

"Things aren't very good, Mr. Rath. Louis is dead. They went to Milan, just as I figured, and he got killed there, only a couple of weeks after he found a job. They had a strike in the plant where he was working. They've got a lot of Commies in Milan, and they make a lot of trouble—there was a riot, and Louis got killed. With that leg of his, he couldn't fight and he couldn't run."

There was a pause. "Did you hear me, Mr. Rath?" Caesar asked.

"I heard. I'm very sorry that Louis died. Are Maria and the boy all right?"

"They're back in Rome with Gina's folks. They need help bad, Mr. Rath. I'd like to see you and kind of talk it over. Gina and I do what we can to help, but you know how it is. We've got three kids of our own. We'd all sure appreciate it if you could do something."

There was a moment of silence before Tom said, "When can I see you?"

"How about lunch today?"

"I'll meet you here in the lobby by the information booth, where we met last time," Tom said. "Twelve-thirty for lunch. Will that be okay?"

"Sure, Mr. Rath. I'll be there."

"Thanks," Tom said, and hung up. I'll have to tell Betsy after all, he thought. I hope this housing project goes through. Then we'd have plenty of money, and it would be easier to tell her.

I won't tell her now, he thought. Not tonight. I might as well wait until the school vote goes through. It would be easier to tell her then, when we knew we were going to be all right ourselves.

What will I do if the housing project fails? he thought. If it doesn't work, we'll just have my salary, and is it fair to ask Betsy to share that with some woman I met during the war? She'd never do that—no woman would!

Tom glanced at the telephone. He wished he didn't have to see Betsy until he could tell her about Maria—he didn't want to have to keep secrets from her any more. The eagerness to go home had left him. He telephoned Betsy and told her he had to stay in town for a business lunch.

"Oh!" she said, sounding disappointed. "Do you really have to?"

"I'm afraid so."

"You sound funny. Is everything all right?"

"Yes."

"Are you angry at me or something? You sound so funny."

"I'm not angry," he said. "I just have to see a guy. This is a thing I simply have to do."

At twelve-thirty Tom got into one of the golden elevators and rode down to the lobby of the United Broadcasting building. Caesar Gardella, dressed in a dark-blue business suit, was waiting for him at the information booth. Caesar smiled embarrassedly when he saw him. "Do you want to go to that Mexican place again?" he asked.

"I guess so," Tom said.

They walked across Rockefeller Plaza in silence. When they got to the restaurant, they sat down in the same booth they had occupied before.

"Two double Black and White's," Tom said to the waiter. When the drinks arrived, he said to Caesar, "Is there anything more you can tell me about Maria?"

"It's just that she and the boy are living with Gina's folks," Caesar

-282-

said. "I guess they're well enough. I don't know whether I should have done it or not, but there didn't seem to be any point in calling you unless . . ."

"What did you do?"

"I told Gina's mother that I had run into you here in New York, and I asked her to talk to Maria about it and see if Maria would take any help from you if you were willing to give it."

"What did Maria say?"

"She sent me a letter to give you. I didn't open it, but Gina's mother says . . ."

"You have a letter for me?"

"Yes." Caesar put his hand in his breast pocket and took out a rather soiled envelope with Tom's full name written in black ink across the front in large, slanting letters. Tom tore it open. He took out a single-page letter folded around a snapshot wrapped in tissue paper. He looked at the snapshot first. It showed a plainly dressed woman, quite stout and almost middle-aged, whom he dimly recognized as Maria, and standing beside her was a boy, a thin little boy all dressed up, with a cap on his head, and a shirt with a wide collar, and a little tight-fitting jacket, and short trousers. With his queer old-fashioned clothes, and his slender big-eyed face, and with his shockingly familiar forehead and nose and mouth, he looked like one of the faded photographs Tom's grandmother had kept of "The Senator" as a child. Tom stared at the snapshot and then with trembling hands quickly stuffed it back into the envelope and unfolded the letter. Apparently Maria had dictated it to someone —the grammar and spelling were all correct.

"Dear Tom," the letter said, "I do not like this, but I don't know what to do. For myself I do not need help, but there is the boy. Anything you could do for him would be from heaven. I am ashamed to ask you, but we were never proud with each other, so perhaps you will understand. The boy needs help. He is a good boy. He studies well. I am sending you this picture that Louis took last year. Do not think we are trying to make trouble for you. I leave this in the hands of God."

The letter was signed, "Maria Lapa." Tom took a drink before folding it carefully and putting it back in the envelope with the photograph. He put the envelope in his inside coat pocket, glanced up, and saw that Caesar was discreetly staring at the wall. There was a heavy silence.

"Caesar," Tom said suddenly, "can I have some time to think this over?"

"Sure, Mr. Rath," Caesar replied. "Nobody's trying to hurry you. We don't want you to do anything you don't think should be done."

"How much do you think I should send?"

"Anything would help. Gina and I have been sending ten dollars a month to her mother. Ten dollars a month is a lot of money in Rome."

"How much would Maria need to raise that boy decently?"

Caesar shrugged his shoulders. "Maria will probably go on living with Gina's mother," he said. "If you sent her a hundred dollars a month, she could do an awful lot with it. She could send the boy to a pretty good school, and everything."

"I've got to have time to work this out," Tom said. "Look, Caesar, you've always been a decent guy. I've got to tell my wife—you can understand that. And it's not going to be easy. I've got to have time."

"Sure, Mr. Rath," Caesar said earnestly. "Maria's all right for now—Gina's mother can take care of her. You've got no need to hurry."

"It might take me a few weeks," Tom said. "I've got to pick the right time to tell my wife."

"It's none of my business, Mr. Rath, but aren't you going to make a lot of trouble for yourself? By telling your wife, I mean."

"Could you send money somewhere every month without telling your wife?"

"No, I guess I couldn't. I sure hope this doesn't make trouble for you, though. I know Maria wouldn't want that."

"I've got a good wife," Tom said. "I don't think there's going to be any trouble. I've just got to pick the right time."

"Mr. Rath, I'd like to say this," Caesar replied awkwardly. "We're grateful to you—Maria and Gina and I. We know you don't have to do it, there's nothing that could make you. I don't know whether it will mean anything to you or not, but Gina and I are going to pray for you, and I know Maria will."

"Maria already has," Tom said. "Now listen. You may not hear from me for quite a while. But I'll get in touch with you, and I'll make some kind of arrangement for Maria. I'll probably do it through a bank or a lawyer. I'll write her a note, but I want to make some kind of permanent arrangement." He paused in confusion. "It would be kind of difficult for everybody if I had to write her every month," he concluded.

"What if your wife won't let you do anything? I better not tell Maria until you're sure."

"No, you better not. We better wait and see."

There was an interval of silence before the waiter came to take their orders.

"You want anything to eat?" Tom asked Caesar.

Caesar shook his head. "I got to be getting back," he replied.

"Me too," Tom said. He paid the check for the drinks. They left the restaurant and hurried off in different directions.

That afternoon Tom had a vicious headache. He threw himself into his work and missed his regular train home. While he waited for another train in Grand Central Station, he went to a drugstore and swallowed two aspirins. Finding that they didn't help much, he went to the Hotel Commodore bar and drank too many Martinis. When he finally got home, Betsy looked at him with astonishment and concern. "Tommy," she said, "what's the matter with you? You look terrible."

"I guess I just got a little stomach upset," he said. "I think I'll go upstairs and lie down."

Without saying more, he walked up to the big bedroom. Taking off only his shoes, he lay down on the wide four-poster bed. All the objects in the room seemed to swirl before his eyes. The paintings of his father and grandfather as children, the old mandolin in its cracked leather case on the top shelf of the corner bookcase, and an electric clock on the bureau blurred and wavered. He shut his eyes. In the quiet room he could hear his wrist watch ticking. A few moments later Betsy came in and looked at him worriedly. "Should I call a doctor?" she asked.

"No," he replied, shaking his head. "I guess I just drank a little too much. I was tired, and when I missed my train, I stopped at the bar in the station."

"You shouldn't," she said. "It's not adult, Tommy! And when you drink like this, I feel as though we were in different worlds. You haven't even told me about your trip to California, and now the kids and I will have to eat supper without you. I wish you'd quit drinking, if only because it makes me feel so lonely."

"I'm sorry," he said. He stretched out and stared up at the crocheted canopy overhead. Betsy left the room. A moment later she came back, and he felt something cool on his forehead. He put his hand up and found a damp towel she had placed there. "Thanks," he said.

"Would an ice bag help?"

"This is fine."

"Did Hopkins say anything to you that worries you?"

"No—everything is fine with Ralph. I'm not worried about my job at all. I'll talk to you about it later."

"Please don't drink any more," she said.

"I won't."

"I don't like to see you like this. It makes me feel awful."

"I'm sorry."

"We've got so much work to do. I promised I'd help mail pamphlets for the school."

"After the school election can I talk with you?"

"What about?"

"Never mind now. It's funny you said you were lonely. We've both been lonely so long."

39

IT WAS INDIAN SUMMER. The day of the school election turned out to be warm and clear. After an early breakfast, Tom and Betsy took the children with them and went to the Town Hall to vote. Ahead of them waited a long line of commuters, the young and ambitious, the old and successful, and the tired of all ages, standing in line to vote yes or no on whether to tax themselves for the construction of a new school. They were polite, excusing themselves elaborately when they jostled each other and pointedly refraining from commenting on the issue at hand.

On the way home after they had voted, Tom and Betsy passed a white sound truck. "Vote *no* on the school!" it was blaring. "Vote against high taxes and poorly planned school programs!" A block ahead was another sound truck shouting, "Vote *yes* on the school! Our children deserve the best!" Apparently the two trucks were following each other around town, blatting like moose in the mating season.

Tom left Betsy and the children at the house and hurried to the station to go to work. On the train he looked once more at the photograph of Maria and her son. Then he read his newspaper, all of it, from headlines about wars and incipient wars to the comics. When he got to his office, he worked all day, getting together plans for the first meeting of the mental-health committee.

At six o'clock he took the train back to South Bay and again examined the photograph, which was becoming stained and creased. Before going home he stopped at the Town Hall, where Bernstein and a group of other officials were about to close the polls and announce the count on the voting machines. A quiet crowd was assembling in the building. Tom saw both Parkington and Bugala. A few last-minute voters hurried in, and then there was a hush while an elderly town councilman consulted his watch and declared the voting at an end. Three rather self-conscious officials began to inspect the voting machines, and there was a long wait. Bernstein walked to the head of the hall, and a small man handed him three pieces of paper. Bernstein cleared his throat. "On machine number one," he announced, "the vote is seven hundred and forty-two *yes* and four hundred and forty-three *no.*"

There was a ragged cheer from the crowd. Bernstein read the counts on the other two machines, which did not differ markedly from the first. "It looks as though the vote on the school is *yes* by a margin of almost two to one," he said.

There was another cheer, and a rising hum of conversation. Old Parkington headed toward the door without comment. Bugala grinned at Tom and shouldered his way through the crowd toward him. "It looks like we got it made," he said.

"I hope so," Tom replied. "Let's get together tomorrow." Hurriedly he headed home. Just as he reached the sidewalk, Bernstein caught up with him. "Say, Tom," he said. "Have a beer with me?"

"Sure."

They went to a bar across the street. When two glasses of beer were before them, Bernstein said, "Well, we got the school. The people in this town have more sense than they're given credit for."

"I guess they do."

"Now about this zoning problem of yours. I'll be glad to call a meeting of the board next week if you want to submit your petition."

"Do you think they'll approve it?"

"I can't tell you that. As a friend of yours, all I can say is that, in my opinion, now would be a good time to submit it."

"Thanks," Tom said. "If you don't mind, I think I'll hurry back and tell Betsy."

The old Ford knocked as he drove it fast up the steep winding hill, past the great outcroppings of rock. When he got to the house, Betsy came to the front door to meet him. She had brushed her hair until it shone and had put on a crisp white blouse. She smiled, and he found he didn't want to keep secrets from her any more. Now is the time, he thought. The housing project's not sure yet, but nothing's ever sure. Now is the time I'll have faith.

"Did we get the school?" she called as he came toward her.

"Yes," he said.

"Wonderful!" she exclaimed. "If Bugala is right . . ."

"I want to talk to you," he said.

"What about?"

"I've got something important I want to talk over with you. Let's go up to our room."

"Is something the matter?"

"Its nothing about the project."

"Can you wait a minute? I'll put the kids to bed."

"I'll wait in our room," he said.

"Is it anything serious? You're acting so strange!"

"I'm all right. I don't want to worry you. It's just something we've got to talk over."

"I've fed the kids, but I've got dinner waiting for you," she said. "Don't you want anything to eat?"

"Later. Come to our room when you can."

As he went upstairs Barbara and Pete, already in their pajamas, ran to meet him. He kissed them and went in to say good night to Janey, who was already half asleep.

"Come on, kids," Betsy said. "To bed!"

"We haven't had a story yet!" Janey said, waking up.

"I'll read you a short one."

Tom went into the big bedroom and sat down nervously on the edge of the bed. He could hear Betsy in the next room quietly reading a story about Winnie the Pooh. He put his hand in his pocket, took out the letter from Maria, and for perhaps the hundredth time examined the photograph. There was the child, big-eyed, serious, dressed with that pathetic and grotesque gentility, staring out at him solemnly, the image of "The Senator" as a young boy. Beside her son, Maria looked proud and serene. He stuffed the photograph and the letter back in the envelope and put them in his pocket.

It was about fifteen minutes before Betsy came in. She was pale and suddenly seemed to him to be as fragile as a girl in her teens. He realized he had scared her. Getting to his feet with clumsy politeness, he said, "I don't want you to be frightened," and immediately realized that those were hardly the words to reassure her.

"Why are you being so mysterious?"

"I don't know if I should talk to you about this. I don't know what else to do. It isn't just the money—I don't like to do things behind your back."

"Behind my back?"

"It was all such a long time ago," he said helplessly.

"What was?"

He had an impulse simply to give her Maria's letter and the photograph, but decided that would be cruel. There was an awkward silence which he realized must be painful to her.

"There was a child," he began.

"A child?"

"During the war. In Rome."

"What child?"

"A child of mine."

"You had a child?"

"Yes."

She said nothing. He had the strange feeling that he had not spoken, that the secret was still his. "I wasn't sure," he said. "I didn't know where she was. I didn't know for sure until I got this letter."

"A letter?"

He gave her the letter. Her face was pale but expressionless as she read it. Then she took the photograph out of the envelope and stared at it.

"Was this the woman?"

"Yes."

"Did you love her?"

"I can't explain it. You can't possibly have any idea what the war was like."

"We've never talked about it."

"I can't. Do you want me to tell you horrors? I wouldn't have brought this up at all if it weren't . . ."

"What do you want to do?"

"I'm going to support this child," he said. "I've thought it over, and I'm going to send him a hundred dollars a month. I guess what I want is your blessing."

"My *blessing!*" she said, her voice rising suddenly.

"Betsy, do you want me to apologize for this child? So much happened during the war! It's strange I should have to apologize for this. I killed seventeen men. I cut the throat of a German boy eighteen years old, and I killed Hank Mahoney, my best friend, because I threw a hand grenade too fast. I'm not ashamed of it, but for having a child I feel terrible. What do you want me to tell you?"

"All of it," she said. "I want you to tell me all of it. You can't just come and tell me you had a child in Italy, and that's that. If you don't tell me now, I'll wonder about it the rest of my life. Where did you meet the girl in that photograph?"

"In Rome."

"*Where* in Rome?"

"In a bar."

"Was it a formal introduction, or did you just pick her up?"

"Goddamn it," he said. "Don't let's make this any harder than it has to be."

"I'm not making it harder than it has to be! Was she just an ordinary pickup? Were you drunk, Tommy?"

"I wasn't drunk. I was scared. And so was she. She was eighteen years old. Her parents had been burned to death before her eyes. She was broke and hungry. Now let this thing alone."

"No," she said. "I want to know. How many times did you sleep with her?"

"I lived with her," he said. "I lived with her for two months."

"When?"

"In 1944."

"When in 1944?"

"December and part of January of the next year."

"The turn of the year," she said. "You know something, Tommy? I almost went crazy worrying about you those months. I suppose that's rather funny. You didn't write. It was the first time I'd gone that long without letters. I didn't hear from you for three months. I'll never forget that. I was so worried that I got your grandmother to try to pull some strings in Washington and find out where you were. It didn't work—we couldn't find out a thing. I used to jump every time the telephone or doorbell rang, for fear it was a telegram for me from the War Department. I can remember trying to write you letters during those months. It isn't easy to write letters when you're not getting any, and when you're sure in your heart that the man you're writing is dead. There wasn't much for me to write about. I can remember trying to be cheerful, not to let you know I was worried. What did you do with my letters when you were living with her? Did the two of you lie in bed and read them together for laughs?"

"Don't," he said.

"No, I want to know. What did you do with my letters when you were living with her?"

"I don't think I got them until I got to New Guinea. The mail was pretty mixed up for us while we were on the move."

"Was she pretty, Tommy?"

"Not as pretty as you. Look at the picture and see for yourself."

"Was she better in bed than I am?"

"Stop it."

"Did she have a good figure? Were her breasts better than mine?"

"Why do you torture yourself?"

"I want an answer."

"I did not love her as much as I love you."

"You're lying a little, aren't you? Do you catch yourself wishing for her when you're making love to me?"

"Try to be adult about this," he said. "I'm not the only man to leave a child behind during the war. There are hundreds of thousands of war children in Japan and Italy and Germany. There are more in France and England and Australia. Anywhere the men were sent out to fight, quite a few ended up becoming fathers. Call it a practical joke of nature. The human race goes on, in spite of itself. That's a dirty thing, I suppose. Wars are full of dirt."

"You sound almost righteous when you talk about it."

"I find it hard to be really ashamed. When I met Maria I thought I was never going to see you again. Do you know what it's like to be scared right down to the bottom of your guts? Do you know what it's like to be sure beyond the shadow of a doubt that you'll be killed on the next jump, or the jump after that? And do you know what it's like to be half afraid of yourself, to know in your heart that the last man you killed was killed with pleasure? Do you know how a corpse grins? When you see enough of that grin, everything decent in the world seems a joke. The dead always have the last laugh— Mahoney, a man I killed, told me that once when we were in Germany together. The dead always have the last laugh. I'm not trying to shock you, Betsy, but you've got to understand that having a child doesn't seem to me to be so bad. Maybe I've got everything twisted backward. Ever since the war, it's been as though I were trying to figure something out. I've never been able to get it quite clear in my mind, but I keep feeling just the way I did when I was about to make a jump and knew a lot of us were going to get killed. I keep having the same feeling I had when I killed Hank Mahoney, the feeling that the world is nuts, that the whole world is absolutely insane."

"And now you've done your bit to straighten things out," Betsy said. "A few more illegitimate children, and everything will be fine."

"All right—I don't make sense. But love, even when it's three quarters lust, does not seem to me to be as bad as lots of things I've seen. I don't love Maria any more—you don't have to worry about that. But she was with me when I didn't have a hope in the world. She was the only good thing that happened to me in the whole war, and we had a child. Dirty or not, that still seems a kind of miracle to me. What do you want me to do, forget it? Maria hasn't got any legal hold on me. I can just tell her to go to hell. Probably if worst came to worst and she sued me, I could prove she was a prostitute. Would that make you feel any cleaner? I can write her now and tell her I don't believe this child is mine. One more act of brutality wouldn't change the world. But I'm not going to do it. I can't do anything about the state of the world, but I can put my own life in order. The only really dirty part about an illegitimate child is that usually the father doesn't support it. This is one decent thing I'm going to do, if I never do anything else, and I hope you'll help me."

"Go ahead and send him money," she said. "I'm not trying to stop you. You have my blessing. That's what you want, isn't it?"

"I didn't think you'd be bitter."

"I'm not bitter, but things haven't been very good since you got out of the service, have they? Is Maria the reason? Let's be honest about it. We haven't had much of a life together. You and I seem to have learned a lot of things since the war—a lot of things I don't want to know. We've learned to drag along from day to day without any real emotion except worry. We've learned to make love without passion. We've even learned to stop fighting together, haven't we? We haven't had a real good fight since you threw that vase against the wall a year ago. We used to fight a lot when we were first married, but we don't really care enough to fight any more, do we? I haven't even cried for months. I think I've forgotten how to cry. All I know how to do nowadays is be responsible and dutiful and deliberately cheerful for the sake of the children. And all you know how to do is work day and night and worry. You give a good sermon on love, but I haven't seen much of it around here. It's a great life, isn't it? Was it that way with Maria?"

He began pacing nervously up and down the room. "I know things haven't been good since the war," he said. "I think they're going to be better. We're not going to have to worry so much about money."

"Did you worry about money when you were with Maria?"

"Maria was part of the war. I can't explain that to you."

"Sure, I don't know anything about war. All I know is the wife's side of it—four years of sitting around waiting, believing that faithfulness is part of what you call love. All I know is that I lived on the belief that everything would be marvelous after the war, and that we've both been half dead ever since you got home."

"Stop it," he said. "We're going to have a good life together." He put his arm around her, but suddenly she twisted free and fled from the room and down the stairs. He followed her. She ran out the front door. There was brilliant moonlight on the tall grass and on the distant waters of the Sound. She ran through the dark shadows of the rock garden toward the old carriage house, where the car was parked. He caught her just before she got there, but she whirled and hit him on the mouth with her clenched fist. He kissed her and she bit him hard. He put his hand up to his mouth. When he took it down, there was blood on it.

"Did Maria kiss like that?" she asked.

Without saying anything, he grabbed her. She twisted away, tearing open the shoulder of her blouse. He caught her around the waist, pulled her down in the tall grass, and lay beside her with one arm imprisoning her.

"We can still fight, can't we?" she said, struggling to free herself. "Is that the one thing we've got left?"

He stroked her hair. "Hush," he said. The grass smelled sweet.

"Let me go," she said, almost wrenching herself free. He threw himself across her and, feeling her fingers digging into his back, kissed her hard. Suddenly she burst into tears and, burying her face in his neck, clung to him like a child. Her whole body was quaking.

"It's all right," he said over and over again. "Everything's all right."

There was no answer but her sobs. It took a long time for them to subside. After an instant of complete silence she said, "Now let me go."

He released her and she lay full length in the grass. Her face, still tear streaked, was bright in the moonlight. Her blouse was shredded at one shoulder, and on her other shoulder there was a dark blood stain on the white cloth, where he had held her. She was breathing hard. "Leave me alone for a little while, will you?" she said. "Go in the house and let me be by myself for a while. I've got a lot to think out."

"Come in the house with me."

She propped herself up on her elbows slowly. "No. I'm not sure what we should do. Maybe you should take a few weeks off and fly over to Italy and see Maria. When you came back, we could decide what's right."

"I don't want to go to Italy. I want to stay here with you."

"Perhaps I should go off by myself for a few days. It might help me to get things clear in my mind."

"I've got a better idea. Let's get Mrs. Manter to take care of the kids for a week. We could buy a new car and take a drive up through Vermont together."

"I don't know. Give me some time to think. Go in the house—I'll be in after a while."

"I don't want to."

"Please."

"All right." He kissed her gently and walked slowly through the moonlight toward the shadows of the house. Just before he went inside, he turned and saw her walking forlornly through the long grass toward the distant row of pines, like a ghost in the moonlight. He started to go after her but thought better of it. After sitting in the living room and smoking a cigarette, he went to the front door and looked out. There was no sign of her. Restlessly he went to the kitchen and put some ice in a glass. He poured a drink, carried it upstairs, and lay down on his bed. Maybe when I finish this drink she'll be back, he thought, and sipped it slowly. He had just drained the glass when he heard the car start. He dashed down the stairs and ran outside. In the moonlight he saw the old Ford back violently out of the carriage house. He ran toward it, but before he got there, it jerked ahead, its lights flashed on, and with its engine roaring in second gear, it careened down the hill. The thought of his father speeding down that same hill toward the waiting rocks at the turn so many years before gripped his mind, and he started running. Ahead of him the red tail light winked in the night. Abruptly it disappeared as the car rounded the first turn. There was no crash. He climbed the great red rocks glistening in the moonlight and could see the car continuing down the road more slowly. He watched until it vanished into the darkness. After standing there a long while to see if she would come back, he returned to the house and lay fully dressed on the bed. There was nothing to do but wait. Maybe she'll telephone and tell me what she plans to do, he thought, but the only sound was the somber striking of the grandfather clock downstairs.

40

It was two o'clock in the morning when the telephone finally rang. He leaped to answer it. "Hello," he said. "Is that you, Betsy?"

"Yes," she said in a small voice. "The car broke down."

He started to laugh with relief. "That's a good old car," he said. "It won't take you away from me."

"I was trying to get home—I was trying to get home as fast as I could. I just wanted to get away by myself and drive for a while. I got everything figured out in my mind and was on my way home when the engine made an awful noise and stopped."

"Where are you?"

"A little way beyond Westport."

"Where are you calling from?"

"The police station. The car broke down on the Merritt Parkway. I was walking along the road trying to find a telephone, when a patrol car stopped and picked me up. I showed them where I had left the car, and they wanted to see my driver's license and registration. I don't have them with me."

"Tell the cops to have the car hauled to a garage, and we'll turn it in on a new one tomorrow. And take a taxi home as soon as you can."

"I don't know if the cops will let me go."

"That's ridiculous. Are there any charges against you?"

"They say they're just holding me for driving without my license and registration, but they seem to think there's something suspicious about me. I guess I'm not very well dressed at the moment. They keep asking me where I got this blood stain on my sleeve and how my blouse got torn."

"They probably think you've been in an accident," he said, laughing.

"Don't laugh. I want to come home. I feel awful and I want to come home."

"Let me talk to the cops," he said.

"Just a minute."

There was a short delay before a gruff voice said, "Sergeant Haggerty speaking."

"My name is Rath, Thomas Rath in South Bay," Tom said. "I want you to call a cab for my wife and let her come right home. If there's any difficulty about it, I'll have Judge Saul Bernstein here get in touch with you immediately and straighten it out."

"No difficulty," the voice said. "We just thought it was peculiar, girl walking along the road alone late at night like that. We just wanted to make sure everything was all right."

"Everything's fine. Please have the car towed to a garage and call her a cab."

"Be glad to. You a friend of Judge Bernstein's?"

"Sure am."

"Give him my best when you see him—name's Haggerty. And tell your wife to bring her license and registration with her after this when she goes out driving alone late at night."

"I will. Let me talk to her again, will you?"

"Okay," Haggerty said. "Just a minute."

"You're out of hock," Tom said when Betsy came on the line. "They're going to call you a cab. Come home. I can't wait to see you."

"I'll be there as soon as I can. I've been an awful fool, Tommy. I know that."

"Anybody can forget a driver's license," he said. "Hurry home and we'll talk then."

He went outside and sat down on the front doorstep. The moonlight was still bright on the long grass and on the water of the Sound, lying ruffled by a rising morning breeze. He lit a cigarette and watched the smoke float lazily off in the moonlight. After about a half hour, he heard a car approaching. Bright headlights flashed across the driveway, and a taxi stopped in front of the house. The back door swung open, and Betsy jumped out. She ran immediately to him. Neither of them spoke. The silence was broken after about thirty seconds by the taxi driver clearing his throat. Tom paid him. When the taxi had gone, he turned to Betsy. "Don't let's go in yet," he said. "It's too nice a night out."

They walked over to the stone wall and sat with their backs against it. He kissed her. "There are some things I have to say," she said. "Don't kiss me again, or I'll never say them."

"Nothing has to be said now."

"This must be said. Tonight while I was driving alone, I realized for the first time what you went through in the war, and what different worlds we've been living in ever since. I'm sorry I acted like a child."

"I love you."

"You're right about helping your boy in Italy. Of course we should do all we can."

"I love you."

"He should have a good education and everything he needs. Do they have trouble getting enough food and medicine and clothes over there? We should find out what he needs and send it. We shouldn't just send money."

"I love you more than I can ever tell."

"I want you to be able to talk to me about the war. It might help us to understand each other. Did you really kill seventeen men?"

"Yes."

"Do you want to talk about it now?"

"No. It's not that I want to and can't—it's just that I'd rather think about the future. About getting a new car and driving up to Vermont with you tomorrow."

"That will be fun. It's not an insane world. At least, our part of it doesn't have to be."

"Of course not."

"We don't have to work and worry all the time. It's been our own fault that we have. What's been the matter with us?"

"I don't know," he said. "I guess I expected peace to be nothing but a time for sitting in the moonlight with you like this, and I was surprised to find that this isn't quite all there is to it."

"I disappointed you."

"Of course you didn't. I was my own disappointment. I really don't know what I was looking for when I got back from the war, but it seemed as though all I could see was a lot of bright young men in gray flannel suits rushing around New York in a frantic parade to nowhere. They seemed to me to be pursuing neither ideals nor happiness—they were pursuing a routine. For a long while I thought I was on the side lines watching that parade, and it was quite a shock to glance down and see that I too was wearing a gray flannel suit. Then I met Caesar, running an elevator. He's the one who knew about Maria—he went through most of the war with me. There was Caesar in his purple uniform, staring at me in my gray flannel suit and reminding me, always reminding me, that I was betraying almost everyone I knew."

"I wish I could have helped you."

"You did help me—you and Caesar. I needed a great deal of assistance in becoming an honest man. If you hadn't persuaded me to play it straight with Ralph, I would be thinking differently now. By a curious coincidence, Ralph and a good deal of the rest of the world have seemed honest to me ever since I became honest with myself. And if I hadn't met Caesar, I don't think I ever would have had the courage to tell you about Maria. I would have gone on, becoming more and more bitter, more and more cynical, and I don't know where that road would have ended. But now I'm sure things are going to be better. I've become almost an optimist."

"I'm glad we're going to have a week to ourselves. Where are we going in Vermont?"

"I know a place where we can rent a cabin by a lake a thousand miles from nowhere. The foliage on the mountains will be beautiful this time of the year. If we get a few more days of Indian summer, it may not be too late for a swim. The nights will be cold, and we'll sleep by an open fire."

"Do you love me?"

"A little."

"Don't tease me. Do you like the way I look?"

"You're beautiful. You never used to like to have me tell you that."

"I want to hear it now. Often. Tell me again that I am beautiful."

"Every time I look at you, you are a delight to me. Every night when I get off the train and see you, I want to tell you that. I haven't for years, because you told me once that you would rather have other compliments."

"I guess when I decided to be a fool, I had to play it big."

"You've not been as foolish as I," he said, and pulled her down beside him in the fragrant grass and kissed her. A sudden puff of wind set the long ends of the grass shivering all around him. She shuddered. "You're cold," he said. "I'll take you in now."

"No. Hold me tight."

"You're trembling. Why?"

"I don't know. I feel as though we almost died and have just been rescued."

"We're not going to worry any more. No matter what happens, we've got a lot to be grateful for."

"When I think of all you've been through, I'm afraid."

"Don't be. The dead don't have the last laugh. It's the children left by the dead and the survivors who laugh last, and their laughter is not sardonic. Ever since you came back to me tonight, I've been remembering a line from a poem that used to sound ironic and bitter. It doesn't sound that way any more. Tonight, for a little while at least, I feel it's true."

"What is it?"

" 'God's in his heaven'," he said, " 'all's right with the world.' "

41

AT ELEVEN-THIRTY the next morning Judge Saul Bernstein got a telephone call from Tom Rath. "I'm just about to leave town for a week, but I'd like to drop down and see you first," Tom said. "I want your help on a very personal problem."

"Come ahead," Bernstein said. "I'll be expecting you." He hung up and tried to concentrate on the tax form he was completing for a client. Tom's call troubled him. He had had many people telephone to ask immediate help on "a very personal problem," and the approaching trip Tom mentioned was also a bad sign. To Bernstein it all sounded like the usual preliminaries to a divorce case. Divorce cases always saddened Bernstein, and the thought of Betsy and Tom Rath dissolving their marriage especially bothered him. He liked them and he thought that with three young children they had no business splitting up. I wonder what I might do to talk them out of it, he thought, and felt a few warning twinges of pain in his stomach.

Ten minutes later when Tom walked into his office, Bernstein was surprised to see that for a man presumably on the verge of divorce, he appeared indecently cheerful. "Good morning!" Tom boomed heartily. "Beautiful day, isn't it?"

"Yes," Bernstein said uneasily. "What can I do for you?"

"Mind if we go into your inner office?" Tom asked, glancing at Bernstein's secretary.

"No," Bernstein said. "Go right ahead." His stomach began to ache quite badly now. People who wanted to go to the inner office even before naming the nature of their business quite often wanted to discuss divorce. He followed Tom into the small book-lined room, and they both sat down.

"I came to you with this because it would be a little embarrassing to discuss with strangers, and I'm sure you'll understand," Tom began.

"I hope so," Bernstein said dubiously.

"The situation is simply this. During the war I had an illegitimate child in Italy. He's been on my mind a lot, but I haven't been absolutely sure of his existence until recently. Now I want to send his mother a hundred dollars a month for his support—they're in real need. When this housing project of ours goes through, I'm going to establish a trust fund, but right now I want to take it out of income. I think it would be less awkward for everyone concerned if we set up some mechanism for having the checks sent regularly by a bank, or perhaps you could do it."

"Are you trying to make this an anonymous gift?" Bernstein asked somewhat guardedly.

"For the sake of propriety I don't want it talked about all over town, and I don't particularly trust the discretion of the local bank, but the person who will get the money will know who it's from. There's no need to keep anything a secret from her."

Bernstein cleared his throat. "You intend this to be a permanent arrangement?" he asked.

"Certainly. At least until the boy has finished his education."

"It might be possible for you to receive considerable tax benefits by having the child legally declared a dependent," Bernstein said. "You ought to look into that if you plan anything permanent."

"I hadn't thought of that," Tom replied. "Fix it up for me if you can, will you? Might as well get all the tax benefits I can."

"It might be necessary for you to admit paternity," Bernstein said. "That might leave you open to further claims by the child's mother, and it might pose certain problems for you in filling out your tax returns."

"I'm not worried about further claims. What would the difficulty be with the tax returns?"

"It might be hard to keep the matter a complete secret here," Bernstein said somewhat embarrassedly. "Especially if you file joint tax returns which your wife has to sign."

"Betsy already knows all about it," Tom said. "She and I are doing this together."

"You are?" Bernstein said, unable to preserve his professional air of detachment any longer.

"I know this must sound a little odd to you," Tom said, "but I met a girl in Italy during the war, and I've told Betsy all about it. The child the girl had needs help, and Betsy and I are going to send it. I suppose that may be a little unconventional, but to us it seems like simple justice."

For a moment Bernstein didn't say anything. Misinterpreting his silence as censure, Tom said a little stiffly, "This is a matter of conscience with me, and I don't intend to try to justify it to anyone. Betsy and I are driving up to Vermont this afternoon, and I would appreciate it if you could arrange to have the checks sent. In this envelope I've brought the money for three months and the name and address I want it sent to. What will you charge me for handling the matter?"

"Nothing," Bernstein said.

"What?"

"No charge."

"Why not?"

Bernstein smiled. "I like what you call 'simple justice,'" he said. "The kind I generally deal with is so complex."

"Thanks," Tom said. Suddenly the air was charged with emotion. Bernstein got up and Tom grabbed his hand. "Thanks!" he said again. "I've got to be running. Betsy's been shopping, but she's probably waiting outside for me now. We're heading up to Vermont!"

He dashed out the door. Bernstein's stomach wasn't aching any more. He walked slowly to the window of his office and stood looking down at the street. Betsy, with her arms full of bundles, was just coming down the sidewalk. Bernstein watched as Tom hurried toward her. He saw them bow gravely toward each other as she transferred the bundles to Tom's arms. Then Tom straightened up and apparently said something to her, for suddenly she smiled radiantly. Bernstein smiled too.

SLOAN WILSON *was born in 1920 in Norwalk, Connecticut, and, in his own words, was educated by "a succession of small Country Day Schools, tutors and boarding schools." Before receiving his B.A. degree at Harvard, he joined the Coast Guard, where he became the commanding officer of first a small freighter and then a tanker in the South Pacific during the war. Of this experience he writes: "Tanker carried aviation gas. Scared me to death, almost. Always thought she was going to blow up. Was only 23 years old when first commanded ship. In my case, that was too young. It was truly a great strain. But I got through war without having anyone on my ships killed."*

Sloan Wilson has written a number of short stories for The New Yorker, *and other works by him have appeared in* Harper's, The Saturday Review *and* The Yale Review.

At present Mr. Wilson is an English instructor as well as Director of Information Services at The University of Buffalo. He writes: "This book was written largely between 7:00 P.M. and 2:00 A.M. and on week ends. It could not have been written at all if my wife hadn't kept the children quiet or away from the place I was working. She also managed all household finances, repaired the children's bicycles, made excuses about why I didn't have any social engagements, was cheerful and ornamental. Without such a wife, writing a book and having a full-time job would have been impossible." And to this his publisher wishes to add that it was Mrs. Wilson who so ably summarized the theme of her husband's book by suggesting the title The Man in the Gray Flannel Suit.

A Just Defense

A Just Defense

The Use of Force, Nuclear Weapons & Our Conscience

KEITH B. PAYNE
& KARL I. PAYNE

MULTNOMAH · PRESS
Portland, Oregon 97266

Acknowledgment is gratefully made to the following for permission to reprint previously published material:

Hamilton Press: Strategic Defense: "Star Wars" in Perspective by Keith B. Payne, copyright 1986 by Hamilton Press, Lanham, Maryland 20706.

Foreign Policy Research Institute: "The Soviet Union and Strategic Defense: The Failure and Future of Arms Control" by Keith B. Payne. Reprinted from *Orbis: A Journal of World Affairs,* Winter 1986, by permission of the publisher. Copyright 1986 by the Foreign Policy Research Institute, Philadelphia.

Zondervan Bible Publishers: For Scripture quotations from the *Holy Bible: New International Version,* copyright 1973, 1978, 1984 by the International Bible Society. Used by permission of Zondervan Bible Publishers.

Edited by Rodney L. Morris
Cover design and illustration by Britt Taylor Collins

A JUST DEFENSE
© 1987 by Multnomah Press
Portland, Oregon 97266

Multnomah Press is a ministry of Multnomah School of the Bible, 8435 NE Glisan Street, Portland, Oregon 97220.

Printed in the United States of America

Library of Congress Cataloging-in-Publication Data

Payne, Keith B.
  A just defense.

  Includes bibliographies and index.
  1. United States—Military policy—Religious aspects.
2. Christian ethics. I. Payne, Karl I. II. Title.
UA23.P375   1987   261.8'73   87-12386
ISBN 0-88070-199-4

87 88 89 90 91 92 93 – 10 9 8 7 6 5 4 3 2 1

This book is dedicated

to wives Beth and Gail, and parents Holland and Vida—

each in their own way made this book possible;

and to Jonathan,

who hopefully will be able to enjoy

a more secure world than we now know.

Contents

Contents

Foreword

"Blessed are the peacemakers," Christ said, "for they shall be called the sons of God." This book is an attempt to apply that very simple calling, in the midst of a very complex world. The authors of this work take seriously the call to God's people to be peacemakers. "But what does it mean," they ask, "to be a 'peacemaker' in relations between countries?" Is it different than promoting peace between individuals? Is the pacifist position the best answer? Is peace at any price a legitimate goal? How should a Christian respond to the issue of military preparedness, nuclear arms, and strategic defense initiatives?

We have all heard the quick and easy solutions on both sides of the issue. And we have heard the prooftexting appeals to Scripture or the absence of any appeal to Scripture at all. As I have carefully read through every page of *A Just Defense*, I have been impressed with the sane and credible approach to the Scriptures that are relevant to the issue, on the one hand, and the balanced and thorough treatment of the various suggested responses to those Scriptures, on the other hand. In not one instance did I detect a tendency to avoid the difficult questions or to prejudice the case with personal biases. The approach is forthright and honest.

In the final analysis, nobody wants a nuclear war. The question is, "What is the best way to avoid it?" I believe *A Just Defense* will give to the genuinely concerned person a thorough awareness of the relevant data so that a credible plan of action can be formulated.

Earl D. Radmacher, President
Western Conservative Baptist Seminary

9

Acknowledgments

The authors would like to express their gratitude to the following individuals for their assistance in the preparation of this book. Each was important to its completion; none, however, is responsible for its conclusions:

Mr. Kurt Guthe, Professor James DeYoung, Mr. Ron Herbig for use of the Cannon Beach conference facilities, Rob and Kathy Hills, Mr. Robert Hosking, Ms. Beth Miller, Mr. Rodney Morris, Miss Sandy Nowack, and Professor Earl Radmacher. Thanks are due to Mr. Paul D'anieri for his help with chapters seven, eight, and nine, and a special thanks to Ms. Jill Coleman for her outstanding and much appreciated help on virtually the entire manuscript.

Introduction

Why write or read a book on the use of force, and U.S. strategic policy? Are not such issues as the role of military force in international relations, nuclear policy, and arms control better left to governmental experts and academic commentators? Why should one become involved in the nuclear debate? This book is a testament to the view that citizens of the United States have an obligation to become involved in such issues. It will attempt to define the fundamental questions for the Christian in the area of military force and, particularly, nuclear arms. With due respect for the sincere views of others on these issues, this book will analyze those views with one purpose in mind: to suggest humbly how the Christian may, in good conscience, deal with the complex issue of the use of military force in a nuclear-armed world.

The questions we have sought to address in this book do not permit easy solutions. The Christian is called to be a peacemaker. That calling is clear. But what does it mean to be a peacemaker in relations between countries? If one opposes U.S. military preparations, does that promote peace as some Christians claim?[1] Or would a militarily weak and reluctant United States simply tempt aggressive states to attack other weaker nations that rely on the United States for their security? If the latter is true, then opposing U.S. military strength can be seen as risking war and promoting injustice. In the international arena the pacifist position is not self-evidently the position that best promotes peace and justice.

The question is not whether Christians should be peacemakers, but what that may mean for the Christian trying

13

to form an opinion on military issues. Does it mean supporting or opposing U.S. military strength?

To be a peacekeeper among states may require different types of behavior than peacemaking among individuals. As individuals we have an entire system of police, courts, and judges to help resolve disputes, protect the innocent, and enforce justice. The individual can call on the power of the state for protection and to provide justice. This is true now, and it was true in New Testament times. For example, as a citizen of Rome the apostle Paul called on the coercive authority and power of the Roman state for protection and justice when he was endangered by a violent mob.[2]

However, at the level of relations between states there does not exist a recognized police force, court, or judges with the power to resolve disputes and enforce justice. Smaller, weaker states often are the victims of stronger, more aggressive states. And millions of soldiers and civilians have died in combat as a result. For example, World War II was set off by the German invasion of Poland in 1939. There was no police force that could come to Poland's rescue or restrain the aggressors, and by the time World War II was over there were fifty million casualties.

One could wish that an international court and police force with the necessary power existed to prohibit such catastrophes; but it does not, and nothing suggests that one will in the foreseeable future. The United Nations was originally conceived around such a hope. But hostility and constant disputes among its members have prohibited the U.N. from playing such a significant role.

Because of this significant difference between the context within which individuals and the states must operate, very different means of promoting peace and justice are likely to be appropriate at the individual and international levels.

In this book we cannot provide quick and easy answers to such complex issues. There are no quick and easy answers. The issue of the proper role of force in U.S. policy, and particularly the proper role of nuclear force according to Christian principles, is not an arena for simplistic solutions. Expressing popular passions and progressive sentiments may please some who are searching for solutions that can be expressed in a few pious-sounding phrases, but we want to provide more.

Most all can agree that Christians must support peace. But repeatedly stating this calling, as if it is therefore clear what Christians should do, is not very helpful. It reflects a commitment shared by all without explaining the implications for how a Christian should act—it does not address the real-world question: What can Christians do to promote peace and reduce the risk of nuclear war? Does the opposition by some Christians to U.S. nuclear arms programs really reduce the risk of war? Or might not such opposition simply encourage the Soviet Union to believe that it eventually can achieve a useful nuclear superiority? A resounding "no" to nuclear war is easy to express; the difficulty is explaining what specific actions can contribute to the preservation of peace, and why.

In this book we examine these issues and pose critical questions. We then suggest answers that respond to fundamental concerns about a world armed with approximately fifty thousand nuclear weapons. We will provide answers that please some but disappoint others. However, we are not seeking to please or disappoint any particular political view; rather we hope to address meaningfully an area of real concern for millions of Christians—the prospect of nuclear annihilation.

WHY BECOME INVOLVED?

But back to our original question: Why should the Christian think about such seemingly arcane and technical issues as nuclear weapons, national security policy, and arms control? Why become involved? There are several answers to that question that deserve consideration.

Christians as Salt and Light

First, Christians have been commanded to be "salt" and "light" in a world that is groping in darkness. If Christians fail to provide answers to peoples' real concerns, they act neither as salt nor light. If Christians refuse to become involved and informed on those problems that pose a real threat to the lives of millions, they will be guilty of failing to express concern and compassion to a humanity overwhelmed by feelings of hopelessness.

Some Christians have adopted the position that because all things are under the control of God, including the prospect of nuclear war, they can simply ignore the problem. This is an attractive rationalization for noninvolvement, but it is not valid. Christians cannot simply throw up their hands and withdraw from earthly responsibilities because they believe God to be in control. If that were the case they would not need to evangelize—but Jesus Christ has given Christians the great commission. Nor would Christians need to work for peace—but Jesus Christ has commanded Christians to be peacemakers. Christians have been commanded to become involved in the world so as to be salt and light—to become involved in support of Christian principles among human relations. As such, there is no excuse for the Christian simply to say that he or she will leave the cause of peace in the capable hands of God. One might as well decide not to wear seatbelts, not to lock doors, or not to be vaccinated against diseases because God is in control. The argument simply is not consistent with the calling of the Christian to be "in" the world but not "of" the world.

Christians as Responsible Citizens

Second, as Americans we live in a democratic society with the rare privilege of participating in the policies our government follows, whether in education, health care, taxation, abortion, or nuclear arms and arms control. Failing to participate in the democratic process is to abandon the responsibility of citizenship. This may mean only that a person become informed on the issues and vote, but it can mean no less; this includes the issues surrounding nuclear policy.

If participation in the democratic process is a responsibility of every American citizen, it is even more so for the Christian. This is so for two reasons. First, Christians are under the direct command of Jesus Christ to carry out their responsibilities as citizens of the state.[3] If Christ had rejected the authority of the state and a citizen's obligation to the state, Christians would have to reject that authority and obligation. But that is not the case. The Christian is under a dual obligation: He has the duty, as an American citizen, to participate in government and is commanded by Jesus Christ to abide by that responsibility to the state.

Second, when Christians have the democratic opportunity to help determine those policies under which they must live, they can abstain from that privilege only at the risk of seeing policies established that are hostile to Christian principles. Such laws and policies may be difficult to imagine in the United States but elsewhere they are often the norm.

In many countries Christians must confront the dilemma and danger of being in opposition to the state. Imagine the joy with which Christians in the Communist bloc would greet the opportunity to shape the policies of their governments—policies that now are openly hostile and repressive toward millions of Christians.[4] Imagine policies that forbid the independent gathering of believers, that send believers to labor camps and "psychiatric" institutes, that forbid the teaching of religion to one's children, that permit the state to take one's children because they are raised in a Christian home, and that ensure that a believer will be denied employment opportunities. These are the sad circumstances of many believers in the Soviet Union.

It has become easy for American Christians to take their liberty for granted. But if these liberties are to be enjoyed by future generations, they must be protected from those who would seek to impose a different set of policies and laws—a set of policies less sympathetic to the Christian conscience. Christians clearly have a special interest in protecting the liberties all enjoy in the United States, and Christian involvement can help ensure that protection.

FUNDAMENTAL ISSUES

The conclusions drawn from the Bible concerning the proper use of force by the government, and the proper role of the Christian in support of the government, have a tremendous bearing on the extent to which Christians can support the government. Many fear they do not have the technical expertise to consider these issues seriously. But the fundamental questions of national security, the use of force, and nuclear weapons are not technical. They rest on value judgments—political and, ultimately, moral judgments. Many secondary issues do involve technical expertise. However, the nuclear debate in the United States is very much a debate over fundamentals. Much of the debate over secondary technical issues overshadows the fact that there does not exist a consensus on fundamental issues, issues that cannot be resolved by technical analysis. Anyone sincerely interested and willing to become informed, even those without technical training, can participate in this critical debate without apology. This book will provide an examination of these critical issues.

Three Basic Questions

Answering three basic questions is the key to any consideration of these issues. Each is important in our attempt to structure a Christian response to nuclear weapons. These questions are:

1. Does the Bible give government a mandate to exercise necessary force in punishing evil and rewarding good, in defending the innocent (protecting civilians)?

2. If government has an obligation to exercise necessary force in rewarding good, punishing evil, and defending the innocent, to what extent can or should the Christian directly participate in and support that process?

3. Of the methods or alternatives available for governments to carry out any divine mandate of protection, reward, and punishment, which are the most consistent with biblical principles and a Christian conscience?

Over the ages Christians have proposed different answers to these three questions. These questions and their answers have become the basis for agreement and disagreement among six major Christian positions concerning the use of force: nonresistance, historic pacifism, radical pacifism, nuclear pacifism, traditional just war, and preventive war. This book will describe these positions and discuss their implications for the nuclear debate.

In assessing each of these positions we have been impressed by the fact they all share a common goal—to avoid nuclear war and promote peace. The real debate over force and nuclear weapons does not concern goals but rather the different methods recommended to pursue those goals. Christians who accept the pacifist position do not desire enslavement under a repressive Soviet-style government—they seek peace on terms compatible with their Christian commitment. Similarly, those Christians who accept the just war position, or an extension of it, are neither cavalier about nuclear war nor looking for some provocation for war—they desire peace with freedom on terms compatible with their Christian consciences. Nevertheless, despite the widespread agreement on goals, there is sharp disagreement on which means for achieving those goals are suitable for Christian support.

This book will outline the distinctions of each position and illustrate how each addresses the three fundamental questions discussed above. It will also examine the important related issues of deterrence, U.S. and Soviet nuclear policy, arms control, and the Strategic Defense Initiative (SDI), popularly known as the "Star Wars" program.

What will be presented in this book is a working proposal concerning an appropriate Christian response to the nuclear dilemma. The position we outline is more compatible with Christian principles than are the pacifist alternatives or the current deterrence policy of the United States, and is less risky than the preventive war position. It offers the prospect of supporting peace, continued liberties such as the freedom of religion, and protecting the innocent, as opposed to promoting one of those goals at the expense of another. The position we outline should appeal to the logic (if perhaps not the emotion) of each of the six major positions; it should respond to the Christian conscience of both the pacifist and the just war advocate. As such we offer this book as an attempt to bring the Christian community together around a single position concerning nuclear policy, and hope that it can facilitate an increased unity of spirit and purpose. To this end, if we are judged successful, all six positions should unitedly rejoice. This would indeed be good news.

Introduction, Notes
_____

1. See the book by Ronald J. Sider and Richard K. Taylor, *Nuclear Holocaust and Christian Hope* (Downers Grove, Ill.: InterVarsity Press, 1982).

2. See Acts 21 and 23.

3. See Romans 13:1-7; Titus 3:1; 1 Timothy 2:1-2; 1 Peter 2:13-17.

4. For a recent discussion of the church in the Soviet Union see, Anita and Peter Deyneka, "The Church Under Gorbachev," *Christianity Today*, 12 December 1986, 26-31.

Chapter 1

Government and the Use of Force

*T*he first critical question that must be answered in any effort to determine the appropriate Christian approach to national security issues is the basic question of the use of force.

Has government been given a divine mandate to exercise necessary force in defending the innocent, rewarding good, and punishing evil? This chapter will consider this fundamental question. If God has given government the prerogative to exercise necessary force in defending, rewarding, and punishing, then it is clear the Christian has a God-given obligation to support government in meeting its responsibilities—even if it means the government must use force in carrying out those responsibilities.

However, Christian radical pacifists claim that government does not have a God-given prerogative to use force for punishing evil or defending the innocent.[1] They claim government should not use force in such functions. If the radical pacifists are correct, then Christians who give their support to the governmental use of force risk doing so in opposition to God.

What does the Bible say about God's intentions for human governments? To help us find answers to this question, we will look at several biblical passages that give indications of the proper role of government. Most biblical commentators concur

21

that Romans 13:1-7 is the key New Testament passage on government's God-ordained responsibilities:[2]

> Everyone must submit himself to the governing authorities, for there is no authority except that which God has established. The authorities that exist have been established by God. Consequently, he who rebels against the authority is rebelling against what God has instituted, and those who do so will bring judgment on themselves. For rulers hold no terror for those who do right, but for those who do wrong. Do you want to be free from fear of the one in authority? Then do what is right and he will commend you. For he is God's servant to do you good. But if you do wrong, be afraid, for he does not bear the sword for nothing. He is God's servant, an agent of wrath to bring punishment on the wrongdoer. Therefore, it is necessary to submit to the authorities, not only because of possible punishment but also because of conscience.
>
> This is also why you pay taxes, for the authorities are God's servants, who give their full time to governing. Give everyone what you owe him: If you owe taxes, pay taxes; if revenue, then revenue; if respect, then respect; if honor, then honor.

The Responsibilities of Government
From this key New Testament passage, we can learn much about the role of government and the relationship of the Christian to government. We find answers here to the question of whether or not governmental authority is God-ordained, and whether the use of force is a God-given prerogative of government. The apostle Paul makes it abundantly clear that government is instituted by God, and that it has the mandate to use force, when necessary, in fulfilling its functions.

Government has specific responsibilities that it is to carry out faithfully for the benefit of those under its authority. Governmental authority is God's ordained servant to do good for that government's citizens (v. 4). Hence, government is to provide protection and care for its people, rewarding their good behavior. Additionally, government is God's ordained agent to punish evildoers by exercising necessary force, including lethal force, for the purpose of bringing his wrath upon evildoers: "for he does not bear the sword for nothing. He is God's servant, an agent of wrath to bring punishment on the wrongdoer" (v. 4).[3]

Christian Responsibilities to Government

These same seven verses teach not only the proper responsibility of the government to its citizens but also proper Christian responses to government as it carries out its God-given responsibilities. Every person (note the inclusiveness of the word "everyone" in verse 1) is to be subject to the governing authorities because government's authority is ordained and established by God (v. 1).

In his classic commentary, *The Epistle to the Romans*, Dr. Charles Hodge succinctly outlines the reasons for this attitude of submission to governing authorities:

> The duty of obedience to those in authority is enforced, (1) By the consideration that civil government is a divine institution, and therefore, resistance to magistrates in the exercise of their lawful authority is disobedience to God, verses 1,2. (2) From the end or design of their appointment, which is to promote the good of society, to be a terror to evil doers, and a praise to them that do well, verses 3,4. (3) Because such subjection is a moral as well as civil duty, verse 5. (4) On these grounds the payment of tribute or taxes and general deference, are to be cheerfully rendered, verses 6,7.[4]

This is an important point for Christians to remember as ridicule and rebellion against governing authorities has become fashionable—even in some Christian circles. Yet Scripture clearly commands Christians to obey their governing authorities because it is God himself who has given government the authority to govern. If some Christians object to this command or attempt to qualify it by saying that Paul intended to tell Christians they are obligated to obey only good governments but not those that fail to qualify as good, two important points should be remembered.

First, there is no such thing as a perfect government, or even one that is normally good. Governments are run by human beings—human beings who have fallen short of the glory of God. Paul was certainly aware of the depravity of man. Yet despite the fact that man and government are less than perfect, Christians are commanded to obey their governing authorities. Paul himself appealed to and submitted to governing authorities even when he knew he was right and they were wrong.

Second, the government that was ruling the Roman Christians at the time Paul wrote this letter was headed by an insane leader named Nero. Nero's government was not only responsible for some of the bloodiest persecutions of Christians in the history of the church, it was also the same leadership that killed Paul and Peter. To say that Roman believers were to obey a government as corrupt as Nero's, and yet Christians in twentieth-century America are not obligated to obey their government because of political corruption, is to imply that America is more corrupt than Rome. A person seriously advocating this position betrays ignorance of history. Comparing the U.S. government to that of Adolf Hitler's Nazi Germany or Nero's Rome, as several radical pacifists have recently done, goes beyond believability to absurdity.[5] Needless to say, if God expected Roman believers who were dying for their faith to obey Nero's government, there is no question that American Christians must obey theirs.

Generally, Christians must be careful not to demonstrate resistance to governing authority (God's ordained agent) because to do so is to resist God's command: "Consequently, he who rebels against the authority is rebelling against what God has instituted, and those who do so will bring judgment on themselves" (v. 2).

The fear of punishment can help motivate Christians to be subject to governing authorities because those who resist will be punished: "But if you do wrong, be afraid, for [the one in authority] does not bear the sword for nothing. He is God's servant, an agent of wrath to bring punishment on the wrongdoer" (v. 4). But Christians should also be subject to governing authorities because of conscience' sake, for subjection to governing authorities is really subjection to God: "Therefore, it is necessary to submit to the authorities, not only because of possible punishment but also because of conscience" (v. 5).

Finally, because Christians receive benefits from the governing authorities, they therefore are responsible to pay taxes to support the functioning of government: "This is also why you pay taxes, for the authorities are God's servants, who give their full time to governing" (v. 6). Paying taxes for the Christians is not an option but a demonstration of obedience to God. The IRS should not have to bother with auditing the returns of Christians.

Support from Additional Scriptures

Additional Scriptures support and corroborate Romans 13:1-7 concerning governmental use of force and the responsibility of the Christian to support governmental authority in fulfilling its roles. It should be recognized, however, that even were there no additional scriptural support for the governmental right to use force in its roles as defender and punisher, Romans 13 is unequivocally clear on the issue. There are, nevertheless, additional Scripture verses that teach Christian subjection to governmental authority and the prerogative of government to use force in fulfilling its role as God's agent to protect the innocent, reward the good, and punish evil.

Jesus clearly recognized the government's right to collect taxes (which at the time helped to pay for its army) when he said in Matthew 22:21, "Give to Caesar what is Caesar's, and to God what is God's."

In John 19:10-11 Pilate claimed he had governmental authority to have Jesus spared or executed. Pilate had been appointed governor of Judea in 26 A.D. by the Roman emperor Tiberius. As such, he was in charge of the Roman occupation army, appointed high priests, had the power of life and death over his subjects, and decided cases of capital punishment. Jesus did not deny Pilate's authority to have him executed. Rather, Jesus reminded Pilate that governmental authority was his only because it had been delegated to him from God:

> "Do you refuse to speak to me?" Pilate said. "Don't you realize I have power either to free you or to crucify you?"
>
> Jesus answered, "You would have no power over me if it were not given to you from above. Therefore the one who handed me over to you is guilty of a greater sin."

The apostle Paul repeatedly accepted and confirmed the government's authority and right to exercise necessary force for the purpose of defense and punishment. Whether before a Roman jailer, city magistrate, military commander, Roman governor, a king, or ultimately Caesar, Paul acknowledged, supported, and taught the God-given role of government to defend the innocent and punish evil—even to the point of the lethal use of force:

> Paul answered: "I am now standing before Caesar's court, where I ought to be tried. I have not done any wrong to the Jews, as you yourself know very well. If, however, I am guilty of doing anything deserving death, I do not refuse to die. But if the charges brought against me by these Jews are not true, no one has the right to hand me over to them. I appeal to Caesar!" (Acts 25: 10-11)

Other passages may be cited that support the thrust of Romans 13:

> Remind the people to be subject to rulers and authorities, to be obedient, to be ready to do whatever is good (Titus 3:1).

I urge, then, first of all, that requests, prayers, intercession and thanksgiving be made for everyone—for kings and all those in authority, that we may live peaceful and quiet lives in all godliness and holiness (1 Timothy 2:1-2).

Submit yourselves for the Lord's sake to every authority instituted among men: whether to the king, as the supreme authority, or to governors, who are sent by him to punish those who do wrong and to commend those who do right. For it is God's will that by doing good you should silence the ignorant talk of foolish men (1 Peter 2:13-15).

It is clear from the Bible that God has delegated to governmental authority the responsibility of rewarding good behavior, defending the rights and freedoms of the innocent, and punishing evil. It is similarly clear that the Bible teaches that governmental authority, as God's agent, may use force if necessary—including lethal force—in fulfilling its responsibilities. Jesus, the apostles, and the early church acknowledged and respected this authority.

Support from History
    It should also be noted that the vast majority of both Catholics and Protestants have historically supported the position that government has not only the God-ordained right but the responsibility and obligation to use necessary force in defending, rewarding, and punishing those under its authority. Even the historical "peace church" (Mennonite, Brethren, and Quaker) has recognized and accepted the government's right and responsibility to use necessary force.
    In short, Scripture is clear that there exists a God-given role for government to act—with force if necessary—on behalf of God to protect, reward, and punish. The overwhelming majority of Christian denominations, Christian writers, and Christian scholars have affirmed this role and the prerogative of government to use necessary force in carrying out its responsibilities.

This discussion may seem far removed from consideration of the Christian response to nuclear weapons, but it is essential to any such consideration. If the New Testament clearly rejected government's authority and responsibilites and stood in opposition to the governmental use of force, then Christians would be obligated to oppose what Scripture has rejected. Such a situation would place Christians squarely against the use of U.S. military power and against the U.S. policy of deterrence. However, because there is a clear biblical position that governmental authority is the agent of God and has the prerogative of using necessary force, there is a biblical basis for Christians to support the necessary use of force by government in fulfilling its responsibilities.

Exceptions to the Instruction to Obey

A very important question with regard to the biblical teaching in this area has to do with the extent of its application. Does the instruction about subjection to governmental authority extend to Christian participation in military service and the potential use of force in defending the innocent and punishing evil? The overwhelming majority of Christian writers and scholars from the early church until the present consistently have concluded that Christian subjection does extend to military service.

The question concerning the extent to which different Christian groups feel they can, in proper Christian conscience, participate in government and its use of force will be addressed in a later chapter. For this discussion it need only be noted that the consistent, dominant Christian position has been to support governmental authority faithfully as unto God. Of course, this should not be taken as Christian endorsement of any governmental policy that itself violates God's direct biblical command.

The only exception to Christian obedience to government comes into play when government participates in actions that are blatantly opposed to God's revealed will. Such would be the case when governmental policy was intended not to defend but to punish the innocent, or perhaps reward the evil. In such a case wherein subjection to the government would be in opposition to God's will, Christians are obliged to act in compliance with God's will rather than governmental authority.

This exception has clear biblical warrant. In Acts 5, Peter tells the Jewish leaders, who had commanded John and him to stop preaching about Jesus, that they must obey God rather than men. While it is true that on that occasion Peter and John opposed the ruling authorities, it is also true they were willing to accept the punishment prescribed for them for their defiance. Scripture does not indicate that the apostles used this injustice to justify freedom fighting, holy wars, or liberation theology; instead, they considered it a joy to be counted worthy to suffer for Christ.

In summary, the types of circumstances that might make it appropriate to stand against governing authorities and accept the punishment that would likely accompany such a decision would be if government purposely kills rather than protects the innocent, punishes rather than rewards good behavior, or rewards rather than punishes evil behavior. However, unless government clearly is behaving in such an unjust fashion, Christians may not use the freedoms they are provided in a democracy to advocate illegal policies. Such action is not biblical behavior no matter how elaborate the rationalizations that can be made.

GOVERNMENTAL AUTHORITY, THE USE OF FORCE, AND NUCLEAR WEAPONS

The question that is important for this discussion is whether the general legitimacy of governmental authority and its use of force extends to nuclear weapons and obligates Christians to support U.S. nuclear policy. However, before the question can be addressed it is necessary to explain briefly the nature of deterrence and the U.S. policy of deterrence.

Deterrence and U.S. Policy

Discussions of the proper Christian response to nuclear weapons often are presented with little apparent understanding of the role the United States intends for nuclear weapons.[6] This is unfortunate because as the verses above indicate, the purpose for which government possesses force is important in determining whether it can be supported by Christians in good conscience. Scripture suggests that the governmental use of force ought to be for the purposes of keeping the peace, protecting the innocent, and punishing the evil.

Can Christians support U.S. policy as consistent with the biblical responsibilities and prerogatives of government? The following discussion will examine the nature of deterrence and how nuclear weapons fit with the U.S. policy of deterrence.

Although academic discussions of deterrence theory often are complex,[7] the concept of deterrence is not difficult to understand. Indeed, it can be seen in some fashion in everyday life. For example, many department stores have signs announcing that, "Shoplifters will be punished to the full extent of the law." That sign is meant to prevent shoplifting (deterrence) by stressing to the would-be shoplifter the legal danger involved. Deterrence can be the most effective means of dealing with such matters because it focuses on stopping the crime before it happens, thereby avoiding all the expense, time, and possible violence that can take place in attempting to catch the criminal after the fact. That, in simple terms, is deterrence.

This notion of deterrence based on the threat of punishment is used by millions of people everyday: Parents hope to deter their children from running in the street by explaining the danger; television ads hope to deter people from drug abuse by presenting facts about its ill effects; teachers attempt to deter their students from cheating on an exam by spelling out the likely consequences; and police hope to deter crime simply by their presence—"walking their beat." As these everyday situations suggest, almost everyone has used deterrence in some instances and been deterred from an action in other instances.

The basic principles of U.S. deterrence are exactly the same as those in the examples from day-to-day living. To be specific, the U.S. attempts to deter the Soviet Union from taking particular actions by clearly presenting the military consequences involved should the Soviet Union take those un-wanted actions. As in the examples cited above, if U.S. deterrence policy works as intended, then the United States can avoid taking the threatened military action. Effective deterrence provides the great benefit of preventing those particular Soviet actions that the United States finds most threatening without the actual employment of military force. Indeed, if the United States is compelled to employ military force, then deterrence has effectively failed.

The notion that the actual need to employ military force means that deterrence has failed follows precisely the same principle as in the example of the department store sign intended to deter shoplifting. If a person sees the sign, is reminded of the possible consequences of shoplifting, and yet does so none-theless, the sign failed in its main purpose of deterring crime. In that case the department store has to go to the trouble, expense, and possible danger of catching the person, turning him over to the police, and pressing charges. The store obviously would rather deter the shoplifting in the first place. Similarly, the U.S. would rather deter threatening Soviet actions than go to the expense and risk of employing military force in response to unwanted Soviet actions.

In most ways effective deterrence is far superior to the actual employment of military force: there are no casualties, there is much less danger to civilians and soldiers, and the costs are less—all because those potential Soviet actions that the United States fears do not take place. Correspondingly, as mentioned above, if military force must be used in response to some feared Soviet action, then deterrence has failed.

It should be noted that although effective deterrence alleviates the need to employ military forces it does not mean the United States can give up its military capabilities. The reason for this can again be illustrated by our example of the sign on which the department store promises to "prosecute all shoplifters to the full extent of the law." If that store has no capability to catch a shoplifter and has no prospect of being able to turn anyone over to the police—in short, there is no

chance anyone will get caught for shoplifting—the sign will
not be an effective deterrent against anyone who knows the
truth. The threat would not provide an effective deterrent because it would be an empty threat.

Similarly, if the United States attempts to deter certain
feared Soviet actions by explaining the military consequences
of those unwanted actions, but in reality has no capability to
back up its threat, that deterrent is unlikely to be effective.
Consequently, to maintain an effective deterrent, the United
States (or a department store) must have the apparent capability
to enforce that deterrent; otherwise its threat will be hollow
and unlikely to deter anyone from anything. In short, effective
deterrence is based on the capability to use force, in the hope
that force will never have to be used.

One of the key differences between the department store
example and the deterrence policy of the United States is that
it may be difficult for the would-be shoplifter to know the
capabilities of the store to enforce its deterrent. Yet if the United
States displayed its deterrent sign without capability for enforcement, the Soviet Union would not likely be fooled for long.
Consequently, if the United States is to enjoy the benefits of
an effective deterrent, it must maintain the military capabilities
necessary to support deterrence.

U.S. Deterrent Objectives

U.S. deterrence policy has specific objectives vis-à-vis
the Soviet Union—that is, there are specific acts the United
States hopes to deter the Soviet Union from ever undertaking.
The United States attempts to deter the Soviet Union from:

1. Highly provocative or coercive behavior that might
erupt into war;

2. Nuclear or conventional attacks on U.S. allies and
friends around the world;

3. Nuclear or conventional attacks on the American
people and homeland.[8]

These goals have remained the constant objective of U.S.
deterrence policy. This is important because the United States

possesses nuclear weapons to support these deterrence policy goals. But it is essential to understand that U.S. policy is built on the view that nuclear weapons are useful as a deterrent primarily if they remain an unused threat, not if they are launched.

Recall the example of the department store: If force must be used in response to the unwanted action, deterrence has largely failed. Similarly, if the Soviet Union takes the unwanted actions described above, despite the best U.S. deterrent efforts, then the deterrent role for nuclear weapons largely would have failed. Ironic as it may seem, it is absolutely accurate to describe U.S. deterrence policy as possessing nuclear weapons as a deterrent so that they will never have to be launched.

When considering the proper Christian response to nuclear weapons and U.S. policy, the basic elements of that policy must be understood and borne in mind. The question of concern in this discussion is whether nuclear weapons can play a legitimate role in U.S. policy from a Christian perspective. Even if government has the God-given prerogative of using force in carrying out its responsibilities of protecting the innocent and punishing the evil, can the actual employment of nuclear weapons possibly fit within that prerogative?

The widespread devastation that could result from nuclear war suggests to some Christians that the employment of nuclear weapons would punish the innocent and the evil equally, protect no one, and therefore could not be legitimate from a Christian perspective—even if government has the right to use force.

Yet if the legitimacy of actually employing nuclear weapons is debatable, what about the possession of nuclear weapons as a deterrent, as is the basis of U.S. policy? Some Christians reject even this role for nuclear weapons. But if, from the Christian perspective, nuclear weapons cannot be possessed for deterrence purposes, what means of security can the United States pursue? How may the American government provide protection for its allies and citizens against the very real Soviet conventional and nuclear military might arrayed against them?

The answers to these questions are not obvious. They are complicated questions on which sincere Christians can and do disagree. The remainder of this book will examine differing Christian views on these questions, searching each for its biblical basis, logic, and comprehension of the issues. Based on this examinaton of the major Christian positions we will suggest alternative answers, answers that we hope will address the legitimate concerns Christians have regarding the nuclear policy of the U.S. government.

Chapter 1, Notes

1. Ronald J. Sider and Richard K. Taylor, *Nuclear Holocaust and Christian Hope* (Downers Grove, Ill.: InterVarsity Press, 1982), 118. "Jesus may have been naive, idealistic or stupid to suggest that we ought to reject retaliation [i.e., retribution] and lethal violence [i.e., force]. But that seems to be what he said.

"But can non-Christians obey Jesus' kingdom ethics? Of course not. But they ought to! . . . God does not have one ethic for Christians and a different ethic for others.

"Certainly non-Christians will be able to follow kingdom ethics only very imperfectly. But they ought to. And to a certain degree, as the story of Gandhi shows, they can. To the limited extent that non-Christian and secular societies actually approximate Jesus' ethical teaching, to that extent they will enjoy greater justice, wholeness and peace."

2. Much has been written on this passage from Romans. Dr. John Murray writes that Romans 13:1-7 should not be considered a parentheses or artificially connected to Romans 12:19-21. (Murray, *The Epistle to the Romans* in *The New International Commentary on the New Testament* [Grand Rapids: Wm. B. Eerdmans Publishing Co., 1982], 145.) R.C.H. Lenski concurs that Romans 13 is the key New Testament unit explaining a Christian's obligations as a citizen under a secular government. (Lenski, *The Interpretation of St. Paul's Epistle to the Romans*, [Minneapolis: Augsburg Publishing House, 1961], 783.) Dr. John Walvoord and Dr. Roy Zuck also conclude that Romans 13 presents the Christian's proper relationship to his government and civil leaders. Walvoord and Zuck also observe that this passage "is the key New Testament passage on the subject," and that it is supported by 1 Timothy 2:1-4; Titus 3:1; and 1 Peter 2: 13-17. (Walvoord and Zuck, *The Bible Knowledge Commentary* [Wheaton, Ill.: Victor Books, 1983], 490.

3. Charles Hodge, *The Epistle to the Romans* (London: Banner of Truth Trust, 1972), 408. Alva J. McClain, the former president of Grace (Brethren) Seminary, has written in a similar fashion as Dr. Hodge concerning the implications of Romans 13: "the moral justification for the institution of human government, and also its power of capital punishment, is based squarely upon the very argument often used against the latter, namely, the sacredness of human life in God's sight—'for in the image of God he made man.' What we call civil or organized government, whether simple or highly complex, exists for only one reason—the protection, conservation, fostering,

and improvement of human life. Genesis 9:6, therefore, becomes one of the most important landmarks in all of human history, for here God not only decrees the beginning of human government in a sinful world but also lays down the moral and social foundation of all such government. As Luther has well said of the text, 'This was the first command having reference to the temporal sword. By these words temporal government was established, and the sword placed in its hand by God.' What we have here, then, is something wholly new upon earth; an institution by which God will now mediate His government over the nations through human rulers who, whether they acknowledge Him or not, are nevertheless 'ordained of God' as 'ministers' of His; and therefore will be held responsible before God for the manner in which they discharge their duties 'for good' to mankind in general and to 'execute wrath' upon those who do evil (Romans 13:1-6)." *The Greatness of the Kingdom* (Chicago: Moody Press, 1968), 46-47.

4. Ibid., 404-5.

5. Sider and Taylor, 178 (citing the arguments of some Christians promoting war tax resistance).

6. See in particular, Committee of Inquiry on the Nuclear Issue, Commission on Peace, Episcopal Diocese of Washington, *The Nuclear Dilemma: A Search for Christian Understanding* (Washington, D.C.: Episcopal Diocese of Washington, 1986); and The United Methodist Church, Council of Bishops, *In Defense of Creation: The Nuclear Crisis and a Just Peace* (Pre-publication print, 1986).

7. For a detailed treatment of deterrence theory see Keith B. Payne, *Nuclear Deterrence in U.S.-Soviet Relations* (Boulder, Colo.: Westview Press, 1982).

8. See, for example, Caspar Weinberger, *Annual Report to the Congress Fiscal Year 1988* (Washington, D.C.: Government Printing Office, 1987), 42-46.

Chapter 2

The Just War Tradition

*C*hristians are confronted by a dilemma. According to Scripture they are to obey and honor governmental authorities as the agent of God; they are to support the government with their taxes and acknowledge the prerogative of government to use force in fulfilling its responsibilities of protecting the innocent and punishing the evil.

Yet Christians must also be willing to disobey governmental authority—and accept any resulting punishment—when government acts contrary to its mandate to protect, punish evil, and reward the good. The dilemma is clear: How can the Christian know if the government is fulfilling its responsibilities legitimately, according to its divine mandate and prerogatives, or if it is transgressing its legitimate role? If government is acting and using force justly, then to oppose that governmental action is to oppose God (Romans 13:1-7). Yet if governmental authorities are violating their responsibilities, then the Christian cannot obey or support such governmental policies.

What kind of guidelines can be followed that will help the Christian discern when government is acting justly and carrying out its responsibilities properly? This is an extremely important question for the Christian, and it is a difficult question because of the following factors:

1. Scripture teaches that governing authorities have been established by God (Romans 13:1-2);

2. Scripture teaches that government is responsible to use necessary force to defend the innocent, reward good behavior, and punish evil behavior (Romans 13:3-4; 1 Peter 2:13-14);

3. Scripture teaches that Christians are responsible to support government in carrying out its divinely mandated responsibilities (Romans 13:1-7; Titus 3:1; 1 Timothy 2:1-2; 1 Peter 2:13-17; Matthew 22:21; Acts 25:10-11);

4. Yet, governmental authorities are human, with human imperfections and the potential to drift toward selfishness, evil, and corruption (Romans 1-3).

Because governments are administered by humans, there is always the possibility that government will use force for evil ends; to support such action would be inconsistent with a Christian conscience. Consequently, the Christian must be aware of governmental policies concerning the use of force—supporting those that are legitimate and opposing those that are not. Much of the debate among Christians regarding the use of force and nuclear weapons stems from basic disagreement over how the Christian can determine, according to the guidance found in Scripture, whether a governmental policy concerning the use of force is proper or improper.

Of the six major positions represented in the Christian nuclear debate (and listed in the Introduction), four fall under the broad umbrella of the just war tradition or some form or extension of it. These four are the nonresistance position, the nuclear pacifist position, the traditional just war position, and the preventive war position.

That all four fall within the basic just war tradition indicates they hold much in common. However, there are also sufficient differences to warrant considering them as four different positions. This chapter will briefly outline the three major variants within the general just war tradition concerning the use of force: the nonresistance position, the nuclear pacifist position, and the preventive war position. We will then focus in detail on the most widely supported view within both the Catholic and Protestant churches—the traditional just war position. Following that, we will examine areas of agreement and areas of disagreement among these four positions, particularly as they seek to address nuclear weapons, nuclear deterrence, and solutions to the nuclear threat issues.

MAJOR VARIANTS WITHIN THE JUST WAR TRADITION

The Nonresistance Position

The nonresistance position acknowledges that government does have the responsibility to exercise force in fulfilling its God-ordained role of protecting the innocent, rewarding the good, and punishing evil. Their support stops short, however, of participation in the taking of life. A person can and should participate in military service, but not as an active combat soldier. The Christian nonresistance position is based on several key Bible passages: Matthew 5:39 teaches that a Christian must personally live a life of nonresistance; a Christian must also support his legal government according to Romans 13:1-7; and a Christian's weapons for warfare are no longer physical but spiritual (2 Corinthians 10:3-4). Therefore, it is argued that Christians must support the government in its God-ordained work, but that support must involve spiritual weapons, not physical ones.

The nonresistance position instructs Christians to remember that they have been charged to serve as Christ's ambassadors, refusing to be conformed to this world system. They must be committed to evangelism and a lifestyle of nonviolence, and they must daily engage in spiritual battle, displaying good will toward all, repaying evil with good, and being ready to suffer for righteousness' sake.[1]

The Nuclear Pacifist Position

As with the nonresistance position, the nuclear pacifist believes that government has the responsibility to carry out its biblically mandated job of protecting the innocent, rewarding good behavior, and punishing evil behavior. Similarly, the nuclear pacifist position teaches that the Christian has a responsibility to become personally involved in that support, including military service.

However, unlike the nonresistance position, the nuclear pacifist does not limit that personal support to noncombatant roles. As the name would indicate, this position does not advocate personal nonresistance or pacifism, but nuclear pacifism. Essentially, the nuclear pacifist teaches that since God has ordained government and its use of force, the obedient Christian must personally participate in that support. Christians cannot refuse to participate in an institution God has established without attacking the character of God himself. The nuclear pacifist does, however, draw the line of support to conventional weaponry; nuclear force is not considered legitimate.

Christians must support their government in the just use of force. Yet, since they argue that nuclear weapons kill indiscriminately (the just would die with the unjust), and a nuclear holocaust would protect no one, nuclear weapons fall outside the just use of force by a government. Therefore, the nuclear pacifist position acknowledges the government's right to use force and the Christian's responsibility to support that right, but rejects the use of nuclear weapons because, it is argued, they would not protect the innocent, but would destroy the innocent with the evil.[2]

The Preventive War Position

Like the nonresistance and nuclear pacifist positions, the preventive war position supports the government's use of force if necessary and the Christian's responsibility to support the government in fulfilling its responsibility. The preventive war position does not, however, limit the extent of a Christian's personal involvement as does the nonresistance position. Rather, it contends that it is not possible for combat military service to be immoral for Christians but a moral responsibility for non-Christians, as the nonresistance position would argue. Nor does the preventive war position limit government's use of military force to conventional weaponry, as does the nuclear pacifist position. The preventive war position says that in a world that has nuclear weapons, many of which could be used against the U.S., the government has a right to threaten the use or actually use nuclear weapons first, if necessary, in meeting its obligation to protect the innocent, reward good behavior, and punish evil behavior.[3]

In noting that all three positions endorse government's right to exercise force and the Christian's responsibility to support the government in fulfilling its responsibilities, it should be understood that this support assumes that government policies protect the innocent, reward good behavior, and punish evil behavior. None of the positions supporting the just war tradition believe that Christians are obligated to support government policy that intentionally destroys the innocent, punishes good behavior, or rewards evil behavior. If this were in fact the official policy of a government, all three positions would teach that a Christian must oppose the evil action and be willing to endure the consequences for choosing to obey God rather than men.

THE JUST WAR POSITION

Moralists, philosophers, and religious writers have established guidelines to ensure that governments exercise force in a just fashion. The rules that have evolved over approximately the last twenty-three hundred years have come to be known as the just war tradition. The just war tradition was not developed to promote warfare, but rather to help guarantee that if a war was fought, it would be for just purposes and would be fought justly, making every effort to protect the innocent.

Just War Guidelines

What are the just war guidelines generally established as the basis for Christians to determine whether their government's decision to use force and the actual use of force can be regarded as morally just? Today, the just war theory is usually outlined by the following eight rules:

1. Just cause. The spread of religious and political ideologies, territorial conquest, and/or revenge are not considered justifiable causes for the use of force. All aggression is likewise condemned. The only basis that war, or the use of force, can be considered just is if it is defensive in nature. If all governments would honor only a defensive policy regarding the use of force, there would be no more aggressive, expansionist wars.

2. Just intent. The objective of a just use of force must always be the restoration of peace and protection of the innocent. Again, revenge, ideological supremacy, conquest, and economic gain are not defensive in nature and, therefore, fail as justifiable bases for the use of force.

3. Last resort. The use of force can be considered just only if all reasonable compromises and negotiations have failed.

4. A formal declaration. The use of force cannot be exercised unless a formal declaration by a properly authorized person or body has been clearly made.

5. Limited objectives. Since the purpose of a just war is peace, an unconditional surrender or the total destruction of a country's political and economic institutions is not a legitimate objective of a just war.

6. Proportionate means. The weaponry or degree of force used must be limited to what is necessary to secure a just peace. Total or unlimited warfare goes beyond establishing a just peace.

7. Noncombatant immunity. Noncombatants (i.e., prisoners of war and innocent civilian nonparticipants) should be guaranteed immunity in a just war. That is, the use of force should discriminate between combatants and noncombatants.

8. *A reasonable hope for success.* A defensive response to an aggressor's use of force must provide a reasonable chance of securing a just peace to be considered justified force.

Dr. William O'Brien of Georgetown University has provided a good summary of the secular justification for the just war theory and its valuable contribution to the contemporary debate over nuclear war and deterrence:

> Although just war doctrine begins with a moral presumption against war, its underlying view of humanity, the state and the international community acknowledges the necessity for war in human relations under certain circumstances. If a political society and the rights of its citizens are threatened by aggression, there is a right of defense that overcomes the presumption against war. (Indeed, in older just war doctrine there was generous provision for offensive wars on behalf of justice.) . . . The greatest attraction of just war doctrine, however, is that it provides an orderly way in which to undertake the moral analyses necessary to judge nuclear deterrence and war as well as other forms of modern war.[4]

The History of the Just War Position

Most just war theorists, religious and secular, point out that their position is not a recent teaching. Many believe it predates even the early Greek philosophers by at least a thousand years.

Although Israel was unique as a theocratic kingdom, and there were consequently exceptions, rudimentary elements of just war principles are evident in Old Testament instruction on warfare. Peace terms were to be offered in order to avoid war if possible (Deuteronomy 20). However if fighting did occur despite attempts to avoid it, the land was to be allowed to remain productive. It is often evident throughout the Old Testament that noncombatants were to be spared. Following the writings of the Old Testament, the just war position is usually traced through the Greek philosophers (e.g., Plato and Aristotle) to Roman jurists (e.g., Cicero). Dr. Robert Culver offers this summary of the thinking of the early Greeks and Romans on the just war position:

> Nature has endowed man with a desire for peace and order and with the power of reason that makes possible an ordered society. True law is right reason in accordance with nature. It is unchanging and universal. It summons us to duty even to our enemies; it precludes treachery; it requires that even war be governed by moral law.[5]

For the Christian, the idea that nature or reason provides universally understood morals and norms for warfare as well as for peaceful living is supported in both Old and New Testaments. Amos 1:3—2:3 states that God would not withhold punishment and vengeance against Damascus, Gaza, Tyre, Edom, Ammon, and Moab because each had violated what they understood from nature and reason regarding universally accepted limits to warfare. Romans 1—3 informs the reader that all men, religious and pagan, know from nature (1:18-20) those things that are contrary to nature and reason (1:21-32).

From the Greeks and Romans, just war history moves to the writings of two early church fathers: St. Ambrose of Milan (c.339-397 A.D.) and St. Augustine of Hippo (354-430 A.D.). Patristic scholars recognize Ambrose and Augustine as the first two Christian writers who tried consciously and systematically to grapple with the difficult job of integrating Christian living and military service. Their thinking and writing has represented the majority position in Christendom, both Catholic and Protestant, from the fourth century until the present day.

Within the Catholic tradition most writers trace the just war position from Ambrose and Augustine to Aquinas in the thirteenth century, to Spanish theologian Francisco de Vitoria in the sixteenth century, to early seventeenth-century philosopher Francisco Suarez, "who systematized the details of the theory to its underlying principles of justice and love."[6] Protestant tradition moves from Ambrose and Augustine to Aquinas, to Martin Luther and his contemporary Ulrich Zwingli, to John Calvin.

Because the just war theory has overwhelmingly held the clear majority position among Christians, both Catholic and Protestant, from the fourth century until the present does not in itself make this position correct. But just as certainly, this near unanimity demands that the thinking Christian weigh carefully any opposing views concerning the use of force.

A second strength of this position is its appeal to the secular moralist as well as the Christian. A person need not be a Christian nor have religious convictions at all to see the virtues and values of this position in dealing with the ever present reality of wars and rumors of wars.

Biblical Basis for the Just War Position

Much of what could be said here has been mentioned in the preceding chapter. The rights and limitations on the use of force by government, as discussed in that chapter, are at the heart of the just war position. However, a concise summary of its biblical support is in order.

Human government has been established by God and given the responsibility to exercise necessary force for keeping order, rewarding good, and punishing evil (Romans 13:1-7; 1 Peter 2:13-17). God has not only condoned war in the past, he has also participated in it and promises to do so in the future. Since we know God is perfect, holy, and good, we cannot say that all wars are inherently evil (Exodus 15:1-18 and 17:8-15; Numbers 10:35 and 31:1-3; Deuteronomy 2:26-31, 3:1-7, and 20:1-4; Joshua 5:13—6:27; and Revelation 6:1-2, 19:11-21, and 20:7-10).

The sixth commandment condemns murder but not all taking of human life. There must be a distinction made between murder, which Scripture clearly condemns, and some forms of killing—such as war, self-defense, and capital punishment—

that Scripture has commanded (Exodus 20:13, 21:12-19, and 21:29). Both the Old and New Testaments condemn taking personal revenge but demand that authorized civil servants exercise just retribution against injustice and evildoers (Genesis 9:6; Exodus 21:23-25; Matthew 5:38-39; Romans 12:17—13:7).

In short, just war advocates teach that a just war may be waged only as a last resort by a legitimate government that has made a formal declaration of its intent. It must reject the use of excessive violence, making every reasonable attempt to protect the safety of noncombatants. The just use of force must have a chance for success, and it must be only defensive in nature. Peace with justice is the goal of a just war. Wars of revenge, territorial expansion, ideology, or religion fail to meet biblical and just war criteria.

Dr. Arthur Holmes provides this apt summary of the biblical evidence for the just war theory:

> On this basis the biblical picture is as follows: (1) The use of force in resisting and punishing violence is entrusted to governments. (2) Believers in both Old and New Testaments are involved in governmental uses of force. (3) Such uses of force are to be drastically limited to what is necessary in securing peace and justice. (4) Vengeance is thereby ruled out, along with all aggression; love and mercy must temper justice.[7]

THE FOUR POSITIONS:
UNDERSTANDING THEIR DIFFERENCES

Before we begin our detailed look at the differences between each of the four positions that fall under the just war tradition, something should be said about those areas in which they are in agreement. As we stated earlier in this chapter, the fact that all four positions accept the basic just war theory indicates they hold much in common. The nonresistance position, the nuclear pacifist position, the traditional just war position, and the preventive war position all agree that government has a right and an obligation to protect the innocent, reward good behavior, and punish evil behavior. They also agree that the Christian, as a disciple of Christ, has a responsibility to support the government in carrying out its God ordained job. As Dr. George Ladd has written:

> If the state has the divinely appointed authority to enforce law and order, it follows that the state has a right to claim my support even to the extent of war when such war is necessary in carrying out justice and enforcing international law.[8]

However, though these four positions hold these elements in common, they also differ significantly when it comes to issues concerning nuclear weapons, nuclear deterrence, and solutions to the nuclear threat. It is important that these differences be understood.

The Nonresistance Position

1. Nuclear weapons and the nonresistance position.

The nonresistance position says very little, comparatively speaking, about nuclear weapons. This position's relative silence is best understood as a result of its plain, literal interpretation of biblical statements regarding the eminent return of Jesus Christ. Obviously, the nonresistance position would not wish for a nuclear conflict. Rather than worry about this, however, time is better spent sharing the Christian message of salvation with as many as possible. Sharing this message, after all, is the Christian's highest priority and should not be sidelined because people are so concerned about this life that they neglect the eternal perspective of the next.

2. Nuclear deterrence and the nonresistance position.

As might be guessed, this position has little to say about deterrence. It is not that deterrence is unimportant, but in light of the Christian's highest priority as commanded by Christ, it must be considered a secondary issue. Those accepting the nonresistance position teach that Christians must support the local government and its policies in any and every fashion except taking another human being's life. If government supports nuclear deterrence, then the person accepting the nonresistance position should support that policy as well. If, on the other hand, the government rejected a nuclear deterrent, it would be necessary for an advocate of this position to reject a nuclear deterrent in support of his government.

3. Solutions to the nuclear threat and the nonresistance position.

The nonresistance position advocates the same solution to the nuclear threat that it advocates for a conventional threat. Christians are set apart for eternal service: they must pray for peace, support government policy in any fashion short of killing, and finally concentrate on reaching as many as possible with the gospel while there is still time to do so. The nonresistance position is consistent theologically if one is willing to accept four very important presuppositions:

1. Christians must support their government (Romans 13:1-7);

2. Christians, while obligated to support their government, cannot kill another human being (2 Corinthians 10:3-4);

3. Christ's promised kingdom of peace is physical and future and will not be realized until he returns in power to rule and reign (John 18:36; Matthew 24; John 14:1-3; Revelation 19:1-4);

4. Until Christ's return, the Christian's highest priority in life, regardless of vocation, is the proclamation of the gospel (Matthew 28:18-20, 2 Corinthians 5:17-21).

Christians are a royal "aristocracy" set apart for divine service. The priorities of this service are twofold: (1) Christians must live a life of personal holiness and purity as children of God, and (2) Christians must evangelize the world with the gospel of Jesus Christ in service for God. Both priorities must be faithfully carried out in anticipation of the rapture of the church and Christ's return to set up his promised millennial kingdom.

The Nuclear Pacifist Position

1. Nuclear weapons and the nuclear pacifist position.
The nuclear pacifist position on nuclear weapons is difficult to summarize. This difficulty is due in part to the lack of unanimity on this topic within the position. There are, however, several areas of agreement around which the nuclear pacifist position clearly unites.

Nuclear pacifists agree that the potential destructive power of nuclear weapons makes them a threat surpassing the worst nightmares of a conventional war. Because of this, nuclear pacifists place nuclear weapons in a special category—they cannot be used. Nuclear pacifists consider nuclear weapons inconsistent with just war guidance for three primary reasons:

1. Nuclear weapons are thought to be indiscriminate in their destruction, failing to distinguish between the innocent and the evil.

2. The use of nuclear weapons, it is believed, would escalate into an unlimited, indiscriminate war.

3. Therefore, if nuclear weapons cannot be limited in their use and if their use will bring about indiscriminate destruction, then there can be no possible beneficial use for nuclear weapons. Without a reasonable hope for success, nuclear weapons eliminate the possibility of a just nuclear war.

Even under New Testament teaching, which authorizes the civil government to use necessary force in rewarding good and punishing evil, governing authorities are expected to protect the innocent. Force must be used discriminatively. Author and pastor John Stott, a nuclear pacifist, writes of the necessity of maintaining the discriminate use of force:

If therefore we are right that a moral defense of the
just war is possible only if it can be seen as an
extension of the administration of justice, then the
distinction between the innocent and the guilty must
somehow be preserved.[9]

Believing that nuclear weapons fail to make these distinctions, nuclear pacifists consider nuclear weapons immoral; they
kill indiscriminately and leave no winner.

Some nuclear pacifists, however, believe that although
the indiscriminate use of nuclear weapons must be considered
immoral, there may be occasions when their limited use could
be considered necessary given our less than perfect world.
Stott again concisely describes this perspective:

There might conceivably, therefore, be a situation
in which it would be morally permissible to use a
very limited nuclear weapon, even though there
would be some degree of radioactive fallout, and
therefore some noncombatants would probably be
killed. It would have to be a situation of the utmost
urgency, in which the only alternative would be the
worse evil of surrender to a godless regime.[10]

2. Nuclear deterrence and the nuclear pacifist position.
    This is another issue that finds divisions within the nuclear
pacifist position. Some nuclear pacifists, believing that nuclear
weapons are immoral, teach that nuclear deterrence must be
considered immoral as well. Jim Wallis, editor of Sojourners
magazine, has written:

The willingness to produce, possess, and use nuclear
weapons must be named for what it is: the chief
manifestation of human sinfulness and rebellion
against God in our age.[11]

On the other hand, Dr. Stott has written:

It seems safer therefore, and more consistent with
both ideal and reality, to retain a nuclear deterrent

while developing the search for a disarmament which is mutual, progressive and verifiable.[12]

This response from a well-known Protestant to the question of nuclear deterrence sounds very similar to the response of a well-known Roman Catholic. Pope John Paul II told the United Nations Second Special Session on Disarmament that the use of nuclear weapons as a deterrent "may still be judged morally acceptable . . . certainly not as an end in itself, but as a step on the way towards a progressive disarmament."[13]

A rather obvious but complex question raised by the issue of nuclear deterrence concerns this distinction between the *possession* and the *use* of nuclear weapons. Most nuclear pacifists seem to agree with John Paul and Dr. Stott that while the use of nuclear weapons must be avoided, the possession of a nuclear deterrent is necessary in the world in which we live until a more satisfactory solution to the nuclear threat can be achieved. Stott, commenting on the possession-versus-use issue, has written:

> For there is a moral distinction between possession, threat, and use. It is probably true that if an action is immoral, then the active threat to perform it is immoral too. But the possession of nuclear weapons is more a conditional warning than an aggressive threat. Indeed, since the intention behind possession is not to encourage use but to deter it, possession cannot be pronounced as immoral as use. Shall we then renounce use but defend possession? This seems to be the conclusion to which we are coming.[14]

This seems to put the nuclear pacifist in the awkward position of endorsing the threat of an action that, if carried out, would be immoral. Most nuclear pacifists accept this awkward position because the failure to make that threat and have a deterrent would create a situation possibly leading to war. Most nuclear pacifists, while wishing that nuclear weapons and nuclear deterrence were not an available option (to anyone), realize that nuclear weapons and nuclear deterrence are a reality and must remain operative until a remedy to the nuclear problem can be developed that will guarantee peace with justice for all.

3. Solutions to the nuclear threat and the nuclear pacifist position.
   Unilateral disarmament. Unilateral U.S. disarmament, although endorsed by some Christians, is soundly rejected by most nuclear pacifists. The majority of nuclear pacifists believe that unilateralism, rather than helping produce lasting peace, is more apt to encourage the Soviet Union to exploit American self-imposed weakness. The Soviets would be able to use nuclear weapons in this case without fear of U.S. retaliation. Consequently, unilateral disarmament would allow the Soviet Union to bully the United States into compliance and surrender if it failed to cooperate with Soviet demands.[15]
   Nuclear freeze. The solution to the nuclear threat advocated by most nuclear pacifists is a mutual and verifiable freeze. The U.S. and Soviet Union would agree to stop producing, testing, and deploying nuclear weapons, and the agreement would be "verifiable" (both sides could monitor the other's actions to catch any cheating). Most nuclear pacifists wisely emphasize the words *bilateral* and *verifiable* in light of the Soviet tendency not only to stretch the wording of a treaty to its limits but also to blatantly break agreements and treaties. Nuclear pacifists, such as Senator Mark Hatfield, Billy Graham, and John Stott, agree that a bilateral and verifiable freeze is a desired first step to world peace—something most just war theorists would agree with—but that a unilateral freeze on the part of the United States is not an acceptable solution to the nuclear problem.
   On the other hand, a minority of nuclear pacifists have indicated their support for a nuclear freeze by the U.S. alone. They reason that the stakes are too high and the danger of global destruction too real to allow both superpowers to remain in a nuclear stalemate. So the U.S. should act unilaterally—it should take that first step as a demonstration of good will and faithful intent. This approach to a nuclear freeze would be

based on the hope that the Soviets would soon follow suit. This minority opinion, however, is viewed by most nuclear pacifists as a dangerous solution with little hope of success.

In summary, most nuclear pacifists advocate the retention of a limited nuclear deterrent, in conjunction with a bilateral nuclear freeze and subsequent reductions, as the most effective working solution for peace in a world faced with options that are less than ideal.

The Traditional Just War Position

1. Nuclear weapons and the traditional just war position.

Advocates of the traditional just war position do not believe nuclear weapons can be labeled immoral a priori. They view nuclear weapons as a needed deterrent against the aggression of the Soviet Union and as the only current means available for ensuring the survival of the United States and its allies as free democratic countries.

Although pacifists and many nuclear pacifists insist that the continued possession of nuclear weapons will lead to a nuclear holocaust, the traditional just war position argues that those weapons have helped provide peace for the last forty years, and that the U.S. must continue to balance Soviet nuclear capabilities.

Traditional just war adherents believe America's nuclear weapons, as a deterrent to Soviet aggression, protect Americans and their allies from living in a repressive gulag. Nuclear weapons are considered an important protection for American political and religious freedoms.

2. Nuclear deterrence and the traditional just war position.

Traditional just war theorists believe nuclear deterrence is ethically and pragmatically superior to other alternatives. It protects political and religious freedom not only for the U.S., but also for our allies, who would be in grave danger if we decided to lay down our nuclear deterrent. The U.S. nuclear deterrent denies the Soviet Union nuclear superiority that would leave America and her allies under the constant threat of nuclear blackmail or destruction. Dr. Carl Henry, a well-known traditional just war theorist, argues that not only is nuclear deterrence moral, it would be *im*moral for America to give up its nuclear deterrent without reciprocal action by the Soviet Union.

> The question of whether weapons and nuclear power can be used morally is not a matter to be prejudged philosophically, but one that depends on the circumstances in which they are used . . . the destruction by Hitler of six million Jews, by Stalin of 15 million people and by Mao of 25 million already represents a quantitative escalation of the disregard of human dignity. Not to use power as a counter balance to that sort of assault on the dignity of man would be immoral and perhaps even a matter of Christian lovelessness.[16]

A key issue for traditional just war theorists regarding nuclear deterrence is the intent for keeping such a deterrent. Why does America have a nuclear deterrent? If the intent is to bully and threaten for expansionist goals, then nuclear deterrence clearly is immoral. However, if the purpose of nuclear deterrence is to protect the American people and our country's allies, then nuclear deterrence can certainly be considered moral.

Traditional just war theorists see nuclear deterrence as a necessary evil. If the world did not possess nuclear weapons, nuclear deterrence would not be necessary. But, unfortunately, the world in which we live does possess nuclear weapons by the thousands, and many of them are aimed at the United States and its allies. Government is commanded in Scripture to exercise faithfully its responsibilities of protecting the innocent, rewarding good behavior, and punishing evil and unjust behavior. In a world that has nuclear weapons, this responsibility does not just allow for nuclear deterrence, it demands it.

3. *Solutions to the nuclear threat and the traditional just war position.*

Unilateral disarmament. Unilateral disarmament is rejected by the traditional just war position as both immoral and ineffective. It is considered immoral because it would place the safety and security of all Americans in the hands of a hostile and aggressive power. This problem becomes compounded when it is realized that an American unilateral disarmament would also undoubtedly place our Western neighbors and allies in great danger.

Just war theorists argue that Christian pacifists may personally choose nonresistance in the face of attack, but they have no biblical right or justification to require others to die with them because of their own personal choice. Kenneth Kantzer, dean emeritus and professor of biblical and systematic theology at Trinity Evangelical Divinity School, warns Christians to beware of those shouting "peace, peace," while leading the United States down a path to conquest and repression.[17] The traditional just war position opposes unilateral disarmament for the very reason that the peace it promotes is thought to be a delusion; unilateral disarmament is therefore considered both ineffective and immoral:

> So then, unilateral disarmament would be unethical and impractical. It denies justice and freedom and opens the door for Soviet and other tyrannical use of nuclear weapons against unarmed opponents, resulting in a holocaust every bit as bad as that which would be caused by a super power exchange. There is no assurance that with unilateral disarmament nuclear weapons will not be used.[18]

Nuclear freeze. Many in the traditional just war position strongly support a bilateral and verifiable nuclear freeze. A nuclear freeze under these conditions would be a good first step in the process of solving the current nuclear threat. The traditional just war position and the nuclear pacifist position are much closer in their support of a nuclear freeze than most people realize. Both agree that a nuclear freeze would be in the best interest of the United States and the Soviet Union if it were bilateral and verifiable. A major difference between the two positions is the willingness of some nuclear pacifists to freeze unilaterally as a demonstration of good will. The traditional just war position insists that a freeze be mutual and encourages the United States to continue to develop its nuclear deterrent until a bilateral and verifiable nuclear freeze actually begins.

Limited and unlimited nuclear retaliation. The traditional just war position soundly rejects an unconstrained use of nuclear weapons. Dr. Kantzer explains clearly that the traditional just war position does not support the intentional harming of the innocent (i.e., noncombatants). Unconstrained nuclear retaliation would harm millions of noncombatants and thus is not an acceptable response. However, the traditional just war position may support the use of a limited nuclear deterrent.[19] The limited use of nuclear weapons against military centers, rather than population centers, may meet the just war criteria of protecting noncombatants. The intent of this type of response would be to retaliate against military opposition, not the civilian populace.

Dr. Robert Culver, himself a former pacifist, provides this summary of the morality of a limited nuclear defense:

> If the present civilized order is to continue, rulers "of good will" must control the effective weapons their moral standards permit them to use. A missile possessed and aimed at Leningrad's residential district will likely never be used, but one aimed at a munitions depot in Russia could be and might be used by men of conscience. The principle of limited war is the same as traditional just war theory. The problems of the nuclear age are no different in principle from any previous age. In a world that never

can eliminate war, limited—that is, *justly waged*—
war is more important than ever before. To propose
that instead we insist on political pacifism, abandonment of war as an instrument of national policy is
utterly unrealistic. If we deny any nation the right
of justified war we condemn it to destruction by
those with no moral scruples at all.[20]

Traditional just war theorists believe that God will and
does bless the peacemaker. They do not believe, however, that
all peacemakers are pacifists, nuclear pacifists, workers in a
pacifist publishing house, or writers of pacifist articles and
books. Some peacemakers deter crime and protect the innocent
by being honest and just police officers. Other peacemakers
may wear a military uniform and help maintain the peace by
deterring the invasion of weaker states by powerful aggressive
states or, if deterrence fails, by helping protect the innocent
and restoring peace.

The Preventive War Position

1. Nuclear weapons and the preventive war position.
Because the preventive war position is primarily an extension of the traditional just war position, much of what could
be said concerning nuclear weapons and the preventive war
position has already been covered in the preceding discussion.

Nuclear weapons are considered necessary for government to fulfill its God-ordained job of protecting its people.
Nuclear weapons are not immoral in and of themselves any
more or less than are conventional weapons. Rather, nuclear
weapons are considered a necessary deterrent against Soviet
aggression and presently represent the key to keeping Western
democracies politically and religiously free.

2. Nuclear deterrence and the preventive war position.
The preventive war position supports the use of a nuclear
deterrent for the same reason the traditional just war position

does. There is a difference, however, in the way both positions view the possible use of nuclear weapons.

The traditional just war position supports the use of nuclear weapons in a strictly defensive or retaliatory response to unprovoked aggression from a hostile enemy. In contrast, the preventive war position not only supports nuclear use in a retaliatory response to aggression, it extends the possibility to the first use of nuclear weapons if an enemy's attack is believed imminent and unavoidable (i.e., a "preemptive" first strike is considered acceptable). Furthermore, it recognizes the recovery of territory or possessions unjustly seized by an enemy as a just cause for the use of force. Unprovoked military action is immoral. But military action in response to an enemy's present or previous unjust provocation is considered morally acceptable.

3. Solutions to the nuclear threat and the preventive war position.
   Unilateral disarmament. The preventive war position rejects unilateral disarmament for much the same reasons as those outlined under the traditional just war position. It is argued that unilateral disarmament is immoral and unethical because it jeopardizes American citizens, who the U.S. government has the biblical responsibility to protect, and America's allies and neighbors, who are to be loved.

Further, unilateral disarmament is considered ineffective and impractical because it does not ensure that the disarmed government's enemies will do the same. This being the case, unilateral disarmament could provoke rather than prevent enemy aggression.

   Nuclear freeze. Most preventive war theorists currently reject the concept of a nuclear freeze. Since the Soviet Union presently holds nuclear and conventional force advantages over the United States in many areas, a freeze at this time would lock America into a permanent position of inferiority. Parity could not be achieved without violating a treaty. Because the United States has allowed itself to be in a position of risk in regard to both nuclear and conventional weapons, the preventive war position advocates a military buildup of both nuclear and conventional weaponry.

SUMMARY

The just war tradition includes four equally sincere Christian positions. All four desire peace on earth and good will for all mankind. All four contain Christians who desire to love God with their whole heart and their neighbors as themselves. The traditional just war position is closest to the center of this general tradition, and historically it has received the strongest numerical support from both Catholics and Protestants. Sixteen hundred years of Christian support for this position does not in and of itself make it true. However, it should encourage the thoughtful Christian to take a long hard look before he decides to deviate from so many Christian witnesses.

Chapter 2, Notes

1. Herman A. Hoyt, "Nonresistance," in *War: Four Christian Views*, ed. Robert G. Clouse (Downers Grove, Ill.: InterVarsity Press, 1981), 25-57.

2. John R.W. Stott, *Involvement: Being a Responsible Christian in a Non-Christian Society* (Old Tappan, N.J.: Fleming H. Revell Co., 1985), 117-50.

3. Harold O.J. Brown, "The Crusade or Preventive War," in *War: Four Christian Views*, ed. Robert G. Clouse (Downers Grove, Ill.: InterVarsity Press, 1981), 151-68.

4. William O'Brien, "Morality and Nuclear Deterrence," in *The Nuclear Freeze Controversy*, ed. Keith B. Payne and Colin S. Gray (Lanham, Md.: University Press of America, 1984), 59-60.

5. Robert D. Culver, *The Peace Mongers* (Wheaton, Ill.: Tyndale House Publishers, 1985), 125.

6. Arthur F. Holmes, "The Just War," in *War: Four Christian Views*, ed. Robert G. Clouse (Downers Grove, Ill.: InterVarsity Press, 1981), 128-30.

7. Ibid., 123-24.

8. George E. Ladd, "The Christian and the State," *Command*, March 1982, 15.

9. Stott, 136.

10. Ibid., 137.

11. Jim Wallis, "A Time to Wage Peace," in *Waging Peace*, ed. Jim Wallis (San Francisco: Harper and Row, 1982), 13.

12. Stott, 140.

13. Ibid.

14. Ibid., 139.

15. Ibid., 140

16. Quoted in Robert F. Swartzwalder, "An Evaluation of Evangelical Perspectives on Nuclear War" (Master's thesis, Western Conservative Baptist Seminary, 1983), 91.

17. Kenneth Kantzer, "What Shall We Do about the Nuclear Problem?" in *Christianity Today*, 21 January 1983, 11. "We must beware of those who cry, 'Peace, peace!' but who would only lead us down a primrose path to slavery or poverty and, in the end, war. Freedom and peace are precious pearls of great price. But they come only to those who are willing to fight for them—and who pray that by God's grace they will not have to."

18. Swartzwalder, 94.

19. Kantzer, 10-11. "It would seem to me, therefore, that we really have only one moral and rational choice. That is to rely upon a strictly limited nuclear defense while at the same time working desperately toward the goal of a nuclear freeze—and then a nuclear cut back, and then an outlawing of nuclear weapons; the ultimate goal would be the destruction of conventional weapons. But those who pray that they will never have to use nuclear weapons must be willing to use them if necessary. Otherwise, there is no deterrent, but only a unilateral disarmament leading through appeasement and surrender to slavery."

20. Robert D. Culver, "Justice Is Something Worth Fighting For," *Christianity Today*, 7 November 1980, 25.

Chapter 3

The Christian Pacifist Tradition

*A*s we have discussed, the just war position has been for the last sixteen hundred years the dominant Christian position concerning the use of force. Because it has been the majority view does not mean it has been the only view sincere Christians have held. Those Christians who oppose the just war position are known as Christian pacifists. The Christian pacifist tradition consists of two primary parts—the historic pacifist position and the radical pacifist position. As one might assume, there are a number of principles both positions hold in common. However, because they do represent distinct groups under the general tradition of pacifism, there are also major differences between them.

We begin this chapter with a brief sketch of the historic roots of the Christian pacifist tradition. We then examine the major areas of agreement and the major areas of disagreement between historic and radical pacifism as well as discuss the main differences between the pacifist tradition and the just war position. Finally, we look at the alternatives historic and radical pacifists offer as working solutions to the problem of nuclear weapons.

THE CHRISTIAN PACIFIST TRADITION

The Historic Roots of Christian Pacifism

Most Christian pacifists assert that pacifism was the common practice of the church during its first three hundred years. Only after Constantine's ascension to power in Rome at the beginning of the fourth century did the church (except for small pockets of believers) compromise its position with the state and lose its pacifist distinction. However, around 1520 A.D., a "numerous minority," which later became known as the Anabaptist church, began to breathe new life into the old pacifist position.[1]

The historic Anabaptist church became the forerunner of today's "peace church" made up primarily of the Mennonite, Brethren, and Quaker churches. Today's peace church includes two very distinct pacifist groups. The first, and numerically the larger of the two, is the group we have called the historic pacifists. This group, by and large, has followed the general teaching of the historic Anabaptist movement. The second group, though much smaller numerically, is the more vocal of the two and is designated in this book as the radical pacifists. This group has made a significant detour from its Anabaptist history and is very active in political and social issues.

Major Areas of Agreement in Historic and Radical Pacifism

Both historic and radical pacifists use the same scriptural basis for their positions. The following passages are among the more prominent ones they use:

> Blessed are the peacemakers,
>   for they will be called sons of God.
>   (Matthew 5:9)

> You have heard that it was said, "Eye for eye, and tooth for tooth." But I tell you, Do not resist an evil person. If someone strikes you on the right cheek, turn to him the other also. (Matthew 5:38-39)

"Put your sword back in its place," Jesus said to him, "for all who draw the sword will die by the sword." (Matthew 26:52)

Do not repay anyone evil for evil. Be careful to do what is right in the eyes of everybody. If it is possible, as far as it depends on you, live at peace with everyone. Do not take revenge, my friends, but leave room for God's wrath, for it is written: "It is mine to avenge; I will repay," says the Lord. On the contrary:

"If your enemy is hungry, feed him;
    if he is thirsty, give him something to drink.
In doing this, you will heap burning coals on his
    head."

Do not be overcome by evil, but overcome evil with good. (Romans 12:17-21)

He will judge between many peoples
    and will settle disputes for strong nations far and
        wide.
They will beat their swords into plowshares
    and their spears into pruning hooks.
Nation will not take up sword against nation,
    nor will they train for war anymore.
(Micah 4:3)

Both pacifist groups teach that killing another human being is never acceptable. They also agree that Jesus Christ is the final (and most complete) revelation of God, and the Sermon on the Mount is the fullest expression of his will for man. This distinctive view of God's unfolding revelation with its culmination in Jesus Christ means that any former instruction from God (the Old Testament) must be subjugated to the New Testament in general and the four gospels in particular. Both pacifist groups believe that verses on nonresistance (Matthew 5:38-39, Romans 12:17-21) are to be applied not only by Christians personally but also by the church corporately. Christ's death and resurrection are the ultimate authentication and example of the superiority of nonviolence and nonresistance over the use of force. New Testament verses that seem to support a Christian, under some circumstances, being justified in using force are superseded by Christ's sacrificial example on the cross. As members of the Kingdom of God, all ultimate ethical norms are to be derived from the life, teaching, and example of Jesus Christ.

The historic and radical pacifists agree that the gospel is transnational, transcultural, and transracial. Christians, regardless of their respective governments' relations, are of one family. The believers' commitment to God and each other must be deeper and more binding than a commitment to any human government or ideology. As a member of the global community, each person is part of a universal nation called the Kingdom of God.

In regard to military obligations, both positions agree that a true Christian should not participate in any form or fashion of military service. Conscientious objection is the only God-honoring alternative to military conscription, and personal pacifism is evidence of a true commitment to Christian discipleship.

Both parties agree nuclear war must be avoided at all cost. Nuclear weapons are immoral and must be dismantled and destroyed; nuclear deterrence likewise is immoral and an invitation to war. Unilateral disarmament must take place immediately, and a nuclear freeze ought to be supported regardless of its terms.

Both pacifist groups have a difficult time agreeing on a precise definition for the Kingdom of God. Some believe this kingdom is physical and future; others believe it is spiritual and within each true believer. Still others believe it is something ultimately future that the church will help usher into existence. Finally, some pacifists use the Kingdom of God synonymously with true Christian conversion. This point is more important than one might think at first glance. Is the Kingdom of God a future home for the Christian to be established by Christ at his physical return? If so, Christians can and should work for world peace, though they realize ultimate peace will not be achieved until Christ returns. However, if the Kingdom of God is spiritual and found within each believer, then it does not demand or expect the physical return of Christ to be inaugurated. Peace will occur only if Christians make it happen as God's peacemakers. That, of course, requires activism.

Major Areas of Disagreement between Historic and Radical Pacifism

A major area of disagreement between these two positions centers around the proper role of government and the Christian's relationship to it. The historic pacifist position recognizes that government has a God-given right and responsibility to exercise necessary force in protecting the innocent, rewarding good, and punishing evil. Historic pacifists believe, however, in a strong separation of church and state. While the state is free to exercise necessary force, Christians are not. Essentially, this position asks government to be concerned about the affairs of government and to allow the church to be left alone to care for its own concerns.

The historic pacifist position does not take offense at its members working for the government, whether in a defense-related or nondefense-related role, if that is their sincere desire. Historic pacifists pay their entire tax liability, believing that Christians have been commanded to support the government with taxes to carry out its job of protecting, rewarding, and punishing.

In contrast, the radical pacifist position rejects the belief that government has a God-given right and responsibility to exercise necessary force for protection, reward, or punishment. Radical pacifists encourage their adherents to become involved in the political process to legislate pacifism and nonviolence as national policy. Radical pacifists however discourage their followers from holding defense-related jobs and encourage those in such jobs to relocate in nongovernmental employment.

Radical pacifists writers also discuss the option of withholding that portion of their taxes that would correspond to the defense department's percentage of the national budget.

Historic pacifists believe man's primary problem is an inherited sinful predisposition that can be remedied only through a personal relationship with God. True freedom is available to all, but only by one means: God's grace through faith in Christ. Because of this, historic pacifists oppose any type of revolutionary "freedom fighting" or other use of force for socioeconomic or political gain. Man's deepest need is a changed heart, which class struggles and guerrilla or freedom fighting cannot achieve.

The radical pacifist's focus is not so clear. Some radical pacifists see mankind's primary problem as economic rather than the sinful predisposition of man's heart. Economic redistribution of existing wealth is considered necessary for government to justly remedy inequalities. This being the case, some radical pacifists appear to openly support third-world class struggles by justifying their use of force.

Other radical pacifists do believe that man's ultimate freedom is found in a personal relationship with Jesus Christ. However, some now claim that this personal relationship with Jesus Christ can be considered genuine only if it is accompanied by a commitment to reject nuclear weapons.[2] As one might guess, the historic and the radical pacifist positions are at an impasse over this extrabiblical, "antinuclear" requirement.

A final area of disagreement is the extent to which the teaching of nonviolence is to be applied. Both positions agree that true Christian discipleship must include a commitment to personal pacifism and nonviolence. Both positions likewise agree that pacifism and nonviolence must be the commitment of the entire church. Where the disagreement arises is in how nonviolence is to be applied to the state.

The historic pacifist position does not believe the secular state can be expected to live by Christian convictions and standards. Thus, while teaching that pacifism and nonviolence extend to Christians personally and the church corporately, historic pacifists do not believe this teaching can or should be applied to the state. The radical pacifist position, on the other hand, teaches that the state should mandate a national policy of pacifism and nonviolence.

Related to this is a disagreement over the issue of resistance. Though both positions agree that violence must be rejected, they do not agree over the issue of nonviolent resistance. The historic pacifist position rejects the use of resistance and violence; they are committed to a position of nonresistance and nonviolence. However, included in the radical pacifist position is the distinction between the use of force and some forms of nonviolent resistance. Thus, within the radical pacifist position is a unanimous commitment to nonviolence but not to nonresistance.

Part of this distinction goes back to radical pacifism's departure from its Anabaptist roots. The radical pacifist seems committed to a type of pacifism that blends biblical pacifism with a humanistic pacifism that emphasizes human capability and asserts that all of society should endorse its position. It also embraces Gandhian pacifism—using nonviolent resistance to pressure government to recognize its cause and adopt its pacifist agenda.

Major Areas of Disagreement between the Pacifist and Just War Positions

The fundamental disagreement between these two positions centers squarely on their theological system of Bible interpretation or hermeneutics. The pacifist position accepts a theological hermeneutic that subjugates the entire Old and New Testaments to the gospels in general and the Sermon on the Mount in particular.

The pacifist argues that although God has in fact revealed his will in the Old Testament, he has progressively revealed more of his will in the New. All Scripture is inspired by God, but the Sermon on the Mount and the life, death, and resurrection of Christ are the most complete and perfect manifestations of God's will for man. Thus, regardless of what a person can learn about Christian living in the Old or New Testament, the Sermon on the Mount and Christ's example supersede all former or later instruction.

If one accepts this presupposition, the historic pacifist position is theologically consistent. According to this view the Old Testament teaching on the use of force was acceptable before Jesus Christ explained more clearly God's will to man. Paul's teaching on government and the use of force in Romans 13, Titus 3, and 1 Timothy 2 must be understood in light of Jesus' teaching on nonresistance in Matthew 5. Similarly, Peter's teaching in 1 Peter 2 on a Christian's response to governing authorities is important for the Christian, but it too must be understood in light of Matthew 5. Verses found in Matthew 3, Matthew 8, Luke 22, and Acts 10 that appear to support the use of force or permit a Christian's participation in military service are once again rejected because of the priority placed on Matthew 5.

Just war advocates do not accept the pacifist's hermeneutical presupposition. Just war theorists teach that although Christ has indeed fulfilled the Old Testament, he has not invalidated the Old Testament. Moreover, although Christ is the most perfect demonstration of God's will to mankind, "All Scripture is God-breathed and is useful for teaching, rebuking, correcting and training in righteousness, so that the man of God may be thoroughly equipped for every good work" (2 Timothy 3:16-17). Just war advocates therefore conclude that inspired Scripture in the Sermon on the Mount discourse must be harmonized with the rest of inspired Scripture.

This leads to a second fundamental disagreement between the just war and pacifist positions: the context of the Sermon on the Mount. Pacifists teach that Matthew 5:38-39 is applicable contextually to individual Christians, the entire church, and, radical pacifists say, to the government as well. If this is true, then pacifism must be not only the personal conviction of individual Christians, but also the corporate commitment of the church and the state.

The just war position argues that the Sermon on the Mount

in general and Matthew 5 in particular addresses personal discipleship, not the corporate church, the secular state, or non-Christians. A few from the just war position would argue further that although the Sermon on the Mount is applicable today for individual Christians, the context concerns teaching about acceptable behavior in Christ's future millennial kingdom.

The just war position recognizing a personal context and application of the Sermon on the Mount has been the overwhelming belief of the church. Additionally, some early church fathers taught that although Christians should be committed to a personal lifestyle of nonresistance, government must be supported in carrying out its God-ordained job of protecting the innocent, rewarding good behavior, and punishing evil behavior. Thus a Christian could be pacifistic in personal lifestyle but, if employed as an authorized agent or civil servant of the government, nonpacifistic in helping government govern justly and fulfill its responsibilities.

One must appreciate the priority of a biblically consistent hermeneutic that gives proper weight to the importance of context. When this fails to occur it is possible for two groups using the same verses to come to very different conclusions. Does the instruction from the gospels and the Sermon on the Mount supersede all other Scripture? Is the context of the Sermon on the Mount private or corporate? A person's answers to both these questions will determine to a large degree his view concerning whether or not a Christian or the state can exercise necessary force or whether both must be committed to a position of nonresistance.

The Christian pacifist position and the Christian just war position also differ over their respective evaluation of the greatest problem facing mankind in the nuclear age and how this problem affects their focus in day-to-day priorities. Many in the pacifist position appear to believe that the threat of a nuclear war is the greatest problem facing mankind in the twentieth century. As a result, some pacifists' primary focus becomes the task of removing this threat to the future of mankind. Much radical pacifist material in particular begins with pictures of the nuclear devastation of Hiroshima and Nagasaki, then moves to pictures of people killed or severely injured by those blasts. A nuclear holocaust is painted in graphic detail, and it is claimed that such a holocaust is inevitable unless Christians unite to remove nuclear weapons.

The Christian just war position, although keenly aware of the nuclear threat, still views man's greatest problem as his alienation from God. It is this alienation from God, with its subsequent greed, pride, selfishness, lovelessness and more, that has placed mankind in the dilemma in which it now finds itself. The nuclear threat is viewed as one more manifestation of this alienation from God and man's resultant inhumanity to man.

Another area where radical pacifists and just war theorists differ is the issue of demonstrating love for one's neighbors, enemies, and self. Most radical pacifist writing is filled with admonitions to love your enemies. Yet demonstrating love for neighbors and for self is almost completely ignored.

In contrast, the just war position at times focuses on the Christian's responsibility to love defenseless neighbors and the innocent, yet love for enemies is nearly forgotten. The pacifist can point to the just war theorist and remind him one is unlikely to express love to enemies by killing them. The just war theorist can remind the pacifist that love for enemies that ignores the consequences inflicted on friends and neighbors is loveless. One is unlikely to express love to one's neighbors by allowing them to be killed if it is possible to protect them. Both positions are partially right, and neither seems to have a consistently clear focus on this issue.

A result of these different views concerning love for enemies and neighbors can be seen in the two positions' emphasis on peace and freedom. Pacifists emphasize love of enemy and nonviolence, even at the expense of innocent neighbors and friends. Some might call this nonviolence at all cost. Just war advocates speak more of freedom than peace, even if that freedom is at the expense of enemies who need Christ. Once again, both positions have a relevant message for each other that needs to be heard: Christians must work toward peace with freedom and express love for enemy, neighbor, and self.

Most pacifists appear to think that if the choice comes down to accepting peace under the dictates of a repressive regime or maintaining freedom by exercising force, the Christian must choose nonviolence at the expense of freedom. In contrast, most just war advocates believe that peace obtained by surrender or subjugation to a repressive power is not the biblical idea of peace. The goal for this group is not peace or freedom but rather peace with freedom.

Concerning the use of force, nuclear weapons, and nuclear deterrence, there is sharp (and obvious) disagreement between the pacifist and the just war theorist. The pacifist position is committed to nonviolence and therefore rejects the use of force by individual Christians or the church. Historic pacifism, in keeping with its Anabaptist history, does acknowledge the government's right to exercise necessary force in carrying out its God-ordained job of protecting, rewarding, and punishing. Radical pacifism does not believe government should use force. Radical pacifists, in contrast to the traditional just war theorists and nuclear pacifists, reject even the possession of nuclear weapons as immoral. Their call is for immediate and complete nuclear disarmament—even if the U.S. disarms alone. The just war position has consistently taught that Christians can personally exercise force in the defense of another and that the exercise of force for the purpose of defense is not an option for government, but a divine mandate.

Historic and Radical Pacifist Solutions to the Nuclear Threat

The historic pacifist position generally provides three alternatives to the nuclear threat. First, Christians can pray for peace by supernatural intervention from God. The Bible is full of stories of how God provided supernatural protection for his people as a result of their obedience to him. If God was willing to provide protection for his people in the past, it is not expecting too much to believe he can or will do so now. It is therefore the Christian's responsibility to pray for peace.

Second, Christians can love their enemies into the saving knowledge of Christ. Christian pacifists forced to live under hostile aggressors can, through their loving and obedient lifestyle, so remind the aggressors of Jesus Christ that they will shamefully renounce their hostile ways and turn their lives over to Christ. Subsequently, rather than viewing each other as enemies, both can understand that they are brothers in Christ who have been commanded to love each other as Christ has loved them.

Third, pacifists teach that Christians can die; they can choose to be killed rather than kill. Since Christian pacifists know they have eternal life in Christ, and that death in this life means life in the next, they have no fear of death. Rather than kill a fellow Christian or a non-Christian (who would then never have a chance for salvation), the Christian pacifist can chose to die.

The radical pacifist position generally advocates three alternatives to maintaining a nuclear deterrent. Following the historic pacifist position, the radical pacifist accepts the view that Christians should choose to be killed rather than kill.

For the radical pacifist who advocates pacifism as national policy, and not just for Christians or the church, this alternative creates an awkward situation. For the individual Christian, the choice of dying rather than killing can be accepted, even if it is not preferred, because eternal life with Christ is a greater gain than the loss of temporal life on earth. However, not all citizens are Christians, and many would likely perish under a national policy of nonviolent resistance. A national policy of nonviolent resistance ought, then, to be unsatisfactory for radical pacifists because it would facilitate the deaths of many non-Christian neighbors. However, the radical pacifist seems to choose the life of the non-Christian attacker over the life of the non-Christian neighbor.

A second alternative for the radical pacifists is willing enslavement and servitude in the hope that the aggressive power will be overthrown. This alternative to nuclear deterrence holds that a nuclear holocaust cannot be undone or changed; its results are permanent. However, volunteer servitude would avoid the permanent problem of a nuclear exchange in hopes that the aggressor would be later converted or overthrown by a country that is more friendly.

A third alternative for the radical pacifist position is civilian based defense (CBD). This alternative to a nuclear conflict advocates organized nonviolent resistance directed at the occupying aggressor. Civilian nonviolent resistance would call the entire country to unite in civil disobedience, causing a political and economic breakdown that would leave the country in chaos and the invading aggressor with a frustrating mess. Besides refusing to cooperate with the invader, civilians would carry banners and signs telling the invaders that they love them, that God loves them, and that they are welcome as brothers and sisters. Hostility, it is hoped, would turn to friendship, and the aggressors would be won over by stubborn love. They would put down their weapons and allow everyone to live in peace.

Two more options that both the historic and radical pacifist positions endorse as alternatives to the nuclear threat are unilateral disarmament and a nuclear freeze. Neither position sees these two alternatives as permanent or final solutions to the problem, but both believe them to be first steps in the long complicated process toward global peace. Unilateral nuclear disarmament would ensure, at least, that the U.S. never used immoral nuclear weapons, and it would provide a testimony of good will and America's desire for peace.

Most pacifists support a nuclear freeze whether it is unilateral or bilateral. As with unilateral disarmament, a unilateral nuclear freeze would demonstrate good will and show enemies they need not fear American's motives or policies. As one might suspect from the radical pacifists' basic attitudes about government and political involvement, they advocate both of these last two alternatives with more enthusiasm than the more isolationist historic pacifists.

This chapter has been an overview of the Christian pacifist tradition. Although numerically this position has represented the conviction of only a small percentage of Christians historically or currently, it still represents the viewpoint of sincere Christians and must be examined in any consideration of the various points of view within the church. Also, in light of the growing popularity of the secular peace movement in our country and the willingness of many Christian pacifists to borrow or incorporate much of that movement's reasoning and assumptions with their own, it is even more important that Christians understand the teaching and rationale for Christian pacifism.

Chapter 3, Notes

1. Robert D. Culver, *The Peace Mongers* (Wheaton, Ill.: Tyndale House Publishers, 1985), 36.

2. Jim Wallis, *Waging Peace* (San Francisco: Harper and Row, 1982), 12. "Christian faith in our day must include a complete turn away from nuclear weapons. It is a sin to build nuclear weapons."
Ron Sider and Richard Taylor appear to support this same type of extra-biblical conditioning to Christian salvation when they write in *Nuclear Holocaust and Christian Hope*: "Just as nineteenth-century Christians came to see the incompatibility of Christian faith and slavery, so twentieth-century Christians are awaking to the enormous danger of nuclear war. Just as for many nineteenth-century Christians conversion came to involve rejecting slavery, so today conversion is coming to include a turning away from nuclear weapons."

Chapter 4

The Early Church

*I*n one sense this chapter is not necessary. As has been demonstrated, Scripture clearly declares that government has the God-ordained responsibility to protect the innocent, reward good, and punish evil. Equally clear is the fact that Christians are under scriptural obligation to support their government. This issue should be settled for Christians committed to Scripture as their final authority.

However, since the Christian pacifist position consistently appeals to the "unanimous" support of the early church for its position, it becomes necessary to examine the evidence for this claim. Much of this chapter consists of extended quotations from the early church fathers. This appeal to primary sources is necessary in order to show whether or not the assertions made about the church fathers' stance on this issue is supportable from the evidence.

But before we determine just what the early church fathers did or did not have to say about military service, war, and the use of force, let's see how two pacifist writers, Ronald Sider and Richard Taylor, portray the position of these fathers in their book *Nuclear Holocaust and Christian Hope*. Under the heading "The Early Church's Attitude toward War," Sider and Taylor write:

Modern historical scholarship indicates that for three centuries, all known Christian writings condemned war. In his careful scholarly study entitled *Christian Attitudes Toward War and Peace*, Roland Bainton notes that until the early fourth century there is not a single existing Christian writing which supports Christian participation in warfare. . . .

When the Emperor Constantine baptized his troops and adopted Christianity in A.D. 313, however, rapid change occurred. Christianity became the official religion of the Empire, and masses of people flocked into the church. Theologians rethought the *unanimous* stance of the previous three centuries in order to allow Christians to fight for the "Christian" emperors. By the early fifth century, only Christians could serve in the army. . . .

Why were the *unanimous* teaching and the predominant practice of the church in the first three centuries opposed to Christian participation in war? Some have argued that it was because of widespread idolatry (worship of the emperor) in the army rather than opposition to killing. But only officers had to sacrifice to the emperor. Since the church allowed soldiers who became Christians to remain in the army as long as they did not kill, idolatry in the army was not the main problem. . . .

. . . A constant stream of Christian writers in the second and third centuries—Titian, Athenagoras, Irenaeus, Clement of Alexandria, Cyprian, Minucius Felix, Lactantius—*all unanimously* condemned Christian participation in war. . . .[1] [emphases added]

This claim for unanimity among the early church fathers in their condemnation of Christian participation in warfare is easily asserted, but is it supportable from the evidence? Just what did the fathers actually teach about military service, war, and Christian participation? The remainder of this chapter will seek to answer this question.

WARFARE AND THE EARLY CHURCH FATHERS

In the introduction to their book, *Christians and the Military—The Early Experience*, professors John Helgeland, Robert Daly, and J. Patout Burns give us an initial glimpse at a possible answer to this question:

> Overly broad and uncritical pacifist assumptions often serve, ironically, to discredit pacifism and non-violence and weaken the cause of peace. Among the more damaging of these is the assumption that the call to nonviolence has the identical meaning and extension as the call to avoid military service. *This is simply not so.* Early Christian attitudes toward military service seem to be at least ambiguous.[2] [emphasis added]

Christians and the Military is mainly an introduction to and interpretation of primary texts from the early church. As a result of their analyses, the authors argue that early Christians apparently knew no general theory of pacifism, and their so-called pacifist writers were "anything but consistent or convincing supporters of pacifism."

One other secondary source, *The Early Fathers on War and Military Service*, is written by Dr. Louis Swift, an expert on social and cultural issues in the patristic era. Dr. Swift makes a telling summary statement in his introduction to the book:

> In sum, the whole question of war, violence and military service must have seemed quite irrelevant for Christians in the early Church, and this fact undoubtedly accounts for the paucity of evidence on the issue during this time.[3]

With this as our backdrop, let's look now at what the early church fathers themselves had to say about Christian involvement in military service and the use of force. Included within the church fathers to be examined are several generally claimed by pacifists as supporters of their position.

Clement of Rome (first century)

Clement wrote his epistle, *The First Letter of Clement*, to the Corinthian church near the end of the first century. He writes:

> Let us then, men and brethren, with all energy act the part of soldiers, in accordance with His holy commandments. Let us consider those who serve under our generals, with what order, obedience, and submissiveness they perform the things which are commanded them. All are not prefects, nor commanders of a thousand, nor of a hundred, nor of fifty, nor the like, but each one in his own rank performs the things commanded by the king and the generals.[4]

Dr. Swift makes the following observations and comments about this text:

> If the text does not endorse Christian participation in war, one would nonetheless have difficulty in reconciling it with a pacifist stance. The fact that the author is not at all embarrassed by such imagery very likely indicates that the problem of Christians serving in the army was not an issue for him.[5]

In commenting on this same passage along with a passage from Ignatius using similar military metaphors, Helgeland, Daly, and Burns write:

> Both Clement and Ignatius are ethically and theologically neutral when they use these metaphors, nor is there any analysis of Christians in a militaristic world. As with the New Testament, there is not one

comment regarding evil of military life whether the evil be from the morality of combat or from contamination of the idolatrous military religion.[6]

Justin Martyr (c.100-165)

Justin Martyr, writing around A.D. 150, declared:

And everywhere we, more readily than all men, endeavour to pay to those appointed by you the taxes both ordinary and extraordinary, as we have been taught by Him, for at that time some came to Him and asked Him, if one ought to pay tribute to Caesar; and he answered, "Tell Me, whose image does the coin bear?" And they said, "Caesar's." And again He answered them, "Render therefore to Caesar the things that are Caesar's, and to God the things that are God's." Whence to God alone we render worship, but in other things we gladly serve you, acknowledging you as kings and rulers of men, and praying that with your kingly power you be found to possess also sound judgement.[7]

Surely Justin knew that the Christians' taxes and prayers supported Roman armies.

Athenagoras (second century)

Athenagoras, writing around A.D. 177 in a letter to Emperor Marcus Aurelius, states:

Who are more justified in receiving what they ask for than people like ourselves? We pray for your reign in order that the succession may pass from father to son, as is most fitting, and that your sway may increase and expand as everyone becomes subject to you. Such a development benefits us, too, inasmuch as we can both lead a life of quiet and peace, and do willingly everything that is enjoined upon us.[8]

Regardless of what this does or does not say about Christians and military service, it certainly does indicate that Athenagoras recognized the Christians' responsibility to pray for and be in subjection to the civil government under which they lived. He also understood that the continued increase and expansion of the emperor's rule (this must have assumed military campaigns) guaranteed a peaceful existence for Christians as well as for pagan people.

Tertullian (c.160/70-c.215/20)

Tertullian is said to be the "first articulate spokesman for pacifism in the Christian Church."[9] He is often regarded by Christian pacifist writers as a staunch initiator and defender of their position. In *Nuclear Holocaust and Christian Hope*, Sider and Taylor quote and comment on Tertullian's writings:

> Again and again the sources make it clear the early church believed that Jesus' teaching excluded killing. Tertullian (A.D. 160-220) taught that Jesus' summons to love enemies was the "principal precept." He believed that in disarming Peter in the garden of Gethsemane, Jesus "ungirded every soldier." He asked, "How shall a Christian wage war? Nay, how shall he even be a soldier in peacetime without the sword which the Lord has taken away?[10]

Such a statement certainly does sound unambiguously pacifistic in nature. Had Tertullian consistently made only these kinds of statements, the pacifist position would have a champion. However, in other of his writings noted by Swift, Helgeland, Daly, and Burns, the confusion begins to mount. Included are quotations such as:

> We are but of yesterday, and we have filled every place among you—cities, islands, fortresses, towns, marketplaces, the very camp, tribes, companies, palace, senate, forum,—we have left nothing to you but the temples of your gods. For what wars should

we not be fit, not eager, even with unequal forces,
we who so willingly yield ourselves to the sword,
if in our religion it were not counted better to be
slain than to slay? . . .

Without ceasing, for all our emperors we offer
prayer. We pray for life prolonged; for security to
the empire; for protection to the imperial house; for
brave armies, a faithful senate, a virtuous people,
the world at rest, whatever as man or Caesar, an
emperor would wish. . . .

So we sojourn with you in the world abjuring neither
forum, nor shambles, nor both, nor booth, nor work-
shop, nor inn, nor weekly market, nor any other
places of commerce. We sail with you and fight with
you, and till the ground with you; and in like manner
we unite with you in your traffickings—even in the
various arts we make public property of our works
for your benefit.[11]

And again:

We know that Rome's continuance holds back the
great force which menaces the world, that is, the
very end of time which threatens frightful
calamities. We have no desire to experience these
things, and while we pray for their deferral, we are
promoting the continued existence of Rome.[12]

Swift observes that other Christians contemporary with
Tertullian did not agree with him concerning the issue of
pacifism since they appealed to both the Old and New Testament
as justification for serving in the army.[13] That Tertullian may
personally have leaned toward a pacifistic position is a legitimate possibility. But to hold Tertullian up as an example of a
universally accepted pacifistic standard for the early church is
not warranted.

Helgeland, Daly, and Burns finish their section on Tertullian with this penetrating and thought-provoking paragraph.

In conclusion, what should be said about the position that holds that Tertullian was a pacifist? First, a few statements about regretting killing in connection with the army do not add up to a pacifist stance. Some of the most ruthless generals have been known to make such statements. Nowhere are these developed into an argument of any kind. In all the hundreds of pages of Tertullian's work one cannot find even one whole paragraph devoted to that topic. In view of the recondite topics he developed, it would seem that if he thought at all about pacifism he would presumably have written a great deal about it. Second, nowhere is there any statement that a soldier should not enlist because killing in combat is wrong. It would seem that one such statement, if not many, would be a necessary condition for establishing in Tertullian's theology a principle of Christian pacifism. Third, statements such as "Christians would rather be killed than kill" have to be seen in their wider context dealing with the military; to use them to build or support a theory of Christian pacifism is totally irresponsible to the text.[14]

Cyprian (c.200/10-258)

Cyprian is one of the early fathers cited by pacifist writers as a supporter of their position. However, in speaking of Cyprian's writings, Dr. Swift notes:

> In absence of direct evidence, however, we should be cautious about putting Cyprian in the pacifist camp, especially in light of his profuse use of military metaphors for the Christian life.[15]

Clement of Alexandria (c.155-c.220)

Clement was Tertullian's Greek contemporary. Dr. Swift indicates that he was "a theologian of stature who was much concerned with the integration of pagan and Christian culture."

After quoting several paragraphs to give the reader a sampling of his writings, Swift concludes:

> It would appear that Clement no more expected the Christian soldier to abandon his profession than he expected the farmer or the sailor to do so, and it seems safe to conclude that the Alexandrian writer would not follow Tertullian in claiming that military service and Christian faith are mutually exclusive.[16]

Origen (c.185-c.254)

Origen is credited with being "the most articulate and eloquent pacifist in the early Christian Church."[17] This being the case, it is ironic that this eloquent pacifist provided a basis for the medieval Bishop Gelasius's two swords theory, and also a major foundational point for the just war tradition. The majority of Origen's views on this topic are found in his treatise *Against Celsus*, written around A.D. 248. Celsus was an anti-Christian writer who composed a piece called *The True Story* around A.D. 178. Essentially, Celsus contends that because worship of the emperor and the defense of the empire must go hand in hand, and because Christians refused to worship the emperor, they could not be considered loyal servants or citizens.

Origen's response is an attempt to demonstrate that although the Christians could not support Rome through military service, their contribution of intercessory prayer for the empire and against her enemies and their financial support (taxes) provided a far greater benefit to Rome than soldiering. Origin goes on to say:

> And to those enemies of our faith who require us to bear arms for the commonwealth, and to slay men, we can reply: "Do not those who are priests of certain shrines, and those who attend on certain gods, as you account them, keep their hands free from blood, that they may with hands unstained and free from human blood offer the appointed sacrifices to your gods? And even when war is upon you, you

never enlist the priests in the army. If that, then, is a laudable custom, how much more so, that while others are engaged in battle, these too should engage as the priests and ministers of God on behalf of those who are fighting in a righteous cause, and for the King who reigns righteously; that whatever is opposed to those who act righteously may be destroyed!"[18]

Origen is a delight and a disappointment to the religious pacifist position. Pacifists appreciate the fact that Origen makes no exceptions concerning Christians fighting in military service. Christians are priests whose greatest contribution is prayer. Origen, however, becomes a problem for radical pacifists when he concedes outright that there is such a thing as a just and righteous war. Although in his view the Christian cannot do the actual fighting, he must actively support those who do.

Lactantius (c.240-c.320)

Lactantius is one more early Christian writer claimed as a supporter for the pacifist position. Yet Lactantius seems to take an ambiguous position on this issue, as an examination of two different sections of his writing will demonstrate. Let's call this first section the early Lactantius:

Thus it will be neither lawful for a just man to engage in warfare, since his warfare is justice itself, nor to accuse any one of a capital charge, because it makes no difference whether you put a man to death by word, or rather by the sword, since it is the act of putting to death itself which is prohibited. Therefore, with regard to this precept of God, there ought to be no exception at all; but that it is always unlawful to put to death a man, whom God willed to be a sacred animal.[19]

However, the later Lactantius appears to have changed his earlier position when he writes:

These things which God in his wisdom has instilled in man are not evil in themselves. They become so through improper use but are by nature good because they have been given to us for preserving life. Just as courage is good if you are fighting for your country but evil if you are rebelling against it, so too, with the emotions. If you use them for good ends, they will be virtues; if for evil ends, they will be called vices.[20]

It is really quite amazing that even with a quotation from Lactanius such as the one just cited, he is still claimed by some pacifists as a staunch supporter of pacifism.

Eusebius of Caesarea (c.265-c.339)

If pacifism were the common practice of the early church, you would assume it would be clearly spelled out in the history of the church. Eusebius's history of the early church has long been considered a major authoritative source in discussing early Christian and church practices. What does Eusebius write of pacifism in the early church? Helgeland, Daly, and Burns observe:

Eusebius does not mention in all of his work any general theory of pacifism in the church as a whole. There is in fact little significant evidence that there was one.[21]

Dr. Swift adds this telling comment:

Eusebius implies that spiritual support in the form of prayer is appropriate for the clergy; but that the Christian soldier on the battle line is expected to do his part no less than his pagan colleague.[22]

SUMMARY

Pacifism claims the support of the early church for its convictions. As has been demonstrated, this claim of absolute support from the early church is an erroneous assertion. The early church had no standardized policy regarding pacifism. The writings of the church fathers during the first three hundred years of the church are ambiguous at best regarding pacifism.

A number of writers have ventured educated guesses as to why the church fathers wrote so little concerning the use of force. These writers generally point out that until the early fourth century, Christians had neither position nor opportunity to be concerned about the proper use of force. Until the Roman government officially accepted Christianity, believers were spending more time dodging the illegitimate use of force being exercised against them than they were considering how they should be justly exercising force. It was not until the early fourth century that Christians had to come to grips with how they would function within a secular government that now embraced rather than persecuted Christians.

Ambrose and Augustine became the first two fathers to address this problem directly. The result of their efforts grew into what commonly is called the just war position, which has been the dominant view in both the Catholic and Protestant church for a least the last sixteen hundred years.

When pacifists claim that Christians practiced pacifism until Constantine's ascension to power so entangled them with secularism and politics that they polluted their convictions, it must be remember that this script is based more upon wishful thinking than historical facts. The early church did not turn its back on a previously pure position of pacifism. Rather, it was finally confronted with the need to develop a policy toward the just use of force by government and a Christian's proper response. There were, of course, Christian pacifists during the first three hundred years of the church. Yet, there was no standardized theology for the church concerning the proper use of force.

After taking this brief look at several of the major writers from the early church, it is easy to see why four prominent scholars—Swift, Helgeland, Daly, and Burns—agree that the teaching and practice of the early church concerning military service and war were ambiguous at best. What is difficult to understand is why Christian pacifists continue to write about "unanimous" support from the early church for their position. The evidence shows such a claim is simply not true. Arthur Holmes, well-known spokesman for the just war position, summarizes well the position of the church fathers:

> [The church fathers] do not deny to government the right to use force, and for all their aversion to violence they do not assert that killing is under all circumstances morally wrong. Their overt objection to soldiering is to the imposition of pagan rites and oaths. Their attitude to war is different from popular pagan attitudes; instead of excitement and glorying in war, they lament its tragic character and yearn for peace. Yet they are grateful for military action that secures both peace and order.[23]

Do the early Christian fathers provide "unanimous" support for the pacifist position as asserted by pacifist writers? Clearly they do not.

Chapter 4, Notes

1. Ronald J. Sider and Richard K. Taylor, *Nuclear Holocaust and Christian Hope* (Downers Grove, Ill.: InterVarsity Press, 1982), 89-90.

2. John Helgeland, Robert J. Daly, and J. Patout Burns, *Christians and the Military* (Philadelphia: Fortress Press, 1985), 1.

3. Louis J. Swift, *The Early Fathers on War and Military Service* (Wilmington, Del.: Michael Glazier Inc., 1983), 27.

4. *St. Clement: Epistle to the Corinthians*, vol. 1 of *The Ante-Nicene Fathers* (Grand Rapids: Wm. B. Eerdmans Publishing Co., 1973), 15.

5. Swift, 33.

6. Helgeland, Daly, and Burns, 19.

7. *Justin Martyr: The First Apology*, vol. 1 of *The Ante-Nicene Fathers* (Grand Rapids: Wm. B. Eerdmans Publishing Co., 1973), 168.

8. Swift, 35.

9. Ibid., 38.

10. Sider and Taylor, 90.

11. *Tertullian: The Apology*, vol. 3 of *The Ante-Nicene Fathers* (Grand Rapids: Wm. B. Eerdmans Publishing Co., 1973), 42, 45, 49.

88   **The Early Church**

12. Swift, 39.

13. Ibid., 42.

14. Helgeland, Daly, and Burns, 29.

15. Swift, 49.

16. Ibid., 50, 52.

17. Ibid., 60.

18. *Origen: Against Celsus*, vol. 4 of *The Ante-Nicene Fathers* (Grand Rapids: Wm. B. Eerdmans Publishing Co., 1973), 667-68.

19. *Lactantius: The Divine Institutes*, vol. 7 of *The Ante-Nicene Fathers* (Grand Rapids: Wm. B. Eerdmans Publishing Co., 1973), 187.

20. Swift, 65.

21. Helgeland, Daly, and Burns, 69.

22. Swift, 88.

23. Arthur F. Holmes, "The Just War," in *War: Four Christian Views*, ed. Robert G. Clouse (Downers Grove, Ill.: InterVarsity Press, 1981), 127.

Chapter 5

Why the Pacifist Position Must Be Rejected

*T*his chapter will present several major reasons why the Christian pacifist position, sincere as it may be, is in error and must be rejected.

Problems with Christian Pacifism in General

The greatest single problem from a theological perspective with the Christian pacifist position is its system of biblical interpretation (hermeneutics). This system subjugates both the Old and New Testament to the Sermon on the Mount. As we discussed in chapter 3, if one is willing to accept this hermeneutical presupposition, then the pacifist position is consistent.

However, with the exception of the "peace church," it is nearly impossible to find serious Bible students, Catholic or Protestant, who believe this is a valid method of biblical interpretation. Scripture, not a person's preconceived philosophical or ideological bias, must be allowed to interpret Scripture.

By accepting the pacifist's hermeneutic, a person can reach a consistent pacifist position. However, the price one must pay is great. Old and New Testament passages that deal with war, military service, or the use of force are either ignored, forced out of their context, or reinterpreted to fit that preconceived position. A clear example of this problem is found in Matthew 5:38-39.

> You have heard that it was said, "Eye for eye, and tooth for tooth." But I tell you, Do not resist an evil person. If someone strikes you on the right cheek, turn to him the other also.

Christian pacifists contend that these verses not only teach that Christians must live a life of personal nonresistance, but also that the corporate church should universally endorse nonresistance as well. Bible students generally acknowledge that these verses should be applied personally. However, few believe the context of these verses is applicable to the corporate church as do the pacifist churches. In addition, the pacifist position fails to make a proper distinction between personal revenge and just retribution. Personal revenge has never been an acceptable option for the faithful believer. Matthew 5:38-39 is not a new command to prohibit the Christian, the church, or the state from exercising necessary force in just retribution. Rather, it is a reminder to Christians of an old command that prohibits an individual from taking personal revenge, and a reminder that just retribution must always be limited by proportionality— the punishment must fit the crime. To maintain otherwise is to wrench these verses out of their proper context and legitimate application.

There are several additional problems beyond biblical interpretation that confront Christian pacifists. First, by refusing to support the government in its necessary exercise of force, Christian pacifists raise a serious question about God's character. Would God command Christians to support an institution whose basic purpose is morally suspect? If pacifists do believe there is something morally or ethically wrong in personally supporting government, what are they saying about the One who has given government its job description? How can personal support of government on the part of non-Christians be considered moral, while that same support on the part of a Christian be considered immoral? Has God ordained two moral standards, one for Christians and another for non-Christians?

Second, in acknowledging government's responsibility to exercise necessary force but refusing to participate personally, pacifists are found guilty of the charge that they use the religious and political freedoms others (both Christians and non-Christians) were willing to pay a great price for but which they are unwilling to secure for others. Just how much is political and religious freedom worth? Christian martyrs have demonstrated for centuries that religious freedom is worth more than life itself.

Finally, Christian pacifism leaves much to be desired for non-Christian friends, allies, and neighbors. What are these people to think were their Christian neighbors to stand by passively rather than help protect the political and religious freedoms of millions of others so that they too might have the opportunity to respond to the gospel? Theologically, the Christian's goal of peace is peace with justice, not peace at any price.

Problems with Historic Pacifism

Historic pacifism is committed to the same system of interpretation—Old and New Testament are subjugated to the Sermon on the Mount—discussed at some length earlier. As such, it is open to the same criticism.

Problems with Radical Pacifism

Radical pacifism utilizes the same hermeneutics as historic pacifism. Yet the radical pacifist goes far beyond the historic pacifist when it comes to applying the teaching of Matthew 5:38-39. The radical pacifist avers that not only should nonresistance be practiced by Christians and the corporate church, but also by the secular state as well. Applying these verses to the church as historic pacifism does is an interpretational error. Applying this teaching to a non-Christian secular government is even more mistaken.

How can the radical pacifist expect a secular government to live by teachings that are given to Christians, which even they fail to live by consistently? Pressing a secular government to adopt Christian pacifism is unbiblical and utopian. To their credit, historic pacifists disagree with radical pacifism over this issue.

Concerning the legitimate extent of the use of force, historic pacifism and radical pacifism again disagree. Both positions teach that Christians and the corporate Christian church cannot legitimately exercise force—they are both committed to nonviolence. But once again the radical pacifist position goes far beyond historic pacifism.

Where the historic pacifist believes that government has the God-given responsibility to exercises necessary force in carrying out its job description, the radical pacifist denies that government should exercise necessary force in protecting the innocent and punishing evil behavior. This radical pacifist teaching must be rejected as biblically unsound for its refusal to acknowledge and support the government's right to exercise necessary force. This right was instituted in the Old Testament and has never been rescinded.

New Testament teaching on government's proper role of protecting the innocent, rewarding good behavior, and punishing evil behavior is unmistakably clear (Romans 13:1-7, 1 Timothy 2:1-4, Titus 3:1, 1 Peter 2:13-17). How does the radical pacifist respond to the call in Romans 13:1-7 for government to protect, reward, and punish, and for Christians to support government in carrying out this job?

First, some radical pacifists insist that this command is directed at local civil leaders (not state or federal leaders) and is specifically addressed to local police work, not military service. However, attempts to explain away this passage by making distinctions between police work and military service are artificial and cannot be maintained historically. Local police work was performed by the military. As patristics scholar Dr. Swift has written,

> I am not persuaded that the distinction between police work and military campaigns was ever a meaningful one for Christians in the early centuries

of the church. The physical violence involved in both activities is indivisible and the idea of Christians serving during periods of relative calm but deserting when war threatened is simply not credible.[1]

Second, radical pacifists maintain that the primary thrust of this passage is found in verse 13:1b—"for there is no authority except that which God has established." Apparently one is to believe that God's primary message to the Christian in this section has little to do with the government's right to exercise necessary force (vs. 1,3,4) and the believer's responsibility to support the government in accomplishing this job as God's servant (vs. 2,4,5,6,7). Rather, the primary message is to remind Christians that all government authority is from God, subject to God, and that the Christian is to obey God, the highest authority, rather than government, which has only delegated authority. This type of textual manipulation stretches the context and normal reading of this passage beyond recognition.

Finally, some radical pacifists not only refuse to acknowledge government responsibilities of protection and punishment, but also sympathetically discuss the notion that Christians refuse to pay that portion of their tax liability that would go to the military service. This action not only undeniably violates Romans 13:6-7, it also refuses to follow the personal command and example of Christ, who commanded that believers pay taxes to Caesar—taxes he no doubt knew would help pay Roman soldiers' salaries (Matthew 22:15-22).

The radical pacifist position fails to deal adequately with numerous verses that clearly add support to the government's justified use of force or the Christian's responsibility to government. These verses include those dealing with soldiers, taxes, swords, and military metaphors. For example, Jesus (Matthew 8), John the Baptist (Luke 3), the apostle Peter (Acts 10), and the apostle Paul (Acts 16) all had the opportunity to explain to believing soldiers the evils of military service and the inherent immorality of a Christian exercising force personally or as an agent of the government. In all of these cases recorded in Scripture, military men received praise, instruction, or acknowledgment of their righteous faith, but no condemnation for their military status.

It is interesting to note that when the writer of Hebrews was giving examples of faithful, godly men in chapter 11— sometimes referred to as the Bible Hall of Fame—a large number of those were soldiers.

If Christians must adopt pacifism, would not at least one of these instances involving Jesus, John the Baptist, Peter, or Paul have demonstrated a clear-cut rejection of military service? Rather than receiving rebuke, when it would have fit the context perfectly, we read John the Baptist's reply to repentant soldiers:

> Then some soldiers asked him, "And what should we do?" He replied, "Don't extort money and don't accuse people falsely—be content with your pay." (Luke 3:14)

John did not tell these soldiers that military service is immoral and that government has no right to exercise force; he did not instruct the soldiers to throw down their swords because followers of Jesus Christ must abstain from such government service.

In Matthew 8 we read of a soldier's confidence in Jesus' supernatural authority:

> The centurion replied, "Lord, I do not deserve to have you come under my roof. But just say the word, and my servant will be healed. For I myself am a man under authority, with soldiers under me. I tell this one, 'Go,' and he goes; and that one, 'Come,' and he comes. I say to my servant, 'Do this,' and he does it." (vv. 8-9)

Jesus' response is interesting indeed:

> When Jesus heard this, he was astonished and said to those following him, "I tell you the truth, I have not found anyone in Israel with such great faith." (v. 10)

He certainly could have told the centurion to lay down his sword and reject the military so that his faith could be honored. But Scripture records no such comment.

In describing the Roman soldier Cornelius in Acts 10, Scripture tells us he was "devout," "God-fearing," and one who "gave generously to those in need and prayed to God regularly." Why would Peter tell Cornelius, "God does not show favoritism but accepts men from every nation who fear him and do what is right"? (vv. 34-35). Why did Peter not tell Cornelius that military service is improper, and that he should leave the service because it is immoral? Scripture gives no such rejection of Christian service to the government in carrying out its God-given responsibilities.

Some radical pacifists argue that Jesus and Peter may well have instructed these centurions to leave the Roman army in dialogue not recorded in Scripture. However, arguing for an unrecorded and hypothetical conversation is weak and unconvincing; but in this case it is the only "evidence" the radical pacifist has.[2]

Because Scripture clearly gives government the right and responsibility to exercise necessary force, and since it also commands that Christians support their God-ordained government, the burden of proof is on the pacifist to explain why there is no scriptural evidence that Jesus and his apostles corrected these God-fearing soldiers. Imaginary conversations do not qualify as scriptural support for pacifism.

Radical pacifists also fail to deal adequately with verses regarding the Christian's responsibility to pay taxes—taxes the writers undoubtedly knew would help fund the Roman army (Matthew 22:15-22, Romans 13:6-7). Jesus and Paul clearly and undeniably command believers to pay taxes. It is difficult to understand how some radical pacifists can assert that the church and state should follow Jesus' example of nonresistance in his death on the cross, yet ignore his direct command and example of paying taxes. Is the Christian to follow Jesus' example only if it agrees with his or her political ideology?

In Luke 22 Jesus commands his disciples to buy swords

(vv. 35-37; cf. Matthew 26:51-52 and John 18:10-11). Some radical pacifists insist that Jesus never intended this command to be taken literally, only figuratively. However, it appears that Peter, who was there and not nineteen hundred years removed, took Jesus' command literally:

> Then the men stepped forward, seized Jesus and arrested him. With that, one of Jesus' companions reached for his sword, drew it out and struck the servant of the high priest, cutting off his ear. "Put your sword back in its place," Jesus said to him. (Matthew 26:50-52)

If pacifists were correct in their figurative interpretation of Jesus' earlier command, one would think Jesus' response to Peter's action would have made that clear. Yet Christ's words reflect no surprise that Peter had a sword. Further, if pacifism was the rule, does not Peter's being armed seem quite out of order?

This passage has nothing to do with personal revenge or personal defense. Peter was trying to protect Christ, not himself, from would-be attackers. Jesus' rebuke was not over Peter's desire to protect him, but rather over Peter's attempt to "save" him from going to the cross—which, of course, was necessary to complete the first part of his messianic mission. This explanation is supported in John 18:11: "Jesus commanded Peter, 'Put your sword away! Shall I not drink the cup the Father has given me?'"

Finally, passages using military metaphors abound in the New Testament (1 Corinthians 9:6-7, 2 Corinthians 6:7, Ephesians 6:10-18, Philippians 2:25, Philemon 1-2, 1 Timothy 6:12, and 2 Timothy 2:3-4). Military metaphors do not prove that Christians supported the government's use of force or that they personally participated in military service. However, their frequent usage would be inappropriate if Jesus, the apostles, and the early church taught that the military was evil, immoral, and ungodly.

Radical pacifists need convincing support from Scripture

to give biblical credibility to their position. Yet that support is not forthcoming, calling into question radical pacifism's theological credibility.

As with Christian pacifism in general, radical pacifism fails to make a proper distinction between personal revenge and just retribution. Similarly, the "unanimous" support of the early church, so often referred to in radical pacifist material, in reality does not exist.

The radical pacifist also has trouble explaining Christ's second coming and the establishment of his millennial kingdom of peace. The radical pacifist is vocal about the role of man, the church, and government activism in establishing world peace. Yet has Christ not promised that he alone will establish his kingdom of peace, and that there will be wars and rumors of wars until his return? Clearly the answer is yes. Then are not some of the objectives of radical pacifist activism (i.e., world peace orchestrated by man) an exercise in dangerous delusion?

It is easy to understand the radical pacifist's relative silence when it comes to biblical eschatology. Yet to remain silent on these issues is to ignore Scripture—something Christians ought not do. And to promote Scripture's teaching on these subjects is to undermine the majority of the causes of this position—something political and philosophical activists cannot afford to do. The radical pacifist is between a rock and a hard place.

Finally, radical pacifism does not provide a reasonable, realistic, nor acceptable solution to the nuclear threat. Unilateral disarmament often is advocated by radical pacifists as the only sensible solution to the nuclear threat facing the world. Yet, U.S. unilateral disarmament would deny protection to its citizens, people who the American government has been commanded by God to protect, and leave U.S. allies weak and vulnerable to Soviet aggression.

Unilateral disarmament cannot ensure a reciprocal response on the part of the Soviet Union. In all likelihood it would guarantee only a tremendous Soviet military superiority. Given Soviet history since World War II it is easy to understand that such superiority would lead to great danger for America, her neighbors and allies.

Another alternative to military defense advocated by the radical pacifist position is to be killed rather than kill. For the radical pacifist to say sincerely that as an alternative to defense "we can die," is less than a satisfactory solution to the nuclear threat. What kind of solution or security does this provide for the millions of non-Christians who will certainly die with them? Does this response really demonstrate love for one's neighbor? For the Christian radical pacifist, heaven is his eternal destiny. But what about the millions of non-Christian neighbors who did not volunteer to die?

Despite its sincerity, radical pacifism fails to consider the consequences its policies will produce for others. This isolationist thinking demonstrates less than biblical compassion for friends, neighbors, or enemies. We are indeed a global family, and America's actions, or lack thereof, affect the entire world. "We can die" is not a responsible answer to the nuclear problem.

Some radical pacifists propose a civilian based defense as an alternative to America's current nuclear deterrence. A civilian based defense would call upon all Americans to reject current military defense and deterrence by dismantling and destroying all existing U.S. nuclear and conventional weapons.

While rejecting current military programs, a civilian based defense would enlist Americans into an organized civilian non-violent movement that would resist an occupying power through noncompliance. This noncompliance would include: work shut-downs, carrying picket signs and banners that tell the enemy of their love for them, and other nonviolent demonstrations. This opposition would continue until the invaders voluntarily decided to give up their hostile aggression in utter frustration.

This suggested alternative to nuclear deterrence is, in reality, a dangerous delusion. Given Soviet treatment of its own citizens, let alone its enemies, civilian based defense would threaten either the subjugation or the destruction of the United States and its allies.

It is difficult to understand how unilateral disarmament or civilian based defense can be considered morally superior to a policy that has maintained peace and freedom for the last forty years. All three of the major alternatives proposed by the radical pacifist position must be viewed as failures from both a scriptural and strategic point of view. The radical pacifist alternatives would abrogate government's responsibility to defend and protect the innocent and put Americans and allies at great risk.

It must be emphasized again that the Christian concept of peace is not the historic or radical pacifist's peace at all cost—it is not the forced peace of servitude. Biblical peace is peace with justice. "Shalom" meant wholeness, well being, and good health. The pacifist peace without justice has absolutely nothing to do with Shalom peace.[3]

Neither the isolationism of historic pacifism nor the blatant danger of radical pacifism is a biblical policy for human government. The Christian pacifist response to the nuclear threat is not consistent morally or biblically.

Chapter 5, Notes

1. Louis J. Swift, *The Early Fathers on War and Military Service* (Wilmington, Del.: Michael Glazier, Inc., 1983), 91.

2. Ronald J. Sider and Richard K. Taylor, *Nuclear Holocaust and Christian Hope* (Downers Grove, Ill.: InterVarsity Press, 1982), 153. "How valid is this argument? Like all arguments from silence, it is weak. There is, to be sure, no evidence of condemnation. On the other hand, there is also no evidence that Jesus and Peter did not go on to teach both centurions that they ought to leave the Roman army. Many more things must have happened in both cases beyond what the text includes."

3. Charles W. Jarvis, "The Hall of Deadly Mirrors: Peace and Nuclear Arms" in *The High Cost of Indifference*, ed. Richard Cizik (Ventura, Calif.: Regal Books, 1984), 152. "In Hebrew, the word *shalom* means 'peace' and has a variety of rich meanings. The root word means 'solidity,' 'wholeness,' 'well-being' and can suggest 'prosperity,' 'integrity' and 'physical health' as well."

Chapter 6

Deterrence, Nuclear Weapons, and a Christian Conscience

*I*t is clear that Scripture supports the conclusion that government has been given the responsibility of protecting the innocent, punishing the evil, and rewarding the good. From a scriptural perspective, these are not responsibilities governments have a choice about—to fulfill only if they are so inclined. Rather, protection, reward, and punishment are the fundamental purposes for government.

Scripture also supports the view that government has the prerogative to use force, if necessary, in carrying out its responsibilities, and that Christians are to support the government in its efforts to fulfill its responsibilities properly. Only when government itself acts in an unjust fashion, directly violating its scriptural mandate, is the Christian to oppose its policy and actions. Scripture does not support the notion that pacifism is the proper mode of operation for government. Indeed, Romans 13 states that it is the responsibility of government to protect the innocent and to punish evil "with the sword."

A Christian certainly can make a personal commitment to pacifism. But how can a Christian suggest that his personal pacifist commitment should apply to governmental policy when government has been given a scriptural mandate to protect the innocent and punish the evil? How could a government be just if it abandoned its responsibilities and allowed an innocent individual—perhaps an individual deserving reward—to be harmed by those deserving punishment? For the Christian to pressure government to adopt pacifism risks attempting to compel government to abandon its biblical responsibilities and to behave contrary to its scriptural mandate.

It is not difficult to see how an individual Christian, knowing that his destiny is secure, would rather accept death than kill an attacker in self-defense. Self-sacrifice is indeed a Christian virtue, and pacifism in response to threats against oneself could indeed give evidence of a Christian conscience.

But pacifism also suggests that one willingly avoid the use of force even if it means that one's innocent neighbor will perish in an attack. Here the individual Christian must consider how to condition love for an aggressor with love and justice for an innocent neighbor: Christians are called upon to love both. Likewise for the government official, love must be compatible with the demands of justice. Are government officials, even Christian government officials, to so love an invader that they leave undefended those citizens threatened with death by that invader? How to condition love of enemy with love of neighbor may be left to the discernment of the individual Christian, but government cannot abandon its scriptural calling to protect the innocent and punish the evil; that would reflect neither love of neighbor nor support for justice.

This conclusion applies to the protection of the innocent whether they are threatened by a fellow countryman, foreign terrorist attack, or direct foreign invasion. The U.S. government has the responsibility to protect its citizens from the death and destruction associated with aggression. The government can no more abandon the responsibility of protecting innocent citizens from foreign attack than it can abandon the responsibility of protecting them from the murderer.

America has, of course, had a most unusual and fortunate history. Its geographic position has placed it away from any powerful and aggressive neighbors. The last bloody war fought on the American homeland took place over a century ago, and that, of course, was the Civil War. Almost no country in history has been so fortunately unfamiliar with the evil of foreign invasion. This history and position tend to cast an idealistic shadow over American thinking. A consistent trend in American thought about international relations is that conflict and war come only when a country misunderstands another, and becomes involved where it ought not. Much pacifist thinking follows the line that if we only better understood those countries we now see as opponents we would understand that our fears simply are mistaken—they really want to be our friends, and only our "Cold War" attitudes stand in the way.[1]

However, world history, unlike American history, is filled with examples of well-understood hostility and real aggression—invasions causing incredible suffering and millions of civilian deaths. The sorrowful histories of Poland, Czechoslovakia, and Hungary in this century alone give a sad reminder of the fate of weaker countries at the hands of stronger, aggressive nations. The recent history of Afghanistan, and the ongoing Soviet military campaign there to kill civilians and destroy the agricultural base is a sad example of the Soviet policy of aggression against innocent civilians. Aggressive and powerful countries do pose a real threat of suffering and death to innocent civilians. This threat is not the figment of a "Cold War" imagination, but the unfortunate reality of international politics and international conflict.

Christians should well understand that full peace in this world will never be achieved. Even toward the end of the age "wars and rumors of wars" will continue (Matthew 24:6). Or, as the prophet Daniel states, "War will continue until the end" (Daniel 9:26).

The U.S. government has the scriptural obligation to protect innocent Americans from such aggression; and the U.S. government has accepted the responsibility of helping allied governments to protect their citizens against foreign threat. Following World War II the United States provided vast financial assistance through the Marshall Plan to rebuild the shattered economies of Europe. The Soviet Union and the countries of Eastern Europe were invited to accept this aid, but rejected it. In 1949 the U.S., Canada, and ten Western European countries signed the North Atlantic Treaty committing each to the common defense. The North Atlantic Treaty Organization (NATO) now consists of sixteen countries of North America and Europe that perceive the Soviet Union to be a common threat. The U.S. also has come to the defense of non-European countries such as Korea and Israel in time of grave threat.

To a large extent the United States and NATO have used nuclear deterrence as a substitute for a sufficient military capability to stop potential Soviet aggression in Europe. The U.S. has hoped that a limited conventional (nonnuclear) defensive capability, complemented by a powerful nuclear deterrent, would ensure that a Soviet attack would never come. This strategy, it was believed, would ensure that the West would not have to spend the enormous sums of money necessary to provide a nonnuclear defensive capability necessary to stop a Soviet attack. (Despite what seems to be common wisdom, nuclear weapons generally are much cheaper than conventional forces—which is a primary reason why the U.S. and its NATO allies have come to depend on them so heavily.) As a result, NATO has never planned for a completely effective conventional defense, and at present almost certainly could not defend Western Europe against a concerted Soviet attack without recourse to nuclear weapons.[2] U.S. forces have been deployed in Europe to help ensure that Western Europe would not be seen as easy prey, and that any Soviet invasion would be fraught with the prospect of a major war that could escalate to a massive nuclear war.[3]

It is this fear of nuclear escalation that is intended to provide an effective deterrent to any Soviet thoughts of aggression in Europe. The point made by General Norstad over twenty years ago concerning the role of NATO conventional forces remains the underlying principle followed by NATO: "The function of [NATO] forces is really not to fight, not even to defend, but to complete the deterrent."[4]

Indeed, when faced with the concern of a Soviet invasion of Iran to seize Persian Gulf oil fields in 1980, the West's conventional force weakness and resultant nuclear dependence was clearly demonstrated. There are few U.S. forces in the area during peacetime, and in the event of attack the U.S. would have to move forces to the area rapidly. Because of conventional force limitations and the difficulty of moving such forces long distances, the U.S. would have been limited to inserting lightly armed parachute troops into the region in response to a Soviet invasion. Without nuclear weapons, such conventionally armed forces would clearly have been incapable of halting mass Soviet tank armies. As a result, it reportedly was the view of U.S. military planners at the time that if the Soviets had moved rapidly to seize the Gulf, the U.S. would have had no other recourse but to initiate the use of tactical nuclear weapons—or give up the primary source of energy for the Western democracies and Japan. Either of these options could have had drastic consequences—yet our own lack of conventional preparedness, and thus nuclear reliance, would have compelled the West to make such a choice.[5]

In short, nuclear deterrence has been the great crutch the U.S. has used to help ensure the security of numerous weaker states that consider the Soviet Union to be a real threat. However, because the U.S. has intended to use nuclear deterrence for a just purpose (i.e., discouraging aggression and protecting the innocent) does not necessarily mean that U.S. nuclear policy can fit within the guidance provided by the Christian just war theory. An important question to be answered is whether government can use nuclear force justly in fulfilling its responsibilities. Are nuclear weapons in a special category that must be excluded from consideration, or can they be considered a legitimate part of a government's arsenal to defend the innocent and punish the evil?

What are the implications of the just war theory for nuclear deterrence? The various positions endorsed by Christians suggest different answers. As discussed earlier, radical and historic pacifists reject the notion that the Christian can support any use of force—consequently their rejection of nuclear weapons goes without saying.

However, even some within the just war tradition reject nuclear weapons. These nuclear pacifists argue, in effect, that nuclear weapons are a special case and are incompatible with just war principles. Because of the widespread destruction that could result from nuclear weapons, their use could never fit within the scriptural guidelines for the just use of force by government. Nuclear pacifists argue that the use of nuclear weapons would be almost inherently indiscriminate, killing both combatants and innocent civilians.

The just war tradition recognizes and accepts the fact that because no military force can be controlled perfectly and accidents in the use of military force are not uncommon, some innocent civilians will likely fall victims in any type of war; there is virtually no way to ensure that all innocent civilians are unharmed in the midst of combat. However, the just war tradition requires that even if military force is used by the proper authorities and for the right purpose (protection of the innocent), care must be taken so as to minimize as much as possible the likely effect of military force on civilians. That is, the good served in protecting the innocent through the use of force must outweigh the unintended and unwanted destruction that always goes along with war. The use of force cannot be considered just if the suffering of the innocent is actually increased as a result of governmental efforts to protect them.

This, according to nuclear pacifists, is the certain result of any nuclear use, and the primary reason why nuclear weapons could never be used justly. Nuclear pacifists accept the just war theory but, in effect, deny the possibility that a nuclear war could ever be sufficiently limited so as to protect the innocent.[6] Consequently, they claim that the use of nuclear weapons must be rejected as inconsistent with the scriptural basis for the governmental use of force reflected in the just war tradition.

Some Christian nuclear pacifists within the just war tradition have made a moral distinction between possessing nuclear weapons for deterrence purposes, and the actual employment of nuclear weapons in war.[7] They claim the actual employment of nuclear weapons can never be considered an acceptable use of military force, but they do not oppose the possession of nuclear weapons. This seemingly inconsistent position is not as peculiar as it may seem. The morality of possessing, but not ever using, nuclear weapons is based on a recognition of their deterrence value. That is, while it is believed the actual employment of nuclear weapons would represent an unjust use of force, their possession is considered acceptable as the basis for deterring the Soviet Union from taking aggressive actions. Consequently, these nuclear pacifists conclude that the possession of nuclear weapons is important for deterrence and morally acceptable, provided there is no intention of actually launching them in war.

In short, these Christian nuclear pacifists conclude that possessing nuclear weapons, without an intention to use them, would provide a deterrent to Soviet aggression without placing the U.S. in jeopardy of violating the legitimate purposes for which governments may use force. Thus nuclear weapons can play a role in U.S. defense policy without violating just war principles.

Unfortunately, the "possession but no use" solution probably would increase the risk of nuclear war because it represents, in effect, a "nuclear bluff" approach to deterrence. The problem with the nuclear bluff approach to deterrence is that it is unlikely to be effective—especially if attempted by the United States. Because a deterrence threat must be believed in order to be effective (remember the department store analogy discussed in chapter 1), the Soviet Union could not be allowed to know that the U.S. never intended to use its nuclear weapons. If the Soviet Union ever discovered that the U.S. deterrent threat was really a bluff, it would undoubtedly be a very weak deterrent.

Given the openness of American society, it would seem almost unimaginable that the U.S. adoption of a nuclear bluff could be kept secret. The U.S. has difficulty keeping defense secrets; this grand bluff would require the utmost in secrecy over a long time on an issue that attracts a high level of public attention (and Soviet espionage).

This problem would be compounded by the fact that even with a nuclear bluff, the U.S. could not stop maintaining its nuclear arsenal or its policy would become obvious. The administrations promoting this bluff would have to deceive the country and Congress every year by declaring that U.S. nuclear weapons had to be maintained for use in the event of Soviet attack—all the while knowing their use was never really intended. Requests to Congress for funding deterrent forces would have to continue to be justified on the grounds of maintaining a retaliatory threat against the Soviet Union; no hint could be given that this was all just a bluff. Even those people responsible for targeting and launching U.S. nuclear forces would have to be kept in the dark. This would indeed have to be the best kept military secret of all time—an extremely difficult task in a nation where "leaks" seem to provide newspapers with highly classified information every day, and Soviet espionage seems to be more successful than ever.[8]

This is not to say the U.S. should ever "use" its nuclear forces in any way other than in the "non-use" of deterrence. For deterrence to work (so that the U.S. never actually has to launch its nuclear force) the Soviet Union must believe that the U.S. would indeed be willing, under certain circumstances, to launch a strike. If the Soviet Union ever suspected the truth of the bluff, U.S. nuclear forces would provide as useful a deterrent to war as a cardboard police car would provide a deterrent to crime or speeding.

In the curious world of nuclear deterrence, as with any concept of deterrence, the threat must at least appear credible to be effective. As Herman Kahn, the late grandfather of deterrence theory once noted: "If we wish to have our strategic air forces contribute to the deterrence of provocation, it must be credible that we are willing to take . . . actions. Usually the most convincing way to look willing is to be willing."[9] To this maxim could be added that even if the U.S. is unwilling to use its nuclear weapons, it must at least look willing for the sake of deterrence. Consequently, for deterrence purposes the U.S. actually must plan for nuclear war, even while being extremely reluctant and cautious about the prospect. In this way the U.S. will help ensure that it never has to employ nuclear weapons. It is highly doubtful, however, that the U.S. could maintain the appearance of willingness to use nuclear forces if it secretly was planning just a bluff.

The fact that a bluff deterrent would be likely to increase the risk of nuclear war has led the U.S. government and defense experts to reject the Christian nuclear pacifists' "possession but no use" proposal.[10] While criticism from the community of strategic experts has not been based on scriptural considerations, it has been based on the view that the United States ought not follow a nuclear policy that would be likely to increase the probability of nuclear war.

Although the "possession but no use" approach to American policy has not received much support from U.S. officials, it does reflect an appreciation by nuclear pacifists of the important role nuclear weapons play in deterrence. The question these nuclear pacifists struggled with was, How can Christians deal justly with the terrible destructiveness of nuclear weapons, yet preserve the beneficial deterrent to aggression that nuclear weapons provide? Their answer of a nuclear bluff, while not likely to provide an effective deterrent, at least recognized the need to maintain deterrence.

The nuclear bluff solution may not be acceptable to U.S. defense officials, but it does reflect a more sophisticated understanding of the realities of international relations than do the pious-sounding but ultimately shallow statements coming from other parts of the Christian community. These statements typically follow such simplistic reasoning as: Nuclear weapons are terrible; therefore we must say no to nuclear war and begin the disarmament process—unilaterally if necessary.[11] While such sentiments sound appropriately progressive, and please members of the antinuclear lobby, they ignore the deterrent role nuclear weapons play in the preservation of international stability. If the United States actually endorsed such a simplistic solution, it would almost certainly increase the risk of nuclear war by weakening the U.S. side of the deterrence balance. Because those who support U.S. unilateral nuclear disarmament and put pressure on the U.S. to disarm can exert no similar pressure on the Soviet government, their solutions run the risk of actually increasing the likelihood of nuclear war.

Those Christian nuclear pacifists proposing a nuclear bluff have avoided this simplistic solution of unilateral disarmament and have recognized the importance of deterrence for international stability. However, they have based their suggested Christian response—"possession but no use"—on the same questionable political and military assumptions made by secular antinuclear groups. Note the argument: Because nuclear escalation is likely to follow even intentionally limited U.S. nuclear use, innocent civilians will suffer disproportionally; therefore the U.S. could never employ nuclear weapons justly.

Limited Nuclear Use and a Just Defense

If the assumptions of this nuclear pacifist position can be challenged legitimately, then the conclusion that nuclear weapons are outside the just war tradition is also suspect. Upon careful examination, it appears that many of the assumptions of the nuclear pacifists are open to question.

For example, the "nuclear bluff" view assumes that virtually any use of nuclear weapons would be sure to escalate beyond control, and beyond any just use of force. Yet this assumption is little more than an educated guess. Fortunately, there is no previous experience in this area on which to base any confident prediction about how a nuclear war would unfold.

Nevertheless, there are some reasons to believe that a nuclear war could remain limited following a limited start. If so, the limited use of nuclear weapons need not lead to the indiscriminate destruction of innocent civilians (which would violate the proper role of government). First, the U.S. has long officially discussed and planned for the possibility of restricting its use of nuclear weapons if war ever comes. In fact, the U.S.

has plans specifically to avoid targeting Soviet population centers in the event of war. Secretary of Defense Caspar Weinberger recently acknowledged this: "We believe that threatening civilian populations is neither a prudent nor a moral means of achieving deterrence; nor, in light of Soviet views, is it effective. But our strategy consciously does not target population and, in fact, has provisions for reducing civilian casualties." President Reagan adds, "In implementing this strategy, the United States does not target population as an objective in itself and seeks to minimize collateral damage through more accurate, lower yield weapons."[12]

Soviet military writers have also stressed the importance of limitation more than massive destruction in the event of war.[13] In the new authoritative Soviet study, General Gareyev, Deputy Chief of the General Staff of the Soviet Armed Forces, indicates the need for limitation because, "The improvements in and accumulation of nuclear-missile weapons have reached such a level that the mass use of these weapons may result in catastrophic consequences for both sides."[14]

Avoiding the destruction of unrestricted nuclear warfare is one key reason both the U.S. and the Soviet Union would prefer to keep any nuclear war very limited. As Professor Albert Wohlstetter, one of the most respected military experts, has observed:

> The Soviets have always had strong reasons of self-interest not only to be wary about using nuclear weapons at all, but to try [if nuclear weapons are used] to keep the risks from getting completely out of hand. It is absurd to suppose that the Soviets would totally disregard the risk of disaster to themselves. . . . the Soviets have compelling incentives to use nuclear forces selectively if at all. They have recognized this interest, as can be abundantly documented both from recently available materials of the Voroshilov General Staff Academy as well as from fresh evaluation of Soviet military writings

during the last 20 years. Moreover, they are able to
use nuclear force selectively and keep it under control, and have been greatly increasing this capability.

The same incentives that impel the Soviets to be
able to use nuclear weapons selectively impel them
to *keep* the use of nuclear weapons under continuing
control. In fact, the notion that Soviet political leaders would casually let nuclear weapons slip out of
their hands is even less plausible than the notion
that they might use them indiscriminately.[15]

Both sides thus have great incentive to keep a cap on any
nuclear use and thereby avoid unlimited and unintended destruction. And, in accordance with this view, both sides have been
changing their nuclear arsenals to make them more controllable
and less likely to cause unwanted damage (by lowering their
overall destructiveness and improving their accuracy).

Nevertheless, there can be no guarantee that nuclear use
would remain limited even if it started out that way. If, in
response to attack, the United States used nuclear weapons in
a limited and discriminate way—for example, against Soviet
warships at sea and isolated military installations—it could
never be absolutely certain that the Soviet Union would respond
in kind. As long as the Soviet Union retains control over its
vast arsenal of nuclear weapons, and the United States is pow-
erless to defend against nuclear arms, the Soviet Union could
respond to the limited U.S. use of nuclear weapons with a
massive nuclear strike causing millions of casualties. It must
be acknowledged that if war occurs, one or both sides might
escalate and thereby permit little or no distinction between
protection of the innocent and punishment of the evil. Such
massive and indiscriminate use of nuclear weapons clearly
cannot fit within the restrictions on force set forth by the Christian just war theory.

However, nuclear weapons are not inherently indiscriminate and disproportionate. If used indiscriminately nuclear
weapons would indeed kill the innocent rather than protect

them. But that fact ought to determine how the government may justly deter and seek to protect the innocent—involving the use of particular types of nuclear weapons, only if necessary, and then with great caution. It is clear that newer technologies, with lower yields, higher accuracy, and improved control capabilities, would permit discriminate nuclear use.[16] Consequently, the Christian is not compelled to adopt the completely antinuclear or nuclear bluff positions.

This view that nuclear weapons need not violate the just war guidelines of proportionality and discrimination is rejected by both Christian nuclear pacifists and secular antinuclear groups. They base their argument on the assertion that if any nuclear weapon is ever used, there will follow certain escalation to indiscriminate destruction. But, as we have shown, there is no certainty behind that argument. Why some Christians have so willingly endorsed that particular political line is open to question; it is no more particularly Christian than it is particularly true. Worse yet, if the political agenda of the antinuclear groups was endorsed by the U.S. government, it could actually increase the risk of war by weakening deterrence. As Professor Wohlstetter has noted:

> But then there is nothing inevitable about the escalation by a democratic government of the use of nuclear weapons to universal ruin, though it sometimes seems that ideologues in the West would like to make it so. They would like, at any rate, to foreclose any Western options for responding to nuclear attack other than the extremes of bringing on the apocalypse or giving up. Those who conjure up a vision of an imminent apocalypse to lend urgency to the potential surrender of Western autonomy would not eliminate that nightmare by subordinating the West to totalitarian power.[17]

If the NATO response to a Soviet attack on Western Europe included, for example, the restricted use of nuclear weapons,

it could meet the key restraints on the use of force required by
the just war tradition:

- The use could be authorized by the proper authorities;
- it could be for the right purpose—to help stop invading Soviet tanks and troops from inflicting terrible destruction on innocent civilians, as they have done in Afghanistan;
- it could be for limited objectives—to stop or slow down the Soviet invasion to facilitate the eventual removal of hostile forces from allied territory, not a counteroffensive against the Soviet Union;
- nuclear weapons could be used that would minimize unintended and unwanted casualties among innocent civilians;
- there would be a chance for success—indeed, many knowledgeable military experts claim that the *only* realistic chance of stopping a Soviet invasion of Western Europe is in the early and limited use of nuclear weapons.[18]

Some types of nuclear weapons have been designed
specifically to minimize unwanted casualties among innocent
civilians, while also providing an effective means of stopping
aggression. For example, the so-called "neutron bomb" (officially known as an "Enhanced Radiation Weapon") is one such
nuclear weapon. Its production by the United States was desperately opposed by the Soviet Union and American antinuclear
groups in the late 1970s. Little wonder the Soviet Union opposed the Enhanced Radiation Weapon so vehemently—it
threatens the heavily-armored Blitzkrieg style of Soviet warfare
that would be used in any Soviet invasion of Western Europe.[19]
As two American military experts have noted,

> The immediate issue, however, remains the most
> effective means by which [NATO] forces could
> counter the threat of multiple, surprise Soviet-

Warsaw Pact armored thrusts. Toward this end the deployment of an enhanced radiation weapon might well be the single most important potential contribution in providing for the defense/deterrence of Western Europe . . . providing the basis for a weapon system that could defend against the threat of a Soviet-Warsaw Pact armored attack upon Western Europe. . . . What enhanced radiation weapons mean for the NATO defense posture is the development of systems capable of destroying an enemy armored advance with much less physical collateral [civilian] damage and radioactive wastes.[20]

Soviet propaganda denounced the Enhanced Radiation Weapon as an immoral "capitalist bomb" because it supposedly would "kill people but not destroy the buildings." What the Soviet propaganda did not point out, for obvious reasons, was that the people who would be particularly vulnerable to a neutron weapon would be invading Soviet tank armies, and the buildings that would be saved would be those in villages and towns (with their sheltered inhabitants) about to suffer from invasion.[21] This Enhanced Radiation Weapon reflected a clear intention to protect the innocent by stopping those ready to carry out aggression, and to avoid the type of indiscriminate destruction generally associated with nuclear weapons. Yet, ironically, it was denounced on moral grounds.

The "capitalist bomb" rhetoric about the Enhanced Radiation Weapon was given massive play in the U.S. (and European) media, and President Jimmy Carter decided to shelve plans to produce and deploy the weapon. This weapon, which NATO allies had agreed to accept, would have provided a significant deterrent against any Soviet plans to invade Western Europe. Since the Enhanced Radiation Weapon would help to ensure that a Soviet Blitzkrieg attack would fail, the Soviet Union would be less likely to attempt an attack. However, the opposition of antinuclear groups was successful in stopping this weapon's deployment. Subsequently, the United States has decided to produce but not deploy the neutron bomb, and France has shown interest in deploying it independently of the United States.[22]

We have argued that the U.S. and its nuclear-armed allies could use nuclear weapons in a restricted way that would be compatible with the strictures of the just war theory. Of course, nuclear pacifists would reply that the Soviet response to even a restricted and discriminate use of nuclear force could escalate to all-out nuclear war, and thereby overshadow any efforts to protect the innocent. Nuclear pacifists would conclude, therefore, that the U.S. could not use any nuclear weapon, even if discriminately and for a just cause such as defending innocent civilians.[23]

However, the reasoning of the nuclear pacifists falls apart at this point. The Soviet Union could respond to *any* U.S. or allied use of force with an indiscriminate nuclear strike— whether the U.S. action first involved nuclear weapons or not. Indeed, it is not possible to predict what actions might lead to a massive Soviet nuclear strike. There simply is not sufficient useful data to allow anyone to claim that he knows what actions would or would not precipitate an indiscriminate Soviet nuclear strike; no one knows what the "thresholds" are. Many commentators, including Christian nuclear pacifists, make pronouncements based on the presumption that they have a good grasp on what would lead to massive nuclear escalation. But such a grasp is beyond any human's reach because fortunately we have no experience with nuclear war to provide the data to support any claims of knowledge.

What we do know is that the Soviet Union *could* initiate such an attack in response to any Western political, economic, or military development it found unacceptable. And as long as the U.S. and its allies are undefended against nuclear attack, massive civilian casualties would be certain to occur. That is the unfortunate reality of the strategic balance and our current condition of defenselessness against nuclear attack.

If the U.S. is to avoid any action that might precipitate an indiscriminate Soviet nuclear strike, it would be completely constrained from *any* use of force, or any action that might be interpreted as highly provocative by the Soviet Union. By the reasoning of the nuclear pacifists, if an ally of the Soviet Union engaged in a terrorist action against U.S. civilians, the United States could not use any force to save the civilians' lives because such action *could* erupt into a nuclear crisis. Similarly, if the Soviet Union invaded Western Europe, the Persian Gulf, Canada, or America itself, the U.S. could not use force in an attempt to halt the invasion and to stop the massive civilian suffering because that might lead to nuclear escalation.

Opposition to any use of force clearly is not advocated by the nuclear pacifists, but it is the logical outcome of their position because *any* U.S.-Soviet military confrontation could lead to a nuclear catastrophe. Indeed, Soviet military planners readily acknowledge that a worldwide nuclear war could "begin with the use of only conventional weapons."[24] To be consistent, Christian nuclear pacifists would have to reject any action that might lead to Soviet nuclear escalation. Yet they do not make such an assertion because that would rule out any legitimate military action that the U.S. might have to take to protect itself or its allies.

The primary assumption of the nuclear pacifists is that nuclear weapons are inherently indiscriminate and must cause unacceptable civilian suffering, while the use of conventional, nonnuclear weapons may be accepted. Justness, however, does not depend on the type of weapon—nuclear or conventional; rather it depends on how force is used. There are many past examples of the unjust use of conventional force with terrible results for innocent civilians, and now, of course, the use of conventional force could precipitate an indiscriminate nuclear war.

The use of conventional force alone caused forty-seven million casualties in the First World War, ten million of which were civilian. World War II witnessed approximately fifty-five million casualties, and German civilian deaths alone numbered well over two million—all from a conventional war. The Battle of Britain in 1940 inflicted approximately fifty thousand casualties on the British, while allied bombing of the German cities of Hamburg and Dresden caused over a hundred thousand deaths, and virtually destroyed Dresden.[25]

These numbers of casualties are mind-numbing, almost incomprehensible. Yet they were inflicted almost entirely by now-obsolete conventional weapons. Even calculations by scientists critical of the notion of limited nuclear force demonstrate that a nuclear conflict *could* involve casualty levels comparable to those resulting from the use of conventional force during World War II—a war most agree was just and necessary to stop the evil of the Nazi dictatorship.[26]

In short, a basic assumption of secular antinuclear groups has been adopted uncritically by some Christians and has led them to nuclear pacifism. This assumption—that the use of conventional weapons can be permissible while nuclear weapons must inexorably involve unlimited destruction—is simply incorrect.

It is easy to be misunderstood. This discussion is not an argument in favor of using nuclear weapons. It is an argument against war of any kind, whether conventional or nuclear. Yet nuclear pacifists, both Christian and secular, threaten to destroy the basis of nuclear deterrence upon which U.S.-Soviet peace has been built over the past four decades. Before accepting the antinuclear views of these nuclear pacifists (and the potentially grave risks involved), we should at least require that their position be based on airtight logic and fact. It is not. Rather, Christian nuclear pacifists, by adopting sloppy thinking and questionable assumptions, threaten to undermine deterrence and increase the probability of war.

There simply is no rational basis for taking a pacifist position toward nuclear weapons only. The nuclear pacifist argument that nuclear weapons could never be used to protect the innocent clearly is wrong. Nuclear weapons could be used by the U.S. or one of its allies in a way that would discriminate between protecting the innocent and punishing the evil. The "neutron bomb" is just one example of a nuclear weapon that could be used to defend innocent civilians from suffering devastating casualties at the hands of invading armies without itself causing indiscriminate destruction. And the possibility of terrible nuclear escalation exists whether the U.S. responds to an attack with nuclear or conventional weapons, or does not respond militarily at all.

Can Restricted Nuclear Defense Be Just?

There are, of course, some ways in which nuclear weapons are very different from conventional weapons. Yet some Christians write as if nuclear weapons themselves are evil—as if an unthinking, inanimate object could have a moral character. But to put nuclear weapons in some sort of special immoral category—as if responding to an invader with a neutron bomb is less moral than responding with conventional bombing raids—is less than honest. Neither action is preferable to peace. But in the event of aggression by a powerful military foe, the alternative of peace and security no longer exists. The aggressor has taken away that preferred condition. In that case, governmental leaders must decide how best to carry out their scriptural mandate to protect the innocent and punish the evil. Only in this case can the use of force, including the limited use of nuclear force, be considered acceptable.

One can adopt a completely pacifist position and claim that the government must renounce any use of force, including nuclear weapons, because of the peril of nuclear escalation. This position tells government to give up its purpose and prerogative of just force as discussed in Scripture, but it is logically consistent. Or, one can say that government can use force, including the highly restricted use of nuclear weapons, to protect the innocent and punish the evil. This latter position is biblical in that it recognizes the duty of government to use force, if necessary, in a just way to protect the innocent. It would allow the U.S. to retain a type of nuclear deterrent other than "bluff." It also acknowledges recent nuclear weapons technology that could help a nation stop an aggressor while minimizing its own unintended and unwanted civilian casualties. Illogical mental gymnastics are required to achieve a position that accepts just war principles but rejects any nuclear force.

The popular and progressive-sounding nuclear pacifist position combines the worst of all worlds. It does not logically apply just war restriction on the use of force, and it almost certainly would increase the probability of a nuclear war by unilaterally weakening the U.S. deterrent. Those who advocate such a position ought to recognize the inconsistency and great risks in their views.

There is yet another problem with the position of the nuclear pacifists. If we are to accept their logic, not only is the U.S. morally responsible for its own actions regarding nuclear weapons, it is morally responsible for Soviet actions. It seems to assume that the U.S. leadership is in a position to determine the actions of the Soviet leadership, and therefore is morally responsible for Soviet behavior. If NATO responds to Soviet aggression in Western Europe by attempting to protect innocent Europeans through a restricted use of nuclear weapons, and tries realistically to minimize the civilian destruction associated with that nuclear use, NATO would appear to have met the key requirements placed on governmental use of force by the just war theory. Yet nuclear pacifists would respond that NATO could never justly use nuclear weapons because the Soviet Union might escalate to unjust massive nuclear war. But this returns to the question of why a U.S.-NATO action, if itself just, can be considered unjust because of the possible Soviet response. If an otherwise just use of force must be considered unjust because the aggressor may respond in an unjust way, then the U.S. could never use any force to defend the innocent.

During World War II Nazi Germany sometimes responded to local partisan efforts to expel invading German soldiers from occupied territory by executing local civilians. Did this unjust use of force by the invader against civilians make local efforts to resist the invaders unjust? Does Soviet military action against civilians in Afghanistan, such as mass executions, render the prior use of force by Afghan resistance fighters against invading

Soviet troops unjust? Does terrorist retaliation against civilians render the prior use of force to stop terrorism unjust? It seems clear that the just use of force cannot be considered unjust because the aggressor may continue or escalate his evil in response. If that were the case, then those innocent civilians whose governments care about the just use of force would be completely at the mercy of those who care nothing about such limitations—and the innocent would only suffer more.

The position of the nuclear pacifist is therefore mistaken for at least three reasons. First, there is no reason to place all forms of nuclear use in a special unjust category. Some very limited forms of nuclear use could, in principle, help protect the innocent from an aggressive invasion within the just war guidelines of discrimination and proportionality.

Second, if we were to judge the use of force by the U.S. as unjust because the Soviet Union might respond with the indiscriminate use of nuclear weapons, then the United States truly would be unable to use any means to protect the innocent against possible aggression. Such a situation is both unscriptural and dangerous: if the Soviet Union believed that actual U.S. policy was driven by such a view, the probability of aggression would almost certainly increase because the U.S. and those it protects would be seen as easy prey.

Third, it is not consistent with a Christian understanding of moral responsibility to suggest that the United States, if it uses force justly, would then be morally responsible for the possible subsequent unjust use of force by the Soviet Union. The United States would not have compelled the Soviet Union to use nuclear force unjustly. Indeed, if the United States used nuclear force in a limited way to protect innocent citizens from invasion, and sought to minimize any further escalation, it would be no more responsible for subsequent unjust Soviet actions than a bank guard is responsible for the unjust actions of the bank robber. If U.S. defensive acts can be rendered unjust because the Soviet response is unjust, then the United States truly would be paralyzed from taking *any* defensive actions—a situation clearly inconsistent with just war tradition and Scripture.

It has been suggested here that there could, in principle, be a just use of nuclear force, as there can be the just use of other types of force. What kind of nuclear use might be compatible with the just war restrictions on the use of force? Obviously, it would have to be in defensive response to an aggressive act. No aggressive use of force (i.e., having a goal other than justice and defense of the innocent)—whether nuclear or conventional—can be condoned by just war restrictions. It would have to be with the intention of protecting the innocent and restoring peace. Yet even if defensive and with the right intent, nuclear use would have to be limited so as not to violate just war discrimination and proportionality guidelines. Even in retaliation for aggression there could be no indiscriminate use of nuclear weapons against an invader's cities, or the cities that had been occupied by the aggressor; both would likely contain many innocent civilians. And even the use of Enhanced Radiation Weapons confined to the battlefield would have to be controlled carefully so as to protect millions of refugee civilians who would be on the roads fleeing the invader. Finally, nuclear use, as with any use of force, would have to hold some promise of success, helping to halt or turn back aggression.

Some of these restrictions could weaken the purely military utility of nuclear weapons. For example, invading Soviet armies might use "city-hugging" tactics to avoid nuclear strikes, staying as close as possible to cities knowing that the U.S. and its allies would not strike them. If military effectiveness were the only guideline for nuclear use, the just war restrictions could only be seen as an unnecessary obstacle. But there can be no excuse, from a Christian perspective, for government to ignore its responsibility to protect the innocent and punish the evil. Government is not to threaten all indiscriminately in exercising its prerogative to use force. Threatening all indiscriminately is what the aggressor's invasion does and is why it should be stopped.

The possibility of U.S. and allied nuclear use could indeed

help in defense because it would compel the invading armies to make difficult choices. Basically, if invading armies converge for an offensive drive to break through NATO defenses they become targets for nuclear attack. If those same invading forces disperse to avoid being targets, it is more difficult to cut a path through American and allied defenses. The mere prospect of a nuclear strike against the invading armies compels them to disperse and slow down their Blitzkrieg. In this regard, the so-called "neutron bomb" would pose a special problem to Soviet attack planning because it would be particularly helpful in stopping tank columns and other armored forces.

This is extremely important because NATO, in particular, has become so dependent on nuclear weapons that it is generally agreed there is little chance the Alliance could now defend itself successfully with nonnuclear weapons alone. To alter this situation would require considerably increased spending on conventional forces, an expense NATO does not appear willing to bear. There also is concern within NATO that if a stronger conventional military capability were mounted in Western Europe, the Soviets might believe the West would not use nuclear weapons, thereby eroding nuclear deterrence. As one European defense correspondent noted recently, there is a possibility that conventional force improvements could reduce NATO's reliance on nuclear deterrence, but the European allies have not supported such a transition:

> All it would take would be a bit more artillery here, a few more aircraft there and a few more men, tanks and command-and-control equipment almost everywhere. Why do the NATO countries take such a risk when a little more money would make a nuclear war that much less likely?
>
> The essential answer is, first, all countries of NATO Europe find it hard either to raise taxes or to cut into their social programmes by enough to buy the extra "insurance"; and, second, there is a feeling among many Europeans that they do not

want to be able to fight a long conventional war on
their soil, successful or no. They believe their security lies in a conventional force that is strong enough
to last for a few days, but weak enough to indicate
clearly to the Soviet Union and its allies that any
attack on the West would soon encounter the nuclear
might of the United States.[27]

It should be noted, in addition, that NATO policy is very
much defensive in nature. This, of course, is easy to say; the
Soviet Union claims the same for its forces. However, not all
military forces are alike. Unlike Soviet forces in Europe, NATO
forces are not well suited for the offensive. For example, NATO
emphasizes forward defense over a long defensive line, and
small, conventional antitank weapons particularly oriented for
defense against invading tank armies. In contrast, Soviet forces
emphasize heavy armored tanks and mechanized infantry units
that are most compatible with and trained for a Blitzkrieg
offensive strategy. Indeed, even planning for a major counteroffensive into Soviet bloc territory following attack has been
opposed within NATO.[28]

The point here is not that nuclear weapons are morally
"good" in any way. Rather, they are a military force that may,
under certain circumstances, be used in a just way. This is
especially important since NATO in particular has become so
dependent on nuclear deterrence for its security, and NATO-
Europe, in general, prefers nuclear deterrence to the cost and
uncertainty of trying to replace nuclear deterrence with increased conventional capabilities.

Similarly, at the intercontinental level, the U.S. possession of a limited and discriminate retaliatory capability is essential. It is important to establish, however, what the use of
nuclear weapons in response to a Soviet attack would be for,
and why such a response would be morally justifiable.

The principal objectives of U.S. nuclear retaliation would
be twofold: to minimize future loss of American and allied
lives; and to restore a secure peace. With regard to the first

objective, it is likely that following an initial Soviet nuclear attack against the United States, whether limited or unlimited, a large number of Americans (somewhere between 20 to 200 million) will survive. The maintenance of a strategic nuclear capability to attack directly some of the opponent's remaining means of waging war (a "counter force" strike against enemy strategic forces) could permit the U.S. to reduce the capacity of the Soviet Union to further threaten U.S. or allied lives if the war progresses. A limited and discriminate U.S. response of this type, intended to defend American and allied populations, would therefore not only be necessary in order to reduce the wartime threat to Western populations, but also morally justifiable in the event of a Soviet first strike.

A discriminatory strike against Soviet strategic forces would also intentionally seek to spare the lives of the Soviet population. This is an extremely important objective from a moral perspective, since the minimization of casualties among enemy noncombatants is a just war requirement. And, importantly, technical analyses demonstrate clearly that U.S. restrictions on the targeting of its nuclear weapons would make a dramatic difference in the number of Soviet civilian casualities, saving as many as 100 million lives that otherwise would perish.[29]

Christians are commanded to love neighbors, enemies, and self. It must be remembered that although the Soviet government is guilty of repressing political and religious freedom, the Christian must view her people not as the enemy but as those for whom Christ died.

Limitation in targeting is also extremely important from a strategic perspective: by limiting U.S. retaliation to selected Soviet military installations and specifically avoiding population centers, the U.S. would not only reduce the threat to the lives of its own citizens, but also improve the likelihood that escalation during a nuclear war could be controlled and deterrence restored. Because the U.S. response would reduce the Soviet capability to engage in subsequent strikes but would avoid large population centers, it would provide Soviet leaders with a powerful incentive to terminate the conflict, without further escalation, while their domestic political control was still intact. Of course, in order to effectively carry out such a strategy, it is necessary for the U.S. to possess a strategic force capable not only of discrimination, but also of survival. The force itself must be extremely difficult to attack.

Above all, however, the very possession of the capacity to remove a large portion of Soviet military forces should serve to deter a Soviet first strike in the first place. If Soviet leaders are convinced the U.S. has the capacity to withstand a Soviet strike and survive with a large enough force to destroy Soviet military forces, they should be deterred from ever undertaking a first strike. This type of discriminating deterrent threat posed by surviving U.S. forces could serve to convince Soviet leaders that they can never be better off following a first strike and thus should not undertake an attack.

In sum, such a strategy for retaliation with these attributes would allow the U.S. to restore deterrence once the war was under way and minimize civilian casualties—American, Soviet, and allied. It should also provide an effective deterrent against war in the first place.

U.S. Nuclear Policy: An Emphasis on Restricted Options

Is U.S. nuclear policy compatible with just war restrictions? The answer to this question is not entirely clear because U.S. nuclear policy, especially nuclear targeting and employment policy, is one of the most closely guarded aspects of U.S. military information. However, U.S. nuclear policy is broadly discussed by current and former government officials and outside experts, providing some basis on which to make a judgment.

Public information suggests that U.S. nuclear policy is intended to be sufficiently flexible so as to allow the option for the limited and discriminate use of nuclear force in response to attack.[30] The U.S. could, in principle, employ nuclear weapons in a highly restricted, discriminate fashion. However, the number and types of U.S. and allied nuclear weapons certainly allow the possibility for massive nuclear use that could not reflect proportionality and discrimination. In short, whether U.S. nuclear weapons could be used in compliance with just war restrictions depends on how employment decisions might develop in an actual war—there appears to exist the capability for both strict limitations and massive use.

There has been in effect since the mid-seventies an official trend toward flexibility, limitation, and discrimination in U.S. nuclear targeting, as opposed to the single capability of unleashing a massive nuclear attack. The desirability of limited nuclear options was first officially recognized in the sixties. This trend toward limitation requires weapons of reduced yield, improved accuracy and strict control so that unintended damage is minimized. In 1970 President Richard Nixon indicated a desire for such flexibility and limitation when he asked, "Should a President, in the event of a nuclear attack, be left with the single option of ordering the mass destruction of enemy civilians in the face of the certainty that it would be followed by the mass slaughter of Americans?"[31]

In 1974, then Secretary of Defense James Schlesinger announced the introduction of more limited and flexible nuclear options as part of official U.S. policy. This new policy was immediately labeled the "Schlesinger Doctrine." It was intended, according to Dr. Schlesinger, to move the U.S. away from a nuclear policy that involved the use of "thousands of [nuclear] weapons" to a policy that stressed the development of more accurate and controllable forces that would allow the U.S. to use only a "handful" of weapons.[32] Since then, accuracy, discrimination, limitation, and flexible options have been the key ingredients in the development of U.S. nuclear policy and forces.

U.S. policy now reportedly has numerous limited nuclear options and attempts to avoid unintended damage to civilian centers. Indeed, the revision in U.S. nuclear policy was intended to allow for the possibility of greater discrimination, even at the price of military effectiveness. As an "insider," Air Force General Jasper Welch noted that this revision "took residential areas off the target list explicitly—and provided even for residential area avoidance under certain circumstances, where one would reduce the effectiveness of the strike in order to avoid residential areas."[33] In short, U.S. policy has accepted military disadvantages under some circumstances in order to avoid unintended damage to centers of population.

Furthermore, U.S. and NATO nuclear planning also appears to be driven by a concern for discrimination. As General Bernard Rogers, the commander in chief of NATO forces, recently stated,

> I place certain constraints on myself in regard to collateral [civilian] damage. I will not fire a nuclear weapon into a city. I am concerned about those targets that are militarily significant, that we need to strike because it will have an impact on the battlefield, but which are close to cities. I will not strike those targets if a large percentage of civilians are going to be killed.[34]

This does not ensure, however, that such limitations would always prevail in the event of war. But from all appearances U.S. nuclear policy *allows for the possibility* of discrimination and proportionality by the U.S., as is required by the just war theory. Of course, because we are genuinely concerned with issues of morality, more must be done to improve the U.S. capacity to employ nuclear weapons in a discriminate and limited fashion. This will involve changes in aspects of current strategy, operational plans, and force posture, particularly the strengthening of command and control systems. The U.S. is indeed continuing to move in this direction.[35]

In short, the evolution of U.S. nuclear policy over the last decade has largely been in support of a limited and discriminate nuclear deterrent and employment capability. This can be seen in the focus on improved control, accuracy, and planning for selective and discriminate targeting options.

One might imagine that nuclear pacifists would applaud efforts to provide more discriminate nuclear capabilities and plans for limited nuclear options, since such efforts are required by the just war tradition. Yet, ironically, Christian nuclear pacifists and most secular antinuclear groups have *opposed* development by the U.S. of more discriminate and limited nuclear forces.[36] Consequently, while decrying the lack of discrimination possible with nuclear weapons, they have opposed the development of plans and capabilities that respond to their criticism.

Limited U.S. nuclear capabilities, of course, undercut the argument of the Christian nuclear pacifists that there is only one choice—either total destruction or nuclear pacifism—and only one solution—U.S. rejection of nuclear weapons and nuclear disarmament. The existence of an alternative weakens their absolutist argument against U.S. nuclear programs and takes some of the emotional wind out of their sails.

The usual approach of antinuclear groups, even some Christian groups, is to shock people with mind-numbing descriptions of nuclear war, and then argue that because the results would be so completely destructive the U.S. must disarm—even if the Soviet Union does not.[37] As Professor Paul Hollander of the University of Massachusetts has noted concerning the connection between peace activists and the fear of nuclear war, "The peace and anti-nuclear movements themselves stimulate such fears by constantly dwelling on the horrors of nuclear destruction and their likelihood unless the policies they advocate are introduced."[38] Imagine how much more difficult that particular approach to the nuclear debate would be if they acknowledged that some types of nuclear weapons could help prevent the mind-numbing horror hostile invasion brings. But that admission, of course, would complicate the issue; it would not be the simple black and white "nuclear disarmament vs. total destruction" choice they prefer to present. Consequently, many Christian nuclear pacifists and antinuclear groups simply deny, incorrectly, the existence of any other option.[39]

The Nuclear Pacifists and MAD Theory—Unlikely Allies?

Christian nuclear pacifists have borrowed the questionable arguments of the secular antinuclear groups, endorsed them as their own, and placed a Christian nameplate on them. Yet, as demonstrated above, their rejection of discriminate and limited nuclear options is illogical. As Christians accepting the just war tradition, they should support any effort that might make weapons less threatening to civilians.

Why do these Christian nuclear pacifists oppose the pursuit of a limited and discriminate nuclear capability? Because, they believe, it would "destabilize deterrence." With this kind of reasoning Christian nuclear pacifists have adopted a line of antinuclear argumentation they probably would avoid if they understood it in its entirety.

Generally, those who oppose limited and discriminate nuclear options say that such options make nuclear war more "thinkable," and, therefore, more likely.[40] If nuclear war is considered controllable as a result of limited options, leaders might be less deterred from using nuclear weapons. Consequently, they argue that the capability for limitation and discrimination weakens deterrence.

Of course, the logic of this view of deterrence is that the potential destructiveness of nuclear weapons ought to be maximized—the more the potential destruction the better the deterrence. Although few are willing to admit it, such a conclusion is the logical result of the argument that the capability for limitation must be avoided because it might make war more "thinkable." Of course, arguing for the threat of nuclear annihilation as a deterrent would not fit well with the progressive-sounding rhetoric generally coming from the antinuclear groups.

However, the mutual threat of annihilation is the basis of the notion of deterrence that has come to be called "Mutually Assured Destruction" (usually shortened to MAD by its critics). The idea is simple: If both sides' population and industry would be destroyed in a nuclear war, then neither, logically, would ever consider starting such a war. This notion of deterrence became part of official declared U.S. policy during the sixties. Then Secretary of Defense Robert McNamara discussed high levels of Soviet civilian casualties and industrial damage as the best basis for deterrence. McNamara defined the U.S. goal of "assured destruction" of the Soviet Union as 25 percent population destruction (fifty million people at the time) and 50 percent industrial destruction.[41] Of course, part of this MAD concept of deterrence includes American vulnerability to similar levels of destruction. It may seem odd, but the official declared U.S. policy of deterrence until the Reagan Administration was not to oppose the Soviet capability to destroy much of the United States. This vulnerability was seen as the basis for "mutual deterrence."[42]

Even U.S. arms control goals came to be dominated by the notion that nuclear weapons should threaten both sides grievously. If this is hard to believe, consider the following quote from Dr. Herbert Scoville in reference to the Reagan Administration's proposal to protect America and its allies with a defensive shield. Dr. Scoville was the president of the Arms Control Association and assistant director of the U.S. Arms Control and Disarmament Agency—no novice concerning U.S. arms control goals:

> Star wars will put an end to any hope for progress
> in arms control. It will also destroy the best arms
> control agreement we have, the ABM Treaty, which
> by forbidding defense ensures that every retaliatory
> warhead is able to reach its target.[43]

It is important to recognize what Dr. Scoville is saying: The "best" arms control agreement is one that ensures that the nuclear warhead will always "reach its target." This, of course, reflects the MAD notion of deterrence—mutual vulnerability through "assured destruction" is "good" for deterrence.

The fact that such a theory of deterrence came to dominate even U.S. thinking about what arms control should accomplish is not well appreciated. It is not difficult to imagine how most Americans would feel if told that their government had been pursuing arms control as a means of perpetuating mutual vulnerability to nuclear attack. Yet under the MAD theory, American and Russian civilians play an important role in the name of deterrence—that of nuclear hostages. Altering that hostage relationship by limiting the destructiveness of nuclear war would, according to the MAD approach to deterrence, be destabilizing.

Advocates of MAD have long opposed limited and discriminate nuclear capabilities and planning. In their view, limited capabilities endanger deterrence by making nuclear war more "thinkable."[44] They assert that limited capabilities are intended for "warfighting" instead of for deterrence. Because in their minds deterrence is based on horrendous threats to people and industry, any notion of trying to restrict the possible damage cannot support deterrence; rather, it must be for the purpose of fighting a nuclear war.

Despite the prevalence of these views, the trend in U.S. policy away from the massive attack plans of MAD and toward flexible options for limitation and discrimination has been explicitly intended to support deterrence. The concern has been that a MAD deterrent is not entirely credible. The Soviet Union would never believe that the U.S. would use nuclear weapons massively because this would simply beget a massive Soviet reply. Consequently, MAD is seen as suicidal for the U.S.; it is not a credible deterrent. The solution to this credibility problem, pursued gradually by the U.S., has been to revise the U.S. deterrent threat in a more flexible, limited, and discriminate direction, not because of an opposition to deterrence but precisely to restore the sagging credibility of the U.S. deterrent.

Those U.S. officials (such as former Secretary of Defense Schlesinger) who have advocated limitations are no more interested in fighting a nuclear war than MAD advocates are of seeing to it that "mutual assured destruction" takes place. They simply present a different view of how best to ensure deterrence. The labels that came to be attached to these two positions, "warfighting" vs. "deterrence" (i.e., a policy of nuclear limitation and flexibility vs. MAD), are unhelpful and superficial.

They suggest that the MAD approach, emphasizing threats to civilians and industry, is the only possible basis for deterrence, and that planning for limited and discriminate capabilities can come only from a rejection of deterrence and a cavalier attitude toward fighting a nuclear war. Numerous articles and books actually present these different views of deterrence in such superficial terms.[45] In truth, both sides have deterrence as their goal.

Christian nuclear pacifists, in their rejection of limitation and discrimination, have placed themselves in a curious position. They rightly reject the MAD notion of massive nuclear war as inconsistent with Christian just war requirements. Then, on the basis of MAD thinking, they oppose developing capabilities for limitation and discrimination, conditions required by the just war theory. The result is a Christian nuclear pacifist position that, in the name of deterrence, opposes limited nuclear options yet substantially destroys any basis for deterrence because it opposes all types of potential nuclear threat.[46]

Secular advocates of MAD have the luxury of opposing limited nuclear options while still arguing for their own version of deterrence based on massive threats to people and industry. They can talk of threatening to destroy cities as the basis of deterrence because they are not bound by the Christian moral strictures of just war. However, Christians cannot consider the purposeful destruction of civilian centers as acceptable. Christian nuclear pacifists, by rejecting both MAD and notions of limitation and discrimination, occupy an intellectual "twilight zone," lacking any logical consistency or basis for deterring nuclear war. They have chosen to pursue an antinuclear political agenda over all other considerations, and to apply just war principles selectively and incoherently.

This elevation of an antinuclear political agenda over Christian principle is clear in the way nuclear pacifists have treated just war requirements. First, they claim the use of nuclear weapons would be so destructive that it would violate just war requirements. Although deterrence is a worthy goal, it cannot justify nuclear means. However, they object to limited and discriminate nuclear capabilities, as required by just war considerations, because they believe such capabilities would "destabilize" deterrence. Just war principles are now rejected on the basis of deterrence considerations. This inconsistent and selective application of just war principles suggests that a political agenda rather than adherence to Christian just war principles has dominated their thinking.

If the U.S. government actually accepted the advice of these nuclear pacifists, the basis for nuclear deterrence would be destroyed:

- U.S. forces could not be used against cities because of the just war requirement to minimize civilian casualties;
- capabilities for limited strike options against military targets must be avoided because they are "destabilizing";
- limited, discriminate nuclear strikes must not be undertaken because they could lead to escalation.

The problem for deterrence, of course, is that this reasoning achieves the intended goal: There could be no operational justification for nuclear weapons. Yet this conclusion can be reached only by inconsistently placing deterrence considerations first on some issues and just war considerations first on others. The result is a position that would, if adopted, lead to the undercutting of deterrence and an increase in the likelihood of nuclear war.

Recently, a report from the Episcopal Diocese of Washington followed this line of reasoning by applying just war requirements to nuclear weapons, finding them unacceptable, and then opposing capabilities for discrimination:

We also wish, at long last, to close out the empty quest to fine tune nuclear weapon designs and effects. We understand that one purpose of continued [nuclear] testing is to make future nuclear weapons increasingly discriminating in their effects, perhaps even to make them less powerful than some conventional ordinance. But what useful purpose is served by trying to blur the distinction between conventional and nuclear weapons?[47]

Of course, the need to make nuclear weapons ever more discriminate is obvious to anyone interested in maintaining a deterrent against war, and doing so in a manner compatible with the Christian mandate to protect the innocent. Why make nuclear weapons "increasingly discriminating in their effects"? Obviously, to provide the U.S. with a just deterrent that both deters and minimizes the risk to innocent civilians. That some Christians use just war requirements to argue against nuclear weapons and then turn around and oppose capabilities for discrimination demonstrates an unfortunate shallowness of thought and the wholly political orientation of their antinuclear position.

Summary and Conclusion

There is an inherent tension between the need for nuclear capabilities to support a credible deterrent and the Christian just war principle that the use of force be limited and discriminate. The power of nuclear weapons is such that notions of limitation and discrimination seem not to fit, and no indiscriminate targeting of cities, as is suggested by MAD, is acceptable. However, limitation and discrimination are possible, particularly with recent advances in accuracy and controlled nuclear effects (such as the neutron bomb). Deterrence need not be based on an incredible "bluff." The U.S. could never maintain such a bluff, and attempting to do so would only weaken deterrence and increase the probability of war. A highly restricted and discriminate threat against Soviet military capabilities could be the basis for a credible deterrent threat that would fit within just war guidelines. And U.S. nuclear policy has been evolving in the direction of such limitation and discrimination since the mid-seventies.

There is a sound reason for the U.S. to possess nuclear weapons and not to resort to planning that calls for a grand bluff. That rationale is deterrence, the foremost goal of which is to ensure that war, and particularly nuclear war, never occurs. The Christian who recognizes that governments have the scriptural responsibility to protect the innocent and punish the evil need not endorse the antinuclear political platform, whether in its secular or Christian guise. Endorsing nuclear pacifism ought not be a litmus test of one's Christian faith as some Protestant denominations are now claiming.[48]

The just war tradition defines guidelines for the governmental use of force that can be accepted by the Christian. These guidelines have been in existence for more than a thousand years. The development of nuclear weapons has not done away with the relevance of just war guidelines, as nuclear pacifists, in effect, argue. Indeed, because nuclear weapons do pose such a grave threat to mankind and do have the potential for indiscriminate slaughter, Christian just war guidelines have become all the more important in the nuclear age. Fortunately, although there is serious tension between the needs of deterrence and just war considerations, the two are not totally incompatible given the possibility for limited and discriminate nuclear planning.

Any unnecessary governmental use of force is unjust and wrong. But Scripture confirms that it is the God-given responsibility of government to protect its innocent civilians from unjust attack and repression. The view of nuclear pacifists that nuclear weapons are inherently immoral and outside just war restrictions is simply wrong.

Nevertheless, there is no comfort to be found in a nuclear deterrent not based on bluff. Indeed, there is little satisfaction in arguing for the acceptability of nuclear deterrence as the basis of security for the American people, Soviet citizens, and the citizens of allied countries. Nuclear pacifists are correct in their basic view that the danger inherent in mutual nuclear threats cannot but leave one fearful of the future.

Horror scenarios demonstrate the danger of relying on nuclear deterrence for our security, even if the U.S. pursued a deterrent based only on limited and highly discriminate nuclear planning: What if an irrational leader came to dominate the Soviet Union the way Stalin did in the thirties and forties? Or what if nuclear weapons were somehow launched accidently or without proper authorization or by terrorists? If cities were targets, then millions could perish from the detonation of only a handful of weapons. While the probability of such situations is remote, they are possible. There is indeed little satisfaction in arguing that the U.S. could, by limitations and restrictions, pursue nuclear deterrence in accordance with the just war tradition. The Episcopal Report notes quite rightly that, "No system or situation is satisfactory, however, which cannot survive a failure of machine or human intelligence."[49]

Indeed, although U.S. nuclear policy and capabilities over the past decade have been moving toward greater discrimination, flexibility, limitation, and control, this does not guarantee that nuclear war could be so controlled. Undoubtedly, many U.S. nuclear targeting options would not be compatible with just war restrictions. For example, official U.S. discussions of nuclear targeting have recently focused on a retaliatory deterrent threat against the Soviet leadership—those primarily responsible for any Soviet aggression.[50] Such planning, although compatible with the scriptural mandate to punish those responsible for the evil of aggression, could entail aiming at targets in and around Moscow. If many leadership targets in cities were struck in retaliation for a Soviet attack, many millions of innocent civilians could be casualties. It is difficult to imagine how such planning could be compatible with just war principles.

The U.S. appears to have a capability for the limited and discriminate use of nuclear weapons; however, the U.S. and the Soviet Union both retain the capability for massive nuclear attacks. The possibility that those capabilities could be used for some reason someday is both the driving force behind the need to maintain a credible deterrent and the need to look for realistic alternatives.

An additional problem is that the reliance on offensive nuclear arms for deterrence involves an offensive arms competition that has led to the manifold increase in nuclear arms on both sides since the early seventies. Deterrence through an offensive nuclear threat is hardly a policy to inspire great confidence, and the American public continually questions the need to maintain so massive a threat. "Enough is enough" is the usual and understandable feeling concerning the nuclear arms competition.

Such feelings are entirely understandable. It would be much nicer were there an end in sight to the need to maintain a nuclear deterrent. Yet the continuation of deterrence offers little other prospective than that the American people must continue to carry the burden of maintaining an offensive nuclear deterrent so that a nuclear war never takes place. That is the reality of the current situation; it also is the reason almost any alternative appears more attractive and can generate great emotional appeal—no matter how incoherent or unrealistic.

Unfortunately there appear to be few realistic alternatives to avoiding nuclear war by threatening to wage nuclear war. Abandoning nuclear deterrence without first achieving a realistic alternative for the prevention of nuclear war would be the most irresponsible of governmental actions. Any group rejecting credible nuclear deterrence must also suggest an alternative means of avoiding nuclear war. The problem with much of the nuclear debate—whether secular or within the church—is that all can agree they do not like nuclear weapons and nuclear war would be a horror; yet few of those who express their moral outrage about nuclear weapons suggest a reasonable alternative to deterrence.

However, if alternatives to nuclear-armed deterrence exist, they deserve our utmost attention. Some Christian radical pacifists and nuclear pacifists have suggested alternatives to deterrence, such as the nuclear bluff; unfortunately it hardly seems a useful suggestion. The following chapters will identify and examine other suggested alternatives to nuclear deterrence, and propose an alternative that could serve to unite the Christian body.

Chapter 6, Notes

1. For an example of how this notion is presented to American school children as part of "peace education" curricula in the United States see, André Ryerson, "The Scandal of 'Peace Education'," *Commentary* (June 1986):37-46.

2. As General Bernard Rogers, commander of NATO forces, recently lamented, "Because of the failure to meet commitments in the conventional area . . . we have mortgaged our defense to the nuclear response." And, "It is not being able to fight more than X number of days that has put us into the position of having to ask for the release of nuclear weapons fairly quickly." Quoted in, George Wilson, "Nunn to Broaden Debate on NATO by Arguing War Plans Are Flawed," *Washington Post*, 21 February 1985, 8; and, William Beecher, "General Outlines Plan to Avert Nuclear War," *Boston Globe*, 16 December 1984, 26.

3. This "extended deterrence" theory is the basis of NATO's "Flexible Response" doctrine, officially labeled "MC 14/3."

4. Quoted in, Glen H. Snyder, *Deterrence and Defense: Toward a Theory of National Security* (Princeton, N.J.: Princeton University Press, 1961), 22-29.

5. Benjamin Schemmer, "Was the U.S. Ready to Resort to Nuclear Weapons for the Persian Gulf in 1980?" *Armed Forces Journal International* (September 1986):92-105.

6. See for example, Ronald J. Sider and Richard K. Taylor, *Nuclear Holocaust and Christian Hope* (Downers Grove, Ill.: InterVarsity Press, 1982), 32, 57-58; and, The United Methodist Church, Council of Bishops, *In Defense of Creation: The Nuclear Crisis and a Just Peace* (Pre-publication print, 1986), 3.

7. See the U.S. Catholic Bishops' Pastoral Letter on this subject in, "The Challenge of Peace: God's Promise and Our Response," *Origins* 13 (19 May 1983):1-32; and, Committee of Inquiry on the Nuclear Issue, Commission on Peace, Episcopal Diocese of Washington, *The Nuclear Dilemma: A Search for Christian Understanding* (Washington, D.C.: Episcopal Diocese of Washington, 1986), 73. It should be noted that the U.S. Catholic Bishops do not explicitly rule out any use of nuclear weapons. However, their Pastoral Letter does not present any discussion of an acceptable option and contains numerous statements that strongly imply that no use could be acceptable.

8. For a recent journalistic discussion of this problem see, "Can Anything Stay Secret?" *Newsweek*, 9 June 1986, 16-18.

9. Herman Kahn, *On Thermonuclear War* (Princeton, N.J.: Princeton University Press, 1961), 287.

10. See for example the discussion in, Francis X. Winters, "Bishops and Scholars: The Peace Pastoral Under Siege," *The Review of Politics* 48 (Winter 1986):31-59; and Albert Wohlstetter, "Bishops, Statesmen, and Other Strategists on the Bombing of Innocents," Commentary (June 1983):15-35.

11. See for example, *In Defense of Creation*, 2, 4, 18, 69; and *The Nuclear Dilemma*, 65.

12. Caspar Weinberger, *The Potential Effects of Nuclear War on the Climate: A Report to the United States Congress* (Washington, D.C.: Government Printing Office, 1985), 11; and President Ronald Reagan, *National Security Strategy of the United States* (Washington, D.C.: The White House, January 1987), 21.

13. See for example, Joseph Douglass, "Soviet Nuclear Strategy in Europe," *Strategic Review* (Fall 1977):19-32.

14. M. A. Gareyev, *M.V. Funze—Voyennyy Teoretik* (Moscow: Voyenizdat, 1985), excerpted in "Updating Sokolovskiy," *Strategic Review* (Fall 1985):103.

15. Albert Wohlstetter, "Between an Unfree World and None," *Foreign Affairs* (Summer 1985):975-76, 981, 985.

16. As is emphasized in Wohlstetter, 990-94; S. T. Cohen and W. R. Van Cleave, "Western European Collateral Damage and Tactical Nuclear Weapons," *RUSI* (June 1976):32-38; S. T. Cohen, "Enhanced Radiation Warheads: Setting the Record Straight," *Strategic Review* (Winter 1978):9-17; and the testimony of Dr. James Schlesinger in U.S. Senate, Committee on Foreign Relations, *Briefing on Counterforce Attacks*, 93rd Cong., 2nd sess., 10 January 1975, 12. Although the calculations presented by Dr. Schlesinger were later revised, even as revised it is clear a limited nuclear exchange would not necessarily be any more, and possibly less, destructive than conventional wars in the past.

17. Wohlstetter, 994.

18. As General Bernard Rogers, commander of NATO forces, has lamented: "The continually widening gap between NATO and Warsaw Pact conventional capabilities impacts the credibility of NATO's deterrence because it compels the alliance to rely excessively on the early first-use of nuclear weapons." Quoted in *Soviet Aerospace* 43 (11 March 1985):59.

19. For a detailed discussion of Soviet strategy see, P. H. Vigor, *Soviet Blitzkrieg Theory* (New York: St. Martin's Press, 1983).

20. Jacquelyne Davis and Robert Pfaltzgraff, *Soviet Theater Strategy: Implications for NATO*, USSI Report 78-1 (Washington, D.C.: United States Strategic Institute, 1978), 49-50.

21. See the discussion of these weapons in William R. Van Cleave and S. T. Cohen, *Tactical Nuclear Weapons: An Examination of the Issues* (New York: Crane Russak, 1978).

22. David Yost, *France's Deterrent Posture and Security in Europe Part 1: Capabilities and Doctrine*, (London: IISS, Winter 1983-84), 50.

23. See for example, *The Nuclear Dilemma*, 26, 72; "The Challenge of Peace," 11, 16, 18; and *In Defense of Creation*, 18.

24. Gareyev, 102.

25. Martin Sorge, *The Other Price of Hitler's War* (New York: Greenwood Press, 1986), 102.

26. See for example, William Daugherty, Barbara Levi, and Frank Von Hippel, "The Consequences of Limited Nuclear Attacks on the United States," *International Security* (Spring 1986):3-45.

27. James Meacham, "NATO's Central Front," *The Economist*, 30 August 1986, survey-22.

28. See for example the discussion in Jacquelyne K. Davis, "Europe's Edgy Approach to Strategy," *Air Force Magazine*, December 1985, 82-88. One of the leading British military analysts notes this steadfastly defensive perspective of NATO, in Lawrence Martin, *NATO and the Defense of the West* (New York: Holt, Rheinhart, and Winston, 1985), 119. Andreas Von Bulow, the head of the Commission on Security Policy for the SPD (one of Germany's two major political parties), provides a recent example of this prominent view within NATO that NATO must not seriously prepare plans for any other than defensive operations; see, Andreas Von Bulow, "Defensive Entanglement: An Alternative Strategy for NATO," in *The Conventional Defense of Europe: New Technologies and New Strategies*, ed. Andrew Pierre (New York: Council on Foreign Relations, 1986), 112-51.

29. See, Office of Technology Assessment, *The Effects of Nuclear War* (Washington, D.C.: Government Printing Office, May 1979), 140.

30. See for example the discussions in, Desmond Ball, "Counterforce Targeting: How New? How Viable?" *Arms Control Today* (February 1981):3-7; Jeffrey Richelson, "Population Targeting and U.S. Strategic Doctrine," *The Journal of Strategic Studies* (March 1985):11-14; Leon Sloss and Marc Millot, "U.S. Nuclear Strategy in Evolution," *Strategic Review* (Winter 1984):19-20, 22; Leon Sloss, "The Evolution of Countervailing Strategy," a lecture at the National War College, February 1982, 2; Desmond Ball, *Developments in U.S. Strategic Nuclear Policy under the Carter Administration*, ACIS Working Paper No. 21 (Los Angeles: UCLA, Center for International and Strategic Affairs, February 1980), 5.

31. Quoted in U.S. Senate, Committee on Foreign Relations, *Briefing on Counterforce Attacks*, Hearings, 93rd Cong., 2nd sess. 1975, 5-6.

32. James Schlesinger in, U.S. Senate, Committee on Foreign Relations, *U.S./U.S.S.R. Strategic Policies*, 93rd Cong., 2nd sess., 1974, 9.

33. Quoted in Gregg Herken, *Counsels of War* (New York: Alfred Knopf, 1985), 261-62.

34. Quoted in Bob Furlong and Macha Levinson, "SACEUR Calls for Research on a European ABM System," *International Defense Review* (February 1986):151.

35. See Caspar Weinberger, *Annual Report to Congress Fiscal Year 1987* (Washington, D.C.: Government Printing Office, 5 February 1986), 74.

36. See for example, Herbert Scoville, "A New Weapon to Think (and Worry) About," *The New York Times*, 12 July 1977, 29; *In Defense of Creation*, 11, 68; *The Nuclear Dilemma*, 66; and "The Challenge of Peace," 18.

37. Sider and Taylor, 213, 273-92.

38. Paul Hollander, "Enduring Misconceptions about the Soviet Union," *The World and I*, October 1986, 647-64, reprinted in *Current News*, April 1987, 9.

39. As the Episcopal Committee observes, "the Committee does not believe that any limits can or would be set on the conduct of nuclear war, nor do we see any strategy for the use of such weapons on a limited basis, no matter what the technological improvements." (*The Nuclear Dilemma*, 72.)

40. See Scoville, 29; and "Flexible Madness," *Foreign Policy* (Spring 1974):175-76; *The Nuclear Dilemma*, 29; and David Dessler, " Just in Case— the Danger of Flexible Response," *The Bulletin of the Atomic Scientist* (November 1982):55.

41. See a discussion of "assured destruction" in, Donald Brennan, "The Case for Population Defense," in *Why ABM*, ed. Johan Holst and William Schneider (New York: Pergamon Press, 1969), 100-101.

42. For an official statement to this effect coming from the secretary of defense during the Carter Administration, see Harold Brown, *Department of Defense Annual Report FY 1980* (Washington, D.C.: Government Printing Office, 1979), 61.

43. "Is There a Way Out?" *Harper's Magazine*, June 1985, 41.

44. See the long discussion of this in Wohlstetter, 962-94.

45. This superficial thesis is most clearly presented in Robert Scheer, *With Enough Shovels: Reagan, Bush and Nuclear War* (New York: Random House, 1982).

46. This is most clearly demonstrated in *The Nuclear Dilemma*, 84; "The Challenge of Peace," 16-18; *In Defense of Creation*, 30-31; and Sider and Taylor, 56-57.

47. *The Nuclear Dilemma*, 66.

48. In August 1982, the leaders of West Germany's Reformed (Calvinist) Church elevated one's views on nuclear weapons to a litmus test of one's Christianity. (See the discussion in, "The Pain of Being Christian in a Nuclear World," *The Economist*, 5 February 1983, 20-21.) In summarizing some of their points, Sider and Taylor say, "Christians must, we have argued, reject the possession and use of nuclear weapons." (Sider and Taylor, 169.)

49. *The Nuclear Dilemma*, 75.

50. Jeffrey Richelson, "Population Targeting and U.S. Strategic Doctrine," *The Journal of Strategic Studies* (March 1985):12.

Chapter 7

Disarmament and World Government as Alternatives to Deterrence

*I*f one argues against the possession of nuclear weapons, or against the potential use of nuclear weapons, as do Christian nuclear pacifists, one is virtually obliged to suggest an alternative to deterrence for keeping the peace. Merely criticizing the current deterrent means of avoiding nuclear war is not very helpful. Arguing against deterrence and the maintenance of a credible nuclear threat without also pointing to a realistic alternative for preventing nuclear war could actually increase the probability of war by undermining that one existing mechanism for peace. Unfortunately, most of the criticism of U.S. nuclear policy simply notes the same point in different ways: Nuclear weapons pose a terrible threat to mankind. Yet how helpful is that observation? Few people are unaware that nuclear weapons are dangerous. Addressing the issue of nuclear weapons requires more than merely observing that they represent a terrible threat; that much is well known. We need less self-righteous rhetoric and more hardheaded thought about how the problem can be treated.

Most Christian nuclear pacifists suggest two ultimate alternatives to deterrence: nuclear disarmament, and some form of world government. Nuclear pacifists claim the system of nuclear deterrence can be dismantled as one or both of these alternatives takes its place to prevent war. Armed with these alternatives to deterrence, nuclear pacifists believe they can press the U.S. to give up nuclear weapons without undue risk. If nuclear disarmament and world government are realistic alternatives to the current nuclear-armed standoff, they certainly deserve serious attention. This chapter will examine both as possible alternatives to deterrence.

NUCLEAR DISARMAMENT

Discussions about nuclear weapons often end with heartfelt cries for nuclear disarmament. Nuclear disarmament is seen by some as an immediate imperative given the threat posed by nuclear weapons. As American scientist Dr. Lewis Thomas recently suggested, "We simply must pull up short and soon, and rid the earth once and for all of those weapons that are not really weapons at all but instruments of pure malevolence."[1] This same call for nuclear disarmament is repeated in many Christian discussions of nuclear weapons. Could this be the solution to our problem?

Disarmament is contrasted with more common notions of arms control in that its goal is not just the regulation of arms, but their wholesale abandonment. There are many sincere calls from the Christian community for complete nuclear disarmament. The Methodist Bishops Pastoral Letter, for example, presents a "vision" for moving "toward a nuclear-free world."[2]

It certainly seems that national leaders should be able to sit down, reason together, and agree to rid the world of these weapons. They should be able to recognize that nuclear weapons pose a common threat, and that ridding the world of them would increase everyone's security.

Christian nuclear pacifists place great hope in disarmament as a means of addressing the threat of nuclear weapons. As the Methodist bishops concluded, "Our hope is that Europe and the whole world may find ways to combine nuclear and conventional disarmament so that our common defenses against war itself may be strengthened."[3] Such disarmament would mean, according to some Christian pacifists, that "War would no longer be possible because nations would no longer have the necessary weapons."[4]

Obviously, if all nuclear weapons are dismantled their threat will have been brought to an end—at least until any new weapons are produced. But what are the prospects for such a happy ending to our problem? Is nuclear disarmament a realistic alternative to deterrence? If so, it would be reasonable to begin the process even if at some modest risk to the existing system of deterrence. Indeed, many Christian proponents of nuclear disarmament suggest that the U.S. should begin to disarm itself unilaterally—which could easily threaten the existing deterrence stability. Ronald Sider and Richard Taylor claim that "it would seem imperative to call for a complete, unilateral and immediate renunciation of [nuclear] weapons."[5] This would, of course, entail the risk that the Soviet Union would not follow along, leaving the U.S. alone in its nuclear disarmament. Nevertheless, argue its proponents, because nuclear disarmament would be so beneficial if it succeeded, the U.S. ought at least be willing to start the process.

Who does not agree that a reliable and global agreement for nuclear disarmament would be a wonderful development and a preferable alternative to nuclear-armed deterrence? There is little argument against what, in effect, would be a step back to the age of nuclear innocence.

Unfortunately, there is virtually no chance that nuclear disarmament can succeed in the current world order. The international system of independent and sovereign states works against any realistic prospect for nuclear disarmament. This is not a situation where leaders of good will and reason need just to be convinced of the rationality of nuclear disarmament and they will rush to embrace it. The situation is far more complex than that. Indeed, there is every reason for leaders of the United States, the Soviet Union, and all other existing or potential nuclear-armed states to be extremely wary of proposals for nuclear disarmament.

The International Order and Nuclear Disarmament

The reasons why the international system undercuts the hope for nuclear disarmament are clear, and have long been recognized in professional writings on international relations.[6] It is not just because some states can legitimately be labeled as aggressive and uncooperative that complete nuclear disarmament will remain an illusion; even leaders earnestly seeking a solution to the nuclear threat must be skeptical of nuclear disarmament proposals.

The very nature of the international system works against the prospect for nuclear disarmament. The main ingredients missing from relations among countries are security and trust. There is no international police force and court system to prevent aggressive and powerful countries from threatening the security of others. There ultimately is no basis of enforcing agreements that have been achieved or ensuring that states cooperate and live up to promises. Each country ultimately is dependent on its own resources for security and survival. On issues of security, the international system is close to an uncontrolled "state of nature" wherein the survival of the fittest is the order of the age.

The international arena within which states exist is quite different from that within which most individuals live. As individuals we have an entire system of laws, police, courts, and judges to help resolve disputes, protect the innocent, and enforce the law. The individual can call on the power of the state to provide protection and to dispense justice. This is true now, and it was true in New Testament times. The apostle Paul, as a citizen of Rome, called on the authority and power of Rome for protection and justice.

However, in relations among states there are no recognized police force, court, or judges with the authority and power to resolve disputes, enforce justice, and protect the innocent. Consequently, weaker states often are the victims of stronger and more aggressive states. And hundreds of millions have died in combat as a result. For example, World War II was ignited by the German invasion of Poland in 1939. There was no police force to come to Poland's rescue or to restrain the aggressors, and by the time the war was over, millions had died.

One could wish the international system was different, having a system of police protection and justice similar to what now exists within individual countries. But it is not, and nothing suggests that the current system is likely to change much soon. The United Nations was originally conceived around the hope that international law could bring an end to war. But hostility and constant disputes among its members have prohibited the U.N. from playing such a role. As Brian Urquhart, U.N. general undersecretary, remarked at ceremonies celebrating the organization's fortieth anniversary, genuine unification and agreement within the U.N. will never be realized "until an invasion from Mars takes place."[7]

One might ask what all this discussion of the international system has to do with nuclear disarmament. It has everything to do with nuclear disarmament. Because there is no international government to enforce a nuclear disarmament agreement, it would be up to each individual state to determine whether, how, and when it would comply with such an agreement. Such decisions would be easier if it were possible for every government to know reliably whether and how every other government was disarming. However, given the ease with which even several hundred nuclear weapons could be stored secretly, it would be virtually impossible to know whether every other state had or had not complied with nuclear disarmament. Because of this lack of central control and the inability of individual countries to know whether every other state was or was not actually disarming, there would have to exist a high level of trust among all states before any could disarm. Yet mutual trust is precisely what is not to be found in the international system.

The absence of mutual trust among states is why it would be so vital for those considering nuclear disarmament to be absolutely certain other countries would comply and disarm.

Yet, in the system of sovereign states, such a precise capability to verify an agreement reliably is impossible. Even with sophisticated verification capabilities the U.S. does not know what the Soviet Union has done with hundreds of huge intercontinental missiles and nuclear warheads that have been decommissioned and replaced by newer systems. Dr. James Wade, Assistant Secretary of Defense for Acquisition, observed during testimony before Congress that, "[the Soviet Union] has hidden missiles. For example, where are the SS-9s that came out of the silos? We don't know where these force elements are."[8] Similarly, Dr. Richard Wagner, Assistant to the Secretary of Defense for Atomic Energy, observed that, "It is worthwhile to note that, when Soviet SLBM [submarine launched ballistic missiles] launchers are dismantled, we have no indication what actions are taken with their associated nuclear warheads."[9]

Imagine how the leadership of the Soviet Union or the United States could possibly approach the prospect of nuclear disarmament when it could never be sure the other side had actually disarmed. Or even if a trusting leadership believed the other had disarmed, it could never be certain the opponent had not rearmed in secret. Unless an international government existed with the power and authority to ensure and enforce disarmament by all, Soviet and American leaders would simply have to trust one another. Such trust cannot come easily to national leaders; a mistake could risk millions of lives that leaders are responsible to protect. And, understandably, the lack of trust is even more severe when the two sides consider each other "the enemy." Of course, if the level of trust and friendship required for disarmament were achieved, there would be no need for nuclear disarmament. The two sides would have already put aside their differences. Nuclear disarmament in the present international system would become a possibility just when it had become largely irrelevant.

The example of U.S.-British relations is instructive. The United States and Great Britain have no war plans or armaments prepared for use against one another. This is not because these earlier warring enemies were able to come to a disarmament agreement; indeed, while they saw each other as enemies such disarmament was unthinkable. It was only after hostility gave way to détente, and the existence of common opponents during the twentieth century solidified an alliance, that the existing level of amity could be achieved. Could such a change occur in U.S.-Soviet political relations? Over the long-term it certainly is possible (although as Brian Urquhart suggested in the above quote, that would probably require the emergence of some new and common enemy, raising new problems for general nuclear disarmament).

The point, of course, is that given the nature of the international system, political relations between the U.S. and the Soviet Union would have to change drastically before nuclear disarmament could occur. Yet once U.S.-Soviet relations had improved from being enemies to allies, a nuclear disarmament agreement between the two would be irrelevant.

The international system makes nuclear disarmament virtually impossible even if one assumes cooperation by every state for a period, something no leader can ever assume. Even if the U.S. believed it could trust one group of Soviet leaders to abide by a nuclear disarmament agreement, what about subsequent Soviet leaders? Unless some international authority existed to ensure continued compliance, how could U.S. or Soviet leaders be certain the other would stay disarmed? They could not, and the support for disarmament could last only as long as friendly political relations allowed for mutual trust.

The above discussion simply considers the prospects for nuclear disarmament in light of the realities of the international political system. If one ignores these realities then proposals for nuclear disarmament can seem very reasonable; unfortunately, when one ignores these realities disarmament proposals become either irrelevant or dangerous. Nuclear disarmament is not a matter of reasonable "good guys" who want disarmament being opposed by sinister "bad guys" who just like those "nukes." This "enlightened good guy" vs. "militaristic bad guy" view is reflected in much of the disarmament discussion by Christian nuclear pacifists; yet it has virtually nothing to do with reality.

Many Christian disarmament activists tend to point an accusing finger at the U.S. government for the lack of progress toward disarmament, as if disarmament could occur if only American policy were more enlightened. But the international system severely constrains those who have the grave responsibility of government. American leaders could greatly increase the prospect for war if they engaged in nuclear disarmament in the belief that all other states would follow suit. If the Soviet Union chose instead to maintain even a fraction of its nuclear arsenal in secret, those American leaders would have given up the U.S. deterrent without having resolved the nuclear threat. That would be a prescription for disaster. Governmental leaders—whether American or Soviet—are behaving in a reasonable fashion, given their responsibilities, when they approach the notion of nuclear disarmament with great caution.

In short, because of the tremendous roadblocks to general nuclear disarmament under the current international system, it can hardly be seen as an alternative to deterrence for the foreseeable future. A reliable agreement for nuclear disarmament would indeed be preferable to the current nuclear standoff; but deterrence is here and now, and it appears "to work." In the real world of international relations, nuclear disarmament is not a realistic alternative. Those Christians who pressure the U.S. government to pursue nuclear disarmament ought to recognize the genuine danger of their actions, especially when their pressure tactics have little if any impact on the Soviet Union. Jeopardizing the U.S. capacity for deterrence in pursuit of unilateral disarmament, as is suggested by some Christians,[10] would almost certainly increase the probability of nuclear war in the vain pursuit of a goal that cannot be achieved in the system of imperfect sovereign states.

WORLD GOVERNMENT

This situation leads to one obvious question: If the nature of the international system constrains even leaders of good will to be wary of disarmament, why not change the international system? That question is absolutely on the mark. The absence of a central government with the necessary authority and power to enforce rules for the common good undercuts the reality of proposals such as nuclear disarmament. If the current system of independent, sovereign, and self-seeking states could be reorganized along the lines of a more centrally directed state, then the problem of war and nuclear weapons could be handled much more easily.

An international authority could monitor compliance with agreements, enforce compliance with rules for the common good (such as general disarmament), and provide protection and justice for member states. Such a central authority could, in effect, outlaw war. It also could prove much more effective in solving important nonmilitary problems that are impossible to handle without international cooperation. For example, it could require that member states work together to solve common problems of pollution and hunger. This would necessarily mean the demise of individual sovereignty for independent states—but that, of course, is the point. U.S. policy in these important areas would no longer be determined through the current independent democratic system based on the U.S. Constitution. Rather, an international authority would make and enforce policy to ensure pursuit of the common good. Similarly, Soviet policy would no longer be determined solely in Moscow, British policy in London, French policy in Paris, and so on. Indeed, on many issues there would no longer be an independent American, Soviet, British, or French policy; decision-making would be the prerogative of the international authority. This, in short, would be the result of moving away from the current system of sovereign states and toward an effective international authority.

The fact that the international system of sovereign states is a roadblock to disarmament has led many Christians to advocate changing the international system. An international authority with real power, a type of world government, is seen as a far better alternative for maintaining peace than the current deterrent stalemate. Interestingly, both the U.S. Conference of Catholic Bishops and the United Methodist Bishops have endorsed a move toward an international authority with real power. The Catholic Bishops explained their hope for such an "international authority":

> There is a substitute for war. There is negotiation under the supervision of a global body realistically fashioned to do its job. It must be given the equipment to keep constant surveillance on the entire earth. Present technology makes this possible. It must be empowered by all the nations to enforce its commands on every nation.[11]

The United Methodist bishops have made an appeal for a similar institution with similar authority, calling for

> global systems of governance with effective authority to assure common security with regard to environmental perils, scarce resources, financial instability, trade inequities, food and hunger, and flagrant abuses of human rights. Only such a broadened view of security can do justice to peacemaking.[12]

Calls for a world government are not limited to Christian nuclear pacifists. Secular antinuclear opinion has often advocated a similar solution to the issue of nuclear weapons.[13] It is clear, of course, that if an effective world government or "international authority" came into being and consistently pursued peace and justice, the current situation of nation threatening nation with vast nuclear arsenals would no longer exist. Many other global problems would likely be more easily treated because cooperative action could be required of the states by the central authority. Is this, at last, a potential alternative to deterrence for maintaining peace in a dangerous world?

International Authority: An Alternative to Deterrence?

Since the Treaty of Westphalia in 1648 the international system has consisted, by and large, of independent sovereign states. Yet that system now stands in the way of solving international problems, including the threat of nuclear war. It certainly seems reasonable to propose that the sovereign state system be revised to promote an international authority capable of dealing with such problems. A type of world government with real enforcement powers, in place of existing sovereign states that encourage mistrust and self-interested policies, could provide peace and justice. In effect, Christian and secular nuclear pacifists have proposed that such a world government replace deterrence as the means of controlling or eliminating nuclear weapons and avoiding nuclear war.

We have shown that the nuclear disarmament alternative to deterrence is an idealistic vision—virtually impossible in the current international system of sovereign states. What is the prospect that this system could be replaced by an international authority through international agreement and cooperation? Could world government be the alternative to deterrence that Christians and non-Christians alike ought to support?

The cooperative creation of an international authority capable of enforcing "its commands on every nation" would, by definition, remove the current U.S.-Soviet nuclear stalemate because it would have to be more powerful than both superpowers to ensure the effectiveness of its authority. Indeed, both superpowers would have to transfer their military capabilities to the central authority so that it would be capable of its peacekeeping responsibilities. An international authority lacking such enforcement power would alter the current situation little—indeed such an organization already exists in the United Nations.

An international authority could not ensure that nuclear

weapons would never be used unless it had the coercive power necessary to preclude all potential wars and prohibit any unauthorized production or use of nuclear weapons. Such a central authority would have to be powerful indeed, perhaps totally so. It is unclear whether the possibilities of repression and coercion inherent in such a global authority (one that could "keep constant surveillance on the entire earth," as the Catholic Bishops call for) would provide a safer and more secure world for its citizens. Nevertheless, the potential risks of a new world order may seem less threatening than the current risk of nuclear war in the existing deterrence stalemate.

But even if one assumes that a world government would be good—seeking peace, justice, and prosperity for all—there is a fundamental problem with this alternative. In short, an effective international authority is beyond any realistic hope of coming into being. The existing international system virtually precludes the possibility of the cooperative creation of such an international authority.

As is the case with proposals for nuclear disarmament, the problem stems from the lack of any effective central authority that could guarantee the security of individual states. As a result, individual states could cede their means of protection to a central authority only if they were relatively certain others had done likewise and were confident the central authority could protect them. It is incredible to expect the Soviet Union, the United States, or any other state to give up sovereign control of its means of protection unless it could be certain that the threat posed by opponents could be handled by the central authority. Indeed, such behavior could be seen as an irrational abdication of a state's primary responsibility of protecting the innocent.

Yet, the level of certainty concerning the ability of the central authority to protect each state's interest could not be high, particularly during its critical formative period. To ensure that the world government would provide protection to all, each state would have to give, virtually simultaneously, most, if not all, of its military capabilities to the central authority.

How could the Soviet Union be confident that the United States would give over control of all of its nuclear weapons, or how could the United States have such faith in the Soviet Union? That level of precise verification and monitoring simply does not exist, and as nuclear weapons become even smaller and more mobile (and thus more easily hidden), it is not at all clear that such verification capabilities ever could exist.

The existing lack of trust inherent in the sovereign state system, and the rational limitations this lack of trust places on each state's willingness to cooperate, renders virtually impossible the cooperative establishment of a "new world order."

If some revolutionary changes were to take place and leaders no longer needed assurances of security for their citizens, or states came to trust their existing and potential opponents, then the formation of a world government would become a viable option. But if such changes were to take place, the establishment of a world government to maintain peace would be unnecessary. The "new world order" would have already arrived.

One must be cautious of predicting the feasibility of any proposed alternative to deterrence that requires a prior miraculous change in the behavior of states and their leaders. Divine intervention could, of course, cause a simultaneous, revolutionary, and enduring change in the hearts of all current and future world leaders so that all were trustworthy and trusting. We must not limit what could be done beyond the hand of man. But that type of perfection has not been granted to mankind yet, and Christian world government proponents must be asked on what basis they anticipate such divine intervention in the near future? Short of the millennial reign of Christ, it certainly is not an expectation based on Scripture.

One supposes that a world government could be established through global conquest by a superpower or an alliance of powers. In the event of such an occurrence the new world leadership presumably could enforce new edicts and policies upon the rest of the world, as the Roman Empire once ruled much of the world and enforced stability within its ever-expanding borders. Yet such a new world order could be even more destructive of justice and peace if that world government was brutal and repressive. Indeed, conquest and the creation of a world empire almost certainly would involve the use of nuclear weapons given the current number of nuclear-armed (or near nuclear-armed) states. Thus, this avenue to a new world order would probably lead to the very threat we seek to avoid.

Some who propose a new world order as the solution to the threat of nuclear war recognize its creation would not be a simple thing. The analogy of the abolition of slavery is often drawn. The cooperative creation of an effective international authority would, it is suggested, require the "same kind of imagination" that led to the abolition of slavery.[14] However, it must be noted that the abolition of slavery in the United States did not come about through cooperative agreement; abolition was part of the bloodiest and most costly war ever fought by Americans (sometimes involving casualties of more than fifty thousand in a single battle). Similarly, the end of serfdom in Imperial Russia in 1861 did not occur through cooperation and the "enlightened consciousness" of those concerned. Rather, it came about largely as a result of the Crimean War, and was forced on the nobility by the absolute power of Czar Alexander II, not without much acrimony. Ironically, Christian pacifists call for a "new abolitionist movement" against nuclear weapons[15] but renounce military force, that which brought slavery to an end in the United States.

There is an interesting element in the proposal by some Christians that a powerful international authority is a feasible alternative to deterrence for the preservation of peace—and that is the basis for their view that such an authority can be established. Some nuclear pacifists note that such an international authority can come about through the "genius of man" and "world public opinion."[16] This view implies that all that is necessary for the creation of an effective and just world government is for mankind to apply reason and public pressure to the problem. However, as discussed above, the absence of trust is the key characteristic of the international arena. This is not because all states are foolish and simply refuse without reason to be trusting, but because international politics has proven that leaders, and through them states, can be untrustworthy. A national leader, acting responsibly and reasonably, simply cannot afford to conduct international relations on the basis of trust.

For example, Soviet leader Joseph Stalin trusted Adolf Hitler to some extent to abide by the terms of their friendship and mutual nonaggression pact signed in 1940. Yet Hitler turned around and attacked the Soviet Union in June of 1941 and inflicted approximately twenty million casualties. In September 1938, British Prime Minister Neville Chamberlain trusted in an agreement signed by Adolf Hitler (the Munich Pact) and returned to Britain declaring that he had succeeded in achieving "peace in our time." World War II began the next year with the German invasion of Poland.

Mistrust has been inherent in the international system not because mankind lacked "genius" in the past, but because national leaders, like the rest of mankind, are not perfect beings; they are subject to the same flaws as the rest of mankind. As a result, the behavior of states has historically not led to trustworthiness in international relations. It is not some newly discovered "genius" that could lead to the creation of an effective, peaceful, and just new world order, but the perfection of mankind (or at least all current and future leaders of mankind). It should not be seen as the voice of an unreasonable pessimist to suggest that such a transformation ought not be expected in this age.

The problem is not that some nuclear pacifists have pointed to world government as an alternative to deterrence. They are absolutely correct to point to the current system of "international anarchy" (as described by one group of nuclear pacifists)[17] as at least partially responsible for the lack of trust and cooperation in international relations. The problem is with their suggestions as to how it will become possible to "get from here to there." Clearly, the "genius of man" cannot solve the problem. This is not a problem similar to landing a person on the moon—one that will yield to enough money and scientific talent. Achieving the cooperation and trustworthiness of all national leaders is not a problem of intellect but of character.

"World public opinion" is another source of change suggested by many nuclear pacifists as the basis for the formation of a new international order. Suggesting that world public opinion is likely to lead to the formation of a world government reflects an incredibly optimistic view of what world public opinion can accomplish. While it is true that democratic governments are sensitive to public pressure on various issues and to varying degrees, it should be recognized that even democratic governments are unlikely to be persuaded by world public opinion on issues involving national sovereignty.

For example, the U.S. invaded the island of Grenada in October 1983 despite the certainty of subsequent international protest (even from U.S. allies). The U.S. government did so because Americans on the island were in danger and because the government in Grenada was quite friendly to Cuba and the Soviets and hostile to the United States. The U.S. attacked Libya in 1986 despite the certainty of subsequent international outrage (again coming from some U.S. allies) because of the terrorist threat Libya posed to Americans. The British waged war against Argentina over the Falkland Islands in the spring of 1983 despite an outpouring of protest from much of the world. And, despite the prospect of international outrage, in July 1985 the French government bombed and sank the private Greenpeace ship "Rainbow Warrior" while it was in port in New Zealand because the ship was scheduled to interfere with French nuclear testing. This brief list of recent actions by democratic governments suggests that even democracies, which one might suppose would be most responsive to world public opinion, appear to be undeterred if issues of security and sovereignty are involved.

Another problem with the notion that world public opinion will lead to a world government is the fact that it is impossible to know what world public opinion is on any particular issue.

No worldwide public opinion polls exist, and it is the height of arrogance to presume that one knows what world public opinion would be on the specific issue of giving up national sovereignty to a central world government.

In spite of advances in international transportation and communications, there is little if any evidence to suggest that world public opinion is becoming less nationalistic—caring less about loyalty to the individual nation-state and more for some concept of a global central government. Indeed, some of the most obvious evidence—peoples around the globe seeking self-determination based on nationalism—suggests just the opposite. Even in the U.N., where the loyalty of U.N. employees is supposed to be to that global organization, the divisive effects of nationalism are pervasive in virtually every aspect of U.N. activities.

While democratic governments are sensitive to domestic public opinion and thus might indirectly be responsive to world public opinion (if it could be measured in any realistic way), democratic governments are a distinct minority in the international system. Most of the peoples of the world are governed by authoritarian and (by democratic standards) repressive regimes. These tend to be largely unresponsive to their own domestic public opinion, much less world public opinion. One need point only to the continuing Soviet military occupation and extermination campaign in Afghanistan to illustrate the unresponsiveness of authoritarian governments to international outrage. Similarly, the Soviet Union brutally invaded Hungary in 1956 and Czechoslovakia in 1968 to put down popular uprisings demanding liberal reforms. The Soviet Union pursued these actions *against its own allies* despite the certainty of worldwide outrage. And perhaps most instructive is the Soviet Union's infamous "Gulag" system of forced labor camps for political prisoners—mostly Soviet citizens—despite the occasional international outpouring of opposition to such practices.

In short, on issues of perceived national security and sovereignty neither democratic nor authoritarian governments appear to allow their decision-making to be determined by world public opinion. Consequently, it is not realistic to conclude that world government is going to be built on the basis of world public opinion, as suggested by Christian and secular proponents.

The dean of U.S. international relations scholars, Professor Hans Morgenthau, noted the continuing disillusionment of those relying on world public opinion for change in the international system:

> Modern history has not recorded an instance of a government having been deterred from some foreign policy by the spontaneous reaction of a supranational public opinion. There have been attempts in recent history at mobilizing world pubic opinion against the foreign policy of a certain government—the Japanese aggressions against China in the thirties, the German foreign policies since 1935, the Italian attack against Ethiopia in 1936, the Russian suppression of the Hungarian revolution in 1956. Yet, even if one supposed for the sake of argument that these attempts were successful in a certain measure and that a world public opinion actually existed in those instances, it certainly had no restraining effect upon the policies it opposed. But the supposition itself, as we shall see, is not supported by facts.
>
> . . . The confidence with which all the antagonists in the international arena believe themselves to be supported by world public opinion with respect to one and the same issue only serves to underline the irrationality of the appeal. In our century, as we have seen, people want to believe that they champion not only, and perhaps not even primarily, their own national interests but the ideas of humanity as well. For a scientific civilization that receives most of its information about what people think from public opinion polls, world public opinion becomes the

mythical arbiter who can be counted upon to support
one's own, as well as everybody else's, aspirations
and actions.[18]

This discussion should not be read as a criticism of the
ideal of a responsible world society, a world community based
on justice and law, or the creation of a benevolent world government. The current sovereign state system, dominated as it
is by nationalistic drives and balance-of-power considerations,
is not conducive to the type of international cooperation that
could solve many problems. Changing the sovereign state system in favor of a just world government certainly sounds like
a preferable alternative to the current nuclear deterrent stalemate. However, it is not responsible for Christian proponents
of world government to present their ideal as a realistic alternative to deterrence while completely sidestepping the issue of
feasibility. If the creation of an effective and just world government is not feasible for the foreseeable future, as it almost
certainly is not, then it should not be considered an alternative
to deterrence.

What about the United Nations?

The history of the United Nations provides an excellent
example of the problems that occur when the ideal of creating
a just world government meets the realities of international
politics. The U.N. was originally conceived as a "new international order," and was intended to render war obsolete and
provide for the common security. Yet the forces of nationalism,
self-interest, and individual sovereignty have led to its failure,
and such forces show no sign of weakening in international
relations.

There were several reasons why Americans tended initially to see the U.N. as the solution to war. The alliance that
called itself the "United Nations" in the early forties had won
the war against Nazi Germany, demonstrating that heroic deeds
were possible. Furthermore, the earlier League of Nations had
failed, it was thought, largely because the United States had

not participated; the United States was now the principal figure behind the U.N. Finally, the U.N. Charter contained elements of a democratic constitution and commitments for collective security. These provisions were thought to help ensure that differences could be resolved peacefully; yet if an aggressor did emerge, the Charter's procedures for collective security would protect the innocent. Although the U.N. did not itself mirror the Constitution, Americans believed the Charter would be seen as a sacred legal foundation for relations among states, as the Constitution is the legal foundation for U.S. domestic relations. International disputes would be settled through legally established channels and war would become outmoded. As President Roosevelt said in 1942 with regard to the role of a United Nations, "This time we are determined not only to win the war, but also to maintain the security of the peace that will follow."[19]

At the Moscow meeting of Foreign Ministers in 1943, the Soviet Union, Great Britain, and the United States agreed to create an international organization to prevent war. It was thought at the time, at least by the Americans, that the same spirit of cooperation that was winning the war against Nazi Germany would stop any potential aggressor following the war.[20]

A few realists recognized that such a cooperative approach to collective security would be possible through the U.N. only if the great powers, particularly the U.S. and the Soviet Union, could first cooperate. But Americans generally assumed that the Soviet Union would cooperate with the United States and Great Britain in maintaining world order. U.S. Secretary of State James Byrnes believed that "the Russians made up their mind to take their place in the world and support the world organization." Averell Harriman, U.S. ambassador to the Soviet Union, anticipated difficulties with the Soviet Union, as did British leader Sir Winston Churchill, who asked repeatedly, "But can we trust the Russians?"[21] President Roosevelt, confident he could "handle old Joe [Stalin]," responded to Churchill's question, "We have to trust someone."[22]

American policy makers in general were extremely optimistic about the prospects for cooperation with the Soviet Union in the U.N. This optimism remained even after the Soviet Union demonstrated a distinctly self-interested approach to the U.N. Stalin demanded sixteen votes for the Soviet Union in the U.N. General Assembly, and settled for three. He demanded and received veto power for the Security Council, and attempted to get individual veto power even over debate in the Security Council. Yet Americans remained optimistic. As chief U.S. negotiator and acting Secretary of State Edward R. Stettinius said about the signing of the Charter in San Francisco in 1945, "I believe that the five major nations proved at San Francisco beyond the shadow of a doubt that they can work successfully and in unity with the other United Nations under this Charter."[23]

American policy makers appear to have had confidence in world public opinion as a mechanism to ensure cooperative action within the U.N. and corrective action in the unlikely event of aggression. Senator Tom Connally, chairman of the Senate Foreign Relations Committee at the time, stated that "a compelling world opinion . . . would make it very difficult for a single member of the Security Council to veto the peaceful settlement of a dispute."[24] Even future Secretary of State John Foster Dulles, not known as an idealist, claimed that the U.N. General Assembly would play, "the role of a 'town meeting of the world,' where public opinion is focused as an effective force."[25]

It was considered unlikely that serious conflict would present a problem because the very existence of the U.N. would be enough to discourage aggression. Yet, in the event conflict did occur, there was little doubt that the U.N. Security Council would abide by the Charter and resolve the problem swiftly.[26]

In short, there was bold optimism in the United States regarding the U.N.'s potential to prevent war. This optimism stemmed from the assumptions that "world pubic opinion" would be an effective force in international relations, and that the U.N. Charter would become a de facto world constitution. Hopes were high that a "new international order" had been created that would redress the problems of the old system of self-seeking states.

Discussions in the U.S. Congress certainly reflected this optimism: Senator Connally called the Charter "the greatest document of its kind that has ever been formulated"; Connally's counterpart in the House of Representatives, Foreign Relations Committee Chairman Sol Bloom of New York, spoke of "this new Magna Carta of peace and security for mankind"; and Charles Eaton, representative from New Jersey, talked of "inexorable tides of destiny" carrying the world "towards a golden age of freedom, justice, peace, and social well-being."[27]

The history of the U.N. is an example of what happens when the ideal of a cooperative new world order, even when sincerely pursued, meets the realities of international politics. In the more than forty years after the signing of the U.N. Charter there have been hundreds of wars, and the U.N. has been able to play a significant role in only a handful. It is not an overstatement to assert that the U.N. has come nowhere near the hopes expressed for it in the forties. The unfortunate but understandable drive of self-interest operating among states has shattered those hopes.

Even those few peacekeeping operations the U.N. has pursued have involved disputes over who should pay the bill. Members such as France, China, and the Soviet Union have refused to pay as a result of disputes over the legality or appropriateness of U.N. peacekeeping operations. The United States, in fact, has been the largest financial supporter of U.N. peacekeeping.[28]

Even in those cases that might be cited as legitimate examples of successful U.N. peacekeeping—in Zaire, the Middle East, and Cyprus—the U.N. has been unable to maintain the peace. In Zaire, additional peacekeeping operations had to take place outside U.N. auspices (conducted primarily by France). In the Middle East the only major relevant peace agreements took place between Israel and Egypt; these were the Camp David accords sponsored by the United States and condemned by the U.N. General Assembly. In Cyprus the U.N.

established a peacekeeping force specifically to "prevent a recurrence of fighting and, as necessary to contribute to the maintenance and restoration of law and order and a return to normal ·conditions."[29] Yet, although the U.N. had been in Cyprus since 1964, a war broke out in 1974 between Greek and Turkish Cypriots and their respective patrons. And now, over a decade since that war, there still has been no settlement of the issues that have led to conflict there.

This is not to suggest that the U.N. provides no benefit to member states or their populations. Some U.N. functions have value, particularly in the health area. But it does point to the virtual impossibility of establishing an international authority with the necessary power to end war. The U.N. has failed in this regard for the same reason that the League of Nations failed a generation earlier: The system of sovereign states does not permit mutual trust as the basis for cooperative relations among potential opponents.

The creation of a just world government hardly can be considered an alternative to deterrence for keeping the peace. The suggestion of such an alternative by Christian nuclear pacifists reflects a lack of understanding of the basic characteristic of international relations—mistrust. We can and do lament the nature of the international system, but that does not alter the reality of the situation.

SUMMARY AND CONCLUSION

Christian nuclear pacifists often have proposed world government and nuclear disarmament as their preferred alternatives to deterrence. If one argues against deterrence or advocates policies that would weaken it, it is, of course, proper to suggest an alternative. Yet, in proposing world government and nuclear disarmament as their favored alternatives, Christian nuclear pacifists have failed to provide anything helpful. The cooperative creation of a just international authority that could outlaw war is no more a realistic alternative to deterrence than is the prospect for complete nuclear disarmament. Both proposals suffer from the same root problem: Either would require the prior transformation of mankind and the international system before becoming feasible. And, following that necessary but unlikely transformation, neither would be necessary to keep the peace because national leaders would have become trusting, cooperative, and trustworthy.

These Christian nuclear pacifists simply have transferred the hard question, "How can we solve the problem of nuclear weapons?" to the equally if not more difficult question, "How can we achieve nuclear disarmament or the creation of a just and effective international authority?" Unfortunately, they provide no answers. Nuclear pacifists seem not to recognize that their suggested alternatives to deterrence are neither new nor feasible and that merely pointing to infeasible alternatives is not very helpful.

What would be helpful would be some useful advice on how we can move from where we are now to either vision of international authority or nuclear disarmament—and this Christian nuclear pacifists do not provide. This is not to single out Christian nuclear pacifists for criticism; no one else has been able to provide a roadmap from here to there either. Serious efforts to examine these alternatives show that we cannot get there from here.

There is no pleasure to be found in concluding that the two alternatives suggested by nuclear pacifists are not at all realistic. As was noted in the previous chapter, deterrence is far from an ideal mechanism for avoiding nuclear war. Yet until a realistic alternative is presented, crusades against deterrence and the means for maintaining deterrence ought to be seen for what they are—actions that potentially do more to increase the risk of war than lessen it.

If complete nuclear disarmament is not feasible, what about the notion of moving piecemeal toward nuclear disarmament? Perhaps the United States and the Soviet Union could agree to cut their forces gradually without incurring the unacceptable risks that abrupt nuclear disarmament would entail. This notion, of course, reflects the hope of arms control—a gradual and agreed reduction in the number of nuclear forces. We know arms control is possible because agreements have been signed by the United States and the Soviet Union. Is it possible that here is a realistic solution to the problem of nuclear weapons? The next chapter will examine arms control as an alternative to deterrence.

Chapter 7, Notes

1. Lewis Thomas, "TTAPS for the Earth," *Discover*, February 1984, 34.

2. The United Methodist Church, Council of Bishops, *In Defense of Creation: The Nuclear Crisis and a Just Peace* (Pre-publication print, 1986), 10.

3. Ibid., 42.

4. Ronald J. Sider and Richard K. Taylor, *Nuclear Holocaust and Christian Hope* (Downers Grove, Ill.: InterVarsity Press, 1982), 214.

5. "International Aggression and Nonmilitary Defense," *The Christian Century*, 6-13 July 1983, 644.

6. For the classic discussion see, Kenneth N. Waltz, *Man, the State, and War* (New York: Columbia University Press, 1959).

7. Quoted in George Spieker, Deutsche-Presse Agenture, "Einigkeit in der UNO erst bei einer Invasion vom Mars," *Washington Journal*, 15 July 1985, 1.

8. Quoted in the testimony of Dr. James Wade, House of Representatives, Subcommittee of the Committee on Appropriations, *Department of Defense Appropriation for 1983, Hearings*, 97th Cong., 2nd sess., part 4, 1982, 545.

9. Quoted from the written testimony of Dr. Richard Wagner, United States Senate, Subcommittee on Strategic and Theater Nuclear Forces of the Committee On Armed Services, *Department of Energy Fiscal Year 1986 Authorization for Defense Programs, Hearings*, 99th Cong., lst sess., 1986, 151.

10. See for example Sider and Taylor, 273-92.

11. See the U. S. Catholic Bishop's Pastoral Letter in "The Challenge of Peace: God's Promise and Our Response," *Origins* 13 (19 May 1983):30.

12. *In Defense of Creation*, 71.

13. See for example Jonathan Schell, *The Fate of the Earth* (New York: Alfred Knopf, 1982).

14. Saul Mendlovitz, "Is There a Way Out?" *Harper's*, June 1985, 44.

15. Sider and Taylor, 228.

16. See, for example, "The Challenge of Peace," 30.

17. Joseph Fahey, "Pax Christi," in *War or Peace? The Search for New Answers*, ed. Thomas Shannon (Maryknoll, N. Y.: Orbis Books, 1982), 68.

18. Hans J. Morgenthau, *Politics Among Nations* (New York: Alfred Knopf, 1960), 261-69, 271.

19. Quoted in Clark M. Eichelberger, *Organizing for Peace* (New York: Harper and Row, 1977), 196.

20. W. Averell Harriman, *America and Russia in a Changing World* (New York: Doubleday, 1971), 33.

21. Harriman, 42; and Eichelberger, 266.

22. Eichelberger, 266.

23. Quoted in Thomas M. Franch, *Nation Against Nation* (New York: Alfred Knopf, 1985), 22.

24. Ibid., 22-23.

25. John Foster Dulles, "The General Assembly," *Foreign Affairs* (October 1945):1.

26. An American assessment of the U.N. published by the World Peace Foundation in 1946 reflects this optimism. It expressed the widely shared view that a decision by the Security Council to use armed forces to remedy a situation would create, "obligations for members of the Organization which they must faithfully carry out according to Article 25." (Leland Goodrich and Edward Hambro, *Charter of the United Nations: Commentary and Documents* [Boston: World Peace Foundation, 1946], 163.) Article 25 states: "The Members of the United Nations agree to accept and carry out the decisions of the Security Council in accordance with the present Charter." A prominent American analysis of the U.N. published in October 1945 reflected the view that the only limits on the Security Council's effectiveness as a peacekeeper would be irreconcilable disagreements among the great powers or a lack of sincerity in how they used the Security Council. This view was proven correct, of course, but what is of interest is that neither of these problems was considered likely to occur. (See R. Keith Kane, "The Security Council," *Foreign Affairs* (October 1945):12-25.)

27. See respectively, 23 July 1945, *Congressional Record* (Senate) No. 91, 7953; 6 July 1945, *Congressional Record* (House) No. 91, 7299; and 6 July 1945, *Congressional Record* (House) No. 91, 7299-7300.

28. See the discussion in Dr. Patrick J. Garrity, "United Nations and Peacekeeping," in *A World Without a U.N.*, ed. Burton Yale Pines (Washington, D.C.: The Heritage Foundation, 1984), 140.

29. Quoted in Garrity, 151.

Chapter 8

Arms Control as an Alternative to Deterrence

*M*any Christian discussions of nuclear issues endorse arms control as a critically important part of the solution to the nuclear problem. Many Christian commentators, particularly those from the nuclear pacifist camp, decry the lack of progress in arms control and quickly point to the U.S. government as the stumbling block. As the Episcopal report admonishes, "Until the American people consistently demand success in arms control from our elected officials, success will elude us. . . . the principal difficulty lies not in negotiating agreements, but in getting them ratified by the U.S. Senate."[1]

It would be easy for virtually any U.S. administration, whether Democrat or Republican, to get an agreement. All that need be done is to agree to Soviet terms, and a treaty would be available on short order. The great difficulty in arms control is not in getting an agreement, but in achieving a treaty that is equitable and supports the goals of arms control. It is often forgotten that arms control does not exist as a goal unto itself; it is supposed to accomplish something. The three classical goals of arms control are:

1. Reduce the probability of war;
2. Reduce the destruction of war;

3. Minimize the cost of maintaining an adequate military establishment.

The U.S. government is flooded with clever suggestions for controlling arms. Some suggest starting with 10 or 50 percent reductions; other proposals boast scholarly titles such as the United Methodist bishops' "Ethic of Reciprocity." But in many suggestions the objective seems to be to "get an agreement," rather than to examine carefully what type of agreement will be both helpful and possible in negotiations with the Soviet Union. It is true that any agreement could, in principle, help to further arms control goals and alleviate the threat posed by nuclear weapons. However, it is not true that every proposal that goes by the name of "arms control" would be helpful. Many could actually reduce the prospects for peace.

Arms Control: Will Getting Any Agreement Do?

Christian nuclear pacifists who admonish the U.S. government for the lack of arms control progress seem to have forgotten that arms control negotiations are just that—negotiations. And negotiations with the Soviet Union tend to be long and difficult. Yet at least one group of Christians has actually demanded a "system of public accountability that demands elected officials to produce arms control agreements every two years. . . ."[2] It is difficult to imagine how U.S. elected officials could be put in a worse negotiating position. Soviet negotiators would be aware that they need only remain inflexible as U.S. negotiators would have to give in to the Soviet position before the allotted two years were up. The negotiations would become a farce.

Imagine labor-management negotiations wherein one side must have an agreement within a known and set time period. If the union representatives were required to negotiate a new contract within some set number of days, and management was under no such constraint, management could simply wait out the union and get the terms it demanded. Similarly, if the U.S. was unilaterally under a near-term time constraint in arms control negotiations, it takes little imagination to realize the type of unequal agreement that would result.

Of course, if arms control negotiations are simply about getting an agreement, then it does not really matter much what the terms of the agreement are. So why not require one every two years? However, that type of thinking is likely to produce highly one-sided and even dangerous agreements. Negotiations about nuclear weapons are too important to allow concepts of just getting an agreement to dominate our thinking.

Much of the lobbying for arms control by Christian groups, despite their sincerity, is likely to be counterproductive. Only one side of the negotiating table feels the effects of those lobbying efforts—U.S. government officials. The Soviet government is not subject to pressure from Americans, and there is no similar unofficial arms control lobby operating within the Soviet Union to put similar pressure on the Soviet government. The small number of unofficial peace proponents within the Soviet Union have been systematically harassed, arrested, sent to psychiatric camps, or deported.[3] Consequently, the pressure exerted on U.S. officials by Christian arms control activists is not balanced by similar pressure on the Soviet government. While nuclear pacifists claim, and undoubtedly believe, that they are furthering the cause of peace by their arms control lobbying efforts, they are in fact undermining the prospects for equitable and successful arms control negotiations.

Neither Christian nor secular arms control and antinuclear activists appear to recognize this problem. All too often they reflect a chilling naivete. On at least one occasion the leader of Physicians for Social Responsibility, an influential secular organization, suggested that activists in the West could indeed affect both the U.S. and the Soviet governments—the U.S. directly and the Soviet Union indirectly through world public opinion.[4] That response can hardly be considered reasonable: Such activists spend most of their energies criticizing U.S. policies and programs while rarely mentioning Soviet policies and programs; secondly, as discussed in the previous chapter, the Soviet government is relatively impervious to world public opinion on such issues.

Perhaps the most recent example of the cynical Soviet attitude toward world public opinion involves their use of "butterfly bombs" against civilians in Afghanistan.[5] These bombs are small explosives intended primarily to maim. As used by Soviet forces they are made to appear as pens or small toy trucks, birds, or airplanes, and as such are particularly attractive to children. For years the Soviets simply denied the existence of such devices. However, after years of accumulated evidence of their use by Soviet forces, the Soviets could no longer deny that such butterfly bombs are being used. Rather than denying their existence, the Soviets have most recently simply blamed the use of such weapons on the Mujahadin resistance fighters. However, in making such a preposterous charge and continuing the use of these anti-personnel mines against civilians, the Soviet government has once again demonstrated its lack of interest in world public opinion. Is this the type of government that can be persuaded by American activists? It hardly appears likely.

According to those who have actually worked within the official Soviet arms control establishment, virtually the only arms control concepts seriously considered by the governing Politburo are those developed by, or in accordance with, the Soviet military. As Igor Glagolev, current U.S. resident and former chief of the disarmament section of the Soviet Academy of Sciences, observes of the Soviet system, "Scholars who desire to limit or reduce the armaments of the U.S.S.R. are not represented in the Politburo and do not participate in decision-making within this main organ. Nor do they have direct access to the Defense Council."[6] As such, the Soviet system is hardly one wherein the protests of American citizens will have a moderating impact. Rather, those protests demonstrate to Soviet leaders that U.S. weapons programs are likely to face political problems at home whether or not the Soviet Union agrees to arms control.

The Strategic Arms Limitations Talks (SALT)

The question remains whether arms control is a reasonable alternative to deterrence—an ultimate solution to the nuclear problem. Is it not possible that by reducing existing nuclear arsenals—say, by 10 percent per year—the problem would be solved in a decade? There is, of course, nothing wrong with the arithmetic involved in this question, which is why such proposals are always so popular. And if the solution to the nuclear problem is so simple, why not just agree with the Soviet Union to start reducing the weapons?

In any examination of arms control as a solution to the nuclear problem, however, it is important to note the almost two decades of negotiations that have taken place. The history of SALT provides valuable lessons concerning what is and is not feasible in the world of arms control. It may also provide some insight as to how real arms control progress may be facilitated in the future.

Unfortunately, the record of the Strategic Arms Limitation Talks (SALT) provides virtually no hope that a deep arms reduction agreement can be negotiated. Following almost twenty years of negotiations, strategic arms control has, thus far, coincided with a tremendous increase in the number of U.S. and Soviet nuclear weapons. For example, the number of strategic ballistic missile warheads deployed by the U.S. and the Soviet Union at the end of the first year of SALT negotiations was 1,874 for the U.S. and 1,716 for the Soviet Union. By the time the Soviet Union walked out of negotiations in November 1983, the Soviet number had grown to 8,377, while the U.S. figure reached 7,292.[7]

Of course, the history of arms control need not be judged solely by the growth in the number of strategic nuclear weapons; its impact on specific, so-called "destabilizing" counterforce weapons ought also to be considered. The results here, however, have been equally distressing. The number of Soviet counterforce ICBM warheads grew from approximately 228 in 1970 to well over 5,000 in 1986.[8] The U.S. increase in the same category was from approximately 54 in 1970 to about 900 in 1986.[9]

Given such results, to say that strategic arms control has been unsuccessful in stopping the arms race is an understatement. As Leslie Gelb, one of President Carter's chief architects of the SALT II agreement, has noted, "Arms Control has essentially failed. Three decades of U.S.-Soviet negotiations to limit arms competition have done little more than to codify the arms race."[10] Or, as a recent study for the Arms Control and Disarmament Agency by Harvard University's John F. Kennedy School of Government reportedly concludes, arms control has had virtually no success in controlling nuclear arsenals despite the lavish attention given it for more than two decades.[11]

Given the conflicting objectives of the U.S. and the Soviet Union with regard to arms control, however, this type of failure is almost assured.[12] The U.S. and the Soviet Union have worked at cross-purposes in arms control negotiations, and these cross-purposes have virtually guaranteed a continuation of the arms competition. Unless there is a significant change in U.S. and Soviet objectives, there is virtually no prospect for arms control to reduce the number of nuclear weapons to such low levels that civilian populations are truly safe from nuclear attack. (And, of course, it must always be borne in mind that even were both sides to agree to deep reductions, unless a powerful world authority existed to guarantee compliance, a small and unverifiable amount of cheating could render such an agreement worthless for actually removing the nuclear threat.)

U.S. SALT Objectives: "To Dream the Impossible Dream"

As discussed briefly in the previous chapter, the MAD approach to deterrence and stability has driven U.S. arms control objectives in SALT. The dominant concept of "stability" in the U.S. has been based on the notion that if the U.S. and Soviet Union are mutually vulnerable to devastating nuclear retaliation, then neither side will be willing to strike first for fear of that retaliation. Ironically, mutual vulnerability to nuclear destruction came to be seen in the U.S. as beneficial because it was believed to virtually guarantee stability. The U.S. sought to use strategic arms control to help ensure the continuity of stability based on mutual vulnerability. There are two relatively simple requirements to maintain such a deterrent. First, neither side ought to be capable of using offensive forces to strike first and destroy the other side's retaliatory potential (a so-called first-strike capability). If one side were to develop such an offensive capability, it would deny the other its retaliatory deterrent, and the balance would be destabilized. Second, neither side ought to be capable of defending itself against a nuclear attack since this would also deny the other its retaliatory deterrent and destabilize the balance. To sustain a MAD strategic relationship both sides must have nuclear forces that could survive a first strike and retaliate effectively against the opponent. In short, weapons should be survivable but society should not be secure.

The U.S. attempted to use SALT to ensure that these MAD conditions were sustained with the minimum number of nuclear weapons necessary to threaten catastrophic retaliation. It undoubtedly is not well appreciated by Christian arms control activists that strategic arms control has largely been structured so as to perpetuate a condition of mutual vulnerability to nuclear holocaust. Why did this goal come to dominate U.S. arms control policy? Probably because the difficulty of negotiating deep offensive reductions with the Soviet Union was clear to those Republican and Democratic administrations negotiating SALT, and because MAD stability seemed to be beneficial and might be facilitated by arms control. Thus, rather than attempting to reduce drastically the number of nuclear weapons so that they no longer posed a threat, arms control was intended to support the MAD approach to stability.

This particular (and some might add peculiar) American approach to SALT explains why a dean of American arms control such as Dr. Herbert Scoville would state (as discussed in chapter 6) that the best fruit of SALT had been to ensure that a retaliatory strike could always get through. This sentiment has been echoed by other American arms control notables. Professor Thomas Schelling, a founding father of U.S. arms control theory, praises the 1972 SALT I agreement specifically because it helped to ensure that "human and economic resources were to be hostages left unprotected." Schelling considers this achievement the "high point" of arms control.[13] Indeed, he goes one step further and questions the value of arms control if MAD can be sustained without it:

> But who needs arms control if economic and reliable retaliatory weapons are available that are neither susceptible to preemption [i.e., a first strike] nor capable of preemption? There may be an answer to this question, but it has not been given.[14]

This notion that MAD is the goal has become part of the popular wisdom in the United States. It has been translated from the idea that arms control can help facilitate MAD stability to the view that success in arms control requires that the U.S. endorse a continuation of U.S. and Soviet capabilities to inflict a holocaust. Indeed, some of the arms control proposals coming from Christian churches are based on an explicit acceptance of MAD. The United Methodist bishops actually endorse a condition of "mutual vulnerability" as the basis for arms control.[15] In so doing, they endorse what had, by 1972, already come to be the officially accepted approach to arms control.

In short, arms control in the U.S. came to be seen officially as a tool for sustaining a pristine condition of mutual assured destruction. This was rationalized by the assumption that such a condition was stabilizing and would minimize the probability of nuclear war. In effect, the arms control goal of reducing the destructiveness of war was rejected because this very destructiveness was the key ingredient for MAD stability. As a result, the U.S. sought to structure an agreement that would ensure that the strategic balance continued to meet the two MAD conditions outlined above—the denial to either side of a first-strike offensive capability or an effective defensive capability against nuclear weapons.

SALT was intended, by the U.S., to support this goal in two ways—by an agreement limiting offensive forces and an agreement limiting defensive forces. SALT I set ceilings on launchers for intercontinental ballistic missiles (ICBMs) and submarine-launched ballistic missiles (SLBMs). It did not actually limit the missiles themselves, only the missile launchers. The key U.S. goal regarding offensive forces—consistent with the MAD theory driving it—was to limit "destabilizing" counterforce capabilities. Limiting such systems that might threaten to destroy retaliatory forces (through a combination of sheer blasting power and accuracy) would help to ensure that the stability of mutual vulnerability would not be undermined by "first-strike" threats. And, again consistent with the MAD requirements for mutual vulnerability, the U.S. sought to ensure that nationwide ballistic missile defense (BMD) systems would not be deployed and thereby undermine mutual vulnerability.

Two separate parts of the SALT I package were intended to achieve these goals: the Anti-ballistic Missile (ABM) Treaty to limit ballistic missile defense; and the Interim Offensive Agreement to limit offensive forces (and particularly counterforce capabilities). These separate parts were presented as an integrated arms control package that would help ensure stability by limiting any potential offensive or defensive threat to the condition of mutual vulnerability.

The ABM Treaty (as amended in 1974) effectively prohibits any useful deployment of ballistic missile defense. This was intended to help preserve the stabilizing condition of mutual vulnerability. It was also thought at the time that limiting defense would set the stage for offensive limitations. If both sides were sure to be defenseless, a relatively small number of offensive nuclear weapons could ensure the vulnerability of both to catastrophic retaliation, and neither would need additional offensive forces, or even as many forces as had already been accumulated. As one of the participants in SALT observed, those "negotiations were premised on the assumption that limitations on strategic offensive forces would not be possible without extensive constraints on strategic defenses."[16]

Thus, limitations on defenses against ballistic missiles were thought to serve two useful roles: (1) to help ensure the continuity of the MAD condition; and (2) to provide the basis for offensive force limitations. A key participant in SALT, Ambassador Paul Nitze, observed that the U.S. position was based on the belief that, "with defensive systems severely limited, it would be possible in the following few years to negotiate comprehensive limits on strategic offensive forces, and to establish a reliable deterrent balance [i.e., mutual vulnerability] at reduced levels."[17]

Many people are surprised the U.S. agreed in SALT I to leave itself defenseless to nuclear ballistic missile attack. Yet as Article I of the ABM Treaty states:

> Each party undertakes not to deploy ABM systems for a defense of the territory of its country and not to provide a base for such a defense, and not to deploy ABM systems for defense of an individual region. . . .

The ABM Treaty was, therefore, intended to facilitate the mutuality of vulnerability.

The offensive force limitations of SALT, and particularly the SALT II negotiations following 1972, were specifically intended to limit counterforce ICBM systems that might pose a threat to retaliatory forces. The reason for this goal was clear. It was feared that Soviet heavy ICBMs would pose a preemptive first-strike threat to U.S. forces and that such offensive capabilities might thereby undermine the mutuality of vulnerability. Consequently, the U.S. sought to limit and control the offensive first-strike capabilities of ballistic missiles through SALT. Indeed, U.S. Unilateral Statement "A" attached to the ABM Treaty stressed the need for limitations on offensive forces, and emphasized that the goal of those limitations was "to constrain and reduce on a long-term basis threats to the survivability of our respective strategic retaliatory forces."

The goal of protecting retaliatory forces by limiting the offensive threat to them was to help preserve the mutual threats of retaliation. The point of this MAD-driven approach to arms control was clear: Neither side was to have defensive capabilities that might upset mutual vulnerability, and neither was to have offensive first-strike capabilities that might threaten the other's forces. In this way the condition of mutual vulnerability could not be threatened by defensive or offensive first-strike capabilities. SALT offensive and defensive limitations, in the form of the Interim Offensive Agreement and the ABM Treaty, were to help ensure this condition of mutual vulnerability. U.S. goals in SALT did not seek to end vulnerability to nuclear attack—indeed the very intention was to perpetuate MAD. The U.S. sought to support the stability that was thought to reside in a condition of mutual vulnerability to retaliatory nuclear attack.

Through the SALT process the U.S. pursued one goal of arms control—reducing the probability of war—at the expense of another goal—reducing the destructiveness of war. Although it may seem bizarre that American officials would, in effect, purposely use arms control to help perpetuate the vulnerability of the American (and Soviet) peoples to nuclear attack, it should not be considered foolish. American officials simply were following the then-current accepted wisdom as how best to stabilize deterrence. The MAD notion of deterrence, by linking stability directly to a condition of mutual vulnerability, led American policy-makers to believe that reducing the probability of war and reducing its destructiveness significantly could not be pursued simultaneously. The reigning wisdom in the U.S. at the time was that when both sides accepted their mutual vulnerability, and neither took steps to jeopardize the opponent's threat (i.e., attempted to reduce their own vulnerability), then stability could be preserved. The U.S. sought to provide for such a "stable" situation with the help of arms control, and as a result, U.S. SALT goals were driven by the MAD approach to deterrence.

The Soviet Approach to Strategic Forces and Arms Control

As the quote by Leslie Gelb cited above suggests, even those identified as liberals acknowledge that U.S. arms control goals have not been met, and from the U.S. perspective, arms control has largely been a failure. Ambassador Paul Nitze recently remarked:

> The 1972 SALT Interim Agreement purported to freeze the offensive balance at the then-existing level. In fact, it did no such thing. . . . It is hard to make a case that the Interim Agreement of SALT II met any of the principal objectives for arms control; one would truly be hard-pressed to demonstrate how they embodied rough equivalence, lowered armaments, enhanced crisis stability, or reduced the risk of war.[18]

A principal reason for this arms control failure from the U.S. perspective is that the Soviet Union has not shared the U.S. approach to the strategic relationship. Soviet arms control objectives have not been driven by the notion that mutual vulnerability is a condition that ought to be accepted and perpetuated as the basis of stability. Because the Soviet Union has never endorsed the MAD notion of deterrence, U.S. arms control objectives were bound to go unfulfilled.

Some in the U.S. recognized that the Soviet Union did not share the American endorsement of deterrence based on mutual vulnerability. Consequently, it was hoped that the U.S. could use SALT as an opportunity to persuade the Soviet Union to accept American views about nuclear weapons and stability, making the U.S. approach to arms control more likely to bear fruit.[19]

However, just as the U.S. saw arms control as a means of supporting the U.S. notion of deterrence, the Soviet Union has pursued arms control as a means of supporting its particular approach to strategic forces. That approach could best be characterized as one emphasizing the limitation of damage to the Soviet Union in the event of war. MIT professor Stephen Meyer, an expert on Soviet strategic thought, observes:

> First and foremost, Soviet military doctrine holds that the primary mission of the Soviet armed forces is to prevent the nuclear devastation of the Soviet homeland—i.e., the armed forces must deter strategic nuclear war, and yet be able to limit damage should deterrence fail.[20]

The Soviet Union does indeed appear to deploy strategic forces largely to contribute to its damage-limitation potential; and a capability for deterrence is thought to inhere in such a strategy.[21] This, of course, is very different from U.S. notions of mutual vulnerability.

Although this Soviet view concerning offensive and defensive preparations for surviving nuclear war comes as quite a surprise to many Americans, official Soviet spokesmen have not been entirely shy in discussing it. A member of the high-level Soviet Central Committee and general of the army observed that "under present conditions . . . the preparation of the country's rear for defense against means of mass destruction [i.e., nuclear weapons] has become, without a doubt, one of the decisive strategic factors ensuring the ability of the state to function in wartime, and in the final analysis, the attainment of victory."[22] Similarly, in his book *Razvitie Protivovozdushnoi Ovorony,* Soviet Marshal G. V. Zimin, chief of the Military Command Academy, has emphasized the importance of damage-limitation in Soviet strategic thought:

> When nuclear missiles are utilized, the focal point of the conflict can spread to the very depths of the country, leading to the destruction of the material means of the state. . . .

All of these conditions pose complicated problems
for air defense, the solution of which is determined
by weapons but also from ballistic weapons. . . .

These conditions also make it necessary to further
perfect civil defenses, the primary purpose of which
is to prepare the population for defense against a
massive attack from modern weapons and to guarantee a working stability for all branches of the
economy in wartime. . . .[23]

Another Soviet commentator has stated the matter simply:
"To save just one percent of the Soviet population would mean
to save three million people. No one in this country would
understand the government if it failed to strive for this."[24]

This Soviet view is extremely important for understanding
why U.S.-Soviet arms control efforts are of such disappointment. Rather than reducing the destructiveness of nuclear war,
the U.S. has pursued arms control as a means of perpetuating
mutual vulnerability. In contrast, the Soviet Union has never
seen deterrence stability and the pursuit of a capability to limit
damage to itself as incompatible. Indeed, the Soviet Union
pursues a strategic capability for damage-limitation and deterrence simultaneously. Consequently, U.S. efforts to "educate"
the Soviet Union to the notions of MAD and arms control
based on MAD were met with hostility. As Igor Glagolev notes,
"The scale of strategic (and conventional) armaments in the
U.S.S.R. is limited by the capacity of the Soviet economy, not
by the exhortations of foreign diplomats."[25]

The two sides have been working at cross-purposes in
arms control—the U.S. seeking to ensure that vulnerability is
mutual, and the Soviet Union seeking to limit the U.S. threat
by achieving a capability to limit damage to itself. Consequently, the structure of the U.S.-Soviet strategic relationship
has not allowed for effective limitation, much less force reductions. The Soviet Union followed its doctrinal requirement to
build forces capable of limiting damage to the Soviet Union,
and the U.S. followed its doctrinal requirement of ensuring

that it had enough capability to threaten the Soviet Union with catastrophic retaliation. The objective of each side has been to deny the other side its goal.

The Soviet Union has sought to deploy strategic offensive weapons capable of destroying U.S. nuclear forces in a first strike. This task would be the responsibility of the Strategic Rocket Forces, particularly the Soviet ICBM force. As Professor Meyer has observed of this "defensive" role for Soviet strategic offensive forces, "This emphasis on destroying the enemy's [i.e., American] military forces before they can reach Soviet territory and carrying the attack to the enemy's homeland is . . . a strategic goal shared equally by the political and military leaders."[26]

The Soviet Union has also attempted to provide for defensive capabilities intended to reduce the damage that might be inflicted by those U.S. forces surviving a first strike. This would be the responsibility of the Air Defense Forces, including ballistic missile defenses, fighter interceptors, and surface-to-air missiles, in addition to the large-scale Soviet civil defense program.

Consequently, the Soviet Union has followed an offensive/defensive "combined arms" approach to damage limitation. This approach attempts to use strategic offensive forces to destroy U.S. nuclear weapons before they could be launched and to use defensive forces to reduce the damage resulting from those U.S. forces that escape attack.

Because the Soviet approach to deterrence and arms control stresses the importance of damage limitation in the event of war, there was almost no likelihood they would sign on for the U.S. notion of arms control based upon mutual vulnerability. Indeed, the Soviet force requirements worked in precisely the opposite direction. This is not to condemn Soviet views of deterrence and arms control. They simply are very different from the U.S. perspective, and this difference has served to undermine U.S. arms control objectives, including U.S. expectations for SALT.

U.S. officials anticipated that the signing of SALT I in

1972 would be followed by reductions in counterforce offensive forces. Yet the Soviet Union pursued an extensive buildup of ICBMs with counterforce capabilities during the seventies. Similarly, with the exception of ballistic missile defense (BMD), the Soviet Union increased its defensive programs following SALT and increased research and development devoted to BMD. The U.S., consistent with the mutual vulnerability concept of deterrence, did not build up its offensive counterforce capabilities and abandoned much of its defensive capabilities.

Had the Soviet Union accepted U.S. "education" regarding stability and arms control, then SALT could have been a success. Both sides could have settled into a "stable" relationship of mutual vulnerability based on the limited number of nuclear weapons necessary for threatening terrible retaliation. While this approach to deterrence and arms control is endorsed by some Christians, particularly nuclear pacifists, it was never adopted by the Soviet Union. Secretary of Defense Caspar Weinberger has summarized the problem:

> The primary U.S. goal in [SALT] negotiations was to enshrine forever the strategic doctrine of mutual vulnerability. By putting caps on each side's strategic nuclear arsenals and foregoing the deployment of all but the most limited anti-ballistic missile systems, strategic stability was to be enhanced. . . . This view, of course, held that the United States and Soviet Union could remain perfectly safe so long as both populations remained perfectly vulnerable. And it is obvious that in order for this doctrine to create stability, each side would have to subscribe to it. . . . Needless to say, things did not work out as planned. For not only did the Soviets refuse to buy into our concept of stable deterrence through mutual vulnerability, they also engaged in one of the most dramatic arms buildups in history.[27]

Arms Control: The Expectation versus the Reality

Had U.S. government officials understood that damage limitation is a fundamental goal of Soviet strategic force programs, what has happened might have been expected to happen. The Soviet Union has continued to improve its civil and air defenses unconstrained by treaty and has pursued a vigorous research and development program for BMD. It also has engaged in a major buildup of offensive counterforce capabilities. Each of these activities is, of course, in contrast to what one would expect if the Soviet Union followed a mutual vulnerability approach to arms control and strategic doctrine.

These developments were predicted by some SALT I participants and commentators who were not persuaded that the Soviet Union adhered to mutual vulnerability notions even in general terms.[28] The Soviet damage limitation objective precluded any possible arms control success. And indeed, it has been this driving objective behind Soviet behavior that has made a mockery of U.S. arms control objectives.

Below is a summary of how U.S. participants in SALT interpreted, according to the mutual vulnerability approach to arms control, what SALT I was all about, and what was to be expected in SALT II. Note that the expectations of U.S. officials were tied to an implicit belief in mutual vulnerability as the guide to arms control.

Claim. "The [ABM] Treaty, by permitting only a small deployment of ABMs, tends to break the offense-defense action-and-reaction spiral in strategic arms competition. . . . In view of the low ABM levels agreed on, it should be possible in the future to agree on mutual reductions in offensive weapons without impairing strategic stability. . . ."[29]

Reality. In the context of strict BMD limitations, Soviet ICBM warheads increased from 1,547 in 1972 to 6,420 in 1985; Soviet SLBM warheads increased from 497 in 1972 to 2,122 in 1985. Figure 1 shows this steady increase in Soviet offensive warheads following the 1972 ABM Treaty.

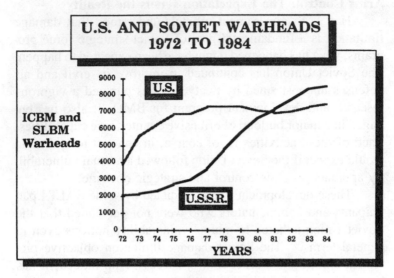

Figure 1

Claim. The ABM Treaty reflected Soviet endorsement of the U.S. concept of deterrence through mutual vulnerability: "This [ABM Treaty] is a general undertaking of utmost significance. Without a nationwide ABM defense, there can be no shield against retaliation. Both nuclear powers have recognized—and, in effect, agreed to maintain—nuclear deterrence [i.e., mutual vulnerability]."[30]

Reality. There is a tremendous amount of evidence that the Soviet Union has never given up its pursuit of a damage limitation capability nor accepted the U.S. concept of mutual deterrence. Figure 2 demonstrates that following SALT I, U.S. strategic defense procurement, as is consistent with mutual vulnerability, fell off dramatically; in contrast, Soviet strategic defense procurement stayed at very high levels, as is consistent with an objective of damage limitation.

COMPARISON OF U.S. STRATEGIC PROCUREMENT EXPENDITURES WITH THE ESTIMATED DOLLAR COST OF SOVIET STRATEGIC DEFENSE

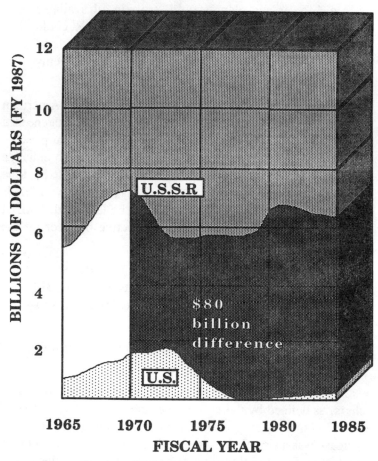

Source: Secretary of Defense Casper W. Weinberger, Annual Report to the Congress, Fiscal Year 1987, p. 59.

Figure 2

As much as Americans do not understand or want to believe it, achieving a capability to reduce damage and survive a nuclear war is a priority Soviet objective. As Fritz W. Ermarth, a foremost expert on Soviet strategic thinking has observed,

> Soviet strategic doctrine stipulates that Soviet strategic forces and plans should strive in all available ways to enhance the prospect that the U.S.S.R. could survive as a nation and, in some politically and militarily meaningful way, defeat the main enemy [i.e., the U.S.] should deterrence fail. . . .[31]

Consequently, the inability of arms control to realize American objectives and stop the dramatic buildup in Soviet capabilities needed to destroy U.S. retaliatory forces ought to come as no surprise.

Claim. A key American goal of SALT I was to enhance the survivability of U.S. retaliatory forces. This was to be done by limiting the increasing Soviet capability to use heavy ICBMs to destroy U.S. forces before they could be launched. SALT I was thought to have achieved that objective by freezing the number of Soviet heavy ICBMs:

> Within the overall limitation [SALT I], the Soviet Union has accepted a freeze of its heavy ICBM launchers, the weapons most threatening to our strategic forces.
>
> There is also a prohibition on conversion of light ICBMs into heavy missiles. . . .[32]

Reality. The number of Soviet heavy ICBMs and launchers, as defined by the U.S. at the time of SALT I, increased from 308 in 1972 to over 660 in 1985. The direct result of this increase was a significant increase in the threat to U.S. retaliatory forces. Figure 3 illustrates this growth of Soviet "destabilizing" heavy ICBMs; in contrast, as is consistent with the notion of mutual vulnerability, the number of U.S. heavy ICBMs has been low (approximately 50 Titan IIs) and those are being deactivated. Even the new large U.S. ICBM, the MX, is to be deployed in comparably low numbers (i.e., 50).

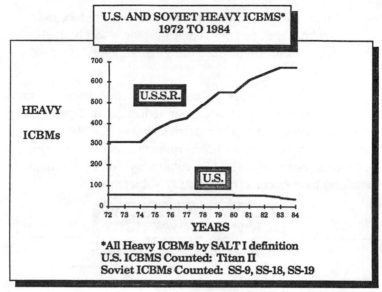

Figure 3

Claim. Within two to five years following SALT I, further negotiations would lead to definitive and specific restrictions on offensive forces that would provide "long-term" survivability for retaliatory forces. That was said to be the primary objective of further negotiations. This objective would be realized, it was suggested, by reductions in the number of missiles, especially those with high throwweight (heavy ICBMs):

> What we are trying to do is to set up a useful device that will hold the situation while we negotiate, hopefully, a matching treaty; that is to match the treaty in the ABM defense field. I think that the measures that we have succeeded in spelling out in this interim agreement with the Russians will do just that. There will be a commitment on their part not to build any more of these ICBMs that have concerned us over the years. That commitment will extend to not building such things as SS-9 [the Soviet heavy ICBM].
>
> I think [the Soviets] are interested in getting a more definitive missile limitation than at present. . . . I

have reason—I have hope that they will reduce the numbers and, perhaps, enter into some sort of qualitative limitations affecting size, yes, throwweight.[33]

Reality. The years of negotiations that have followed SALT I did not lead to a cap or reduction in Soviet heavy ICBMs. Indeed, the number of Soviet heavy ICBMs, according to the U.S. SALT definition, has more than doubled (see Figure 4). As a direct result, U.S. retaliatory forces (particularly ICBMs) have become increasingly vulnerable.

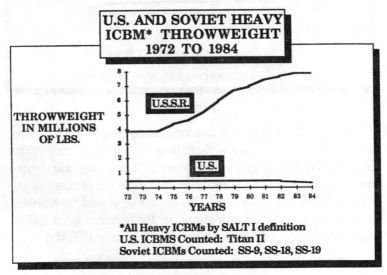

U.S. AND SOVIET HEAVY ICBM* THROWWEIGHT 1972 TO 1984

THROWWEIGHT IN MILLIONS OF LBS.

U.S.S.R.

U.S.

YEARS

*All Heavy ICBMs by SALT I definition
U.S. ICBMS Counted: Titan II
Soviet ICBMs Counted: SS-9, SS-18, SS-19

Figure 4

Each of these claims by U.S. officials about SALT was a logical expectation from the mutual vulnerability approach to arms control. The U.S. expected arms control to ensure mutual deterrence through mutual vulnerability and to control the Soviet offensive threat to U.S. retaliatory forces. It was assumed that the Soviet Union would have an interest in accepting such offensive restraints and reductions as long as BMD could, in effect, be banned.

Yet the Soviet Union perceived its self-interest differently and proved unwilling, even in the absence of BMD, to accept the type of restraint on its counterforce offensive capabilities that would have validated the U.S. mutual vulnerability approach to arms control. A misunderstanding of Soviet interests and strategic objectives ensured that U.S. arms control objectives would not be realized.

Many Christians, commenting on the prospects for arms control, seem to ignore two decades of arms control history. They talk as if the Soviet Union follows a mutual vulnerability approach to arms control and that arms control agreements can be built on that basis. The Episcopal Diocese in Washington, D.C., is critical of the U.S. government for a lack of arms control progress, and proposes that arms control can and ought to be built on the concept of mutual vulnerability: "We should subscribe publicly to the principle of the interdependence of United States and Soviet security, the permanence of the nuclear stalemate, [and] the mutual suicide of weapons use. . . ."[34]

Those in the Christian community making such comments appear genuinely to believe Soviet public pronouncements about arms control, and ignore the history of real negotiations. This contrasts sharply with the views of those who have actually worked within the Soviet Union on arms control issues. Dr. Glagolev discusses the Soviet approach to arms control when he was chief of the disarmament section of Soviet Academy of Sciences:

> During that period, the government of the U.S.S.R. proposed the liquidation of all nuclear delivery vehicles as part of the first phase of a general and complete disarmament. This unrealistic proposal was made entirely for propaganda purposes and was never discussed seriously in the Soviet Union. Actually, the opposite policy was followed to increase the number of intercontinental missiles as rapidly as possible.[35]

Another former high-ranking Soviet official, Arkady Shevchenko, confirms that the Soviet military High Command domi-
nates the Soviet approach to arms control, and that this fact
has important implications:

> Sophisticated [Soviet] military officers approached
> SALT as a means to achieve by negotiation what
> the Soviets feared they could not attain through com-
> petition: a restraint on America's ability to translate
> its economic and technological strength into military
> advantage. . . .[36]

It is clear, after so many years of negotiations, that the
Soviet Union does not accept the mutual vulnerability notion
of arms control. And, of course, because arms control is a
public issue in the U.S., the Soviet Union is able to use arms
control to encourage American public opposition to U.S. military programs. As a recent blue-ribbon panel of independent
military and arms control experts concluded concerning the
Soviet view of arms control,

> Current Soviet policy on arms agreements is domi-
> nated by the Soviet Union's attempt to derive unilat-
> eral advantage from arms negotiations and agree-
> ments, by accepting only arrangements that permit
> continued Soviet increase in military strength while
> using the negotiation process to inhibit Western in-
> creases in military strength. There is no evidence
> that Soviet emphasis on competitive advantage over
> mutual benefit will change in the near future. . . .
> If such a change occurred, the possibilities for reach-
> ing much more substantial arms agreements might
> increase.[37]

Without that change, successful arms control based on mutual
vulnerability will not happen.

Fritz Ermarth has observed that if U.S. officials had understood the nature of Soviet strategic thought,

We would have been less sanguine than we were about prospects that the Soviets would settle for a strategic parity comfortable for both sides. We would not have believed as uncritically as we long did that the SALT Process was progressing toward a mutually desired strategic stability based on already tacitly accepted, shared principles.[38]

Overkill

The fundamental distinction between U.S. and Soviet strategic views helps to explain some of the myths that have grown up around nuclear weapons and arms control. For example, many Christian commentators propose that the U.S. pursue unilateral arms control measures, in the hope that the Soviet Union will follow suit. This can be done safely, so they say, because there already exists such a high level of "overkill" that there could be little risk in unilateral restraint. The usual method of demonstrating the level of overkill is to add up the explosive power of U.S. and Soviet nuclear arsenals in terms of pounds of TNT, and then divide that figure by the world's population. The result is said to be enough TNT per person to destroy the entire population several times.

Yet this is an extremely superficial and misleading calculation; the power of nuclear weapons ought not be analyzed this way. It ignores the fact that the power of nuclear weapons could not be spread out evenly over the population. Some areas would receive tremendous levels of explosive yield, others none at all. This method of thinking about nuclear arms makes no more sense than suggesting that there existed a tremendous overkill potential during World War I because there were an estimated nine billion rifle bullets in existence—six for every person on earth.[39] As with nuclear yields now, those nine billion bullets could never have been spread evenly over the population. Overkill did not exist in this sense then, and it does not exist now.

There is a more reasonable version of the overkill concept. This notion suggests that the U.S. and the Soviet Union have so many nuclear weapons, each could destroy many of the other's cities with a small fraction of the existing arsenals. As such, the U.S. could easily give up some of its forces in a unilateral effort to demonstrate goodwill and reduce tensions. Though it is true that the U.S. and the Soviet Union have about ten thousand strategic nuclear weapons each, and a far smaller number could inflict terrible destruction to each side's society, this overkill thesis is based on those facts alone. It fails to account for differing U.S. and Soviet views of nuclear weapons and, as a result, is extremely misleading.

As discussed above, U.S. notions of deterrence require that the U.S. maintain a "catastrophic retaliatory" capability against the Soviet Union, while the Soviet objective is to destroy U.S. forces before they could be used and to defend against those that survived the Soviet first strike. Because the U.S. calculates its deterrent based on *retaliatory* requirements, it must take Soviet first-strike capability and planning into consideration when determining "how much is enough" for the U.S. deterrent. Consequently for deterrence, it is not simply the number of existing weapons that is important, but the number of weapons that could survive a first strike and threaten retaliation. Because much of the U.S. arsenal would be destroyed in a Soviet first strike, the number of U.S. forces that can be counted on for deterrence is much smaller than the simple number of existing forces.

When this factor is included in the calculations, it is clear the U.S. has little if any overkill capability. As many as 90 percent of U.S. ICBMs and a high percentage of U.S. strategic bombers and submarine-launched ballistic missiles could be destroyed in a Soviet first strike. Although the U.S. may possess ten thousand strategic weapons, approximately 75 percent of those forces could be destroyed in a first strike.[40] Given the continued Soviet development of more counterforce first-strike capabilities and defensive capabilities for damage limitation, the U.S. must correspondingly modernize its retaliatory capabilities if it wishes to maintain a deterrent. One simply cannot say that because the U.S. possesses thousands of nuclear weapons it has an overkill capability—unless one chooses to ignore the fact that many, and possibly most, of those forces would be destroyed in a first strike.

Some might think that if two to three thousand U.S. weapons could survive a first strike, then the U.S. still has an overkill capability and could safely pursue unilateral arms control initiatives. Since much of the Soviet population resides in about two hundred urban areas, why would the U.S. need several thousand survivable nuclear weapons for deterrence? A few hundred reliable weapons could threaten the bulk of the Soviet population, and every U.S. program to expand its arsenal beyond that level is just adding to the overkill.

If the U.S. based its deterrent on a single massive threat to the Soviet population, then several hundred survivable and reliable nuclear weapons could be enough to maintain its deterrent. However, as discussed in chapter 6, the U.S. actively attempts to avoid Soviet population centers in planning its deterrent threat. The U.S. deterrent is not based on a plan to purposely inflict horrendous casualties on the Soviet population. Rather, it focuses on military facilities and political control of the Soviet government.

The great difficulty of this type of deterrent threat is that it requires many more survivable and capable nuclear weapons than does a simple threat to population. Indeed, maintaining such a deterrent is extraordinarily difficult to achieve because—consistent with the Soviet goal of damage limitation—the Soviet Union continues to improve its capability to protect these assets. Nevertheless, official U.S. policy is that the most effective and moral deterrent possible is one that is not, as was declared about U.S. policy in earlier years, based on MAD and its intentional targeting of some high percentage of the Soviet population.

When one takes into consideration that the U.S. deterrent is not intended to be "counter-city" but must appear capable against the numerous Soviet military and political-control targets, and the likelihood that many existing U.S. forces would be destroyed in a first strike, the number of weapons possessed by the U.S. cannot be considered overkill. Because the Soviet Union never accepted the Western "wisdom" of MAD and continues to try to counter the U.S. deterrent by improving its offensive and defensive capabilities,[41] the U.S. must continually improve its forces to ensure that they are capable of supporting deterrence. Rather than some "mindless momentum" of nuclear buildup, virtually all U.S. strategic modernization programs are the product of this problem. Consequently, when Christians press the U.S. government to pursue unilateral arms control on the basis of overkill, they are reflecting a deep misunderstanding of U.S. and Soviet policies and the realities of the U.S.-Soviet deterrence relationship.

Arms Control and a Nuclear Freeze

In the early eighties American churches strongly supported a grassroots movement for a nuclear freeze. The nuclear freeze proposal was straightforward. It advocated "a mutual freeze on the testing, production and deployment of nuclear weapons and of missiles and new aircraft designed primarily to deliver nuclear weapons."[42] Many denominations formally endorsed this proposal or ones similar. They simply equated a nuclear freeze proposal with peace, opposition to nuclear war, and reductions to the nuclear threat.

While there is everything to be said for promoting peace, opposing nuclear war, and striving to reduce the nuclear threat, an understanding of U.S. and Soviet policies reveals why a nuclear freeze would not promote those goals. Indeed, a freeze would be more likely to increase the probability of a nuclear war—just the reverse of what its proponents hoped and believed. This is true for several reasons.

First, both sides have the capability, even following a first strike, to destroy most of the major population centers of the other. A freeze would not much alter that situation for the foreseeable future; indeed, it could "freeze in" that dangerous situation. Actually reducing the nuclear danger to population centers would require deep reductions in offensive weapons, the deployment of effective defenses against nuclear weapons, or some combination of the two. A freeze would do nothing in this regard.

Second, a freeze would be likely to undermine the deterrence of nuclear war. The reason for this is simple: Many of the U.S. nuclear programs are intended to maintain the U.S. deterrent in the face of Soviet nonnuclear defensive programs. If U.S. (and Soviet) nuclear programs are frozen but Soviet nonnuclear programs to counter the U.S. deterrent are not frozen, the U.S. deterrent will erode. This weakening of the U.S. side of the deterrence balance would likely increase the probability of war.

As discussed above, the Soviet Union continually improves its defensive capabilities to counter the U.S. deterrent; much of this improvement is nonnuclear. For example, over the last two decades it has spent up to $56 billion on the construction and equipping of war survival shelters and bunkers for the political leadership alone.[43] This massive nonnuclear program of hardened shelters and relocation sites for the political and military leadership would not be limited by a nuclear freeze, but it does drive up U.S. weapons requirements for the maintenance of deterrence.

Similarly, the enormous Soviet air defense program intended to defend against U.S. bombers has many nonnuclear elements, and has had a real impact on U.S. bomber requirements. As Dr. William Perry, under secretary of defense for research and engineering during the Carter Administration noted: "Sometime in the mid-1980s, [the B-52 strategic bomber's] ability to penetrate the air defenses of the Soviet Union will be problematic. In fact, to put it more strongly, it will be doubtful."[44] As a result of the continuing Soviet investment in nonnuclear air defenses, the U.S. has been compelled to pursue new alternatives to the B-52 bomber to maintain the deterrence balance. Yet the freeze, while not stopping any of the Soviet nonnuclear defensive programs meant to counter the U.S. deterrent, would prohibit the U.S. from improving its deterrent capabilities. Because the U.S. does not have a comprehensive defensive program similar to that of the Soviet

Union, this problem is not faced by the Soviet Union. The problems brought on by a nuclear freeze would largely be unilateral for the U.S., and would easily threaten to upset the deterrence balance and increase the probability of war. This critical problem is not relevant to strategic bombers alone; it confronts every element of the U.S. deterrent. For example, ballistic missile-carrying submarines constitute an important element in the U.S. deterrent "Triad" of bombers, ICBMs, and submarine-launched missiles. These submarines, when on patrol, are considered the most survivable segment of the deterrent (i.e., they are the least vulnerable to a first strike). Indeed, because of its survivability, the submarine fleet is regarded by many as essential to stable deterrence. What would be the implications of a freeze for this critical part of the U.S. deterrent? The freeze would not prohibit the Soviet Union from continuing to invest heavily in its nonnuclear defenses against the submarine portion of our deterrent. In this case, the Soviet Union would be free to expand its anti-submarine-warfare (ASW) program because those systems are generally nonnuclear. It would, however, greatly restrict the U.S. potential for maintaining the survivability of the submarine force, undermining the U.S. side of deterrence and the basis of the deterrence relationship.

Exacerbating the problem of the Soviet nonnuclear threat to U.S. deterrent forces is the fact that the Soviet buildup of nuclear forces during the seventies already posed a threat to some U.S. forces prior to the freeze proposal. Consequently, a freeze not only would prohibit the U.S. from responding to Soviet nonnuclear programs to counter the U.S. deterrent, it would lock in an existing Soviet nuclear threat to the deterrent. For example, as a result of the truly massive Soviet buildup of counterforce weapons during the seventies, U.S. ICBMs became highly vulnerable to a nuclear first strike by the early eighties. This problem was readily recognized by the Carter Administration.[45] A freeze would lock in that dangerously destabilizing situation by denying the U.S. options for enhancing the survivability of its ICBMs. That is, the Soviet first-strike threat to U.S. ICBMs already exists, and a freeze on any new U.S. ICBM program would help perpetuate that dangerous situation.

The most dangerous effect of the freeze is that it would degrade the avenues of survivability for each part of the U.S. deterrent. Our ICBMs are already vulnerable to preemption; a freeze would deny the U.S. the most feasible means of addressing that problem. The aging U.S. strategic bomber force has had to stay ahead of advances in the continually improving Soviet air defenses for two decades. A freeze would stop the U.S. from keeping up any longer. As for the submarine-launched missiles, the freeze would cap their modernization while giving free rein to Soviet anti-submarine capabilities.

By degrading the survivability of all U.S. deterrent forces in the short and long term, a freeze would threaten deterrence and stability. Consequently it would increase the probability of war—just what everyone, including freeze proponents, is anxious to avoid. This is not an argument against the freeze based on a cavalier attitude toward nuclear war; it is an argument against the freeze based on the fact that a freeze would be likely to jeopardize peace.

Another problem with the freeze is that it would prohibit the U.S. from moving increasingly toward the discriminate and controlled nuclear capabilities required by just war considerations (as discussed in chapter 6). This appears of little concern to freeze proponents because they generally support the MAD approach to deterrence. Randall Forsberg, one of the originators of the freeze proposal, claims that the U.S. deterrent should be based on the threat to destroy Soviet cities and kill millions of Soviet citizens.[46] This concept of deterrence is, of course, most consistent with the freeze proposal because it is the "easiest" deterrent to maintain, and because a freeze would prohibit the U.S. from pursuing increasingly discriminate nuclear capabilities.

However, as discussed above, U.S. deterrence policy is not intended to be a "counter-city" but a "counter-military" threat. This discriminate approach to deterrence is far more compatible with just war guidance than the MAD "counter-population" notions endorsed by freeze activists. As Roman Catholic bishops, in following just war considerations, observed,

> The lives of innocent persons may never be taken directly, regardless of the purpose alleged for doing so. . . . Just response to aggression must be discriminate; it must be directed against unjust aggressors, not against innocent people caught up in a war not their making."[47]

Yet a freeze would hinder the development of a discriminate and controlled deterrent because it would stop the development, testing, and deployment of increasingly controllable, discriminate, and survivable deterrent forces. A freeze would stop this development in U.S. deterrence policy not because a counter-military approach requires more weapons—indeed this approach could be based on fewer nuclear weapons than current force levels. Rather, the pursuit of an increasingly discriminate and controllable deterrent requires the modernization of U.S. forces, modernization that would be prohibited by a freeze.

In short, a freeze not only would weaken stability by increasing the vulnerability of U.S. deterrent forces to a Soviet first strike, it would deny the U.S. the ability to move increasingly away from the unacceptable counter-population threat favored by freeze proponents but opposed by just war considerations. As such, the freeze proposal ought to be considered carefully on both moral and deterrence grounds.

It is unfortunate that American churches did not examine the freeze proposal more closely before providing such a blanket endorsement. That a freeze would likely prove destabilizing and generally is predicated on an unacceptable MAD notion of deterrence should have led to a different position by the churches. It appears this is another example of many Christian churches being led, uncritically, by the concepts of the anti-nuclear side of the secular strategic debate. Of course nuclear war must be avoided, but it must be recognized that a nuclear freeze would likely not achieve that good goal and, in fact, would likely erode the deterrence balance.

The Action-Reaction Arms Race

Another myth is that the arms race is an ever-spiraling accumulation of nuclear firepower. Each side supposedly is driven by a desire to match the other missile for missile, warhead for warhead. U.S. spending for strategic forces is said to climb ever higher each year in this mindless race, and spending for social services has been reduced as a result. If we could only break this action-reaction arms race cycle, so the argument goes, the arms competition would end. As Christian pacifists Taylor and Sider assert,

> The arms race between the United States and the Soviet Union has proceeded in an upward spiral. We build a missile, and they build a missile to counter it. They increase their military spending; we increase ours. The freeze stops this spiral. It hits the brakes. It gets both sides to stop.[48]

Based on this particular notion of the arms race, many Christian nuclear pacifists have recommended that the U.S. take unilateral steps to reduce its arms and break the action-reaction cycle. Yet virtually every aspect of these typical notions about the arms competition is mistaken.

The notion that the U.S. has pursued ever-spiraling defense budgets and nuclear firepower in competition with the Soviet Union simply is wrong. If one looks at a comparison of U.S. and Soviet spending for the acquisition of strategic nuclear forces from 1965 through 1987, it is clear that the Soviet Union has continually outspent the U.S. by a significant margin—amounting to almost $230 billion over twenty years (see Figure 5).

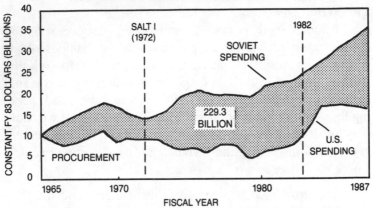

**U.S. AND SOVIET SPENDING
ON ACQUISITION
OF STRATEGIC FORCES (1965-1987)**

From the signing of SALT I in 1972 through 1982, the total difference in spending on acquisition of strategic forces is approximately 140 billion.

Soviet spending estimated in equivalent dollars.

SOURCE: U.S. Congress, Senate, Committee on Armed Services, department of defense Authorization for Appropriations for Fiscal Year 1984, Hearings, Part 5, 98th Cong., 1st Sess. (Washington, D.C.: U.S. Government Printing Office, 1983), p. 2418.

Figure 5

If one looks at the more comprehensive comparison of U.S. and Soviet strategic force expenditures the difference is even more pronounced. By this comparison, for twenty years the Soviet Union has outspent the U.S. on strategic forces by approximately $390 billion (see Figure 6).

COMPARISON OF U.S. STRATEGIC FORCE EXPENDITURES WITH THE ESTIMATED DOLLAR COST OF SOVIET FORCES

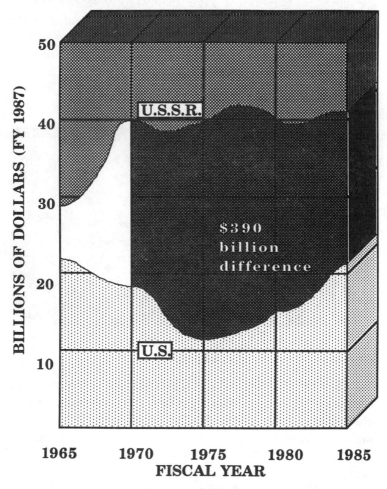

Source: Secretary of Defense Casper W. Weinberger, Annual Report to the Congress, Fiscal Year 1987, p. 58.

Figure 6

In addition, if one compares total federal outlays for defense and nondefense spending, it is clear that the usual view of ever spiraling defense spending choking off nondefense spending also is incorrect. Over the last forty years real U.S. spending for defense has showed little growth, and actually declined during most of the seventies. In contrast, nondefense spending has steadily increased and has gone well beyond defense spending (see Figure 7).

TOTAL FEDERAL OUTLAYS

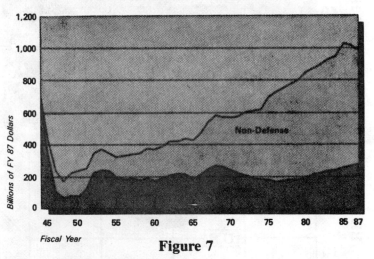

Figure 7

Similarly, if one looks at most indexes of strategic force capability, U.S. capabilities have declined and continue to decline relative to those of the Soviet Union.[49] Indeed, in comparing the overall U.S. and Soviet nuclear warhead stockpiles since 1965, it is clear that the U.S. stockpile has steadily declined while the Soviet stockpile has increased, surpassing that of the U.S. around 1975, and growing steadily since. If one compares U.S. and Soviet nuclear stockpile yields (i.e., cumulative explosive power in megatons), it is also clear that the Soviet Union surpassed the U.S. around 1972 and has gone well beyond U.S. levels since. Comparison of virtually all other categories of strategic nuclear force reveals that the U.S.

has not pursued the action-reaction, ever-spiraling arms race as described by Sider and Taylor.

Serious studies of U.S. and Soviet strategic nuclear programs continually show that the action-reaction explanation of the arms race does not stand up to historical facts.[50] Yet the notion persists among some Christians that to solve the nuclear threat the U.S. must move first to stop the action-reaction cycle through arms control. Yet, as Dr. Harold Brown, secretary of defense under Jimmy Carter, observed about the history of the arms competition, "When we build, they build—when we stop, they continue to build."[51] Consequently, even though the U.S. demonstrated considerable unilateral restraint throughout the entire decade of the seventies, there has not been the positive response hoped for from the Soviet Union.

This is not to suggest that the U.S. has not spent large sums of money on strategic nuclear forces over the last three decades; clearly it has. But the perspective of the arms race reflected in much of the discussion by Christian nuclear pacifists does not acknowledge the history of strategic arms competition. History does not support those Christians who suggest that the U.S. take risks to initiate a break in the arms race cycle and then await "reciprocal deeds by the U.S.S.R."[52] That theory has already been tested and found wanting.

Proposing that the U.S. take unilateral, even risky, initiatives to stop the arms race simply fails to take into account why the Soviet Union and the U.S. deploy strategic forces. It is not a senseless international "keeping up with the Joneses." On the Soviet side it is to provide the Soviet Union with a capability to deter, and if deterrence fails, to survive and preferably win a nuclear war. Such objectives require tremendous offensive and defensive strategic capabilities, and do not leave much margin for "reciprocal deeds" of arms control. In contrast, the U.S. historically has deployed strategic forces to maintain the U.S. side of the deterrence balance—to ensure a capability to threaten the Soviet Union with catastrophic retaliation. Yet, as the Soviet Union pushes to reduce its vulnerability and the U.S. tries to maintain Soviet vulnerability for deterrence purposes, there is little room for American notions of unilateral reductions to stop the arms race at a "stable" level of mutual vulnerability. That concept simply has not been acceptable to the Soviet Union. As John Collins, senior national defense specialist for the nonpartisan Congressional Research Service, has observed,

> The U.S. concept of parity has no visible Soviet corollary. On the contrary, Moscow places a premium on preponderant forces designed to afford a favorable edge for political, deterrent, and warfighting purposes. . . . Offensive weapons that we consider unstable are Soviet staples, especially large land-based missiles . . . which would be most effective against U.S. counterparts in a first strike. Defense of the homeland is a high priority. Soviet leaders scarcely see arms control as the central issue of our time. It is an important tool in their strategic kit bag, but deployed military power consistently takes precedence.[53]

Arms Control Violations

A final arms control myth presented by some Christians as fact is that the Soviet Union has abided by the arms control agreements it has signed.[54] Even when the Episcopal report *The Nuclear Dilemma* notes that the Soviet Union "may" have violated the SALT I ABM Treaty, it goes to great lengths to blame the event on "strained" political relations between the U.S. and the Soviet Union. Duplicity is not even discussed as a possible basis for Soviet cheating.[55] One is reminded of the observation by Professor Paul Hollander of the University of Massachusetts: "While peace activists refrain from criticism of the Soviet Union, they are inclined to criticize the United States . . . there is a striking contrast between the willingness to give the benefit of the doubt to Soviet policies and the readiness to hold the American government responsible for a wide-range of global problems, including the arms race."[56]

To view arms control as holding out the promise of solving the nuclear threat and providing an alternative to deterrence, one must somehow deal with the indisputable fact that the Soviet Union has violated or circumvented many of the strategic arms control agreements already signed. How can one propose a bright future for arms control when the Soviet Union is cheating on existing agreements? This is a difficult question to answer and is perhaps why the issue is generally skirted by those Christian activists proposing arms control as an alternative to deterrence. It might also be the case that the facts of Soviet violations simply are unfamiliar to those Christians. They should not be.

The Soviet Union has shown a pattern of violating arms control agreements. It has violated long-standing agreements and the more recent agreements on strategic forces as well. For example, the 1936 Montreux Convention prohibits the passage of aircraft carriers through the Turkish Straits. The Soviet Union has violated this agreement recurringly from 1976 to the present with its Kiev Class carriers.[57] The Geneva Protocol of 1925 prohibits the use of chemical weapons against treaty signatories. The Soviet Union appears to have circumvented the treaty by using chemical weapons against countries such as Afghanistan which are not signatories.[58] There also is considerable evidence that the Soviet Union has retained, produced, stored, transferred, and used biological weapons in violation of the Biological Weapons Convention of 1972.[59] The Soviet Union also has violated the multilateral agreement of the Helsinki Final Act (1975) by not providing the required notification for military exercises.[60]

Perhaps most relevant to this discussion, however, is Soviet violations and circumvention of U.S.-Soviet agreements governing strategic nuclear weapons. This fact obviously raises the question as to whether the Soviet Union can be trusted to negotiate in good faith, rather than using arms control to pursue strategic advantages.

The most militarily important example of Soviet circumvention of the SALT I agreement involves the "light" versus "heavy" missile distinction. In SALT I the U.S. was most concerned to limit Soviet heavy ICBMs because those were the weapons capable of threatening the U.S. deterrent in a first strike. The U.S. requested agreement on a clear definition of the difference between a light versus a heavy ICBM. This was important because a clear definition was essential to any agreement effectively limiting heavy ICBMs. Consequently, the U.S. offered a specific definition. Yet, according to American chief negotiator Gerard Smith, the Soviets refused any specific definition of the light/heavy ICBM distinction; they argued that a clear definition was unnecessary because both sides knew what was meant by heavy and light, and could distinguish between them.[61]

This refusal to come to a clear definition now appears to have been purposeful deceit. During the negotiations the Soviets had their SS-18 and SS-19 ICBMs under development, both of which would be heavy ICBMs under the U.S. definition and therefore strictly limited under the agreement. Yet in order to avoid such limitations, the Soviets cynically told the U.S. a specific definition was not necessary. As a result, the Soviet Union was able to circumvent the clear purpose of SALT by deploying over 350 SS-19s above the agreed SALT limits on heavy ICBM launchers.

This action by the Soviet Union is an extremely important circumvention of SALT because it has significantly increased the Soviet capability to destroy U.S. ICBMs in a first strike. This was perhaps the most destabilizing strategic development of the seventies and completely contrary to what the U.S. thought SALT was all about. U.S. negotiators clearly believed that SALT I had capped heavy ICBMs in 1972. As then Secretary of State Henry Kissinger stated when defending SALT I before Congress,

> Within the overall limitation [of SALT I] the Soviet
> Union has accepted a freeze of its heavy ICBM

launchers, the weapons most threatening to our strategic forces. There is also a prohibition on conversion of light ICBMs into heavy missiles. . . .[62]

Soviet deployment of the SS-19 as a light ICBM ensured that this critical expectation of SALT could not be met. It is important to note that this light/heavy ICBM issue is not some unimportant detail of SALT. It represents circumvention of the very heart of SALT—to cap destabilizing offensive first-strike capabilities and to limit ballistic missile defenses. Such circumvention of the object and purpose of a treaty is a material violation of the agreement according to the Vienna Convention of the Law of Treaties (1969). Soviet behavior regarding the deployment of the SS-19 clearly was a purposeful and fraudulent circumvention of SALT.

The Soviet Union has violated two other SALT I offensive limitations. First, the Soviet Union has placed its new SS-25 ICBM (which itself violates the SALT II agreement as is discussed below) in facilities formerly used for SS-7s. This action is a direct violation of SALT I.[63] Second, the Soviet Union has used several means to disrupt U.S. capabilities to verify SALT. It has encrypted critical information (telemetry), and it has used deliberate concealment measures to confuse U.S. monitoring of Soviet military activities relevant to arms control agreements.[64] These activities are themselves a violation of SALT I and SALT II, and reduce the ability of the U.S. to monitor Soviet activities that might be in violation of agreements.

The Soviet Union has also violated the ABM Treaty. One of the prohibitions of the ABM Treaty is the deployment of strategic ballistic missile early warning radars other than on the periphery of the country and oriented outward (see Article VI of the treaty). The Soviet Union has violated this prohibition by its construction of a large phased-array radar at Krasnoyarsk in Central Siberia.[65] This radar is not located on the periphery of the Soviet Union, and it is oriented toward much of the interior of the Soviet Union. The ABM Treaty also prohibits ballistic missile defense (BMD) radars that are not of a permanent, fixed type. Yet the Soviet Union has developed transportable BMD radar that are rapidly deployable. These radars are listed officially as "potential violations" of the ABM Treaty.

An action of the Soviet Union listed officially as a "highly probable" violation of the ABM Treaty is the testing of surface-to-air missiles (i.e., defenses against bombers) as systems for ballistic missile defense. This is a real concern for the United States. Limiting the testing of surface-to-air missiles was important to American negotiators because of the existing huge numbers of Soviet anti-bomber surface-to-air missiles. It was considered critical that the Soviet Union not be able to circumvent the ABM Treaty limitations on ballistic missile defense by upgrading its systems for bomber defense into systems for missile defense. Thus, the U.S. required that the ABM Treaty include a prohibition on the testing of anti-bomber defense systems for anti-ballistic missile missions. The Soviet Union appears willfully to have violated this important prohibition.

It should be noted in this review of Soviet arms control violations, probable violations, and acts of circumvention, that the U.S. has not been careless or hasty in its official discussions of this issue. Official statements about Soviet cheating have followed extremely detailed and thorough reviews of the available data, and have indeed been rather cautious given the apparent scale and continuity of Soviet cheating.[66]

The Soviet Union has also violated the SALT II agreement of 1979. Although this treaty was never ratified, both sides agreed to abide by its provisions. Yet at least four important provisions of this treaty may have been violated by the Soviet Union.[67] One of these—the production and deployment of the SS-25 ICBM—has been cited officially as a "clear and irreversible" violation and "particularly disturbing."[68] Article IV of the Treaty states that only one new type of ICBM may be deployed by either side. The Soviet Union has claimed the SS-24 as their one new ICBM, while the U.S. has claimed the MX as its new missile. Yet the Soviet Union has also built and deployed the new SS-25 ICBM—clearly a prohibited new missile according to the Treaty.

It is difficult to provide an exact number of Soviet arms control violations because that number depends on how precisely "violation" is defined and how much evidence must be marshaled before a violation is cited. The Reagan Administration has been rather cautious in this regard.[69] Nevertheless, it is clear that the Soviet Union has engaged in purposeful cheating on some arms control provisions, and pursued extremely dubious actions on others. (See the Appendix for a partial listing of such Soviet behavior.)

Some Christians minimize the significance of Soviet arms control violations.[70] Others, such as the United Methodist bishops, virtually dismiss the entire issue by declaring that discussions of "alleged treaty violations" amount to "incendiary propaganda" as opposed to matters of genuine importance.[71] It is amazing that these Christians trivialize the issue and even criticize discussion of it. These same groups expect arms control to carry the heavy burden of replacing the current approach to nuclear deterrence, yet they appear unconcerned about the clear fact that the Soviet Union is cheating on existing agreements.

If cheating on agreements is not important, then it is difficult to claim that the agreements themselves can be very important. Yet some Christians claim the political effect of achieving an agreement is more significant than the agreement itself. The Methodist bishops claim that "the technical details of particular arms accords are less important than the political achievement of such accords and the direction in which they point."[72] If so, whether the letter of an agreement is followed or not is of less importance than the political "spirit" of an agreement. Yet what kind of *political* signal does Moscow send about the entire arms control process when it willingly and repeatedly violates agreements? And how much confidence can we place in future arms control agreements given this Soviet perspective?

In addition, what kind of political signal is sent to Moscow when blatant arms control violations are ignored or swept under the carpet in the U.S.? Moscow must conclude that the U.S. is not really serious about Soviet compliance with arms control agreements. This fosters an extremely poor basis on which to proceed with negotiations because it tells Soviet leaders they can sign agreements without a clear requirement to abide by them. Arms control may be able to contribute to beneficial changes in the strategic nuclear balance, but not if we have indicated to Soviet leaders beforehand that it is not essential for them to comply with agreements put into effect.

The U.S. decision in October 1986 to move beyond the SALT II limits in one category of weapons can only be understood as a response to Soviet arms control violations. In fact, for many years the U.S. tried quietly to use diplomatic channels to bring the Soviet Union into compliance with its commitments. These efforts did not bear fruit. Consequently, under international law the U.S. has the right to void any part or all an agreement the other party has violated. In fact, there is little else the U.S. could do other than to demonstrate the age-old diplomatic principle of reciprocity: if the Soviet Union continued to refuse to consider itself bound by every aspect of an agreement, the U.S. could not remain in total compliance either. This principle is extremely important to arms control because if the Soviets believe they could continue to violate agreements and the U.S. would take no serious action in response, there is no basis for enforcing compliance. The U.S. decision vis-à-vis the SALT II agreement can only be understood in this context. It is worth noting just how far the U.S. went, over a thirteen year period, to try to pursue Soviet violations quietly and through diplomatic channels. As Secretary of Defense Weinberger noted in a letter to President Reagan, those diplomatic efforts in the Standing Consultative Commission (SCC), the U.S.-Soviet body established to consider such matters, "failed to resolve any significant compliance issue in the approximately 1500 days that it has been in session over the past 13 years. A less productive forum for the resolution of disputes would be difficult to find."[73] A good example of how poorly the quiet diplomatic efforts in the SCC have fared involves the Soviet Kraznoyarsk radar, a blatant violation of the ABM Treaty. The U.S. and Soviet Union have spent over 220 hours discussing the radar at Krasnoyarsk without any apparent Soviet efforts to dismantle it or even acknowledge that it is a violation.[74] Another example involves the illegal Soviet testing of air defense components. Although the U.S. brought the issue to the SCC, over one hundred suspicious tests were conducted by the Soviet Union over twelve years. When these tests were completed, the Soviets announced they would cease. However, after a brief interval, the tests were resumed, and the U.S. once again brought the issue back to the SCC.[75] As the unclassified summary of the report by the General Advisory Committee of the Arms Control and Disarmament Agency observes,

> U.S. verification capabilities have not deterred the Soviet Union from violating arms control commitments. Furthermore, the near total reliance on secret diplomacy in seeking to restore Soviet compliance has been largely ineffective. The U.S. record of raising its concerns about Soviet noncompliance exclusively in the Standing Consultative Commission and through various high-level diplomatic demarches demonstrates the ineffectiveness of this process.[76]

As a result of the continued pattern of Soviet treaty violations and the ineffectiveness of diplomatic efforts over many years to resolve violations or suspicious behavior, the U.S. was compelled to reconsider its commitment to the SALT II limitations. Such an action was only common sense. The U.S. could not responsibly continue with business as usual regarding an agreement the Soviet Union was violating, and when established diplomatic channels proved ineffective in addressing noncompliance issues. No arms control agreement is likely to be helpful if only one side abides by it.

SUMMARY AND CONCLUSION

Christian nuclear pacifists have recommended arms control as a superior alternative to maintaining nuclear forces for deterrence. In addition, these same Christians criticize the U.S. for the lack of progress in arms control. Some Christian groups go so far as to demand that U.S. officials "get an agreement" within a set time period.

However, it should be recognized that such lobbying of the U.S. government puts pressure only on American officials, and likely undermines the U.S. position in any ongoing negotiations. This is due to important differences in Soviet and U.S. political systems: The American democratic government is influenced to a considerable degree by sustained domestic public pressure; the authoritarian Soviet government is influenced to a far lesser extent by peace activists and is under no similar pressure. Indeed, the Soviet government has systematically suppressed and arrested independent peace activists in the Soviet Union.

The Soviet leadership is keenly aware of the powerful domestic pressure on the U.S. government to achieve an agreement. This asymmetrical pressure on the U.S. government can only encourage the Soviet leadership not to bargain in good faith. Why bargain when the opportunity is there for the U.S. domestic situation to force the U.S. into making concessions without any Soviet reciprocity. Those Christians who pressure U.S. government officials to get an agreement, and even suggest that those officials be given a time frame within which they must achieve an agreement, can only hurt the prospects for any useful arms control.

In addition, the differences in U.S. and Soviet strategic objectives have virtually ensured that strategic arms control negotiations could not bear the hoped-for fruit. The U.S. has intended to use SALT to stabilize the strategic balance around the concept of mutual vulnerability. This has guided the U.S. toward trying to achieve limits on defensive capabilities and offensive first-strike capabilities. Likewise, the Soviet Union has attempted to further its own strategic objectives, which have nothing to do with *mutual* vulnerability. Soviet strategic objectives are to combine offensive and defensive capabilities to ensure that the Soviet Union could survive, recover, and possibly win a war if one were to occur. And, as former high-level Soviet officials have stressed, the Soviet Union attempts to use arms control primarily to further its strategic objectives. With these conflicting strategic concepts and objectives, it is not surprising that U.S. goals in SALT were not achieved. Indeed, the strategic balance has developed very differently from what American officials hoped and expected.

This is not to suggest that genuinely helpful arms control agreements are impossible. Yet for arms control to actually reduce the nuclear threat would require a very different approach by the U.S. and the Soviet Union. Unfortunately, there is little to suggest that the type of drastic changes necessary are coming in the foreseeable future.

The Episcopal Report notes that "with a concerted effort and with both U.S. and Soviet leaders committed to succeed, a framework which limits deployments of intermediate-range and strategic nuclear forces can be erected."[77] It is of course true that if both sides want arms control to succeed, and define success in the same way, then an important agreement should emerge. Yet expecting this to occur does not take into account the reality that the U.S. and Soviet Union do not share the same definition of arms control success. They have, in fact, been working at cross purposes. Nor does it seem to take into account that a "framework" limiting weapons may or may not be helpful in reducing the nuclear threat. The SALT "framework" agreements have neither reduced destabilizing first-strike capabilities (such Soviet capabilities increased by over 1,500 percent during the SALT period) nor reduced the number of strategic nuclear weapons in each side's arsenal. In contrast, to really reduce or end the nuclear threat would require very deep reductions in the roughly ten thousand strategic nuclear weapons on each side—and the assumption that both sides would comply with an agreement. Such an agreement may be possible in the future, but the history of arms control does not suggest that anyone hold his breath until it happens.

In addition, even if the U.S. and Soviet Union agree to drastic reductions in their respective offensive strategic arsenals, the nuclear threat would not necessarily be eliminated. As long as the U.S. is defenseless against nuclear attack, even a small number of Soviet covertly deployed nuclear weapons could threaten millions of lives. That is one reason why the issue of cheating and compliance is so important to any long-term future for arms control as a means of dealing with the nuclear threat. The Soviet record does not support high hopes.

Many myths about arms control and the arms race have arisen, due in part to a general misunderstanding of the different U.S. and Soviet approaches to deterrence, strategic weapons, and arms control. For example, the most popular notion about nuclear weapons is that the U.S. and the Soviet Union could blow up the world many times over, so the U.S. should start the arms reduction process by unilaterally reducing some of its "overkill" capability.

Yet the U.S. deterrent is not based on the notion of blowing up the world even once. Rather, the U.S. deterrent is based on a *retaliatory* threat to Soviet political and military capabilities—targets which tend to be numerous and well defended. Soviet strategic doctrine focuses on striking first at U.S. deterrent forces, then defending against those forces that might survive and retaliate. Consequently, the U.S. deterrent requires many more weapons than could actually be used simply because many of them will be destroyed early on by Soviet capabilities. Superficially reasonable-sounding notions of overkill simply fail to take this key factor into account.

Of course, if the U.S. planned its deterrent around the mutual assured destruction (MAD) concept of purposefully targeting the largest Soviet cities and threatening population, then the U.S. would have an overkill capability; such a deterrent requires a minimum nuclear capability to support it. But intentionally threatening to destroy cities and kill a large percentage of the Russian population is not the U.S. deterrent concept, and according to just war considerations it is something that the U.S. ought never plan to do. When one understands U.S. and Soviet strategic doctrines and looks at current U.S. capabilities, it becomes clear that an overkill capability does not exist. Indeed, in order to maintain a retaliatory deterrent, the U.S. must continually modernize its nuclear forces to ensure that the continual Soviet nuclear and nonnuclear defensive programs do not erode the U.S. side of the deterrence balance. This is one of the main reasons why a nuclear freeze, despite all the rhetoric about how it would promote peace, would in actuality increase the risk of war. It would allow Soviet nonnuclear defensive programs to continue unchecked, yet it would freeze U.S. nuclear programs, denying the U.S. the capability to maintain its deterrent in the face of Soviet nonnuclear countermeasures. Such a situation could only be destabilizing as the U.S. deterrent eroded.

In addition, the notion of the arms competition as an action-reaction process whereby each side strives to match the other side in every strategic nuclear force category and every dollar (or ruble) spent, simply is historically inaccurate. U.S. spending for such forces has trailed well behind that of the Soviet Union for two decades, and Soviet nuclear capabilities matched and surpassed those of the U.S. in most categories by the late seventies.[78] In fact, the U.S. has purposefully practiced self-restraint in many areas of strategic capability—particularly during the seventies. Yet, the hoped-for moderation of Soviet strategic nuclear programs has not been forthcoming. When we build, they build; when we do not build, they build. Clearly, the history of the arms competition and the particular approach of the Soviet Union to arms control undermines the argument that we ought to reduce some of our deterrent forces, even if at some risk, in order to provide a good example to the Soviet Union and in anticipation of a similar Soviet restraint.

Finally, the Soviet Union has violated and purposefully circumvented existing arms control agreements. This strikes to the very heart of what can be expected from arms control. If the Soviet Union willfully violates arms control agreements, how much hope can there be that arms control can reliably replace the need for deterrence? The answer is self-evident.

This discussion of arms control is not meant to lead to the conclusion that arms control is useless or without hope. However, what it can accomplish, given the long-standing and unique U.S. and Soviet approaches, has been quite limited. Arms control may have slowed the growth of strategic nuclear weapons, but even that is uncertain. Given almost two decades from which to judge, it is virtually unimaginable how arms control alone could ever lead to the elimination of the nuclear threat—the movement has been entirely in the other direction. And if arms control somehow did lead to deep reductions in nuclear weapons, as long as the U.S. is defenseless (and recall that this has actually been an objective of U.S. arms control policy), then even a small amount of cheating by the Soviet Union at any future time could again place millions of lives in nuclear danger.

Arms control, as practiced by the U.S. and Soviet Union and as advocated by some Christian peace activists, cannot be considered an alternative to deterrence for the foreseeable future. In chapter 10, however, we will discuss how arms control could play an important role in reducing the nuclear threat. But before we explore that possibility, we want to examine briefly one last alternative to deterrence suggested by some Christian pacifists—civilian based defense.

Chapter 8, Notes

1. Committee of Inquiry on the Nuclear Issues, Commission on Peace, Episcopal Diocese of Washington, *The Nuclear Dilemma: A Search for Christian Understanding* (Washington, D.C.: Episcopal Diocese of Washington, 1986), 53, 58.

2. Ibid., 57.

3. See the discussion in Stanley Kober, "The Other Side of the Soviet Peace Offensive," in *The Nuclear Freeze Controversy*, ed. Keith B. Payne and Colin S. Gray (Lanham, Md.: University Press of America, 1984), 131-45.

4. Jane Wales, luncheon presentation, Nuclear War Education Conference, sponsored by George Mason University, 12 April 1986.

5. James B. Curren and Phillip Karber, "Afghanistan's Ordeal Puts a Region at Risk," *Armed Forces Journal International* (March 1985):97.

6. Igor Glagolev, "The Soviet Decision-Making Process in Arms-Control Negotiations," *Orbis* (Winter 1978):778.

7. John Collins and Patrick Cronin, *U.S./Soviet Military Balance: Statistical Trends, 1970-1983*, Report No. 84-163 S (Washington, D.C.: Congressional Research Service, The Library of Congress, 27 August 1984), 28.

8. Ibid., 14; and *The Military Balance: 1985-1986* (London: International Institute for Strategic Studies, 1985), 21.

9. Collins and Cronin, 14; and *The Military Balance*, 158.

10. Leslie Gelb, "A Glass Half Full," *Foreign Policy* (Fall 1979):21.

11. Cited in R. Jeffrey Smith, "Arms Talks: 20 Years of Duds?" *Washington Post*, 5 November 1986, sec. A.

12. See Keith Payne, "The Soviet View of Strategic Defense: The Failure and Future of Arms Control," *Orbis* (Spring 1986):1-17; and Keith Payne *Strategic Defense: "Star Wars" in Perspective* (Lanham, Md.: Hamilton Press, 1986), 141-78.

13. Thomas Schelling, "What Went Wrong with Arms Control?" *Foreign Affairs* (Winter 1985-86):222, 223.

14. Ibid., 229.

15. The United Methodist Church, Council of Bishops, *In Defense of Creation: The Nuclear Crisis and a Just Peace* (Pre-publication printing, 1986), 35.

16. Thomas K. Longstreth, John Pike, and John Rhinelander, *The Impact of U.S. and Soviet Ballistic Missile Defense Programs on the ABM Treaty* (Washington, D.C.: National Campaign to Save the ABM Treaty, 1985), 3, 4.

17. Paul Nitze, "The Objectives of Arms Control," *Survival*, May-June 1985, 102.

18. Ibid., 102, 103.

19. See Richard Pipes, "Why the Soviet Union Thinks It Could Fight and Win a Nuclear War," *Commentary* 64 (July 1977):27; Raymond Garthoff, "SALT and the Soviet Military," *Problems of Communism* 24 (January-February 1975):33-34; Raymond Garthoff, "SALT I: An Evaluation," *World Politics* 31 (October 1978):1-25; and John Newhouse, *Cold Drawn: The Story of SALT* (New York: Holt, Rinehart and Winston, 1973), 4.

20. Stephen Meyer, "Soviet Strategic Programmes and the U.S. SDI," *Survival*, November-December 1985, 278. See also, Peter King, "Two Eyes for a Tooth: The State of Soviet Strategic Doctrine, *Survey* (Winter 1979):48.

21. See, for example, Fritz Ermarth, "Contrasts in American and Soviet Strategic Thought," *International Security* (Fall 1978):138-55; Robert Legvold, "Strategic 'Doctrine' and SALT: Soviet and American Views," *Survival*, January-February 1979, 8-13; Peter King, "Two Eyes for a Tooth: The State of Soviet Strategic Doctrine," *Survey* (Winter 1979):45-56; Benjamin Lambeth, *How to Think About Soviet Military Doctrine*, P-5939 (Santa Monica, Calif.: Rand, February 1978); John Erickson, "The Soviet View of Deterrence: A General Survey," *Survival*, November-December 1983, 242-51; William Odom, "Soviet Force Posture: Dilemmas and Directions," *Problems of Communism* July-August 1985):6; Meyer, "Soviet Strategic Programmes," 274-92;

220   Arms Control as an Alternative to Deterrence

and Michael Deane, *Strategic Defense in Soviet Strategy* (Washington, D.C.: Advanced International Studies Institute, 1980), 17-22.

22. General A. Altunin, "The Main Direction," *Voennye Znaniie*, (December 1973):4-5.

23. Marshal G. V. Zimin, *Razvitie Protivovozdushnoi Ovorony* (Moscow: Voennoe Izdatel'stvo, 1976), 191-92.

24. Quoted in Caspar Weinberger, "Strategic Defense Initiative Opponents Show Reluctance for Self-Defense," *ROA National Security Report* 4 (November 1986):3.

25. Glagolev, 768.

26. Stephen Meyer, "Post Iceland: No Change in Soviet Buildup," *Washington Post*, November 1986, sec. A-2.

27. Weinberger, 2-3.

28. Several participants in the SALT I process were accurate in their relatively pessimistic estimates of what would occur over the next fifteen years. See for example, William R. Van Cleave's testimony in *Military Implications of Anti-Ballistic Missile Systems and the Interim Agreement on Limitation of Strategic Offensive Arms, Hearings*, 92nd Cong., 2nd sess., 1972, 569-92; and Senator Jackson's statements throughout those hearings; Donald Brennan, "When the SALT Hit the Fan," *National Review*, June 1972, 6685-92; and Mark Schneider, "Problems of SALT: 1972," *Survive*, July-August 1972, 2-6.

29. Statement by Gerard Smith, head of the U.S. SALT I delegation, before the Senate Armed Services Committee in 1972. Quoted in *SALT I Reconsidered* (Washington, D.C.: Institute of American Relations, 1979), 13.

30. Secretary of State William Rogers, Statement to Senate Foreign Relations Committee, 19 June 1972, quoted in *SALT I Reconsidered*, 99.

31. Fritz W. Ermarth, "Contrasts in American and Soviet Strategic Thought," in *Soviet Military Thinking*, ed. Derek Leebaert (London: George Allen & Unwin, 1984), 51.

32. Henry Kissinger in *Military Implications*, 121.

33. Gerard Smith, *Military Implications*, 100, 395.

34. *The Nuclear Dilemma*, 90.

35. Glagolev, 772.

36. Arkady Shevchenko, *Breaking With Moscow* (New York: Alfred Knopf, 1985), 204.

37. Fred Hoffman, Study Director, *Ballistic Missile Defenses and U.S. National Security*, prepared for the Future Security Strategy Study, October 1983, 11-12.

38. Ermarth, 51.

39. James Child, *Nuclear War: The Moral Dimension* (London: Transaction Books, 1986), 47-48.

40. Keith Payne, *Nuclear Deterrence in U.S.-Soviet Relations* (Boulder, Colo.: Westview Press, 1982), 165-82; and Keith Payne, "What If We Really 'Ride-Out' a Soviet First Strike," *Washington Quarterly* 7 (Fall 1984):85-92.

41. For a summary of the continually improving Soviet defensive programs see, *Soviet Strategic Defense Programs* (Washington, D.C.: U.S. Departments of State and Defense, October 1985).

42. See Randall Forsberg, "Call to Halt the Nuclear Arms Race." (*Reprints from the Nuclear Weapons Freeze Campaign*, 4144 Lindell Boulevard, 2nd Floor, St. Louis, MO 63108.)

43. Department of Defense, *Soviet Military Power* (Washington, D.C.: Government Printing Office, 1985), 51-52, 90.

44. U.S. House of Representatives, Committe on Appropriations, Subcommittee on the Department of Defense, *Department of Defense Appropriations for 1980, Hearings*, part 3, 96th Cong., lst sess., 1979, 29.

45. See the speech by Harold Brown at the Naval War College, 20 August 1980, in U.S. Department of Defense, News Release No. 344-80, 20 August 1980, 2.

46. Presentation at, "In/Security: Facts and Figures about the Nuclear Age," a conference at Sarah Lawrence College, Bronxville, New York, 7 May 1983. For another freeze-oriented endorsement of MAD see, Stansfield Turner, "The Folly of the MX Missile," *New York Times Magazine*, 13 March 1982.

47. U.S. Catholic Bishop's Pastoral Letter in, "The Challenge of Peace: God's Promise and Our Response," *Origins*, 19 May 1983, 11.

48. Ronald J. Sider and Richard K. Taylor, *Nuclear Holocaust and Christian Hope* (Downers Grove, Ill.: Intervarsity Press, 1982), 226.

49. See, for example, John Collins *U.S.-Soviet Military Balance 1980-1985*, Report No. 85-89 S (Washington, D.C.: Congressional Research Service, Library of Congress, 1985), 301-18.

50. Colin Gray, *The Soviet-American Arms Race* (Lexington, Mass.: Lexington Book, 1976).

51. Quoted in Joyce Larson and William Bodie, *The Intelligent Layperson's Guide to the Nuclear Freeze and Peace Debate* (New York: National Strategy Information Center, 1983), 19.

52. *The Nuclear Dilemma*, 65.

53. Collins, 98.

54. Sider and Taylor, 223.

55. *The Nuclear Dilemma*, 64.

56. Paul Hollander, "Enduring Misconceptions about the Soviet Union," *The World and I*, October 1986, 647-64; reprinted in *Current News*, 17 April 1987, 11.

57. See, The General Committee on Arms Control and Disarmament (GAC), *A Quarter Century of Soviet Compliance Under Arms Control Commitments: 1958-1983* (October 1984), 7.

58. Ibid., 6-7.

59. Ibid., 6.

60. *Soviet Noncompliance with Arms Control Agreements*, Unclassified President's Report to the Congress, 1 February 1985, 4.

222   Arms Control as an Alternative to Deterrence

61. Ambassador Gerard Smith, statement in *U.S. Senate, Committee on Armed Services, Military Implications of Anti-Ballistic Missile Systems and the Interim Agreement on Limitation of Strategic Offensive Arms, Hearings*, 92nd Cong., 2nd sess., 1972, 289, 294, 363, 364.

62. Henry Kissinger, Ibid., 121.

63. U.S. Department of State, Bureau of Public Affairs, *U.S. Interim Restraint Responding to Soviet Arms Control Violations*, Special Report No. 147, 27 May 1986, 5.

64. *The President's Unclassified Report On Soviet Noncompliance with Arms Control Agreements*, 23 December 1985, 4.

65. Arms Control and Disarmament Agency, *Soviet Noncompliance*, 1 February 1986, 1-2.

66. For a much more extensive listing of Soviet treaty violations and circumventions than the Reagan Administration has cited see, *A Quarter Century of Soviet Compliance*, 1-15; for a summary review of many more alleged Soviet violations see Statement by Senator McClure, *Congressional Record* (Senate), 6 March 1986, S2180-99.

67. *President's Unclassified Report*, 8-11.

68. *U.S. Interim Restraint*, 5.

69. See the discussion in Colin Gray, "Moscow Is Cheating," *Foreign Policy* (Fall 1984).

70. *The Nuclear Dilemma*, 55, 64.

71. *In Defense of Creation*, 67.

72. Ibid., 66.

73. Quoted in "Reports on the Standing Consultative Commission," *Congressional Record*, 23 March 1987, E 1080.

74. Press conference by Richard Perle, assistant secretary of defense, 12 March 1987.

75. "Standing Consultative Commission," E 1080.

76. General Advisory Committee on Arms Control and Disarmament, *A Quarter Century of Soviet Compliances Practices under Arms Control Commitments: 1958-1983*, Summary (October 1984), 14-15.

77. *The Nuclear Dilemma*, 57.

78. For a thorough study of U.S. and Soviet capabilities see, *Measures and Trends: U.S. and U.S.S.R. Strategic Force Effectiveness*, DNA 46022, Prepared for the Director, Defense Nuclear Agency (Alexandria, Va.: Santa Fe Corporation, March 1978).

Chapter 9

Nonmilitary Defense as an Alternative to Deterrence

Civilian Based Defense

A final alternative to deterrence suggested by some Christians is civilian based defense (CBD), which is essentially a concept for nonmilitary defense. This alternative is associated most closely with Ronald Sider and Richard Taylor and is developed in their book *Nuclear Holocaust and Christian Hope*. Sider and Taylor define their notion of nonmilitary CBD as follows:

> Nonmilitary defense might be defined as systematic, organized, active, nonviolent resistance against a power which is regarded as evil, unjust or contrary to a particular way of life. Its purpose is to protect a nation's freedom and sovereignty and to thwart the goals of an invading enemy.[1]

Sider and Taylor recommend that the U.S. and its allies adopt a civilian based, nonmilitary defense approach to security. It would, they claim, provide a means of protecting our freedoms and values in a nonviolent manner acceptable to the

223

conscience of a Christian pacifist. Sider and Taylor provide numerous examples of CBD to illustrate the basic concept, which involves American unilateral disarmament. They say, for example, that by adopting CBD

> we would publicly announce our intention to disarm regardless of the response of others. We would embark on a massive national program of CBD. . . . During the several year process of preparation for CBD, we would get rid of all nuclear and conventional weapons.[2]

In the absence of military means for defense, CBD would allow an aggressor to invade and occupy America. As Sider and Taylor note,

> In CBD enemy occupation is considered the *beginning*, not the end of the battle. The distribution of enemy soldiers and functionaries throughout the country is seen not as defeat, but as "the initial stage for a longer struggle at close range."[3]

Rather than using military means to resist aggression, CBD would be based on active but nonviolent noncooperation by the population. This active noncooperation would be done while demonstrating "good will" toward the invaders.[4] The population would not follow unjust orders or policies; it would not recognize the invader's power. It would strike, mount boycotts, and simply not cooperate with the invader. Sider and Taylor characterize CBD noncooperation as follows:

> This noncooperation takes many forms. People commit acts of *omission* by refusing to do things that the enemy commands. . . . The people commit acts of *commission* by doing things the enemy forbids. . . . Through a thousand acts they defy the enemy, dramatize public disapproval of the occupation and maintain allegiance to their way of life.

> Even when the enemy punishes citizens with
> prison, exile, torture and death, they remain firm.
> They will *never* do the enemy's will.[5]

Sider and Taylor note quite rightly that the nonmilitary defense they recommend ought not be in any way equated with cowardice. Indeed, it would take great courage for unarmed civilians to defy the armed might of an invader and "accept arrest, exile or even death rather than assent to tyranny or oppression."[6] The death and destruction resulting from such noncooperation would likely be horrible to behold.

Another important element of Sider and Taylor's concept of CBD is that noncooperation would be done with good will, even agape love. An important result of this expression of concern and love for the invader would, according to Sider and Taylor, be the development of sympathy among the invading forces. The expression of good will and love, even toward those torturing and killing civilians, would moderate the invader's repression:

> It is not surprising, then, that the expression of such
> love can have enormous impact on the enemy. Love
> compels him to question the rightness of what he
> is doing. Love softens his heart. Love touches his
> conscience. Love awakens in him a longing for rec-
> onciliation with his neighbor and with God.[7]

This nonviolent and loving resistance would include active measures to convince the invading forces of the wrongness of their actions. Sider and Taylor recommend that Americans climb onto tanks and talk with the soldiers, questioning why they had come; that demonstrators hand out leaflets in the occupation force's language explaining "that the invaders will not be harmed, but that Americans will suffer and die rather than give up their democratic way of life."[8]

Civilian based defense offers a clear answer to the question of whether it would be better to be "Red than dead." Under

CBD the population would choose death rather than submission to or collaboration with a Soviet invasion force.

Critical Concerns Regarding Civilian Based Defense

Several points need to be made about this concept of nonmilitary defense. First, it does not offer a bloodless response to invasion. The type of resistance suggested would likely meet with terrible destruction to the civilian population. However, that in itself does not mean CBD is inferior to military defense; military defense *could* involve many civilian casualties as well.

Second, CBD is completely incompatible with its primary stated purposes—the protection of American values and "way of life." An occupying Soviet force is not going to respect the individual American freedoms of free press, assembly, worship, and speech just because Americans still claim them. These rights are not granted to Soviet citizens at home, much less to occupied territories. Even a brief glance at the countries the Soviet Union has occupied since World War II—from East Germany to Afghanistan—demonstrates that personal liberties would not be respected. Indeed, following Soviet occupation independent religious and political institutions are often the first to come under stark repression.

Sider and Taylor approvingly cite three examples of non-military resistance against the Soviet Union: Czechoslovakia (1968), Hungary (1956), and East Germany (1953). In each case, Soviet troops marched in to suppress largely nonviolent worker and student liberalization movements, and in each case, the bulk of the population did not gain and does not now have the personal freedoms generally taken for granted in the U.S. Ironically, in those examples of nonviolent resistance to Soviet troops cited by Sider and Taylor, the liberalization process appears to have had no chance of surviving Soviet occupation. Other instances of Soviet military occupation, such as that in Latvia, Estonia, and Lithuania after World War II, led to the loss of personal freedoms and the actual incorporation of these states into the Soviet Union.

Of course, Americans could choose to ignore the invader's authority (such as any martial law curfew) as Sider and Taylor suggest, but they would likely be arrested or shot in any attempt to exercise freedoms. This can hardly be called protection of freedoms; indeed, CBD is the planned absence of such protection in the hope that the invader will stop his repression and simply go away.

Third, CBD represents the planned rejection of government's scripturally mandated duties to protect the innocent, preserve justice, and punish the evil. Of course, the government would be responsible for organizing and preparing for CBD. But it would, in effect, be preparing to leave innocent civilians defenseless in the face of aggression, murder, torture, rape, and all the other evils that often occur during invasion. It is planned defenselessness in the hope that the mercy of the invader will soften the blow, and that he will eventually grow so weary of the occupation that he will give up and go home.

This is an important difference between military defense and CBD. Military defense generally involves plans for active resistance against those who would bring harm to innocent civilians. Of course, it is not always successful, as the Nazi invasion of Western Europe in 1940 illustrates. But protection of innocent civilians is the intent and basis for much military planning, whether by deterrence or direct defense—it is government's attempt to fulfill its scriptural calling. Civilian based defense would entail governmental rejection of that calling by purposefully planning for citizens to subject themselves to the invader's potential brutalities. Individual citizens may, of course, follow their consciences and pursue peaceful resistance in the face of repression and suffering. But how can a government responsible for the defense of those very citizens plan *not* to protect them when protection may be feasible?

Fourth, CBD would not discriminate between combatants and noncombatants. Indeed, it encourages mass participation by the population and requires that innocent civilians be subject to repression. As such, the bulk of the population would willfully be set up by the government to endure the terrible evils of a conquest and occupation. This, of course, might occur in the context of a failed military defense. But it is not the planned and purposeful objective of military defense to allow the citizenry to be the target of hostilities.

Fifth, CBD is predicated on the notion that the bulk of the population can effectively execute a plan of nonviolent, loving, noncooperation. Sider and Taylor write of participation in CBD by "70 million management and blue-collar workers and 4 million farmers. . . . nearly 3 million teachers, 60 million students, and a half-million radio, TV and newspaper workers."[9] Yet, Sider and Taylor note quite rightly that agape love is a key to the expression of such loving and nonviolent noncooperation. It is difficult to accept the notion that virtually all of the American population would be willing or able to express "good will" and agape love to an invader who may well be abusing, torturing, and murdering their families. Such a calling would be difficult for even the most spiritually mature Christian to answer. Are we to expect 200 million persons of different faiths or no faith to comply?

These are difficult questions for those promoting CBD as the Christian alternative to military defense and deterrence. In short, by willfully placing the bulk of the civilian population in harm's way, CBD appears to violate the scriptural requirement of governments to protect the innocent. It also violates the just war requirement that the use of force discriminate between combatants and noncombatants. Civilian based defense willfully renders civilians the target of the invader's aggression, and then refuses to provide them protection. In effect, it turns citizens into the undefended and unarmed focus of aggression. And while the consequences of a military defense against invasion can involve tremendous suffering by the civilian population, CBD provides no basis for believing the consequences of an attack would be any less stark. Whereas military defense prepares to resist aggression and protect the innocent (and is successful in many instances), CBD does not.

Conventional Invasion and Civilian Based Defense

The likelihood of a conventional invasion of the U.S. appears remote. The great oceans separating the U.S. from potentially hostile powers have isolated the U.S. from direct threats. Indeed, one of the overriding themes of American statecraft during the twentieth century has been to stop potential enemies before they could represent a direct threat to the American homeland. Consequently, U.S. battles for more than a hundred years have been waged almost exclusively on other continents, and few living Americans have had to suffer the terror of a war fought at home.

This, of course, is in stark contrast to the peoples of Europe and Asia, many of whom were compelled to live through the horrors of war fought at home, followed by military occupation. In World War II, total deaths from allied bombing of Germany and Japan were far fewer in number than the 1.5 million deaths resulting from the German siege of Leningrad. In the 1937 Japanese "Rape of Nanking," as many as 250,000 Chinese civilians were killed brutally over the course of a few days.[10] In contrast, American defense policy and geographic position combined to create an almost unprecedented condition of security from invasion for almost two centuries. Civilian based defense, of course, would be a complete reversal of that policy, and could actually invite military invasion by making the U.S. appear to be easy prey.

In addition, CBD would not allow the U.S. to do much to prevent the domination of all Europe by Soviet bloc forces. Indeed, a U.S. military withdrawal from Western Europe consistent with CBD would likely encourage Soviet military adventure by easing the military conquest of Europe. And because the U.S. would have disarmed itself of nuclear weapons as well, there would be no nuclear deterrent to inhibit Soviet attack on U.S. allies.

The Soviet Union, if in control of the technical and human resources of Europe, would represent a direct threat of invasion to North America. Such vulnerability is not at all realistic today; CBD could make it so. As a result, in addition to the rejection of government's scriptural mandate to protect, defend, and punish, implementation of CBD would likely increase the threat of conventional invasion to the U.S. and its allies.

The words *invasion* and *occupation* may convey little meaning to those who have not faced the prospect of a hostile invasion. A brief review of Soviet actions in Afghanistan provides some insight into what invasion and occupation would really mean.

Afghanistan and the Soviet Occupation

On Christmas day in 1979 the Soviet Union invaded Afghanistan and brought a puppet Afghan leader in with the invading forces. Approximately 85,000 Soviet troops invaded Afghanistan to support this new puppet government. The Afghan resistance, lead by the Mujahidin freedom fighters, has proven much stronger than anticipated by the Soviets, leading to increased Soviet troop levels (there are now 115,000 to 125,000 Soviet occupation troops in Afghanistan) and the pursuit of a long-term strategy for prevailing in the war.

Militarily, the Soviet long-term strategy is to destroy the basis of resistance. Socially and politically, the Soviet Union is trying to create a new Afghanistan in the image of the Soviet Union. This strategy is not intended to bring about a rapid victory. Rather it is intended to ensure eventual victory without significantly increasing Soviet troop requirements.

The long-term Soviet strategy involves more than fighting the Mujahidin—it includes fighting against the civilian population that supplies and shelters the Mujahidin. In an attempt to separate the Mujahidin from this essential popular support base, the Soviet tactic has been "aimed specifically at depopulating areas of strategic importance."[11] There are several methods of this tactic. The first method is massive bombing to kill villagers or force them to relocate. The second is invasion of villages with armored columns and the terrorizing of the population. Third is to destroy crops and slaughter livestock in an attempt to deny food to the population and ultimately the Mujahidin.

Finally, the Soviets use antipersonnel mines that maim and kill in order to demoralize the population and discourage resistance. The goal of all these tactics appears to be to create enough terror among the population to discourage resistance and support for the resistance.

The use of heavy bombing against Afghan villages increased in 1985. These air raids generally bypass military objectives and instead attack civilian targets.[12] As one expert on Soviet actions in Afghanistan has observed, "The Soviets apparently made a conscious decision to go after civilian targets in areas of strong resistance."[13] Eyewitnesses have described a typical attack as three jets dropping fifteen to twenty bombs, enough to destroy small villages.[14] Other witnesses confirm this Soviet strategy, noting that these bombing raids cause few casualties among the Mujahidin, but that "the casualties in the villages were pitiful."[15]

A tactic of the Soviets that is used less frequently now than during the early stages of the war is terrorizing villages by attacking them on the ground instead of simply leveling them with bombs. A typical ground attack begins with most villagers fleeing and Soviet tanks entering the village unscathed by the Mujahidin. Soviet forces stay several days burning crops and buildings, then take any remaining civilians to be interrogated or simply executed. Soviet forces leave antipersonnel mines behind, resulting in injuries and deaths to the returning residents days after the Soviets have left.[16] A 1985 United Nations report states that thirty-six such massacres were known to have taken place since the war began.[17] Since tanks can be ambushed and cannot reach all areas due to the mountainous terrain, recent attacks have made more use of aircraft.

Attacks against Afghan civilians are being carried out in conjunction with a policy of destroying the Afghan food supply. Yahya Massud, brother of the leader of the resistance in the Panjshir Valley, says "the Russians are applying a scorched earth policy. They are burning the crops, the houses, everything."[18] Sometimes fields and livestock are targets of bombing raids, antipersonnel mines are scattered in fields to kill and scatter livestock, and chemical and biological weapons are used to kill and create disease in people and livestock.

Soviet tactics have caused a large number of people to flee Afghanistan. Estimates vary, but approximately 4 million Afghans are now refugees in Pakistan and Iran. This is equal to one quarter of the prewar population. About 3.5 million of these are in Pakistan, forming the largest group of refugees in the world. In addition to the refugees in Iran and Pakistan, many Afghans have fled from the countryside to the cities to escape the war. Thus official estimates of refugees underestimate the total number of people displaced by the war.[19]

Finally, there may have been as many as 500,000 Afghans killed between 1979 and 1985.[20] A large percentage of these have been civilians.

The Soviet intervention in Afghanistan often is compared to the American intervention in Vietnam. Some comparisons are accurate, but with respect to treatment of civilians, U.S. and Soviet strategies are quite different. The U.S. attempted to win indigenous support by reaching out from the villages to set up local rule; the Soviet approach is to use major towns as garrisons and destroy the rest—to terrorize the residents and break their will. Apparently the Soviets learned from their Ukrainian extermination campaign of 1933 that victory may be to whoever can "make terror reign."[21]

An additional important point to note is the Soviet practice, since the beginning of the war, of bringing more than twenty thousand Afghan youths to the Soviet Union for indoctrination. These efforts focus on the very young, and the education process they receive there could last up to ten years.[22] The goal of this program is not only to control the teaching environment but to acclimate Afghans to life with the Soviets. In some cases, children are taught to spy or to sabotage and then sent back to Afghanistan to help the war effort.[23]

In attempting to bring Afghanistan into the Soviet bloc, a two-front battle is being waged on the civilian population. The first front is against the Afghan population—to brutalize and terrorize them. The second front is against the youth—to create a reliable and well-trained elite who could eventually run the country.

The result of these tactics has been, in the words of a United Nations reporter, the "massive and systematic violations of human rights in Afghanistan," including the loss of many lives, imprisonment in intolerable conditions, torture, and the disappearance of many people. A 1986 United Nation's report on human rights in Afghanistan states that the killing of civilians and general disregard for civil rights persist and that Soviet forces appear largely responsible. The U.N. report goes on to say that there is continued evidence of the Soviet use of gas and chemical weapons and booby-trapped toys to maim children. As analysts examining the Soviet behavior in Afghanistan have noted, the Soviet use of booby-trapped toys "heralds a class of weaponry—the antichild device—not previously seen in the annals of war."[24]

Simply because the Soviet Union has behaved in such a brutal fashion toward the Afghan population does not mean it would behave in a similar fashion toward the American population. However, there are indications, found in both historical examples and Soviet writings, of what Soviet occupation of the U.S. would entail.[25] There would likely be mass arrests, deportations, and executions. Personal freedoms (including the freedom of worship) would be prohibited, and a Soviet-style political system would be established—based on Soviet forces, Soviet administrators, and American "realists" who would be willing to collaborate. As a world-renowned expert on the Soviet Union, Robert Conquest, has observed,

> The Soviet authorities will not, of course, be able to arrest everybody, but since it will be necessary to repress and deter hostile thought and action, the number of arrests will obviously run into millions.
>
> In a "difficult" country like America, where the tradition of liberty has been strong, the probability is that, apart from executions, about 25 percent of the adult population will ultimately be sent to forced-

> labor camps or exiled under compulsory settlement
> in distant desert and arctic regions or in the U.S.S.R.
> If past performance is anything to go by, around 5
> percent of the prisoners in the labor camps would
> be women. . . .[26]

In addition, Dr. Joseph Douglas, after a long study of
Soviet strategy, suggests that the Soviet Union may engage in
some nuclear attacks on cities and other nonmilitary targets
for the sole purpose of demoralizing the American people and
discouraging resistance and noncooperation.[27] Douglas notes
this may be what is meant by such writings as this example
by a Soviet military authority: "In a number of cases it is
possible that attacks will even be made against objectives which
are not of great military and economic importance, but which
are advantageous from a political viewpoint."[28]

It is difficult for Americans, accustomed as we are to
personal freedoms, to comprehend that many people live under
extremely different conditions. We are accustomed to mass
demonstrations in support of or opposition to various issues,
to public presentations of grievances and public debate of sensitive issues, and to a democratic political system in which the
rights and cares of the general public are taken seriously. It
often is not appreciated that these political conditions are rare
in the international system.

When Sider and Taylor discuss civilian based defense,
they write as if Americans could pursue their noncooperation
against an opponent practicing an American-style political system. They write of the effectiveness of mass civilian demonstrations in response to a Soviet military invasion:

> Instead of American soldiers . . . the invaders would
> see tens of thousands of unarmed people carrying
> signs with messages in the invader's language: Go
> Home! We Won't Harm You; Don't Shoot—We Are
> Your Brothers and Sisters; Your Life Is Precious;
> You Are a Child of God. . . .

> Demonstrators would hand out leaflets in the invaders' language, countering the propaganda they had been fed about the reasons for the invasion. The leaflet would explain that the invaders will not be harmed, but that Americans will suffer and die rather than give up their democratic way of life. Each demonstrator would also carry a bilingual pamphlet giving a nonviolent code of discipline. . . .[29]

Sider and Taylor write as if resistance to Soviet invasion could be a replay of the successful and just American civil rights movement of the sixties. Yet CBD would not take place in an American political context—that would have been changed drastically by Soviet invasion. The Soviet government does not allow unauthorized mass demonstrations or the passing out of leaflets by Soviet citizens in the Soviet Union, much less by the population of an occupied country. Anyone attempting to participate in such demonstrations would undoubtedly be subject to severe repression. If one imagines crowds continually dispersed by gunfire, and those attempting to pass out leaflets being arrested or shot, then one has a better idea of CBD under Soviet occupation. Civilian based defense would likely result in millions of casualties; it could not protect the American "way of life."

This is not an overly harsh estimate of Soviet occupation. It must be recalled that the Soviet Union has a very different political system with different values. This point is illustrated repeatedly by Soviet behavior, including the continuing Soviet extermination campaign in Afghanistan or the 1983 Soviet military destruction of a civilian airliner (KAL-007) in international airspace. Historically, the Soviet Union simply has not regarded human rights in any sense recognized by Americans. A review of how the Soviet leadership consolidated its own rule at home and treated its own "noncooperative" citizens perhaps best illustrates this point and demonstrates the brutality of Soviet power.

The Consolidation of Political Power: The Soviet Experience

Between 1928 and 1938 the Soviet Union, under increasing control of Joseph Stalin, undertook to eliminate all opposition to the ruling regime. When difficulties arose in implementing the "New Economic Policy" and the first Five Year Plan in 1928, Stalin dealt harshly with those not cooperating. All outspoken opposition groups were arrested and Russian agriculture was forced into collectivization. Stalin then set out to eliminate opposition within the Communist Party and state offices, and among the peasantry. Consequently, the Soviet Union carried out collectivization and waves of purges, ultimately including the military and secret police. These action resulted in many millions of deaths.

The first phase of the purges—the collectivization of agriculture—was initiated under the guise of the New Economic Policy. In 1928 the Soviet government announced the acceleration of the Five Year Plan, so that it would be fulfilled in four years. According to the official Soviet history, "Socialist emulation" was "encouraged."[30] This meant that crops were taken from the peasant farmers to increase supplies to the cities to facilitate industrialization. The wealthier farmers—referred to as *kulaks*—were arrested as enemies of socialism, and anyone who opposed moving to an agriculture collective was considered a kulak. Necessary force was provided by urban party members, who had little sympathy for the peasants.[31]

Many peasants killed their livestock rather than having the government seize them, further exacerbating a developing food shortage. The collectivization, combined with a bad harvest in 1932, resulted in widespread famine in which as many as ten million perished.[32] The collectivization—involving mass arrests and killings—and the famine virtually eliminated noncooperation and dissent among the peasantry.

In 1934, with the Communist Party's control over the peasantry established, Stalin sought to establish control over the Party. Stalin evidently viewed Leningrad party boss Sergei Kirov as a possible contender for power, and thus had him assassinated. Stalin then used the political crisis over Kirov's assassination to justify a political purge.[33] In the security panic following the assassination, political and state organs were purged—first those allegedly responsible for Kirov's murder, then those who were connected with the assassination but did not stop it, and then any whose loyalty to the party might be questioned.[34]

People were caught alone, either at home or while traveling and away from their local party organization, and forced to confess to a crime and implicate others.[35] Regional heads of the NKVD (the internal security force which was the forerunner to the KGB) were actually given quotas of "enemies of the state" to be apprehended and executed.[36] The great purge moved from creating a brutally enforced allegiance to Stalin's regime, to a stark reign of terror against virtually every segment of society.

Estimating who and how many were killed during the collectivization and purges is difficult given the secrecy and general lack of information about internal events in the Soviet Union. However, from 1928 to 1933 the targets were the wealthier peasants, the kulaks, and anyone who resisted collectivization. In addition to those arrested were the millions killed by the famine caused by the collectivization. Estimates of the total killed ranged from five to ten million.[37]

From 1934 to 1936 the primary targets were political workers whose loyalty was in any way suspect. This included virtually all party leaders (100 of the 139 members of the 17th Party Congress), party and state leaders from the republics, managers and scientists, and those associated with someone who had been arrested.[38] Even the military could not withstand the purge. The great purge from 1937 through 1938 was set against much of the military command, and continued against earlier victims until about 50 percent of the political workers had been purged, and between 25 and 50 percent of military commanders and of the NKVD leadership as well (which itself had implemented earlier purges).[39]

Many of those purged were simply executed, while others were sent to prisons or concentration camps. There were between 7 and 9 million arrested from 1934 to 1938. Between 800,000 and 3 million of these resulted in executions, depending on how the estimation is done.[40]

Soviet policy in this period was to eliminate all internal opposition, beginning with the weakest and moving to the strongest. Dimitri Simes, a noted expert on the Soviet Union, places the number killed in the collectivization, purges, and famine at 20 million. He concludes that

> what the Communist government did to its people was genocide —pure and simple. But the most frightening thing which emerges . . . is that there was no rationale for the crime. At least there was no rationale Westerners could comprehend. . . . Stalin and his associates were obsessed with building the machinery of totalitarianism control, the machinery which was prepared to tolerate neither the economic power of Kulaks nor the ethnic peculiarity and pride of Ukranians. Both had to be broken at all costs.[41]

While this type of behavior may seem to be an aberration of politics, even for the Soviet Union, it ought to be recognized that purges of elite government officials were implemented in the Soviet-sponsored Communist takeovers of Eastern European states after World War II and an extermination campaign is taking place now in Afghanistan at the hands of Stalin's successors.[42]

This discussion points to the brutal Soviet approach to the consolidation of political authority. The Soviet regime under Stalin was willing to inflict millions of deaths on the Russian people to establish its power base. This occurred despite the fact, as Dimitri Simes notes, that the victims of this horrible repression did not present a violent threat to the Soviet government. Indeed, many of the kulaks killed supported the Communist government and had fought in the Red Army.[43]

Given this historical precedent, it is not difficult to recognize that Soviet occupation of the U.S. would involve terrible repression of any civilians who refused to cooperate as Soviet forces attempted to consolidate political power. Yet civilian noncooperation is the sole avenue recommended by Sider and Taylor to preserve American freedoms. It is virtually impossible to imagine how civilian based defense and noncooperation could possibly protect the American way of life from a Soviet-style occupation, as Sider and Taylor claim it could.

Nevertheless, from a Christian perspective, the *consequences* of adopting CBD as opposed to military defense cannot be the only criteria for judging between the two. The behavior of government must be examined in light of the responsibilities outlined for government in Scripture. Those responsibilities are protection of the innocent, the pursuit of justice, and the punishment of evil, "with the sword" if necessary. CBD, in fact, constitutes the virtual rejection of those responsibilities.

It must be acknowledged that military defense might be no less a failure in protecting American freedoms than CBD (i.e., military defense could fail), and might involve no fewer casualties among the American population. This critique of CBD is not meant to suggest that nonmilitary defense is necessarily foolish, would cause more civilian casualties than military defense, or would always be inappropriate as a means of resisting an occupation force. Nevertheless, what is clear is that a U.S. policy of CBD would not protect the innocent, preserve justice, or punish evil—indeed, it is a plan *not* to protect or punish. CBD also can not promise to preserve lives that would otherwise be lost, particularly if one assumes that the Soviet Union is the occupying force in question.

In some cases CBD may be the only means available to resist a powerful opponent; the military option simply may not exist, as has been the case in most of the postwar Soviet invasions of Eastern European countries. However, pursuing CBD because there are no other options for resistance is much different than willfully giving up all other options in order to pursue CBD, as Sider and Taylor recommend.

Civilian Based Defense as an Alternative to Deterrence

Although CBD may be considered as a possible (but un-scriptural) option for resistance to Soviet occupation, it cannot logically be suggested as a replacement for nuclear deterrence. CBD completely fails in any discussion of the nuclear threat. It simply does not address the problem.

As Sider and Taylor discuss CBD, the U.S. would abandon all nuclear and conventional arms whether or not the Soviet Union did the same. As such, there would be little incentive for the Soviet Union to disarm, since it would not have to give up forces in order to get reductions in the U.S. arsenal. Also, the Soviet Union would still face nuclear-armed opponents; at a minimum it would still have to contend with Chinese, French, and British nuclear systems. The Soviet Union would have genuine reasons to retain nuclear weapons. Consequently, one must consider the potential CBD condition where the Soviet Union possesses nuclear weapons and the U.S. does not.

In such a condition there would be no basis for nuclear deterrence: there would be no deterrent to discourage the Soviet Union from a nuclear strike against the U.S. Such a situation could be exceedingly dangerous for the U.S. population. Sider and Taylor suggest that the danger of a Soviet nuclear strike would be slight because the U.S. would have disarmed. They ask, "What would be the use" of a Soviet nuclear strike on "a nation so committed to liberty?"[44] Sider and Taylor write as if the U.S. commitment to liberty against Soviet rule would some-how appeal to Soviet leaders—champions of liberty that they are. However, simply because the U.S. would no longer possess nuclear weapons is no reason to believe that the U.S. would no longer be a nuclear target.

There is considerable inconsistency in arguing, as do Sider and Taylor, that CBD would render the U.S. extremely difficult to occupy, and that the U.S. would not be a nuclear target. To the extent that the U.S. could not be handled easily by conven-tional forces, it would become an even more important nuclear target. Being unarmed would not save the U.S. from being a nuclear target.

If the Soviet Union decides, for whatever reason, to wage a large-scale war in Eurasia, it will certainly attempt to ensure that the U.S. could not become involved, even if the U.S. had a policy of CBD. But the Soviet Union would just as certainly not want to employ millions of soldiers in the occupation of America; those same soldiers could be doing important duty against Western Europe or China. And, as Sider and Taylor note, fraternization between peaceful Americans and Soviet soldiers could create discipline problems for Soviet military authorities. Soviet leaders might want to avoid such potential problems by avoiding direct conventional occupation of the U.S. Indeed, Sider and Taylor endorse CBD as a way of making life miserable for Soviet occupation authorities, encouraging disintegration and mutiny within the Soviet military, instigating an "epidemic of freedom" within the occupation forces, and tying down troops that would be needed elsewhere. Yet, for those very reasons, and because the movement of so many troops thousands of miles would be such a difficult undertaking, the Soviets could initially prefer a nuclear alternative to the conventional occupation of the U.S.

More importantly, Soviet leaders would realize that the U.S. would be under great political pressure to rearm and enter an ongoing fray, particularly in the context of a new world war wherein democracy's very existence was threatened. The U.S. entered World Wars I and II on a similar basis. And, of course, from the Soviet perspective, just because the U.S. claimed (and even appeared) to be unarmed, does not mean the U.S. had not covertly stored nuclear and conventional weapons just in case. And even if the U.S. had not secretly stockpiled nuclear weapons, the U.S. government obviously would not have forgotten how to make them. The U.S. would still pose a threat to the Soviet war effort, and the Soviet Union would have every incentive to ensure that the tremendously powerful American industrial potential could not be mobilized for military purposes and brought to a new world war. Under such conditions a nuclear strike, not an attempt to occupy the U.S. militarily, would not be out of the question.

In short, when Sider and Taylor suggest there would exist no incentive for the Soviet Union to strike the U.S., and that the Soviets would prefer to occupy the U.S. conventionally, they are entirely unconvincing and, indeed, argue against their own thesis that conventional occupation could be a military and political disaster for the Soviet Union. In reality, the Soviet Union would have significant incentives to strike the U.S. in the context of a large-scale war in Europe or Asia, and significant disincentives for attempting conventional occupation.

The U.S. now has many nuclear weapons, in large part, to ensure that a Soviet nuclear strike against the U.S. can never make sense to Soviet leaders, the risk of U.S. retaliation being too great. However, under CBD that deterrent would be abandoned without the corresponding removal of the possible incentives for a nuclear attack against the U.S. This prospect is one reason why CBD would be likely to increase the danger of nuclear destruction for the U.S., increasing the existing risks of a nuclear disaster for the American people. This truly fearful danger in the CBD proposal should be recognized by its supporters.

Sider and Taylor suggest that the Soviet Union would not use nuclear weapons against the U.S. for fear of "increasing the resistance movement."[45] Yet if the Soviet Union used nuclear weapons against the U.S., it could positively ensure there would be no resistance movement. How do noncooperation, mass demonstrations, and handing out leaflets stop nuclear warheads? They do not. Unfortunately the reverse is not true: Enough nuclear warheads would be very effective in stopping noncooperation, mass demonstrations, and the handing out of leaflets, along with any other organized activity in the U.S.

Finally, Sider and Taylor suggest that the Soviet Union would not strike the U.S. because domestic and world public opinion "might be broadly negative" if it did so, and the Soviet Union would look poor "in the eyes of the world."[46] Here again, when no other rationale appears convincing, "world public opinion" is called on to explain why the Soviet Union would behave in a moderate way.

It is difficult to imagine a context wherein world public opinion would be less likely to determine crucial Soviet military and political decisions: The Soviet Union could be involved in a large-scale war with Western Europe and China, terrible levels of destruction would be taking place, perhaps even nuclear destruction from British, French, and Chinese weapons. Even in the context of lesser crises, such as in Afghanistan and the liberalization movements in Eastern Europe, world public opinion has not had a powerful influence on Soviet military actions. As Robert Conquest has observed regarding the Soviet approach to world public opinion, "They are still somewhat sensitive to presenting too repulsive an appearance to international audiences. But when the world is looking the other way (as to some degree in Afghanistan today), or during wartime, or in the turmoil of postwar circumstances . . . complete ruthlessness has been and will be the order of the day."[47] Why would one expect world public opinion to play a determining role in the context of World War III?

The late Professor Hans Morgenthau, world renowned as one of this century's foremost scholars of international politics, noted the tendency, particularly among Americans, to believe that world public opinion would act as a restraining force in international politics. It has continually failed to do so.

> World public opinion becomes the mythical arbiter who can be counted upon to support one's own, as well as everybody else's, aspirations and actions. . . .

> Does such a world public opinion exist at present, and does it exert a restraining influence upon the foreign policies of national governments? The answer is bound to be in the negative. Modern history has not recorded an instance of a government having been deterred from some foreign policy by the spontaneous reaction of a supranational public opinion. . . .

Wherever one probes beneath the surface of popular phraseology, one finds that a world public opinion restraining the foreign policies of national government does not exist.

A world public opinion retaining the international policies of national governments is a mere postulate; the reality of international affairs shows as yet hardly a trace of it.[48]

Basing America's security against nuclear attack on the hope that world public opinion would determine Soviet military actions in a time of acute military crisis, as do Sider and Taylor, should be recognized as extraordinarily dangerous. And the U.S. government would be irresponsible (from a scriptural and strategic perspective) were it to adopt such a policy.

Sider and Taylor present two possible U.S. options under CBD in the event of a Soviet nuclear ultimatum: (1) "strategic surrender" or "apparent capitulation" with continued, but much reduced, levels of noncooperation; and (2) "calling" the Soviet nuclear threat by informing the Soviet leadership that, "You can create scorched earth and dead cities, but you cannot make us give in to tyranny. You can kill the innocent, but their blood will cry out against you. . . ."[49] Sider and Taylor, in effect, present two responses to a Soviet nuclear ultimatum under CBD—surrender, or an invitation for the Soviets to inflict a nuclear strike on America.

Of course, it cannot be assumed that the Soviet Union would give the U.S. an ultimatum and the chance to surrender— the nuclear strike could just come. However, even assuming that the U.S. is given an ultimatum and the prerogative to surrender, neither of the alternatives presented by Sider and Taylor is acceptable from a Christian or a strategic perspective. With regard to surrender and capitulation, individuals can practice pacifism and self-sacrifice, but Scripture tells government that its duties include defense of the innocent, not preemptive surrender. This is a particularly important point when one considers that the Soviet government to which we would surrender is a brutal regime and virtually certain to repress individuals' rights to worship, impart their faith to their children, or share their faith. As to the second alternative of "calling" the Soviet nuclear threat, government is not given the prerogative to abandon its defensive duties and then, in response to subsequent and inevitable threats, declare that its citizens are ready to die. The U.S. government would be in violation of its constitutional and scriptural duties were it to open its doors to an opponent's nuclear wrath, and then actually call that wrath down on U.S. citizens.

Sider and Taylor defend CBD by noting that although it would involve some risk, the alternative of military defense and deterrence also involves risks. CBD and deterrence, however, do not involve equal levels of risk. Whereas deterrence acts to reduce the probability of nuclear attack, CBD would actually increase the likelihood of nuclear holocaust by destroying deterrence. Similarly, CBD could encourage conventional aggression from even moderate-sized military powers (such as Cuba) by making America appear to be easy prey, and then would provide no protection for innocent civilians if invasion came. In contrast, military defense would provide some means by which the U.S. could stop or slow an invasion and protect its innocent civilians, thereby helping to deter such an invasion in the first place. In short, CBD would serve to increase the probability of nuclear attack against the U.S.; and, in contrast to a credible military defense, it would also increase the probability of invasion and then provide no protection if invasion took place. It is difficult to imagine a more unsound and dangerous approach to government policy.

Sider and Taylor finally observe that even in "the worst possible outcome" CBD is preferable to "an American decision to go down the nuclear road that leads to mass murder by the hundreds of millions."[50] They then define "the worst possible outcome" of CBD as Soviet conquest of the U.S. and the world, followed by widespread repression and the disappearance of democracy "for years into the future." This result, they argue, would be preferable to nuclear war, and therefore CBD is seen as the lesser of two risk-laden alternatives.

Whether Soviet global conquest would, in fact, involve fewer casualties and less misery than a nuclear conflict is at least open to question. But, even assuming that to be the case, it must be recognized that CBD does not in any way ensure that nuclear war will not occur. Indeed, by disarming America and destroying the nuclear deterrence balance, CBD increases the prospects for both Soviet conquest *and* nuclear war. CBD would tear down the barriers to this truly "worst possible outcome." For all Sider and Taylor's concern to get away from the nuclear threat, and their ringing proposal of CBD as an alternative to nuclear deterrence and military defense in general, the net result of their proposal would be to increase the risk of nuclear misery and political repression for the U.S. and its allies.

Ironically, CBD suffers from the same flaws as the MAD approach to deterrence. It leaves defenseless millions of innocent civilians and provides no protection in the event of war; in effect, both involve the purposeful absence of protection. An important difference, however, is that CBD does not offer the single redeeming feature of MAD. It does not provide a deterrent to the use of nuclear weapons. Although MAD may be effective as a deterrent, it is unacceptable for the Christian because it envisages the indiscriminate destruction of combatants and noncombatants, providing no protection for either. CBD also leaves innocent civilians exposed to nuclear and conventional attack. It willfully places them in a position of great risk, and provides no basis for deterrence. CBD thus offers the U.S. the worst of both worlds.

SUMMARY AND CONCLUSION

Civilian based defense is proposed by Christian nuclear pacifists as a nonviolent alternative to military defense and nuclear deterrence. CBD involves complete military disarmament, and mass noncooperation and resistance in response to attack. It is preferable, according to its proponents, because it would not involve American use of nuclear or conventional weapons, but could preserve the American way of life if the U.S. were attacked. Consequently, two Christian pacifists, Ronald Sider and Richard Taylor, claim that although CBD entails some risks to the population, the worst possible outcome under CBD (Soviet conquest of the U.S. and its allies and widespread repression) would be preferable to the risks involved in nuclear war.

Upon analysis, however, CBD does not provide anything like a preferable alternative to deterrence and military defense from a Christian or a strategic perspective. Indeed, there is no inconsistency in this case between Christian and strategic considerations. CBD deserves to be condemned from both perspectives for numerous reasons.

Despite the nonviolent orientation of CBD, it could not prevent widespread violence and bloodshed. Those Americans involved in resistance, mass demonstrations, and the handing out of leaflets would become targets of harsh repression. Repression would be particularly hard if the country occupying the U.S. was the Soviet Union. The historical record, including current Soviet actions in Afghanistan, reflect extremely brutal Soviet tactics toward those carrying out "active noncooperation," which is, of course, what Sider and Taylor recommend for virtually the entire American population.

CBD would not hold out any hope for protecting American freedoms and our way of life, which is, according to Sider and Taylor, one of its primary purposes. Under CBD the population would ignore the unjust rules of the occupation force and acknowledge only the laws of the true U.S. government. Yet, if Americans cannot exercise their constitutional rights for fear of arrest, harassment, or execution—which almost certainly would be the case during Soviet occupation—the American way of life would not be protected.

CBD would violate the scriptural mandate that government protect the innocent, maintain justice, and punish evil.

The basis of CBD is to leave the bulk of the population defenseless before the opponent's monopoly of military power, but active in their resistance to Soviet occupation. As a result of CBD, millions of civilians would be targets of repressive violence without the benefit of government protection. CBD would, in effect, violate the just war principle of discrimination between combatants and noncombatants. Indeed, it would purposefully place millions of unprotected civilians in harm's way.

CBD, as discussed by Sider and Taylor, is predicated on the notion that the bulk of the population would be capable of expressing good will and agape love toward those who were inflicting terrible suffering on family and friends. If the population reacted violently and with understandable bitterness, the logic of CBD would collapse. One must wonder whether it is reasonable in this age to assume, as a part of government planning, that the bulk of the population could express good will and agape love to those who would be inflicting such suffering. Can it be assumed as part of official government planning that the vast majority of the population had attained that level of Christian maturity?

CBD fails to provide the one advantage that Sider and Taylor claim makes it far preferable to deterrence: They assert that CBD would virtually preclude the nuclear threat. However, CBD could not in any way prevent a nuclear holocaust. The U.S. and its allies would still be vulnerable to nuclear destruction (and the Soviet Union would still be vulnerable to allied or Chinese nuclear attack). Under CBD there still would exist incentives for Soviet nuclear attack, but the U.S. would have abandoned its deterrent. This is one of CBD's greatest weaknesses—it would abandon our nuclear deterrent without addressing the problem of the nuclear threat. It can scarcely provide an alternative to deterrence since it does not even address the nuclear problem. Sider and Taylor's advice in the event of a Soviet nuclear threat is either U.S. surrender, or a readiness to accept 160 million American casualties. For the U.S. government to adopt such a position would be the height of irresponsibility and in direct violation of its scriptural mandate to protect the innocent.

CBD not only would leave the U.S. open to the nuclear threat, it would almost certainly increase that threat. By destroying the U.S. side of the deterrence balance CBD could serve only to increase the probability of nuclear attack. And, by abandoning all U.S. means for self-defense, CBD would also increase the likelihood of a conventional attack. Ironically, to the extent that CBD would appear to be an effective means of disrupting and absorbing a potential aggressor's conventional forces, it would increase that aggressor's incentives to use nuclear weapons. Consequently, even if CBD would work as described, it would be exceedingly dangerous for the American people.

CBD suffers from the same problems that afflict the unacceptable MAD concept: It willfully exposes to threat those millions of lives the government is charged with protecting. But CBD does not even provide the single benefit of MAD—it provides no deterrent to nuclear attack under any circumstances, and even increases the probability of attack.

In summary, CBD is not an alternative to deterrence. It opens the door to nuclear and conventional attack and invites any would-be aggressor to step through that door. It leaves the U.S. government vulnerable to nuclear coercion, and the American people naked not only to nuclear destruction, but to harsh repression by conventional forces. CBD would be appropriate in a perfect world, but that world does not and will not exist during this age. Governments are meant to protect the innocent in a dangerous world; CBD suggests that government abandon that responsibility. As such, it is not an acceptable alternative to deterrence and military defense.

Chapter 9, Notes

1. Ronald J. Sider and Richard K. Taylor, *Nuclear Holocaust and Christian Hope* (Downers Grove, Ill.: Intervarsity Press, 1982), 259.

2. Ibid., 273-74. See also, Ronald Sider and Richard Taylor, "International Aggression and Nonmilitary Defense," *The Christian Century*, 6-13 July 1983, 643-47.

3. Sider and Taylor, *Nuclear Holocaust*, 261.

4. Ibid., 259-70.

5. Ibid., 262.

6. Ibid., 260.

7. Ibid., 269.

8. Ibid., 275.

9. Ibid., 279.

10. For a discussion of these and other incidents, see James Child, *Nuclear War: The Moral Dimension* (London: Transaction Books, 1986), 41-43.

11. John C. Whitehead, "Afghanistan's Struggle for Freedom," *Department of State Bulletin*, February 1986, 1.

12. Sandy Gall, *Behind Russian Lines* (London: Sidgwich and Jackson, 1983), 92.

13. Zalmay Khalilzad, "Moscow's Afghan War," *Problems of Communism*, January-February 1986, 5.

14. Gall, 74.

15. Mike Martin, *Afghanistan Inside a Rebel Stronghold* (Poole, England: Blandford Press, 1984), 138.

16. C. Malhuret, "The Soviets in Afghanistan: Report from Afghanistan," *Current History*, May 1984, 31.

17. *Situation of Human Rights in Afghanistan*, United Nations Document A/40/843, 5 November 1985, reprinted in Craig Karp, "Afghanistan: Six Years of Soviet Occupation," *Department of State Bulletin*, February 1986, 15.

18. Quoted in Gall, 83.

19. Khalilzad, 1.

20. Reported in *The New York Times*, 10 December 1985.

21. Mulhuret, 31.

22. Paul Trottier, "Soviet Influence on Afghan Youth," *Department of State Bulletin*, March 1986, 47.

23. Khalilzad, 9.

24. Trottier, 46; and John Tagliabue, "Russians Pressing Afghan Campaigns," *The New York Times*, 21 November 1986. See also, James B. Curren and Phillip Karber, "Afghanistan's Ordeal Puts a Region at Risk," *Armed Forces Journal International* (March 1985):97.

25. See for example, Joseph Douglass and Amoretta Hoeber, *Soviet Strategy for Nuclear War* (Stanford, Calif.: Hoover Institution Press, 1979),

22-33; and Robert Conquest and Jon White, *What To Do When the Russians Come* (New York: Stein and Day, 1984).

26. Conquest and White, 36.

27. Douglas and Hoeber, 27.

28. Col. M. Shirokov, "The Question of Influences on the Military and Economic Potential of Warring States," *Voyennaya mysl*, No. 4 (April 1968), FPD 0052/69, trans. 6 April 1970, 39.

29. Sider and Taylor, *Nuclear Holocaust*, 275.

30. M. P. Kim, et. al., *History of the USSR: The Era of Socialism* (Moscow: Progress Publishers, 1982), 264.

31. Alec Nove, *Stalinism and After* (London: George Allena and Unwin, 1975), 42.

32. Robert Conquest, *The Great Terror* (London: Macmillan, 1968), 22-25.

33. Ibid., 37, 41, 48.

34. Ibid., 53.

35. Timothy J. Colton, *Commissars, Commanders, and Civilian Authority: The Structure of Soviet Military Politics* (Cambridge, Mass.: Harvard University Press, 1979), 142.

36. Conquest, *The Great Terror*, 528.

37. Ibid., 23-24.

38. Nove, 54-59.

39. Colton, 142.

40. Conquest, *The Great Terror*, 525-28.

41. Dimitri Simes, "Stalin and His War Against the Peasantry," *The Washington Post, Book World*, 19 October 1986, 3, 14.

42. Adam Ulam, *Stalin: The Man and His Era* (New York: The Viking Press, 1973), 485.

43. Simes, 14.

44. Sider and Taylor, *Nuclear Holocaust*, 286.

45. Ibid., 284.

46. Ibid., 285, 286.

47. Conquest and White, 19.

48. Hans J. Morgenthau, *Politics Among Nations* (New York: Alfred A. Knopf, 1960), 271, 261, 269, 270.

49. Sider and Taylor, *Nuclear Holocaust*, 285, 286.

50. Ibid., 287.

Chapter 10

A Just Defense

*P*receding chapters have examined Christian views concerning nuclear weapons. In many cases those views have been hostile toward deterrence, ranging from grudging and conditional acceptance to outright rejection. Pacifists, nuclear pacifists, and traditional just war theorists have suggested alternatives to deterrence: disarmament, world government, arms control, unilateral disarmament, and civilian based defense (CBD). None of these suggested alternatives is new; each has a history beginning well before the nuclear age as a suggested alternative to international conflict. None of them, however, appears realistic, and pursuit of them in disregard of deterrence requirements would likely be very dangerous for Americans, Russians, Europeans, and perhaps the rest of the world.

Those Christian pacifists and nuclear pacifists who reject deterrence generally have suggested alternatives that would almost certainly increase the risk of a nuclear holocaust. They have been unable to offer alternatives to deterrence that are relevant to the real world of international relations. And in this case, unrealistic proposals can truly be dangerous if they incite opposition toward deterrence based on unobtainable expectations. The consequence of abandoning deterrence before establishing a reliable alternative could be the nuclear holocaust we all want to avoid.

A condition of world peace, justice, and security, without any military expenditures or plans, would be ideal. Unfortunately that option does not present itself in this world. Peace, justice, and security must therefore be protected from those who would violate those conditions. In this regard, deterrence based on restricted capabilities and plans, while far from ideal, does appear to be compatible with Christian just war considerations; and it "works" in the real world.

In contrast, calls for alternatives to deterrence, such as world government and complete nuclear disarmament, ring hollow when given a reality test. No matter how beautifully described, visions of an effective world government or a completely disarmed world cannot answer the question of how the "genius of man" might get us there from where we are now. This is not to say that such a condition will never occur. Rather, it is to note that institutions established by man will continue to fall short of those visions. For the Christian it ought to be important that the prophet Micah tells us when such peace and justice will prevail on earth:

> In the last days
>
> the mountain of the LORD's temple
>   will be established
>   as chief among the mountains;
> it will be raised above the hills,
>   and peoples will stream to it.
>
> Many nations will come and say,
>
> "Come, let us go up to the mountain of the LORD,
>   to the house of the God of Jacob.
> He will teach us his ways,
>   so that we may walk in his paths."
> The law will go out from Zion,
>   the word of the LORD from Jerusalem.

He will judge between many peoples
and will settle disputes for strong nations far and
wide.
They will beat their swords into plowshares
and their spears into pruning hooks.
Nation will not take up sword against nation,
nor will they train for war anymore.

(Micah 4:1-3)

Can we anticipate that mankind itself will establish such a perfect vision of peace and security before "the last days" and by its own power and initiative? It appears that Micah and the "realist" school of international relations agree that the answer is no.

In addition, many, including those accepting the just war tradition, seem to place their hope in arms control.[1] Yet the prospect for negotiations to end the nuclear threat appear almost nonexistent if the U.S. and Soviet Union continue to follow their respective strategic and arms control policies. And even if two leaders could agree to drastic offensive reductions through negotiations, unless those reductions were very deep—bordering on 100 percent—*and could be verified reliably,* they would not end the nuclear threat. A small number of nuclear weapons can cause high levels of destruction to undefended targets, especially cities. And it is likely to become increasingly easier to hide a relatively small number of nuclear weapons as they become smaller and more mobile.

These problems suggest why arms control has not been pursued by the U.S. (or the Soviet Union) as a means of abolishing nuclear arms and transcending deterrence. Rather, the U.S. has pursued strategic arms control as a means of preserving deterrence stability.

For arms control to provide the final answer to the nuclear threat, a combination of extremely deep reductions and reliable and precise verification measures would be necessary. Neither of these conditions appears to be feasible. Even the reported arms control breakthroughs at the Reagan-Gorbachev summit in Reykjavik, Iceland, in the fall of 1986 could not meet these standards necessary for arms control to solve the nuclear threat. The proposals discussed at Reykjavik have been acclaimed as representing the greatest potential breakthrough in arms control history. Yet, even that potentially radical arms control agreement has not been considered a replacement for nuclear deterrence by arms control enthusiasts, but as reinforcement for the stability of deterrence.[2] And it now appears that a comprehensive agreement based on Reykjavik is unacceptable to either side.

Finally, nonviolent noncooperation in the form of CBD does not provide an acceptable alternative to deterrence. Indeed, as described by Ronald Sider and Richard Taylor, CBD would likely increase the risk of nuclear conflict by unilaterally disarming the U.S. and thereby destroying the deterrence balance. The U.S. and its allies would be confronted with no alternatives to Soviet nuclear attack or coercion other than capitulation or holocaust.

Each of the suggested alternatives to deterrence is, at best, a distant prospect, and more likely a romantic dream given the ingredient of mistrust that pervades the international system. This mistrust is based on an enduring feature of international politics: Humans, and therefore leaders of states, cannot always be trusted to act in a cooperative fashion, and often do pursue aggressive, self-interested policies. Additionally, there is no international authority to protect weaker states from the stronger. Recognition of these facts constrains each state severely in the policies it may safely pursue, and ultimately ensures that the suggested alternatives to deterrence will remain visionary.

This is not to say that change in the international system is not possible. But radical change, so as to make disarmament or world government realistic, would require the virtual perfection of mankind—or the intervention into history of a powerful judge to arbitrate all disputes fairly and enforce justice. Suggestions of CBD, nuclear disarmament, and world government are unlikely to become useful policy options until such a time, when, of course, they will be unnecessary altogether.

Are we stuck with deterrence? As discussed in chapter 6, the purpose of deterrence and U.S. strategic forces is to help ensure the avoidance of war, particularly nuclear war and nuclear coercion. And it appears to have worked for four decades. Deterrence provides a vital service that cannot now be filled by any other means; to be without that service while still facing nuclear and conventional force threats would be dangerous indeed. As Professor James Child of Bowling Green University notes in his discussion of deterrence and morality:

> The simple truth is that we don't know what the Soviets would do should we unilaterally disarm. . . . But they surely could make these kinds of threats, and there would be nothing but their own sweet disposition to stop them. . . . There simply is no viable resistance of any kind to a nuclear monopolist equipped as the Soviet Union is. Slavery is slavery, pure and simple! It is sobering at moments like this to reflect that it is only the men and women of the Strategic Air Command and the United States Navy's ballistic missile submarines fleet who stand between us and slavery. . . . The equation is simple: The only deterrence in the nuclear age is nuclear deterrence. Life without a nuclear deterrent on the same planet with a well-armed nuclear monopolist is slavery.[3]

We have concluded that nuclear deterrence can be consistent with Christian just war considerations under specific and strict conditions. Nevertheless, nuclear deterrence and weapons can be accepted only with great reluctance. The existence of thousands of nuclear weapons poses a danger to millions of people, and nuclear deterrence does not itself offer a means for ridding the world of those weapons. Indeed, the continuation of deterrence based on mutual offensive threats implies a continuation of the arms competition and an enduring possibility of nuclear holocaust.

Consequently, there exists a dilemma: The continuation of deterrence does not terminate the possibility of a nuclear holocaust; it is not a complete solution to the nuclear problem, only a "holding action" that may fail one day with terrible consequences. Nevertheless, it at least addresses the problem realistically. Nuclear deterrence provides one benefit—it is the basis for avoiding a nuclear war in a self-serving international arena where at least five nations (and probably more) are nuclear-armed. In a world where complete and reliable nuclear disarmament is not politically feasible, deterrence provides a measure of safety. Deterrence is far from perfect, but the other alternatives discussed so far do not address the problem, are simply irrelevant in the current world, and would make matters even worse than they now are.

This chapter will present an alternative that may not suffer from these problems, yet could satisfy the consciences of those Christians sympathetic to the pacifist and just war traditions, including Christian nuclear pacifists, perhaps even radical Christian pacifists such as Sider and Taylor. We call this proposed alternative to mutual offensive deterrence a *just defense*.

Just Defense as an Alternative to the Current Deterrence Balance

Although deterrence can be considered acceptable under just war considerations, it would be far preferable to preserve security while also removing or greatly reducing the nuclear threat. This is impossible under a deterrence policy of mutual vulnerability, of course, because that approach to deterrence is based on the existence of mutual nuclear threats. A just defense would be intended to end the current condition of mutual vulnerability and thereby provide a means for security other than deterrence.

A just defense would reject the mutual vulnerability approach to deterrence that has so dominated U.S. strategic and arms control policy. Rather than attempting to perpetuate a stable mutual vulnerability, just defense would promote mutual defensive capabilities against nuclear weapons and seek to reduce offensive arsenals through formal or informal arms control agreements. Ultimately, the U.S. and Soviet Union would no longer be capable of threatening one another with strategic nuclear weapons, and their respective defensive systems would provide protection against reduced strategic nuclear threats. The termination of mutual threats under a just defense would not be based on a nuclear disarmament agreement; indeed, mutual trust (that element lacking in international relations) would not be required.

Such a defensive orientation would require a significant change in the current politics of both sides. The Soviet Union would have to give up its "combined arms" approach to damage-limitation. It could no longer rely on an offensive threat against the U.S. to support its goal of damage-limitation; defensive systems would be the order of the day. The U.S. would have to reverse its past preferences for a condition of stable mutual vulnerability and (ironically) adopt the Soviet goal of strategic defense.

In short, a just defense would replace the current offensive-based deterrence concept. It would not rely on mutual offensive threats for security but on mutual defensive capabilities for mutual security. This would be a major change from past U.S. and Soviet practices. In the past such significant U.S. and Soviet policy changes appeared to be almost unthinkable. However, recent technical and policy developments render a defensive-based relationship sufficiently feasible to deserve consideration as a preferred alternative to the current form of deterrence.

Because just defense focuses on mutual defensive capabilities instead of mutual nuclear threats, it would ultimately get the U.S. out of the offensive deterrence business—of threatening nuclear strikes as the route to security. It would also move the U.S. government toward a policy of protecting Americans in the event of war, as opposed to sustaining "stability" on the basis of a mutual hostage relationship.

Consequently, just defense should appeal to those Christians of all perspectives who are rightly concerned about the lives of innocent Americans and Russians in the event of war. It would avoid the entire issue of what conditions might justify a U.S. nuclear strike. The U.S. would no longer be capable, as a result of Soviet defenses, of threatening the Soviet Union with strategic nuclear attack. Similarly, as a result of American defenses, the Soviet Union would no longer be capable of threatening the U.S. with strategic nuclear attack.

Pacifist and just war objectives are supported by the overarching goal and means of just defense: the protection of innocent civilians via defensive capabilities instead of threatening the opponent with military strikes.

A condition of mutual defensive capabilities and a mutual inability to engage in offensive nuclear strikes could reassure those Christian nuclear pacifists who cannot accept any U.S. use of nuclear weapons but are still gravely concerned with the defense of the innocent in the event of war. A just defense should also satisfy those Christian preemptive war advocates who, quite understandably, are concerned about protecting the American people from a Soviet nuclear attack. Yet it does not require the recommendation these preventive war advocates feel compelled to make—to launch a nuclear strike first upon strong evidence that the Soviet Union is about to attack. Just defense would, in short, provide protection for the American innocent under attack and protect Soviet civilians from nuclear retaliation.

A just defense could do what the current offensive-oriented deterrence cannot: It could address the various concerns of Christian pacifists, nuclear pacifists, and just war advocates. For example, a priority pacifist concern is to avoid violent resistance if under attack. A just defense would involve the protection of the American population against those nuclear weapons launched toward the U.S., but it would not involve violence against the aggressors. As such, it could protect the innocent without causing violence against those carrying out the attack. (The sole exception to this could be the crews in

Soviet strategic bombers and submarines attacking the U.S.; they could, indeed, be casualties in U.S. attempts to stop their nuclear arms from striking Americans. Consequently, even a just defense may not completely satisfy a total pacifist.) However, much of the nuclear pacifists' concern would be addressed by a just defense. The U.S. would no longer base its security on offensive nuclear threats and would not be capable of effectively striking the Soviet Union with strategic nuclear arms. Yet, unlike the various alternatives to deterrence suggested by nuclear pacifists, just defense could provide a means of security in the absence of deterrence.

Just Defense and Recent U.S. Policy

Even though strategic defense as an alternative to offensive-based deterrence would be a radical change from past American thinking, U.S. policy is already moving in this direction. A new "Strategic Defense Initiative" has been presented officially as the future direction of U.S. policy. As Caspar Weinberger stated in the 1987 *Report of the Secretary of Defense to the Congress*:

> The President's Strategic Defense Initiative stuns many traditional thinkers who seem incapable of thinking beyond the conventional and accepted wisdom. In fact, strategic defense represents a natural extension, the capstone of an array of changes in our strategic nuclear forces, motivated by the search for a more secure deterrent. It offers a far safer way to keep the peace. . . . We hope that strategic defense will eventually render nuclear missiles obsolete. That is our long-range vision.[4]

This move toward defense capabilities as an alternative to offensive deterrence is most closely associated with the Reagan Administration's Strategic Defense Initiative (SDI). The SDI (or as it has become known in the press, the "Star Wars" program) was announced in a speech to the nation by President Reagan on 23 March 1983. During that televised speech the president asked American scientists to begin a serious investigation of the technical feasibility of strategic defense against nuclear weapons. The president criticized the notion that security is best preserved by deterrence through mutual offensive threats, and suggested a defensive alternative:

> Would it not be better to save lives than to avenge them? Are we not capable of demonstrating our peaceful intentions by applying all our abilities and our ingenuity to achieving a truly lasting stability? I think we are—indeed we must.
>
> After careful consultation with my advisers, including the Joint Chiefs of Staff, I believe there is a way. . . . It is that we embark on a program to counter the awesome Soviet missile threat with measures that are defensive. Let us turn to the very strengths in technology that spawned our great industrial base. . . . I know this is a formidable technical task, one that may not be accomplished before the end of the century. Yet, current technology has attained a level of sophistication where it is reasonable for us to begin this effort.

This speech marked the beginning of a major policy debate in the U.S. As might be guessed, many former government officials and opinion leaders who were the architects of the mutual vulnerability notion of deterrence have been highly critical of a "defensive transition." Professor Thomas Schelling has given the following conclusion to his negative comments regarding SDI:

> Most of what we call civilization depends on reciprocal vulnerability. I am defenseless against almost everybody that I know, and while most of them would have no interest in harming me there must be some that would. I feel safer in an environment of deterrence than I would in an environment of defense.[5]

It may be unsurprising that those former officials considered "fathers" of the mutual vulnerability approach to deterrence and arms control oppose an official move toward a defensive alternative. But the debate following the announcement of SDI has been even more heated than might have been expected. It leads to several important questions for this chapter: What is SDI, and why has the debate been so sharp?

There has been a great deal of misunderstanding about SDI. Much of the commentary following President Reagan's speech implied that the president had called for the immediate deployment of "death rays" in space. But note the primary focus of Reagan's now famous speech:

> I call upon the scientific community in our country, those who gave us nuclear weapons, to turn their great talents now to the cause of mankind and world peace, to give us the means of rendering these nuclear weapons impotent and obsolete.

This focus was repeated during the president's second inaugural address on 21 January 1985, when he said,

> I have approved a research program, to find, if we can, a security shield that will destroy nuclear missiles before they reach their target. It wouldn't militarize space; it would help to demilitarize the arsenals of Earth.

The president called upon the scientific community to examine the feasibility of defenses against nuclear weapons. That may not seem like such a radical idea—poll data suggest that most Americans are unaware that the American homeland is virtually defenseless against nuclear attack. But it should be recalled that for nearly twenty years established wisdom ordained that mutual vulnerability was stabilizing and unavoidable.

As with most challenges to conventional wisdom, the president's speech was met with skepticism and criticism, even ridicule. Much of the initial derogatory labeling of the SDI centered around "Star Wars" and was meant to discredit this program by making it seem fanciful. The label has stuck and may have had some of its intended effect of discouraging public support for the program.[6] Nevertheless, virtually all opinion polls demonstrate that public support for SDI is high. Indeed, self-identified Democrats, Republicans, and independent voters support strategic defense with an equal level of enthusiasm.[7]

In short, what the president called for was a bold new effort by the scientific community to examine the feasibility of using defensive forces to remove the threat of nuclear weapons. The speech noted that such a task would be extremely difficult and could take decades to achieve, but it reflected a basic optimism about the capacity of U.S. science to handle the technological problems.

Following his speech, the president directed two studies to be conducted—one to examine the technology necessary for ballistic missile defense (BMD), the other to assess the strategic and arms control policy implications of BMD. These classified studies were conducted from June through October 1983.

The technology study, called the Defensive Technologies Study, was conducted by more than fifty scientists and engineers, and called on the technical aid of hundreds of individuals from academia and industry. The Defensive Technologies Study team was led by Dr. James Fletcher, then of the University of Pittsburgh and recently appointed the new head of the National Aeronautics and Space Administration (NASA). An assessment of BMD policy implications was conducted under the auspices of the Future Security Studies Study. It was led by Fred Hoffman, director of Pan Heuristics, a research organization based in Los Angeles. The conclusion of the policy study was that strategic defenses—even of modest effectiveness—could help stabilize the U.S.-Soviet relationship.

The conclusions of the Defensive Technologies Study set the basis for the SDI program. The study concluded that "powerful new technologies are becoming available that justify a major technological development effort offering future technological options to implement a defensive strategy."[8] The study team outlined a long-term technology approach for BMD on a scale similar to that of the Apollo lunar landings program. It recommended a long-term research and development plan to evaluate and demonstrate the feasibility of key BMD technologies, The outcome of that research would, in turn, facilitate informed decisions on whether engineering, and later deployment, of effective BMD systems would be feasible. The Defensive Technologies Study Team also concluded that the most effective systems for BMD would use multiple layers, or tiers, and that a strong control management was needed to focus the development of technology for a comprehensive BMD capability.

Following the Defensive Technologies Study Team's recommendation for a strong central management, the U.S. structured a focused research program to pursue the new technologies concepts emphasized in the study. The program established by the Department of Defense continued the work of the technologies and policy studies and combined previously planned defensive research into a single program. On 6 January 1984, the president reportedly signed National Security Decision Directive-119, authorizing a national research program to assess and demonstrate the technological feasibility of intercepting attacking nuclear missiles.

The SDI is, in a sense, "simply" a research and development program. But it includes a long-term goal of protecting the American people from nuclear attack. To note that SDI is now a research program, however, is not to downplay the major change in thinking that the president's 23 March 1983 speech initiated; that speech brought a new official commitment to the concept of strategic defense for the American people. There is virtually no prospect for any defensive systems to be deployed during the Reagan Administration; rather, the Reagan Administration has initiated the coordination and acceleration of research and development on strategic defensive technologies. This will allow a future president and Congress—possibly early in the 1990s—to make a more informed decision concerning the deployment of ballistic missile defense. The SDI research program should help answer such questions as: Are defenses against Soviet ballistic missiles feasible, how effective might they be, and how much might they cost?

Why did President Reagan decide to pose such a direct challenge to conventional wisdom about arms control and strategic relations? It is difficult to piece together the exact sequence of events that led to SDI or to know the true importance played by particular individuals in the president's decision. Nevertheless, it appears that a number of converging influences and factors led to the March 1983 speech.

Although several advisers appear to have played important roles in initiating the SDI proposal, President Reagan was sympathetic to the notion of strategic defense long before the SDI speech. During his bid for the Republican presidential nomination in 1976, candidate Reagan voiced a hope to his military adviser, General Daniel Graham, of finding a way out of the "trap of deterrence based on mutual vulnerability."[9] He likened the U.S.-Soviet strategic relationship to two men aiming cocked pistols at each other—a prelude to catastrophe. During his 1980 presidential campaign, Ronald Reagan commented on a visit to NORAD (the North American attack warning center located inside Cheyenne Mountain near Colorado Springs, Colorado):

> NORAD is an amazing place. . . . They actually are tracking several thousand objects in space, meaning satellites of ours and everyone else's, even down to the point that they are tracking a glove lost by an astronaut that is still circling the earth up there. I think the thing that struck me was the irony that here, with this great technology of ours, we can do all of this yet we cannot stop any of the weapons that are coming at us. I don't think there's been a time in history when there wasn't a defense against some kind of thrust, even back in the old-fashioned days when we had coast artillery that would stop invading ships if they came.[10]

The seeds of SDI clearly existed before Reagan became president. And by the early eighties, events were taking place that would increase the president's appreciation for a dramatic change in strategic policy. First, it had become increasingly clear that the long-term trends in strategic offensive forces were running against the U.S. Further, the public mood seemed to be moving in an increasingly "anti-nuclear" direction. The "nuclear freeze" movement was attracting significant grassroots support. A draft of the American Catholic Bishops' Pastoral Letter on nuclear war criticized U.S. offensive force programs and endorsed a freeze. The arms control negotiations in Geneva did not appear to offer great hope for a serious reversal of these distressing trends, nor did they provide a solution to the "trap of mutual vulnerability." Finally, several advisers and influential scientists suggested to the President that technology had advanced to the point where an effective ballistic missile defense had become a real possibility.

These factors combined to convince Reagan that the strategic dilemma could not be solved by continuing to travel along the same old path. That path—trying to compete with the Soviet Union in offensive arms to maintain the deterrent while attempting to negotiate limits on the same arms—had led only to ever-increasing numbers of nuclear weapons and offered no hope of moving away from the mutual vulnerability trap. But now a potential solution had appeared in the form of new technologies for defending against ballistic missiles—a potential solution to the unfavorable long-term trend in offensive forces, and a potential avenue leading away from mutual vulnerability.

An additional motive for the origin of SDI must be acknowledged. It is clear that the president saw the replacement of mutual vulnerability (and deterrence based on mutual vulnerability) by a defensive-oriented policy as a moral requirement. He indicated a strong preference for a government policy intended actually to defend the American people and their allies, rather than a policy that presented them as hostages for deterrence purposes. When the president announced SDI in his March speech, he asked: "Wouldn't it be better to save lives than to avenge them?" Since that speech, the Reagan Administration has often referred to a defensive policy as a more moral alternative to the existing policy of deterrence through mutual vulnerability.[11] Indeed, official U.S. discussions rapidly came to endorse the notion that the American and Soviet populations should be defended. As President Reagan has said more recently, "Today, the only defensive weapon we have is to threaten that if they kill millions of our people, we will kill millions of theirs. I do not think there is any morality in that at all."[12]

This moral preference for both sides being protected is not some public relations ploy by the U.S. government. It is the basis of the Administration's view concerning a defensive transition. Rather than striving always to maintain a strategic nuclear threat against the Soviet Union, and leaving itself vulnerable to attack as part of the deterrence balance, the U.S. is now considering the actual defense of its population and endorsing Soviet defenses. This amazing redirection of policy thinking is viewed by the U.S. administration as a morally preferable alternative to the current deterrence relationship.

Some SDI Concepts: "Defensive Architectures"

Although it is uncertain what types of future systems might constitute a comprehensive ballistic missile defense system (or "defensive architecture" as it has been discussed by those doing the research), the potential components of a possible nearer-term BMD "architecture" are better known.[13] These could include, for example, three layers of defenses.

The first layer could consist of approximately one hundred satellites armed with numerous small, heat-seeking rockets. These nonnuclear rockets would attack Soviet ICBMs in the "boost phase" of their flight. The boost phase is the first of four distinct phases of a Soviet missile's flight toward the U.S. (See the illustration on the next page for a display of these phases.) During the three-to-five-minute boost phase, the rocket engines burn and "boost" the missile until it leaves the atmosphere. The intense heat produced by the rocket engines during this boost phase provides space-based sensors with a means of detecting the missile launch.

BALLISTIC MISSILE TRAJECTORY PHASES

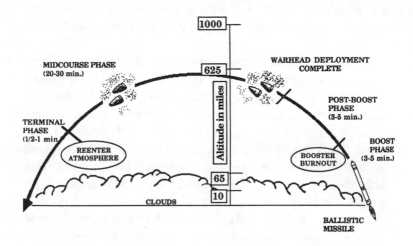

Interception of the missile during its boost phase is important to the effectiveness of a BMD system because the missile would not yet have released its complement of multiple warheads (multiple independently targeted reentry vehicles, known as MIRVs). Consequently, a single intercept could destroy numerous warheads. If the largest ICBM in existence, the Soviet SS-18, could be destroyed during its boost phase, all of its potential twenty to thirty warheads would be neutralized. A capability for boost-phase interception would give defensive interceptors important leverage because a single interceptor could destroy many offensive warheads; in theory it could give BMD a 100-to-1 advantage over the offense.[14]

A second defensive layer could consist of ground-based nonnuclear BMD interceptors. This second layer would be derived from the BMD technology tested successfully by the U.S. Army in June 1984. These nonnuclear "exo-atmospheric" interceptors could be launched from the U.S. and would operate in outer space during the long midcourse of an attacking missile's flight trajectory. Sensors based in space would observe the separation of the multiple warheads from their "bus," and facilitate midcourse interception by ground-based, nonnuclear interceptors. This second layer of defense would further thin-out the attacking force, and reduce the number of offensive weapons against which the next layer of defense would have to contend.

The third layer in this hypothetical BMD system would attack Soviet warheads in their last phase of flight. This is the terminal phase (lasting about one minute) when the warhead reenters and then descends through the atmosphere on the final leg of its ballistic trajectory toward the intended target. Terminal phase BMD would intercept warheads within the atmosphere (that is, it would use "endo-atmospheric" interceptors). This defensive layer could utilize ground-based BMD missiles with nonnuclear homing interceptors.

A more futuristic and effective BMD "architecture" would likely incorporate interceptor systems to attack Soviet ICBMs and warheads throughout their entire flight path. In addition to intercept during the boost, midcourse, and terminal phases, a future BMD system could strike at the "bus" that carries and releases a missile's MIRVs immediately following the boost phase. Interception during this three- to five-minute "postboost" phase of flight could also provide defensive leverage if the defense can destroy the bus before it has released all of its MIRVs. Following the boost and postboost phases, the released warheads travel along the midcourse of their trajectories above the atmosphere. In this midcourse phase the warheads rise over a long arc to an altitude of about a thousand kilometers. The midcourse phase of flight lasts twenty to thirty minutes. Future defenses might have more than one tier of interceptors ready to destroy attacking warheads during the midcourse, given its relatively long duration.

The "exotic" means for intercept in a futuristic BMD might include directed energy weapons (DEW), such as laser or particle beams. DEW components could be space-based, utilizing satellite platforms to strike at Soviet ICBMs as they rise in their boost phase from their launch sites in the Soviet Union. Ground-based (or space-based) lasers could use space-based relay and "battle" mirrors to direct the beam to Soviet boosters. Space-based weapons capable of propelling small homing interceptors at speeds far greater than the 10,000 mph of current rockets might also provide an effective boost, post-boost, and midcourse means of intercept. This would be an "electromagnetic railgun" which would use an intense magnetic field to propel a homing interceptor at the Soviet missile or warhead at speeds greater than 50,000 mph. Railgun tests already have exceeded speeds of 10,000 mph.[15]

Although it is far from clear at this point, given the early stage of SDI research, a highly effective defense probably would include multiple defensive tiers and multiple means of intercept. A defensive architecture for effective BMD might include ground-based interceptors such as the one tested by the U.S. Army in June 1984, ground-and space-based homing rocket interceptors, and space-based particle beams and electromagnetic railguns.

In short, a near-term system could include three layers of nonnuclear homing interceptors—a space-based tier for boost phase intercept and ground-based layers for midcourse and final phase intercept. A more distant comprehensive defense might include several additional tiers of interceptors making use of space-based DEWs and electromagnetic railguns.

There are, of course, uncertainties involved in a number of SDI technical areas. For example, the unclassified summary of the 1983 Defensive Technologies Study noted, "There are several critical technological issues that will probably require research programs of ten to twenty years." These issues include:

- Will it be possible to intercept missiles in their boost and postboost phases?
- Will midcourse discrimination become sufficiently precise to permit useful discrimination between warheads and penetration aids?
- Can defense systems be rendered sufficiently survivable to counter Soviet defense suppression tactics?

- Will defenses be able to achieve a sufficiently favorable cost ratio vis-à-vis Soviet offensive countermeasures?
- Can battle management (i.e., the computer "brains" of the system) be effective, survivable, and capable of rapid response?[16]

Of course, because such technical feasibility questions exist does not in the slightest imply that SDI is a bad idea; SDI is a research and development program specifically to help resolve such important technical questions.

Since SDI research is necessary to determine the technical feasibility of a highly effective BMD system, it is not possible to specify now, other than in a general way, the systems that might be used if a decision were made to deploy such defenses. However, the defensive advantages of multiple types and tiers of BMD suggest that any future BMD system would consist of multiple layers and types of intercept systems.

Of course, to achieve comprehensive protection against nuclear weapons, even a highly effective defense against ballistic missiles would have to be complemented by air defenses against bombers and cruise missiles. The West already has some appropriate air defense systems in production and deployed in Western Europe, and these systems could be modified to provide greater effectiveness against cruise missiles.[17] Additionally, some of the systems useful for BMD would also contribute to the mission of defending against bombers and cruise missiles. Recent policy developments in the U.S.—the Air Defense Initiative (ADI) in particular, intended to address the threat posed by bombers and cruise missiles—indicate that the U.S. recognizes the need for increased air defense as an element in any future comprehensive defensive effort.

In summary, SDI is a program for research and limited development of ballistic missile defense systems. SDI concepts include exotic beams and more conventional rockets for the defensive mission. If SDI actually leads to the deployment of a defensive system, some of its components may be space-based, while others could be ground-based. As yet, it is too early in the program to suggest any firm conclusions. SDI remains a research and development program intended to facilitate an informed decision during the early-to-mid-1990s as to whether the U.S. ought actually to build and deploy an operational BMD "architecture." SDI represents the most serious effort in decades to move beyond deterrence by mutual offensive threats of annihilation. It is not yet clear whether SDI research will lead to effective defenses, but it is the first step in that direction and reflects radical rethinking of official U.S. policy from protection through mutual threats to protection through defense.

The Churches' Response to SDI

It might be assumed that the church would have come out fully in support of SDI. The notion of a movement away from deterrence based on offensive nuclear threats and toward security for both sides through defenses would seem, almost self-evidently, to be the Christian preference. However, there has been a debate among Christians concerning SDI and strategic defense.

For example, a coalition of religious leaders and organizations—the Religious Coalition for a Moral Defense Policy—has been established in support of SDI. This coalition includes, among others, Bill Bright, head of Campus Crusade for Christ, and Ben Armstrong, executive director of the National Religious Broadcasters. The coalition clearly rejects deterrence through mutual vulnerability calling it "militarily questionable and ultimately immoral." They have endorsed SDI as a morally superior alternative and asked Americans "to seek God's intercession, guidance and wisdom" for the cooperative beginning of a transition away from offensive deterrence and toward defensive systems.[18]

In contrast, some Christian denominations and organizations have come out in opposition to SDI. In 1985 the General Assembly of the Disciples of Christ denomination issued a resolution condemning both nuclear deterrence and SDI. In October 1984 the Church of the Brethren—one of the historic "peace" churches—issued a resolution against the SDI research program.[19] Similarly, the 1986 Pastoral Letter of the United Methodist bishops, *In Defense of Creation: The Nuclear Crisis and a Just Peace*, strongly denounces SDI, as does the Episcopalian report on *The Nuclear Dilemma*.

It is easy to understand why Christians would support the goal of moving toward a defensive transition and away from nuclear deterrence threats: It would provide a means of security in the nuclear age without threatening widespread nuclear destruction, and other alternatives to deterrence do not appear possible. A defensive alternative also seems to be far more compatible with traditional Christian just war considerations than any concept of nuclear deterrence. Because SDI is a first step in any future transition, many Christians have come to its support.

It may seem amazing that any Christians would oppose the SDI defensive research program. However, some Christian organizations opposing SDI have presented the following reasons for their opposition: (1) cost; (2) goals and technical feasibility; (3) deterrence stability; (4) arms control; (5) the ABM Treaty; and (6) defense effectiveness. Each of these will be examined in some detail.

SDI Cost

Some churches oppose SDI and the concept of strategic defense because they judge the financial cost of defensive research and a future defensive system to be too high. This charge generally comes from those who have expressed the greatest moral outrage about nuclear weapons and the dangers of deterrence. Yet, now that the U.S. has officially initiated a major research program to assess the prospects for defending against nuclear weapons and transcending deterrence, the charge is, "We are appalled at the probable costs."[20] It is rather curious that those so vocal in their opposition to nuclear weapons and deterrence would be so concerned about financing a potential solution. If SDI demonstrates that a defensive transition is technically feasible and that millions upon millions of lives

(American and Russian) could be protected against the nuclear threat, moving in that direction would seem to be worth a large percentage of our national budget. One must wonder how cheap the potential solution to the nuclear threat must be to be considered "worth it" by these critics.

In fact, the SDI research program amounts to a small percentage of the Department of Defense budget and a far smaller percentage of the entire federal budget. The total budget requests for SDI between 1985 and 1989 was expected to amount to approximately $26 billion. This amount would be for research and development, not deployment of a system. That amount of money is large anyway one looks at it. But even $26 billion should be put into context: That's roughly $5 billion per year over a five-year period, less than two percent of the defense budget at current rates and about one-half of one percent of the federal budget at current rates. Is defensive research, intended to determine the potential for ending or drastically reducing the nuclear threat, not worth that amount?

By way of comparison, in 1984 *alone* Americans privately spent over $53 billion on alcoholic beverages and over $30 billion on tobacco. Such spending, if continued, would add up to over $410 billion over a five-year period. Averaged over a five-year period, the money requested to investigate the capability to defend against nuclear ballistic missiles per year would amount to about one-sixteenth of what Americans spent on tobacco and alcohol in 1984.

Of course, it should be recognized that the Congress has not actually provided the amount of money requested by the president for SDI. Consequently, the $26 billion figure does not reflect actual spending—that will be significantly lower. Indeed, the sums Congress has provided for SDI funding are not much higher than would have likely been spent by the Departments of Defense and Energy in research on defense technologies had the president never initiated SDI.[21]

What SDI has done is to accelerate and organize various existing defensive research projects under one program. It also has provided policy guidance concerning the long-term goals of strategic defense, demonstrating serious interest in using defensive technologies to move away from mutual vulnerability.

Actually deploying effective defensive systems would undoubtedly take many years and require much more than $26 billion. It is virtually impossible to provide an accurate estimate of what such systems might cost because it is not yet clear what their characteristics would be in any detail, or how many of what types of components would be involved.

Nevertheless, it is possible to make some assumptions about the defensive systems and estimate costs from there. Many unofficial cost estimates have been offered for BMD systems. According to some, deployment of a partially effective defense—one that could be available in the 1990s and would intercept 90 percent of attacking Soviet nuclear warheads—would cost about $60 billion; other estimates for a partial system range between $60 and $90 billion. Other estimates for a complete BMD "architecture" using multiple layers and space-based components range from $300 to $750 billion.[22]

Such enormous figures must be put into context to be understood. First, it should be noted that the U.S. has pursued large military spending programs in the past to safeguard peace and security. The U.S. spent well over $1 trillion on strategic nuclear forces over the past thirty years, and over $300 billion on National Guard and Reserve forces alone.[23] Such expenses typically are spread out over many years or decades; expenses that would not be bearable over a short period can be undertaken over a longer period (much like a family purchasing an automobile or a house). And a longer-term perspective certainly applies to any future defensive system, the cost of which might run into the hundreds of billions of dollars. For example, even if the cost of effective defensive systems were as high as suggested by some critics, say $500 billion, that cost averaged over a thirty-year period would represent about 5.5 percent of the defense budget, or under 2 percent of the federal budget at current rates. The United States now spends more than that amount per year on strategic offensive programs to maintain deterrence.

If the systems for effective BMD and air defense appear to be technically feasible (a question that cannot be answered now), then spending a relatively modest percentage of the defense budget for the potential to protect millions of lives does not seem unreasonable. Of course, if one does not consider the current condition of mutual nuclear vulnerability to be serious, then such spending would not seem reasonable. However, it is difficult to consider the nuclear threat with such complacency.

What does seem unreasonable, however, is the position many Christian critics of SDI have taken by expressing great concern about the current nuclear condition and then criticizing as too expensive a responsible attempt to transform that condition.

Defensive Goals and Feasibility

Another reason some church organizations oppose SDI is the supposed official confusion over its technical characteristics and goals. For example, the United Methodist bishops write:

> We observe, first of all, that the moral promise of SDI seems to have shifted from replacing deterrence to "enhancing" deterrence. . . . There have also been confusing and contradictory claims about the kinds of weapons proposed: whether they will actually protect people or only protect missiles; whether they will be non-nuclear or require a nuclear weapon component; whether they will be space-based or ground-based, or both.[24]

Of course, since SDI is a research and limited development program intended to assess the technical prospects for BMD, it is not realistic to expect a blueprint for the system to already exist. As discussed above, SDI, if it progresses, will help determine whether comprehensive BMD is feasible and the characteristics of the most effective systems. Because those characteristics are not yet known is hardly a reason to criticize the research or the defensive goal; if our knowledge of defensive systems was already so mature there would be no reason for an SDI research program.

As to the charge that there is confusion regarding the objectives of SDI, the bishops quoted above simply are mistaken. There is no confusion as to the goals of SDI. It is precisely the purpose of SDI to help determine, through a research and limited development program, the technical potential for BMD; that has been and remains its purpose.[25]

The charge that the goals of possible future BMD deployment have somehow shifted from protecting people to protecting missiles is similarly mistaken. It is quite true that many proponents of strategic defense and SDI have proposed using BMD in the near-term to lower the vulnerability of U.S. strategic forces to a first strike, and thereby enhance the stability of deterrence. One reason for such a view is that proponents (and critics) of SDI believe that current BMD technology could provide a limited defense for limited objectives, such as protecting U.S. strategic forces. That much appears now to be technically feasible.[26] Consequently, there is interest among many SDI supporters to go ahead and deploy the type of defense that is feasible.

However, the long-term goal of U.S. strategic defense policy is not confined to limited defenses to enhance the current deterrence balance. If U.S. defensive objectives were limited to protecting U.S. strategic forces, then they would indeed represent only a reinforcement of the current deterrence relationship (which, of course, could be valuable in itself). Yet the Reagan Administration has been clear that its long-term goal is to provide protection for the American people and their allies against nuclear-armed ballistic missiles. There is no ambiguity concerning that goal or why the Administration wants to move in that direction, if it is technically feasible. As Secretary Weinberger has stated,

> Deterrence must some day rest on the protection of our population and that of our allies. . . . To give up this hope, to give in to those who would merely

extend deterrence through retaliation into the next century by protecting only military assets, would in no way satisfy the moral and security obligations we have to our citizens.

. . . We have no defense, and to embrace a policy that pledges never to provide such a defense would be unconscionable.

. . . The goal of SDI must be to discover a thoroughly reliable defense for our country and our allies. Anything short of that would simply serve to continue the current mutual suicide pact.[27]

As discussed above, many questions remain concerning the technical feasibility of such a difficult task. This issue of technical feasibility is another criticism leveled at SDI by some churches. For example, the "Committee of Inquiry on the Nuclear Issue" for the Episcopal Diocese of Washington, D.C. stated that it is technically impossible to provide effective defenses for people. Despite their clear lack of technical expertise and the inability of any human to predict now what will or will not be technically feasible twenty to thirty years from now, the Episcopal Committee states:

We concluded, therefore, that there is no possibility of building an effective full-scale defense system (an "Astrodome" defense in the current jargon) that has any prospect of protecting people and cities. . . .[28]

Although such criticism reflects a curious certainty about the future of technology, some technical analyses do indeed support such a judgment.[29] In April 1984 a paper prepared by Dr. Ashton Carter for the Office of Technology Assessment concluded with the following "principal judgment":

The prospect that emerging "Star Wars" technologies, when further developed, will provide a perfect or near-perfect defense system . . . is so

remote that it should not serve as the basis of public
expectation or national policy about ballistic missile
defense (BMD).[30]

And in a paper for the Johns Hopkins School of Advanced
International Studies, former Secretary of Defense Harold
Brown stated, "Technology does not offer even a reasonable
prospect of a successful population defense."[31]

On the other hand, a number of other highly credible
scientists have been much more optimistic. In 1983 the Defensive Technologies Study Team consulted with hundreds of technical experts, and following 100,000 man-hours of study,
reached an optimistic conclusion regarding the potential for
effective defense. The head of the study, Dr. James Fletcher
of NASA, described the team's conclusions:

> Although enormous hurdles remain; the technologi-
> cal advances of the past two decades show great
> promise for ballistic missile defense. . . . In the
> Defense Technologies Study, we took an optimistic
> view of the emerging technologies and concluded
> that "a robust, multi-tiered ballistic missile [defense]
> system can eventually be made to work."[32]

Dr. Fletcher's own conclusions are optimistic about BMD technology:

> A complete four-phase system . . . has the potential
> for protecting nearly all the population—perhaps
> even greater than 99 percent, in my opinion—against
> massive nuclear attacks.[33]

Similarly, Professor Robert Jastrow, founder of NASA's
Institute for Space Studies, has testified before the Senate that
the U.S. could have a two-layered BMD system for about $60
billion by the early 1990s, and that a conservative estimate of
such a system would place its effectiveness against Soviet
ballistic missile attack at 90 percent.[34]

Given this debate within the scientific community concerning whether or not the potential exists for an effective and

comprehensive BMD system, it is reasonable to be cautious in anticipating what technology can achieve. However, one also should be reluctant to accept the judgment, even from experts, that a particular technological task is impossible, particularly in reference to a decades-long project such as building a comprehensive defense system. Expert opinion in the past concerning the impossible can be quite humorous. Several examples are instructive:[35]

> Rail travel at high speed is not possible because passengers, unable to breathe, would die of asphyxia.
>
> *Dr. Dionysus Lardner (1793-1859),*
> *professor of natural philosophy and*
> *astronomy at University College, London*

> Heavier-than-air flying machines are impossible.
>
> *Lord Kelvin, British mathematician,*
> *physicist, and president of the*
> *British Royal Society, c. 1895*

> I can accept the theory of relativity as little as I can accept the existence of atoms and other such dogmas.
>
> *Ernst Mach, professor of physics,*
> *University of Vienna, 1913*

> This is the biggest fool thing we have ever done. . . . The bomb will never go off, and I speak as an expert in explosives.
>
> *Admiral William Leahy, advising*
> *President Truman on the impracticality*
> *of the atomic bomb, 1945*

Although the scientific opinion that receives most of the media attention is critical of SDI and strategic defense, there are many highly respected scientists who are enthusiastic about it. In May 1986 a new organization of such scientists, the Science and Engineering Committee for a Secure World, announced its establishment at a press conference in Washington,

D.C. The Committee is chaired by Dr. Fred Seitz, former president of the National Academy of Sciences and president emeritus of Rockefeller University. It includes such prestigious members as Dr. Hans Mark, chancellor of the University of Texas system, Nobel Prize-winning physicist Dr. Eugene Wigner of Princeton University, and Dr. Harold Agnew, former director of the Los Alamos National Laboratory. At the press conference, Dr. Martin Hoffert, chairman of the Department of Applied Science at New York University, presented the Committee's policy statement. Part of that statement is presented below:

> At the present the American people, by past government policy and to some extent by previous limitations of science and technology, have essentially no defense whatsoever against a nuclear attack. . . . The genius of American scientific and engineering professionals, however well-meaning, helped create this world of nuclear terror. But today scientists and engineers from America and around the world have the opportunity to play a positive and critically important part in reducing and perhaps eventually eliminating the threat of nuclear war by means of America's Strategic Defense Initiative program. . . . New technological breakthroughs have significantly increased the prospect that the U.S. can successfully devise effective systems which will destroy attacking Soviet nuclear missiles long before they can come close to their targets in America, Europe or elsewhere. . . . The Strategic Defense Initiative (SDI) undertaken by President Reagan and the Congress seeks to utilize such new technological means to turn America's strategic military policy away from the unreliable, outdated MAD doctrine and its death-dealing nuclear missiles, to a Mutually Assured Survival policy based on new, life-protecting defensive systems. . . . For the above reasons, therefore, it is our judgment that the Strategic Defense Initiative

program is worth pursuing and deserves the full support of the scientific community, Congress, and the American people.[36]

Of course, one ought not rush to endorse every new claim for technically exotic BMD systems. However, there surely is some basis, given historical precedent, to be skeptical of those who stamp "impossible" on what future technology might achieve. We are not talking here of changing the nature of man or international relations, such as would be required for nuclear disarmament or a benign world government. These are questions of defensive technology that may be solved by technological progress.

Although there is presently no consensus concerning the future potential for BMD, this is not a conclusive indictment against SDI. The purpose of SDI is to help determine the technical potential for comprehensive strategic defense. A negative conclusion, such as has already been pronounced by some Christians, ought not to be rendered until the necessary research and development program provides a better basis for conclusions. That is a primary purpose of SDI.

Dr. Fletcher put the technical critique of SDI in the proper perspective when he observed,

> There are many uncertainties as the United States embarks on its strategic defense effort. We could not now with confidence construct effective ballistic missile defenses. Conversely, we have not been presented with any compelling technical means that show that such defenses are not possible. The technical issues surrounding the development of effective defenses have many possible solutions and should not at this stage be the primary focus of the debate.[37]

Deterrence Stability, SDI, and Strategic Defense
    Another criticism of SDI and strategic defense coming from some churches is that it would destabilize the current

deterrence balance. As the Episcopal report observes, "This is, in fact, the most dangerous implication of the SDI; it strikes at the core of the stability of the strategic balance."[38] Of course, if SDI leads to the deployment of defensive systems, it would challenge the core of the current deterrence relationship precisely because that core is based on mutual vulnerability to nuclear weapons. The primary goal of such defenses would be to change that condition of mutual vulnerability.

Interestingly, the Episcopal report argues in support of the *mutual vulnerability* of cities as the basis of deterrence stability:

> Thus, mutual vulnerability breeds prudence, restraint, caution. It deters not all troubling actions, but aggressive actions that threaten those things which both sides hold most dear. . . . A small retaliatory capability able to destroy Soviet cities, thereby deterring the outbreak of nuclear war—has intrinsic logic.[39]

Of course, mutual vulnerability means not only that Soviet cities would be vulnerable to "small" nuclear strikes, but that American cities would be similarly vulnerable. Ironically the Episcopal report, which expresses such concern about nuclear weapons, criticizes SDI because it might help alter the condition of mutual vulnerability. It actually appears to argue for the targeting of Soviet and American cities and against efforts to alter the vulnerability of those cities. It is not surprising then that this report would find fault with SDI.

If one's assumption is that mutual vulnerability is a beneficial and necessary precondition for stability, as appears to be the assumption of the Episcopal report, then SDI must appear destabilizing. However, history suggests that mutual vulnerability is not a requirement for stability. During much of the early nuclear age the U.S. was relatively invulnerable to a Soviet nuclear strike, yet the situation appears to have been quite stable.

In addition, it is important to consider the Soviet position regarding defense and stability. After all, as discussed in chapter

2, deterrence stability is, to a large extent, in the eye of the beholder. And in this case it is the view of Soviet leaders that is important. Does the Soviet Union consider strategic defense to be destabilizing?

If we judge the Soviet view by recent Soviet statements about SDI, then we must reach the conclusion that Soviet leaders *do* believe U.S. strategic defenses to be destabilizing. However, the recent Soviet statements against strategic defense are quite different from earlier statements. For example, Major General N. Talensky, who held important positions on the Soviet General Staff and later served as the arms control and disarmament liaison between the Soviet Ministry of Defense and the Soviet Academy of Sciences, made the following statement about strategic defenses:

> The danger of nuclear attack continues to threaten humanity, and this makes Governments look for sufficiently effective ways and means of decisively reducing the danger of nuclear rocket attack and if possible to neutralize it altogether.

> Thus, anti-missile systems are defensive weapons in the full sense of the word: by their technical nature they go into action only when rockets of the attacking side take to their flight paths, that is, when the act of aggression has been started. . . .

> It is quite illogical to demand abstention from creating such weapons in the face of vast stockpiles of highly powerful means of attack on the other side. Only the side which intends to use its means of attack for aggressive purposes can wish to slow down the creation and improvement of anti-missile defense systems. For the peace-loving states, anti-missile systems are only a means of building up their security.[40]

Premier Aleksei Kosygin made similarly favorable comments about the role of strategic defense:

Which weapons should be regarded as a tension factor—offensive or defensive? I think that a defensive system which prevents attack is not a cause of the arms race but represents a factor preventing the death of people. . . . An anti-missile system may cost more than an offensive one, but it is intended not for killing people but for saving human lives.[41]

It is most important to examine what the Soviet Union does in the area of strategic defense, not just the negative comments coming from Soviet leaders since SDI was announced. Soviet leaders have purposely misled the West concerning their real views about military matters in the past. Indeed, entire bureaucracies in the Soviet government and military have the formal responsibility of misleading and misinforming the West on military and political issues.[42] Consequently, it is important to test what they say against real world experience.

If Soviet actions with regard to their defense programs are taken into account, it is clear that Soviet leaders are much less opposed to strategic defense than their recent statements would indicate. Indeed, Soviet strategic defensive programs are of such scope and cost, that it hardly appears likely that Soviet leaders could genuinely consider defenses as anything but an essential military capability.

Soviet spending for strategic defense in general is approximately ten times greater than what the U.S. spends.[43] Specifically, over the last ten years the Soviet Union has spent almost $150 billion on strategic defense—nearly fifteen times more than the United States has spent.[44] And Soviet spending in the area of laser defense is three to five times what the U.S. spends.[45] Indeed, over the past decade the Soviet Union has spent more on strategic defense than the U.S. has on strategic offense,[46] and all the while the U.S. allowed most of its strategic defenses to dwindle to virtual nonexistence.

What this means in real terms is that Soviet strategic defense programs far outstrip U.S. defensive programs. This is not an attempt to paint a fictitious Soviet menace. It simply is the case that Soviet programs for strategic defense, from civil defense to ballistic missile defense, far surpass those of the U.S.

For example, Soviet air defenses (intended to intercept bombers and cruise missiles) include approximately 10,000 surface-to-air missiles, over 2,000 interceptor aircraft, and about 6,000 air defense radars. Comparable U.S. figures are: zero surface-to-air missiles; fewer than 300 interceptor aircraft; and about 100 air defense radars. The Soviet BMD site—the only operational one in the world—has recently been increased to include one hundred interceptors, and Soviet civil defense spending has run about $3 to $4 billion per year. In contrast the U.S. deactivated its single BMD site in 1975, and spends about $150 million per year for civil defense.[47]

Finally, Soviet research and development of exotic BMD systems has been on-going for decades in some cases. Soviet laser weapon programs date back to the mid-sixties and are much larger than the U.S. effort;[48] and since the early seventies the Soviet Union has had a research program to explore the feasibility of placing particle beam weapons in space. Soviet programs to develop directed energy weapons for strategic defense—including BMD, antibomber, and antisatellite weapons— have been in the past and will continue to be pursued vigorously. U.S. programs for directed energy weapons are much smaller and may trail the Soviet Union by years.[49] The Soviet laser program alone, if replicated in the U.S., would cost approximately $1 billion per year.[50] In short, Soviet programs for strategic defense are extensive and have been much more serious than U.S. programs for years.

The Soviet Union pursues strategic defense very seriously. Consequently, there is no indication in their behavior that Soviet leaders genuinely believe strategic defenses to be destabilizing; rather, they give every appearance of believing strategic defense to be an inherently reasonable objective. Actual Soviet programs betray no change in the historic Soviet view that strategic defenses are desireable—a view often expressed by Soviet leaders prior to SDI. For example, at the Glassboro Summit in 1967, Soviet Premier Aleksei Kosygin told President Johnson "that the idea of not engaging in defense was one of the most ridiculous propositions that he had ever heard."[51] Of course, Soviet leaders now criticize the new U.S. defensive program; but there is no reason to accept the position, in effect, that Soviet defenses are acceptable but the recent U.S. defensive effort is destabilizing.

The United Methodist bishops also reject SDI on stability grounds and offer a commonly cited view as to why they believe that BMD deployment could be destabilizing.[52] They suggest that a combination of U.S. offensive and defensive capabilities might cause the Soviets to fear that the U.S. was preparing to launch a first strike and then hide behind its limited defenses. In such a condition, Soviet leaders would be tempted to preempt the expected U.S. first strike by striking first themselves. Consequently, initial defenses would be destabilizing. This argument appears on the surface to be logical, but deeper examination reveals its flaws.

If both sides have moderately effective offensive and defensive capabilities, neither could count on striking first and then surviving the other's certain retaliation. Even moderately effective defenses could easily protect many U.S. (or Soviet) offensive strategic forces from a first strike, and thus permit retaliation. The essential point the "instability argument" does not acknowledge is that the Soviet Union could hardly feel compelled to strike first, as this argument posits, when U.S. strategic retaliatory forces would be well defended. In the event of a Soviet first strike, those defended U.S. nuclear forces would retaliate; the Soviet Union would be committing suicide by striking first. Assuming that Soviet defenses are no more effective than U.S. defenses, Soviet leaders certainly could not count on striking the U.S. first and then defending themselves effectively—particularly when military planners use conservative assumptions in their planning (i.e., Soviet leaders would underrate their own defenses and overrate U.S. offensive capabilities). Suggesting that such a situation would lead to a Soviet first strike is to suggest that the Soviet Union would commit suicide for fear of death.

If one assumes that Soviet leaders would be willing to commit national suicide, then the current situation must be considered terribly unstable—either side could strike first *now* and ensure its own destruction; adding limited defenses to the deterrence balance would not change that situation. Indeed, limited defenses could stabilize that balance by protecting retaliatory capabilities from first-strike threats, and thereby add to the deterrence of any first-strike considerations. Thus, it is not at all clear why the Soviet Union would have significantly greater incentives to strike first in the context of mixed offenses and limited defenses than it has now. Indeed, the incentives would appear to work in the opposite direction—even limited defenses should be stabilizing.

More distant prospects for strategic defenses also should not cause instability. If both sides were well defended, as fits SDI's long-term goal, the incentives to strike first would be greatly reduced. Highly effective defenses would simply act to disarm the attacking side, while the defender would retain whatever retaliatory capability it possessed. Assuming both sides are well defended, the value of strategic offensive forces is greatly reduced as there would be little sense in striking first or second. That would be a highly stable condition.

There may be a more serious potential for instability generally not discussed by the critics of SDI. The Soviet Union already has BMD radars, launchers, and interceptors operational and in production, and functioning models of ground-based laser BMD systems may be available within the decade. While the United States may be ahead of the Soviet Union in some areas of high technology that could be applied to future BMD systems, the Soviet Union is, without doubt, far ahead of the United States in its capability to deploy a near-term (within ten years), operational, nationwide BMD system. If this near-term BMD deployment potential were combined with *existing* Soviet air defense and civil defense programs, the Soviet Union could have formidable deployed defenses in advance of a comparable U.S. capability. A potential danger of instability stems from the fact that the Soviet Union could hit the ground running with its existing strategic defense programs, and the U.S. could not.

This Soviet defensive advantage could be highly

destabilizing. This point often is misstated as a suggestion that a U.S. BMD would be stabilizing while a Soviet BMD would be destabilizing. The point rather is that a unilateral Soviet capability for strategic defense would be destabilizing. It could reduce Soviet concern for the U.S. nuclear deterrent without the compensating factor of U.S. and NATO defenses. Unilateral Soviet strategic defense, including BMD, could indeed make the world safer, from the Soviet perspective, for war. The Soviet Union might not choose to exploit this advantage militarily or politically, but the fact of its availability could prove highly destabilizing.

In addition, the United States cannot determine whether or not the Soviet Union will deploy nationwide defenses. It simply is mistaken to assume that the Soviet Union will deploy nationwide BMD only if the United States moves in that direction first. The Soviet Union may well add to its existing BMD system regardless of U.S. actions concerning SDI and BMD. After all, the Soviet Union began deploying its BMD system when the United States had none, and it continues to operate and modernize the world's only BMD system despite the fact that the United States deactivated its only operational BMD site in 1975. To oppose SDI and any future American BMD deployment on the premise that the Soviet Union would expand its BMD system only in response to U.S. deployment is erroneous and inconsistent with historical precedent.

Nevertheless, if the United States does decide to deploy BMD, the Soviet Union almost certainly will expand its current system. Such Soviet BMD deployment could have destabilizing consequences given their early advantage in BMD and other forms of strategic defense. Two potential solutions to the problem spring to mind. First, if the United States and Soviet Union could achieve even a modest arms control agreement limiting offensive capabilities and regulating BMD deployment, the probability of a destabilizing unilateral advantage would be reduced. A second possible solution would be for the United States to maintain a limited strategic offensive capability for a short time until U.S. defensive programs could achieve sufficient effectiveness to counter the likely initial Soviet defensive advantage. In effect, U.S. offensive forces would have to counter Soviet defense advantages until U.S. defenses could catch up.

The issue of stability and defensive systems is quite complex, and this discussion considers only three of several potential conditions: limited offensive and defensive capabilities (as posited in the Episcopal report); mutual highly effective defenses; and a Soviet defensive advantage. Much speculation about the prospects for stability and instability is possible, but strategic defenses ought not automatically be considered destabilizing simply because they would reduce or eliminate mutual vulnerability.

Simply because the U.S. has followed a policy of deterrence through mutual vulnerability for many years does not mean that deterrence stability *requires* mutual vulnerability, as some Christian critics of SDI appear to believe. Defenses may, in the future, alter the current condition of mutual vulnerability, and we know historically that there are stable defensive conditions.

There are more and less dangerous ways to pursue stability. Unless one believes that deterrence can function perfectly forever, basing stability on the mutual vulnerability to nuclear attack should be seen as extraordinarily dangerous; if it ever fails, we will have ensured, by our own policy, the greatest holocaust possible. That is the basic problem with stability based on MAD. Ironically, it is this approach to stability that is endorsed by some Christian groups most vocal about the nuclear threat.

Perhaps the best reason for proceeding with SDI is directly related to the issue of stability. As discussed in chapter 6, there is no reliable data on which to base confident predictions of what may or may not cause a strategic nuclear war; because we can never be sure we will always be able to deter a nuclear war, we ought to plan to minimize its death and destruction. This is not an expression of support for "war fighting" as opposed to deterrence; it is recognition that we may not know how to avoid nuclear war and therefore should plan to protect innocent lives if it is thrust upon us. SDI should help us to determine whether and to what extent BMD could contribute to such protection.

Arms Control

The U.S. has already officially presented one means of alleviating any instability that might be associated with the deployment of defenses: to pursue deep reductions in offensive forces prior to and in conjunction with the deployment of defensive systems. This is the basic thrust of the so-called "cooperative" defense transition proposed by the U.S. If both sides have greatly reduced offensive forces but capable defensive systems, the fears of a first strike should be virtually nonexistent because there would be no incentives or capabilities for a first strike.

Under the notion of a "cooperative defense transition" the U.S. has developed an arms control position far different from those of the past; it now pursues deep offensive reductions while opening the possibility for future defenses. In the past, mutual vulnerability was the guide for U.S. arms control policy. Now mutual defensive capabilities and offensive reductions appear to be the goal. Such a condition should be highly stable; but if deterrence ever failed, defenses would prevent the terrible destruction that is now certain.

However, some Christian groups oppose SDI and strategic defenses because they believe that strategic defense and arms control are incompatible. Both the United Methodist bishops' pastoral letter and the Episcopal report claim that SDI will prohibit success in offensive arms control.[53] And the Episcopal report goes on to claim that offensive arms reductions depend on first limiting strategic defenses.[54] This view was, of course, the official perspective of the U.S. during the SALT negotiations: The U.S. expected offensive reductions to follow from the ABM Treaty, and has been sorely disappointed since. As discussed above, the history of SALT has clearly demonstrated that limiting defensive systems has not established the basis for reducing offensive arms.

In contrast to earlier assumptions concerning BMD and arms control, it is quite possible that the deployment of strategic defenses will provide the basis for success in offensive arms control that has eluded us for almost two decades. Indeed, as is discussed below, the deployment of defenses could be a necessary precondition for real offensive arms control.

It was once accepted wisdom within the community of strategic experts to claim, as some Christians still do, that arms control and strategic defense are incompatible. Yet history now calls that view into question. SDI already has contributed to progress in the arms control process. The Soviet Union walked out of negotiations in November 1983, yet over a year later it returned to negotiations for the self-expressed purpose of halting the American SDI. At the very least, SDI persuaded the Soviets to abandon their ongoing boycott of negotiations.

In addition, there is little doubt that the new Soviet arms control proposals presented since their return to negotiations reach further than any serious Soviet proposals of the past. These proposals have one common bargaining point: The Soviet Union is now willing to give up some offensive forces in return for the U.S. abandonment of its SDI program. SDI has already acted as a catalyst for progress in arms control negotiations—we are now talking about real reductions instead of simply codifying planned increases.

In principle, reductions in offensive forces and the deployment of BMD could go hand in hand in support of arms control objectives. This would be a complete reversal of the U.S. approach to arms control established at SALT (i.e., strict BMD limits and relatively loose constraints on offensive forces). But in terms of freezing or reducing the number of strategic nuclear weapons, or reducing the destruction in the event of war, the traditional approach to arms control still advocated by some Christian groups as the alternative to deterrence has shown less than stellar success. From the time of SALT I until the Soviets walked out of negotiations in 1983, the Soviet strategic nuclear arsenal grew from 1,716 weapons to 8,377; the U.S. arsenal grew from 1,874 to 7,292.[55]

A new approach to arms control that reverses the traditional pattern of ineffective constraints on the offense and strict limits on defenses could be a more effective means of pursuing the objectives of arms control. And this admittedly new approach to arms control could give real significance to modest offensive limitations that otherwise would have little meaning.

Limits on offensive forces would reduce the burden on the defense and thereby make Soviet and U.S. BMD systems more effective. In general, the fewer the number of offensive objects the defense must try to identify and intercept, the more effective the defense. Consequently, even the type of modest arms control agreements that have proved possible so far could facilitate the effectiveness of the defense.

Why is arms control, by itself, unlikely to make a significant difference in the nuclear threat? In America's current condition of total defenselessness to attack, and given the high numbers of strategic nuclear weapons available to both sides (approximately ten thousand for each), even a 75 percent reduction in the number of weapons would not necessarily reduce the vulnerability of the American population in the absence of defensive systems. But more modest (and realistic) offensive limitations could be extremely useful if assented to as part of an arms control agreement that permitted or encouraged defenses. Indeed, an offensive arms control agreement that did not achieve reductions, but only placed ceilings on existing offensive capabilities, could facilitate the effective functioning of the defense. A nuclear freeze that would not be of benefit if mutual vulnerability is perpetuated as policy could take on great value as part of a defensive transition.

In short, the history of the traditional approach to arms control does not offer hope that it can actually reduce the vulnerability of the United States to nuclear attack. Similarly, the traditional approach has not proved stabilizing in placing effective constraints on counterforce weapons; under SALT the number of Soviet counterforce ballistic missile weapons grew from about three hundred to well over five thousand. A defense-oriented approach to arms control should offer more hope. The Soviet drive for a combined arms (offense and defense) damage-limitation potential and the U.S. drive to maintain a nuclear deterrent leaves little scope for offensive reductions under the traditional approach to arms control. Each side, in effect, is driven to deploy forces to deny the other its goal. However, in the context of a defensive transition, mutual offensive limitations would serve U.S. *and* Soviet self-interests because they would facilitate the effectiveness of U.S. and Soviet strategic defenses. Both U.S. and Soviet self-interest could therefore be served by accepting mutual offensive force constraints and moving toward a much greater emphasis on strategic defense. If compelled to make a choice between mutually devastating offensive threats or reliable damage-limitation through the combination of strategic defense and arms control, the latter should be much more attractive. This assumes only that if the choice must be made both the United States and the Soviet Union will be more interested in limiting damage to themselves than in inflicting damage on each other. Nothing in Soviet or U.S. strategy suggests otherwise.

To persuade the Soviet Union to agree to serious offensive arms control and to move more toward strategic defense, it is unnecessary to convince Soviet leaders that a damage-limitation capability is a priority goal; they have believed that for years. Rather, the U.S. must demonstrate that damage-limitation is best achieved when offensive forces are constrained and BMD deployed. This new strategy for arms control would not require the Soviet Union to give up its damage-limitation objective. As the SALT experience has demonstrated, the Soviet Union is unwilling to accept significant reductions in its counterforce offensive weapons—those forces now most important to the Soviet damage-limitation goal—in deference to the mutual vulnerability approach to arms control and deterrence. Such an expectation has been, and almost certainly will remain, without promise.

The approach to arms control suggested above is, in principle, far superior to the mutual vulnerability approach of the past. If implemented, it would lead to a more defense-oriented environment and to a U.S.-Soviet strategic relationship wherein both sides could feel more secure because the prospect of a nuclear holocaust would have abated. A new framework for arms control that endorses rather than prohibits defenses and reduces offensive forces would have several advantages over the current offense oriented framework:

1. The U.S. and Soviet Union would, for the first time, have compatible self-interest in the negotiated limitation of counterforce offensive capabilities; both could more easily achieve their respective damage-limitation objectives with the benefit of mutual offensive limitations.

2. The Soviet Union would not be required to give up its priority objective of damage-limitation as a prelude to achieving deep offensive reductions; consequently, such reductions would become possible.

3. The negotiated phasing down of offensive forces as a complement to the negotiated phased deployment of defensive systems would allay fears that strategic defenses could lead to strategic superiority for either side.

There is an additional and very important reason why the deployment of defenses will be essential to successful offensive reductions. As discussed in chapter 8, a fundamental problem of pursuing only deep offensive force reductions is that even modest levels of cheating could undermine their value. Indeed, an agreement to eliminate all strategic nuclear weapons could be rendered meaningless by the covert retention of even a few hundred missiles. And the Soviet Union does not have a good track record when it comes to treaty compliance. Consequently, the verification requirements for deep offensive reductions are severe, yet such monitoring precision is virtually impossible.

This is a particularly critical problem from the U.S. perspective, but Soviet leaders have also acknowledged it. Neither trusts the other enough to draw down their strategic arsenals drastically without some form of "insurance." And, of course, if that much trust did exist, we would no longer need agreements to feel secure.

The deployment of even modest strategic defenses could provide the insurance necessary to permit deep offensive reductions. Despite the existing questions about the feasibility of defenses against a large and growing Soviet nuclear arsenal, it is clear that defenses could be effective against a relatively small number of covert forces that might be the result of cheating. Strategic defenses could, in effect, render such cheating meaningless and therefore of much less concern. Without this defensive insurance against possible cheating, it is extremely difficult to imagine how the U.S. could agree to deep offensive reductions.

This notion of using defenses to solve the verification problem was part of the U.S. position at the 1986 Reagan-Gorbachev Iceland summit. However, it is not originally an American suggestion. Soviet Premier Andrei Gromyko presented this same concept to the United Nations in 1962.[56]

Rather than inhibiting successful offensive arms control, strategic defense may well be the key to real offensive reductions. It would allow the U.S. and Soviet Union to pursue compatible strategic objectives, and solve the otherwise intractable verification problem associated with deep offensive reductions.

Many who criticize SDI on arms control grounds appear to be conversant with only two concepts about things strategic: (1) mutual vulnerability means stability; and (2) strategic defense is the enemy of stability and arms control because it threatens mutual vulnerability. Unless U.S. strategic thinking can transcend those two pervasive and probably misguided shibboleths, there will be little prospect for serious arms control or strategic defense.

Some members of the arms control and antinuclear community do appear to recognize the compatibility between strategic defense and the objectives of arms control. Jonathan Schell, whose book *The Fate of the Earth* was a catalyst for the antinuclear movement in the early eighties, seems to have recognized this potential benefit of strategic defense:

Building defenses, depending on what else you do, could make it a lot easier to achieve the abolition [of nuclear arms]. I think what arms control people are afraid of is that Star Wars is a shield that will allow Reagan to fight a nuclear war. But what if, while you build up the defenses, you reduce the offenses. . . . Then Star Wars isn't a threat at all. If you're afraid of the sword and the shield, OK. But then you should attack the sword—not the shield.[57]

An ideal strategic defense/arms control solution to the nuclear threat would see the reduction of nuclear offensive capability (down to whatever minimum level would be acceptable to the superpowers) and a corresponding increase in strategic defenses. At a future crossover point, defensive capabilities would surpass those of the offense. This, of course, is an ideal and may not occur even if effective defenses are feasible and deployed—it certainly will not occur in the absence of deployed defenses. The chart below reflects such an ideal process.

AN IDEAL STRATEGIC DEFENSE/ARMS CONTROL SOLUTION TO NUCLEAR WEAPONS

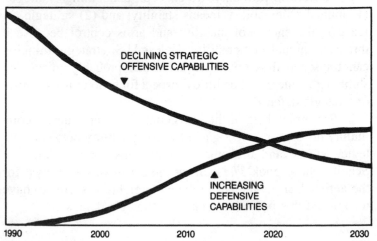

A defensive transition appears to be the only means by which deep offensive reductions can become a reliable avenue to security. And such a transition should, ultimately, appeal to the Soviet Union, which would no longer be asked to abandon its drive for a damage-limitation capability (as was required under the SALT approach); that goal would be affirmed by this approach to arms control. By providing an alternative and nonoffensive means of achieving a damage-limitation capability, defenses could be perceived by both sides as being in their self-interest. Reducing the value of offensive capabilities, particularly counterforce weapons, by rendering them increasingly ineffective should facilitate agreements controlling those weapons. And, of course, controlling offensive weapons would allow both sides' defensive systems to function more effectively.

However, a mutual defensive transition cannot guarantee success in offensive arms control. It logically should provide a more effective basis for offensive reduction, but arms control negotiations are influenced by so many international and domestic political issues that even such logic cannot promise success.

The bottom line of this discussion is that strategic arms control has not been effective under the U.S. "offense-only" approach of the past. There is no reason to believe it will be any more fruitful in the future without a significant change. A defensive transition, providing security through defensive measures instead of through Soviet offensive and defensive preparations or U.S. deterrence preparations, could provide the necessary change.

The ABM Treaty

Some Christian opposition to SDI is based on the view that it threatens the ABM Treaty.[58] However, SDI has been structured to remain consistent with the ABM Treaty. The program is not in violation of any treaty.

Nevertheless, it must be recognized that if SDI demonstrates defense to be affordable and technically feasible, then the U.S. may (one would hope) decide to deploy defensive systems. Any deployment of BMD beyond the token numbers allowed in the ABM Treaty would indeed violate that treaty. There is an inherent inconsistency between remaining within the ABM Treaty and deploying strategic defenses.

However, the ABM Treaty has specific provisions for modification and/or withdrawal (Articles 14 and 15). The U.S. need not violate the ABM Treaty to deploy BMD; it can exercise its rights under the Treaty to attempt modification or ultimately withdrawal. In addition, U.S. Unilateral Statement "A" attached to the Treaty in 1972 states specifically that if the offensive reductions expected by the U.S. were not achieved within five years, the U.S. could be compelled to reconsider its obligations under the treaty. Those expected offensive reductions, which would have given meaning to the ABM Treaty, were never realized. Indeed Soviet offensive forces increased in a way SALT was intended to preclude.

The question of real importance is which would be the proper course: to maintain the ABM Treaty and mutual vulnerability, or change the treaty and reduce vulnerability? The ABM Treaty, from the U.S. perspective, is very much a product of the mutual vulnerability notion of deterrence. If that approach to deterrence is now considered unacceptable for technical or moral reasons, we should not feel compelled to perpetuate a treaty that reflects acceptance of mutual vulnerability. Of course, the U.S. must not violate a treaty, but it certainly should consider its options for legal modification and withdrawal. Indeed, under international law the U.S. now has the prerogative of voiding the ABM Treaty in part or entirely because the Soviet Union is in violation of it.

The U.S. already has ample reason to reconsider its commitment to the ABM Treaty. The conditions that spawned that treaty have changed drastically: The Soviet Union has since built up a tremendous counterforce offensive capability, which is precisely what the ABM Treaty was intended to preclude through its limits on defense. And the Soviet Union is in violation of the treaty. Finally, emerging defensive technologies appear to present the possibility of highly effective defenses:

Mutual vulnerability may, thus, be avoidable. With such a drastic change of conditions, the ABM Treaty must not be considered sacrosanct. International law fully recognizes that if the circumstances surrounding an agreement change so radically that the purpose of the treaty is undermined, reconsideration of the agreement is legitimate.

It simply is not reasonable to reject SDI, as some Christian groups have, because the deployment of BMD would be inconsistent with the ABM Treaty. SDI is not a BMD deployment program, and is consistent with the treaty. In addition, that view completely ignores the larger question of whether the condition of mutual vulnerability (and thus, the ABM Treaty) ought to be reconsidered. If that condition is unacceptable, then ultimately the ABM Treaty must also be unacceptable if the technology for defense is feasible and affordable. And it is the mission of SDI to answer the feasibility and cost questions about BMD. Opposing the SDI research program on the basis of the ABM Treaty simply is unwarranted.

Defense Effectiveness

There are curious considerations regarding strategic defense in some Christian treatments of the issue. For example, the Episcopal committee opposes SDI because it judged that strategic defense must function almost perfectly to be worthwhile and such effectiveness is impossible.[59] This view reflects a tenet of the secular anti-SDI argument that even a few weapons penetrating the defense and attacking cities could cause millions of casualties, and because no system is likely to be 100-percent effective, the entire concept of strategic defense is flawed.

Why such an argument would come from Christian groups is difficult to understand. It may well be that no defense will provide "perfect" protection in the event of war—it is difficult to find examples in history of any defense always promising perfect protection against an attack. However, rejecting a defense because it is unlikely to be perfect appears to be far removed from any Christian perspective. Are those lives that would be saved by even imperfect defenses of no account because other lives could be lost? How many lives would have to be saved before they become important enough to save? In principle, if strategic defense could save one innocent life that otherwise would be lost in the event of war, it should be considered. But the difference in lives saved or lost could be in the tens or hundreds of millions, depending on how effective the defense ultimately might be.

This is not an issue of some level of casualties being "acceptable." If the choice is between a secure peace or war, the choice is clear. Protecting lives by maintaining peace with security obviously is the best alternative. But that alternative is not always available. The U.S. may not be any more able to prevent World War III than Britain was able to prevent World War II—in which case we must be prepared to save as many innocent American and Russian lives as possible.

Consequently, although most would agree it is preferable to avoid war rather than defend people during war, that preference should not prohibit considerations of feasible defenses. Because a defense may not protect everyone does not mean we ought not try to protect anyone. The U.S. government has the obligation to defend. It hardly seems likely that this scriptural mandate can be followed by the advice: but if you cannot do it perfectly, forget it. Professor James Child's comments are cogent:

> Obviously, our first moral obligation is to avoid nuclear war. However, if war comes, we are under a strict obligation to those who survive to maximize their numbers and, if possible, make tolerable the quality of their postwar lives. They do not, by virtue of what has happened to their society, become moral ciphers. [60]

It is not clear yet whether defensive technologies will be capable of providing the public protection against nuclear attack, and if so, at what level of effectiveness. But to suggest that the effort is not worth the candle because the defense will not be 100 percent is strange logic for Christians to follow.

SUMMARY AND CONCLUSIONS

Strategic defense appears to be an alternative to deterrence that does not suffer from the problem of certain infeasibility. The other options suggested by Christians opposed to deterrence, world government, disarmament, and civilian based defense are not viable alternatives. And, arms control alone, without the complement of strategic defense, also appears to be of limited value.

Strategic defense may prove to be technically infeasible, but unlike the other suggested alternatives, it does not require the impossible—the moral perfection of leaders and the achievement of continuing cooperation and trust within the international arena and among hostile powers. This ultimately is an issue of man's character, not a thing easily fixed. In contrast, strategic defense poses technical and economic questions, and SDI is a program to help determine the technical and economic feasibility of strategic defense.

Some Christian groups have declared their support for SDI and strategic defense, others their opposition. However, none of the issues raised against SDI or strategic defense necessarily leads to opposition. Each issue raised—cost, feasibility, stability, arms control, the ABM Treaty, and defense effectiveness—if examined closely, can indeed lend support to SDI and the goal of strategic defense.

The British development of radar and interceptors to defend against air attack, which arguably prevented Nazi air superiority over Britain during World War II, was preceded by a similar debate over the virtues of offensive deterrence over defense.[61] Ironically, during this most recent version of that debate, some Christian groups have taken the side of mutual vulnerability.

Nothing within the just war or even the Christian pacifist

tradition stands against a defense that does not threaten the opponent. Such a defense appears to be compatible with both traditions. Indeed, it is the hope that strategic defense could provide a just defense—a means of dealing with the nuclear threat—that could be supported by these two very different Christian traditions. The examination of emerging defensive technologies deserves enthusiastic support because it is the first step in what may be a long road toward ending the current condition of mutual nuclear threats.

If the technology for strategic defense proves to be a disappointment, we are likely to be stuck indefinitely with some form of offensive nuclear deterrence. As discussed in chapter 6, the just war tradition can accommodate nuclear deterrence, but only in a conditional and highly restricted sense. Continued reliance on mutual vulnerability for stability is not a preferable future, and we should be highly skeptical of those Christians who suggest that it is. The promising alternative of a just defense deserves our support.

Chapter 10, Notes
---

1. See for example, "A Proposal to Tilt the Balance of Terror," *Christianity Today*, 9 April 1982, 16-19.

2. See for example the discussion in Stansfield Turner, "Reagan Is Right: No ICBMs Means No First Strike," *The Washington Post*, 26 October 1986, sec. B.

3. James Child, *Nuclear War: The Moral Dimension* (London: Transaction Books, 1986), 112.

4. Caspar Weinberger, *Report of the Secretary of Defense to the Congress on the FY 1987 Budget, FY 1988 Authorization Request and FY 1987-1991 Programs* (Washington, D.C.: Government Printing Office, 5 February 1986), 74-75.

5. Thomas Schelling, "What Went Wrong With Arms Control," *Foreign Affairs* (Winter 1985-86):233.

6. The level of popular support reportedly decreases considerably when the label "Star Wars" is used to describe the program. See "The High Frontier," *Washington Times*, 25 June 1985, sec. A.

7. Most opinion surveys show 70 percent to 90 percent public support for the SDI program. See Keith Payne, *Strategic Defense: "Star Wars" in Perspective* (Lanham, Md.: University Press of America, 1985), 233-47.

8. U.S. Department of Defense, *The Strategic Defense Initiative Defensive Technologies Study* (Washington, D.C.: Government Printing Office, 1 April 1984), 4.

9. Interview with General Daniel Graham, 26 March 1985.

10. Quoted in Robert Scheer, *With Enough Shovels: Reagan, Bush and Nuclear War* (New York: Random House, 1982), Advance Reader's Edition, 104.

11. See for example, Caspar Weinberger, "Morality Demands the SDI as Only Alternative to U.S.-Soviet Suicide Pact," *New York City Tribune*, 2 January 1986, 9; and Caspar Weinberger, "Ethics and Public Policy: The Case of SDI," *The Fletcher Forum* (Winter 1986):1-4.

12. Quoted in "Keep Space Defense Option," *Colorado Springs Gazette Telegraph*, 30 December 1984.

13. See the discussion in Robert Jastrow, *How to Make Nuclear Weapons Obsolete* (Boston: Little, Brown, and Co., 1985), 100-106; and Report of the Technical Panel, *Missile Defense in the 1990s* (Washington, D.C.: George C. Marshall Institute, 1987).

14. *Strategic Defense Initiative*, 6.

15. Jastrow, 92.

16. These issues are derived from *Strategic Defense Initiative*, 11-12; and James Fletcher, "Technologies for Strategic Defense," *Issues in Science and Technology* 1 (Fall 1984):23-25.

17. For discussion of the U.S. Patriot air defense system and possible modifications see Michael Bearce, "The Tactics," *Air Defense Artillery* (Winter 1985):24-27; "Expensive But Necessary: The PATRIOT Surface-to-Air Missile System," *Military Technology* (1986):1-11; and Thomas Enders, *Missile Defense as Part of an Extended NATO Air Defense* (Bonn: Konrad-Adenauer-Stiftung, 1986), 73-78.

18. See the discussion in "Christians Take Sides on Proposed Defense System," *Christianity Today*, 4 April 1986, 43. See also, Richard Sincere, "What the Churches Are Saying about Star Wars," *This World*, Spring-Summer 1986, 3-11; "1,000 Clergymen Back 'Star Wars' Defense Plan," *Washington Times*, 23 August 1984, 4; and "Group Opposes 'Star Wars' Funding," *Washington Post*, 14 May 1985, sec. A.

19. See Sincere, 6; and "Christians Take Sides," 43.

20. The United Methodist Church, Council of Bishops, *In Defense of Creation: The Nuclear Crisis and a Just Peace* (Pre-publication print, 1986), 39.

21. Source: SDIO and the Department of Energy, reported in, "The SDI Spending 'Explosion,'" *Detroit News*, 1 November 1986.

22. See, respectively, Zbigniew Brzezinski, Robert Jastrow, Max Kampelman, "Defense In Space Is Not 'Star Wars'," *New York Times Magazine*, 27 January 1985, 29; Pat Friel, "An Exchange on BMD Technology," *Comparative Strategy* 5 (1985):216; statement by Gen. Abrahamson in, John Cushman, "Senate Democrats May Curb 1988 ABM Research Spending," *New York Times*, 20 March 1987, sec. A; *Defense Daily*, 29 November 1983, 137; *Soviet Aerospace*, 18 October 1983, 43; and Barry Blechman and Victor Utgoff, *Fiscal and Economic Implications of Strategic Defense*, prepared for the project on "The Military Uses of Space," The Johns Hopkins Foreign Policy Institute, July 1986.

23. See Department of Defense Cost Summaries by program in, Department of Defense, Office of the Assistant Secretary of Defense (Comptroller),

National Defense Budget Estimates for FY 1986 (Washington, D.C.: Department of Defense, March 1985), Table 6-5.

24. *In Defense of Creation*, 36-37.

25. Weinberger, *Report of the Secretary of Defense*, 287-92.

26. See Jastrow, 41-43; Patrick Friel, "U.S. Ballistic Missile Defense Technology: A Technical Overview," *Comparative Strategy* 4 (1984):319-47; Harold Brown, "The Strategic Defense Initiative: Defensive Systems and the Strategic Debate," (paper for the Johns Hopkins School of Advanced International Studies, The Johns Hopkins University, 1984), 13-16; Harold Brown, "The Strategic Defense Initiative: Defensive Systems and the Strategic Debate," *Survival*, March-April 1985, 59-60; Harold Brown, "Is the SDI Technically Feasible?" *Foreign Affairs* 54 (1986):436-37, 451-52; and, Union of Concerned Scientists, *Space-Based Missile Defense* (Cambridge, Mass.: Union of Concerned Scientist, March 1984),61.

27. Quoted in Caspar Weinberger, "Strategic Defense Initiative Opponents Show Reluctance for Self-Defense," *ROA National Security Report* 4 (November 1986):2-3.

28. Committee of Inquiry on the Nuclear Issues, Commission on Peace, Episcopal Diocese of Washington, *The Nuclear Dilemma: A Search for Christian Understanding* (Washington, D.C.: Episcopal Diocese of Washington, 1986), 31.

29. See, for example, *Space-Based Missile Defense*.

30. Ashton B. Carter, *Directed Energy Missile Defense in Space—A Background Paper* (Washington, D.C.: U.S. Congress, Office of Technology Assessment, April 1984), 81.

31. Brown, "Strategic Defense Initiative," (1984), 4. For a similarly negative view see Richard Garwin's prepared statement, "The President's Strategic Defense Initiative," Testimony for the Senate Armed Services Committee, 24 April 1984.

32. Quoted in Fletcher, 15, 25.

33. Ibid., 26.

34. Jastrow, 100-106; see also *Soviet Aerospace* 43 (29 April 1985):1. For a more recent study reaching similar conclusions about potential effectiveness, see the study by the Washington-based George C. Marshall Institute issued in December 1986. This study was discussed in, Warren Strobel, "Missile Shield Called Deployable by 1994," *The Washington Times*, 23 December 1986, sec. C.

35. Quoted in Christopher Cerf and Victor Navasky, *The Experts Speak* (New York: Pantheon Books, 1984), 232, 236, 299, 252.

36. 15 May 1986, *Congressional Record* (Senate), S5986-87.

37. Fletcher, 29.

38. *Nuclear Dilemma*, 31.

39. Ibid., 34, 84.

40. N. Talensky, "Anti-Missile Systems and Disarmament," *International Affairs* (October 1964):16, 19.

41. Quoted in "Vazhnye Problemy," *Pravda*, 11 February 1967, 1.

42. See Richard Schultz and Roy Godson, *Dezinformatsia* (New York:

A *Just Defense*   307

Pergamon Press, 1984), 17-40; and American Bar Association, "How the KGB Operates: Answers from a KGB Defector," *Intelligence Report* (July 1981):3-6.

43. U.S. Department of Defense, *Strategic Defense Initiative, Authorization for Appropriations for Fiscal Year 1985*, Hearings before the Committee on Armed Services, U.S. Senate, 98th Cong., 2nd sess., (March 8, 22, and 24 April 1984), 2974.

44. Spending figures from Robert Gates (Deputy Director of Central Intelligence), *The Soviets and SDI*, an address to the World Affairs Council of Northern California (Bay Area International Forum), 25 November 1986, 4.

45. See Richard DeLauer, statement by the Under Secretary of Defense, Research and Engineering, *The FY 1986 Department of Defense Program for Research, Development and Acquisition*, 99th Cong., 1st sess. (Washington, D.C.: Government Printing Office, 7 March 1985), IV-7.

46. Department of Defense, *Strategic Defense Initiative*, 2929-30.

47. For graphic illustrations of this difference in the Soviet and American approaches to strategic defense, see Payne, *Strategic Defense*, 48-49.

48. See *Soviet Strategic Defense Programs*, 12-13. See also George Wilson, "Soviets Reported Pushing Laser Arms," *Washington Post*, 3 April 1985.

49. See the testimony of Richard DeLauer in U.S. Department of Defense, *Strategic Defense Initiative*, 2928-29.

50. *Soviet Strategic Defense Programs*, 13.

51. Cited in Henry Kissinger, "NATO: The Next Thirty Years," *Survival*, November-December 1979, 267.

52. *In Defense of Creation*, 38.

53. Ibid., 38; and *The Nuclear Dilemma*, 61, 84.

54. *The Nuclear Dilemma*, 84.

55. See John Collins and Patrick Cronin, *U.S./Soviet Military Balance*, Report No. 84-163-S, Congressional Research Service, Library of Congress, 2 August 1984, 28.

56. Address by A. Gromyko to the U.N. General Assembly, 21 September 1962, 17th sess., 1127th plenary meeting, reprinted in, United States Arms Control and Disarmament Agency, *Documents on Disarmament*, publication 19, vol. 11, July-December 1962 (Washington, D.C.: Government Printing Office, released November 1963), 896-917.

57. Quoted in Gregory A. Fossedal, "A Star Wars Caucus in the Freeze Movement," *Wall Street Journal*, 14 February 1985, 30.

58. *In Defense of Creation*, 38, 67; *The Nuclear Dilemma*, 32. See also, "Christians Take Sides on Proposed Defense System," 43.

59. *The Nuclear Dilemma*, 30.

60. Child, 64.

61. See, Benson Adams, "An Early SDI That Saved Britain," in *Promise or Peril, The Strategic Defense Initiative*, ed. Zbigniew Brzezinski (Washington, D.C.: Ethics and Public Policy Center, 1986), 9-16.

Conclusion

The use of force and nuclear weapons is a complex issue. Although many concerns demand the attention of the global Christian body, this subject in particular demands deep consideration because simplistic solutions do not exist. That Christians must work for peace is obvious, and peace is a goal shared by all. All six positions examined in the preceding chapters—nonresistance, nuclear pacifism, traditional just war, preventive war, historic pacifism, and radical pacifism—share the same goal. All would like to see world peace and justice for all. But simply stating that Christians must be peacemakers does not provide a means to this common goal. The means by which world peace might actually be achieved are not as obvious as many appear to believe. As this book has outlined, many of the usual answers, such as disarmament or a nuclear freeze, could actually hinder the prospects for peace. Much of the slogan-making of Christian peace activists does not provide solutions to the real security problems that must be faced.

As citizens who share the rare privilege of living in a country that allows its people to determine not only who will govern but also the policies by which their country is run, Christians must be actively and intelligently involved in the governing process. Christians must be responsible in their role as citizens in helping to determine which candidates and policies this country will follow. It is not just a good idea; it is mandatory that Christians be involved.

It is clear from Scripture that government has been given the responsibility to exercise force when necessary in protecting the innocent and punishing evil or unjust behavior. It is equally clear that Christians have been commanded to support their government in carrying out its God-ordained responsibilities. The just war position rightly recognizes the government's responsibility to exercise necessary force, the necessity to constrain that use of force, and the Christian's personal obligation to help government carry out its job.

The just war position has and continues to represent the majority view among both Catholics and Protestants. In addition to providing a scriptural basis for evaluating the use of force and the extent to which a person can support that use of force, the just war position also provides a basis for protecting neighbors. Biblically, a person may refuse to defend himself in the face of aggression, choosing instead to accept and endure hostility, but government does not have this option. It must defend the innocent, reward good behavior, and punish evil behavior.

Although the pacifist position is endorsed by sincere Christians, its scriptural support is less than convincing. Not only does the pacifist position fail to endorse personal support for an institution God has ordained, it also does not provide the same love and protection for neighbors that it does for enemies. Christians, of all people, must be cognizant of the fact that personal choices often affect those around them. In choosing to exercise personal liberties a person must consciously put the principle of love for others first. Making choices that allow others to be harmed as a result of one's personal liberty does not demonstrate love for others but disdain.

The theological basis for the pacifist position rests squarely upon the a priori acceptance of nonresistance. For those willing to accept nonresistance and to subjugate the rest of Scripture to that belief, this position is an option. However, for those not willing to accept nonresistance or the subjugation of the entirety of Scripture to nonresistance, pacifism may be viewed as sincere, but sincerely in error.

In spite of pacifist claims to the contrary, it is clear from the writings of the church fathers that the early church had no standardized policy of pacifism. It is wrong for pacifists to continue to teach that it did. Pacifism fails to receive the theological and historical support it needs to give it credibility.

Although many Christians have expressed their opposition to nuclear weapons, the need for nuclear deterrence is generally recognized. Even many nuclear pacifists, although opposing any use of nuclear weapons, endorse the possession of nuclear weapons as a deterrent. The argument is, of course, that for deterrence purposes the U.S. merely needs to possess a nuclear capability but not ever plan to use that capability. This has been described as "deterrence by bluff."

This position suffers from two serious flaws. First, it is almost impossible to imagine that the U.S., with its open political process, could maintain a credible bluff. And second, in the event of a Soviet nuclear attack, the U.S. government has the obligation to protect American citizens as best it is able. Even if the Soviet first strike were large and killed many, those surviving the first strike deserve whatever protection can be given; they are not "moral ciphers."

Consequently, there would be a legitimate role for limited U.S. nuclear retaliation. The use of U.S. strategic nuclear forces against remaining Soviet military capabilities, especially nuclear capabilities, could serve to save many in the West from the threat of subsequent strikes.

U.S. retaliation would, of course, have to be restricted and controlled. It would have to minimize the number of Russian noncombatant casualties. Such a requirement necessitates highly controlled and accurate nuclear capabilities, and a highly restricted targeting policy. U.S. policy and strategic capabilities have been moving in such a direction since the midseventies. The indiscriminate use of nuclear weapons is not acceptable, and the effects of nuclear weapons must be controlled so as to minimize Russian casualties. Of course, more can and must be done by the U.S. in pursuit of such capabilities, and such endeavors should be supported by Christians.

Strict restrictions on targets and excellent accuracy are required by just war considerations, and thus are essential on their own merit. But they should also help to discourage continued escalation, and thereby help to restore peace. U.S. retaliation that specifically excluded Soviet population centers should provide Soviet leaders with a powerful and continuing incentive to avoid escalation to the cataclysmic levels of destruction so many antinuclear activists postulate.

In addition, the type of retaliatory actions the U.S. could legitimately pursue—targeting military capabilities so as to minimize noncombatant casualties—should also support an effective deterrent against nuclear attack in the first place. And, as long as U.S. forces are highly invulnerable to a Soviet first strike, U.S. counterforce capabilities should not give the Soviets destabilizing incentives to strike first.

Consequently, there is a deterrent that should be effective in preventing war, but could legitimately be carried out if deterrence fails. A threat to selected Soviet military capabilities should provide an effective deterrent. And, if the Soviet Union attacked the United States nonetheless, selective and discriminate retaliatory strikes could help to reduce the possibility of further American and allied casualties. With the existence of this type of potential deterrent the Christian is not forced to choose between either the nuclear bluff or nuclear pacifist position.

Indeed, the Christian nuclear pacifist position is built on sand. Its primary failing is its assumption that the use of nuclear weapons could never be discriminate, and that nuclear escalation to indiscriminate destruction would be virtually certain to follow any type of nuclear use. This assumption compels the conclusion that there can never be a justifiable resort to such use. However, new technologies have opened the door to increasingly discriminate nuclear options. Thus the Christian reasonably can suspect the validity of the assumption that any and all nuclear use is inherently indiscriminate and escalatory.

In addition, nuclear escalation could stem from the use of only conventional forces. Consequently, if one adopts the reasoning of the nuclear pacifists and rejects behavior that *might* escalate to indiscriminate nuclear destruction, one would have to reject any and all use of force. Such a position must lead to complete pacifism. It would deny the West any means of opposing Soviet power, and it would deny government any means of fulfilling its mandate to protect the innocent.

There is no reasonable basis to distinguish between nuclear and conventional weapons with regard to their ultimate potential for escalation. We simply do not understand the nature of nuclear war well enough to know, with any certainty, what are the thresholds for escalation. Consequently, there is no reason to consider nuclear weapons any more or less escalation prone than many other types of force. One logically can hold a completely pacifist position because of the fear that any conflict could lead to indiscriminate nuclear destruction—there is a logical but scripturally unacceptable case for pacifism. There is, however, no logical rationale supporting the Christian nuclear pacifist position.

In addition, while Christian nuclear pacifists endorse just war requirements in building their case against nuclear weapons, they abandon those requirements when they argue against technologies for greater discrimination and control of nuclear weapons. Taking such an inconsistent position seems to reflect an antinuclear political agenda rather than a coherent application of the just war tradition to the nuclear issue.

Although a policy of nuclear deterrence can be accommodated by the just war tradition, it is hardly a policy to be preferred if there exist any feasible alternatives. Unfortunately, the alternatives suggested by some Christians are romantic fiction. They ought not be held out as alternatives to deterrence, and the U.S. certainly should not be encouraged to abandon deterrence in favor of them. In this category of "romantic fiction" belong complete disarmament, nuclear disarmament, the creation of a world government, or disarmament followed by planning for nonviolent resistance (civilian based defense).

The proposals that world government or disarmament will provide an alternative to deterrence suffer from similar fallacies. Either would require the prior transformation of man and the international system before becoming possible. And, of course, if such a transformation took place, a world government or disarmament would be unnecessary for security. Any suggested alternative to deterrence that requires a radical change in human nature or the international political system has no hope of succeeding in this age.

The suggestion that the U.S. should disarm and follow a policy of public nonviolent resistance also cannot be accepted. It would increase the risk of attack and purposely place civilians in harm's way. That is a complete reversal of the role given to government in Scripture. In addition, civilian nonviolence would not, in any way, avoid the prospect of a nuclear attack against the U.S. This pacifist notion of civilian based defense suffers from the same dangers inherent in the current condition of vulnerability, but it does not permit the one benefit of the current situation—the U.S. possession of a deterrent to nuclear attack. Moreover, if one examines past and current Soviet behavior toward Soviet citizens and occupied countries, there ought to be little hope that CBD could protect American freedoms. Civilian based defense promotes a dangerous combination of abandoning the means of protection and increasing the risk of attack. Government should in no way be encouraged to consider such a policy.

Arms control—the notion that the U.S. and the Soviet Union can gradually negotiate away nuclear weapons—is another suggested alternative to deterrence. This alternative is supported by members of each Christian position. Unfortunately, arms control as practiced by the Soviet Union and the U.S. over the past two decades provides no hope for such an outcome. The offensive structure of the strategic relationship has, in effect, not allowed for the possibility of success. Indeed, the competing strategic objectives of the two sides virtually ensure the continuation of the arms competition.

Christians ought not blame the U.S. government for the obvious failure of arms control to reduce or even stem the arms competition. This is not a matter of one side or another needing to be prodded. Christian disarmament activists' efforts have a grossly asymmetrical impact. They have virtually no impact on the Soviet leadership, largely because they can be ignored by that leadership, but also because their activities focus so overwhelmingly on U.S. policies and programs alone. This can only serve to undermine the U.S. position in negotiations. If those same activists would learn more about Soviet policies and weapons programs so as to include them in their focus, this problem might at least be eased somewhat.

There are many arms control myths. Perhaps the most serious misunderstanding, however, has to do with traditional U.S. arms control goals. Most Americans equate arms control with reducing vulnerability to nuclear attack—but that has not been the objective or the result of negotiations. The U.S. approach to strategic arms control has been to stabilize deterrence by reducing the probability of nuclear war through the maintenance of mutual vulnerability; it has nothing to do with reducing the vulnerability of Americans to nuclear attack. Consequently, many American proponents of this now traditional arms control agenda praise the ABM Treaty of 1972 specifically because it ensured that the "retaliatory warhead would always get through."

The Soviet approach to arms control has been directly contrary to the U.S. approach. Soviet arms control policy is driven by the Soviet concept of security, which has never endorsed deterrence built on mutual vulnerability. Rather, the Soviet Union has sought to attain a capability to limit damage to itself in the event of war.

Consequently, while the U.S. has attempted to maintain an offensive deterrent threat, the Soviet Union has attempted to limit that deterrent threat, primarily through offensive counterforce capabilities. This type of strategic relationship does not lead to a realistic expectation that arms control, if it follows the established path, will produce deep offensive force reductions in the future.

Finally, the Soviet Union does not have a good track record with regard to abiding by its arms control commitments. Unfortunately, those Christians who place the greatest confidence in arms control seem also to ignore this behavior or even blame it on the U.S. Yet the issue of Soviet noncompliance is critically important if one considers arms control an alternative to deterrence. Even if the U.S. and Soviet Union could agree to deep reductions—approaching zero nuclear weapons—such an agreement would be undermined by even a relatively small number of covertly deployed forces. Modest cheating "at the margin," such as practiced by the Soviet Union, would become highly significant.

It is clear these suggested alternatives to deterrence are either without hope or cannot solve the nuclear problem alone. An alternative that is a cause for hope, and the one advocated here, is a just defense—a transition to defenses that would move the U.S. away from reliance on offensive forces while building up defensive forces. A defensive alternative intended to protect Soviet, American, and allied citizens should appeal to all Christians.

There are questions, of course, about the technical feasibility of such a transition. It is not clear that effective defense against the nuclear threat is possible. However, the Strategic Defense Initiative has, since 1983, been attempting to address these technical questions.

Surprisingly, some Christian groups have come out against SDI. The reasons for this opposition do not vary from the secular debate; they involve issues of cost, stability, arms control, the ABM Treaty, and defense effectiveness. However, on closer examination each of those issues can be seen as a reason for supporting SDI.

For example, the SDI research program costs a tiny fraction of the defense budget and a minuscule fraction of the federal budget. Such levels of funding appear to be reasonable to determine if and how we might be able to defend ourselves against the nuclear missile threat. *Deploying* a comprehensive BMD system could, ultimately, cost hundreds of billions of dollars. Yet the U.S. has spent even greater sums on other long-term military programs, including strategic offensive forces. Even the cost of deploying a defensive system would represent a modest fraction of the defense budget, and a very small fraction of the federal budget. Such a system, if feasible, could save millions of lives. A government charged with the protection of its population could not reject such an option based on such cost considerations.

The Reagan Administration has proposed that both the U.S. and the Soviet Union be defended and that reductions in strategic offensive forces take place as part of a defensive transition. This would undercut the Soviet offensive counterforce approach to damage-limitation, and this is why, perhaps, the Soviet Union has opposed SDI. However, it should not be thought that the Soviet Union is opposed to strategic defense. Soviet programs and past performance in this area speak louder than current words. The Soviet Union historically has been, and shows every appearance of continuing to be, very supportive of its own programs for strategic defense. This appears to be a case of Soviet leaders approving of strategic defense for the Soviet Union but not for the U.S.

Although technical feasibility remains to be seen, it is clear that a defensive alternative to offensive deterrence would be preferable in every way; it would represent a means by which the government could carry out its obligation to address the nuclear threat without simultaneously threatening the attacker with destruction. As such, it should satisfy the consciences of Christian pacifists and just war theorists of all varieties, including nuclear pacifists.

If a defensive alternative to deterrence ultimately is shown to be technically infeasible, we are likely to be stuck with nuclear deterrence as the only available means of addressing the nuclear threat. That would be unfortunate. It would be even more ur.fortunate if the defensive research program that might lead us to a just defense were abandoned now in pursuit of an unrealistic panacea. A just defense is the most realistic and moral alternative on the horizon and deserves the backing of all who desire to be peacemakers in the nuclear age.

Appendix

Soviet Arms Control Noncompliance: A Partial Listing

TREATY/AGREEMENT	ISSUE	U.S. GOVERNMENT FINDING
Unilateral Commitments		
1. Moratorium on nuclear testing, 1958	Breach of Moratorium, Sept. 1961—Sept. 1962	Breach of commitment
2. No offensive weapons in Cuba, 1962, 1970	Missiles, 1962 Subs, 1970-74	Breach of commitment
3. Moratorium on SS-20s in Europe, Mar. 82	Continued deployment of SS-20s in Europe	Breach of commitment

Multilateral Agreements		Recurring violations
1. Montreux Convention, 1936	Passage of carriers through Turkish straits	Violation
2. Geneva Protocol, 1925	Production, transfer, and use of trichothecene mycotoxins for hostile purposes in SE Asia and Afghanistan	Violation
3. Biological Weapons Convention, 1972	Continuing production and storage, 1972-1986	Violation
4. Conventional Weapons Convention, 1982	Failure to observe between signing and ratifying	Violation
5. Conventional Weapons Convention, 1982	Use of mines and incendiary weapons against civilians in Afghanistan	Violation
6. Helsinki Final Act, 1975	Failure to give prior notification of military exercises	Violation

Test Ban Treaties

1. Limited Test Ban Treaty, 1963	Extraterritorial venting of radiation	Numerous violations
2. Threshold Test Ban Treaty, 1974	Weapon tests exceeding 150 Kiloton yield	Likely violation

Salt I Interim Agreement

1. Ban on missiles at dismantle sites	Deployment of SS-25s at former SS-7 sites	Violation
2. No hindrance of National Tech Means of Verification	Deliberate concealment of activities	Numerous violations
3. Limit to 740 SLBM Launchers	Deployment exceeding 740	Violation
4. Ban on replacing light ICBMs with heavy ICBMs	Replacement of SS-11 with SS-17s and SS-19s	Circumvention of purpose

Salt I ABM Treaty

1. Restrictions on Ballistic Missile Early Warning Radars	Krasnoyarsk radar location and orientation	Violation

	Development and deployment of prohibited systems	Violation
2. Ban on development and deployment of ABM radars other than permanent fixed types		Violation
3. Ban on concurrent testing of SAM	Testing SAM and ABM concurrently	Highly probable violation
4. Ban on ABM abilities of other weapons	ABM capabilities of SAM-5, -10, -12	Probable violation
5. Ban on rapid reload ABM systems	Automatic or semi-auto reload ABMs	Ambiguous situation
6. Ban on nationwide ABM defense	All of the above ABM issues	May be building prohibited defense

Salt II

1. One new missile limitation	SS-25 as second new missile	Irreversible violation
2. Ban on deliberate concealment measures	Encryption of ballistic missile telemetry	Violation
3. Agreement not to produce, test, deploy SS-16	Deployment of SS-16 at Plesetsk	Probable violation

4.	RV to throwweight ratio	Testing warhead less than 50% throwweight	Violation
5.	SNDV ceilings	All ceilings exceeded	Violation
6.	Backfire Bomber Range	Arctic basing gave international range	Not consistent with commitment
7.	Backfire production limit to 30 annually	Excess production until 1984	Violation
8.	Ban on concealing launcher/missile assoc.	Concealed SS-25 mobile launchers and tests	Violation

SOURCES: *The President's Unclassified Report on Soviet Noncompliance with Arms Control Agreements*, 23 December 1985.

Soviet Noncompliance With Arms Control Agreements (unclassified President's report), 1 February 1985

The General Advisory on Arms Control and Disarmament, *A Quarter Century of Soviet Compliance Under Arms Control Commitments: 1958-1983: Summary, October 1984*, 10 October 1984.

United States Arms Control and Disarmament Agency, *Soviet Noncompliance*, 1 February 1986.

Scripture Index

Subject Index

ABM (Anti-ballistic missiles), 177, 185, 186, 209
ABM treaty, 299-301
Afghanistan, 103, 159, 230-35
Ambrose, St. (c. A.D. 339-397), 44
Anabaptist movement, 62
Antinuclear groups, 109, 113, 115, 118, 129, 130, 171
Aquinas, St., 44-45
Arms Control and Disarmament Agency, 131
Arms control. See also Deterrence.
 versus disarmament, 144
 expectations versus reality, 185-93
 failure, 174
 history, 191-93
 and just defense, 292-99
 negotiations, 170-72
 and nuclear freeze. See Nuclear freeze.
 progress in, 169
 and SALT. See SALT.
 and Soviet Union, 172, 180-84, 192, 206-13
 strategic, 255, 278-79
 treaty, 169
 unilateral. See Unilateral disarmament.
 violations, 206-13
Athenagoras (second century), 79-80
Augustine, St. (A.D. 354-430), 44
Authorities
 biblical teaching, 22, 25-26
 obeying, 24-25

Biological Weapons Convention of 1972, 207
BMD (Ballistic missile defense), 184, 185, 264, 269, 270, 272, 278, 280, 289, 290, 293, 294, 300
Byrnes, James, 162

Calvin, John, 45
Carter, Jimmy, President, 115

CBD (Civilian based defense)
 alternative to deterrence, 240-46
 alternative to radical pacifism, 73, 98
 conventional invasion and, 229-30
 critical concerns regarding, 226-28
 objections to, 246-49
 Sider and Taylor on, 223-25, 234-35, 240-46
Christian pacifism. See Pacifism, Christian.
Churchill, Winston, Sir, 162
Citizens, Christians as responsible, 16-17
Class struggle, 66
Clement of Alexandria (c.155-c.220), 82-83
Clement of Rome (first century), 78
Cold War, 103
Commandment, sixth, 45-46
Connally, Tom, 163
Conscientious objection, 64
Culver, Robert, 56-57
Cyprian (c.200/10-258), 82

Defensive Technologies Study, 264-65
Deterrence. See also Arms control.
 just defense and, 258-61
 nonmilitary defense and, 223-49
 nuclear
  alternatives to, 72-74, 144-50, 153-61, 240-46
  basis of, 118
  bluff approach, 107-10
  first strike and, 125-26, 176-77, 195, 208
  NATO use of, 104
  and nonresistance, 47-48
  and pacifism, 50, 72
  and preventive war position, 57-58
  and traditional just war, 53
  U.S. use of, 104-5
 principles of, 30-31

327